Praise for Tracy Wolff's Crave series

charm

ALSO BY TRACY WOLFF

charm

#1 *NEW YORK TIMES* BESTSELLING AUTHOR
TRACY WOLFF

Entangled Publishing, LLC
644 Shrewsbury Commons Ave., STE 181
Shrewsbury, PA 17361
rights@entangledpublishing.com

Entangled Teen is an imprint of Entangled Publishing, LLC.

Visit our website at www.entangledpublishing.com.

Edited by Liz Pelletier
Cover art and design by Bree Archer
Stock art by Renphoto/gettyimages and Dem10/gettyimages
Interior endpaper design by Elizabeth Turner Stokes
Interior design by Toni Kerr

ISBN 978-1-64937-149-2 (Hardcover) ISBN 978-1-64937-363-2 (B&N)
ISBN 978-1-64937-300-7 (BAM) ISBN 978-1-64937-301-4 (TARGET)
ISBN 978-1-64937-364-9 (WALMART) ISBN 978-1-64937-129-4 (Ebook)
ISBN 978-1-64937-382-3 (B&N BF Signed Edition)

Manufactured in the United States of America

First Edition November 2022

10 9 8 7 6 5 4 3 2

an imprint of Entangled Publishing LLC

For Andrea Deebs,
the most badass mother a girl could ever ask for.
Thank you for being mine.

At Entangled, we want our readers to be well-informed. If you would like to know if this book contains any elements that might be of concern for you, please check the back of the book for details.

Nearly Gutless Grace

—Grace—

My head feels strange.

Actually, *every part of me* feels strange, and I don't have a clue what's going on.

I think back over the last few minutes as I try to figure out why I feel so hollow and unmoored, but all I can see is Jaxon's face. He's smiling at me as we walk down the hall, and we're joking about—

Just like that, it all comes flooding back. A scream tears through me, and I instinctively jerk away from Hudson's blade.

Except there is no blade, I realize as I arch backward.

There is no Hudson.

No Jaxon.

No hallway—and *no Katmere Academy*. In their place is a vast, dark emptiness that has panic clawing at my insides as I struggle to figure out what's happening.

Where am I?

Where did everyone go?

What is this odd weightlessness that fills my every cell?

Did Jaxon's brother actually kill me with that sword?

Am I dead right now?

The idea slinks into the corner of my mind and seizes the breath in my lungs.

Panic grows into full-blown terror as my eyes strain to see more than an inch into the inky-black nothingness that surrounds me. I frantically run my hands over my body in an effort to find the death blow. To confirm—or please God, debunk—the idea that I am dying *or already dead.*

Oh God, I don't want to be dead. The thought slams through me. *Please don't let me be dead—or worse, a ghost.*

Dating a vampire is one thing, but *please, please, please* don't make me a ghost. Getting stuck haunting Katmere Academy's hallways for an eternity as

Nearly Gutless Grace is *so* not my idea of a good time.

But as I finish my personal inspection of myself, I notice there is no wound to find.

No blood.

Not even any pain. Just this weird numbness that refuses to go away as it turns me colder with every second that passes.

I try blinking fast a couple of times to clear my vision, and when that doesn't work, I rub my eyes, and then I force myself to look around again, ignoring my sweaty palms and shaking hands as I do.

But nothing's changed. Darkness still surrounds me on every side—and not just any darkness. The kind that only happens when there is no moon, no stars. Only a sky as black and empty as the terror growing inside me.

"Seriously? As black and empty as the terror growing inside you?" a sarcastic voice with a very proper British accent asks from deep in my head. *"Melodramatic much?"*

I've gotten used to a voice in my head sometimes telling me how to survive over the last couple of weeks, but this is totally different. This guy sounds like he wants to hurt, not help me.

"Who are you?" I ask.

"Really? That's your big question?" He yawns. *"Soooo original."*

"Fine, then will you just tell me what's going on?" I demand in a voice that is way more high-pitched—way more frightened-sounding—than I would like. Then again, *truth in advertising* is a saying for a reason…

Still, I clear my throat and try again. "Who are you? What do you want from me?"

"I'm fairly certain I'm the one who should be asking those questions, Princess, considering you're the one dragging me along for this ride."

"Dragging you?" My voice breaks. "I'm the one trapped here with no clue about where *here* even is, let alone who I'm trapped with. Of course I have questions, especially since it's too dark for me to see anything."

He makes a noise that should sound sympathetic but is actually anything but. *"Yeah, well, there is a solution for a large part of that—"*

Hope leaps in my stomach. "Which is?"

He gives a long-suffering sigh. *"Turn on the fucking light. Obviously."*

A quick, sharp click of a switch being flicked echoes through the emptiness. A half second later, brightness floods the world around me.

Head Space, Talk Space, Give Me Some Space
—Grace—

Pain assaults my eyeballs, and I spend a few interminable seconds blinking like a mole just emerging from the earth. But when I can finally see again, I realize I'm in a room. A very large loft, at least half the size of a football field, with floor-to-ceiling bookshelves stretching the entire length of the wall in front of me.

The top shelf is crowded with candles of every size and shape imaginable, and for a moment, a new worry creeps in. But a quick glance around shows that there's no altar in sight. No jars of blood. No creepy spell book meant to hasten my journey to the afterlife.

Which I take as a very good sign. I mean, there are only so many times a girl can handle being the human sacrifice du jour. And I'm pretty sure I've already reached my limit...plus one.

Another quick glance around reveals nothing scary at all about the room I'm in. In fact, the entire area looks like one of those fancy furniture-catalog showrooms.

The three main walls not covered in bookshelves are painted a bright white, with lamps and chandeliers bathing the entire space in soft, warm light. My gaze bounces around the space, a gorgeous mix of modern and rustic furniture in white, tan, or black arranged into eight distinctive areas by the strategic placement of rugs and seating.

There's an area filled with albums crowding two giant black metal shelves and an impressive media cabinet. Farther down is an exercise space, a target-practice area, and then a gaming section dominated by a massive flat-screen TV and a super-comfy-looking couch with game controllers scattered on the white cushions. There's a bedroom area with a big white bed, library space with rows and rows of books filled to bursting on too many bookshelves to count, a reading nook with a black accent wall, kitchen, and what must be the bathroom in the rear.

Everything feels almost soothing. Like coming home.

Well, unless, of course, you count the disembodied voice that keeps talking in the back of my head. A voice that, very definitely, does not belong to me *or* my conscience.

"Do you like the accent wall? It's Armani black," he says, and I have to grit my teeth against telling him what he can do with his *Armani black*, not to mention the condescension he's got dripping from every proper British syllable. But antagonizing whoever this guy is doesn't seem like the best bet right now, especially not when I still have to get my bearings.

Instead, I settle for trying—one more time—to get some answers. "Why are you doing this to me?"

A heavy sigh. *"There you go again, stealing my line."*

I'm so freaked out that it takes a moment for his words to register. When they do, I can't help squawking and throwing my hands wide. "I already told you, I'm not doing this! I don't even know what *this* is."

"Yeah, well, sorry to contradict your self-delusion, but it's got to be you. Because vampires can do a lot of things, but we sure as fuck can't do this."

The way he says "fuck" this time comes out more like "fook," his accent growing heavier with each word, and I have the inane urge to giggle.

"Yeah, well, neither can I. In fact—" I break off as the rest of his words sink in. "You're a vampire?"

"Well, I'm sure as shit not a werewolf. And since I'm not breathing fire or waving a magic wand out of my arse, you do the maths."

"I don't know what you're waving—out of your ass or otherwise—because I can't *see* you," I snap. "Where exactly are you, anyway? And, more importantly, *who* are you?"

He doesn't answer—big surprise. But before I can say anything else, there's a small sound behind me, like the whisper of expensive fabric brushing against itself.

I whirl around, fists raised and heart pounding, only to find a very tall, very good-looking guy with a modern pompadour and excellent taste in clothing, if the black silk shirt and black dress pants are any indication. He's leaning a shoulder against a bookshelf as he stares at me through narrowed arctic-blue eyes, his hands shoved deep into his pockets.

It takes a second for what I'm seeing to register, but when it does... Oh my God. Oh. My. God. This is *Hudson*. Wherever this room happens to be—*whatever* it happens to be—I'm trapped in it. With Jaxon's *sociopathic older brother.*

3

Just the idea has my stomach clenching and drops of nervous sweat rolling down my spine. But if my very short time at Katmere has taught me anything, it's to never show fear to a paranormal…at least not if I hope to get out of the situation alive.

So instead of screaming my head off—which part of me totally wants to do—I narrow my eyes right back at him. Then brace myself for God only knows what as I say, "Looks like the devil really does wear Gucci."

He snorts. "I already told you I'm a vampire, not a devil—though I suppose you could be forgiven for confusing the two, since you know my wayward little brother. Also, to be clear, *this* is *Armani*."

He says the last with the same reverence I usually reserve for cherry Pop-Tarts and Dr Pepper in the middle of a long study session.

I nearly laugh, and probably would have if I wasn't still reeling from the knowledge that this guy really *is* Hudson. In the flesh. Which means that whole moment in the hallway when I stepped in front of a sword wasn't a hallucination. Lia's plan worked—Hudson really is back. And for reasons I don't understand, I'm trapped with him in a Pottery Barn catalog.

As thoughts of everything I've heard about him these last couple of weeks race through my head, I choke out, "What exactly do you expect to get from doing this?"

"I already told you, this is your little soiree, not mine." He glances around with disdain. "And it's not exactly hopping, now, is it?"

"God, you are such a jackass." Frustration races through me, overwhelming the fear I should probably be feeling. I know this guy is a stone-cold killer, but he's also annoying. As. Fuck. "Could you just forget for one second that you're a psychopath and tell me what you want?"

At first, it looks like he's going to keep arguing with me. But then his face closes up, his eyes going blank as he answers, "Isn't it obvious? I want to have a tea party." His British accent is as sharp as a switchblade as it skates across my skin. "I do hope you like Earl Grey."

I barely resist telling him what he can do with his Earl Grey—and his sarcasm. But I have bigger fish to fry. "If you think I'm going to help you hurt Jaxon, that's not going to happen." I'd rather he just kill me now than let him turn me into a weapon against the boy I love.

"Please. If I wanted to hurt that little bastard, he'd already be dead." His voice is flat, his eyes bored, as he pulls out a cobalt-blue pocket square and starts to polish the face of his *very* expensive-looking watch.

Because polishing jewelry really is of the utmost importance right now.

"Correct me if I'm wrong," I say, shooting him a skeptical look. "But isn't *he* the one who killed *you*?"

"Is that what the tosser is telling people? That *he* killed *me*?" He gives a very proper sniff. "Not bloody likely."

"Considering it's been about a week and a half since I participated— unwillingly, mind you—in a ceremony to bring you back from the dead—"

"So that's what all that racket was?" he interrupts with a yawn. "And all this time I thought you were auditioning for the werewolves' yearly howl-a-thon."

My eyes narrow at the insult. "You know, you're an even bigger asshole than they said you were."

"To be fair, what's the point of being a small arsehole?" he asks, brow raised. "Mummy dearest always taught me if you're going to do something, you might as well be the best at it."

"Is that the same 'mummy dearest' who assaulted Jaxon when you died?" I respond, voice scathing.

He stills. "Is that how he got that scar?" He's still staring down at his watch, but for the first time since we began talking, his voice is devoid of its usual sarcasm. "He should have known better."

"Better than to kill you, despite everything you did?"

"Better than to trust her," he murmurs, and he sounds a thousand miles away. "I tried to—" He breaks off in the middle of the sentence, shaking his head like he wants to clear it.

"Tried to what?" I ask, the words slipping out even as I tell myself to let it go. It's not like I can believe anything he says anyway.

"Doesn't matter now." He shrugs and goes back to polishing his watch.

And smirking in that way that makes me want to scream and get the best of him at the same time.

I shove my hands into my pockets—so I don't try to strangle him with them—and my right hand brushes up against something that makes my heart sing. I tug the phone from my pocket and hold it up triumphantly. "I'll just call Jaxon to come get me—and take care of you once and for all!"

Hudson mutters something under his breath, but I don't pay him any attention. My pulse is racing as I tap open my messages app. I can't believe I didn't think about my phone before now. I bite my lip as I ponder what to say. I don't want to send Jaxon into a complete panic for my safety, but I really want him to come fast. In the end, I settle on a short message.

Am fine. Trapped with Hudson though. Sending location.

I hit send, then scroll down and tap "share my location." And wait.

After several seconds, a message pops up saying the text couldn't be delivered, and I nearly cry when I notice I have no bars. I blink away tears as I shove my phone back into my pocket and say the only thing that matters. "I want to go back to Katmere."

"By all means." Hudson must realize my phone isn't working because he gestures to the elaborately carved wooden door that's several feet away from us. "Feel free."

"You didn't bring me here through that door." I don't understand how I know that, considering everything between Katmere and here is a blank, but I do.

"Once again, *I* didn't bring you here at all," he answers, and the smug amusement is back.

"Don't lie to me," I grate out. "I *know* you did this."

"Do you?" He lifts one dark, perfectly arched brow. "Well, then. Since you know *everything*, enlighten me. Please. How precisely am I supposed to have managed all of *this*?"

"How the hell am I supposed to know how you did it?" I shoot back, and by now my fingernails are digging into my palms so hard that I'm afraid I'll draw blood...which will lead to a whole new slew of problems. Especially considering, "I just know that you did. You're the vampire, after all."

"I am, indeed. And that matters because...?" This time both brows go up.

"Because you're the one with the power. Obviously."

"Obviously," he repeats with just a hint of scorn. "Except I already told you. Vampires can't do this."

"You don't actually expect me to believe that, do you?"

"Why not?" But the look he shoots me is somehow both condescending and accusatory. "Oh, right. Because if something strange happens, it must be the vampire's fault."

No way I'm going to fall for the "poor little vampire" routine he seems to be taking out for a spin right now. I know exactly what he did. And exactly how many people he's hurt with his actions.

Including Jaxon.

"The reason I don't trust you has nothing to do with you being a vampire," I tell him. "And everything to do with you being a psychopathic prick with a god complex."

That startles a laugh out of him, followed by an amused, "Don't hold back. Tell me how you really feel."

"Oh, I'm just getting warmed up." I put as much badass into my voice as I can muster up. "Keep me here much longer, and I promise I'll make sure you regret it."

It's obviously an empty threat, considering there's not much I can do that will hurt Hudson.

Something he is very much aware of, judging by the look in his eyes—not to mention the "oh yeah?" grin he's wearing as he pushes off the bookcase to stand to his full height. Right before he says, "Tell me, Grace. How exactly do you plan on doing that?"

4

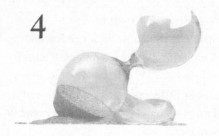

Every Little Thing He
Does Is *Not* Magic
—Grace—

Hudson crosses his arms over his chest as he waits for me to answer. The only problem? I don't have an answer. Partly because I haven't been in this new world long enough to understand how anyone's powers work, even Jaxon's or Macy's. And partly because Hudson is being so jerky about the whole thing that it's impossible for me to think.

I mean, how can I come up with a plan when he's staring at me like that, his bright blue eyes amused and his ridiculous lips twisted into that obnoxious smirk I'm growing to know all too well?

There's no way. I can't. Not when he's just waiting for me to fail. Or worse, to ask him for help.

As if.

I'd rather go another round with Cole and his not-so-merry band of werewolves than ask Jaxon's brother for help. Besides, it's not like I can trust anything he says anyway. He is a known murderer, liar, sociopath, and God only knows what else…

It's the last thought that gets me moving, that has me racing toward the door. Hudson says that he's not the one to blame for us being here, that I'm the one doing this. But isn't that what any sociopathic liar would say if he wanted to convince someone to stay put?

It is, and I'm not falling for it one second longer. I'd like to get out of here with my skin—and everything else—still intact.

"Hey!" For the first time, Hudson sounds a little alarmed—which is only more proof in my mind that I'm doing the right thing. "What are you doing?"

"Getting away from you," I snarl over my shoulder as I pull open the door and dash outside before I can let the nerves skittering down my spine change my mind.

It's dark out, so dark that my heart starts pounding and my stomach clenches in fear. For a moment, I think about changing my mind, about turning around and going back inside. But the only way to get back to Katmere, and to Jaxon, is to get the hell away from Hudson. Besides, I'm never going to figure out where I am—or anything else for that matter—when I'm stuck in that room.

So I force myself to keep running straight into the dark, despite the uneasiness that has my heart pumping much too fast. The night sky remains pitch-black and empty above me, no stars or a moon to help lead me to safety, which is terrifying enough as it is.

But as long as this path takes me away from Hudson, that's good enough for me.

Except, all of a sudden, something makes a rustling noise behind me. Fear clogs my throat even as I push myself to run faster. Not that I'll be able to outrun a vampire—Lia taught me that—but I'm still going to try.

But the rustling sounds again, followed by a flapping noise directly above me. I have one second to glance up, one second to register that a vampire—even Hudson—is the least of my worries, before a sharp, terrifying shriek splits the night air.

5

Hot and Not
So Heavy
—Hudson—

The way Grace is running straight toward the giant, flame-shooting plonker of a beast currently tearing through the sky directly at her tells me the anti-Hudson propaganda machine has obviously been hard at work in the time I've been gone. I mean, how bad could she possibly think I am that she's willing to risk an attack by *that* instead of staying in here with me, where it's safe?

The way she glances over her shoulder at me like she's terrified that I'm about to rip her throat out with my fangs when she should be focused on the threat directly above her pretty much proves my theory, in my opinion.

I move to go back inside—no skin off my arse if she gets herself eaten—but then the bloody beast screams as it swoops down toward her. I wait, certain that she'll finally figure out that I'm not the bad guy here and turn around.

Instead, she glances up at it and *keeps running* away from safety.

Forget the queen. God save girls who believe everything they hear. And leap before they look.

This time when the beast roars, it spits a stream of fire that turns the sky in front of her into an inferno. She still doesn't turn around, though. Instead, she freezes, turning herself into a giant human-size target. One the beast—or is it a dragon?—seems more than chuffed to aim for.

Big surprise.

Another streak of flames rips through the night. Grace manages to dodge them as she jumps to the left, but it's a near-miss. Way too close for comfort, which is proven by the smell of singed hair that fills the air between us.

It's a nauseating scent.

Again, I think about going back inside. After all, who am I to interfere with her newfound career as barbecue? Especially when she's made it abundantly clear that she'd rather be burned alive than spend any more time with me.

I nearly manage it. I even make it over the threshold. But then she screams.

It's a thin, high-pitched sound that sends a chill straight to my bones. Fuck. Just fuck. She might have brought this on herself, but I can't ignore her fear, no matter how much she bloody well deserves it.

And she does deserve it. She's the one who got us into this bloody mess to begin with. But much as I might wish otherwise, being a pain in the arse isn't enough of a reason to let someone die. If it was, I would have let my little brother go belly-up a long time ago.

I turn back around in time to see the dragon encircle her in flames. I give myself a moment to grieve—this *is* my favorite Armani shirt I'm wearing, after all—before I fade straight to her.

I feel the flames before I even reach her. They're sizzling hot as they lick at my face, my skin, but I'm in and out so fast that a few burns are all I get. They sting like hell—dragon flames will do that to a guy—but it's nothing I can't handle.

And it's nothing compared to my monthly training sessions with dear old Dad.

It's hard to win with a man who thinks the only wounds that matter are the ones you can't see.

I grab onto Grace as the dragon gears up for another round, pulling her into my arms. As I do, I stumble over a rock on the ground and end up grabbing her more tightly than I intend to as I struggle to keep my balance.

She stiffens against me. "What are you—"

"Saving your arse," I snarl, wrapping as much of me around her as I can manage in an effort to protect her from the fire. Then I fade straight back to the room where we started. The dragon's on my arse the whole way, flying faster than any dragon I've ever seen.

I cross the threshold with Grace in my arms and slam the door behind us.

I barely have a chance to set her on her feet before the dragon crashes into the door so hard, he rattles the entire structure.

Grace yelps, but I'm too busy lunging for the dead bolt to notice. I slide it into place just before the bloody dragon crashes against the door again. And again. And again.

"What does he want?" Grace asks.

"Are you serious?" I shoot her an incredulous look. "I don't know where you're from, but in this world, things eat you the second you drop your guard."

"Yourself included?" she asks snidely.

And there it is. More proof that no good deed goes unpunished. Somehow I keep forgetting that.

"Why don't you push me a little further and find out?" I lean forward, snapping my teeth together with a loud click. "You're welcome, by the way."

She looks at me incredulously. "You really expect me to thank you?"

"It is customary when someone saves your life." But apparently that doesn't matter to her.

"Saves my life?" Her laugh grates like nails on a chalkboard. "You're the reason I was in danger to begin with."

I'm getting damn sick of this girl accusing me of shit I haven't done. "Are we seriously back to that?"

"We never left it. It's kind of the whole reason I..." She pauses as if searching for the right word.

"Ran outside and nearly got flame-roasted?" I supply in my most helpful tone.

She narrows her eyes at me. "Do you always have to be such a jerk?"

"My apologies. Next time I'll let you burn." I start to move past her, but she steps in front of me, blocking my way, her gaze remaining fixed on something over my shoulder.

There's a flicker of fear deep in her eyes, but all I see is a vast, empty black sky framed by a window reflected in her gaze. And just like that, I get my first inkling about where we might be. And it's not pretty.

6

In One Head and
Out the Other
—Grace—

"Yeah, well, it's your fault I nearly burned to begin with." I drag my gaze from the window and snark at him. If he hadn't trapped us here, none of this would be happening.

Instead of running for my life from some kind of fire-breathing dragon monster, I'd be hanging out in Jaxon's tower instead. Maybe curled up on the couch with a book or tucked up next to him in his bedroom, talking about—

"Oh, for fook's sake. Tell me I'm not going to get treated to another litany about how much you like being in bed with my brother." He clutches his hand to his chest in what I assume is some kind of bizarre imitation of me. "Oh, Jaxy-Waxy. My goth little vampire. You're so strong and sooooo fooked up. I just love you soooo much." He rolls his eyes as he says the last.

"You know what? You're disgusting," I growl, pushing past him.

"Yeah, like that's the first time I've been called that," he answers with a shrug. "Then again, your judgment *is* seriously impaired."

"*My* judgment? You're the one who murdered half of Katmere A—"

"It wasn't anywhere near half." He yawns. "Get your facts straight."

I start to make another comment about how less than half doesn't make it any better, but there's something in his eyes, in his voice, that makes me think he's not quite as immune to my observations as he'd like to be.

Not that I should care—the guy is a mass murderer, after all—but I've never been one to kick someone else when they're down. Besides, it's not like insulting him is my best way out of this place.

"Go ahead and insult me all you want," Hudson comments as he tucks his hands into his pockets and leans a shoulder against the nearest wall. "It still won't solve our problem."

"No, only you can do that—" I break off as I realize something. "Hey! Stop that!"

"Stop what?" he asks, brows raised.

I narrow my eyes at him. "You know exactly what you're doing!"

"Au contraire." He gives a guileless shrug that makes me wish I believed that violence actually solved problems. "I know what *you're* doing. I'm just along for the ride."

"Yeah, well, if that ride involves reading my mind, *stop it*."

"Believe me, nothing would thrill me more," he answers with that ridiculous smirk of his. I'm beginning to *loathe* that smirk. "It's not like there's anything interesting going on in there anyway."

My hands tighten into fists as outrage tears through me at the admission—and the insult—implicit in his words. I want nothing more than to tell him off, but no matter what he says, I'm smart enough to have figured out that that will only egg him on.

And since the last thing I want is for Hudson Vega to take up full-time residence in my head, I grit my teeth. Force my annoyance back down. And half whisper, half shout, "Well, then you should have no trouble staying out of it, should you?"

"If only it were that easy." He gives a mock-sad shake of his head. "But since you've trapped us in here, it's not like I've got a choice."

"I already told you. I'm not the one trapping us in this room—"

"Oh, I'm not just talking about this room." The gleam in his eye turns predatory. "I'm talking about the fact that you've trapped us inside your head. And neither of us is getting out of here until you accept that."

"Inside my head?" I scoff. "Are you flat-out lying or are you delusional?"

"I don't lie."

"So delusional, then?" I ask, knowing I sound obnoxious and not caring in the slightest. God knows, Hudson has been obnoxious from the second he told me to turn on the *fooking lights.*

"If you're so sure that I'm wrong—"

"I am," I interrupt. Because he is.

He crosses his arms over his chest, continuing like I haven't just interrupted him. "Then why don't you come up with a better explanation?"

"I've already told you my explanation," I snarl. "You—"

It's his turn to interrupt. "One that doesn't involve me being responsible for this. Because I've already told you that isn't the case."

"And I've already told you that I don't believe you," I shoot back. "Because if this was all in my head, if I actually had a choice of who to be trapped with, you would be the last person on that list. Not to mention I sure as shit wouldn't bring a fire-breathing hell beast along for the ride. I don't have a clue what that thing is, but I do know that my imagination isn't twisted enough to have thought it up."

I look around at the room. At the ax-throwing target-practice area. At the couch littered with gaming controllers. At the wall filled with record albums. At the billion and one weights scattered around a black leather bench.

At Hudson.

Then continue. "My imagination would not have thought *any* of this up for a prison."

As if to underscore my point, the dragon—or whatever that thing is—crashes into the door with enough power to shake the whole room. The walls shudder, the shelves rattle, the wood creaks. And my already pounding heart starts to beat like a metronome on high.

Taking a page out of Hudson's book, I slide my hands into my pockets and lean against the closest chair. If I do it to hide the fact that my hands are trembling—and my knees are so shaky that I'm not sure they'll support me much longer—then it's nobody's business but mine.

Not that he'd probably notice anyway. Right now, he's too busy trying to sell me on his twisted version of events to pay attention me just barely fighting off the beginning stages of a panic attack.

"Why on earth would I make this up?" I ask after clearing my throat to get rid of the sudden tightening there. "I assure you I don't need an adrenaline rush to feel alive. And I'm *not* masochistic."

"Well, then, you really did pick a piss-poor mate, didn't you?" Hudson replies caustically. But he's moving, and I'm paying more attention to that than his actual words, as every cell in my body is screaming for me not to take my eyes off him. Screaming that I can't afford to have him where I can't see him.

"Yes, I'm the threat here," he sneers as the monster crashes into the wall directly behind where he's walking past. "Not whatever the hell is out there."

"So you admit that I'm not doing this! That that thing—whatever it is—is not of my making," I crow, and yes, I'm aware that celebrating that win while a monster circles us is a little like the dance band on the *Titanic* playing "Nearer My God to Thee" as the ship went down. But small—and by small, I mean *minute*—victories have been in short supply in my life since I got to Katmere

Academy, so I'm going to hang on to every one I get.

Hudson doesn't answer right away. I don't know if that's because he's trying to think up a good rebuttal or if it's because my stomach chooses that moment to growl—loudly. But whatever his reason is, it ceases to matter as the dragon lets out a blood-curdling roar. Right before he makes another attempt to get inside.

And this time he doesn't go for the door. He goes straight for the giant window directly in front of me.

Burning Down
the Louse
—Hudson—

I'm already fading several feet to the left as Grace opens her mouth to scream.

I grab hold of her for the second time tonight, pulling her flush against me just as the shite dragon slams his powerful head through the window behind us. Glass shatters, flying everywhere, but I stay where I am, doing my best to block the shards careening through the air in all directions.

Of course, Grace thanks me by screaming loudly in my ear. Huge surprise.

Pain radiates through my supernaturally sensitive eardrum and, not for the first time tonight, I think about leaving her to her own devices. This whole clusterfuck *is* her fault, after all. But several streams of fire have immediately followed the exploding glass, and I don't have it in me to just fade away and leave her here, at the dragon's mercy.

As we rush away from him, the beast roars loudly enough to drown out Grace's screams—a small blessing—but that doesn't last long. The girl certainly has a set of lungs on her.

More's the pity.

"Pipe down for a minute, will you?" I demand as I fade us toward the small bathroom at the end of the room. She may think screaming is some kind of protection against getting fried, but I know differently. If anything, it will just get the arsing dragon more pissed off.

Vampires aren't the only ones with sensitive hearing. And this dragon seems a little more sensitive—and a little more everything—than most.

Fire whips by us as we head through the narrow bathroom door, followed closely by a loud crash. Once again, the room shakes violently.

I glance behind me to see what the damn creature is up to now. I half expect to have to dodge more fire, but the flames are gone as suddenly as they appeared.

As is the dragon itself. Not through any choice of his own but because the window he just broke through has disappeared as well. In its place is a series of painted bricks, the same color as the wall around them.

"Not doing this, my arse," I snort, dropping Grace down on the bathroom counter with a thump. Windows don't wall themselves off. Someone has to *do* it. And in this case, that someone is Grace.

Whether or not she wants to admit it—to herself or to me—is something only time will tell.

At least she's stopped screaming. I may be trapped here with her for the foreseeable future, but I'm still counting that as a win. Especially if the silence lasts for more than five minutes.

"How did you get him to stop?" she asks, well before my hoped-for five minutes are up. But she doesn't scream it, so I'm still calling it a success.

"I didn't." I nod to the bricked-up window. "You did."

"That's impossible." But she's staring at the newly built wall, eyes wide. "Walls don't just form out of thin air."

"Apparently, they do." My back is burning like hell itself—a nice little by-product that comes with being struck by dragon fire. I whip off what's left of my shirt in an effort to get a look at the damage. And to stop the edges of the fabric from brushing against the wound.

"What are you doing?" Grace squawks, once again entirely too close to my eardrum.

Apparently, five minutes was extremely optimistic on my part. Which is saying something, considering I'm not exactly known for my sunny outlook.

"Do you have to keep shouting?" I growl as I take a large step away from her. "I'm right here."

"Do you have to take your clothes off?" she mimics with a shudder of disgust. "I'm right here."

Has any one human *ever* been more annoying?

I grind my teeth together in an attempt to stop myself from sinking them into her—and not in the good way. I've never drained anyone dry before, but there's always a first time. And right now, Grace Foster seems like the perfect candidate on which to pop that particular cherry.

Of course, I might be trapped here forever if I do, but that won't be anything new. I've spent most of my life trapped somewhere. At least it will be quiet again.

"Next time, I'll let that dragon have you." I turn to look over my shoulder, trying to figure out how much damage the damnable flying beast did. But despite the more fanciful paranormal lore out there, vampires aren't equipped with the ability to rotate their heads 360 degrees.

More's the pity. That trick would come in handy in here, especially since it's not like I can exactly check myself out in the mirror. But I've been in worse scrapes than this and managed to get myself fixed up and through them. Why should this be any different?

"What are you doing?" Grace asks again—and this time it's at a normal decibel. Thank God.

Maybe that's why I tell her the truth. "The dragon got me."

"What?" she gasps. "Let me see!"

"That's really not nec—"

"You don't get to tell me what's necessary," she answers, grabbing my shoulders before I can finish the protest.

I'm so surprised that I don't fight her as she spins me around like vinyl on my favorite turntable.

"Oh my God!"

And we're back to yelling. I swear this girl's voice only has two pitches. Normal and excruciating.

It's a miracle Jaxon can put up with it.

Then again, having someone who cares enough about you to get upset probably eases the eardrum pain. Not to mention the rest of the pain, too.

"The dragon did this to you?" she asks, still loud enough to make my ears ache.

This time I don't bother to hide my wince—maybe she'll finally get the message and quiet down a decibel or ninety—as I put a little more distance between us. "Well, I sure as shite didn't do it to myself."

"Yeah, but I thought vampires healed quickly? Isn't that one of the upsides of being one?"

"To be fair, there aren't a lot of downsides," I say with a smirk.

I'm facing the mirror now, and though I can't see myself in it, I can see her roll her eyes at me very clearly. "Yeah, okay. Maybe not. But that doesn't answer my question. Shouldn't one of those special powers of yours have healed most of this damage already?"

"I'm a vampire," I tell her, my voice dry as dust. "Not a superhero."

She laughs. "You know what I mean."

I do, actually. Which is probably why I give in and explain when I've made it a habit to *never* explain anything about myself.

"If I was burned by regular fire, it would hurt, but it would heal in a couple of minutes. These burns came from dragon fire, though. Which means they hurt a lot more than regular burns would. And they'll take longer to heal."

"How much longer?" she asks.

I shrug, then regret it as the action sends another wave of burning pain through my back. "A couple of days or so."

"That sucks," she whispers, and this time when she glances over my back, the hard look in her eyes is gone. It's replaced by something softer. Something that looks an awful lot like concern—or pity.

Either way, it makes me uncomfortable. And that's before she reaches out a gentle hand and smooths it over my aching, burning back.

I brace myself for pain, but it doesn't hurt. In fact, it feels nice. A lot nicer than it should.

And fuck. Just fuck.

Because everything about this situation just keeps getting *so much worse*.

Eat, Drink,
and Be Wary
—Grace—

Hudson shivers as I slide a finger down the edges of his damaged skin. "I'm sorry." I yank my hand back, feeling like a monster. "I tried to be gentle. Did I hurt you?"

"No." His answer is short, but his voice isn't snarly for once. Just empty. I don't know why that seems so much worse.

His back is to me, so I glance in the mirror to see if I can read his expression. Except there's nothing reflected in the mirror but me. There's definitely no stony-faced vampire with the personality of a caged tiger who also somehow still manages to have the most expressive eyes I've ever seen.

Because vampires have no reflections...

The realization washes over me, and not for the first time, it hits me how different my life is at this moment from a couple short weeks ago. Not just because of my parents and Katmere Academy and *Jaxon* but because I really am living among monsters.

Well, one particular monster at the moment, I think as I stare at Hudson's back. And not just any monster. I'm stuck here with the one monster the other monsters are afraid of.

The one monster who managed to destroy so many of them with just a thought. Just a whisper.

It's a terrifying realization. Or it should be. But as I stare at Hudson's hurt back, he doesn't seem nearly as scary as everyone has made him out to be. He seems like any other damaged boy.

And an attractive one at that.

The thought slips into my brain unbidden, but once it's there, I can't help but acknowledge the truth of it. If you somehow find a way to discount his sociopathic and psychopathic tendencies, Hudson is a very attractive guy.

Not as attractive as Jaxon, obviously—no one is—but he's definitely good-looking. In a purely objective, "never going to be interested in him" way, of course. Then again, how could I be, when I've got the sexiest, and the best, guy in the world waiting for me back at school?

Waiting for me and probably freaking out because he doesn't know what happened to me.

Tears burn behind my eyes at the thought.

I hate that Jaxon is worrying about me right now. Hate that Macy and Uncle Finn probably are, too. I've come to love them all so much in the short time I've been at Katmere, and I can't stand the idea that my absence is hurting them. I especially hate that it's hurting Jaxon, who is more than just my boyfriend. He's my mate.

I still don't know exactly what it means to have a mate, but I know that Jaxon is mine. It hurts to be away from him, but I at least know he's safe. I can't imagine how much worse it must be for him, not knowing where I am or if I'm okay. Especially since the last person he saw me with is *Hudson*.

"Poor little Jaxy-Waxy. He must be suffering so." I don't have to be able to see Hudson's face to know he's rolling his eyes again.

Which makes me annoyed enough to huff, "Just because you can't possibly understand what he's going through doesn't mean you need to make fun of him."

"Afraid his fragile ego can't take it?" he shoots back.

"More like afraid I'll strangle you if you keep being an ass."

"By all means." Hudson bends his knees just enough to make his neck accessible to me. "Do your worst."

Part of me wants to take him up on the offer, to show him that he should be afraid of me even though he clearly isn't. Another part of me is too scared to even try, though. I may have gotten out of that trap Lia set for me with the help of Jaxon, but there's no way I'm strong enough to take on a vampire alone. Especially not one as strong as Hudson.

Being human definitely has its downsides in this world. Then again, I guess it has a downside in any world. Look at my parents.

For a moment, my mom's face dances in front of my eyes. But I slam the door shut on it—on her—before I can sink into the sadness. Sink into the pain of missing her, especially when I'm trapped in this place with a—

"So sorry to interrupt your pity party before it becomes downright maudlin," Hudson says in a voice that is anything but. "But I've got to ask.

If you're going to spend all night feeling sorry for yourself, can you give me ten minutes to get cleaned up first? I'd like to at least grab a shower before you bore me to sleep."

It takes a moment for his words to register. When they do, outrage explodes through me. My hands shake, my stomach twists, and it takes every ounce of self-control I have not to lash out at him. But I won't give him the satisfaction of knowing he got to me. He doesn't deserve it.

"Hate to be the one to break it to you, Princess. But I'm in your head. I already know I got to you." He sounds even more bored, if possible.

Which only pisses me off all over again. It's bad enough I have to put up with this guy in my head, but having him pick apart my every thought is freaking me out.

Still, even knowing that's what he's going for can't stop me from snarling, "I despise you."

"And here I thought we were getting to be best mates," he deadpans. "I was so looking forward to making friendship bracelets and exchanging dating tips with you."

"Oh my God." This time my fingers curl all the way into fists. Fists I want nothing more than to plow into his sanctimonious, too-perfect nose. "Don't you *ever* get tired of being an ass?"

"It hasn't happened yet." He pauses, as if to consider. Then shrugs. "Keep us here long enough and maybe we'll both find out."

"Are we seriously back to that again?" I ask with a resigned sigh. I'm already freaked out and tired—who wouldn't be in my situation?—and arguing with Hudson is only making me more of both. "You sound like a broken record."

"And you sound completely naive."

"Naive?" I repeat, and I know there's insult in my voice.

He raises a brow. "It's either naiveté or willful ignorance. Which one do you prefer?"

"Whichever one gets me away from you faster," I shoot back.

I'm pretty proud of the comeback—or I would be if my stomach didn't choose that exact second to growl again. Loudly.

My cheeks flush with embarrassment, and they only grow hotter when Hudson smirks.

"You know," he muses, rubbing a hand over the back of his head, "there's a way to settle this argument once and for all."

"Oh yeah?" I speak a little too loudly, trying to cover up the fact that my stomach is grumbling again. "And what's that?"

He walks out of the bathroom and over to the tiny kitchen near the front corner of the room. "Figure out what kind of food is stocked in this place."

"What will that show?" I ask even as I follow him.

He tosses me a look that asks if I'm being deliberately dense. But in the end, he answers, "I'm a vampire."

As if that explains everything—and it kind of does, because he's obviously referencing the blood thing—he opens a kitchen cabinet. "If I was doing this, I'm pretty sure I wouldn't have filled this cabinet with..." He pulls out a rectangular blue box. "Cherry Pop-Tarts?"

9

From One Blink to the Necks
—Grace—

"**I** don't even know what a Pop-Tart is," he continues as he turns the box over and over in his hands, as if staring at it will give him some clue what he's looking at.

Judging from the continued question in his eyes, it doesn't. And for the first time, I wonder if maybe—just maybe—Hudson is telling the truth. It goes against everything I know about him, everything I want to believe about him, but as I pull open a couple more cabinets, it's hard to think that there's another explanation for what's going on here.

Especially since the cabinets are filled with more of my regular snacks. Peanut butter crackers. Popcorn. Salt and vinegar chips. And half of a twenty-pack of my beloved Dr Pepper. Which seems curious—at least until I open the small fridge next to the stove and find ten cold Dr Peppers lined up in the door, not to mention several Liquid Death sparkling waters—lime flavored, of course—and a few of my favorite Pamplemousse La Croixs.

There's also a drawer full of my favorite apples, a bunch of red grapes, some pears, and the makings for several different kinds of grilled-cheese sandwiches.

Either whoever stocked this kitchen has eerily similar tastes to mine or I'm somehow in charge of this whole thing. Considering I'm human, with absolutely no power of my own, such a thing seems completely impossible. But here we are.

And since two weeks ago, none of this seemed possible—especially being in love with a vampire and being related to a bunch of witches—I decide to withhold judgment. For a little while at least.

After grabbing an apple and a La Croix from the fridge, I turn to Hudson, who's just wandered back into the kitchen sporting a new shirt. Thank God.

I expect him to gloat, or to at least shoot me a triumphant look or ten, but instead he's just standing there, head bowed and hands braced against the counter as if it's the only thing holding him up.

Even worse, he's shaking. It's a fine tremor, one I might have missed if I wasn't watching him so closely. But I am watching him closely now, and it's impossible not to see it. His face might be blank and those expressive eyes of his focused downward, but if these last few weeks have given me nothing else, they've given me the ability to recognize pain when it's right in front of me.

And while some people might go so far as to say that Hudson deserves whatever pain he's feeling after all the shit he's done, I can't help remembering that he got those dragon burns trying to rescue me. Which means it really is up to me to help him, whether I want to or not.

Not giving myself time to think—or him time to say something that would make me change my mind again—I stride back to the bathroom and pull out a bottle of peroxide from beneath the sink. I don't give myself a chance to question how I knew the first aid supplies would be there, along with a bottle of Tylenol and some pain-numbing antibiotic cream. Instead, I just grab everything, plus some gauze and a few bandages, then head back to the kitchen.

To Hudson.

"Take off your shirt," I tell him in the most no-nonsense voice I can manage as I twist off the top of the peroxide bottle.

He doesn't budge. Though his lips twist into a snarky grin as he answers, "No offense, Curly, but you're really not my type."

"Look, Hudson, I know those burns hurt. I'm offering to help. And this time I won't change my mind."

"Don't worry about it." He stands up, shoving his hands into his pockets in a move I know he wants to look nonchalant. It would probably be more effective if he wasn't still trembling a little. "I can take care of myself."

"I'm pretty sure if that was true, you would already have done it," I answer. "So can you just cut the bullshit and take off your shirt so we can get this over with?"

He arches one brow at me. "Now, how can I resist a charming offer like that?" He glances down at the medicine in my hands. "Look, I appreciate the thought, but none of that is going to work."

"Oh." I hadn't considered that. "Are vampires immune to human medicine?"

"No. But we are immune to just about everything we might need human medicine to cure." Hudson nods toward the Neosporin in my hand. "Like the bacteria that antibiotic cream is designed to kill. I don't need the cream because the bacteria can't hurt me."

"Fair enough." I incline my head in a touché kind of gesture. "But I picked this out because of its numbing qualities, not its germ-killing abilities. And I still think it's worth a shot. Unless you really don't think this kind of medicine will work against something supernatural, like dragon fire."

He starts to shrug, then catches himself with a wince. "I don't know if it works or not. Leave it here, and I'll give it a try."

"You'll give it a try?" I eye him doubtfully. "I know vampires can do just about anything—or so they say—but I'm pretty sure you're going to need a little help reaching your own back."

"I'm used to doing things on my own. I don't need any—"

"Help," I finish for him, ignoring the flash of pity that tears through me at the thought of anyone—even Hudson—being so alone in their life that they've learned to do everything by themselves. "Blah, blah, blah. Save it, Tick Boy. I've heard all the excuses."

"*Tick boy?*" he repeats in his very proper British accent. I've only known him a few hours, but I'm pretty sure he's never sounded more offended in his life.

Good. The last thing I want to do is make friends with Jaxon's evil older brother. But I don't have it in me to watch him suffer if he doesn't have to. I'd do the same for anyone.

Besides, if he's lying to me and he *is* the one doing this to us, I figure it's better to keep him alive. How the hell am I going to find my way out of this place on my own?

"Don't look so surprised," I say as I open the packages of gauze so I have easy access to them. "You both suck blood, don't you?"

"It's not the same thing," he growls.

I twist off the top of the antibiotic cream so that it's ready, too. "You only say that because you don't know what it's like being fed on."

"And you do, hmm?" There's a new look in his eyes, one that has me shaking in my shoes.

Not that I'm about to let him know that. Give a guy like Hudson an inch, and he'll take about twenty miles.

"Will you just turn around?" I tell him in the most bored voice I can muster as I hold up the peroxide.

Thankfully, the strange look is gone as quickly as it came. And now his only response is to cross his arms over his chest and glare down at me in annoyance. He still looks intimidating as fuck, even with obvious pain in his eyes.

But this is an intimidating I can work with. After all, I spent most of my first week at Katmere having Jaxon glare at me in the exact same manner. I'm pretty much immune at this point.

"You're going to have to show a lot more fang if you want to scare *me*," I tell him in the most bored voice I can manage.

"That can be arranged." And in the space from one blink to the next, he's covered the distance between us. And his fangs are at my neck.

"Don't tempt me," he growls, so close that I can feel his breath brush my ear. "You're not the only one who's hungry here."

Terror has my heart beating like a hummingbird's wings, fast and thready and just a little bit painful. But there's no way I'll give Hudson the satisfaction of knowing just how terrified I am.

Of him, of this place, of never seeing Jaxon again.

So I shove a hand through my curls and turn my head until we are eye to eye, nose to nose. And say, "Bite me!" just before I dump half the bottle of peroxide onto his back, shirt and all.

Burning Your Britches
—Hudson—

"**W**hat the everlasting fuck did you do that for?" I roar as my back catches fire in a whole new way, the wet shirt clinging to the burns now.

"Stop being a baby," Grace tells me as she ducks out of my hold. "Your back needs to be cleaned."

"I already told you that shit doesn't matter," I bark, reaching down to grab the hem of the shirt and whipping it over my head. As the cool air hits the burns, I wince. "We can't get infections!"

"Yeah, well, you aren't exactly the most trustworthy person I've ever met," she answers as she moves around behind me. "I'm not sure the peroxide helped anything, but it didn't make anything worse."

"Says the woman whose back doesn't currently burn like hellfire itself."

"Could you please stop whining for ten seconds?" I can't see the bloody girl, but I can still hear the eye roll in her voice. "It's getting old."

Two dozen retorts dance on the tip of my tongue, but I snap my teeth together. Knowing Grace as I am getting to, I'm fairly certain anything I say will be called whining.

Which is rich considering she's mated to my mealy-mouthed little brother, whose every word is either a whine or a complaint. But I guess the mating bond makes even the worst shit look like rainbows and confetti. More's the pity.

Grace pulls some gauze out of the package on the counter, and I eye her warily. "I can take it from here."

"Yeah, I can tell."

For once, her voice is as dry as mine. And as unimpressed. I have to say, that doesn't exactly instill confidence in her nursing abilities.

I brace myself for her to scrub at my burns with the gauze, as compassion over competence seems to be her deal. But her touch is surprisingly gentle as she brushes gauze against my back, blotting the excess peroxide off instead of wiping at it in a way that would further irritate my burned skin.

Her gentleness doesn't stop the pain radiating through my muscles into my bones, but it doesn't make it worse, either. Which is why I stay where I am and let her do whatever she's going to do. Well, that, and having someone else touch me—even if it is platonic, even if she is my brother's mate—feels good after so many decades of solitude.

"I'm going to put the cream on now," Grace tells me after she's dried off my whole back. "Hopefully it will help."

I'm not counting on it, but I stay where I am as she squeezes the salve onto her fingers. The moment her fingers brush against my back, though, I stiffen.

"Does it hurt? I'm trying to be as soft as I can."

"It's fine," I answer. Because, shockingly, it is. Everywhere her fingers touch, the burn lessens. It doesn't disappear, but any downgrade from excruciating to annoying feels bloody brilliant to me.

Her fingers continue to slide over my charred skin, and a not-unpleasant coolness takes the place of the burn. It's followed by a new kind of warmth that has me glancing over my shoulder. Because Grace can insist that she's human all she wants, but there's no way some human cream—pain-relieving or not—is making this much of a difference.

No, the healing, or whatever it is, has to be coming from Grace. Whether she knows it or not.

I'm not in the mood for another dissertation on all the reasons I don't know what I'm talking about, though, so I keep what I'm still figuring out to myself. I've got no intention of giving her any knowledge she could try to use against me anyway.

Two hundred years at the mercy of my father's whims have taught me the folly of that.

"Okay, I think I've got them all covered." Grace steps back. "I don't think we should bandage them. They already look better, but we should probably let them breathe for a little while."

I watch as she twists the cap back on the cream and try to ignore the fact that my back hurts more now that she's not touching me. It pisses me off, even though I know it's only because she's got some kind of healing gift she's unaware of. But I don't like needing anyone for anything. And I sure as shit don't like feeling indebted to my brother's mate.

Which is why I don't thank her for her help. And I don't stick around for any more chitchat, either. I fade to the bedroom area at the other end of the room as Grace moves to the small kitchen sink to wash her hands.

"Hey! What are you doing?" she squawks as I start gathering up a truly copious amount of throw pillows from the bed and toss them onto the floor.

As I consider what I'm doing fairly self-explanatory, I don't bother to answer. Instead, I look around for something else to do and settle for grabbing the top of the quilt and dragging it to the foot of the bed.

Grace can't fade, and her legs are ridiculously short—much like the rest of her—so it takes her a good minute to make the same journey that took me about three seconds. But eventually she makes it to the bedroom area and slaps her hands onto her hips as she asks, "Are you seriously going to go to bed? Now?"

"It's been a long week, Princess. I'm tired." I keep my back to her as I turn down the sheets.

"Yeah, but we still haven't figured out what to do!" She's so indignant that her voice actually squeaks a little at the end.

"And we're not going to tonight." As if to underscore my statement, the dragon chooses this moment to crash into the roof. The whole room shakes as a result.

"You don't really think we're going to be able to sleep with that thing circling, trying to find a way in?" She looks up at the ceiling like she expects it to collapse in on us at any minute.

"He's not getting in," I answer with more confidence than I actually have. "And if he does, we'll handle him."

"Handle him?" She's gone from squeaking to outright screeching. "How exactly do you think we're going to do that?"

"I've got a few tricks up my sleeve," I answer, glancing at the bricked-up window yet again. "And so do you."

"You're not seriously back to that again, are you?" she demands. "I didn't do that."

"Okay." Because I really am exhausted—being brought back from "the dead" isn't exactly easy on a guy—I don't fight her. Instead, I reach down and unbuckle my belt.

I figure it will be enough to make her run, but Grace just narrows her eyes at me. Apparently, she's dug in and ready for another fight.

Too bad I'm not. Which is why I reach down and unbutton the waistband of my pants.

But all that does is make her cross her arms over her chest as she pulls a card out of my deck and leans a shoulder against the nearest wall.

I'll admit, I'm a little impressed and a lot amused. I'm also not about to back down from the dare implicit in her eyes.

So I'm left with only one option at this point.

I slide the zipper down and let my wool Armani dress pants fall to the ground at my feet.

Sleep Like
the Undead
—Grace—

udson Vega wears boxer briefs.

And not just any boxer briefs. *Versace* boxer briefs in red and green and blue and peach and *gold*, which cover nowhere near as much as a pair of shorts would.

Not that they look like any shorts I've ever seen. No, these boxers are gaudy as hell, and they know it. No, they celebrate it. They've got a coat of arms on one side, an elaborate crown on the other, with color blocking and a sword—a freaking black-and-gold-and-blue sword—over the crotch.

I don't know if it's truth in advertising or delusions of grandeur, and I have no intention of ever finding out. But even I have to admit, Hudson might be the only person on the planet who actually looks good in them.

Not that I'll ever let him know that—especially since how good or bad he looks in a pair of boxers doesn't matter to me in the slightest.

So instead of gawking at the flashiest pair of underwear I have ever seen, not to mention the vampire currently wearing them, I ask instead, "So, what? You think you automatically get the bed because you're the vampire and I'm the pathetic little human?"

"I just want to point out that those are your words, not mine." He gives me a smile designed to piss me off—arrogant, insouciant, and just dangerous enough to have the little hairs on the back of my neck standing straight up.

All of which should have been warning enough, but somehow it still surprises me when he turns to plump a pillow—and oh my God there's an actual castle on his ass. Or is that supposed to be a Greek temple à la Mount Olympus? It's so hard to tell—and he tosses casually over his shoulder, "Besides, I figured you'd join me in it."

Okay, maybe I *am* naive because I really, really wasn't expecting that. "I'm your brother's *mate*," I snap out when the shock finally wears off. "There's no way I'm ever going to sleep with you. *Ever.*"

"Oh no, not that," he answers, totally deadpan. "However will I survive the devastation?"

"You're a real jerk, you know that?" I tell him with a snarl.

"I do believe the subject's come up before, yes." He stretches to plump the pillows on the other side of the bed, totally unconcerned with anything I'm saying.

Which doesn't stop me from speaking. If we're going to be stuck here together for God only knows how long, we need to be clear on a few things. Including, "I don't know what you think is going to happen here, but I can assure you, it isn't."

He turns back to look at me, and gone is the sarcastic ass I've been dealing with all night. In his place is a very, very tired-looking guy.

"Sleep, Grace. What I want is to sleep." With that, he climbs into the bed and pulls the covers over himself, before rolling so that his back is to the center of the bed.

Just one more way for him to show just how little—and by little I mean not at all—he feels threatened by me. Embarrassment washes over me, even before he says, "You're welcome to take the other side. I promise not to sink my fangs into you while you sleep."

"It's not your fangs I'm worried about," I shoot back before I can think better of it. Embarrassment turns to full-out humiliation as the words hang in the air between us.

Oh my God. Seriously? I can't believe I just said that.

My cheeks are burning, my stomach turning, even before he mutters, "Yeah, well, you don't have to worry about that, either." For the first time, he sounds as tired as he looks. "Good night, Grace."

I don't answer him, but then it's obvious that he doesn't actually expect me to. At least not if the way he closes his eyes and goes immediately to sleep is any indication.

The part of my brain that was screaming at me to run earlier is back in full force. If I have any chance at all of getting away from him, it insists, this is it. When he's exhausted and off guard and in too much pain to care if I decide to make a break for it or not.

But the dragon is still out there. I can hear the flapping of his wings as he circles the roof, can feel his primal cries deep inside my soul.

Which means I'm trapped between two apex predators.

Whoever said humans were top of the food chain was apparently a cockeyed optimist.

Grace on a Platter

—Grace—

I don't know how long I stand there watching Hudson sleep. Seconds that feel like minutes?

Minutes that feel like hours?

But as the time passes, it becomes more obvious to me that Hudson really is asleep. And that, for all intents and purposes, he plans to stay that way.

It's good news—great news, really—and I finally let myself take my first real breath since we ended up here. Then I take another and another until I'm well clear of the area that functions as a bedroom.

I'm still starving—I never got to eat that apple I picked up earlier—so I continue back toward the kitchen area. I move slowly, steadily, making sure not to bump into anything or make any sudden movements that might startle Hudson awake. Or worse, set him off.

My stomach growls the instant I step foot in the kitchen, almost as if it's been waiting for the moment it feels safe—the moment *I* feel safe—to draw attention to itself. But safety is a relative thing when you're sharing space with a sociopath, so I don't let myself get too comfortable.

Instead, I keep my head turned toward him as I search quietly through the drawers, finding a few other essentials like a can opener and a cell charger, until I find what I'm really looking for. A knife. And not just any knife. An extra-sharp butcher's knife.

I think about grabbing one of the axes from his ax-throwing station instead, but there are only four of them. The odds that he'll notice one of them missing are pretty high, and that's the last thing I want.

Of course, I know that if Hudson comes at me, neither an ax nor a knife is going to provide me much protection—if any at all. But I'm not just going to serve myself up to him on a platter, either.

Grace's blood—and the rest of me, too—is off the freaking menu, thank you very much. I'd rather die fighting than just roll over and let Jaxon's older brother kill me. He's already hurt my mate enough. No way I'm going to let him take me away from Jaxon, too.

Not without one hell of a fight, anyway.

I keep the knife next to me on the counter as I grab some bread and make a quick cheese sandwich. I eat it standing up, my eyes focused on Hudson's sleeping form on the bed. He doesn't stir.

When I'm done eating, I grab a Dr Pepper from the fridge and head toward the couch that's closest to the door—and farthest away from the bed. I settle into the corner of the sofa and set the can of soda on the table but decide to tuck the knife in between the two cushions nearest to me. I stretch out and pull my phone from my pocket again.

As I play with the apps on my phone—the only things that still work, since I can't call or text anyone—I wait for Hudson to give up whatever game he's playing and become the predator I know he is. The predator he didn't even try to hide from me.

But an hour passes, and he doesn't make the move. In fact, he doesn't make *any* move at all. Instead, he's so still as he lays in that bed that more than once I have to look closely just to make sure he's still breathing. Unfortunately, he is.

Tiredness washes over me like a tsunami pulling me under. Drowning my determination to stay awake—to stay vigilant—in wave after wave of exhaustion. The last thing I do as I finally fall asleep is pull up a pic of Jaxon and me.

I took it three days ago, when we were hanging out in his room. My study session with Macy and Gwen had finished up faster than we'd planned, so instead of heading back to our room with Macy, I stopped by the tower to tell him good night.

He'd just been getting out of the shower, and he looked and smelled delicious. His black hair was wet and plastered against his cheek, his bare chest was still a little damp, and his smile was completely contagious.

Which is why I'm pressed up against that chest—my back to his front—with a grin on my face brighter than the aurora borealis peeking through the window behind us. He'd been trying to talk me out of the selfie and into the rumpled bed to the right of us, but I held my ground.

Despite everything we've been through together, our relationship is new.

Which means there are precious few pictures of the two of us together. I wanted this one and made sure Jaxon knew it.

And now, as I sit here on this couch alone, I'm so glad that I insisted. Because it gives me something to focus on in the middle of this huge, confusing mess. Something to try to find my way back to.

So I hold on to the phone—on to the picture of us—as tightly as I can.

And try to remember what Jaxon sounds like when he says he loves me.

13

My Life Is an Open Phone
—Grace—

I wake up slowly to the feeling of being toasty warm and the sound of my cousin's voice telling me she can't wait until I come to Katmere Academy.

It takes me a minute to get my bearings—to remember where I am and who I am with. But as every horrible thing that happened yesterday floods my brain, I sit up so fast that I nearly fall off the couch.

"Macy?" I call, shoving my wild curls out of my face as I pray that it was all just a dream. That every messed-up thing that happened yesterday was part of the most elaborate nightmare I've ever had. "What's going o—"

I break off as three things hit me at the exact same time.

One, I'm covered with what might very well be the softest, warmest blanket ever made.

Two, Macy is not in this room with me.

And three, Hudson Vega has my phone.

Even worse, it appears he is taking liberal advantage of me sleeping to scroll through every piece of content that he can get his thumbs on. The bastard.

"Hey!" I shout, making a lunge for the phone. But my throat is dry, my eyes are barely open, and my just-woke-up coordination is nothing compared to a vampire's. Especially when that vampire is Hudson.

He's off the couch and halfway across the room before I can do much more than get myself out from under the ridiculous blanket he obviously covered me with. For a second, it seems like a confusing gesture—Hudson actually doing something nice for me—as I do have a vague recollection of being cold in the middle of the night.

"What the hell do you think you're doing?" I demand, ignoring my pounding heart and the knife I still have stashed in the couch as I race across the room to him. One part of my brain is screaming at me that confronting him is a very bad idea, but the other half is yelling at me to get my damn phone back.

It's the second half that I listen to, because I refuse to spend however long we're trapped in this place terrified of Hudson all the time. No matter how terrifying he is.

"Give that back," I insist as I make a grab for my phone.

"Chill out, Princess," he answers as he holds it just out of reach. "I was only looking through it to see if there was anything in it we could use to get ourselves out of here."

"Like what? A secret code I just happened to forget about?" I ask in disgust.

"Maybe." He shrugs. "Stranger things have happened."

"Yeah, well, did you ever think to ask me about it instead of just invading my privacy?"

"Considering you don't seem to have a clue what you're doing?" he answers, leaning a shoulder against the nearest wall. "No, it never occurred to me."

And then he lowers my phone and plays another video—this one of the day Jaxon and I made our snowman together.

My heart trembles a little at the sound of my boyfriend's voice. Deep, warm, happy. Seeing Jaxon happy is one of my favorite things in the world—he's suffered so much—and this memory was one of the best in my whole life. Everything about it was perfect.

"Damn it!" I consider going back to the couch for that knife as I make another grab for my phone, but he deflects it without even looking up from my screen. "Stop watching my stuff!"

"But Jaxy-Waxy looks so cute with that little vampire hat. Did you make it for him?"

"No, I did not." But I love it. Love that he brought one for our snowman and love even more the look on his face when we stepped back to survey the final result.

And now Hudson is watching it with impassive eyes, combing through my most personal memories and looking for clues that don't exist. Judging Jaxon and judging me on something that is none of his business. It makes me hate him just a little more.

This time when I reach for the phone, Hudson pivots, giving me his back, and I lose my temper. I just lose it. I grab his shoulder and yank him back as hard as I can, seething, "Just because you don't have anyone who wants to build a snowman or make a video with you doesn't mean you've got the right to creep on other people."

The fact that I used every ounce of strength I have and Hudson doesn't so much as budge pisses me off more than I ever imagined possible. As does the brow he raises as he looks down at me, as if to ask what I think I'm doing.

Which is rich, considering what he's up to at this very moment.

But as our gazes meet for the first time since I woke up this morning, I can't help taking a step back. Because there's a pent-up rage burning in his eyes like nothing I have ever seen before. It makes the predatory look he gave me last night feel like child's play.

I stumble back another step, my heart in my throat as I glance around for a weapon.

"It's in the drawer," Hudson tells me in a bored voice. And just like that, the rage is gone from his eyes and in its place is the blankness—the emptiness—I'm growing used to.

My stomach twists sickly. "What is?" I ask, even though I'm afraid I already know what he's talking about.

"Don't play ignorant, Grace. It just makes us both look like fools."

He pushes from the wall and tosses me my phone. I catch it in numb fingers as he saunters away.

"Where are you going?" I ask as panic crawls through me. I hate being trapped here with him, but the idea of him walking out and leaving me trapped here alone suddenly feels infinitely worse.

"To take a shower?" His voice drips with disdain. "Feel free to join me if you'd like."

The panic turns right back into anger. "You're disgusting. I would never get naked with you."

"Who said anything about you getting naked?" he answers as he opens the door. "I just figured the distraction would give you the perfect opportunity to bury that knife of yours right in my back."

14

Diary of a Vampire Kid
—Grace—

I stare at the closed bathroom door as something that feels an awful lot like shame crawls through my belly. Hudson sounded bored, not hurt, but I can't help flashing back to that moment of rage in his eyes.

Rage that I would dare try to kill him?

Or rage that I would think I might have to?

Something tells me it's the latter, and the shame grows deeper, more pronounced.

Although I have absolutely nothing to be ashamed of, I assure myself as I force my feet to get moving.

He's the one who killed all those people at Katmere.

He's the one who nearly killed Jaxon.

And he's the one who thought nothing of flipping through my phone like he had some kind of right to invade my privacy.

Of course I have the right to try to protect myself against a killer. Anyone with any common sense at all would do exactly the same thing I did.

Exactly the same thing I'm going to do again. He can act all pissed off anytime he wants. But that just means he's more dangerous, not less.

It's that thought that propels me across the kitchen to the couch where I hid the knife last night. Half of me expects the weapon not to be there, but it is exactly where I left it. Of course, it's been bent into a circle, so that the tip of the blade is touching the end of the handle. And when I go to check the drawer again, so is every other knife in there, except the paring knife, which is bent in half.

Hudson destroyed every single one of them, leaving them useless and me defenseless. The fact that they would have done very little against him if he chose to attack me doesn't matter. All that matters is he went out of his way to destroy any small modicum of security I might have found. And that is fucking vile.

I start to slam the drawer closed, but I won't give Hudson the satisfaction. Even with the shower running, he'd probably hear and I don't want him to know just how pissed off—and how scared—I really am.

So I close the drawer slowly and focus on what I *can* control, which isn't much. My stomach is growling again—stress always makes me hungry—so I grab a pack of cherry Pop-Tarts and an apple and head back toward the sofa I slept on last night.

It was cold, at least until Hudson covered me with a blanket—and what's that about anyway, considering how angry he was this morning?—and then it was super comfortable. I need a little comfort right now.

It's with that thought in mind that I stop to peruse the bookshelves. Books have been a solace for me my entire life, and how lucky am I that if I'm stuck in this place, wherever *here* is, that I'm surrounded by thousands and thousands of books?

I eat my apple as I wander up and down the shelves, discovering a ton of old favorites—*The Catcher in the Rye*, *The Hunger Games*, Sylvia Plath's *Collected Poems*—along with a bunch of books I've wanted to read but haven't gotten to and even more that I've never heard of.

I stop when I get to a row of wine-colored books bound in softly worn leather. There are at least a hundred of them, and though some look much older than others, they're obviously part of a set—not just because they are the same color but because they all have identical markings on the spine and, when I pull a couple off the shelf, identical gold edges as well.

Plus, each one has a lock on the front. Journals? And if so, whose? I don't think I'll ever know, considering they're locked, but it's interesting to speculate about.

The locks themselves are beautiful—ancient-looking and ornate—and as I turn the first book over in my hands, I can't resist running a finger over the small keyhole. To my shock, the moment my finger comes in contact with it, the lock slides open.

The book is mine for the reading.

I hesitate for a second—these are someone's journals. But judging from the age of this journal, that someone is probably long dead, I rationalize, and won't care at all if I spend some time looking through their thoughts.

I open the book carefully—it's lasted a long time, and I don't want to be the one to damage it. The first page is blank, except for the inscription: *To my brightest pupil, who deserves so much more from this world. Sincerely, Richard.*

It's a strange inscription, though a fascinating one, and I spend a moment tracing the lavishly written letters with my fingertip. But my curiosity has gone from piqued to burning at the words, and it isn't long before I turn the page to see what this star pupil has written.

I turn to the first page, and at the top of it is the date May 12, 1835. It is followed by an entry in childish scrawl.

I got into a fight today.

I shouldn't have. I know I shouldn't have, but I couldn't help it. I was ~~prove~~ provoked.

Richard says that that doesn't matter. He says that self-control is the mark of a ~~cival~~ civilized man. I told him I didn't know what that meant and he told me that "self-control is the ability of a man to control his emotions and desires even in the face of great ~~provaca~~ provocation." I told him that was well and good but that anyone who said that didn't have an annoying little brother.

Richard laughed, then told me that future kings must have self-discipline at all times and do only what they think is best for their people even if their people are annoying little brothers. Even super-annoying little brothers? I asked. And he said especially them.

Which makes sense, I guess, except my father doesn't seem disciplined at all. He does whatever he wants whenever he wants and if anyone questions him he makes them ~~disape~~ disappear sometimes for a little while and sometimes forever.

When I said that to Richard, though, he just looked at me and asked if I really want to be the kind of king my father is. I told him the answer to that is <u>NO!!!!!!!!</u> I never want to be the kind of king or person or vampire or <u>ANYTHING</u> that my dad is. He may have a lot of power, but he's also really mean to everyone.

I don't want to be that kind of king. And I don't want to be that kind of father. I don't want everyone, including my family, to be afraid of me all the time. Especially my family. I never want them to be afraid of me. And I never want them to hate me the way that I hate him.

Which is why I never should have done what I did. I never should have punched my brother in the face, even though he punched me first.

And kicked me. And bit me twice, which really, really hurt. But he's my little brother and it's my job to take care of him. Even when he's super super super annoying.

Which is why I'm writing this here. So that I don't ever forget. And because Richard says a good man always keeps his vows, I vow to ALWAYS take care of Jaxon, no matter what.

I freeze when I see Jaxon's name at the bottom of the page. Tell myself that it's a coincidence, that no way the person writing this journal, the person vowing to always take care of his little brother, is Hudson.

Except there's a lot of things in this entry that make me think that it really is him. *Vampire. Future king. Big brother…*

If this is Hudson's journal and not some long-dead prince, I should stop reading. I really should. But even as I tell myself that I'm going to close the book, I flip the page to the next entry. Just to see if it really is him. Just to see how things could have changed so much that he would go from vowing to always protect his brother to trying to kill him.

I start to read the next journal entry, something about learning to whittle so he can make a toy for his little brother, but I have to stop after only a couple of paragraphs.

How could this sweet, earnest little boy become the monster who caused so many deaths at Katmere?

How could the child who vowed to protect his brother forever turn into the sociopath who tried so hard to kill that same brother?

It doesn't make sense.

A million more questions race through my mind as I turn the page and keep reading…just as the bathroom door opens and Hudson walks out.

My stomach jumps as his gaze finds me, then immediately narrows in on the book in my hands. Terrified to make any sudden move, I swallow slowly. And wait for all hell to break loose.

15

The Best Defense Is
More Defense
—Hudson—

Well, fuck. I sure as shit didn't see *this* coming.

Which, in retrospect, makes me as shortsighted as I keep accusing Grace of being. Of course she found my damn journals while I was in the shower. And of course she saw nothing wrong with reading them after spending the morning watching me flip through her phone without her permission.

Talk about being hoisted with my own petard. But knowing the hoisting is justified doesn't make it any easier to handle the aftermath. In fact, I think it might just make it harder, considering it leaves me with no recourse. And absolutely no argument.

Fuck, fuck, fuck.

I consider walking over to her and grabbing the damn thing out of her hands, but that would only make everything worse. Not to mention hand her more power than she already has, and I've got no intention of doing that. Not when she already looks at me like I'm something she wants to squish beneath her shoe.

Nothing left to do but brazen it out, then. Even if what I really want to do is set fire to the whole lot of journals. Fuck the sentimentality that's had me keeping them all these years. The damn things need to burn.

Just not tonight.

"So, what volume are you starting at?" I ask as I cross the room toward her.

Because there's no way I'm sitting down on that couch with her right now, I lean a shoulder up against the closest wall, determined to look like I don't give a fuck. About anything.

When she doesn't answer right away, I cross my arms and my ankles and prepare to wait her out. After all, the best defense is *more* defense.

It's a lesson I learned at the feet of my dear old dad, even if he'd spent years trying to teach me just the opposite. Not to mention turn me into the same kind of monster as he was.

Too bad I decided a long time ago to be my own kind of monster and fuck the consequences.

Obviously, it's going brilliant so far.

"I didn't know they were yours."

Considering the guilty look she's been wearing from the second I walked out of the bathroom, I'm calling bullshit on that one. "Maybe not when you picked it up. But you didn't put it down once you figured it out, did you?"

She doesn't answer, just looks back down at my journal.

"Not that it matters. Read away. Though I would suggest skipping the volumes in the middle. My tween years were very…" I pause for effect, even go so far as to shake my head a little ruefully, just to show her how little I really care. "Emo."

"Only your tween years?" she asks without missing a beat, brows raised.

"Touché." I incline my head in a half bow. "But eventually they get better. I didn't really hit my stride until after I'd read Plato's *Apology*. Rigorous self-reflection à la Socrates and all that."

"And here I thought you learned everything you knew from the Marquis de Sade."

I look away, hide my grin behind my hand. Grace is quick, I'll give her that. A definite pain in the arse but really quick. And pretty funny, too.

"I do have a question, though," she says, and she's back to looking at the open journal in front of her.

I stiffen, my whole body going on red alert as I wait for a question I'm damn sure I'm not going to like. Something about Jaxon's and my relationship, probably, which pretty much guarantees I won't have an answer. I've been trying to figure shit out between my brother and me for most of my life, but it's like beating my head against a brick wall.

Or at least it was, right up until he decided killing me was the only way to solve our differences. Then I pretty much decided he could go fuck himself. Even thought about killing the little arsehole while I had the chance. It's not like he had any compunction about doing the same to me.

In the end, I couldn't do it, though. Truthfully, I didn't even try. It just seemed better for everyone if I disappeared for a while. Maybe even forever.

"What's your question?" I ask, bracing myself for the worst.

Grace holds up my journal. "If you're so convinced that I'm the one doing this—that I'm the one holding us here in this place—how on earth could I be sitting here reading your journal?"

"Seriously? We're back to that? That's your big question?" I don't know whether to be relieved or insulted.

"It's a valid question," she answers. "I mean, I didn't even know these things existed before I grabbed one off the shelf. How on earth could I possibly know what's in them?"

"The same way I know that chocolate chocolate chip cookies are your favorite kind."

"Aren't chocolate chip cookies everybody's favorite kind?" she counters.

"How the hell would I know that?" I ask, exasperated. "I'm a vampire."

"Oh, right. Well, trust me. Chocolate chip cookies are everybody's favorite."

"Not everyone's," I answer. Because in this situation, she's not the only one who can see more than anyone should have access to. I can, too. That's how I know that, "Some people like oatmeal raisin cookies best. And other people really like Dalí sketches and John Morse collages."

Her big brown eyes go huge. "How do you know about that?" she whispers.

It's a loaded question, one whose answer might send her screaming straight into the dark outside that never seems to lift if I'm not careful. But it's also the perfect distraction from that damn book in her lap.

And the perfect way to convince her, once and for all, that she really is the one in charge of keeping us here. Well, her and that dragon outside, but that's an issue for a different time.

For now, I'm more focused on show-and-tell—just not the kind that takes place in a kindergarten classroom.

No, for this lesson we've got to go somewhere else entirely. Except...not really.

So as not to scare her, I reach over slowly and take the journal from Grace's hands.

"What are you doing?"

I don't answer her. Why should I when her distraction provides me with the opening I've been looking for?

So instead of answering, I take advantage of the opportunity she gave me to breach her defenses. And just like that, I reach in and grab a memory.

16

No Vamp Is
an Island
—Grace—

W e're on the beach.
And not just any beach. Coronado Beach in San Diego. I'd recognize it anywhere. Partly because the very iconic, very recognizable, red-roofed Hotel del Coronado is right in front of me and partly because it's my old stomping ground.

I used to come here all the time—sometimes by myself and sometimes with Heather. Even before we had our driver's licenses and could cross the bridge whenever we wanted, we'd hop the ferry and ride it over to the small island in the San Diego Bay. Then we'd get off the boat and walk down Orange Street to the beach, stopping along the way to look in the shops and art galleries that line the small boulevard.

When we got hungry, we'd buy ice cream cones at MooTime or cookies from Miss Velma's Bakery, then wander down to the beach. We would swim in the summer when the water finally got warm enough and just wade in to our knees during the other seasons.

Coronado is pretty much my favorite place on earth, and so many of my best memories are right here on this street. I haven't been here since a week before my parents died, and it's strange to be back now, with Hudson of all people.

"I don't understand," I whisper as a young mother in a bright yellow sweatsuit rolls her baby carriage by right in front of us. "How did we get here?"

"Does it matter?" he responds, looking up at the sky.

And I get it. Even though we were trapped in that room for only a day, it somehow feels like so much longer.

It feels like it's been forever since I walked under the bright blue sky, counting fluffy clouds as the warmth of the sun beats down on me.

Forever since I've felt the wind slide past me, flirting with the edges of my clothes and ruffling my curls.

Forever since I've breathed in the salty sea air, listening to the endless crash of the ocean against the shore.

I've missed this—missed home—more than I ever imagined possible.

"I guess not," I whisper as I pause to look in the window of my favorite gallery.

And breathe a sigh of relief when I realize nothing has changed. The Adam Scott Rote *Alice in Wonderland* painting still hangs in the front window, a beautiful, grown-up Alice staring out at us as the Red Queen towers over her from behind.

"I fell in love with this painting when I was fourteen," I tell Hudson. "My mom kept me home from school for a half-birthday celebration, and she brought me here to Coronado to hang out. She told me we could do anything I wanted for the whole day, and it turns out what I wanted to do most was explore this gallery and stare at all the incredible artists on its walls."

"This is where the John Morse collage is, too, isn't it?" Hudson asks as we wander inside.

"It is," I tell him. "But it's on the other side of the gallery. Or at least it used to be." I take off past a display of other Rote works into the small enclave where I used to spend so much of my time. Hudson doesn't hesitate to follow me.

And yes! "It's still here," I murmur, barely resisting the urge to press my fingers to the cool, protective glass that overlays the most stunning collage print of Einstein I ever could have imagined.

His face is a million colors, and his wild hair is made of shreds from all kinds of different boxes like Hot Tamales, Lunchables, Cheez-Its, and parchment paper.

"I've never seen anything like that," Hudson says from a spot beside me.

"Me neither." I curl my fingers into my palms, just to make sure I don't touch. "I'm so glad it's still here."

"Me too." Hudson smiles at me and it's softer, sweeter, than I would ever have expected.

Once again, something uneasy tugs at the back of my mind, but it's easy to ignore it when I'm surrounded by so much beauty.

We take our time wandering the gallery, Hudson making pithy comments about the art he doesn't like while I wax rhapsodic about the pieces I love. Eventually, though, we've seen everything there is to see and wander back onto the street.

"Are you hungry?" I ask as the smell of fresh-baked cookies fills the air. "Miss Velma's bakery is right over there."

"She's the one who makes the oatmeal raisin cookies, isn't she?" Hudson asks.

"She is," I answer as I eye him curiously. "How do you know about those cookies?"

"Does it matter?" He gives a little shrug. "I thought the point was to eat cookies, not talk about them."

"Oh, believe me, we can do both."

I hustle the hundred feet to Miss Velma's place, Hudson right behind me.

A bell chimes as we pull open the door, and Miss Velma looks up from where she's arranging a fresh batch of cookies in the display case to wave us over.

She's a tall Black woman, with a narrow face and the most beautiful curly gray hair bouncing around that face. For a second, relief flashes through me that she's still here. She's old and fragile-looking, her shoulders stooped and her fingers gnarled with time. But her smile lights up the whole shop the same way it always has.

"Grace!" she squeals, and for a moment she sounds—and looks—like a girl as she bounces on her toes and reaches for me. "My girl! I wasn't sure I'd ever see you again."

"You should have known a few thousand miles would never keep me away from your cookies, Miss Velma," I tell her.

"You're right. I should have known," she answers with a laugh, even as she eyes Hudson curiously. "Who's your friend?"

"Miss Velma, this is Hudson. Hudson, this is Miss Velma."

"The best cookie maker in all of San Diego," he tells her with a smooth smile.

"The best cookie maker in the whole country," I correct him as Miss Velma laughs and laughs.

Then she picks up a small box from the counter behind her and starts filling it with chocolate chocolate chip cookies before I even say a word.

"We want a couple of oatmeal raisin ones, too," Hudson says, and Miss Velma beams at him.

"Wonderful choice. Those are my favorite! They were always my favorite customer Lily's choice, too. Sadly, they're my worst sellers, so I haven't made these in weeks," she says as she closes the box top. "Everyone wants chocolate chip or snickerdoodles or chocolate chocolate chip. Nothing that pretends to be a little bit healthy, even if it isn't. But something told me to whip up a batch this morning, and I'm so glad I did."

"Me too," Hudson tells her fervently. "I've never had one before, and I can't wait to taste it."

Something niggles at the corners of my mind, a feeling that something isn't quite right here. But before I can figure out what it is that's bothering me, Miss Velma reaches for Hudson's hand and squeezes it. "When you eat it, I hope you feel all the love I put into it."

Hudson doesn't say anything for a moment, just looks down to where her old, arthritic hand is clutching his young, strong one. When the silence stretches on a bit too long, he clears his throat and whispers, "Thank you."

"You are very welcome, dear boy." She squeezes his hand again before reluctantly letting him go. "Now, get on out of here and go down to that beach. It's supposed to rain later, so you should take advantage of the good weather while you've got the chance."

"Rain?" I say, but Miss Velma has already walked into the back of the shop.

"Shall we?" Hudson says, pushing the door open, then stepping aside so I can walk through it first, leaving me little choice but to grab the cookie box and walk back outside.

As I do, I look up at the sky and see that Miss Velma is right. In the space of this one short little stop at the cookie shop, the sky has gone from bright blue to ominous gray. The sun has disappeared and the world around me now feels dark and dingy, something San Diego has never felt to me.

I don't like it. At all. And as Hudson moves to join me on the street, I can't help wondering if it's an omen.

And if so, what exactly is it warning me about?

17

This Is How My
Cookie Crumbles
—Grace—

The wind picks up as we walk toward the beach. The ocean is directly in front of us, and I can see the waves building up, can hear them crashing harder and faster against the shore with each second that passes.

My stomach tightens a little as nerves twist deep inside me, but I take a deep breath and try to ignore it as Hudson asks, "What happened to Lily?"

I sigh. "She died of cancer eighteen months ago. She was nine, and Miss Velma's oatmeal raisin cookies were her favorite things in the whole world. As she got closer to the end, they were the only things she would eat."

Hudson's jaw works as he looks out at the sea. "I don't know if that's amazing or awful."

"Yeah." I give a watery little laugh. "Me neither. I'm going to go with amazing, because she was such an amazing little girl. Always happy, no matter how sick the chemo made her or how much pain she was in."

"You knew her?" He looks surprised.

"Only because her mom used to bring her into the shop a lot. They would sit at the corner table and Lily would color while Miss Velma made her her own batch of oatmeal raisin." I can't help but smile as I remember how industriously she used to color her pictures.

When I grow up, Grace, I'm going to be an artist just like the ones whose paintings hang in Mr. Rodney's gallery.

I have no doubt, Lily. You draw the most amazing flowers I've ever seen.

Because I'm a flower. The prettiest flower. That's what my mama says.

Your mama is absolutely right.

The snippet of one of our last conversations comes back to me, and I swallow hard. Hudson doesn't ask me what I'm thinking about, but then, I guess it's pretty obvious. Especially considering he shifts the box of cookies to the hand that's farthest away from me as he starts walking a little faster toward the beach.

"Hey! We've got to eat a cookie before we reach the water," I tell him as I push my shorter legs to move faster. "It's tradition."

"I thought maybe you wouldn't want to eat one after that story," he answers. He must see that I'm struggling to keep up, because he slows his stride again.

"You're not wrong," I answer. "But we have to."

He lifts a brow. "Tradition is tradition?"

"That's what I'm saying." I grin back at him.

He looks like he wants to argue, but in the end, he just nods before reluctantly opening the cookie box.

I take the oatmeal cookies off the top, then hand him one and say, "To Lily."

"To Lily," he echoes, right before we both take a bite.

The familiar taste hits my tongue, and tears burn the back of my eyes. I've never been a fan of oatmeal raisin cookies, and these are no different, but I still eat one every time I visit. For Lily. For my own mom, who used to love oatmeal raisin cookies, too. For my dad, who hated them but used to eat them all the same because he knew Mom wouldn't make them only for herself.

I miss them so much. It's strange, really. Some days I wake up, and it doesn't feel so terrible. But somehow those days are worse than the ones that start out really bad. Because on those days, I'm just going along, doing my thing, and then something will trigger a memory out of the blue, and I'll be unprepared for it.

I'll feel crushed all over again.

It's how I feel now, like I've been run over by grief yet again.

"Hey. You okay?" Hudson asks, and then he's reaching for me like he wants to comfort me. Or hold me up.

I jerk away instinctively. Remind myself that just because he's being nice at the moment doesn't mean he's not a sociopath. A murderer. A monster.

"I'm fine," I tell him, swallowing down the remnants of my sorrow, because I can't handle being vulnerable. Not right now, and not in front of him. "Let's just eat our cookies."

To emphasize that I'm serious, I take a large bite of the oatmeal cookie. Then chew enthusiastically, pretending it hasn't turned to sawdust in my mouth.

Hudson doesn't say anything, just watches me with serious eyes as he, too, takes a bite of the cookie.

He chews for a few seconds, and then his whole face lights up. "Hey! This is actually really good."

"You should try the chocolate chocolate chip," I tell him after finally choking down the cookie I chewed for what feels like forever.

"I'm going to," he answers as he reaches into the box and pulls out my favorite of Miss Velma's cookies. He takes an enthusiastic bite, his eyes going wide at what I know from experience is the perfect ratio of cookie dough and chocolate on his tongue.

"That's..."

"Amazing," I fill in for him. "Delicious. Perfection."

"All of those," he agrees. "And more."

He smiles at me before taking another bite of cookie, and as the wind blows past us, ruffling his perfect pompadour for the very first time, he looks different than usual. Younger. Happier. More vulnerable.

Maybe that's what has everything inside me freezing as questions begin to dance around the edges of my mind. "Wait a minute," I murmur as things I learned at Katmere start filtering through all the emotions that have been bouncing around inside me because I'm *home*.

"How can you eat that cookie?" I ask. "Jaxon ate a strawberry in front of me once, and he said it made him completely sick. How can you stand here eating two huge cookies like it's nothing?"

Hudson doesn't say anything. Instead, he just looks at me as the happiness drains from his eyes only to be replaced by a wariness I don't understand.

Until suddenly I do.

"None of this is real, is it?" I whisper as horror washes over me. "This is just another trick? Just another way for you to—"

"It's not a trick," Hudson interrupts, and his voice sounds strange, almost pleading. And maybe I could focus on that if Miss Velma's cookie shop wasn't flickering like a bad wifi connection right behind him.

For a moment, the roar of the ocean gets louder in my ears, so loud that it feels like it's going to come crashing down on us at any second. But even as I brace myself to get soaked, the roaring fades away to nothingness.

As does the cookie in my hand.

As does Miss Velma.

As does everything and everyone but Hudson and me.

Even worse, we're back in the dark. At least until Hudson flips a switch and the lights come back on.

Even before my eyes adjust, I know where we are. And I finally know what happened.

"It was all just a memory, wasn't it?" I ask him. It's not even an accusation at this point, just a statement of fact. "Somehow you got in my head, and you stole a memory."

"I didn't just get in your head, Grace. And I didn't steal anything. You gave it to me."

His words hit me like a match hits gasoline, and a fire races over my skin, pours through my body, fills me up until all I can see or taste or feel is red-hot rage. "I would never do that!" I spit at him. "I would never just give you something precious to me like this."

"Oh yeah?" Now his eyes narrow to slits. "And why is that exactly? Because I'm not worth it?"

"Because you're my—" I break off before I can say the word "enemy." Not because it isn't true, not because he isn't exactly that, even if I did forget for a minute or two. But because the word itself sounds so old-fashioned and melodramatic, while all the emotions whipping through my body feel like neither of those things.

But it looks like I don't actually need to say the word for him to know what I'm thinking. It's written all over his face, even before he says, "I'm not your enemy. I thought you'd figured out that we're in this together."

"Really? Together? That's why you think it's okay to look through my phone and steal deep, personal memories right out of my head? Because we're in this together?"

"Not out of your head," he reiterates.

"I don't have a clue what that means."

"You sure about that?" He raises a brow as he leans his shoulder against the wall and crosses his arms over his chest. "Because I'm pretty sure you do."

"That's absurd!" I say. "How could I—" But once again I break off as the pieces scattered inside me begin to slowly fit together the only way that makes any sense.

Horror washes over me. "You can see my memories because none of this is real. You can see into my head because none of this"—I wave my arm to encompass the room—"really exists."

But Hudson shakes his head. "It is real, Grace. Just not the kind of real you're used to."

But I'm too far down the rabbit hole to concentrate on anything he's saying. Too far into my own personal nightmare to concentrate on anything but the truth that is shining like a beacon inside me.

I know he's told me this before, several times, but I didn't believe him then. Why would I? But now I can't help but see the truth right in front of me. And it scares the hell out of me.

But hiding from it won't solve the problem, and it sure as hell won't get Hudson and me out of this mess that I've created. But maybe talking about it will.

Work the problem, my sophomore-year algebra teacher always used to tell us. *Look at the information you have and let it guide you to the solution.*

"I can read your journals because somehow, some way, you were right and you're trapped inside my head." It's the hardest thing I've ever said, and it sets everything inside me to trembling. "I can read your journals, but not your mind. But you know what I'm thinking and can see my memories."

I glance around again at the space we're trapped in, a space that is clearly more his than mine. "You made this room, but I can control it, which means..."

But Hudson doesn't so much as blink. Instead, he just raises his brows. And waits for me to speak.

And waits.

And waits.

And waits.

Silence presses between us, but for once I don't feel honor bound to break the silence. Not when my mind is still racing with the implications of what I've finally come to accept.

So I wait until Hudson sighs, looking for all the world like a teacher trying to get the right answer from a recalcitrant student. "And?" he prompts.

I've never considered myself bratty in my life, but perhaps in this moment— on this subject—that's exactly what I've been. I think back to the journal entry I read today, to the little boy who was so determined to do right by his brother, his tutor, his people.

I don't know where things went wrong. I don't know how or when that earnest little boy turned into a guy who could make people kill each other with just a whisper.

But I do know that somewhere deep inside this Hudson, that little boy still exists. I saw him for just a moment last night, when I was trying to patch up his back. And I saw him again today, standing outside Miss Velma's store, eating an oatmeal raisin cookie that, for all intents and purposes, should have made him sick.

And if he was there for those moments, he's probably there at other times, too. Like right now, watching me with those blue, blue eyes as he waits for me to catch up. Waits for me to take a giant leap of faith.

And while a leap is out of the freaking question—this is Hudson Vega, after all—I decide that maybe, just maybe, I can take a tiny little hop.

Which is the only reason I pull in a deep breath and then let it out slowly.

The only reason I unclench my fists and open my posture.

The only reason I reach deep inside myself and say the one thing I never thought I'd say. The one thing I'm more terrified of than any other.

"I really want to get out of here. And the only way I can see that happening is if we work together."

Hudson's grin flashes for a moment, transforming his whole face. "I thought you'd never ask."

18

Trying to Lair Low

—Hudson—

Grace looks like she's going to be sick.

Not that I blame her. One bite of that oatmeal raisin cookie, and I'm feeling pretty shite myself. The fact that the cookie wasn't real—and that I didn't actually eat any of it—doesn't seem to matter to my queasy stomach.

"I do have a question for you," Grace says after several awkward seconds. "You knew almost immediately that we were trapped in my head."

"Is that the question?" I ask with a smirk. Not because I don't understand what she's getting at but because it's fun to rile her up—because she gets all prissy and dictatorial when I do and because she's really cute when she's prissy and dictatorial.

Not that it should matter to me how she looks when she's my brother's mate, but for some reason, it does. Besides, I've spent the last hundred years of my life living down to people's expectations of me.

I don't see why I should stop now.

Grace rolls her eyes at me, but she doesn't jump down my throat. Progress? I wonder. Or is she just biding her time because she needs something from me?

The cynic in me figures it's the latter, but...we'll see.

"You knew right away that we were trapped in my head," she continues.

I lift a brow. "Still not a question."

"Okay, fine. Here's the question. How did you know?"

It's a good question, and one I've been waiting for her to ask since I figured it out. But just because I've been expecting it doesn't mean I've got an answer for her, because I don't.

I just knew.

But that's not going to help us get out of here, so I dig a little deeper. Try to figure out what it is that tipped me off. But the best I can come up with is, "It just didn't feel real."

"What didn't feel real?" Now she looks confused as well as queasy.

I gesture to the room around us. "All of this. It felt a few degrees off."

"I don't get it. It feels real to me." She glances toward the room's one remaining window. "Especially that dragon."

"Oh, the dragon's real," I assure her. "And so is everything else beyond these walls."

"Okay, I'm even more confused than when we began this conversation. How can the dragon and outside be real and everything in here be fake?" She throws her hands up in exasperation. "I've never even seen this place before, so if I'm imagining it, how could it feel off?"

"Because it's my lair," I tell her, then watch in amusement as her eyes go wide.

"Your lair?" she whispers, looking around at everything in here. Especially the ax-throwing station in the center of the room. "Seriously?"

"Right down to the books on the shelves. Except for the kitchen and the windows, everything in here is exactly the same as in my lair. Except it's not."

"What the hell does that mean?" She starts to pace—out of nerves or because she wants to get away from me, I can't quite tell.

Either way, I don't try to move with her. The last thing I want to do is get her nervous now that we're finally talking. The more nervous she is, the longer she's going to keep us trapped in here, and I've been trapped long enough, thank you very much.

My whole fucking life is more than long enough.

So instead of pacing with her, I grab a seat on my very comfortable sofa and let her go. She thinks she's human—how long could it possibly take her to wind down?

"Well?" she prompts when I don't rush to answer her question.

"I don't know what you want me to say. Being here is like being in my lair but with minor changes." I nod my head toward the bedroom area. "Like, the bedroom is usually on the other side of the room. And what self-respecting vampire would have windows in his lair? Or need a kitchen filled with Pop-Tarts?" I shrug. "Besides, the art is missing from the walls."

She glances around the room, her eyebrows shooting up. "There doesn't seem to be a space missing a painting."

I shrug again. "You seem to have added more bookcases or shelves. I just assumed you couldn't get it all right."

She shakes her head. "Then why not guess there was a third party trapping us here? Why jump to it being me doing it all?"

Finally, a question that's easy to answer. "Because I can read your every thought and memory, Grace, but you can't read mine."

She stops, eyes narrowed, and I'm thinking she's going to come sit down. But nope, she's off and pacing again, wincing as she does, as if the small act of standing still for ten seconds was actually painful for her.

"So if this is your lair, how did I know to bring us here? I've never been here before." She doesn't even try to hide the suspicion.

Well, that was quick. Gone is the semi-friendliness of the last few minutes and in its place is the same suspicion she's been casting my way since we ended up here together. I'd say it's a record, but that's not exactly true. She lasted at least thirty seconds longer than Jaxon.

Must be a mate thing—hate all the same people, even if you don't have a reason to. Just one more fucked-up version of loyalty, if you ask me.

Not that anyone ever has.

But Grace is obviously channeling her inner Jaxon, because this time when she stops in front of me, the old belligerence is back.

"How would I know what your lair looks like?" she asks again. "If we really are trapped in *my* head, why does it look like *your* room?"

It's a valid question, one I've been thinking about myself. But not the way she asked it. No, that was very definitely an accusation, and I am so over those.

Which is why I make sure my voice is dripping sarcasm when I answer. "That's a great question. When you figure out how to get in touch with your subconscious, you can ask it."

Two can play this game of cordial impoliteness. When you live at the Vampire Court, you learn it really fucking early.

"I'm just saying it doesn't make sense."

"And that's on me?" I ask, annoyance turning to anger in a blink. "I was minding my own business, blissfully unaware of *anything*, when all of a sudden all hell breaks loose. One second my ex-girlfriend is exploding on an altar, and the next I'm back to the moment before my plonker of a brother tried to kill me again, except this time, some girl is getting in the middle of the fight. Before I can even realize what's happening, stop teaching the arse a lesson, that same girl—who is apparently my brother's mate—kidnaps me and locks me back up in some strange facsimile of *my* lair, all while treating me like I'm the one with the problem. Excuse me if I don't have all the fucking answers yet."

Not bothering to wait and see Grace's response to anything I just told her, I storm into the kitchen and grab a bottle of water out of the fridge. I drink it down in a couple of long swallows, then dump the bottle in a neatly labeled recycling bin.

Because of course this girl has a recycling bin in whatever strange fever dream she's got us locked up in. We may kill each other or get eaten by a giant, ugly-ass dragon, but at least we will have fake recycled our fake bottles first.

Makes perfect fucking sense to me.

"You're right," she says.

"Excuse me?" I answer at the closest I get to a shout. Because those are the last two words I ever expected to hear come out of her full lips.

Not that I'm paying any attention to her lips. But the sentiment stands.

"I said, you're right." She makes a point of enunciating each syllable, because this girl can dish it just as well as she takes it. Maybe even better.

Makes me wonder what she's doing mated to a guy like my brother, who definitely isn't the type to appreciate it. And once I start wondering that, I can't stop myself from popping deep in her mind to take a look at the aforementioned bond.

Is it a dick move?

Absolutely.

Do I do it anyway?

Absolutely.

We'll just chalk it up to living down to expectations one more time. Told ya I was good at it.

Except...something isn't right. When I dive deep to take a look at the mating bond, I don't find only one string. I find dozens, in all the myriad colors of the rainbow.

I've never seen anything like it, never even heard of anything like it. I know Grace is convinced she's fully human, but in my mind, this is just more proof that she's anything but.

Just to make sure I'm in the right place, I reach out and stroke one finger across all the different strings. Too bad the second I do, I realize I've made a huge tactical error. One that's going to hurt like hell.

19

Put a String on It

—Hudson—

I yank my hands away from the strings as fast as I can, but it's way too late for that. Instantly, I'm flooded by a cyclone of emotions so powerful that it's all I can do to keep my mouth shut and stay on my feet.

Joy, sorrow, pride, loneliness, confusion, despair, love, fear, excitement, anxiety—so much anxiety that I feel my own heart start to pound. I try to back out of it, but I'm trapped in the whirlwind of so many emotions coming at me so fast that I can't separate them enough to label them.

No wonder Grace is so freaked out *all* the time. No one person can possibly feel all these things simultaneously and be okay. Certainly not for *all* these people. It's unimaginable.

And terrible.

This is *definitely* my punishment for sticking my nose in where it doesn't belong. Especially since it's impossible to find the mating bond in all this cacophony.

I could force myself through the strings—and all the subsequent emotions that come with them—but that would hurt Grace, which is the last thing I want to do. Despite what she and everyone else seems to think of me, I'm not in the habit of deliberately hurting anyone. And I'm definitely not in the habit of hurting a defenseless girl simply because I made a mistake.

So instead of forcing my way out, I hold myself as steady as I can and wait for the mess I made to settle down.

It only takes a few seconds, but with all the emotions battering at me, it feels like an eternity. Once things quiet down and the hurricane dies away, I finally get my second clear look at the strings.

This time as I lean over them, I make damn sure not to touch a single one. No way in hell am I going through that shite again.

It is tempting, though. If each of these strings leads to a different connection, a different person, then I'm fascinated. Because how does an orphaned girl from San Diego already have this many relationships in my world? And how does a girl like this, who somehow manages to connect to this many people, end up mated to my "I walk alone" little brother?

It doesn't exactly seem like a mating made in paranormal heaven.

Which is why I can't resist looking closer, even though I can hear Grace talking to me in the background. Something about *do you want to take it or leave it.*

I have no idea what she's talking about, and I don't really give a shite. Because as I lean in to get a closer—not tactile—look at all her bloody strings, I notice three things.

The first one is that the black string with strange green ribbons running through it I'm growing more convinced is her mating bond to Jaxon doesn't look nearly as bright as the other strings. In fact, it's almost translucent, which it definitely shouldn't be. At least not if anything I've been taught about this shit—from my tutor and from school—is right.

Second, there's a green string in the middle of all the other strings that twinkles a bit as I approach. I back away slowly, and the string seems to settle down. I have no idea what this string is connected to, but something tells me it's not anything we should be fucking with right now. If ever.

And finally, there's another string I can't pull my gaze from in this tangle of connections. It's a bright, electric blue, and it's gossamer thin, but it is very definitely there. And it's glowing ever so slightly.

And somehow I know, even before I reach out a fingertip to touch it, that it connects to me.

20

All the Sizzle,
None of the Heart
—Hudson—

As the realization sinks in, I recoil so fast that I nearly fall head over heels. "Hey!" Grace reaches out, but I jerk back before she can touch me. "Are you okay?"

I stare at her for several beats, so caught up in what I just saw that it takes a few beats for her words to register.

When they do, I mutter, "I'm fine," and step back another step. As I do, something flashes in her eyes, but my heart is racing and the blood is pounding in my ears and I've got *no time* to figure out what's going on with her.

I'm too busy trying to figure out what the fuck is going on with me. With us.

Not that there is an *us*, I assure myself. And there's nothing to freak out about here at all. Definitely no reason to have all these bizarre, unidentifiable emotions pouring through me. I just saw incontrovertible proof that the girl makes connections with everyone and everything. Just because one has apparently formed between us doesn't mean anything.

It doesn't mean that we're going to be friends or anything like that. And it doesn't mean that we're going to be stuck here for a long time, either. It just means that at this very moment in this very space, there's some kind of *connection* between us.

Which makes sense now that I think about it. After all, I *am* trapped in Grace's head. It'd be weird if we weren't linked somehow. And judging by how thin that string is, it will probably snap the second we actually figure out how to get the fuck out of here.

Relief flows through me at the realization, calms the too-fast beating of my heart and the chaotic tumble of my thoughts.

Just in time, actually, because judging from the look on Grace's face, she's had about enough of my freak-out. No offense, but she can join the fucking club there.

"Seriously, Hudson?" she demands, shoving the wild tumble of her hair out of her face in a way that's rapidly becoming familiar to me. A way that means she's preparing to go into battle. With me, of course, as that seems to be her favorite pastime. "Are you actually listening to anything that I'm saying?"

"Yeah, of course I am," I tell her even as I go back over the last several minutes in my head.

"Oh yeah? What did I say, then?" She crosses her arms over her chest and narrows those big chocolate-brown eyes of hers at me as she waits for an answer.

And why the fuck am I noticing the color of her eyes anyway? And what she does with her hair? Neither of those things matters in the least, so why am I suddenly thinking about them?

I'm not, I assure myself as my heart starts to go crazy again. I'm just freaked out by what I saw. It'll be fine.

It *is* fine. It absolutely is.

Or it will be once I get the fuck away from her for a while. Which is, admittedly, difficult considering we're trapped together. But I'm about to give it the old college try, because whatever the fuck is in my head right now needs to get the fuck out.

"Hudson!" She sounds even more exasperated.

But Jesus, she can get in line. Because exasperation doesn't even touch what I'm feeling at the moment. "What?" I snap.

I didn't think it was possible, but her eyes narrow even more. And her cheeks turn a bright, becoming pink. No. Not becoming. Just regular, plain pink.

What the fuck? I shove a hand through my hair and barely resist the urge to yank it all out. What the everlasting fuck is happening here?

"Oh my God! What on earth are you thinking about? You haven't heard a word I've said."

"Of course I have. You're right, I'm wrong. Take it or leave it. Why aren't you listening to me? Blah, blah, blah."

"Blah, blah, blah?" Her eyebrows shoot up so hard and fast, they nearly hit her hairline. "You are *such* a jerk! You know that, right?"

"*I'm* a jerk?" I echo. "All I'm doing is trying to figure this mess out."

"Really? Because it looks to me like all you're doing is either ignoring me or making fun of me. I thought you were going to take this seriously."

She starts to move away, but I stop her with a hand to her arm. Then let go as soon as I feel a strange sizzle in my fingertips.

"Ow!" Grace yanks her arm away, then gives me a "what the hell" look. "You shocked me."

"Is that what that was?" I ask, staring down at my hand. Which now feels like it belongs to someone else.

Then again, this whole experience feels like it belongs to someone else. If only I could get so lucky.

Of course, luck has never been my strong suit.

"What do you mean?" For the first time in several minutes, Grace sounds less aggressive and more curious. "How have you never been shocked before?"

Because I'm pretty sure I'd have to be touched for that to happen, I want to tell her. Which is something that's been few and far between in my life. Lia was the last person to touch me like that, and it's not as if there was ever a lot of electricity between us.

But that just makes me look pathetic, and I happen to think I've done enough of that in the last few minutes to last a lifetime. Besides, there's no actual electricity between Grace and me. At least, not *that* kind.

It's got to be the rug we're standing on. Or the weather conditions outside. Or—

"Ouch!" It's my turn to yelp as Grace's arm brushes against me and lightning zips up my arm.

"Sorry!" she exclaims, jerking backward.

But when she seems like she's going to say something more, I just shake my head and mutter, "Maybe it's a human thing."

She looks like she wants to argue, but in the end she must decide we've got bigger things to talk about, because she lets it go.

Thankfully.

"So, what I was trying to tell you earlier is maybe you're right." She tucks a flyaway curl behind her ear and waits expectantly for my response.

But I need a little more to go on than that. "In what way?"

"When you said that thing about my subconscious doing all this."

"I didn't think that was in question." I lift a brow and try not to note how close we're standing to each other. "Unless you're consciously doing this?"

"Why would I be?" She looks offended. "Believe me, I want to get out of here even more than you do. Jaxon and Macy are probably worried sick about me."

Now it's my turn to roll my eyes. "Of course. We wouldn't want to worry little Jaxy-Waxy, would we?"

"Why do you always have to be so obnoxious about him?"

"You think this is obnoxious?" I ask. "Believe me, I haven't even gotten started yet."

"Why doesn't that surprise me?" she mutters, then takes a deep breath and says, "but if you think you can hang on to your self-control for a few more minutes, I think I might actually have an idea to get us out of here."

21

I'm Not RSVPing
for This Pity Party
—Grace—

I don't know what the hell is wrong with Hudson, but something definitely is. He looks like an animal that's been frightened and is getting ready to run the second anyone makes any kind of move toward him. And by anyone, I of course mean me.

I take a step closer to test the theory, and yep. He's definitely freaking out. If the wild look in his eyes wasn't evidence enough, the fact that his pupils are completely blown out definitely is.

"Hey, it's going to be okay," I tell him. "We'll figure this out."

Hudson nods, but when I go to place a comforting hand on his shoulder, he jerks away again. Which…okay. Message received. He really, *really* doesn't want to be touched by me. I was trying to comfort him, but it's not like I want to touch him anyway.

Working together to get out of here doesn't mean that we're suddenly going to be best friends. He is who he is, after all.

Although…if my plan actually works, maybe he won't be like this forever.

He nods, then leans a shoulder against the nearest wall. I can't decide if it's because he thinks it makes him look cool—which it does, though I'd die a million deaths before I admit that to him—or because dealing with the *human* is *just so exhausting* that he needs a way to hold himself up.

"So, what's this fantastic plan of yours?" he asks with a smirk.

"I never said it was fantastic. I said I thought it might work."

"Same thing, isn't it?" he asks. "Or do you just not want to own it?"

God, he is such a jerk. Suddenly I'm not so sure my plan *will* work after all. I mean, if you want to mold someone into a halfway decent person—and yes, I know I'm setting the bar low, but this is Hudson I'm talking about here—you need some fairly malleable clay to start with.

And right now, with that stupid smirk and closed-off body language, he looks anything but malleable.

Still, it's worth a shot. Anything if it gets me out of here and back to Jaxon. So I take a deep breath and say, "I've been thinking. It's not all your fault that you're the way you are."

That wipes the smirk off his face. Now he's just staring at me with an inscrutable expression. I look at his eyes for a clue, but they're blank, too.

I wait for him to say something to clue me in to what he's thinking, but he doesn't say a word. And since I really, really can't stand uncomfortable silences, it only takes a few seconds before I'm babbling.

"I'm just saying, I read that journal entry of yours, and you sounded like a really good kid. So, obviously, something happened between then and now to make you like this."

"Like this?" he asks quietly.

"You know." I wave a hand, encompassing him from head to toe. "I think we can both agree you exhibit a whole lot of sociopathic behavior, right?"

He adjusts his shoulder against the wall, crosses one ankle over the other. Raises a brow. "Oh, we can, can we?"

I note the warning in his tone, but I don't stop. I've got to get this out if we have any hope of ever getting out of here. "But that's just because you've had a shit upbringing. Or at least I'm guessing you have if it was anything like Jaxon's."

He laughs then, but there's nothing humorous about the sound. "Well, there's your first mistake. Believe me, Jaxon and I were brought up very differently."

I'm not sure what to say to that, considering the sudden bitterness in his voice. I know Jaxon had it rough growing up—and still has it rough. His mother scarred him because she was furious at him for what happened to Hudson. So it stands to reason that he had it even rougher than Hudson did, even if they weren't raised together.

But looking at Hudson, with his lips pressed together and a faraway look in his eyes, I can't help reevaluating that opinion. But that only makes my plan more important. I don't know what happened to Hudson in his childhood, and I can't change it even if I did know. But I can help him deal with it so he can become a better person.

"Just hear me out," I tell him, positioning myself in front of him when it looks like he's going to walk away. "Think about the cookie shop."

"Believe me, I've done nothing but think about that damn shop for the last half an hour." He shifts slightly, as if it hurts to stand still.

From the way he's looking slightly green around the gills, I'm guessing imaginary cookies don't go down for vampires any better than real strawberries do. Note to future Grace: Don't let Hudson eat anything, even in dreams or memories.

"I'm so sorry if the cookie made you sick," I tell him softly. "That wasn't my intention."

"I'm not sick," he answers, even as he presses a surreptitious hand to his stomach.

I don't believe him, obviously, but I'm not about to call him on his lie. Not when I'm in the middle of trying to convince him that my plan will work.

Please, God, let it work.

"Remember how happy you were at the cookie shop, though? And the art gallery? Before you ate the cookie?"

"I don't have dementia," he snaps. "I think I can remember an hour ago fairly easily."

Okay, so that's obviously a touchy subject, though I don't know why… "I was just thinking. What if we do that more often?"

"Go to the beach?" he asks sardonically.

"Visit some of my memories together. So you can see what a life filled with love is like."

"That's your big plan? Show me happy times and that will somehow set us free?"

"When you say it like that, you make it sound ridiculous."

He pretends to think about my words for a second. Then says, "Nah. You did that all on your own."

"Well, I was thinking that, you know, if it really is my subconscious trapping us here… Well, the only reason I'd keep us here instead of going home is to protect Jaxon from you." The muscle along Hudson's jawline tightens. "So, umm…maybe if you weren't a…*threat*…maybe my subconscious would free us."

His gaze narrows on mine, but he doesn't say a word.

I shrug. "We could give it a shot, you know. See what happens."

And yeah, I get that it sounds ridiculous to think showing him what it is to be loved and happy—helping him feel it—will change the trajectory of his life. But I only read a few pages of his journal yesterday, and it's obvious his father is a shit person who cares only about himself. Add that to what I know of Jaxon's mother, and there's no way this guy ever had a chance. At least these journals make it look like Jaxon got out early. Hudson had to stay there his whole life.

He never had a chance. I want to give him that chance and, in doing so, get us the hell out of here. If my mind is truly a prison, then rehabilitation is exactly what Hudson needs to free us both.

"It could work," I tell him, and this time he lets me put a hand on his shoulder. "You just need to trust me. It will work."

For long seconds, he looks from my face to my hand and back again. When he finally speaks, his voice is much milder than it was a few seconds ago. "Just to be clear about what you're suggesting. You think the way to get us out of here is to trick your subconscious into believing I'm a good person?"

"Not trick it. Obviously, the plan is to make you a better person."

"Oh, right. Of course." He looks down at his hands. "Because I'm a shite person right now."

Alarm bells are going off in the back of my head, a warning that maybe I didn't handle this as well as I could have. "I didn't say that, Hudson."

"Oh, I'm pretty sure you did." His voice is still calm, but it's colder than the air in Denali. "And I have to say, I choose to leave it."

I shake my head. "I don't know what that means."

"At the beginning of this conversation, you told me to take it or leave it. And I'm telling you that I'm leaving it."

He straightens up from his perennial "lean against the wall" stance, and I have a moment to realize just how much taller he is than I am. A shiver works its way down my spine as he steps closer to me. Then he's snarling, "Fuck the 'poor little rich boy' narrative you've built around me. Fuck you riding in on a white horse to save me."

He leans down until our faces are only inches apart and I can see the rage burning in the depths of his eyes. "And fuck your opinion of me. You can keep it and your little tour of Grace's happy times far the fuck away from me."

22

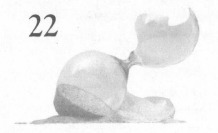

All Cry,
No Punishment
—Grace—

The fury in his eyes is overwhelming, and it takes every ounce of courage I have to stand my ground. This is too important. So I lift my chin and go toe to toe with him, even after he flashes his fangs at me.

"You're a real jerk, you know that?" I glare at him. "I thought maybe there was something else—something better—behind the facade, but there really isn't. You're just an asshole."

"I tried to tell you that," he says, his grin as sharp as the regrets currently shredding my insides. "You're the one who wouldn't listen. Looks like we both have issues."

"Yeah, well, at least my issues still show I have faith in people. Versus yours, which just make you mean."

"Your issues will get you killed," he bites back. "Don't say I didn't warn you when you finally find your way back to brother dearest."

"Jaxon would never hurt me," I tell him.

"Yeah, that's what I used to tell myself, too. Now look where we are."

"That's not fair," I tell him. "You know why he did that."

"You're right. I do know." He shoves a hand through his hair before leveling me with a look that has my stomach spinning, twisting, and turning. "The question is, do you?"

I want to call his bluff, want to tell him that I know he's just bullshitting me. But there's something in his eyes that has the words lodging in my throat.

When I don't answer, silence stretches taut as a circus wire between us. I hate the heaviness of it, the discomfort—it makes my skin crawl and my throat itch. But he's the one who's being unreasonable, the one who's finding fault with everything I have to say.

If he wants to move this conversation forward, he's going to have to be the one to do it.

Except before he can say a word, there's a loud screech from outside, followed by the sound of something large and heavy banging against the door.

"He's back," I whisper, forgetting my determination not to speak with the absolute horror of that realization.

"Of course he's back," Hudson says. "You didn't really think he was gone for good, did you?"

"No! Of course not." I had hoped the dragon was gone, but that didn't mean I believed it. I was counting on him giving us a little more time between attacks, however. Looks like he didn't have the same plans.

"What do we do?" I ask as the thing screams in rage. Seconds later, I can hear the flap of his giant wings. I want to believe he's leaving—that that's the sound of him flying away—but I'm not that optimistic, no matter what Hudson says.

"I don't have a clue what you're going to do," he answers. "But I'm going to read a book."

"A book?" I gape at him. "Do you really think that's a good idea right now?"

"It's a better idea than standing here wondering if the dragon is going to get in," he shoots back. "If he does, we'll deal with it. If he doesn't, then I'm sure he'll keep coming back until he does."

"Which means what exactly? That there's no way we'll survive?"

"I guess that depends on how quickly you can figure out what you did to get us here so that you can undo it."

"I already told you, I don't know how we ended up here. And if I knew how to get us out of it, believe me, we'd already be back at Katmere."

"That's why I said you need to figure it out," he says. Then turns his back on me and walks straight to the closest bookshelf.

I thought he was just messing with me when he said he was going to read, but it turns out Hudson doesn't say things he doesn't mean. So I watch as he peruses three bookshelves before picking out a pristine copy of Albert Camus's *The Stranger*. Then he settles down on the nearest couch, kicks his feet up, and proceeds to read as a pissed-off, screaming dragon continues to circle us.

I, on the other hand, pace back and forth, waiting for the thing to leave. I mean, how am I supposed to relax when there's a monster outside determined to kill me?

Especially when I'm pretty sure the monster inside feels the exact same way?

Eventually, though, the panic slowly abates. My heart rate slows down, fatigue sets in, and it becomes nearly impossible to keep my eyes open. Adrenaline is all well and good when it comes to saving your life, but the crash that comes after it sure is a bitch.

But just because I've calmed down doesn't mean I'm ready to go to sleep with that thing hovering in full seek-and-destroy mode.

Out of desperation, I make a dive for the bathroom.

After I close and lock the door, I lean back against it and sink slowly to the floor. And, despite every effort I make to the contrary, I start to cry.

I cry out of terror, because I have no idea what's happening here—or if I'm going to survive it.

I cry out of sadness, because in this moment I miss my mom and dad more than I ever imagined possible. I miss Jaxon and Macy and Uncle Finn.

And, maybe most of all, I cry out of resignation, because never has it been more obvious that I'm not in Kansas anymore. This is my new life, and it's always going to be my life.

I wouldn't trade Jaxon or Macy for anything, but I'm so tired of not understanding how things work here. So tired of having more questions than answers. So tired of having to depend on other people to explain things to me that I never dreamed existed.

Like right now, there's a part of me that wants nothing more than to march out there and ask Hudson how this whole thing is happening. He says I've locked us up in my head somehow—I have no clue how that's possible, but after that flash to Coronado, I'm willing to believe it.

But why would I choose to wall us up in his lair of all places? Why not Katmere Academy? Or my old house in San Diego? Or pretty much anywhere else on earth? Why the hell would I pick this place, where he's obviously got home-field advantage—and plans on taking full advantage of it?

Plus, if we are in my head, where did that dragon out there come from? I guarantee I've never thought anything like that up in my life. And if I somehow managed to create him, how the hell did he break that window? How did he burn Hudson, who should be safe in my mind?

None of it makes sense—at least not to me. Hudson seems to know what's going on, but he's way more familiar with this world and its rules than I ever will be.

Which is just another thing that sucks. I don't trust this guy, at all. And now, here I am, stuck with him as pretty much my only source of information. And there's no way to know when he's telling the truth and when he's telling one more giant lie. Not to mention, he's not exactly been forthcoming with the information he does decide to give me.

Ugh. Can I just say fuck. My. Life.

Then again, I'm pretty sure it's already fucked. And so am I.

I swipe a hand at the tears rolling down my cheeks, wipe them away. No matter how much I want to stay right here on this bathroom floor for the rest of the night—or eternity—I can't. When I was growing up, my mom always had a rule about crying. She'd give me ten minutes to cry, sob, yell into a pillow, do whatever I had to do. Ten minutes to feel sorry for myself and whine about how terrible whatever I was going on about was. But when those ten minutes were up, I had to pick myself up and move on.

Of course, what picking myself up looked like varied depending on the situation and what it was that had made me cry.

Sometimes, I had to find a solution.

Sometimes, I had to get my scraped knee or cut arm taken care of.

And sometimes…sometimes I just had to suck it up and accept that life isn't always fair, and there's nothing we can do about that fact. Those were the times I hated most of all, and today—right now—is definitely one of those.

But rules are rules, and my ten minutes are up.

So I climb to my feet.

Wash my face.

Take a deep breath.

And tell myself that I can do whatever needs doing. Even if what needs doing is kicking the ass of a two-hundred-year-old vampire with a personality disorder. It may not be easy and it may not be pretty, but—one way or another—I can find a way to get it done.

The thought makes me feel better, or at least steadier, as I make my way back into the main room. Until I get my first look at Hudson, who is watching me with a look in his eyes that can only be described as "gleeful."

Which, when it comes to him, is *never* a look I want to be on the receiving end of. And yet here it is. Panic hits me even before he says, "New plan, Princess."

"Oh yeah?" I shoot him a skeptical look. "What exactly do you have in mind?"

"Instead of convincing you I'm a decent person, as you so helpfully suggested, I'm going to take the low road instead."

Well that sounds…terrifying.

Swallowing down the instinctive fear, I cross to the bookcases and stand with my back against the biggest one. Just in case.

Then I give him my best "tell me something I don't know" look. And answer, "Here I thought you already were."

He returns my look with one of his own—only his says, *You haven't seen anything yet.*

And, as if to prove it, he reaches over and flips on the state-of-the-art stereo he's got taking up a whole lot of space in the media area of the room. The second he does, Guns N' Roses' "Welcome to the Jungle" comes blaring through the speakers so loudly that the windows rattle—right along with my brain.

23

Welcome to
My Jungle
—Hudson—

"**A**re you serious right now?" Grace squawks loudly enough to be heard above the music. But it barely registers, as I've got my earbuds in to muffle the sound.

Not that I need to hear her to see how pissed she is. The outrage written all over her face has me grinning. I'm not normally the type to torture others—I'm more of a "live and leave alone" kind of guy—but I'm not going to make it through too many more of Grace's earnest suggestions on how to "save" me without losing my shite.

So really, this is safer for both of us. She can try to redeem me all she wants, and I won't hear enough to get pissed off.

She may think I'm a sociopath, and maybe I am. But the fact that she said all that shit to me and I didn't do a damn thing about it should qualify me for something. Sainthood, maybe. Or at least a 99 Flake—and you know I don't do dairy.

Besides getting a little of my own back, annoying her might just have the nice, ancillary benefit of getting her to let us go. She thinks she needs to trick whatever part of her has us locked up here into thinking I'm not a threat. Maybe I just need to infuriate her enough that that part decides that whatever it's got going on here isn't worth it and lets us go in self-defense.

Is it a long shot? Sure. But so is everything else I've thought of, and at least this way I'll get to have a good time.

"Turn the music down, Hudson!" she shrieks again.

I simply smile vacuously and mime that I can't hear her.

Which only pisses her off more, judging by the way her eyes narrow and her fingers curl into a pretty good facsimile of claws.

Nice to know I haven't lost my touch.

"I'm serious!" she screams as Axl Rose goes on about watching us bleed.

"Do you really think this is going to help anything?"

Again, I pretend not to understand her. Then, when she's still sputtering with outrage, I walk over to my quiver of axes and pick one out.

Grace's eyes go wide, and her complaints turn to squawks of alarm. I feel bad for a second—I don't want her to think I'll actually hurt her—so I rush my throw as I send the ax hurtling toward the large target on the wall.

Because I rushed it, the ax lands several inches wide of the bull's-eye. Which has me grabbing two more and sending them soaring through the air. Both hit dead center of the target.

A quick glance out of the corner of my eye shows her gaping at the target like she's never seen one before. "You really throw axes?" she asks.

It's the first thing she's said to me that's not a shout since she came out of the bathroom, so I don't pretend not to hear her. At the same time, though, the answer's pretty obvious, so I just shrug.

Then throw another ax.

This one slides right in between the other two. Direct bull's-eye.

Grace watches with what looks like interest, but when I hold one out to her to throw, she shakes her head vigorously as she backs away.

"Just turn down the music, will you?"

She phrases it like a question, but it's not a request. Which leaves me with only one thing to do. I walk back to the stereo and turn the music up, just as The Halo Effect's "Shadowminds" starts to play.

It's heavy on drums, heavy on bass, and absolutely obnoxious when played this loud. In other words, perfect for what I'm trying to accomplish.

Grace is so angry now that she can barely speak, which is fine by me. About time she joined the club.

She storms over to the kitchen, and I pretend not to watch as she grabs a bottle of water from the fridge. But it's hard to play innocent when she opens one of the cupboards and pulls out a box of those Pop-Tart things she likes so much.

An *empty* box.

What can I say? I used my time wisely while she was in the bathroom.

I throw another ax, but I don't have a clue if it hits or not. I'm too busy watching her out of the corner of my eye.

She looks confused, but not upset—or should I say not any more upset than she originally was—as she tosses the cardboard box into the recycling bin.

But when she reaches for another box, one that is sealed on top, and opens it to also find no Pop-Tarts, she slams it down on the counter and looks at me with narrowed eyes.

In response, I calmly walk to the target to retrieve my axes, then set up to throw them again—all without so much as acknowledging she exists. But once she reaches into the cabinet a third time, I can't help but watch as she opens yet another empty Pop-Tart box.

At that point, she doesn't even bother to throw the box away. Instead, she slams it down on the kitchen counter with a primal shout before making a beeline straight toward me.

"What is your problem?" she yells, and this time she's loud enough that there's no pretending I don't hear her over the music. Which...damn. The girl has one hell of a set of pipes on her.

"You're the one screaming," I reply calmly. I'm pretty sure she didn't hear me, but she gets angrier anyway. And this time when she screams, I reach over and turn the music down—leaving her suddenly yelling into a quiet room.

"Why do you have to be so—" Her words bounce off the walls, and she freezes mid-tirade. "Seriously?" she demands. "Now you turn the music off?"

"You looked like you had something to say," I answer with the most innocent expression I can muster.

For a second, it looks like Grace is going to wrest one of my axes out of my hand and beat me with it, but in the end she just takes a deep breath and blows it out slowly. More's the pity. I was looking forward to the entertainment.

"Where. Are. My. Pop-Tarts?" she asks after blowing out another breath.

"Pop-Tarts?" I try to pretend confusion, but I'm pretty sure the amused look in my eyes gives me away. "Are you talking about those rectangular pink biscuits you're always eating?"

She lifts her chin. "First of all, I am not *always* eating them. I've had two packs since we've been here. And—"

"Looks to me like you had three whole boxes," I interrupt. "Maybe more."

"Secondly," she continues, but she's forcing the words out between clenched teeth now.

And maybe I should be ashamed of myself for getting her this riled up, but it's hard to be ashamed when I'm getting this much entertainment out of the whole thing. And also because I can still hear her sounding all serious when she offered to help me become a better person.

"Secondly," she repeats when she realizes she doesn't have my full attention. "They aren't biscuits."

"Oh, right. What's the American word for biscuits again?" I snap my fingers like I'd forgotten, even though we ate cookies together just a few hours ago. "Cookies! You call them cookies, right?"

The sound she makes comes from deep in her throat. It's low and dangerous and just a little bit primal. Which only makes me grin wider.

This is going better than I'd ever anticipated. If I can keep this up a little longer, we'll be out of here by morning.

"And thirdly," Grace growls. "Keep your hands—and everything else of yours—off my Pop-Tarts."

It's a warning and a threat rolled up into one, and I can tell she's deadly serious about it. But that just makes it more fun to poke the bear.

So I do. I lift a brow, give her the most insouciant smile I can manage. And ask, "Or else?"

Then step back and wait for the fireworks.

It doesn't take long.

24

Dividing the Room in Styles
—Grace—

"**A**re you a toddler?" I ask him, because who else responds to justified outrage like that?

"Is that the best you've got?" he says with a raised brow. "Because I was looking forward to a real threat."

"You want a real threat, you overgrown child? How about you lay one more finger on my Pop-Tarts, and I'll file your fangs down while you sleep?"

Now both brows are up. "Damn, Grace. That's harsh." There's real surprise in his eyes—as well as some amusement—as he continues. "Who hurt you?"

As he waits for my answer, Hudson rubs an absent thumb over the pointiest part of his fang. And looks surprisingly good doing it. So good, in fact, that I take a step back. And snipe, "Don't worry about who hurt me. Worry about how I'm going to hurt you if you don't keep your hands off my stuff."

"Your stuff?" His glance around the room is zero parts remorse and one hundred percent Lord of the Manor. "We're currently living in *my* lair."

"I don't see why that matters."

"Sure you do." His lips twist in that superior smirk that drives me nuts. "My lair, my things."

"In normal circumstances, I might be tempted to agree. But, as you've told me numerous times since we've gotten here, we're not actually in your lair at all. We're in my head."

"So?"

"So…" I shrug like it's the most obvious thing in the world. "My head, my things."

"Wow, Grace. I didn't know you felt that way." There's a wicked gleam in his eyes that I don't trust, but I've got no choice now but to brazen through this. Whatever this is.

Which is why I tell him, "Sorry, *Hudson,* but a girl's got to do what a girl's got to do," before I start walking back to the kitchen.

"You know, that's a very good point," he agrees as he follows me across the lair. "Which leaves me with only one more question for you, then."

I'm getting tired of this cat-and-mouse game. Getting tired, period, if I'm being honest. Trying to stay one step ahead of Hudson is an exhausting job, one I don't know that I'm up for.

Maybe that's why I answer, "What's your question?" without thinking it through.

The wicked gleam has turned into a full-out grin as he leans against the counter and stares down at me from his ridiculous height. "Now that I'm yours, what *do* you plan to do with me?"

Ugh. I walked right into that one. And now I'm blushing, my cheeks turning red-hot despite my best attempt not to react to the innuendo in his words. This is just one more way he's trying to get to me—like the music and the Pop-Tarts—but I'm not going to give him the satisfaction.

So, ignoring the blush that is making my whole face feel like it's on fire, I look Hudson straight in the eye and answer, "I thought I'd already explained this to you. I'm going to file down your fangs."

He grins. "There's that mean streak again. I've got to admit, it's growing on me."

"Yeah, well, I think it's pretty obvious that I don't want to grow on you," I snap back.

"Hey, I'm just calling it like I see it." He stretches then, and the T-shirt he changed into after his shower rides up a little bit, showing off a swath of exceptionally ripped abs.

Not that I care what kind of abs he has—ripped or otherwise. It's just hard to ignore when he's standing right in front of me.

"There's no need to be shy, Grace," he continues, and as he leans back, I swear his shirt shows even more skin. And a tiny little bit of the happy trail that leads into the low waistband of his workout pants. "A woman needs to know how to ask for what she wants."

I keep my eyes stubbornly on his face. "I know exactly what I want."

"Oh yeah?" he answers in a voice like a secret. "What's that?"

"To get the hell away from you." Deciding I don't need to eat tonight, I push past him and walk back to the couch I slept on last night.

He follows me, because of course he does.

And all of a sudden, I've had it. I'm sick of his attitude, sick of his juvenile tricks, sick of him always getting the better of me. And I'm sure as hell sick of him always being three feet away from me. This room is huge. Why does he always have to be exactly where I am?

As if to prove my point, he sits on the couch and kicks his feet up on the coffee table. And that's it. That's freaking it.

"No!" I shout.

He looks startled. "No what?"

"Get up!"

When he just stares at me like he doesn't understand the words coming out of my mouth, I grab his arm and tug at him. "Get up! Get up, get up, get up! This couch is mine!"

"Are we back to everything in here being yours?" he asks. "Because if so—"

"No!" I cut him off, because I am not going there again. "No, no, no!"

"You okay?" he asks, brows raised. "Because you're looking a little flushed—"

"The couch is mine. The bed is yours." I point to the bed at the end of the room, just in case he pretends to misunderstand me. "In fact, you can have that whole side of the room."

"Excuse me?" He's looking a lot less confident and a lot more confused. Good. It's about time he feels as off balance as I do, about time I find a way to gain back the upper hand.

"You heard me," I tell him as an idea finally starts forming. "You can have this whole side of the room—the bed, the ax throwing, the stereo, the TV."

I look around for a roll of duct tape and am shocked to find one in my hand. And not just any duct tape—no, this is a limited-edition One Direction roll of duct tape, like the kind my dad bought me when I was a kid. Harry, Louis, Niall, Zayn, and Liam all stare happily back at me as I make my way to the far end of the room.

"And I get everything on this side. Couch, books, kitchen—"

"And the bathroom?" he asks, brows raised at me laying the duct tape right down the center of the room.

"The bathroom's the only neutral ground," I tell him while I roll the tape right past my couch. "Everything else in here belongs to either you or me. And neither of us gets to cross this line."

I take the line all the way to the wall on the opposite side of the loft and tear it off the roll. When I turn around, it's to find Hudson resting with a shoulder against the wall, arms crossed over his chest. The wicked look in his eyes is gone, replaced by the empty expression from earlier.

I'm pretty sure that means I got to him.

I'm about to pat myself on the back for finally getting under his skin when the universe hands me another present. He mutters, "All the books are on your side of the room."

"Why, yes. Yes they are." I shoot him my best facsimile of an evil grin and head straight toward the bookshelf that holds all his journals. "And I know just what I'm going to read first."

25

I Mo, You Mo, We All Emo
—Grace—

Apparently, Sartre knew what he was talking about when he wrote *No Exit*. We've been trapped here for eight of the longest, most interminable weeks of my life, and every time I think it can't get any worse, I read another one of Hudson's journal entries and find out that it can.

Each journal entry reminds me that Jaxon's and Hudson's parents really are the worst people on the planet. Which makes me think of both brothers.

Which sucks on so many levels, mainly because I'm trying very hard not to think of either Vega brother. The first because I'm trapped with him and he is on my very last nerve. And the other because I'm starting to admit I might never see him again.

When we were first trapped here, I constantly looked through the photos of Jaxon on my phone, cried myself to sleep every night, *ached* to see his face just one more time. Tell him how much I love him one last time. But as the days have turned to weeks, and the weeks to months, I've made myself stop.

No more quick looks at my phone to remind myself of his smile.

No more grinning at the memory of a corny knock-knock joke we'd share.

No more imagining his arms wrapped around me as I fall asleep.

Because I know if I don't let him go, my subconscious might do anything to see Jaxon again, including give in and release Hudson from this prison. And if Hudson then killed Jaxon, I'd never forgive myself.

I would give Jaxon up a thousand times if it meant saving his life.

And no matter what Hudson's said to the contrary, I still believe that's exactly why I've trapped us here in this prison with a roll of tape stretched down the middle. I still believe I could let us free if he'd give in and at least *try* to be rehabilitated.

Because the more I read Hudson's journals, and as much as I'm convinced that both boys got the shit end of the stick in the parent department—Hudson's stick was used to beat him with it. I'm finding myself feeling a whole lot of sympathy for him. Which is not something I ever thought I'd say—and definitely not something I ever wanted to feel.

But it's hard not to imagine the little boy with the cut finger, rushing to finish a carved horse in the one day a month he has aboveground, just so his little brother won't feel as alone as he does. Even harder not to feel bad for him.

And not to wonder when he gave up. When he went from this sweet boy determined to protect his brother to the sociopath who tried to kill him instead.

I know a lot went on in the last hundred and fifty years, and I've got dozens of journals to fill in the time. But I still want to know how. I still want to know if it was one defining moment or a lot of little moments.

Not that it matters—the end result is the end result. Except, sitting here, holding this boy's journal in my hands, it suddenly feels like it matters a whole lot.

I glance down at the latest journal entry. I'm well into what Hudson called his "emo years" now, and I can tell why he advised me to skip them—although not for the reason he implied. Because these are the most heartbreaking stories I've ever read. Even the amusing entry titles can't make me smile anymore.

Today I saw the most amazing invention. It was incredible. A telephone.

It's a device with a knob-like object to listen from and another to hold in your hands and speak into. There's a cable that connects the contraption to the wall, and Richard says the cables go all over the city and connect to other homes.

I asked him what you do with it, and he said you can talk to anyone anywhere they are as long as you both have a device, too. Imagine that!

I begged him to let me try it, but Father walked in and demanded to know why I wasn't in the training yard. For the first time, I thought about giving him exactly what he wants. A demonstration of my powers. Maybe he'd stop making me Transcend.

Maybe I wouldn't only get one day a month to note how the world is changing while I stay trapped in that dark crypt.

But I glanced back at the telephone before heading out to the training area and knew it wasn't worth it. I'd shown Father what I could do one time, when he'd taken Jaxon from me, and ever since, he's not stopped dreaming up new ways to torture the power out of me again.

If he knew the other thing I could do...he'd never let me go. Ever.

Besides, who did I have to call anyway?

26

Re-Tweeting

—Grace—

As I finish the journal entry, I can't stop myself from looking over at Hudson. He's currently draped over the chair in front of the TV, playing *Demon's Souls*. But after eight weeks of alternating between that and *Call of Duty*, he doesn't seem that into it.

Maybe that's why he chooses this exact moment to turn his head and look back at me. Our gazes lock, and for a second, he looks inquisitive.

But then his gaze drops to the journal in my lap, and his whole face closes up. Anger flares briefly in his eyes, but then they go blank. And we're left staring at each other—me caught between the sweet boy he used to be and the obnoxious guy he is now and him...who the hell knows where he is. Nowhere good, from the look of it.

After a minute, he goes back to his game. But it turns out, that's only to shut it off. Then he's standing up and stretching, like he's getting ready to throw axes or do his daily round of five hundred push-ups.

Instead of reaching for his axes, though, he looks straight at me. Raises one dark brow. And lets out the most bizarre sound I have ever heard.

It's earsplitting and terrible and like nothing I've ever heard before. I stare at him, shocked, as he does it again. And again. And again.

"What the fuck are you doing?" I finally manage to gasp out.

This time, the look he gives me is so innocent, it's amazing a halo isn't shining right above his head. "I'm practicing my birdcalls."

"Your what?"

"I'm an amateur ornithologist. Since we've been trapped in here for weeks, I haven't had a chance to go birdwatching, but that's no reason to neglect my birdcalls."

"Your birdcalls?" I get up from the couch and put his journal back on the shelf. "There is no way that ridiculously creepy sound is made by a bird."

"It absolutely is," he informs me, then makes the strange cackling sound one more time. "The Australian kookaburra, in fact. It's the largest of the kingfisher birds, even though it only weighs up to about one pound. It has an average life span of fifteen years and takes about twenty to twenty-two days to incubate as an egg."

He rattles off the facts like they're right there at the front of his brain—or like he's making them up. I think it's the latter, but since I haven't been able to google anything since we landed here two months ago, I guess I'll never know.

"That's…fascinating," I say in a tone that tells him birds aren't really my thing. Normally, I'd have a few more caustic things to add, but that last journal entry is still fresh in my mind. And it's hard to be snarky to someone who obviously suffered so much.

So instead of saying something cutting, I just smile at him and head toward the kitchen. But I only make it a couple of steps before Hudson makes another obnoxious sound—albeit very different than the first one.

This one is an eerie, high-pitched *oooooo* that has shivers shooting down my spine.

But I'm determined to take the high road here, so I just keep walking. Which Hudson, unfortunately, seems to take as encouragement to keep going.

"Ooooooooooooooo. Ooooooooooooooo. Ooooooooooooo."

The sound is like fingernails scraping down the wall, but I do my best to ignore it—until somewhere around the fifteenth time he does it.

"Okay, seriously. What kind of bird sounds like that?" I ask, grabbing a Dr Pepper from the fridge. Because if I'm going to have to put up with this for the next who knows how long, it's going to require something stronger than water.

"It's the common loon, actually. Some people find its call relaxing." He does it again. "Ooooooooooooo."

"How nice for them," I answer as I pull out the fixings for a grilled-cheese sandwich. And count backward from one hundred. Surely he'll be done with the scary-ass loon sounds by then.

Turns out, I only need to get to seventy-six before he gives up on the ooooooos. I let out the breath I've been holding in a long sigh of relief, only to jump about a foot in the air when he follows the loon call with a loud, deep croak that sets every nerve in my body on edge.

Don't react, I tell myself.

"Croooooooak."

It will just encourage him if he gets a rise out of you. You know he's only doing it because he's bored.

"Croooooooooooooooooooooooooooak."

Don't react, don't react, don't react.

"Croooo"—he's interrupted from his warble by a cough, and I think that's the end of it. But nope, he's committed, because the second he's able, he goes right back to it. "Crooooooooooooooooooooooooooooooooooooooooooooo oak."

"Okay, I get it. Jesus! You don't have to pretend a bird sounds like a damn frog just to annoy me—"

"I'm not pretending anything," he answers, sounding highly affronted. "That is the song of the South American toucan—"

"You're just making shit up now," I tell him. "No bird sounds like the cross between a dying frog and a pissed-off pig."

"The toucan does," he answers, and again he looks so innocent that it's hard to believe he's fucking with me. But I've been trapped in this hellhole with him for way too long, and I am well aware that he's just trying to piss me off. Even before he continues. "I know it's an acquired taste, but some ornithologists think it's the most beautiful call of all birds—"

"Bullshit!" I explode. "I have put up with the kookaburra and the loon. But there is no way I am putting up with some fake-ass toucan snort—"

"Not fake," he interjects.

"Fake, not fake. I don't give a shit. Knock it off with the birdcalls."

"Okay."

"That's it?" I ask suspiciously. "Just okay?"

"Sure, if it bothers you that much—" He shrugs and smiles sweetly.

Wondering if maybe we're calling a truce after eight weeks of open warfare, I smile back. Then pick up my Dr Pepper to take a drink as I turn back to the stove.

"Crooooooooooooooooooooooooooooooooooooooooooooooooooooooo oooak!" Hudson howls at the top of his lungs.

I choke on my drink, spew Dr Pepper everywhere, and spend the next two minutes coughing soda out of my lungs.

Fuck my life. And fuck Hudson Vega.

27

De-Briefing

—Hudson—

"**D**o you have to take forever in the shower?" Grace snarls as I walk out of the bathroom.

I give her a deliberately mild look. "Someone certainly got up on the wrong side of the bed this morning."

"I got up in a fine mood, thank you very much." She moves past me with a glare. "But I've been waiting to pee for an hour now."

Good. It's nice to know all the time I wasted in there actually paid off. But all I say is, "Sorry."

"No, you're not. If you were, you wouldn't do it every freaking day." She looks me over with a scowl. "And could you please put some clothes on while I'm in the bathroom? You look ridiculous."

"I'm wearing clothes," I answer, glancing down at myself in confusion. "How is what I'm wearing ridiculous?"

"You're wearing sweatpants, not clothes. It's not the same thing." As if to underscore her point, she slams the bathroom door in my face.

As soon as she does, I drop the innocent, confused look. I've been wearing it so much lately that I'm afraid my face is going to freeze like this. And then what the hell am I going to do? It's hard to scare people away when you look like a damn Boy Scout.

But I've found that—next to birdcalls—pretending innocence as I play a dirty trick on her is the best way to get under Grace's skin.

For the love of God, may I please get under her skin soon.

I have to admit, the girl's got more staying power than I ever expected. I was sure we'd be out of here that first night after I made the moves on her *and* annoyed the shit out of her at the same time.

Instead, we've been here for six of the longest months of my life, and there doesn't seem to be any end in sight. Which is why I've recently taken to hogging the bathroom for hours on end. Surely that will get old quickly, right?

But as I make my way to the closet—which is firmly on my side of the room—I gather that I'm not the only one who was in the mood to screw with my roommate this morning. Because while I was in the bathroom, Grace rearranged all my stuff.

And by "rearranged," I mean made a total and utter disaster out of any and all semblance of order my side of the room once had. No wonder she was bitching about my lack of a shirt when I walked out of the bathroom. She wanted to hurry me down here so I could see *this*.

My shirts and pants, which are normally hanging, are tossed into my drawers.

My pajamas and boxers are hanging on hangers in the closet.

And all of my bedding has been stripped off my bed and piled underneath it.

What the everlasting hell?

And the fuckery doesn't stop there, either, I realize as I stride over to my album collection. They are still on the shelves where I have always kept them, but she has completely rearranged them. Instead of sections alphabetized by type—with albums in the section alphabetized by artist's last name—they are all mixed up together. With absolutely no rhyme or reason to the madness.

She destroyed the entire system.

I turn to glare at the bathroom door. This is some first-class-level treachery she's got going on here. There's no birdcall or shaken/exploding Dr Peppers (a particularly clever prank, I must admit as I remember the soda dripping down her face) that's ever going to be payback enough for this.

The bathroom door opens as I'm glaring at it, and it hits me why she showered last night—so she could be around to see the result of her devil's handiwork.

She is going to pay for this. Oh, is she going to pay. As soon as I figure out how.

None of that shows on my face, though, as she walks out of the bathroom with a gleeful gleam in her eyes. Instead, I adopt the innocent look I am so damn sick of and say, "Someone was busy while I was in the shower."

"Do you like it?" she asks, and she's giving me the innocent look right back—all wide eyes and sweet grin. But I practically invented this shit, and there's no way I'm going to be beaten at my own game. Not now, not ever.

"I love it. I was getting bored with that filing system for my vinyl anyway." I nearly choke on the words, but somehow I manage to get them out. "This way, every time I reach for an album, it will be a surprise."

"That's exactly what I was thinking," she agrees enthusiastically. "I knew you'd like it."

"I really do. So much."

Then, because my eye is actively twitching by this point, I turn and walk back toward my bedroom area. As I do, I will her to leave it at that. To not try to push any more of my buttons.

But Grace and I have been cooped up in here for months with that damn dragon circling and slamming against the walls and roof every chance he gets. We've pulled every prank in the book on each other up until this point, so of course she doesn't leave it alone.

I wouldn't, either.

"Do you like what I did to your closet?" she asks sweetly.

"Love it," I answer from between clenched teeth. "Hanging the boxers up was especially ingenious."

"I think so, too. I mean, I figured peacock underwear like that needs to be displayed where you can see it every day."

"I see it every day when I open my drawer." I reach for a pair. "But this is nice, too."

As I hold it up, I see she's done more than just put the bloody things on a hanger.

For a second, I'm too shocked to do anything but stare at the pair in my hand. Then I start pulling all of them down and checking them. Sure enough, she's done the same thing to all of them.

She's used black Sharpie to draw on every single pair of Versace boxer briefs I own.

On the ones with faces, she's drawn mustaches and for several of them, she's also added devil's horns. On the ones without faces, she's drawn in lightning bolts and stars and some comic-book sound effects. Bam. Pow. *Splat.*

I am particularly offended by the ones that say *splat* directly over my crotch.

"Those were Versace," I tell her, and no matter how hard I try, I can't keep the horror out of my voice. What kind of a monster does something like this?

"They still are," she responds cheerfully.

And I swear, if I was a different kind of vampire, her throat would be ripped out right now. As it is, I take a moment to fold my boxers and stack them on my bed.

Because two can play at this game.

28

It Dunks to Be Me

—Grace—

The look on Hudson's face is priceless. In fact, I wish I had my phone on me because I would totally take a picture and save it for posterity. Apparently, he was even more attached to those boxers than I thought.

I consider poking him a little bit more—God knows, he loves to poke me when he's got the upper hand—but then he turns around, and I realize that I'm in trouble.

And not just any trouble. Big freaking trouble. And there's absolutely nowhere for me to go.

His bright blue eyes are shining with calculation, and his mouth is twisted into that ridiculous smirk that always means he's up to something. Even worse, the tips of his fangs are gleaming against his lower lip in as much threat as promise.

Six months ago, I would have been convinced I was about to die. Now I'm only partially convinced.

He takes a step toward me, and for a second my eyes dart to the door. For the first time since the night we got here, I'm seriously thinking of taking my chances with the dragon. Because sure, he'll kill me, but at least it will probably be fast.

That's more than the look on Hudson's face says at the moment.

"Don't even think about it," he growls, and he's right. I know he's right. But that just means there's only one place for me to hide.

"Wait a second," I tell him, holding a hand out as if to ward him off. "We can talk about this."

"Oh, I intend to," he answers as he very deliberately takes another step toward me.

"It was a joke. I was just trying to—" Fuck it. I make a mad dash for the bathroom.

Seven more steps, four more steps, two—

Hudson slams into me from behind, and the momentum of him crashing into me while I'm running carries us through the bathroom doorway. I start to fall—again from the power of him slamming into my back—but he catches me at the last second. Picks me up in his arms.

As he takes a step toward the shower, I don't know whether to laugh or scream. When he reaches into the stall and turns on the water, I end up doing both as I wrap my arms around his neck and hang on for dear life.

"Oh, fook no," he tells me, and outrage has his British accent sounding even more pronounced—and more formal—than ever. "You can scream all you want, but after ruining every pair of underwear I have, you're going in."

"They're not ruined!" I try to tell him between shrieks of laughter. "I used eyeliner. You can wash them—"

"No, *you* can wash them. After you get a dunking." Again, he tries to thrust me away from him and into what I know is an ice-cold shower. Again, I hang on like a limpet, wrapping my arms and legs around him and clutching as tightly as I can.

"Don't do it, Hudson!" I screech, still laughing, as he tries to peel me off him. "No, don't! I'm sorry! I'm sorry."

"For fuck's sake," he mutters under his breath, two seconds before he steps into the shower with me still in his arms.

The instant the freezing cold water hits us, I scream and he curses, low and long and vicious.

"I told you not to do it!" I say when I finally catch my breath from laughing so hard, my sides ache.

"And I told you that you were going in," he answers with a sniff. "Any person worth her salt would have taken her well-deserved punishment like a woman instead of caterwauling about it loudly enough to wake the dead."

"I did not *caterwaul*! In fact—"

It hits me in that moment that I'm still in Hudson's arms. And now we're soaking wet, which means I can feel a whole lot more of him than I could a couple of minutes ago. And he can definitely feel—and see—a whole lot more of me.

He must realize it, too, because by the time I'm pulling away, he's already letting me go—or at least sliding me down his body until my feet can touch the ground.

"You okay?" he asks, and though he's stepped back a little, he's still got his arms wrapped around my waist to steady me.

And suddenly, the look in his eyes doesn't make me want to run. It makes me want to stay right here.

Panic roars through me at the thought, has my stomach twisting and my blood pounding in my ears. "I'm fine," I tell him, and I shove away from him so hard, I go flying out of the shower stall and nearly land on my ass.

He catches me, this time with hands as gentle as a whisper, as he sets me back on my feet. "Grace—"

"Get off me!" I shout, and this time when I push him away, he lets me go.

29

How Do You Say Good-Pie?
—Hudson—

"**A**re you okay?"

I say the words begrudgingly, since it's not like we're on the best of terms at the moment. Not that we ever have been, but it's been especially bad since the great shower incident of last spring.

Ever since that morning, Grace has kept her distance. And I've done the same. Which has made the last several months of reorganizing my vinyl collection, studying new birdcalls, and throwing axes exceedingly boring. Once a month, we sit on opposite ends of the couch and watch one of my DVDs together while she munches on popcorn. It's the best day of the month.

The only other highlight to my days that stretch like a desert between film nights has been her daily wake-up call at seven a.m., followed by, believe it or not, an unspoken star-jumping—or as Grace calls it, jumping jacks—contest. Most days, I win, but every once in a while, I like to shake things up and give her a chance.

This doesn't feel like she's pissed off at me, though. This feels like something else.

"Grace?" I prompt when she doesn't answer. But she doesn't look up from the book she's staring at. In fact, I don't even think she heard me.

Still, I wait for a few more seconds, just in case I'm wrong.

But when a minute comes and goes and she still hasn't said a word, I clear my throat. Loudly. And ask again, "Hey, Grace. Are you all right?"

She doesn't say a word—which I'm pretty sure is an answer in itself.

Something's been wrong with her all day, which I can further tell by the way she's currently holding herself. Like she's afraid she'll shatter if she makes any sudden moves. And maybe she will. I don't know.

I've seen a lot of different facets of Grace over the last year that we've been locked up here.

Angry Grace, who is usually determined to see me suffer.

Competitive Grace, who refuses to give an inch.

Mischievous Grace, who likes to cause as much trouble as possible.

Conflicted Grace, who doesn't know what she wants or why she wants it.

I'm used to those Graces, will take any one of them anytime. But this... this is Sad Grace, and I don't know how to deal with her at all. I definitely don't know how to make her better.

But surely leaving her to stew in her own sadness isn't the way. Not this time.

So instead of walking away, I take my first unauthorized step over her ridiculous One Direction duct tape in months (except to grab the odd bottle of water) and sit down on the couch next to her. The fact that she doesn't shove me away or tell me to get lost is the final clue that something really is wrong with her.

Which only leaves me with one thing I can do to try to help her. I slip inside her mind and sneak a peek at the memory that's right at the forefront.

. . .

"I want to see the baby seals, Daddy! Let's go see the babies!"

Young Grace—maybe six or seven—is strolling down a beachfront street in a frilly white dress with red polka dots all over it. She's holding the hand of a man in his mid-thirties, who's also dressed up.

"We can't, Grace. They aren't here this time of year."

"What do you mean? They have their babies here, so they should live here." Grace looks all upset and, for a second, I think she's going to stomp her foot until her father takes her to see the seals.

But her dad just leans down and tickles her until she laughs, a joyous sound that fills up the whole memory and makes my chest tighten.

"Things don't work like that," he tells her after she finally stops giggling. "Everything has a season, and right now, it's the season for them to be in their other home, where the water is warmer."

"Because it's winter and it's going to be cold here soon?" Grace asks.

"Exactly. They don't have a house where they can warm up like we do. So they need to go where the water is warm enough for them to be comfortable."

Grace seems to think about that for a little while as the pair keeps walking, swinging their hands back and forth.

"When they come back, they'll stay for a while?" she asks. "And have babies of their own?"

"They sure will," her dad says.

"And you'll bring me down to see them—as long as we don't get too close. Seals need their space so they can feel safe." She says the last as if it's something she's been told a million times before. Which—judging from how headstrong I know her to be—she probably has.

"Absolutely. I love to see the babies, too."

"I can't wait!" She claps her hands, then looks up at her father with big brown eyes. "How long will I have to wait?"

He grins and bops her on the nose. "Five or six months, honey. They'll be here at the end of April or beginning of May."

"April is after March!" she tells him in a singsong voice. "And March is after February and February is after January."

Her father is laughing full-out now, shaking his head like she's the cutest thing he's ever seen. And maybe she is. Parents are weird about their offspring. Not my parents, obviously, but most parents.

"You're absolutely right. That is how the months go."

"But that's a long way away. It's going to take *forever*." She looks utterly disappointed.

"You'd be surprised how short forever can be when you're busy," her dad answers. "The babies will be here before you know it."

"And you'll bring me to see them?" She studies his face like a poker player looking for a tell.

He laughs again. "Yes, I promise. I'll bring you to see the seals in April." He holds out a hand to her. "Deal?"

She thinks about it for a second, then shakes his hand. "Deal!"

She's got a wide smile on her face, and for the first time, I notice she's missing her two front teeth. It's a good look on her—ridiculously adorable— something she uses to her advantage when she continues. "Can we go down now, Daddy? I know there aren't any seals, but I want to see the tide pools."

"Not today, honey. I'll bring you back this weekend, and we'll check out all the tide pools. But first we have to go to the store for Mommy. Remember? She needs us to pick up more cream so she can get it all whipped up for the pumpkin pie."

Grace claps her hands. "I like pumpkin pie!"

"So do I, precious. So do I." Her dad reaches down to ruffle her hair. "What do you say we race to that store on the corner there? Whoever wins gets the biggest piece of pie."

Grace rolls her eyes—a move I'm intimately acquainted with. "You always get the biggest piece of pie."

"Do I?" Her father pretends to be surprised. "Maybe that's because I always win."

"Not this time!" Grace takes off running as fast as her little legs will carry her.

Her dad catches up in no time, swooping her into his arms and putting her on his shoulders. "This way, we both win," he tells her as they duck to get into the store.

"Yay! That means we get all the pie!"

"You don't think we should leave a small piece for Mommy?" They start cruising down the convenience store aisles to the dairy refrigerator.

"A really small piece?" she asks, looking down at her father with suspicion.

He chokes back a laugh. "The smallest piece ever."

"Okay. I guess that will work." She sounds so begrudging that both her dad and I crack up.

"I love you, sweetheart."

"I love you, too, Daddy," she answers sweetly. Then, "Oooh, can I get some bubble gum?"

Her father shakes his head even as he reaches for a pack of gum and hands it to her. "Give you an inch and you'll take three miles, won't you, Gracie-girl?"

"Three's my lucky number," she tells him as she turns the pack of gum over and over in her hands.

"I bet it is," he answers. "I bet it is."

30

Uneasy as Pie

—Hudson—

Today is Thanksgiving, I realize as I slip out of the memory. When we'd first discovered we were trapped here, Grace had opened a kitchen drawer and pulled out a calendar. Marking off another day was my signal she was ready to do her daily jumping jacks. How could I not have noted what day it was this morning?

No wonder Grace is so upset. Today's the start of the second holiday season she's going to have to spend without her parents, the second holiday season she's had to spend locked up in my lair with no end in sight.

I'm not American—Thanksgiving means nothing to me—but even I understand the sucker punch she's feeling right now. I just don't know what the bloody hell to do about it.

"You want to make a pumpkin pie?" I ask, because that's what she was thinking about in her memory. *And* because a turkey seems well beyond our culinary skills.

"I don't know how to make a pumpkin pie," she answers, and even though it's a negative response, it tells me I'm on the right track. It's the first thing she's said to me all day.

"How hard can it be?" I posture. "Some pumpkin, some sugar—" I assume there's sugar in a pie. "Some crust. We'll be done, just like that." I snap my fingers.

She laughs, and it's one of those sad, sniffling kind of laughs that cuts a man at the knees. "I'm pretty sure there's more to it than that."

"Well, let's find out." I stand up and hold out a hand. She just looks at it— her gaze darting between my face and my hand—until finally she takes it and lets me pull her up. "You are going to have to let me in the kitchen, however."

"You're already off sides," she answers. "What's another hour?"

"My sentiments exactly."

"I want to go on record as saying I think this is going to be an unmitigated disaster," she tells me as we walk toward the kitchen.

"Who cares?" I answer with a shrug. "There's just the two of us here. And it's not like I'll know if it's good or not."

She thinks about that for a second. "Good point."

"I always make good points. You're just not usually in the mood to listen to them," I tell her. "Besides, the pie could be delicious by the time we're done."

"Yeah, well, I'm not holding my breath."

She opens the cupboard and pulls out canned pumpkin, something called evaporated milk that sounds scary as shite, a bunch of spices, some sugar, and some flour. "Maybe that's a good idea," I tell her, eyeing the array of ingredients in front of us that I have absolutely no idea what to do with. "You might pass out."

Grace laughs a little as she crosses to the refrigerator. "What happened to your boundless faith and enthusiasm?"

"Turns out it has bounds."

That makes her laugh harder, exactly as I intended. "Okay, so what do we do?" I ask.

"We're in luck. There's a recipe on the back of the can." She holds it up after adding a carton of eggs and some butter to the pile of ingredients on the counter.

"Well, that certainly feels like cheating," I tell her with a sniff, even as I admit to myself that I'm secretly relieved. "I was planning on winging it."

"Oh, we'll have plenty of chances to wing it," she says with a roll of her eyes. "There's no recipe for piecrust."

"That *does* sound like a problem." I eye the very intimidating bag of flour. "Although, is there any law that says pies actually need crust?"

"Crust is pretty much the defining characteristic of a pie, Hudson." She shakes her head. "Otherwise, it's just...fruit."

"Hmmm." I pretend to consider her words. "You make a solid point."

She pulls out a large mixing bowl. "I know I do. Even though pumpkins are technically gourds and not fruit."

I play her words back in my head a few times. "I don't even know what that means."

"It means—" She shakes her head, shoots me a rueful smile. "Never mind. It doesn't matter to the pie as a whole."

"So why are we even talking about it, then?" I ask, baffled. "Don't we not have enough of an uphill battle with this piecrust recipe we're supposed to pull out of our arses?"

"We do," she agrees. "We really do."

But she doesn't move to do anything. Instead, she just stands next to me, and we both stare at the ingredients.

Eventually, though, I've read everything there is to read on every ingredient at least three times. "Soooo. Are we going to do this?"

"Don't rush me, Vega. I'm just getting warmed up."

"Okay, then." I put my hands up in mock surrender. "Far be it from me to rush genius."

To give her more time, I walk to the fridge and grab a bottle of water.

"I think you mean rush disaster, don't you?" she comments.

I shrug. "Tomato, to-mah-toe."

"I think you mean pum-kin or pump-kin."

"Are you delirious?" I shoot her a faintly aghast look that I don't mean at all. "I think you should leave the wordplay to me."

"Fine." She sticks her tongue out at me. "But when you get bored, don't come crying to me."

Then she rolls up her sleeves and dumps a bunch of flour into the bowl in front of her.

A powdery white cloud rises up and chokes us both.

"Well, I give us a ten out of ten so far," I say when I can finally breathe again. "What's next?"

"Butter?"

I lift a brow. "Are you asking me or telling me?"

"I have no idea." She grins at me.

I grab the butter and unwrap it. "Okay, then. Here goes nothing." I start to throw it in with the flour.

"Wait!" Grace is full-on laughing now, and it's such a change from how she was on the couch that relief sweeps through me. I have no idea how to make a pie or a piecrust, but I'll do this forever if it keeps Grace smiling like that. I'm not sure what that says about me—or us—but I'll have to figure it out later. Pie making is surprisingly arduous work. "We have to cut it into the crust."

"Am I supposed to have any idea what that means?"

"It means—" She shakes her head as she takes the butter from me. "Never mind. Just watch and learn."

"From the expert," I deadpan.

"Of the two of us? Yeah."

"Good point." I watch as she cuts up the butter into little squares and then mashes them into the flour with her fingers. "I thought you didn't know how to do this."

"Well, I've watched my mom a hundred times. But I have no idea if my measurements are right. I figure we're going to end up with either piecrust or Play-Doh at the end of this, so it's a win-win either way."

"Play-Doh?" I ask warily, not sure if I want to know. The name doesn't exactly inspire confidence when cooking.

"Don't worry about it." She goes to the sink and fills a measuring cup with water, then slowly adds it into the flour/butter mess until it becomes some kind of cohesive ball thing.

"So, is that dough?" I ask, peering into the bowl when she finally stops kneading.

"It's something," she answers, poking at the beige-ish lump with a finger. "Whether or not it's dough, I guess we'll find out soon enough."

"Ummm..." I don't know what to say to that.

"Don't sound so worried. It'll be fine. Maybe." She crosses to the sink to wash up. "Why don't you start on the filling while I try to find my hands under all this mess?"

"Me?" I try to seem unfazed, but it comes out sounding like a yelp. I clear my throat before trying again. "You want me to make the filling?"

"It was your idea," she reminds me. "And you did say we were going to make this pie."

I've got no argument for that, so I pick up the tin and read the directions. Then proceed to measure and dump and mix to the best of my ability. Which isn't much, but enthusiasm has to count for something, right?

Finally, it's done, and Grace pours the strange-looking glop into the piecrust she arranged in a baking dish. Then she pops the dish into the oven, and we both stand in front of the glass door and stare at our handiwork.

"That's going to be completely inedible," I say after a minute.

"Have faith," she tells me. "It's supposed to look like that."

"Are you sure?" I ask, brows raised, as we both start to clean up.

"No. But I think so." She sighs, then looks at me with serious eyes from where she's putting away the ingredients. "Thank you."

"For what?" I ask.

"For this." She takes a deep, shuddering breath before whispering, "I used to do this with my dad. Every year from the time I was five."

"I'm sorry," I tell her stiffly, and I want to pat her on the back or something, like they do in shows. But I'm elbow-deep in pumpkin pie remains, and I'm not sure she wants me to touch her anyway. Just in case, though, I wander over to the sink and wash up.

"It's okay." Her sigh sounds watery, which freaks me out more than I want to admit. "You know, when I was five, I lost my first front tooth right before Thanksgiving. It just fell out, but then the other one got knocked out in a bike-riding accident. I looked totally ridiculous."

"No, you looked adorable," I say before I can stop myself.

She stops with her hand on the pantry door, looks at me with confusion, then realization.

Just when I think she's going to yell at me for invading her memories once again, miraculously she continues. "That front tooth, the one that got knocked out, grew in really strange. When I was older, I used to get made fun of for it a lot."

"Kids are the worst," I say, like I have any idea.

She considers me again for a second, then looks down at her hands. When she speaks, it's nearly a whisper. "I'm so lonely."

It doesn't feel great to hear that, considering I'm right here, flour in my hair and pie filling under my nails. Then again, this is the most interaction we've had in months, so do I blame her for being lonely?

Just because I'm not doesn't mean she shouldn't be. Most people haven't spent their entire life in solitary confinement.

"I'll eat the pie," I tell her in desperation. We figured out pretty early on that I don't experience hunger in this place, which—thank God. The only thing worse than being trapped with a Grace who can barely tolerate me is being trapped, barely tolerated, and craving her blood.

"I don't think so. Much as I appreciate your offer to poison yourself for me, I think I'm going to opt out."

"Well, the offer stands," I say as she opens the oven to take a peek. "Just so you know."

I walk over and peer into the oven beside her, and my stomach sinks. No way that pie is going to be edible. It looks more like a Frisbee than food.

"Thank you." There's another hitch in her breathing, and this time when I look at her helplessly, she allows herself to sag against me.

At first, I'm so shocked that I don't know what to do. But then Richard's moments of "societal interaction training" kick in and I put an awkward arm around her shoulders. Pat her back.

She responds by turning into me and resting her head on my chest.

Again, I don't know exactly what to do. So this time I do what feels natural. I wrap my arms around her, cradling the back of her head in my hand, and hold her against me as she cries.

And cries.

And cries.

As I hold her, I note several things. One, she fits surprisingly well in my arms. Two, she smells really good—like vanilla and cinnamon. And three, I kind of like holding her.

I wish she wasn't bloody well crying—I hate that she's hurting—but I definitely don't mind the way she feels against me. It's an odd realization, an odd sensation, considering the last person I hugged was Lia after I'd accidentally told her to love me forever. But that hug was filled with panic and regret and shame. I don't know what this hug is, but it's not that.

"There, there," I tell her, patting her back as delicately as I can manage. "It's going to be okay."

She shakes her head back and forth against my neck, and I try not to notice the fact that I'm pretty sure a little bit of her snot is running down my chest, inside my shirt.

Eventually, she takes a deep, shuddering breath. "I'm sorry."

"Why? Everybody cries sometimes."

She pulls back to look at me with red eyes and blotchy, tearstained cheeks. "Do you?"

The question startles me, and I hold her gaze, trying to decide if she really wants the truth or is just looking for sympathy.

Because honestly, I haven't cried since I was very young.

Not since my sadistic dad locked me in a concrete prison for the umpteenth time that year and told me I either give him the power he craves or I'd be locked away for the rest of my life.

As I lay in the pitch-dark tomb to "think over my choices," alone and scared and angry as all fuck, I'd finally given in to my rage and screamed at the universe at the unfairness of my life, beat my fists against the stone walls of my crypt until my knuckles were shredded and my voice was hoarse. And when the fight drained out of me, the begging started.

I'd pleaded with gods I don't even know exist over and over to just let me disappear. Just let me go. Turn my soul to dust and let the wind carry me away. I already had the power to turn other things to dust, so why couldn't I do it to myself?

I must have wanted it so badly…because I actually did it. I disintegrated myself.

My bones and blood and cells had shattered under the burden of my anger and despair, and my soul broke into a billion tiny pieces that were still me and yet weren't.

I was finally free.

I don't know where I went. I don't think I was dead, but I wasn't exactly alive, either. All I know for sure is the panic and loneliness and anger that had been all I'd ever known had disintegrated with me.

It was the only moment of peace I'd ever felt.

But eventually, because the universe really enjoys fucking with me, I came back together again. Alone in the dark again. But this was oh so much worse.

I'd managed to tough out being entombed the majority of my life because I knew no other way. This was just how it was. But it wasn't. Not really.

There was a place in this world where I could feel safe—I had seen it, lived it. I just wasn't allowed to keep it.

And so I cried.

Because happiness is not something people like me should ever experience. It makes us wish for more than we're allowed.

I shake my head, as much to pull my thoughts back to the present as to answer Grace's question. I think about telling her the truth, but instead I say, "Yeah. Sometimes."

Grace nods, then crosses to the sink to wash her face. I think she's doing better, but when she's drying it, she whispers, "I can't remember what Jaxon sounds like. I've tried, but I just can't."

I start to tell her that's because she's spent a hell of a lot more time in here with me than she ever did with him. But something tells me that won't make us friends. And right now, she looks like she needs a friend a hell of a lot more than she needs a sparring partner.

"Do you want me to look?" I offer after a few awkward seconds go by. "I can check it out, see what's going on."

She seems mystified. "Check what out?"

"The mating bond."

"Really?" Her eyes go wide. "You can see it?"

I nod. "Yeah, of course. I saw it when we first got trapped here."

I don't mention I also looked the day of the great shower incident. And every day since.

I couldn't help myself from checking, confirming that what I'd noticed the day before and the day before that was really true.

The mating bond to Jaxon was gone.

Not thin or translucent. Completely gone.

When I'd first seen it, I'd rushed to the bathroom and dry heaved for ten straight minutes. I'd told Grace I tried one of her Pop-Tarts, but that wasn't it.

Mating bonds are forever. Everyone knows that. The only way for one to disappear is if your mate dies. But as far as I could tell, Grace wasn't dead. Which could only mean one thing. Jaxon was dead.

I've wanted to beat the little bastard's arse so many times, I've lost count. But never, not once, have I wanted him dead. I'd rather die myself, and have, than see him truly harmed.

I struggled with telling Grace, but in the end I decided there was no point. At least she had her memories, and she's mentioned a couple of times she imagines by now he's learned to move on without her and she hopes he's happy.

Still, I couldn't give up hope my brother wasn't dead. So I kept checking for the mating bond every night before I'd fall asleep.

After a month of grieving his death, another option began to grow like a seed inside me. What if the bond was gone because Grace and I were never leaving this place and the magic knew it and let him go? Or what if something was wrong with the bond? They'd only been bonded a little over a week before Grace had ended up in my lair, and honestly, their bond never looked right when I'd first seen it. Something just felt off about it, with two colors woven together like that.

I knew finding a solution other than my brother's demise was like trying to hold grains of sand slipping between your fingers, but I did it. Night after night.

And every night, I'd close my eyes and know I was right in not telling Grace.

As I stare at the wetness slowly drying on her cheeks, I can't help but question if I'm hurting her more by not telling her the truth and giving her a chance to grieve, to move on.

I rub my chest absently, trying to relieve the tightness squeezing my breath. "Will you look?" She swallows hard. "I want you to look."

I take a deep breath and nod, then close my eyes and reach inside Grace.

Immediately, I'm surrounded by dozens of brightly colored strings. I'm careful not to touch any as I weave toward where I'd last seen the mating bond string with Jaxon, the same place I check every night.

I'm not the least surprised it's gone.

I turn to leave, though, and my heartbeat stills in my chest. Just freezes like it's forgotten how to beat at all.

I stand there for a second, then another and another—too afraid to breathe or even blink. I don't know how long I stay rooted to the spot, staring at the scariest thing I've ever seen, but I know it could have been an eternity and it still wouldn't be long enough to take it all in.

Because the thin string I instinctively know connects me to Grace has quadrupled in size since yesterday...and it's now glowing the most brilliant blue I have ever seen.

31

Stalks and Bonds

—Grace—

"You okay?" I ask. "You look like you're about to pass out."

"I'm fine," he murmurs, his gaze looking far away. "Everything's fine."

"Is it going to hurt?"

That seems to pull his attention back, and he smiles at me. "Of course not. Mating bonds aren't designed to be painful." He shakes his head. "If they were, no one would want to be mated."

"I don't mean the bond. I mean…you looking."

"Oh." He gives me a soft smile that is very un-Hudson-like, and all I can think is I must look even worse than I thought. "Nah. I already looked."

"You did?" My heart lets out a few really hard pumps. "What did you find?" He doesn't answer right away, and the nerves I've barely been holding in check start to churn. "Tell me what you found."

It isn't a question, and Hudson seems to know that, because he sighs. But he doesn't hesitate when he tells me, "It's gone."

"Gone—?" I shake my head, trying to clear it. "I don't understand."

"The mating bond's not there, Grace. It used to be, very faintly, but now it's gone. It's like it never existed."

The words hit me with the force of a wrecking ball, slamming through me with a power that levels me. "I don't understand."

"I don't, either," he tells me, and he looks more scared than I've ever seen him. "But it's gone. And there's something else—"

"I don't believe you." The words come from deep inside me.

He draws back like I've slapped him. "Excuse me?"

"I'm sorry, but I don't. Jaxon's my mate." I'm not even sure what that means really, but I know that it doesn't just disappear. If the bond can break so easily, what's even the point of it? "You guys all make such a big deal about mates being forever. So how does that just stop because I'm gone for a while?"

"I don't know." Now he sounds as frustrated as I feel. "I'm just telling you what I saw."

"Or what you want me to believe." The words are out before I know I'm going to say them. But once I do, I don't regret it. Just because Hudson baked a pumpkin pie with me doesn't mean he's magically my best friend. And it definitely doesn't mean I should trust everything he says—especially when what he's saying doesn't make any sense.

"Hey, you're the one who said you didn't feel Jaxon anymore. I was just—"

"That's not true. I said I couldn't remember what he sounded like, not that I don't feel him." I glare at him. "It's not the same thing at all."

"Really?" He lifts a brow. "So you can feel him?"

"I—I just—I don't— It's complicated, okay?"

"Yeah." He laughs, but there's absolutely no humor in the sound. "That's what I thought."

"You don't understand—" I try.

"I understand plenty." The buzzer on the oven goes off, and he pushes off the couch, strides toward the kitchen.

"Make sure you use an oven mitt to take it out," I call after him. Because even though I'm mad at him, it doesn't mean I want him to hurt himself.

He holds his hand up in what looks like a backward-facing peace sign. At first, I think he's saying "okay," but judging from the set of his shoulders, I can't help thinking he just flipped me off Brit-style.

"Seriously?" I demand. "What the hell is that for?"

He shoots me a look over his shoulder that says I should know.

And just like that, our small moment of peace is over.

"I think it's fair for me to question what you say," I tell him, getting off the couch.

"Do you?" He dumps the pie on the stovetop. "So why the fook did you ask me to look if you weren't going to believe me?"

It's a good question, one I'm not sure I have an answer to. "I don't know. I guess I just wanted reassurance that things are okay between Jaxon and me."

"But now that it looks like they're not, you get to shoot the messenger?"

When he puts it like that, I feel like I'm the one in the wrong. "I'm sorry. I'm not saying you're lying. I'm just saying maybe you made a mistake. Maybe you didn't know where to look—"

"I know where to look."

"Okay, fine. But you either made a mistake or you're lying to me. Because Jaxon—" My voice breaks. "Jaxon is—"

"Your mate. Yeah. I got it." He tosses the oven mitt down on the counter. "Enjoy your pie." Then he stalks off toward his bed.

As he walks away, his words about the mating bond seem to reverberate inside me, getting louder and more powerful with every second that passes. The mating bond is gone. Gone. Gone.

Terror that his words might be true wells up inside me until it's all I can think about. And just like that, the tight control I've been keeping on my emotions since I ended up in this place dissolves.

My heart starts to pound.

My mind starts to race.

Sweat drips down my back.

"Hey, are you all right?" Hudson asks from across the room, and this time he doesn't just sound concerned. He sounds alarmed.

"I'm...fine," I manage to gasp out as panic races through me, but I can barely get the words out because it's not true. I'm not fine, and it feels like I'll never be fine again.

I bend over, brace my hands on my knees as I try to suck air into my suddenly starving lungs. It feels like a monster truck is parked on my diaphragm, and the harder I work to breathe, the more difficult it becomes.

I'm shaking all over, and the room is spinning around me as I tell myself to breathe. To just breathe. That it's only a panic attack. That I'm okay. That everything's okay.

But that's a lie. Because right now, Hudson is trapped in my head and we're both trapped God only knows where. It's been more than a year since my parents have died, more than a year since I've spoken to my uncle or Macy or *Jaxon*. And now our mating bond—the one thing I've been hanging on to through this entire mess—might actually be gone?

Macy said mating bonds only break if a mate dies.

Which leads me to think it's one of two things. Either Jaxon is dead or I am, at least in the sense of dead in that world. Lia had said losing a mate was excruciating, so I don't think Jaxon is dead. I am certain I would have felt him dying through the bond. Which means...we're never leaving this place. As far as Jaxon is concerned, I *am* dead.

It's too much. Way too much.

I take a breath, then feel like I'm being strangled as I try to get air into my too-tight lungs. But that's not even the worst problem we've got right now. Because the damn dragon is back *again*.

I can hear him screaming, can hear his giant wings flapping as he circles the roof, looking for an opening. So far, we've been able to shore up any damage that he causes, but at some point soon, there's going to be nothing we can do. I can only fix the walls and the roof so many times before they become unfixable. And once that happens, there will be nothing to keep the dragon out. Nothing to keep him from roasting us alive.

For the moment, he's still outside, I tell myself as my stomach pitches and cramps. As sweat rolls down my spine and my vision turns to gray. He's not going to get in here. He's not going to hurt me.

But it's too late to sell myself on that. Full-blown panic has gripped every part of me. My knees turn to water, and I feel myself pitching forward, and there's nothing I can do to save myself. The panic is too overwhelming, the threat is too real, and I can't rationalize it away.

"Hey!" Hudson sounds more than alarmed. He sounds panicked.

Join the club, I want to tell him, but terror has a stranglehold around my vocal cords, and nothing comes out. He fades toward me—or at least that's what Hudson calls it when he moves ridiculously fast—and even though I throw my arms up in a futile effort to protect myself, he catches me a second before I hit the ground.

32

Some Bonds Can't
Be Unbroken
—Grace—

"I've got you," he tells me.

And he does, despite the fight we just had.

He helps me gently to my feet, then says, "Look at me, Grace. Don't worry about anything else. Just look at me and breathe. In and out. In and out."

It's easier said than done, considering the dragon keeps ramming against the wall right behind us. The bricks are screaming in protest and mortar dust is falling to the ground at our feet.

It's not only the dragon that's got me freaking out, though. I've managed to keep the panic attacks at bay since our first day here by telling myself that everything was going to be okay. By promising myself that we'd find a way out of here and that I'd find a way back to Jaxon. That no matter how long my brain keeps us locked up here, eventually I'd find my way back to my mate—and the new life I had just started to build—again.

Now, if Hudson is right, all that is gone. Just like my parents. Just like my life in San Diego. Even Katmere Academy is over. We've been here for more than a year, which means I should have graduated six months ago. I should be at college or at least figuring out what I want to do with my life instead of trapped with Hudson while some rabid dragon tries to kill us both.

Is it any wonder I'm having a panic attack? The more reasonable question is, why the hell isn't Hudson?

But somehow, he's not. As he talks to me, his face is totally calm. His eyes are steady, his voice is soothing, and the hands he still has wrapped around my upper arms are as gentle as they are supportive.

But I still can't breathe. I still can't get past the terror blanking out the edges of my mind.

The dragon roars right before he crashes into the wall again, and I let out a scream of my own.

"You've got this, Grace," Hudson tells me, and his voice is firmer than it was a couple of minutes ago.

I shake my head even as I try to take a deep breath. Normally I'd agree with him—I can handle these panic attacks and whatever else comes my way—but this feels different. This feels like everything I've worked so hard to gain back since my parents died is crumbling beneath my feet. And I don't think I've got the strength to do it all over again.

"What's the alternative?" Hudson asks. "Give up?"

I look at him, confused. "Wait. Did I say that out loud?"

"You didn't have to. I'm in your head, remember?"

"Don't!" I tell him, throwing up a hand as I stop shaking and my knees decide they're going to support me after all. "Don't you dare say anything about anything you might have read in my mind. You have no right—"

"No right?" His eyes narrow as he drops his hands from my arms and steps back. "You're keeping me prisoner here, and you're telling me I have no right?"

"It's not like I have a choice!" My breathing has evened out in the last minute or so, and I take a deep breath, let it out slowly.

"Yeah, me neither," he snarks back. "You don't see me complaining."

"Are you serious? You're complaining right now!" I huff out a breath. "And it's not like I'm all up in your head, reading *your* every thought."

"No, you just read my *journals*," he shoots back.

"You're damn right I do," I snarl. "And maybe I'd feel more guilty about that if you hadn't spent the last year picking through my memories like they were after-school specials."

"I've got to entertain myself somehow, don't I?" He gestures to the books behind me. "You've hogged every book in the place for the last year."

"Oh, poor baby. You only had the PlayStation, turntable, ax-throwing station, and an extensive DVD collection to keep you busy." I give him my fakest pitying look. "However did you manage?"

Before he can reply, the dragon gives a particularly loud, particularly vicious shriek. I brace myself for the worst—can feel Hudson doing the same—but instead of slamming through the roof or something equally as awful, we can hear his wings flap as he finally gives up and flies away. For now, anyway.

As he leaves, the last of my anxiety goes with him, and I realize for the first time that my panic attack is long gone. Arguing with Hudson made me so mad that I forgot to freak out. Huh. I never saw that one coming.

But as Hudson shoots me a truly obnoxious smirk before making his way back toward his bed, I can't help wondering if he knew exactly what he was doing. If maybe, just maybe, he's been doing it all along.

I want to go after him, but in the end, I don't. Because he's already climbing into bed. And I don't have anything new to say to him anyway.

But as I settle down on the couch, I can't help thinking it's going to be a long, long night as I force myself to come to terms with the fact neither of us wants to say aloud.

We're on borrowed time.

Alive or dead, whatever we are in this limbo is about to come to an end.

Because I know it as surely as I've ever known anything—that dragon came very close to toasting us today, and he won't give up next time.

As I curl onto the couch and pull the blanket up under my chin, I can't prevent the silent tears from rolling down my cheeks.

I cry angry tears for what I've lost with Jaxon.

I cry regretful tears that Jaxon will never know what happened to me.

I cry hopeful tears that one day someone else loves him as much as I did.

I cry every emotion I'm feeling, and as the last tear dries on my cheek, I know it was a tear of joy for being loved so much by someone so wonderful, even if briefly.

It almost makes the fact that I'm going to die soon not suck completely.

33

Fake It or You Don't Make It

—Grace—

Eventually, I'm all cried out, but I still can't sleep.

Hudson of course seems to have had no problem falling right off without saying one more word to me. Which is fine. It's not like I have so much to say to him right now, either. Except maybe *thank you*—for helping with my panic attack and for baking a pumpkin pie with me.

I have to admit, I never saw either of those things coming, but maybe I should have. I've read a lot of his journals over the last year, and they've all been so contradictory to the guy I was told he was. The guy who tried to kill his own brother. The guy who uses mind control like it's the best invention of the twenty-first century. The guy who believes in vampire superiority so completely that he's willing to kill for it.

That's the Hudson his brother knows. The Hudson everyone at Katmere knows. So why am I beginning to figure out that the Hudson I know is a very different person?

He makes ridiculous birdcalls.

Freaks out when I eat next to one of his precious books.

Throws axes like the demons from hell are after him.

And puts himself between a fire-breathing dragon and some girl he has absolutely no reason to want to help.

It doesn't make sense.

Are there really two Hudsons, or does one of us have it wrong? And if one of us is mistaken, who is it? Them or me?

More, how will I ever figure it out?

As I get up to grab a drink—and maybe sample the pumpkin pie Hudson and I made earlier—I can't help but glance at his journals. I'm four from the end now, but maybe that's the problem. Maybe the answer to how he changed from the boy who bought a house for his aging tutor to the sociopath everyone warned me against is in the last journal.

Maybe that's why it's the last journal.

I grab some water, cut myself a piece of pie, and accept that I'm one hell of a hypocrite as I snag Hudson's final journal off the shelf.

I don't know why, but I'm convinced the way to stop the dragon from attacking again is somehow tied to saving Hudson.

Just as I settle myself on the couch and open it, Hudson mutters something indistinguishable in his sleep. I freeze, worried that I've woken him up, but seconds later, he rolls over and one of his pillows flops to the ground.

I breathe a sigh of relief. Not that I'm exactly stressed out that he'll find me—he knows I've been reading them all along. Still, something feels different after our argument, or whatever that thing was this afternoon, and for the first time, I feel a little guilty about doing this.

Not guilty enough *not* to do it, but still. Guilty nonetheless.

I take a bite of pie and surprisingly, it's not terrible. It's not great—the crust has a strangely gummy consistency—but the pumpkin tastes good enough that I take a second bite. My mom's pie is a million times better, but considering what Hudson and I had to work with, I'm going to call it a success.

I take a couple more bites, then shove the plate away. I may be reading Hudson's journal, but there's no way I'm getting crumbs in it. Being trapped with him for more than a year has taught me well.

The first three entries aren't very eventful, but when I turn the page on the fourth, every cell in my body goes on red alert, though I don't know why. Maybe it's the deep gouges his pen made in the paper, like he'd forgotten his own strength when he was writing it, or maybe it's the slashed letters that all but crackle with indignation.

Whatever it is, I brace myself before I start to read.

Well, another day aboveground bites the dust, in the most ignominious manner possible. And to think I used to hope for a time I no longer got shoved in a crypt.

Just had my monthly state-of-my-own-worthlessness meeting with Dear Old Dad, and to say it didn't go well would be quite the understatement. Richard gave me a whole pep talk about how I shouldn't let my father—or my lack of performance—upset me, then seemed shocked that I wasn't more upset.

I didn't have the heart to tell him I probably would have been very upset if I hadn't engineered the whole thing myself...or at least my part in it.

I don't know what makes my father angrier—that his little experiment isn't coming along as nicely as he'd hoped or that he had to find that out in front of his entire council, whom he'd invited to my "demonstration."

After I failed spectacularly—but not too spectacularly, if I do say so myself—he pulled me into his too-opulent office for a "little chat." I'm not sure why he called it a chat, though, considering my only role in the entire proceeding was to listen to him tell me how worthless I am. I suppose it's better than actually having to talk to him.

"Twenty percent is not an acceptable performance rate," he told me in that snooty voice he's got that makes me want to disintegrate his vocal cords every time I hear it. I wanted to tell him that I disagreed. That twenty percent was the perfect performance rate to sell what I was trying to sell—namely that my powers aren't nearly as strong as my father wants them to be.

More, that they aren't nearly as strong as they actually are.

My father's plan was to demonstrate my mind-control abilities to his council today, not only to encourage them to get behind his latest scheme for war but also to let them know that we will be coming for them next if they don't.

My whole life—such as it's been—has been in service of his goal for world domination. There's only one problem with that scheme, however. I've got no interest in it. At all. Which means when I went in there today, I had my own goal—to fail just badly enough for him to think I'm incompetent, but not so much that he thinks I'm a traitor.

If I'd been able to mind control more than fifty percent of his guards, Cyrus would have deemed the demonstration a total success and started moving forward with plans for God only knows what. If I'd failed completely, he would have known I was faking and acted accordingly.

No, twenty percent was the exact right rate to convince my father that I have some power, but not too much. More importantly, it's the right amount to make sure he decides that I'm nowhere near ready to be unleashed on the world. That his perfect plan will fail, just like I have, if he races to execute it prematurely.

Of course, selling this as well as I have means that I can look forward to several more years of being beaten senseless by his men, trying to force powers that I already have to mature. And while I'd do almost anything to avoid a right proper beating by one of his shite soldiers, I'm not about to take the easy way out at the expense of so many other people's lives.

Que será será. Whatever will be will fucking be.

And yes, I am well aware of the fact that I'm quoting a song from a Hitchcock movie. Then again, after more than a few lifetimes of dealing with Cyrus, I've learned horror is always appropriate.

Sacrifices need to be made, and I'm just the guy to make them.

Besides, who doesn't like letting a werewolf drool on them after they kick you in the nuts?

34

I Read You
All Wrong
—Grace—

Oh my God. OH MY GOD.

I stare at the words on the page until they become all blurry and run together. Then I blink and read them again. And again. And again.

They reverberate through my heart, burrow inside my skin to my very soul as the truth strikes home. It can't be true. It just can't be.

I don't know what happened at Katmere the year Hudson died.

I don't know why Jaxon believes what he believes.

I don't know why *everyone* believes what they believe.

But it isn't true.

I flip through the next several journal entries, reading them as quickly as I can. I read about how much Hudson hates his father, about how Cyrus has managed to recruit so many members of high-ranking paranormal families to join him. About how Hudson is determined to stop him, no matter what.

How could Jaxon have gotten it so wrong?

How could all of us have been so shortsighted?

Was Lia—Lia of all people—the only one who saw the truth?

Just the thought makes me sick, has panic setting in. What if Jaxon had just listened to Lia to begin with? Talked to his brother instead of assuming the worst? Maybe that whole big human-sacrifice montage wouldn't have had to happen.

My stomach revolts at the memories and the might-have-beens, and I make a mad dash for the bathroom. I barely get there in time.

My knees hit the ground, and I vomit back up all the pumpkin pie I just ate. I try to do it quietly—the last thing I want to do is wake Hudson while the evidence of what I've been doing is still sitting on the couch. And also, I'm not ready to face him.

I don't know if I'll ever be able to face him, but I know for sure that I'm not ready now.

But vampires have incredible hearing, and for all his pretending otherwise, Hudson is a light sleeper. Which means that by the time I've flushed the toilet, he's standing in the doorway.

"Are you all right?" he asks quietly as he reaches into the small linen closet and pulls out a washcloth.

"I'm fine. Too much pumpkin pie, I think."

"Too much something," he answers, running the rag under cold water. "Here, put this on your neck. It will help with the nausea."

"How do you know?" I ask, curious, not confrontational. "Do vampires have the same problem?"

I move to the sink to get my toothbrush and toothpaste as he answers, "Not really. But we do know when there's really strong blood flow in your carotid artery." His fangs flash when he grins. "So it stands to reason that putting a cool compress there would help you out."

"Oh, right." I smile weakly after brushing my teeth and rinsing my mouth. "The old carotid artery."

For a second, I flash back to Jaxon nuzzling my neck before sinking his fangs in. I can feel my cheeks flush, and suddenly the bathroom feels way too small. It's weird to be thinking about something so personal when Hudson is standing two feet in front of me.

"Can we go back to the main room?" I ask quietly, not wanting to push past him but really, really wanting to be out of here.

"Of course." He steps back immediately. "You sure you're okay?"

"I'm fine. I swear."

But the minute we get back to my couch, Hudson's eyes fall on his open journal. "A little light reading?" he asks with a raised brow.

"I'm sorry. I'm so sorry." And then I throw my arms around him.

I don't know who's more shocked.

"It's…fine," he says, sounding totally bemused.

But I just squeeze him more tightly—my arms seem to be totally outside of my control at the moment—hugging him the way no one has ever hugged him before. Hugging him the way he always should have been hugged.

By his mother.

By his father.

By Jaxon.

By Lia.

By all the people who should have loved him. Who should have taken care of him.

In response, he pats me awkwardly on the head. He even goes so far as to murmur, "There, there." And sounds very British while he does it.

I still don't let go.

Eventually, his arms move around my back. Slowly, tentatively, like he has no idea how to hug someone. And then he's holding me tightly, too. So tightly that I can barely breathe. And that's more than okay.

Eventually, he pulls away.

I let him go, expecting him to put some distance between us. But he doesn't. Instead, he only moves a breath away, so that our skin brushes with every exhalation.

"Hudson—"

"Grace—"

"You first," I tell him with a smile. I don't have a clue what I'm going to say anyway.

But he doesn't say anything. Instead, he puts a finger under my chin and tips my face up to his. Our gazes collide and for one long, impossible moment, everything inside me goes still.

And still Hudson waits. Still he keeps his eyes locked on mine. I don't know if he's waiting for permission or asking for forgiveness.

Eventually, he must get the answer he was waiting for because he starts to move.

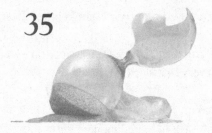

35

Running Down
a Nightmare
—Grace—

Slowly, ever so slowly, Hudson leans forward, and I forget how to breathe. How to think. How to *be*.

I forget anything—and everything—that isn't him. That isn't this moment.

My heart is racing as I try to figure out what is going on. I don't want Hudson to kiss me. I don't. Do I?

And then, just as his lips almost touch mine, a loud, obnoxious shriek sounds from directly over our heads.

Reality crashes into me, and I pull back, horrified by what I've almost done.

I almost kissed Jaxon's brother.

I almost kissed Hudson.

Hudson.

Shame rushes through me, collides with horror and regret and a bunch of other emotions I'm not ready to look at too closely yet.

But that's okay, since I don't have time to look at them, either. Because the damn dragon has decided that this is the moment he's going to take his stand.

His claws rake across the roof as he flies by, bellowing in rage.

Chills skate their way down my spine. This attack feels different. I don't know why, but it does, and a quick look at the concern on Hudson's face tells me he feels the exact same way.

"What do we do?" I ask as the dragon crashes against the roof so hard, he shakes the entire room, toppling one of the bookcases with a thunderous crash.

I don't have time to mourn the volumes of books scattered all about the library area as Hudson grabs my hand and hustles us closer to the door.

"We aren't going out there!" I whisper-shout as terror moves through me. "That thing will kill us!"

"I'm not sure we're going to have a choice," he answers grimly.

"What does that mean?"

But I'm afraid I already know. Because the dragon is pounding on the roof now, hitting it over and over again like the dinosaur from *Jurassic Park*, looking for a weakness he can exploit.

"Isn't there some way we can make it go away?" I hiss.

But even as I ask, there's a loud creaking sound above us. And then shingles and wood are raining down on top of us as Hudson wraps himself around me.

I throw a hand out, try to wall up the damage the way I've done time and again since we've been here. But it's too late. The dragon comes flying through the broken roof, eyes glowing with rage and flames shooting from his open mouth.

"Fook this!" Hudson exclaims. And then we're up and running for the door. Or to be more precise, he's running and dragging me along beside him.

"He'll get us out there!" I tell him again.

"I hate to break it to you," he shoots back in an ironic voice. "But he's going to get us if we stay in here, too."

As he finishes, a stream of fire hits the wall beside us. And I know that Hudson's right.

There's only one way to escape.

"You ready?" Hudson yells as he throws open the front door we've kept locked shut for so long.

"Not even close!" I shout back.

But ready doesn't matter now. Nothing does but staying alive. So I tighten my hold on Hudson's hand and run with him straight into the dark.

36

Please Don't
Start the Fire
—Grace—

"What do we do?" I pant as we run faster than I've ever run in my life. "Duck," Hudson answers grimly, pulling me down just as a whole bunch of flames rip through the air right above our heads.

"Oh my God!" I crouch even lower, trying to put as much distance between fire and me as I possibly can. But ducking so low makes achieving any kind of speed a lot more difficult. As does the weaving back-and-forth pattern Hudson has established.

Not going to lie. I feel a little like I'm in one of those action movies my dad always used to watch, dodging bullets from the bad guy with every bob and weave. Or, more accurately, flames from a flamethrower.

Only this is real life and—

I yelp as a new billow of flames grazes the side of my arm.

"Fuck this!" Hudson growls as he drops my hand. For a second, I think he's just going to leave me here to fend for myself.

Not that I blame him. I've seen him fade many times over the last year, and I know I'm the weak link in this equation. In fact, I'm kind of amazed he's stuck with me this far.

But instead of ditching me like I expect, Hudson grabs me and throws me onto his back. I instinctively wrap my legs around his waist, my arms around his shoulders. "What the—"

"Hold on!" he yells, and then we're fading forward, moving faster than I've ever moved in my life. Faster than a speeding car, definitely. Maybe even faster than a plane.

It's terrifying and exhilarating at the same time. Or it would be exhilarating, if a dragon wasn't literally on our asses.

More flames fly by as the dragon soars overhead, and I hold on even more tightly to Hudson. "Faster," I urge, and he snorts.

"Easy for you to say." But, impossibly, he lays on even more speed. Thank God. Because a glance over his shoulder shows the dragon closing in on us. And seriously—how fast can this thing fly?

Faster than Flint, I'm pretty sure, though I only ever saw him fly through the tunnels. Still, I know he didn't move like this, streaking through the sky like lightning.

Nothing moves like this—not even Hudson, who is breathing heavily as he continues to pour on the speed.

"We've got to find somewhere to hide," I shout to be heard over the roar of the wind *and* the dragon.

"Feel free to pull something out of your arse," Hudson tosses back breathlessly. "Because I'm not exactly seeing anything out here."

For the first time since the dragon crashed through our roof, I look somewhere besides in front of us or behind us. And I realize that he's right. Or at least, I think he is.

It's dark out here—really dark—and it's hard to see beyond a few feet in any direction. But what I can see is completely empty, like we're running in a void.

Dark, wide open, endless.

It's a nightmare I never even knew I had in me.

Even worse, I may only be able to see a few feet in any direction in this darkness, but Hudson's vampire eyes give him way more for distance. And if he doesn't see anything, we are totally screwed.

It's okay. We're okay. The shadows will protect us, right? "The shadows are our friends. The shadows are our friends," I whisper over and over, praying it's true.

As if determined to prove me wrong, though, the dragon swoops so low that I can feel his claws just barely graze across my back. The only reason he doesn't manage to grab me in his giant talons is because Hudson—in a move that feels close to precognitive—chooses that exact moment to drop almost to his belly.

I shriek as pain tears through me, and my left arm goes completely numb. It's so unexpected that I start to slide off Hudson, who curses and reaches behind him to grab on to my legs with both hands.

"Hold on!" he growls.

"That wasn't on purpose," I growl back, thankful when the feeling comes back in my arm as I straighten up and un-pinch whatever nerve had been jabbed for a second.

He just laughs in response, and I swear to God, he doesn't even sound scared. He sounds...exhilarated, like outrunning a dragon is one of the most fun things he's ever done.

Then again, after reading those journals, part of me wonders if it actually is. The thought is so horrible that I try to banish it as soon as it occurs to me, but it's too late. It's already moved in and now it's there, in the back of my head, even as I plaster myself even more tightly to his back. At this point, every inch counts.

Sure enough, the dragon swoops in for another grab.

Instead of ducking this time, Hudson weaves sharply to the right. The dragon screams his annoyance into the endless night and makes yet another try for us.

Hudson goes right again, and the dragon's claws miss my back. They do get tangled in my curls, however, and as Hudson surges forward, I swear I lose a whole fistful of hair.

The back of my head is throbbing almost as badly as my back now, and I'm beginning to think Hudson really has the better end of this deal. Sure, he needs to be the one on the bottom because he's the only one of us who actually has a chance of outrunning this damn dragon, but at the same time, I'm not actually enjoying my current role as human shield.

I open my mouth to tell Hudson as much, but before I can get out more than a, "Hey," the dragon drops low again.

And this time, Hudson doesn't manage to weave in time.

37

You're Dragon
Me Down
—Grace—

I scream as the beast wraps his talons around my arms. Somehow, his nails scrape against my skin as he grabs me, but they don't actually pierce through anything important, something I'm intensely grateful for as the dragon once again starts to climb.

Up until this point, I've been holding on to Hudson as tightly as I can, but as the dragon grabs me, I know I've got two choices. Keep holding on to Hudson and let him die with me. Or let him go and give him a halfway decent chance at escape.

I let go—the last thing I want is for anyone else to suffer whatever fate this dragon has planned for me—but that doesn't mean Hudson does. He still has his arms wrapped over my legs, helping to hold me to his back.

He curses as his feet leave the ground, and I kick out as hard as I can, trying to get him off me. In normal circumstances, I know he'd barely even notice my kick. But he's off-balance and not expecting it, and it sends him tumbling to the ground.

I watch him hit hard and roll. But then the dragon is flying straight up, and I lose sight of Hudson in the dark. "Run!" I scream at him, determined that one of us gets out of this alive. I have kept him locked up in my head for more than a year—helping him escape this monster seems only fair. "Hudson, run!"

He doesn't answer, and relief sweeps through me. At least one of us will survive. At least one of us—

The dragon bellows in rage, and we go spinning through the air. Nausea churns in my stomach—I feel like a yo-yo spinning without a string—and I have no idea what's happening. Except, judging from the dragon's outrage as we spin head over heels, he's not in control of any of this.

Which means Hudson is. Damn it. What did he do?

We're getting dangerously close to the ground—which I might appreciate if I wasn't about to be caught between the ground and I don't know how many thousand pounds of dragon. As it is, I brace myself for what I'm sure is a lot of pain followed by certain death.

But somehow, the dragon finally manages to pull out of the flat spin. With another scream of outrage, he—and positioned where I am, I sadly know for a fact that this thing is a he—turns to climb. Caught between terror and relief, I take a deep breath and will myself not to throw up. I love roller coasters as much as the next girl, but this is a whole other level.

Apparently, Hudson isn't okay with the dragon flying off with me—my sacrificial thoughts be damned. Because the next thing I know, there's a hitch in the dragon's upward motion, like something has grabbed on to him and is dragging him down.

The dragon snorts and spits fire and screams in fury, and it doesn't take a genius to know that that *something* is Hudson freaking Vega. I don't know anyone else who can piss someone off that much.

There's a sickening crunch that sounds an awful lot like bones breaking. It's followed immediately by another scream from the dragon—but this one definitely sounds like pain, not anger.

I have no time to wonder what Hudson did before another cracking sound rends the air. And just like that, I'm falling.

We're high up enough now that the ground seems way too far away. I don't know how far, since I can't see in the dark, but that just makes free-falling like this worse.

Fuck. Just fuck. Somehow I'm back between the dragon and the ground, and this time the ground is definitely going to win.

Except something hard slams into my back just as the ground comes into view. Dragon? But then Hudson is wrapping himself over and around me, covering up as much of me as he can.

I have one second to figure out what he's doing before we hit the ground with a force that shakes me all the way to my bones. And then we're rolling, rolling, rolling.

By the time we finally come to a stop, with Hudson on the bottom and me on the top—my back to his front—I've had the breath knocked out of me completely. And so has he, judging by the fact that his chest isn't rising beneath me, and he hasn't said a word.

I have to say, a speechless, breathless Hudson is something I've prayed for a lot over the last year, but never did I think it would happen like this. And that I would be so anxious for it to pass.

Willing my body to relax even as I can hear the dragon's giant wings flapping above us, I finally manage to draw a couple of breaths. As soon as I do, I roll over and start pushing at Hudson. "Come on, come on! We have to move!" I gasp, trying to stand and pull him up at the same time.

"On it," he gasps right back as we finally manage to stumble to our feet.

"Where is he?" I ask, looking overhead for some sign of the giant beast.

Hudson doesn't need to answer as the dragon immediately comes into view. He's flying straight for us, fire streaming from his mouth.

"Run!" I shout, but before we can so much as turn, the dragon disappears right in front of us.

"Bloody hell!" Hudson curses, looking around wildly.

"Where is he?" I ask again, and I'm looking, too. The only problem is it's still so dark that I can't tell where he went.

"Hell if I know," Hudson mutters, and I realize I didn't just lose sight of him because I can't see in the dark. The dragon actually disappeared.

"We should run," I tell him as a fresh wave of fear slams through me.

He gives me a "no shit" look, but before I can return the favor, the dragon reappears—on the ground right in front of us.

38

Waking Dawn

—Hudson—

Fuck! Just fuck!

What the hell does a guy have to do to get a break around here?

There's no time to run, no time to do anything but die, to be honest, and that's not an option I'm particularly okay with. Then again, the irony can't be avoided, considering how much time I've actually spent playing dead in my life.

There's no time for niceties, so I grab Grace's arm, try to pull her behind me so I take the brunt of whatever the dragon's about to hit us with. But Grace is her usual intractable self, and instead of letting me protect her, she throws herself at me.

Her arms and legs go around me at the exact same second the dragon lets loose a whole new stream of fire and I try to pivot, try to move so that it hits me instead. But it's too late. The fire is already washing over her.

"Grace!" I scream, trying to stumble back. Trying to do something, anything to get her out of the flames.

But I can't move. My feet feel like they're encased in cement, my entire body completely beyond my control. Grace is being burned alive, and there is absolutely nothing I can do about it.

"No, Grace! Fook! No!" How the fuck can I not be able to move? And how the fuck can I help her? I can't let her die. I can't—

"It's okay, Hudson." She doesn't seem to be talking—her face is pressed right next to mine, and it doesn't feel like it's moved so much as a muscle—but I can hear her voice all the same. It's different than it has been the last year, when we were trapped together in my lair. It echoes, sounds far away. But that doesn't matter now. Nothing does but what she says next. "I'm not hurt."

"How can you not be? The flames—"

"I don't know. But I'm fine." I can't see her smile, but I can hear it in her voice. "I swear, I'm fine."

"But—"

The dragon screams. Roars. He paws at the ground. Shoots off more flames. Screams some more. None of it works. None of it disrupts Grace's voice in my head telling me that she's all right. So I take a deep breath and wait.

As suddenly as it started, the fire stops. Seconds later, the dragon disappears. Seconds after that, he's twenty feet up and flying away.

And seconds after that, I'm free. The feeling of being frozen is gone.

"Grace!" I run my hands down her arms, over her back. "Are you all right?"

"I'm fine." She steps awkwardly away. "Thanks for breaking my fall back there."

"Thanks for keeping both of us from turning into that dragon's flame-roasted breakfast," I answer.

She smiles then, just a little. "You're welcome."

I want to ask her what the fuck happened back there, but her lips are trembling and I know she's fighting back tears. Now is not the time to point out that she most definitely is something other than *human*.

Instead, we both watch as dawn is breaking across the sky in streaks of lavender and violet as we both look around, try to get our bearings. And try to figure out one, why we're not dead, and two, what the fuck to do next.

"Is this—?" Grace starts hesitantly.

"The first time we've seen the sun in more than a year?" I answer for her. "Yeah, it is."

She nods before turning her face up to the sky. And I get it. Vampires are designed not to see the sun when we're eating properly (which a sudden growling in my stomach reminds me I have not been)—and I went years at a time without seeing it when I was buried in the crypts—but even I've missed seeing the sun over the last year.

"What do you think it means?" Grace asks as the surrounding area comes more into view.

That includes a range of craggy black mountains several miles in front of and to the sides of us. Mountains we're going to need to cross if we have any hope of getting out of this weird fishbowl valley we're currently standing in the middle of.

Before the dragon comes back.

"I think it means we're not in Kansas anymore," I tell her. Somehow leaving the dubious safety of the lair meant that we've also left her head, if my hunger and the sudden inability to read her mind are any indication. And despite that weird turn-us-both-fireproof thing she just did, I'm afraid we're totally bollocksed.

"So what should do?" she asks as she stares at the strangely foreboding mountains in front of us.

"What do *you* think we should do?" I counter.

She sighs, then glances at the sky behind us where the dragon was just a few short minutes ago. "Start walking."

39

Keep Calm and Don't Carry On
—Hudson—

"**H**op on my back," I tell her, crouching a little so she can do it comfortably. "Umm, I don't think so," she answers, right before she starts walking— exactly as she said she was going to.

"And why is that?" I run a hand through my hair, trying not to pull it out by the bloody fistfuls. "You did it when the dragon was chasing us."

"Yeah, well, those were extenuating circumstances. Now that he's gone, I'm walking on my own two feet."

"Gone for now," I say caustically. Not gone forever. Which is how long it is going to take us to even *get* to those mountains if Grace keeps being this stubborn. Maybe there's another reason she doesn't want me to hold her now that imminent danger has passed… "If this is about that almost kiss—"

"What kiss?" she asks blandly. "If there was a kiss, or almost a kiss, I've already forgotten it."

Well, that certainly lets a bloke know where he stands, doesn't it? Sure, there's a wobble in her voice that says otherwise, but I'm sure as hell not about to call her on it. Not when the absolute last thing I want to do is kiss a girl who's pining over my pain-in-the-arse younger brother. I don't know what the hell I was thinking. She threw me with that hug. That's my story.

I persist. "So there's no reason for you not to hop on my back, then, is there?"

"You mean besides that it's infantilizing?" She winces as she gathers her hair behind her head in a ponytail, then pulls the hair band off her wrist and uses it to gather her curls up into a giant bun at the top of her head. I've seen her do the same thing a hundred times over the last year, and I keep waiting for it to fail. Keep waiting for the weight of all those wild, glorious curls to pull free of the band and come tumbling down.

So far it hasn't happened but, judging from the way her bun is already leaning to the left, today might be the day.

"And you don't think forcing us to do things the longer, harder way isn't a childish tantrum?" I ask. "Because it feels like you're having a strop to me."

"Yeah, well, everything smacks of me 'having a strop' to you," she answers in the most atrocious British accent I've ever heard.

"I don't sound like that," I tell her as we begin to walk. Slowly.

"You sound exactly like that," she shoots back. "Especially when you're angry. Or when you think your precious underwear is in jeopardy."

"My underwear *was* in jeopardy." I narrow my eyes at her. "In fact, it was under attack. And just so you know, I still owe you a more severe payback for that monstrous act."

I mean it as a threat, but I guess I'm not as scary as I used to be, because Grace just grins at me. "I don't know about that. You looked pretty hilarious whining about your precious panties."

"Boxers," I tell her with a roll of my eyes. "And again, they were Versace."

She laughs, then shoots me a curious look. "What is it with you and Versace, anyway? And Armani? Like, I know Jaxon wears Gucci—"

"Of course he does," I interrupt with a sniff. "I'm surprised he doesn't walk around with one of their riding crops, too. Old-world style."

"Oh my God! You are *such* a snob."

It's my turn to give her a look. "I'm a centuries-old vampire prince with more money and power than any one person should have. Of course I'm a snob."

"Wow. Way to own it." She shakes her head as if surprised.

I don't know why. In all the time we've been trapped together, I've never pretended to be something I'm not with her. Not once. "People should always own who they are, flaws and all. The fact that I happen to have more flaws than most doesn't change that."

Grace doesn't say anything. Not that I expect her to—unless she's pissed off, afraid, or plotting revenge, she tends to err on the side of kindness. It's one of the things I like best about her.

We walk for more than a mile in silence, and as we do, I can't help growing more and more curious about where we are. Originally, I put the dark, purplish cast of the world around us down to it being early morning. The sun was just beginning to rise over the horizon in front of us.

But the closer we get to the mountains—and the sun coming up over them—the more it's apparent that the colors around us have nothing to do with dawn at all. And everything to do with the landscape of this world.

Right now, it feels a little bit like Mars—except, instead of being red, the soil is dark purple. And so is the sky. And so is everything else around us. Rocks, hills, even the sun—they're all made up of different shades of purple, from the lightest lavender to the deepest violet. The mountains ahead of us still look black, but as a purple gecko-like creature with six legs runs over my foot, I start to side-eye the hell out of them, too. I could be way off base here, but I'm pretty sure when we get there, we're going to find that they're a midnight violet instead of black.

I have no idea what any of that means, though. I've been racking my brain for the last half an hour, trying to figure out where we might be. But I've got nothing.

Not just because of the color—though the purple thing is strange—but because even the terrain doesn't seem *normal*, for lack of a better word. It's rough and rocky, with jagged edges and steep inclines that lead back down into sunken, cratered valleys.

It definitely seems more like what I imagine another planet would feel like versus anywhere on planet Earth. But since neither of us has strapped our arse to a rocket in the last year, there has to be another explanation. But fuck all if I know what that is.

We're walking down a particularly sharp incline, one loaded with jagged rocks and sharp, shadowed holes, when Grace cries out. It's the first sound she's made, other than some heavy breathing up the steepest inclines, in close to forty-five minutes, and I jerk my head toward her, alarmed.

She's stumbling forward, throwing her hands out for balance, so I fade to her, determined to catch her before she sprains an ankle or impales herself on a rock when she falls. But she surprises me by catching herself before she hits the ground.

"Whoops!" She looks up at me with laughing eyes. "I nearly bit it that time."

"I didn't realize that was something to laugh about." Even I know the words make me sound like a total tool—too stiff and way too formal—but there's something about Grace getting hurt that bothers me more than I want to admit, even to myself. "You really should be more careful."

I want to slap myself even as the words come out of my mouth—and wouldn't blame her for doing the same. But instead of taking offense like she probably should and telling me to mind my own business, Grace just laughs.

"But then what would you have to complain to me about?"

That stings a little, but she's not wrong. "I'm sure I'd think of something."

"True story," she agrees. Then she reaches out and grabs on to my arm as the terrain gets rockier.

It's the last thing I expect from her, but I slow my pace immediately. And try not to note how much I like the feel of her hand on my arm. And the fact that she reached out to me for help when she needed it—even if it is just so she doesn't break her neck.

The second we get to the bottom of the incline, Grace drops her hand. But she doesn't move away, and I find myself checking her out from the corner of my eye, just to see if I can figure out what she's thinking.

I can't, which isn't exactly a surprise considering she becomes more—not less—of a mystery to me with every day that passes. But it's still frustrating.

"You didn't really mean what you said earlier, did you?" Grace asks as we start climbing up yet another hill.

"About you needing to be more careful?" I lift a brow. "I sure as—"

She cuts me off with a look. "I'm talking about what you said about having more flaws than most people. You don't really mean that, do you?"

"Of course I mean it. Have you met me?"

"I have, actually." She looks away. "And I don't think you're nearly as bad as you want everyone to believe."

I'm fairly certain that's the first time anyone has ever said that to me in my whole life. I don't know what to do with it—I sure as shit don't know what to say to it. So I don't say anything, just concentrate on putting one foot in front of the other. And looking out for the dragon that I'm not quite willing to believe has actually disappeared.

Grace catches me looking over my shoulder, probably because she's doing the same thing, and gives me a rueful smile. "Waiting for that thing to come back is making me nervous."

I want to ask why she won't let me fade us the fuck out of here, then, but decide it makes me sound like too much of an arse. So I just nod and say, "Yeah, me too."

"Have you tried to see if your powers work out here?" She blinks up at me, and I nearly smile remembering the fight we had about my powers not working in the lair. She kept insisting I Jedi mind tricked her into eating two entire packages of Pop-Tarts in one sitting. Trust me, this girl needs no one mind tricking her into eating *all* the Pop-Tarts she can. She continues. "Because if they do, if he comes back, maybe you could—"

"Not if, when," I tell her dryly. "That thing isn't giving up anytime soon. And yeah, I tried in the middle of his attack. I've got nothing except my regular bag of vampire tricks."

"That's so strange." She shakes her head. "I thought maybe you didn't have your powers in the lair because…"

"Because you were keeping me hostage in your head?" I finish.

"I wasn't going to put it quite like that," she answers with a roll of her eyes. "But yeah. Maybe."

"You can feel it, can't you?" I don't bother to explain, because either she can or she can't.

But Grace nods. "It's not the same here as it was in the lair, is it?"

"It's not," I agree. "This is something else."

"Yeah." She looks around and shivers a little, despite the fact that it's at least twenty degrees Celsius out. "I'm not doing this."

"I know."

We're close enough to the mountains now for me to see that I was right. They aren't black, but rather a deep aubergine purple that somehow makes them look even stranger than I first thought.

But we're also close enough for me to see something else—a grouping of four small buildings at the base of the mountain. Or four large buildings. Who can tell when they're standing next to a fucking mountain?

Small or big, it doesn't matter. What matters is that—hopefully—someone inhabits those buildings.

Someone who can tell us where the hell we are.

And how the fuck we can escape before we become a midnight snack for the strangest fucking dragon I've ever seen.

40

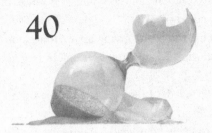

Don't Farm It In

—Grace—

My legs feel like they're going to fall off.

Actually, my whole body feels like it's going to collapse, and we're still at least a mile, maybe more, away from the buildings up ahead.

Hudson spotted them several miles back, but now that we're close enough for me to see them, I just want to be there already.

I hope they have chairs. And a shower. And chairs.

Please God, let there be chairs.

I used to run on the beach in San Diego all the time—Coronado, La Jolla, sometimes even OB if Heather and I went to Belmont Park to ride the roller coaster and bumper cars. But running in sand—or the snow near Katmere Academy—is nothing compared to walking in this weird purple dirt.

Most of the way it's been rocky and difficult to get a foothold, but for the last couple of miles, as we've gotten closer to the mountains, the soil's been different, fine and loamy.

With every step I take, I sink into it a little, which means I also have to struggle with every step to pull myself back out of it. It's not quicksand, but it sure feels like it could be if it spent a few extra days at the gym.

Still, letting Hudson carry me all the way there wasn't an option. It's one thing if we're fleeing for our lives and my very human "slowness" is a liability. It's another thing altogether to let some big, strong guy carry me around like I'm his personal rag doll.

Not to mention I feel awkward—like, so freaking awkward—touching Hudson right now. I did it once on this walk because I didn't want to fall on my ass and cause more trouble, but hanging on him? Our bodies pressed together when we're not in fear for our lives?

I don't freaking think so.

Not after that *almost* kiss.

What even was that, anyway?

I've been thinking about it—and by thinking about it, I mean obsessing about it—nonstop since the dragon decided to leave us alone for God only knows what reason.

What was I thinking?

How could I do that?

I know the mating bond between Jaxon and me is gone.

I know it's been more than a year, and Jaxon and I only knew each other for two weeks.

I know I can't remember what he sounds like, and if I didn't have pictures I'm not even sure I would remember what his smile looks like. Or the way his eyes crinkle. Or the way his hair falls over his eyes.

But I do have pictures. And I do remember what it felt like to be held by him. To be loved by him.

Maybe he doesn't love me anymore—maybe that's why the mating bond is gone. But I don't know that. I don't know anything as long as I'm trapped here. I can't cheat on him—I *won't* cheat on him. And I sure as hell won't do it with his own brother.

Which means Hudson and I need to have a talk, sooner rather than later. Just…not yet. Not when I'm exhausted and smelly and don't have any idea what I'm supposed to say to him.

And maybe he feels the same way. That the almost kiss was some kind of aberration based on loneliness and emotional overload and maybe we don't need to say anything about it at all because he doesn't have any plans on it happening again, either.

But what if he feels differently than I do?

What if he thinks the almost kiss *did* mean something?

Something is happening between us. I'm adult enough to admit that. *Something* keeps tugging at me to seek out his gaze, tease out his smile, reassure myself he's nearby and safe. But that could just be a by-product of being trapped together in such a small space for so long. Maybe we Stockholm syndromed each other. That's a thing, right?

The thought has me feeling all weird inside, in a way I don't exactly recognize. But I don't want to think about it while we're alone in what feels a lot like the middle of freaking nowhere—and I sure as hell don't want to dig into the feeling and try to figure out what it means.

Some things are better left alone.

A sudden thought has me stumbling. Hudson reaches out to steady me, and I blurt, "Umm, you can't still read my mind, can you?"

Hudson's gaze swivels to mine, one eyebrow raised. "No. That's how I know for sure we're not in your head anymore. Why? What evil thoughts are you dreaming up over there about me?"

I let out a breath I didn't know I'd been holding. "Selling you to the first person who offers me a shower."

He chuckles but turns back to gaze into the distance, and I try to will the heat to leave my cheeks.

"Hey, are you seeing what I'm seeing?" Hudson asks all of a sudden, yanking me straight out of the most embarrassing existential crisis of my life and back to reality.

"Probably not, since you have way better eyesight than I do," I answer.

"Really?" He points to the side of the structures. "You don't see the rows carved into the ground? It looks a lot like—"

"Crops!" I interrupt excitedly. "It's a farm!"

"It's a working farm," Hudson corrects me. "As in, there are people there. And food for you. And—"

"Chairs," I whimper. "There are chairs. And maybe even a bed. And a shower. Please, God, let there be a shower."

My stomach chooses that moment to rumble, as if the mention of a farm clues it in that it doesn't have to pretend not to exist anymore.

"And food for you," Hudson repeats firmly.

"What about for you?" I ask, aware of just how much has changed since we left the lair. Because if I'm this hungry, and I ate yesterday, how hungry must Hudson be, considering it's been more than a year since he's eaten?

I know he said it didn't matter in the lair, but we're not in the lair anymore. He's going to have to eat.

The thought makes me all kinds of flushed. All kinds of uncomfortable, though I don't know why. We're heading to a farm. Like the blood in the coolers at Katmere, surely there's something there that Hudson can feed on—besides me, I mean.

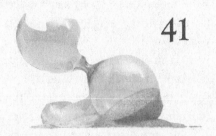

41

Crop Till You Drop

—Grace—

"**A**re you lost?" A voice comes from seemingly nowhere as we reach the fields of crops.

Hudson and I whirl around, trying to figure out who's speaking, only to find a little girl of maybe ten or eleven standing several feet away from us. She's obviously just emerged from the giant stalks of whatever vegetable it is that is growing right over her shoulder and is carrying a basket of what looks like some kind of berry I've never seen before.

It's purple, of course.

Then again, so is she. Completely purple.

Glowing purple skin. Purple irises. Purple pointed ears. Even her very long hair—arranged in two French braid pigtails down her back—is a soft, sweet lavender.

The only thing about her that isn't purple are her peach overalls...and, randomly, her teeth. As she smiles, I can't help wishing her teeth *were* purple instead of white. Maybe the fact that they all gleam with razor-sharp points when she smiles would be less frightening then. As it is, it takes every ounce of willpower I have not to take a big step back—one that hopefully puts me out of range of her very serious bite.

Hudson gives me a "what the fuck" look—one I return with interest, even though I don't know if it's about me or this kid. Mine is definitely about her, or more specifically, about how the hell we get away from her. I mean, she seems nice enough, but it's hard to relax when she just came out of the plants like some paranormal child of the corn.

But standing here staring at her and envisioning every horror movie I've tried not to watch isn't going to solve our problems. So praying that she's as nice as her sparkling eyes and wide smile seem to proclaim, I say, "Actually, we *are* lost. Maybe you can help us?"

"I thought so. Nobody just wanders by our farm unless there's a problem. Certainly no one who looks like you do." She offers me her basket. "Would you like one?"

My stomach growls again, but I've got a rule of not putting anything in my mouth if I don't know what it is. It's served me well through my eighteen years, and I don't plan on violating it now. But it seems rude to ask her what they are, especially when we need help, so I just smile and say, "No, thank you."

She shrugs as if to say, *Your loss*. Then asks, "What's your name? I'm Tiola."

"Hi, Tiola. I'm Grace, and this is Hudson." I gesture to him. "We've been walking all day and—"

"What are you?" she interrupts.

"Excuse me?" My brows go up.

"Well, you're obviously not like me," she answers, holding out one purple hand, in case I've missed the fact that she looks very different than I do. "So what are you?"

"Oh! I'm human," I answer, wondering if she even knows what that means. "And Hudson is—" I hesitate, not sure how much I should say. I don't want to freak her out, and I definitely don't want to scare her away.

But Hudson just rolls his eyes and interjects, "A vampire. I'm a vampire." He makes sure to flash his fangs when he smiles at her.

But she doesn't even glance his way. Instead, her already sparkling eyes light up even more as she moves closer to me.

"I knew it! I knew you were a human." She bounces up and down on her toes like she's gotten the best present ever. "I've read about you in books, but I've never actually met one of you before. Do you really have *red* blood?"

She says it like it's the most amazing thing she's ever heard. Which isn't a concern at all. "Um, yeah. I do."

"Can I see it?" She presses close enough that I start to worry about those teeth of hers again.

"Actually, um, most humans like to keep their blood inside their skin as much as possible. But if I cut myself or something, I'll be happy to show you."

Hudson gives me another look, this one even more "WHAT THE FUCK" than the last one. And I totally get it. This might be—and by might, I mean probably is—the weirdest conversation I've *ever* had. And considering it wasn't that long ago that Hudson spent an entire afternoon bird-calling at me, that's saying something.

"How does he drink your blood if you keep it inside you?" Those inquisitive eyes focus on Hudson for the first time.

"Oh, um. No, he doesn't—"

"Yeah, I don't—" Hudson says at the exact same moment.

We both break off, awkwardness springing up between us like a barbed-wire fence. One that's got a whole lot of high-voltage electricity shooting through it.

Tiola looks back and forth between us for a second, then rolls her purple eyes with such exaggeration that I'm pretty sure it can be seen from space.

"You guys are funny," she tells us. Then, without another word, she turns around and walks right back toward the tall field of plants.

"Should we...?" I look to Hudson for advice, but he just shrugs.

"Are you coming?" Her voice floats back to us on the wind.

Unless we want to stand out here in the middle of nowhere, we don't exactly have a choice. But that doesn't mean I shouldn't feel a little apprehensive following her into a field of periwinkle-colored plants that grow taller than Hudson. Not when every second of my moviegoing experience has taught me that bad things happen in places like this.

But it's not like there are a lot of other options out here. Plus, Hudson's with me, and I'm pretty sure together we can defeat whatever one small purple child can dish out. Please God let that be true.

Tiola moves fast and assuredly through the field, only stopping to glance behind her once to make sure that Hudson and I are keeping up. We are, but my fatigued muscles are burning pretty badly, and I'm praying that we get to wherever she's taking us as soon as possible. Unless where she's taking us is bad, and then... No, even if that's the case, I want to get there fast.

Come what may, I'm ready for today's little jaunt to be over.

I relax a bit when, after about four minutes of walking, Tiola takes a sharp left turn, because at least I think that means we're heading straight toward the farmhouse. And chairs.

And her parents, hopefully? Or at least *someone* who can tell us where we are and point us in the right direction. Although, if we have no idea where we're going, I'm not sure there *is* a right direction.

That's an existential crisis for another moment, however, because right now I can almost feel a warm shower raining down on me, and getting to it is all that matters.

But as we walk through what I'm becoming more and more convinced is the longest field in history, I can't help paying at least a little attention to the crop that's growing there.

"What do you think this is?" I ask Hudson, who's broken a small piece off one of the plants and appears to be studying it. The stalks are tall and slender, almost like blades of grass growing straight up from the soft, fertile soil.

He gives me a look. "Because the vampire knows so much about food, human or otherwise?"

It's my turn to roll my eyes. "Thanks for the help."

His lack of assistance doesn't stop me from looking, though. Or from trying to figure it out.

As we pass plant after plant, I try to find some kind of food source growing on them. Berries, like the ones Tiola has in her basket, or something bigger that maybe looks like corn or sunflowers? But there's nothing. Just the straight, thin stalk growing at least a couple of feet above Hudson's head. Does that mean the plant itself is the crop, like wheat? And if so, what is this stuff?

Finally, curiosity gets the best of me, and I start to call to Tiola to ask. But just as I open my mouth, we burst out of the field and into the front yard of the cutest farmhouse I have ever seen.

"Is this home?" I ask Tiola as she runs toward the porch.

"Yes," she shouts, turning back to face Hudson and me. "Come on. It's almost dinnertime."

But as she whips around to look at us, a giant snake slithers out from behind a rock, right toward her exposed back, and my heart seizes in my chest.

42

She's Giving Me the Smokey Eye
—Grace—

"Look out!" I yell, but Hudson's already moving. He fades to Tiola between one breath and the next, snatching her off the ground and into his arms even as he kicks out at the snake.

Tiola screams, and I rush toward her. "It's okay. It won't hurt you! Hudson will—"

"Don't hurt her!" she screams, struggling against him just as two people, who I assume are her mom and dad, come running down the steps toward us.

"Bollocks," Hudson mutters under his breath, setting Tiola back on the ground while still making sure he's between her and the snake.

But the snake is the least of our problems—and so are her parents—because it only takes a few moments for us to be surrounded by a variety of creatures, from snakes to birds to small, furry mammals. All of which are constantly shifting from dark purple to black to translucent and back again. And all of which are heading straight for Tiola.

"What's happening?" I ask, positioning myself on the other side of Tiola just in case.

"They're my friends!" she tells Hudson, tugging at his arm so he'll step out from in front of her. "They won't hurt me."

"Your friends?" Hudson lowers his arms as her words register, but he doesn't move. "These…"

"Umbras," she fills in helpfully, even as she drops down to a crouch. "And yes, they're mine."

As if to prove her words, the moment her knees hit the ground, the shadowy creatures swarm her. Running, writhing, slithering all over her, they climb into her lap, onto her shoulder, over the top of her head. Dozens and dozens of them are chittering at Tiola as they wrap themselves around her.

She laughs and calls each of them by name. Pets them. Talks to them.

As she does, they lose their forms until there are no snakes. No birds. No squirrels. Until they are all just amorphous creatures that blend into one another in varying shades of deep, dark purple.

I've never seen anything like it, but then I haven't been in the paranormal world very long, the last year notwithstanding. I glance at Hudson, hoping he knows what's going on here, but he looks dumbfounded as Tiola treats these shadowy creatures as if they really are her best friends.

In the meantime, the two adults have finally made it across the front clearing to get to us. A tall man with a big, round face and skin the same color as the rich purple pansies my mom used to grow is wearing a pair of blue jeans and a faded green plaid shirt, and a shorter woman with generous curves and skin like a field of lavender is wearing a beautiful red cotton dress with tiny purple polka dots. Her parents, I assume. I don't know what I was expecting them to wear—but I figured whatever it was, it would be purple. I start to open my mouth, to provide some kind of explanation as to what we're doing with their daughter, when the man looks down at his daughter indulgently.

"What have you brought for us this time, Ti?" he asks.

"This time?" Surprise has the words tumbling from my mouth.

"Our daughter is a penumbra." Her mother smiles fondly at Tiola. "A finder—and keeper—of lost things."

"Like us," I murmur as their reaction begins to make sense.

"Like you," her father agrees. "But usually like these shadows."

The shadows are still wrapped around Tiola, cuddling with her hair, talking to her, even playing what looks an awful lot like hide-and-seek behind her elbows and knees.

One of the larger shadows—about the size of a beach ball—must get bored, though, because it slides off her and plasters itself over and around my feet.

"Oh, sorry," I tell it, stepping back to get out of its way. It takes more effort than I thought, though, and for the first time I realize these shadows have mass. They aren't just shapes caused by something getting between a light source and the ground. They're actual, real creatures.

Something that becomes very obvious as the shadow follows me. It darts between my ankles before sliding around my calves and creeping over my knees.

Despite my jeans, I can feel the chill of it on my skin, and I can't help shivering a little. Partly from the coolness of it sliding over me and partly from the fact that this is one more thing that I can't believe is happening.

Shadows aren't alive. They certainly aren't sentient. But as *this* shadow creeps up my arm to brush against my neck and flutter through my hair, it certainly feels real.

At first, I'm afraid to move—the last thing I want to do is upset this thing that I know nothing about—but eventually it perches on my chest and slaps its hands (if those things can even be called hands) against my cheeks as it chitters on and on at me in a language I absolutely don't understand.

"Hey! That hurts a little!" I tell it, reaching down to pull it away from my face.

As I do, I'm struck by how smooth and almost slimy its surface feels. And how familiar. Which doesn't make sense until I notice it feels an awful lot like the stingrays I used to get to pet at the aquarium near my house in San Diego.

It chitters at me some more in a voice that sounds very much like it's scolding me. And then it slides off my chest and straight down into my shirt.

"Hey!" Surprised and a little afraid—do shadows bite?—I look to Hudson for help.

But he's too busy laughing his ass off to do much of anything else. I shoot him a "thanks for nothing" glare.

"Oh, don't worry!" Tiola tells me. "Smokey's friendly. She won't hurt you."

"Yeah, Grace. Smokey won't hurt you," Hudson piles on with a wicked grin. But he finally comes over to see if he can help. "Hey, Smokey. Why don't you—"

He breaks off as the shadow pulls up the bottom of my shirt to escape and literally launches herself from my belly into his arms. He catches her with a startled, "There's a good girl."

Smokey responds by sliding up his chest to curl around his neck. And then she starts to coo like a freaking turtledove.

Tiola's father laughs. "Looks like you've got yourself a new friend."

"Looks like," Hudson answers, and he doesn't sound disgruntled about it at all. More like bemused, and I can't help thinking about whether Hudson has ever had a pet before. Or a friend, for that matter, who wasn't his tutor. I didn't find evidence of either in his journals, and I wonder about what that must have been like for him.

"Well, Lost Things, let's head on up to the house so you can tell us your story," Tiola's father says with a grin. "I'm Arnst, by the way. And this is Maroly." He nods toward his wife.

"I'm Grace," I tell him with a smile. "And this is Hudson. Thank you so much for your help. I don't know what we would have done if we hadn't happened upon your farm."

"You look resourceful," Maroly says with a gentle smile. "I'm sure you two would have been fine. But we're glad you're here. Tiola loves having company."

We follow them across the front yard to the house with its cheerful front porch filled with pots of flowers and what look like herbs—all in varying shades of purple, of course.

When we get to the doorway—accompanied by Tiola and her dozens of shadow friends—Maroly turns around with a fierce frown. "No! You stay out here!"

"Oh, sorry!" I rear back, embarrassed to have misunderstood. "We'll—"

Arnst cracks up, and his laugh is as big as he is. It fills up the whole covered porch and spills out into the air all around us.

"Oh, not you, Grace!" Maroly tells me with a rueful shake of her head. "The umbras. They aren't allowed in the house, and they know it. They're just trying to take advantage of the fact we have company."

She gives the writhing mass of shadows—the umbras—a stern look. "Go!" Then she turns the look to Hudson. "And that includes you, Smokey. Give that poor boy some peace."

Smokey's only response is a mournful howl that has Arnst laughing even harder. Especially when Tiola joins in.

"Smokey's trouble," Tiola explains through her giggles. "She likes to give Mom a hard time."

"A hard time doesn't exactly cover it," Maroly says with a sniff. "Don't make me turn the water on you, Smokey. Get off that boy."

This time, the sound Smokey makes is more like a wail. High-pitched and shiver-inducing.

"Yes, yes, yes. I know you like him." Maroly reaches over and plucks the umbra off Hudson's neck, which isn't an easy feat, considering she does her best to hang on to his throat.

He makes a slight gagging sound, and Maroly shakes her head. "See now, you just choked your new friend. Is that what you want?"

Smokey quivers in response and lets out the saddest little sob I think I've ever heard in my life. A quick glance at Hudson tells me he feels the same. He looks nearly as sad as Smokey as he crouches down to run a hand over her...head? Back? It's hard to tell what's what, as she is currently a knee-high rectangular blob shape that looks like it's crumpled in on itself.

"It's okay, Smokey," he whispers, petting her a few more times. "I promise I'll come see you later."

She shoots back up into her full oblong glory at his words, a happy mixture of chittering and cooing pouring forth from her mouth as she spins around and around his ankles.

"All right, that's enough!" Maroly says, shooing her back off the porch. "Go get some food at the barn. I promise we'll send him back out to play later."

We watch Smokey race across the clearing to the barn, and I'm a little shocked at how fast she can move. Not quite as fast as Hudson in full fade mode but way faster than me.

Once she disappears from sight, Maroly ushers us into the house. "You've definitely made a friend in that one," she tells Hudson.

"Apparently." He grins. "She's very sweet."

"She's a menace," Arnst corrects him. "But a good-natured one, so there's that."

"That's more than you can say about me most of the time," Hudson tells him with a laugh.

As Arnst and Maroly laugh with him, I can't help looking at Hudson with new eyes. Who is this person he's showing Tiola's parents? It's definitely not the guy who has spent the last year tormenting me with ridiculous pranks.

But is he the guy who helped me make pumpkin pie? Who held me while I cried for all the holidays I'll never get to spend with my parents?

I don't know.

Maybe that's the problem when it comes to Hudson. After reading his journals, I know he isn't the person Jaxon thinks he is. The person he warned me about. But just because I know who he *isn't* doesn't mean I have a clue who he is.

Every time I think I may have an answer to the question of Hudson, I end up with a dozen more questions. But there is one thing I know. One thing I've figured out over the last twenty-four hours.

It's past time that I find out.

43

One Direction
Is Not Just a Band
—Hudson—

Grace is looking at me strangely, and I don't know what I'm supposed to think about that.

Then again, I don't know what I'm supposed to think about any of this. Tiola, her parents, the umbras. When we were in my lair, at least I had a pretty good idea of where we were and what was going on. Now that we're out here, I don't have a bloody clue.

Something about this place is jogging a memory in the very back of my mind, but I can't quite put my finger on what that is yet. I don't even know if it's a true memory or if it's just the memory of some previous piece of information that Richard told me once.

The man loved to impart the most obscure scraps of knowledge—the less known something was, the more he loved to share it. Is this strange purple place something like that, or is it something else entirely? Something I know almost nothing about because it's more important than I ever imagined?

"Dinner's ready," Maroly says, ushering us farther into the house. "There's a bathroom down the hall where you can wash up."

"Hudson's a vampire, Mama," Tiola tells her in a very important voice. "That means he can't eat our food."

"A vampire?" Arnst looks at me with new eyes. "We've heard stories of vampires, of course, but I've never actually gotten to meet one in these parts. Welcome."

It's not the reaction I'm used to, but then, given Tiola seemed excited by Grace's red blood, chances are no one here ever needed to worry about vampires being predators. It's actually kind of refreshing to have someone think of me as anything other than a threat. "Thank you," I say, and I mean it.

Maroly turns to Grace with inquisitive eyes. "Are you also a—"

"Oh, no! Definitely not!" Grace answers so emphatically that it's a little insulting. "I'm just a plain human."

That's not true. The longer we're trapped here, the more convinced I become that there's something more to Grace than the humanity she is so determined to lay claim to. Not that it matters at the moment, considering I don't yet know what it is. And I'm not about to contradict her about it. At least not in front of these seemingly kind people who have opened their house to us.

Then again, a quick look at Maroly's and Arnst's faces tells me I'm not the only one with doubts about what exactly Grace is. But looks like they're not going to say anything, either.

"Well then, you must be starving," Maroly tells her kindly. "Come. I made plenty."

As if on cue, Grace's stomach growls. Her cheeks turn a familiar shade of pink, but I don't know why she's embarrassed. Hunger is normal, especially considering she hasn't eaten all day. Add in the amount of walking/running/fighting we did, and I'm surprised she isn't ready to gnaw on the first edible thing she comes across.

I know I am.

But since Grace is my only option here, I shove that thought down deep. No way am I drinking from her right now. Not when we've finally managed to go a few hours without her looking at me like I'm a cross between a puppy killer and a monster.

"That sounds amazing," Grace answers with a sweet smile I've never once seen aimed my way. Of course, I'd probably keel over from shock if she did.

Grace slips down the hall to clean up, and then I do the same. Part of me wants to dive into the shower first, given I'm not going to eat. But I have several questions I need answered from Maroly and Arnst, and this seems like the best time to get those.

So I satisfy myself with taking off my shirt and washing the grime and grit from our long day slogging through dirt off my hands, face, and torso. After a quick dry with a fresh towel Maroly handed me, I head back to the dining room, where everyone is already gathered around the large, round table.

There's an empty spot between Grace and Tiola, so I slide into it with a smile at the little girl. She smiles back, her sharp teeth gleaming in the light cast by the chandelier that appears to be lit by glowing crystals above us.

"So," Maroly says as she pours ice water into the glass in front of me. "Tell us where you two came from. There's nothing around for miles, and it doesn't look like you have a carriage or other ride." She smiles encouragingly, revealing teeth that are somehow even sharper looking than her daughter's.

"We don't actually know," Grace answers as she spoons what looks like stir-fried vegetables onto her plate. *Purple* stir-fried vegetables. "We were running from a dragon—"

"A dragon?" Tiola bounces up and down on her chair. "A real dragon? I've never seen one of those!"

"He was definitely a real dragon," Grace tells her. "He spit fire and everything."

Arnst doesn't look skeptical so much as shocked when he comments, "You're saying a dragon *chased* you into Noromar? That doesn't make sense. We don't have any dragons."

"None of this makes sense." I take a drink of water, grateful that it seems to be the same here even if everything else is different. Then what he said sinks in. "Wait a minute. Did you say we're in *Noromar*?"

The memory that was tickling the back of my mind stirs to full-blown life as the stories Richard told me all those years ago come roaring back in full color. Or should I say, full purple.

"Yes." Maroly adds salad to her plate and then passes it to her daughter. "You're in what I believe you call the Shadow Realm—Noromar to us. Rumor has it there's a doorway between our two worlds that opens once every thousand years, but it's never happened in our lifetime. We always think of it as more myth than truth. You know, something to dream about but not real. So, honestly, I have no idea how you got here. Or how—" She breaks off, exchanging a long look with Arnst.

It doesn't take a genius to know what she was going to say, though. If the doorway opened to let us through—or even if we just somehow managed to slip through—lightning doesn't strike twice. Which means—

"There's no way for us to ever get back?" Grace's voice breaks on the last word, but her whisper still echoes through the room like a shout.

44

I Can Dish It Out
If You Can Make It
—Hudson—

"We don't know," Arnst says solemnly. "My family's lived here on the outskirts of the realm for seventy-five years, and we've never heard of such a thing happening."

"But maybe if you get over the mountains, farther into the realm to one of the villages," Maroly hastens to add, "you'll find someone who knows more about this."

"Someone like who?" Grace asks, and her voice still isn't back to normal.

"The Shadow Queen," I answer, and Maroly gasps.

"How do you know of our queen?" Arnst asks, and everyone seems to lean a little bit farther away from the table, as if afraid of what I might say next.

I shrug. "Honestly, I don't really know much of anything about her. My tutor used to tell me tales of Noromar when I was young, but I always thought he'd made the place up to amuse me on long, lonely nights."

I glance at Grace, just to see how she's doing. She seems to be holding her own on the panic-attack front, but her face *is* paler than I've ever seen it.

I hesitate, not wanting to offend our hosts, but then continue. "He said there was a realm made of shadow creatures known as wraiths led by a vicious Shadow Queen who is even more power-hungry than the vampire king, and that all she wants is to escape from the Shadow Realm to ours. I got the sense that her power would be insurmountable in our world or something." I pause, then lean toward Tiola with my hands raised in mock attack. "He also said wraiths love to eat vampire children who don't keep their rooms clean."

Tiola giggles, as I hoped she would. The temperature in the room had dropped several degrees at the mention of the Shadow Queen, and I wanted to keep everyone talking to learn why.

Arnst shakes his head. "Yes, there are those of our kind who follow the queen and are constantly testing the barrier for a way into your world."

"But not to worry." Maroly pats my hand across the table. "The barrier cannot be pierced by any wraith—even the queen."

"What about by humans?" Grace asks, then chews on her bottom lip. She didn't ask about vampires, and I'm trying hard not to wonder if that was intentional.

Again, Arnst shakes his head. "I'm sorry, my dear. As far as I know, no one can pass through the barrier back to your world. We've heard stories of others like yourself coming to Noromar but no one ever going back."

Grace looks like she might be sick, and I can't blame her. Just because I don't have a home to go back to doesn't mean I can't understand she might feel differently about staying here. With me.

Hoping it will steady her, I put a hand on her knee and rub it back and forth. Of course, the fact that she doesn't immediately knock it off tells me everything I need to know about her state of mind, and it isn't good.

Which is why I leave my hand where it is as I continue. "So I guess asking the Shadow Queen is pointless?"

"Not if you want to keep breathing, son," Arnst says. "Your tutor at least got that part correct. She is...powerful. And she deals swiftly with...*guests* from your world."

"My husband is right." Maroly shakes her head, but her eyes have a faraway look, like she's lost in thought. "Noromar can be unkind to strangers."

"Well, except for Mayor Souil!" Arnst snaps his fingers. "He is from your world, and his village has managed to keep the queen's army from invading for nearly a hundred years."

"Who's Mayor Souil?" I ask, wary of involving too many people in Grace's and my mess. Especially people I haven't met—and whose trustworthiness I can't judge for myself. The last thing I want is to cause more trouble, for Grace or for these three people who have been so kind to us.

"His village is just over the mountains to the east," Maroly answers. "And honestly, it might be the only place safe for you from our queen. If I were you, I'd travel there as soon as the queen's army passes to the south."

Tiola whines, "But I wanted them to stay with us. Do they really have to go?"

Arnst and Maroly exchange another glance fraught with tension, and I find I'm holding my breath. Is the queen really this dangerous to foreigners? Maybe it has something to do with Richard's story after all—maybe she thinks we know a way through the barrier. If only.

Maroly continues. "I'm sorry, honey, but I think your new friends should probably leave as soon as it's safe to travel. They can stay and visit for another day, two at the most. We wouldn't want Queen Clio to find them, would we?"

Tiola shivers. "She's mean."

And that answers that. If anyone can scare this strong-willed little girl, she must be the devil herself.

I start to ask Maroly another question about the queen, but a glance at Grace has me changing my mind. It's subtle—very subtle—but for someone who has spent the last year with little else to do but stare at her, Grace slightly shaking her head definitely doesn't go unnoticed.

I make a mental note to ask her why later. Then say, "Thank you very much. We appreciate it."

"*Really* appreciate it," Grace echoes.

"Are we done talking about boring stuff?" Tiola asks.

We all laugh, and Maroly reaches one slender purple hand out to cover her daughter's where it rests on the table. "And what is it that you want to talk about?" she asks.

"I want Grace and Hudson to sleep in my room!" she says. "It can be my first slumber party."

At her announcement, Arnst chokes on his water. Which makes perfect sense to me. There's not a semi-decent father on *either* side of the barrier who is going to be okay with letting a strange man—vampire or not—sleep in a room with his vulnerable ten-year-old daughter.

"Grace and Hudson will be sleeping in the spare room," Maroly says in a voice that brooks absolutely no argument—from any of us.

Tiola must hear the finality, too, because she doesn't argue with her mom. She does pout into what's left of her dinner, however.

"Speaking of which, you two must be exhausted." Arnst pushes back from the table and starts clearing away the empty dishes. "Maroly, why don't you show them to their room while I clean the kitchen."

"We're happy to help," Grace says, jumping up and grabbing some plates as well. She might even have sounded convincing, except for the fact that she's listing to the side as if just standing is too difficult for her at the moment.

"I'll help," I say, finishing off my water before gathering up whatever plates are left on the table. "Why don't you take a shower, and I'll be in when Arnst and I finish cleaning?"

"You don't have to do that," Arnst protests. "Tiola and I make a good team."

"Hudson can help you!" Tiola interjects. "And I can help Mama show Grace to her room."

Arnst looks like he wants to argue some more, but I solve the problem by walking through the doorway to the kitchen, arms laden with plates. If Tiola has a case of Grace hero worship, who am I to stand in the way of that?

Arnst must figure out that he's beaten, because he follows after me just a few seconds later. I've never actually done dishes before, but I've seen Grace do them enough this last year that I know the basics. Besides, it doesn't look hard—just tedious. So I grab a sponge, pour a bunch of surprisingly non-purple liquid on it from a container marked DISH SOAP, and scrub.

A *very* large amount of bubbles and one very wet T-shirt later, I finish the dishes. Arnst, who has been putting food away and wiping down the table and counters, takes one look at me and chuckles.

"That's a good look on you," he teases as he hands me a towel to dry off with.

If Grace said that, I'd make a snide comment about the look not even making my top-five best, but with Arnst, I just kind of tilt my head ruefully. "Maybe I need a little more practice with the dishwashing thing."

"You did great," he answers. "Why don't you head on up, and I'll have Maroly bring both of you some pajamas and a change of clothes for tomorrow. They won't be a perfect fit, but they should do well enough until we can get yours clean."

"Thank you. We appreciate it, and everything you're doing for us."

"Well, we couldn't just leave you out there, could we? Besides, when else would we ever have the chance to meet a vampire and a *human*?"

He says "human" like it's the most reverent thing in the world. It's all I can do not to roll my eyes and tell him where I come from, they're like a dime every three dozen. But self-censorship is a good thing, or so Grace assures me, so I just smile and say, "Where else would we get the chance to meet three"—I search my memory again for what Richard called the people of Noromar—"wraiths?"

Something flashes in his eyes so quickly that I can almost convince myself I imagined it, but then he's smiling. "Looks like we'll all have stories to tell for years to come, hmm?"

Then he's shooing me up the stairs to the "second door on the right," but I barely make it to the landing when a loud, terrifying screech fills the air around me.

45

Don't Let the Bedvamps Bite
—Hudson—

"**W**hat is that?" I ask, racing back down the stairs to find Arnst looking out the window with a scowl on his face.

"Tiola!" he calls. "You better get out there and take care of that immediately!"

"Take care of what?" I ask. "Do you want me to go with her?"

"Not unless you want to spend the next three hours with a shadow following you around," he answers. "That's Smokey. She's apparently very upset that you haven't made it back out to see her. Tiola!"

He says the last with a warning edge to his voice that would have made me obey instantly at that age if he were my parent. Then again, by the time Cyrus got upset enough to raise his voice, everyone knew that heads—and more than likely a lot of other body parts, as well—were going to roll.

"I can go," I tell him, raising my voice to be heard above Smokey's sudden caterwauling.

"Absolutely not. Tomorrow is soon enough for you to see the likes of that umbra," Maroly tells me as she joins us downstairs. "Besides, she needs to learn that she can't carry on like this and get her way."

I'm not sure how I feel about any creature carrying on this much just because they want to see me, but I can't leave her to scream in misery instead of at least trying to do something to help her, either. I've been left in misery—not screaming, but definitely in misery—more than a few times in my life, and it's not something I'd wish on anyone.

Before I can decide if I want to say something to Maroly, however, there's a sudden pounding of feet on the stairs. It's followed by an "I've got her, Mama!" as Tiola runs out the front door, slamming it behind her.

"See, I told you. She's got Smokey. You go on up to bed and check on your Grace. She looked like she was about to fall on her face during dinner."

I think about telling her that she's not *my* Grace, that she's not my *anything*, but in the end, I don't really see the point. Besides, she's right. Grace did look extremely tired before she went upstairs. I should probably check on her to make sure she's all right.

It's strange to have that thought. Stranger still to mean it. It's been a very long time since I've cared about one specific person enough to worry about them. Stranger still that that person is Grace.

Not that it's a big deal, because it's not. I care about that bloody shadow outside, too, and I only met her for about ten minutes. No, it's not a big deal at all.

"Thanks again," I tell Maroly before climbing the stairs. "We both appreciate what you've done for us so much."

She waves me away as she heads out the front door, calling for Tiola.

There's a large bank of windows directly across from the stairs, and I glance out them as I step up to the second floor. Immediately, I'm struck by how fast Maroly moves when she wants. Not quite as fast as I can when I fade, but still. She's crossed from the house to the barn in moments.

It's also hard not to miss how bright it still is outside. It's late here—at least late enough to have people getting ready for bed—and the sun is still high in the sky. Like "midmorning on a regular summer day" high.

I've never seen anything like it. Even in the parts of Alaska that have twenty-four hours of daylight, the evenings have civil twilight. Here, that's definitely not the case.

Which means what exactly? That the days are longer in the Shadow Realm? I guess that makes sense, considering shadows only exist when there's light, but how much longer is their day? Is it never dark here? But how is that possible, considering Grace and I ran across full-out darkness to get here earlier?

Or did we just run until we reached a place where the sun was *already* up?

It's an intriguing thought, especially when I consider the darkness outside my lair. It never lifted once in the year we were there. At the time, I assumed it had something to do with Grace's mind, but now I'm questioning whether that darkness was the barrier between our world and this one. When we ran through it, did we somehow cross that barrier?

If so, how did the dragon make it across with us? And why did he stop chasing us once we made it to the light? Where did he go? He can't have just disappeared. At least he couldn't in our world. In this world, though? Who the fuck knows?

This family seems completely unconcerned by the dragon, which is the only reason I agreed we could stay here. I don't know why, but I think we're safe from the dragon in this little farmhouse, and safety isn't something to ever not appreciate when you have it.

"Hey, Hudson. Are you okay?" I turn to see Arnst striding down the hall with a pile of clothes in his hands and realize I've been standing outside the door to my room—to Grace's and my room—for who the fuck knows how long.

"Yeah, sorry. Just thinking." I knock briskly on the heavy wood door and try to pretend this doesn't feel weird. Sharing the lair was one thing. Sharing a tiny bedroom feels a lot more intimate, and I don't know how I feel about that.

"These are for you and Grace," Arnst says, handing me the clothes in his hands. "There should be enough here to get you through a couple of days, so bring your clothes down when you get up tomorrow morning, and we'll get them washed for you."

"Thank you. I'll let Grace know."

He points to a door that's about ten feet down the hallway. "There's the bathroom if you want to take a shower. Otherwise, I guess I'll see you in the morning."

"Thank—" I start again, but Arnst just claps me on the back before walking away.

"Good night," he calls over his shoulder.

"Good night," I call back, just as Grace pulls open the door.

"Did you knock?" she asks.

"Yeah, I didn't want to…" My voice trails off as I note the only thing she's wearing is a white T-shirt.

It's a large T-shirt—one of Arnst's, judging by the way it hits on her lower thigh—but it's still just a T-shirt.

For a second, my mind wanders into "what is she wearing underneath" territory, but I lock that shit down fast. The last thing either of us needs is for me to be thinking like that, especially not when we're sharing a room. And especially not when she's made it clear—in behavior if not words—that she thinks almost kissing me was a mistake.

But, even telling myself that, it's hard to ignore the fact that Grace has very nice legs. And very nice everything else, too.

Fuck. This is never going to work. Living in the very large loft together was one thing. Trying to coexist in this tiny room, with its very big bed, is something else entirely.

Maybe I should just walk right back out. There's a chair on the porch I can sleep on—

"What's all that?" Grace asks, shooting me a strange look I assume is because I took two steps into the room and froze like a deer in headlights.

"Arnst gave them to us for tomorrow." I force myself to walk closer to the bed so I can drop the clothes on it.

"That's really sweet." She begins to go through the pile, separating Arnst's clothes from Maroly's. Hers from mine. "Though these aren't exactly name brand," she teases, holding up a pair of worn jeans. "Hope you don't miss your Armani too much."

"I don't miss it at all, actually," I say, and it's the truth. "When you're a vampire prince, you're expected to dress a certain way—no reason not to do it in style. But that doesn't mean I don't feel more comfortable in jeans."

I see Grace swallow once, twice. Then, "The bathroom's next door," she says as she passes me a pile with a couple of pairs of jeans, some joggers, and a few T-shirts. "In case you want to take a shower."

She must be exhausted, because she doesn't even make a crack about them having the same style clothing as we do in our realm—a question I make a mental note to ask Arnst about in the morning.

"Yeah, Arnst told me." I grab a pair of black joggers and a white T-shirt off the pile and head for the door. The sooner I get out of this room and away from Grace's inviting scent, the better.

What happens after my shower, when I'm back in here with Grace, is another problem. One I'll deal with when I get to it.

46

I Like to Sleep Tight, But Not This Tight
—Grace—

As I wait for Hudson to come back from taking a shower, I put our clothes away in the empty dresser. Twice.

When they are as neat as I can possibly make them, I look around for something—anything—else to do.

I settle on putting on some of the homemade lotion sitting on the vanity tray. It smells like lavender and lemon and feels amazing gliding over my skin, so I take my time, cover every inch of my body. But that still only takes about five minutes.

So I go back to the drawer and rearrange the clothes a third time.

Hudson still isn't back when I plump the pillows on the mattress—and notice for the millionth time since I got up here that there's only one bed.

I'd noted that there were only four doors in the small hallway when Maroly first brought me upstairs, which means their little farmhouse has three bedrooms and a bathroom on the second floor. It felt inhospitable to suggest we'd need separate bedrooms, given there was obviously only one guest room.

I drop the pillows and go back to the dresser to rearrange the clothes. Again.

I also straighten the pictures on the wall—both pretty decent abstracts— lift and lower the blinds until they fall in a perfect row, arrange the curtains several times so that they block as much outside light as possible, smooth out the bedspread, and fold my dirty clothes.

Then I rearrange our clothes again.

Because apparently sharing a room with Hudson has made me completely neurotic.

It's ridiculous to freak out like this. Absolutely, positively ridiculous. I mean, we shared the lair together for more than a year, and we survived. Why should sharing this room for a night or two be any different?

It shouldn't. But for some reason, it is. It really, really is.

Maybe it's because we had that one almost kiss before everything went to hell.

Maybe it's because, since I read those journals, I can't hate Hudson the way I used to. I can't even be afraid of him. Not really.

Or maybe it's because the mating bond with Jaxon is gone.

It shouldn't matter—it *doesn't* matter. I love Jaxon. I want to be with him forever.

But what if what Maroly and Arnst said at dinner is true? What if the barrier between our world and Noromar only opens once every thousand years?

What if that one time was to let us through?

What if there is no fine print, no escape clause, no magic that can change things?

What if Hudson and I are stuck here, in the Shadow Realm, forever?

It's a terrifying thought, one that has me pacing back and forth as I struggle to stave off a panic attack for the second time tonight.

Somehow, I managed not to freak out at dinner when the subject first came up. And I managed to avoid thinking about it after dinner when I took my shower. But now that I'm here in this room with nothing else to do but think, it's impossible to ignore it anymore.

Impossible not to wonder if my entire life has changed forever.

Impossible not to wonder if I have to start all over in *another* new place.

Impossible not to wonder how everyone I love are doing back home. If I'll ever see them again.

Back in Hudson's lair, I'd resigned myself to believing that we were never leaving. I put Jaxon out of my head, wished everyone I knew a great life, and tried to move on. But then we left the lair—and the dragon didn't kill us—and for the briefest moment, I allowed myself to believe maybe I could go home again.

Only to learn that I'm still trapped, still unable to ever go home, if what Maroly said about the barrier between our worlds is true.

Is it any wonder that I'm freaking out?

That it feels like there's a weight on my chest and like the walls are closing in on me from every direction? I miss my family. I miss my friends. And the idea of spending the rest of my life without ever seeing them again is enough to send me spiraling.

I can't breathe. And there aren't enough clothes to straighten in the world to make it so I can.

Bending over, I brace my hands on my knees and concentrate on taking deep breaths.

In, one two three four five, out.

In, one two three four five, out.

The counting doesn't touch it, so I move on to another technique Heather's mom taught me.

Five things I can see: the black rug on the floor, the white curtains with black flowers, the black bedspread with white flowers, the black-and-gold lamp next to the bed, the vase of fresh purple flowers on the dresser.

In, one two three four five, out.

Four things I can touch: the soft blanket draped over the end of the bed, the smooth coolness of the white walls, the lightness of the T-shirt I'm wearing, the firmness of the bed as it springs back against my fingertips.

In, one two three four five, out.

Three things I can hear: a high-pitched whine outside the window, the rush of Hudson's shower, the creak of the stairs as someone walks down them.

In, one two three four five, out.

The panic has receded, and I'm much calmer than I was, so I don't bother with what I can smell or taste. But I do take a couple more deep breaths as I tell myself that it's going to be okay. That I just have to take things one day—one hour—at a time. That somehow, I'll find my way through this like I've found my way through every other horrible thing that's happened to me since my parents died.

As long as that dragon decides to keep his distance, I can handle everything else. Including being stuck in a Shadow Realm indefinitely—and sharing this room with Hudson. It's only for a day or two. I can do anything for forty-eight hours…as long as it doesn't involve human sacrifice.

Ten minutes later, I've finally convinced myself to sit on the bed—which is big progress, considering I haven't wanted to so much as touch it since I got in here—when Hudson knocks on the door again.

"Come in," I call, and when he opens the door, I continue. "You don't have to keep knocking. This is your room, too."

"I know. I just didn't want to…catch you unaware." He pauses in the doorway, looking almost innocent in the soft cotton sweatpants and T-shirt.

I laugh despite the nerves that are still lurking just under my skin. "I promise to change in the bathroom and not in here, okay? Then you don't have to worry about walking in on me naked."

As soon as the words leave my mouth, I regret them. Instead of lowering the tension between us, I've just ratcheted it up. Because now we're both thinking about me naked, and that is absolutely, positively *not* what I wanted to have happen right this moment.

Hudson looks discomfited for a second or three, but then he clears his throat and says, "I'll keep that in mind. And make the same promise—about myself, I mean."

"Okay, good." An awkward silence descends between us, and I blurt out what's been on my mind ever since I walked into this room after dinner. "You can have the bed."

"No." Hudson looks insulted. "You can have it. Obviously."

"Why obviously? You just spent a year sleeping in the only bed—"

"That's not quite the same thing," he interrupts, and there's a flush to his cheeks that I've never seen before.

"Oh yeah?" I can feel myself finally relaxing as we settle back into our normal sparring routine. "And why is that exactly?"

"Because you're the one who divided the room! You gave me the bed. I was just following the rules."

"Oh, nice try," I tell him with a snort. "You slept in the bed the very first night, *before* I divided the room."

He looks at me like he has a response to my argument on the tip of his tongue, but in the end, he just sighs as he leans a shoulder against the nearest wall. "Just take the bed, will you? I'll sleep on the floor."

It's as close to admitting defeat as I have *ever* heard Hudson Vega come, and part of me wants to savor it. God knows, it may never happen again. But at the same time, I'm just sick of this argument. I'm tired, I want to go to sleep, and it seems ridiculous to make him sleep on the hard wood floor when this bed is big enough to fit four people comfortably.

Which is why, despite all my nerves from earlier, I hear myself saying, "You know, we're both reasonable, adult-type people. We can just share the bed."

"I'm sorry. I must not have heard you correctly." Hudson feigns concern. "Aren't you afraid that you'll get vampire cooties if you sleep next to me?"

"If I was going to get *vampire cooties*, as you so eloquently put it, I'm pretty sure I would have them already," I shoot back as the last of the adrenaline from my panic attack dissipates and I'm left feeling even more exhausted than before. "Now, are you going to get in this bed or are we going to spend the rest of the night debating whether or not you're contagious?"

"I can assure you that I am *not* contagious," Hudson says with an insulted sniff. "In *any* way."

"Glad to hear it," I mutter, yanking back the covers on my side of the bed and climbing in before I change my mind. When he still doesn't make a move toward the bed, I roll my eyes and add, "Neither am I, just in case you were wondering."

And then I close my eyes and roll so that my back is to the middle of the bed, determined to fake sleep until Hudson finally gives up and climbs into bed. Or until the real thing comes along.

But we remain at an impasse. Me in bed, refusing to discuss matters any further. Hudson resting his shoulder—and his attitude—against the wall, waiting for who knows what. Eventually, though, he must acknowledge that he's as tired as I feel, because he finally moves to the bed.

There's another brief hesitation—I can feel it even if I can't see it—as he stands by the side of the bed. Then the mattress shifts, and I can feel him climbing in beside me.

"Just so you know, I don't cuddle," I toss over my shoulder as he settles in with several feet between us.

"How*ever* will I survive the disappointment?" he drolls.

"You could probably still go find Smokey," I tease back.

He half chokes, half laughs. "You've got a real mean streak in you, you know that?"

I might have taken offense, but he sounds more amused than annoyed. "I learned from the best."

He snorts out another laugh but doesn't say anything else.

I wait several seconds, just to be sure. Then whisper, "Good night, Hudson."

He doesn't hesitate. "Good night, Grace. Sleep tight."

Why do I feel like neither of us is going to sleep a wink tonight?

47

You Really Stuck
My Landing
—Grace—

Awareness comes slowly in the dimness of the room.

I remember right away that I'm not in the lair, but everything else is kind of a blur. Probably because I'm warm and relaxed and more comfortable than I've been in what feels like forever.

Then again, this is the first time I've slept in a bed in more than a year. Of course I'm comfortable. The couch at the lair was perfectly fine, but the space and firmness of this bed feels like pure luxury. Luxury I have no desire to leave quite yet.

I should probably reach for my phone, see what time it is. But I don't want to know. Not when the idea of crawling out from under these blankets feels like torture. So I wriggle a little bit instead, try to burrow more deeply into their warmth.

And then freak out when *the bed wriggles right back*. Moments before it wraps an arm around me and whispers, "Remind me, Grace. What's the human definition of cuddling again?"

"Oh my God," I screech, try to throw Hudson's very heavy arm off me, but that's hard to do when it's wrapped around my waist, holding me in place. "Get off me!"

"I hate to be the bearer of bad news, Princess," Hudson says in a voice that I swear is the vocal embodiment of an actual smirk. "But you're the one on top of *me*."

I hate that he's right, hate even more that sometime during the night, I draped myself all over him. Like all. Over. Him.

My face is buried in his neck.

My arm is wrapped all the way around his chest while half my torso presses him into the bed.

And my leg—omigod, *my leg*—is thrown over his upper thighs.

I am literally pinning the boy to the bed.

Oh my God.

"I do have to ask, though," he continues in a low, wicked voice that has my heart beating way too fast. "Was it as good for you as it was for me?"

I'm too desperate to put some space between us to answer. Instead, I sit up in a hurry and try to roll off him. Except he chooses the exact same second to move—he's trying to help me by scooting to the side, I know—and it only makes things worse. Because now that I've finally managed to sit up, I'm straddling him, my legs spread and knees resting on either side of his hips.

Now it's Hudson's eyes that fly open in a hurry, and I find myself staring into their surprised blue depths for one long, interminable moment before a bunch of things happen all at once.

Hudson's hands go to my hips, and he starts to lift me off him. But I'm already scrambling away as fast as I can, and the extra momentum has me rolling right off the edge of the bed.

I hit the floor with a *thud* and a very loud squeak. And then I just lay there, because, seriously, where is there for me to go from here? With the way my luck is running this morning, I'll try to sit up and fall face-first into his lap.

As if to underscore my fears, the bed shifts, and I can feel Hudson peering over the edge at me. "Grace?" His voice is filled with concern. "Are you all right?"

"I'm fine," I tell him, though it comes out muffled because I refuse to lift my face from where it's buried in the rug.

"Can I at least help you up?" he asks tentatively.

His hand brushes against my back, and I shrug it off. "Just leave me. I can die here. It's fine."

That startles a laugh out of him. "I don't think that's possible."

"Sure it is," I say, finally turning my head because the rug really doesn't taste as good as it looks. "I just have to lay here long enough."

"Yes, well, I'm pretty sure Arnst and Maroly will come looking for you before you die, and I don't think you want them to see you like this," he answers dryly.

"I'm sure they've seen worse." I press my cheek against the rough wool of the rug and can't help wishing I'd thought to grab a pillow as I fell.

"Worse?" Hudson repeats, choking a little on the word. "Oh, they've definitely seen worse. It's just, umm…"

He must wave a hand over me because I feel a sudden breeze on the backs of my thighs and the bottom of my ass. Because of *course* the T-shirt I'm wearing is all the way around my waist. Of freaking course it is.

Which means that in the last five minutes, not only has Hudson had *all* of my most sensitive parts pressed up against all of *his* most sensitive parts, but he's also had one hell of a view.

Suddenly, the hand I shrugged off a minute ago has a whole new meaning. He was trying to cover me up, and I wouldn't let him. Could this morning get any more embarrassing?

With a groan, I reach up and grab a fistful of sheet and blanket and pull as hard as I can as I flip myself onto my back. Which, it turns out, is yet another singularly unimpressive move on my part, because Hudson comes tumbling down right along with the covers.

And lands directly on top of me.

For a second, we're both too stunned to move. But then he laughs—a warm, amused sound that shakes his whole body against mine.

"So that's a yes, then," he comments when he finally has his mirth under control. "It *was* as good for you as it was for me."

"What. The. Actual. Hell?" I yelp. And by yelp, I mean whisper, since a 180-pound vampire is currently lying on top of my diaphragm. "You have to be doing this on purpose!"

"Um, you are aware that you're the one who pulled me down, right?"

"I was going for the blanket! How could I possibly have even moved you with one hand, let alone pulled you off the bed?"

"I was already leaning off the bed, so I was off-balance," he answers. "You just pulled me the rest of the way."

"How off-balance could you possibly have been?" I gasp out when I finally manage to get my breath back. "You're a freaking vampire. I thought balance was your thing."

"I was trying to convince the most obstinate person I've ever met to let me help her. I didn't expect her response to be to try to strip the whole bloody bed!"

"Yeah, well, a girl's got to do what a girl's got to do," I whisper harshly. "Speaking of which, if you don't get off me in the next thirty seconds, you're going to die here right along with me. Except I'm going to make sure you go first."

"So bloodthirsty, Grace." He *tsk-tsk*s. "Is that any way to treat your cuddle bunny?"

Cuddle bunny? What the hell? Who is this guy and what did he do with Hudson? "I think you meant to say you're my cuddle *buddy*." I stress the *d* sound.

"Aww, Grace, I thought you'd never ask. I'd love to be your cuddle buddy."

"Hudson!" I growl.

"Okay, okay. So grumpy." And just like that, he braces his hands on either side of me and executes a perfect second half of a burpee, from push-up through plank to jumping lightly to his feet. The jerk.

Even worse, he reaches a hand down to me. "Now, will you please let me help you before we end up destroying this *entire* room?"

Part of me wants to say no just to spite him, but in the end, I give in. The faster I get up, the sooner I can pretend none of this ever happened.

Especially the part where I woke up feeling safer and better than I have in a very, very long time. Which isn't terrifying at all.

48

No Farm, No Foul
—Grace—

When we get downstairs, everyone else is already up and gone.

Maroly left a note on the kitchen counter, along with a bowl of fruit and a breakfast pastry for me.

"Hudson and Grace," Hudson starts to read. "We had to head out to the farm, but please enjoy whatever you would like for breakfast. I left you a pravenda roll that Tiola helped me make yesterday, but if it's not to your liking, help yourself to anything in the fridge."

He pushes the breakfast offering over to me, then continues reading. "I spoke to a friend of mine last night, a historian at the university, and she promised she would ask some people about the barrier. She said she would reach out if she uncovers anything. We will be back around one for lunch. Enjoy your morning. Maroly."

"Is it possible that we just happened to find the kindest family in the entire Shadow Realm?" I ask as I pop a cube of something that looks like purple watermelon into my mouth.

Unfortunately, it definitely doesn't taste like watermelon, and I gag a little before I can stop myself. I resist the urge to spit it out, though, because it doesn't taste bad per se. It just tastes different than what I expected. Instead, I concentrate on trying to figure out what it does taste like.

Maybe a mix of carrot and kiwi? Or maybe kiwi and papaya? I take another piece, chewing more tentatively this time. No, not papaya. Dragon fruit, maybe?

"I don't know." Hudson answers my earlier question. "Arnst and Maroly have been absolutely amazing to us, and Tiola's great. It's just been my experience that if something is too good to be true, it's—"

"Usually too good to be true," we finish at the same time.

"Yeah." He sighs, shoving a hand through his un-gelled hair.

It's the first time I've seen him dressed for the day without his perfect coif, and I'm not sure how I feel about it. It makes him look a little less hardened, a little more vulnerable. A lot more like the guy who wrote those journals than the prickly asshole I've gotten to know over the last year.

He's wearing a pair of Arnst's worn blue jeans, and they hang low on his hips. I can't help noticing they're a little baggy through the legs but they reach all the way to his casual loafers. My gaze travels back up his long legs to the T-shirt stretched across his wide shoulders. The soft fabric is dyed almost the exact color of his oceanic eyes—eyes that have clearly noted my full-body inspection, if their mocking look is any indication.

"You need new shoes," I mutter before shoving a pastry in my mouth.

He chuckles but thankfully lets it go as he plops down in a chair next to me.

I glance at the clock above the pantry door. "It's seven thirty now. Do we really want to just sit around here all morning doing nothing when they've helped us so much? It's a farm, right? They must need help doing farmy things."

"Farmy things?" Hudson teases.

"You know what I mean!" I wave a hand to encompass the window—and the rows of crops just beyond that stretch farther than I can see in every direction.

"I don't know if I do." He puts on a serious face. "Maybe you should provide a demonstration, just so I know we're on the same page."

"Maybe you should bite me," I retort without thinking.

Hudson doesn't clap back at me the way Jaxon did when I made that mistake, but then, he doesn't have to. The way his eyes linger on my throat says everything.

The air between us turns heavy, loaded, and swallowing becomes a whole lot more difficult.

Hudson's eyes, dark and haunted—haunt*ing*—move slowly along the column of my throat. From the pulse point at the base of my neck to the sensitive spot under my jaw to the *very* sensitive spot right beneath my ear, he studies them all like he's going to be quizzed later.

Forget swallowing. Breathing just became more difficult. Nearly impossible, really, which is a problem considering humans need air to breathe. And the way Hudson has me feeling right now—like prey to his very hungry predator—is reminding me just how human I am.

Then he blinks and the moment is gone. In place of the predator is the

Hudson who helped me off the floor this morning. The Hudson who let a shadow wrap herself around his neck because it made her happy.

But seeing this Hudson doesn't make me forget the other one. It just makes me feel more off-balance, more keenly aware that the predator is lurking just beneath the surface. It should terrify me—and maybe it does—but not for the reason I thought it would. No, I tell myself as my heart rate takes its sweet time returning to normal, the reason I'm finding myself afraid to be near Hudson has nothing to do with him killing me.

And everything to do with him devouring me, one tiny piece at a time.

49

Re-Veg Is Sweet

—Hudson—

G race is blushing again, her cheeks turning a soft, rosy pink that I've grown to like over the last year despite myself. Not just because it means all that gorgeous blood of hers is flowing just a little closer to the surface—though that is quite the nice little side benefit.

But I also like it because it lights her up. Makes her glow.

Not that I give a shit if she glows or not. I'm just saying she looks good when she does.

"Sooo, back to this farmy behavior," she tells me sternly. But as she speaks, her hand flutters up to her throat, her fingers stroking the exact spots I couldn't help staring at. And I know that she's more affected than she wants to let on. More affected, even, than the blush tells me.

Good. I've been wide awake since she repeatedly climbed on top of me overnight, no matter how many times I gently nudged her aside. I shouldn't be the only one suffering here.

"I don't know why you're looking at me," I answer in the poshest accent I can muster. "I'm from London."

"Yes, I knoooooow you're from London, Hudson. Everyone knoooooows you're from London. I'm just saying you can pick a few vegetables, right?"

"Of course I can." I pause, let her get comfortable. Then ask, "What's a vegetable again?"

"What's a—" For a second, her face goes blank. And then it suffuses with even more color as she starts babbling. "Oh my gosh! I'm so sorry. I didn't even think about the fact that you've never really been around anyone before. Even at Katmere, you were kind of a loner, so you probably don't know that humans eat vegetables. I mostly ate fruit while we were in the lair, so you might not have noticed. There are these leafy green things… Although here, they might be purple. I don't know. Either way…"

Well, that sure as shit was shortsighted of me, wasn't it? I've been standing here the whole time, and I'm still not sure how that went from me fucking with her to me being the object of Grace's pity. Which really fucking sucks, by the way.

She can be as mad at me as she wants, but she sure as hell doesn't need to pity me.

I hold up a hand to interrupt the monologue on veggies she's been giving for what feels like forever but is probably only a couple of minutes. Which actually seems like a really long time to be waxing poetic about shit that grows in the ground, but I'm just a vampire. What do I know?

Except that I never want to see her look at me like that again. Like she feels sorry for me. No fucking thank you.

"For Christ's sake, Grace. I know what a bloody vegetable is." When she still looks skeptical, I list them off. "Lettuce. Cauliflower. Peas—"

"Actually, peas are a legume—"

She cuts off when she sees my "are you serious right now?" look.

"Am I to take that to mean you don't care about legumes?" she asks, eyes wide and innocent.

And fuck. I fell right into her trap. I've been around her long enough to usually know when she's taking the piss. Every once in a while, she gets me, though, and judging from just how wide her eyes are—I've noted that the amount of bullshit she spews correlates exponentially with how much she deliberately widens her eyes—she's been fucking with me this whole time.

Because apparently after a night of cuddling, I'm that bloody gullible. But it's hard not to be when I can still remember what she feels like pressed against me. And how good it is to wake up warm and comfortable and not alone, next to someone who smells and feels as good as Grace does.

And if that doesn't make me the most gullible ass in the world, I don't know what does.

But just because I fell for her tricks doesn't mean she needs to know that. Which is why I look her straight in the eyes and call her bluff. "Actually, I'd love a lesson on legumes. In fact—"

I break off as a sudden, heart-wrenching wail fills the air. It's the kind of cry that stops your pulse, has shivers running up and down your spine, and makes you cringe all at the same time.

"What on earth is—" Grace breaks off as our eyes meet and realization dawns.

"Smokey," we both say at the same time.

Grace takes a minute to clean up her breakfast bowl and grab a couple of bottles of water, but I head straight for the front porch. No one should have to sound like that poor thing sounds right now.

As soon as I open the front door, Smokey rushes me. She slams into me so hard, I have to throw a hand out to keep my balance, then she spins around and between my legs like a cat. If that cat was twenty kilos of solid muscle and on crystal meth.

Her crying has stopped, thankfully, but as I bend down to pet her, she lets out a yowl that splits the air around us.

"I'm sorry!" I yank my hand back immediately. "Do you not want to be petted? I won't if you—"

She hops up then, bouncing her head against the underside of my hand.

"I'm not sure what that means," I tell her.

Smokey yowls again, then hops straight up and onto my still-outstretched hand.

"She wants you to pet her, silly," Grace tells me as she comes through the door.

"I tried that, but she made the most pitiful sound ever." Still, I gingerly place a hand on the top of her...head? blob? and try again.

This time, the yowl she lets out sounds a lot happier than the last one.

"See?" Grace says with a laugh. "I told you that's what she wanted." She reaches a hand out to pet Smokey, too.

But the second Grace's fingers come in contact with the shadow, Smokey hisses like a snake and strikes out at her. Grace immediately jumps back, out of striking zone, but we both look at the sweet little shadow in bewilderment.

"Hey, what was that?" Grace asks.

"I don't know," I answer with a surprised shrug. When I turn back to Smokey, I ask, "Do you want me to put you down?"

In answer, Smokey plasters herself to my chest, thinning out so that she's wrapped around my midsection like a belt. Or more likely a corset, I realize, as she starts to squeeze.

"It's okay," I say, patting her a little awkwardly. "You don't have to get down."

She lets out a soft sigh in response, like everything is right with her world.

"Why don't you try petting her again?" I tell Grace. "Maybe she was just feeling insecure balanced on my hand like that."

"Maybe," Grace says doubtfully. But again, the second she tries to pet the umbra, the little creature goes into full attack mode. Hissing, striking out, screaming like a berserker on a battlefield.

"Okay then!" Grace holds both her hands up in surrender. "I promise I won't touch you again."

Smokey mewls in agreement and settles back against me.

Grace and I roll our eyes at each other, but I can't help grinning just a little. Nothing—no one—in my life has ever chosen me over someone else before. They've certainly never liked me better. It's a good feeling, and I find myself petting and crooning to Smokey as we walk down the porch steps.

Which has her moving up from my waist and resting one of her corners on my shoulder, like a baby rests their head.

"I think that thing's in love with you," Grace mutters under her breath.

"Don't be jealous," I tease her with a grin. "I'm sure you'll find a friend soon."

"I should have known this would make you insufferable." She looks to the heavens. "One shadow picks you, and you think you're the best thing ever."

"I've always known I was the best thing ever," I say. "You're just mad because Smokey's a better judge of character than you are."

"Yeah, that's what it is." Sarcasm drips from her voice. "How'd you guess?"

"I'm just perceptive like that," I answer as I scratch one of Smokey's round blobs poking out on top of her head almost like rounded ears. It must be the right thing to do, considering the way she makes a high, repetitive sound in the back of her throat. If she were a cat, I'd say she was purring. As it is, the closest description I can think of is yodeling.

Because it looks like yodeling shadows are a thing here in Noromar. A quick glance at Grace tells me she's about to jump out of her skin at the noise, but now that I'm past the shock factor, I find it oddly soothing. It's nice to have immediate feedback that I'm doing this whole friend thing right.

Plus, I've seen—and heard—much weirder things at the Vampire Court through the years. This is nothing.

By tacit agreement, we head to the barn, hoping to find Maroly or Arnst to see what we can do to help, but we're barely halfway there when Tiola bursts out of the side of the high, grasslike crops we walked through yesterday.

"Come on!" she calls, beckoning wildly. "Hurry up or you'll miss it."

She doesn't say anything else. Just dives back into the field and starts racing away.

Grace and I exchange a look, and then we take off after her. Because really, what else are we going to do?

50

I'm Oh So Swan-Yay

—Grace—

I race through the field as fast as I can, arms and legs pumping as I weave between rows of crops and try to keep Hudson and Tiola in my sights.

They're both moving fast—really fast—which means I've got to work extra hard. Not to keep up, because that ship has long since sailed, but just to stay close enough that I can follow them.

And this isn't even fading speed, I note as we make another twisty turn through the crop rows. This is Hudson keeping up with a little girl with superhuman but not vampire speed, while also glancing back occasionally to make sure he hasn't lost me, too.

I lay on a final burst of speed, round the corner, and so, so thankfully emerge out of the crop field and into a large clearing.

I realize it's a meadow at the edge of a lake as I watch Hudson and Tiola finally stop about three hundred yards in front of me. Filled with wildflowers in a dozen different shades of purple and knee-high violet grass, the whole clearing looks like something out of *Alice in Wonderland*. Not just because the colors are so different than our world but because everything just looks a little...skewed.

The trees at the edges of the clearing are wide and tall but seem upside down, with their branches growing every direction along the ground and their long purple trunks stretching toward the sky. The boulders near the lake look like rounded-off pyramids—big and heavy on the bottom but narrowing more and more toward the top. Even the nearby creek that feeds into the lake runs differently than at home. It runs up the hill, flowing upstream and into the lake.

It's weird, really weird, and yet also beautiful in an off-kilter kind of way. I like it, a lot, and judging from the look on Hudson's face when he turns around to check on me, so does he.

"What are we looking at?" I ask as I jog up to the lake's edge to meet him and Tiola.

But even as the words leave my mouth, I know. Because there, on the lake, is the most beautiful bevy of swans I have ever seen. There must be two hundred of the birds, ranging from the lightest lemon yellow to the brightest gold, swimming over the surface of the clear purple lake.

"We almost missed it," Tiola whispers so quietly that I can barely hear her.

"Almost missed what?" I ask, keeping my voice low as I step closer to Hudson.

But the second I'm next to him, Smokey hisses in outrage. Annoyed by her possessive behavior at this point—especially since I have no designs, romantic or otherwise, on her new favorite person—I hiss back, twice as loud.

It startles a laugh out of Hudson, which in turn must startle the swans on the lake. Because, as one, they take to the sky.

"This!" Tiola squeals, clapping now that she doesn't have to worry about disturbing the swans. "We almost missed this."

At first, I'm not sure what she's talking about. Because sure, the swans are flying, but— Oh!

As one, they turn over, diving backward until they form two perfectly synchronized circles. As one, they spin around and around—seven times, I count—getting closer to the water after each spin. On the final circle, they pull out from the bottom, one after another, then take off flying across the sky in a perfect V formation.

"That was..." Hudson begins, but then his voice drifts off like he has no words, and I totally understand. Because I don't, either. For the first time in my life, I understand why a group of swans is sometimes referred to as a ballet. *Swan Lake* indeed.

"Told you you'd like it," Tiola says smugly.

"You're right," Hudson agrees, reaching out a hand to ruffle her hair. "Thank you for showing us."

Smokey, who is still on his chest, whines a little at the gesture until he reaches down and gives her a pat as well. Then she goes back to making those weird purring-adjacent sounds that are like fingernails on a chalkboard to me.

"Hey, do you happen to know where your mom and dad are?" I ask. "We were hoping they could point us to something we could help with on the farm."

"You want to help?" Tiola sounds so skeptical that I burst out laughing.

"I know we don't look like much," I answer, wrapping an arm around her shoulders for a quick hug, "but surely there's something we can do that we won't mess up."

"Surely," Tiola agrees, but she sounds about as confident as I feel when I walk near Hudson while he's holding Smokey. Like, maybe it will be fine, or maybe I'll end up getting a giant chunk taken out of my ass by a tiny little shadow. Both feel equally possible.

"Mom's in the garden," Tiola says. "And Dad's in the milk barn. Where do you want to go?"

"Garden," I tell her.

"Milk barn," Hudson answers at the exact same time.

"You think you can *milk* something?" I ask. *"Really?"*

"Stranger things have happened. Besides," he snarks, "humans do it regularly. How hard can it be?"

"*Some* humans do it regularly," I correct. "Most of us stay as far away as we can get."

"Milking's fun." Tiola interrupts our bickering. "I'll take you there, Hudson, and we can show Grace Mom's garden on the way."

As we walk back toward the group of buildings to the left of the main house—thankfully at a much slower pace than we got to the lake—I ask Tiola, "So when you say garden, you mean something different than the crops you guys grow?"

"Oh, yes. Definitely. Mom grows about a hundred different things. It's how she feeds us mostly."

"That's so cool. I can't wait to see it." I'm not a huge gardening fan by any means, but I helped my mom grow and pick the herbs for her teas back home in San Diego. It'll be nice to muck around in the dirt a little, picking food that will immediately be used.

Besides, the real reason I want to garden—or do *anything* that will keep me busy—is so I don't have time to dwell on the fact that this is it. This place, these people, even the nefarious Shadow Queen who will supposedly kill us if she finds us...this is my new life. *Forever.*

I know Maroly asked her friend to find out all she can about the barrier, but I think deep in my soul, I already know the truth. We're never going home.

I'm not even a little surprised when the admission has me gulping to catch my breath, my chest tightening as a panic attack starts to take hold. I glance at Hudson out of the corner of my eye, curious if he can sense my rising panic. I've grown used to him in my head and knowing what's on my mind, knowing exactly how to calm me down.

But he seems completely oblivious to my inner struggle.

A giant smile is stretched across his face as Tiola chatters a mile a minute about the joys of milking some animal called a tago. His right hand absently scratches Smokey behind her...ear?...while his left cradles her against his chest like a baby. Out of nowhere, I get a vision of an older Hudson, walking with his own children one day, a look of pure happiness lighting his electric-blue eyes, softening the creases around his mouth, and I swallow.

He chuckles at something Tiola says and tosses me a conspiratorial look—and winks. I have no idea what she said, but Hudson *winked at me.*

By the time Tiola drops me off with her mom, I'm irrationally pissed and grateful he's heading far away from me for a bit. How dare he be so happy that we're stuck in this purple-on-purple world?

I know his life has been shit. I know this probably all seems like a much better future for him than he ever had back home. *I get it.*

Doesn't mean I can't be upset he's clearly just accepted we're never going home without a care in the world while I'm over here fighting to not pass out. I latch on to my anger and take a deep breath, exhaling on the most long-suffering sigh I've probably ever uttered.

Hudson must hear, because he tosses a questioning look at me over his shoulder. I roll my eyes at him, a clear indication I am not in the mood to discuss my irrational snit, which he thankfully takes as the hint it is, because he shrugs and keeps following Tiola.

"I hope the tago pees on him," I mutter under my breath, then widen my gaze as I finally take in Maroly's "garden."

51

A Not So Savage Garden
—Grace—

Tiola wasn't exaggerating when she said her mom grew a lot of different things.

The garden is huge—so huge that it could be mistaken for another field of crops, except for the fact that so many different things are obviously being grown here. In one section, there is a huge tangle of vines growing together, with large round and squarish fruit growing off them. All purple of course.

I wonder which ones are the melons I had for breakfast as I make my way past a section filled with nothing but leaves poking out of the ground next to another section with giant leaves curling into individual stalks at least two feet tall.

"Grace!" Maroly waves to me from the other end of the garden where she's on her knees. "What are you doing out here?"

I cross the distance between us at a jog. "I thought I'd come see if you needed help. What can I do?"

"Oh, you don't have to do that," she tells me. "Tuesdays I spend all morning in the garden, fertilizing and pulling weeds."

"I can pull weeds with the best of them," I tell her. "It used to be my job in my mom's herb garden."

"Okay, if you insist." She smiles at me. "Thank you."

I join her on the ground and start yanking a couple weeds out of the ground by their roots.

"We live so far from the closest villages that it's impossible for me to shop with any regularity," Maroly says as we work together. "So our garden is pretty much a necessity, which is why I grow so many things."

"Where is the nearest village?" I ask, glancing up at the dark, craggy mountains that seem to loom over everything. "Hudson and I didn't see anything besides your farm out here at all."

"That's because our farm is the only thing on this side of the mountains for many miles." Maroly pulls several thick weeds with giant thorns out of the ground like it's nothing and adds them to the growing pile beside us.

I glance at her hands, expecting them to be torn and bleeding from her efforts, but they're as smooth and perfect as they were yesterday when she was serving us dinner.

How is that possible? The thorns were all over the stalks of those weeds. There's no way she was able to avoid them. Which means what exactly? That her skin is different than human skin? Less easy to puncture?

It's a wild thought, especially considering it looks the same as my skin. But as she pulls up a bunch more weeds of the same type—again without any damage to herself—I figure it's got to be true.

To test my hypothesis, I reach for one of the same kind of weeds. And pull my hand back with a muttered curse as several of the thorns draw blood immediately.

"Oh, be careful!" Maroly tells me as I pop my injured finger in my mouth. "Did it get you?"

"Just a little," I answer. "It was my own carelessness."

"Why don't you stick to that section over there," she says, nodding toward the area I think is lettuce. "Those weeds tend to be a little less aggressive."

I move over to check out that section, and it turns out Maroly's right. So I spend the next hour crawling up one row and down the other, yanking every weed I see.

Maroly does the same, and by midmorning we've got the entire garden free from trespassers. "Now comes the fun part!" she tells me as we carry the weeds to a nearby composting bin.

"Picking the vegetables?" I venture.

"Exactly. Coming out here and pulling stuff for a couple days' worth of meals is one of my favorite things about this farm. For a while, it was the only thing I liked."

"So you didn't always live here?" We head back to the garden, and I watch in awe as Maroly pulls a bunch of purple asparagus-looking things out of the ground.

"Me?" She laughs. "Oh, God no. This farm has been in Arnst's family for generations, but I've only been farming for about twelve years. We met at university and fell in love, but I had no idea what I was getting into when I took the leap and followed him here."

It's her turn to look at the mountains. But unlike my distrust of them, her expression fills with wistfulness the longer she looks at them.

"Where are you from?" I ask. Not that I know one Shadow Realm city from another, but I've got to start somewhere, and this seems like as good a place as any.

"Oh, I'm from the little village about fifty miles east of the mountains, where we think you should look for sanctuary," she answers after a second. "It's called Adarie."

"You miss it?" I prompt as we move away from the asparagus thingies and cut a few large, oddly shaped vegetables off what I'm pretty sure is a vine—the Shadow Realm's answer to zucchini, apparently—as I put it in the basket Maroly gave me to carry. Or something else entirely?

"I do. Very much. But Arnst loves this farm and so does Tiola." She gives a little laugh. "And so do I, most days, even if the hours are killer."

"I've always heard that about farms," I tell her. "That they take a ton of dedication."

I glance around at the baskets of vegetables we've already picked, the sheer size of the garden we have left to work in, and consider if I'd be cut out for the farm life. I guess I'm going to have to think about things like that, what my life is going to be like here in Noromar.

I bite my lip. I had always wanted to be a marine biologist. I bet there's all kinds of interesting marine life in the Shadow Realm. But then my shoulders immediately slump as I remember the queen will likely kill us if she finds us. I don't know much about this place yet, but I'm pretty sure that means travel is off the menu.

"Farms are definitely hard work," she agrees, pulling me from my thoughts. "But tell me something about you, Grace."

"Oh, um, there's not much to tell. My parents died about a year and a half ago." It's the first time I've said it out loud in ages, and it's a gut punch all over again. Partly because it seems impossible that they've been dead so long and partly because I miss them. A lot.

Being around Maroly and Arnst and Tiola, doing things with them that families do, brings it all back. It's hard not to think about my mom when I'm standing here gardening with Maroly. Or my dad when I watch Arnst tease Tiola. It's been a long time since I've been around a family like this, and it's harder than it should be. Definitely harder than I'd like it to be.

Then again, I am in an entirely different world. Or realm. Or whatever they call it here. Is it any wonder I'm feeling homesick when the only things that feel familiar are the people? Everything else seems like another planet in another galaxy in another universe.

"I'm sorry to hear that," Maroly says softly.

"Me too." I give her a smile to cushion the words. Then tell her the whole spiel about Uncle Finn, Macy, and Katmere Academy.

"Is that where you met Hudson?" she asks. "This Katmere Academy."

"Something like that, yeah." I don't know why, but I don't want these people to know what happened with Hudson back home. If anyone deserves a fresh start, it's him.

"And he doesn't mind your power?" She reaches for one of the squared-off melons I noted earlier, uses a scissors to snip it from the vine.

"My power?" I repeat. "Oh, no. I'm not like everyone else at school. I'm human, not paranormal. I don't have any power."

Maroly stops in the middle of snipping another melon and turns to look at me.

I wait for her to say something placating, like *it doesn't matter* or *power is highly overrated anyway*. The things I used to tell myself a lot when I was trying to figure out why on earth someone like Jaxon would want to be with someone like me.

But she doesn't do that. She doesn't downplay the power thing at all. Instead, she narrows those gorgeous purple eyes of hers like she's trying to see inside me and asks, "Are you sure about that?"

"Am I sure about what?" I ask, confused.

"That you don't have any power. Because I'm pretty good at sensing magic, and from where I'm standing, it feels like you've got a whole lot of it inside you."

52

There Has to Be
an Udder Way
—Grace—

I'm still thinking about my conversation with Maroly the next day after spending the last three hours trying to milk a tago—and by trying I mean anything but succeeding. If I had any magic, I'd have ended that misery the first time one of the six-sided udders sprayed me in the face.

The whole idea of my having magic is completely nonsensical, but so is nearly everything else she said about me that morning.

"Oh, I'm not magic," I told her when she brought it up. "Neither were my parents. I guess my dad was technically a warlock, but he lost his power when he married my mother and left his coven. And I've never had any."

"I wouldn't be too sure about that," she said as she moved gracefully between rows and started picking handfuls of eggplant-colored lettuce. "Magic manifests differently in everyone, Grace."

"Maybe it does here in Noromar, but back home, you either have it or you don't. There's no in-between."

"Hmm. It sounds like you come from a very unforgiving world."

I wanted to argue that point, too, but the truth is, she's right. Our world is very unforgiving in so many ways—ways that have nothing to do with magic and everything to do with pain.

But just because she's right about that doesn't mean she's right about everything. Because I don't have any magic, and I definitely don't have any power. I'm pretty sure I would have noticed by now.

My mind flicks back to the dragon attacking and my somehow making both Hudson and me fireproof, but I shake my head. There's probably a very good reason that happened. I don't know what, but I'm sure there's a simple explanation.

Because it's not like any of my friends could hide their magic, even if they wanted to. So how could I possibly hide mine?

As if to prove my point, Hudson fades across the meadow straight to where I am taking a break from milking beneath a grouping of tall willowy trees with leaves the size of chairs fanning out around their thin trunks. He covers three hundred yards in the time it takes me to exhale the breath I took when I first saw him.

Yeah, it's definitely hard to hide that kind of speed.

"I figured I'd find you here," he says, plopping down on the ground next to me and leaning against the huge, gnarly tree trunk. "Shirking your duties."

I start to tell him to bite me, but that went so well last time that I bite my tongue at the last minute. And flip him off instead.

"Is that an invitation?" he asks, brows raised.

"For you to fuck yourself?" I shoot back. "Why, yes. Yes, it is."

"Wow. Not pulling any punches today, huh, Grace? I'm wounded." He gives me his most angelic look. The one that usually has me shaking with trepidation at what he's done now, but he's already screwed me over today.

"If I were you, I'd be very, very worried about falling asleep tonight," I answer, reaching down to wring milk from my T-shirt.

"Hey"—he holds both hands out in mock innocence—"you were the one who made fun of me last night for saying vampires were not cut out to be dairy farmers."

I roll my eyes at him. Hard. "That didn't mean I wanted to be *volunteered* for udder duty this morning."

He chuckles, his eyes crinkling at the corners with mischief. "What can I say? I'm a card-carrying feminist, and I would never want to suggest you couldn't do a better job than a man."

He is ridiculous.

And as much as I want to stay mad at him, I can't, because I remember exactly how the conversation started this morning about chores… With me having a panic attack that this was our last day on the farm. Arnst had said he'd seen a dust cloud to the southwest, which meant the queen's army would be far enough away by tomorrow morning, and we had to try to get to Adarie before anyone could discover—and kill—us.

"You are such a jerk," I mutter without any heat.

Out of nowhere, a loud, low growl fills the clearing. It has the hair standing up on the back of my head as I look around for some heretofore-unseen wild purple animal.

But Hudson just laughs and pats his back. "It's okay, Smokey. Grace doesn't mean to be so cruel. It's just who she is."

Of course. It's the freaking shadow. I haven't actually done anything to her, but somehow she hates me more every minute that passes. Or maybe it's just that she loves Hudson more, and since the two of us are usually trading insults, she hates me on general principle.

Either way, it's no fun to be hated by something that loves everyone else so much.

"Does she seriously have to go with you everywhere?" I groan.

"She is my shadow," he answers with a shrug.

And I can't help it. I burst out laughing, which is exactly what he wanted, if his self-satisfied smile is anything to go by.

"Maroly packed a lunch for you," Hudson says, dropping a small picnic basket between us. "I tried to tell her we'd barely worked and didn't need a break, but she wouldn't stand for it."

"Speak for yourself," I say with a toss of my head. "I spent the whole morning covered in tago milk. It's not a great smell, I have to say. I'm pretty sure it's in my pores."

Hudson leans forward, pretends to take a deep whiff. As he does, Smokey hisses at me in warning, but I ignore her. My new plan for dealing with Hudson's pet is to just pretend she doesn't exist when she does something obnoxious to me—which is pretty much every minute of every day.

"You're right," he says after a few seconds. "There's a definite stench."

"Wow." I toss him a half-amused, half-insulted look. "Thanks."

He pulls several food items out of the basket as well as two bottles of water, then offers me a sandwich. He blinks at me with his full boyish charm turned up to eleven. "Truce?"

"Oh, there will be no truce, Vega. No surrender." I narrow my eyes, make my voice as scary as I can manage. "Only vengeance. And *death*."

"Death? Really? Doesn't that seem a little extreme—"

I leap to my feet before he's finished and take off running toward the small glade of trees at the end of the lake. Hudson follows me, just as I knew he would.

Come on, I urge as he starts to close the gap between us. Just a little closer. A little closer. A little— I jump to the right at the last second.

Hudson's momentum carries him forward, right into the lake—which I already discovered, after exploring yesterday afternoon, does not have a shore. Of course, this means Hudson doesn't just get his legs wet...he immediately sinks beneath the clear lavender water.

53

Suck It Up,
Buttercup
—Grace—

"**W**hat the fuck?" Hudson sputters as he comes up for air and shoves his wet hair off his forehead.

I can barely hear the litany of very colorful curse words leaving his mouth over my own laughter. When Smokey starts yowling at the top of her lungs, too, I can't stop myself from doubling over in laughter. If I wasn't already her least-favorite person on the planet, I'm pretty sure I would be after today.

But hey, Hudson deserved that. I may never get the smell of tago milk out of my hair again.

"I told you I was sorry, Grace!" he growls as he reaches the side of the lake with two powerful strokes.

I cross my arms and send him an evil "I told you so" smile. "And I told you there was no sorry, Hudson."

"Only death. Yeah, I remember." He sighs loudly. "Apparently, I should have taken you more seriously."

"Apparently," I agree. Right before I rub my fingernails against my chest, then blow on them in a total "nailed it" gesture.

"I'm going to get even eventually."

"I'm sorry." I put a hand to my ear. "I can't hear you over all of your whining."

His brilliant blue eyes narrow to slits. "Payback's a bitch, Foster. You know that, right?"

"Is it?" I ask innocently. "I hadn't noticed."

And then I turn and saunter back to my tree—and the picnic basket full of goodies that's waiting for me.

Seconds later, there's a large splash, followed by more screeching from Smokey. Sadly, I don't even get a bite of my tago cheese sandwich before a dripping wet Hudson Vega is standing over me.

"You're blocking my sun," I tell him without bothering to look up.

"Grace." There's a note in his voice that has me dropping the act in an instant.

I spring to my feet, terrified that I inadvertently drowned Smokey or something with my prank. But no, she's right there, wrapped around Hudson's soaking wet jeans. "What's wrong?"

"I …" He heaves a giant sigh. "Think I need some help."

"With what?" I ask, then take a couple of wary steps back. I know this could all be part of some twisted revenge—I wouldn't put it past him—and also, if something is bad enough that Hudson feels the need to ask for help, then the more distance the better.

"I think there's something on my back," he answers, shrugging his shirt off as he turns around.

I scream. I can't help it. It just rips right through me as my entire body wigs out. "Holy shit! Holy shit, holy shit, holy shit!" I take a step closer, just to make sure I'm right about what I'm seeing, and— "Holy shit!"

"A little more clarity would be nice here," Hudson says, and he's admirably calm considering the situation. And the fact that I am being absolutely no help.

Shit. Get it together, Grace.

I take a deep breath, blow it out slowly. And manage to say, "So, it's really not that big of a deal."

"Yeah, I'm pretty sure the ship has sailed on that explanation," Hudson answers dryly.

"Yeah, you're probably right." I sigh and take a second to gird my loins for what's coming next. "First of all, I want to say I'm really, really sorry. I had no idea—"

"What, Grace?" Hudson finally snaps. "What exactly is on my back?"

"Leeches. You've got a couple"—seven, he has seven!—"leeches on your back. I, umm, I need to get them off."

"Can you do it?" he asks, and despite everything, he sounds genuinely concerned. "If it bothers you, I can get Arnst—"

That would require us going all the way back to the farm, and there's no way I want poor Hudson to have those nasty things on him one second more than necessary. "No, it's fine. There were leeches in the lake in California. My dad had to get them off me once when I was younger. I know what to do."

I don't mention that I cried for days afterward every time I thought about the nasty little worms sucking on my blood. Ick.

Since Hudson is facing away from me, I don't even try to repress my shudder. "I'm so sorry, Hudson. I'm so, so, so sorry. I would never have done this to you on purpose."

"It's fine, Grace. Just—"

"Get them off. Yeah. I'm on it," I say, right before I take a deep breath and slide my pinkie fingernail between the leech's nasty mouth and Hudson's very-not-nasty skin.

It comes off easily—thank God—and I throw it as far away from us as I can manage.

"One down," I tell him cheerfully—or as cheerfully as I can manage with my stomach threatening to revolt at any second.

"One to go?" he answers doubtfully. And sure, I told him there were a couple of leeches, but he has to feel the others and know that there's more.

"Maybe a couple more than that," I answer weakly.

I wait for him to freak out, but he just sighs and runs a hand through his wet hair. "Don't say how many. Just tell me when it's done."

"Good plan." I take another deep breath and carefully dislodge another leech. And another. And another.

I save the biggest for last, partly because I'm afraid it's going to give me the most problems and partly because I really, really don't want to touch the thing. It's big and black and currently attached right in the middle of Hudson's left shoulder blade.

I must have made some sound, though, because Hudson turns his head to look at me. "Hey. You okay?"

"I'm pretty sure I should be the one asking you that," I tell him, swallowing down the bile trying to climb its way up my throat. "There's just one left."

"You're looking a little green. You sure—"

"I've got this, Vega. I'm the jerk who did this to you. I'm going to fix it. Especially since you're being so freaking kind about the whole thing."

And when I put it like that, it's easy to just suck it up and grab the leech's body with one hand while I slide the nail of my index finger—this one is way too big for my pinkie nail—under its mouth. It pops off with a loud, obnoxious sucking noise—much louder than any of the others—and I scream a little as I throw it away.

"That's it," I tell Hudson as I breathe a sigh of relief. "But we're going to need to doctor them when we get back to the house."

"Grace—" Hudson tries to interrupt me, but I just talk over him.

"So they don't get infected. I made sure I dislodged them all properly—"

"Hey, Grace—" He's got a worried look on his face, like he thinks I'm going to freak out any second. Or maybe like he thinks I already am. But I just want to get this out so I never, ever, ever have to think about those leeches again. Or the fact that I'm the one who did this to him.

Tears burn in the backs of my eyes, but I refuse to let them fall as I continue. "So they didn't release any extra bacteria into your bloodstream, but you still have open wounds, so—"

"Hey, Grace." Hudson takes hold of my upper arms in a firm but painless grip. "It's all right."

"They can get infected if you aren't careful with them, and I'm sorry. I'm just so sorry—"

He must give up on trying to talk me down, because the next thing I know, Hudson is pressing one still-damp finger to my lips. "My turn to talk," he tells me quietly. "Okay?"

I nod.

"Good." He slowly pulls his finger away, but the look in his eyes warns me that he's not above putting it right back if needed. "First of all, it's okay. It's just a few leeches. They aren't going to hurt me, and their bites aren't going to get infected. That's where the whole vampire thing really comes in handy. Two, I'm not mad at you. I know you didn't do it on purpose. And three, that last-minute maneuver that landed me in the lake? That was a freaking epic prank. I will absolutely, positively be getting you back for it, but it was. Freaking. Epic."

"It was, wasn't it?" I say after a second.

"Absolutely." He gives me a mock-angry look. "Although I'm warning you now that you should be very afraid."

"Oh, I am," I tell him. "Very, very afraid."

Except I'm not. At all. Because who could have imagined that Hudson would have handled this whole disaster the way he has? He got me stuck with the worst milking experience of my life—and I stewed about it all morning. I sent him plummeting into a lake (unknowingly) full of leeches, and he seems more concerned that I'm upset than he is about the prank.

Which leaves me with another problem.

I'm really starting to like this guy, and I don't have a clue what I'm supposed to do about that.

54

He's Got
Hangry Eyes
—Hudson—

Grace still looks pale, but she's not nearly as bad as she was a few minutes ago, so I finally step back. If I'd known she was going to get so upset about the leeches, I would have kept my mouth shut until we got back to the farmhouse. Then again, on a purely selfish front, it's nice to know she cares about me being hurt.

Smokey, who's been shockingly quiet since I rescued her from the lake, must take my stepping back as some kind of cue, though. Because she begins to lay into Grace like it's the end of the freaking world—and Grace is the one responsible for it all.

I can't understand anything she's saying and neither can Grace, but that doesn't stop the small shadow from taking her to task. With each snarl and screech, she advances on Grace a little more until Grace—who has no back down in her for me at all—backs up. Soon, every step Smokey takes toward her sees Grace taking two back.

It's the funniest bloody thing I've seen in a long time. Even before Grace looks at me and says, "A little help here, Hudson?"

"Actually, I think Smokey's got it well in hand," I tell her, leaning back against the nearest tree to enjoy the show. "Don't you, girl?"

Smokey yowls what I'm almost certain is an agreement before turning back to Grace and yelling at her some more.

"Okay, okay, Smokey. I get it!" Grace holds out a placating hand, but the shadow ignores it. "I already apologized to him. Can you get off my back already?"

Smokey hisses in response, which has Grace narrowing her eyes and hissing back.

"She does know that we're friends, right?" Grace asks.

The question itself—and the look on her face when she asks me—surprises me so much that I respond before giving myself a chance to think about it. "Is that what we are, Grace? Friends?"

Her startled gaze collides with mine. I don't know why she's so surprised, though. Not when at least fifty percent of the time I'm convinced she wants nothing more than for me to disappear or die.

"I thought we were," she whispers.

Which gets her another hiss from Smokey. But now the shadow's tirade isn't so funny anymore. And neither is Grace's discomfort.

"Smokey!" I call the shadow with a firmness that has her turning to look at me. "Leave Grace alone."

Smokey gives one loud, annoyed caterwaul in response and then turns her back on me. But she does stop berating Grace, so I'll take it.

"Thank you," Grace says a little stiffly.

I want to apologize, to tell her that of course we're friends. But the truth is, I don't know what we are. And I don't think she does, either. Clouding the issue with some false sentiment isn't going to make it any easier to understand.

"Do you want to head back?" I ask.

"I thought you said Arnst told us to take the afternoon off?"

"He did." I shrug. "I just didn't know if you wanted to spend that afternoon with me."

"I'm pretty sure that should be my question," she says. "I did cover you in leeches, after all."

"Good point. I'll see you later." I start to walk away.

"You should at least take a water," she calls after me.

I burst out laughing. I can't help it. There's the Grace I know and sometimes like. Never giving an inch even when she's trying to make amends.

"What?" Her look is as innocent as it gets. "It's hot out here."

That's a bunch of shit, and we both know it. I don't call her on it, though. Instead, I take the proffered bottle of water and sink down in the grass next to her—much to Smokey's very vocal disgust.

I hold a hand out to the shadow and, at first, it looks like she's going to bite it. But in the end, she crawls up my arm and wraps herself around my left biceps.

In the meantime, Grace pulls her sandwich out of the basket and starts to eat. But she only takes a couple of bites before she wraps it back up and puts it away.

"Not hungry?" I ask.

"That's kind of what I want to talk about."

"So the water bottle wasn't just a peace offering." I feign surprise. "I'm appalled."

She just rolls her eyes. "I'm being serious, Hudson."

"You want to talk about being hungry?"

"I want to talk about *you* being hungry," she answers. "The leeches made me realize—"

"Wait a minute. The leeches made you think about me feeding?" I don't know whether to be amused or insulted. Maybe both. *Probably* both. "What the fuck did Jaxon do to you?"

The blush is back, and this time it goes all the way down her neck to the small bit of skin revealed by Maroly's T-shirt.

"Oh my God!" She slaps her hands onto her cheeks to cool them down, but the red is only getting more pronounced. "That's not what I meant!"

"Okay." I wait for her to say something else—anything else—but she just sits there staring at me all wide-eyed and embarrassed. Until finally, I prompt, "So what *did* you mean?"

"I *meant* that the leeches took blood from you," she finally answers through gritted teeth. "Blood I'm pretty sure you're ill-equipped to give, since you haven't..."

"Fed in two and a half years," I supply helpfully.

"Exactly. That's a long freaking time to go without drinking."

She has no idea. But that's the point, isn't it? I've worked really hard so that she wouldn't know what it's like to be this hungry. "It's fine, Grace. *I'm* fine."

"I know—that's obvious. I just wanted to say. If you..."

"If I...?" I have absolutely no clue where she's going with this.

She takes a deep breath in that way she does when she's super nervous. Plays with the frayed edge of her jeans. Clears her throat a couple dozen times. And then finally says, "I just wanted to say that if you're hungry and you need to feed, you can..." She clears her throat again. "You can feed off me."

55

Afraid of My
Own Shadow Queen
—Hudson—

The second her words register, my fangs explode into my mouth.

The hunger I've been ignoring since we walked out of the lair comes roaring to life deep inside me, and it's all I can do not to take Grace up on her offer, right here. Right now.

Except that's not cool. She's not some random blood donor on the street. And she's not my person, either. Not like that. I may not be able to read her mind anymore, but I can tell she's just someone who's feeling guilty, and there's no way I'm going to take advantage of that. No way I'm going to feed from her when she's so freaked out by the idea that she can barely get the words out.

So even though every cell in my body is screaming for me to drink from her, I shake my head. And say, "You don't have to do that. I already told you, I'm fine, Grace."

"I know I don't *have* to do anything," she answers. "I'm just saying that if you need to feed, I'm here for you."

"Fine. Thank you. I'll keep that in mind." I know I sound abrupt, but fuck. What am I supposed to do when all I really want to say is, *Yes, please.*

Her face closes up at my tone. "I'm sorry if I overstepped. I wasn't trying to—"

Fuck. "It's fine, Grace. I appreciate the offer. Honestly. But I'm good."

Her big brown eyes search my face, looking for I don't know what. For the first time, I notice the gold flecks at the very center of her irises. They're beautiful. *She's* beautiful, stubborn chin and all.

"So," Grace says in a voice that's filled with forced cheer. "What do you want to—" She breaks off at the sight of Arnst running across the clearing, waving his arms like he's trying to guide an airplane in for a tricky landing.

"Grace! Hudson!"

We both leap to our feet, but this time I don't bother to wait for Grace as

I fade across the meadow, my heart pounding in my chest. "What's wrong? Are Maroly and Tiola okay?"

"They're fine," he gasps out, bending over to brace his hands on his knees while his lungs work overtime trying to suck in air.

I have trouble believing that. If he was running out here fast enough to be gasping for air, something is wrong. Very wrong. I just don't know what it is yet.

"What is it?" Grace asks as she comes running up behind us.

I shake my head but note he's carrying a large rucksack over his shoulder. Something uneasy moves inside me at the sight of it. I don't know why it makes me nervous, but it does.

Arnst's gaze goes wide as he gasps, "I'm so sorry." Which I'm nearly certain is code for *you're totally fucked.*

But Grace doesn't see what I see. At least not yet. She's too busy worrying about her friend to notice that something important isn't right. Instead, she pats him on the back and says, "It's okay. Just rest for a minute."

"I can't," he says as he finally straightens up. "And neither can you. You both need to go. Now."

"Go?" Grace repeats as she shoots a puzzled look my way.

"We need to leave the farm," I tell her. Adrenaline's already shooting through my body, and it's taking every ounce of self-control I have not to throw Grace on my back and fade the fuck out of here.

"I don't understand." Grace looks between Arnst and me. "I thought we were waiting to hear from Maroly's friend—"

"She sold us out," Arnst says grimly. "She told the Shadow Queen that two strangers crossed the barrier. The queen sent a unit of soldiers to arrest you and bring you to her."

"Arrest us?" she repeats.

"We told them you'd already gone, but they don't believe us. They're insisting on searching the farm. Maroly and Tiola are giving them the grand tour of the barn right now. They're going to stall them as long as they can, try to give you as much of a head start as possible." He thrusts the rucksack at me. "But you need to go—now."

I nod, but my gaze is focused on the farm in the distance as I try to use my preternatural vision to gauge if the soldiers have seen us yet or not. So far, it looks like Maroly is keeping everyone occupied on the far end of the farm.

Arnst continues. "Go over the mountains, but don't take any of the main roads. You've got to hike your way through them. Once you make it over them, you need to travel another fifty miles east to a village called Adarie. It's the one we told you is run by a foreigner who is able to keep the Shadow Queen away. It's your only hope."

"Adarie," I repeat, wondering if this is a trap. Wondering if it matters if it is. It's not like we've got anywhere else to go.

Something flashes in Arnst's eyes, but it's gone too fast for me to identify it. Anger? Shame? I wish I knew. Maybe I'd have a better idea of what we're supposed to do if I'd gone ahead and asked him those questions I'd had about the Shadow Queen before Grace waved me off.

"It's where Maroly's from," Arnst finally reminds us. "I've spent a fair bit of time there. It's a good town, filled with good people," he assures us. "Her cousin runs the inn. There's a letter in the bag for him. Maroly wrote it herself. When you get there, find him and give him the note. He'll help you."

He starts to back away. "I also put some money in the front pocket. It's not a lot, but it should get you food and some clothes and a few nights' lodging at the inn. Good luck," he tells us, but he looks so grim while he says it that it feels more like a bad omen than a wish for success. And that's before he pauses and says, "May the suns always shine in your path."

Then he turns and runs back the way he came, leaving Grace and me staring at each other over a rucksack that neither one of us knows what to do with.

56

Baby Got Piggyback

—Grace—

"What do we do?" I ask Hudson as panic races through me.

He's still calm—I try to tell myself that's a good thing—but the truth is Hudson is pretty much always calm, so his lack of terror has absolutely no bearing on how much trouble he currently thinks we're in.

Before he can answer, Smokey lets out the most pathetic yowl I've ever heard from her—and that is saying something. She unwinds herself from Hudson's arm and throws herself at his feet, hanging on as tightly as she can.

As she does, he looks at me with abject panic in his eyes, but I don't know what to tell him. If we're going on the run, bringing the loudest shadow in existence is probably not the way to go. At the same time, leaving her here doesn't look like it's going to be easy. And just might break her little heart.

I know the feeling. The Vega boys are very hard to forget.

Finally, out of desperation, Hudson crouches next to her and runs a hand down her little back. "It's going to be okay," he tells her. "I'm going to miss you, too."

Her only answer is to throw herself into his arms and hold on even tighter. She's not crying—which is a surprise—but maybe that's because she knows tears can't fix this. Nothing can.

Nervous, I glance to the edge of the clearing. "She's making too much noise, Hudson."

"I'm aware of that, Grace," he replies, frustration coating every word. "I have to go, Smokey. I'm sorry." Then he leans in close and whispers, "I love you," so softly that I have to strain to hear it.

Then again, maybe that was the point. I wasn't supposed to hear him. I'm sure he doesn't consider it good for his image that he's such a softy for the little shadow who adopted him. And maybe with his family—with the mother who scarred Jaxon so terribly—it wouldn't be.

But with me? It's just one more sign that there's a lot more to this guy than I ever imagined when we first woke up in the lair. A lot more to him than anyone imagines, I think.

Suddenly, there's a noise in the thicket of trees beyond the clearing. Hudson's head comes up immediately and he lets go of Smokey. "Go," he tells her. "Now!"

She looks like she wants to argue, but she must recognize the firmness in his voice because she starts to run across the clearing toward the lake, still howling and crying.

As the crackling in the undergrowth gets louder, I look at Hudson and ask, *"What do we do?"* for the second time in as many minutes.

"Run."

He doesn't bother to ask if I want him to carry me so we can fade. Instead, he just thrusts the very heavy backpack onto my shoulders and pretty much throws me on his back.

The second I've got my arms and legs wrapped around him and he knows I'm secure, he takes off so fast that I almost fall off.

"Hold on!" he yells, and it's like he's building up speed because with each stride he takes, we go a little bit faster until the world around me is nothing but a blur.

As we hit the trees on the opposite end of the clearing, I turn back—just in time to watch a group of soldiers burst into the meadow.

"Did they see us?" Hudson asks as he somehow manages to go even faster.

"They're not heading this way, so I don't think so."

"Good."

I turn to face front again and realize something. "Wait!" I tell him. "You're going in the wrong direction! Arnst said we have to go over the mountains!"

"I know what he said." But he makes no move to turn around.

"You think he's lying?" I ask. "Why would he go through all the trouble of warning us about those guys back there just to screw us over?"

"I don't know," Hudson answers grimly. "But I'm not exactly in a trusting mood right now."

Fair enough. I'm not feeling particularly trusting myself.

"So what's the plan, then? Besides run like hell."

He puts on another burst of speed. "That's pretty much the plan."

"Yeah, I was afraid of that."

Hudson runs flat-out for miles with me as his own personal backpack. I try to make myself as light as I can, but there's not a lot I can do in this situation—except hold on tight so he doesn't have to worry about me falling off.

It's not something I want to worry about, either—not at these speeds. For the first time in my life, I understand what it must be like to be a Formula 1 racer, and I have to say, I don't understand the appeal. Not when one tiny little mistake could mean instant death.

Just thinking like that has panic balling in the depths of my stomach, however, and me freaking out isn't going to help Hudson. It sure as hell isn't going to keep the two of us alive. So I push that thought away and hold on tight, not just to Hudson but to my own personal control, and promise myself it's almost over.

Which it will be at some point.

Just not now.

For the first time since Maroly told me I had power—magic—I wish it were true. If I did, I'd find a way to use it to get the Shadow Queen's henchmen off our back. Find a way to use it to keep Hudson and me safe.

I don't know how long Hudson runs. Time doesn't seem real when the world around you is no more than a blur of streaming light.

At one point, though, Hudson slows down enough for me to notice a crevice in the ground, yawning wide and deep in front of us. My heartbeat is like a jackhammer in my chest as he pours on the speed again, and I figure out exactly what he plans on doing.

"Whoa, what are you do—" I break off as he leaps over the thing like a damn gazelle.

And then he leaps over another crack in the earth, this one even wider than the first.

I scream a little—I can't help it—and bury my face against the top of his shoulder. There are some things a girl really doesn't need to see. Especially one who's a lot more at the whim of gravity than Hudson seems to be.

We have to have been traveling for nearly two hours, but we finally make it through the broken, boulder-strewn terrain. My arms and legs are completely numb, though I don't want to say anything, not when Hudson is the one doing the heavy lifting. But I'm tired, and I really could use a break.

I have to wonder if Hudson really can't read my mind anymore, because he only runs another five minutes or so before he finally stops for a breather.

Which should be exciting to me, but uncramping my legs after my two-hour piggyback ride isn't what I would call easy.

I manage it, though—and, with a little support from Hudson, even manage not to fall on my ass once my feet are back on the ground. It's a close call, though, and Hudson looks at me with remorse.

"I'm sorry. Next time, we'll stop sooner, give you a break."

"I'm more worried about you." For the first time ever, Hudson is sweating. Plus, he looks paler than usual, his cheeks slightly gray and his normally lush red lips a disturbing shade of bluish-purple. "Are you all right?"

"I'm fine." He shrugs off my concern like it's nothing. "I just need to take a breather for a few minutes."

"Take as long as you need," I tell him as we settle on the ground. And by settle, I mean collapse.

The trees around us are like the ones by the lake—upside down, with their branches running against the ground—so there's not a lot of shade for us to hide in. We do our best to find a little bit of protection from the ceaselessly beating sun, but I'm pretty sure I'm going to be burned soon enough.

Or die from thirst.

Although...maybe Arnst thought of that. Sitting up, I reach for the backpack and drag it out from under Hudson's head.

"Hey!" he grouses. "I was using that."

"As a pillow." I roll my eyes. "I've got a better use for it."

He starts to give me more of a hard time, but when he realizes I've got the bag open and am pawing through it, he stops complaining.

"Anything useful in there?"

"Yeah, actually." I toss him one of the six water bottles Arnst packed for us and take one for myself. "Don't drink it all in one go," I tease.

Hudson just unscrews the cap and downs half the contents in one long swallow. "Are there more?" he asks.

"Yeah, a few."

He just nods and finishes his, then lays back down on the ground and closes his eyes.

I'm worried about him.

I've never seen him look tired before, and right now he looks really, really tired. To be fair, for most of our acquaintance, we were stuck in a room together doing almost nothing. Pretty hard to get tired like that.

But even at the farm or after that massive dragon fight, he never looked like this. Just completely worn out.

"Hey," I say after several long minutes pass and he doesn't so much as move. "You doing okay?"

He opens one eye and looks at me suspiciously. "Yes. Why?"

"I don't know. You just look…"

The eye closes again. "Like I ran two hundred miles with another person on my back?" There's just enough snark in his tone to get my back up. But I think it's deliberate on his part—a distraction to get me off the scent.

But I'm not falling for it. Not now, when our entire escape—our very safety—depends on him being healthy enough to get over those mountains. There were a few times Hudson had slowed enough for me to tell that he'd run north most of the way but eventually he'd headed east toward Adarie. I don't know how far we are from the town, but my best guess is we're still about thirty miles west and fifty miles north—and a rugged mountain range still sits squarely between us.

"You need to feed." Unlike earlier by the lake, it's a statement and not a question.

He sighs heavily. "I'm fine."

"You're not. Obviously. And I know I was only at Katmere Academy for a couple of weeks, but I never once saw a vampire there look like you do right now."

That has him sitting up in a hurry. "So sorry if I don't live up to the standards set by your precious Jaxon."

"That's not what I meant, and you know it!" I tell him. "I'm just worried about you—"

"Yeah, well, don't." He pushes to his feet and what? I'm supposed to pretend I don't see the fact that he's swaying back and forth? "I've got this."

"Why are you being so stubborn?" I demand. "Is it really such a hardship to consider feeding from me? I promise I won't read anything into it."

"Yeah, that's what I'm worried about." He rolls his eyes. "In case you haven't noticed, Princess, we're on the run."

"I am well aware of that," I tell him through clenched teeth. I'm not going to fight with him. I'm not going to fight with him. I'm not going to fight with him. I make those seven words my new mantra as I take a deep breath and let it out slowly. "I also know you're doing all the heavy lifting for this run, which means you need to replenish the energy you're putting out. That's just basic science."

"It is," he agrees. "You know what else is basic science?" He points at the sky. "The fucking sun that never fucking sets in this fucking realm. And since you're obviously the expert on vampires after two whole weeks at Katmere, tell me, please, how this whole feeding plan of yours is supposed to work if the sun never sets."

Oh, shit. I blink up at him. "I forgot about the 'not going out in the sun when you drink human blood' thing."

"Yeah, apparently." He shoves his hands into his pockets and looks out over the mountains, jaw working.

"We still have a problem, though. You're not going to make it all the way over the mountains if you don't eat. Not without hurting yourself."

"I'm aware. Once we get into the mountains, I'm sure there'll be some wildlife or something I can drink from. It'll be fine." He doesn't sound enthused, and I don't blame him. Drinking from some wild animal we just happen upon probably sounds as appetizing to him as eating it sounds to me.

But desperate times, desperate measures, or so they say. At least Hudson acknowledges the problem and understands that we have to deal with it. That's what matters.

"You ready to go?" Hudson asks as he picks up his discarded water bottle from earlier.

"Yeah. Do you want me to walk for a while?"

He glances up at the mountains looming in front of us, large and deep purple and intimidating as fuck, then back at me with a small smirk on his face.

And I get it. I really do. Even a non-hiker like me can tell these mountains have a lot of sheer rock faces that need to be climbed and not hiked. And considering we have absolutely no climbing gear, I'm at least ninety percent certain I'll die in the first hour.

But I'm still willing to give it a try—especially if Hudson is on the bottom to catch me when I fall, which I have absolutely no doubt that he will do. Probably more than once.

"Don't worry about it, Grace," he says after a second. "I'm not going to collapse on you quite yet."

"I'm glad to hear that," I answer dryly. "Considering if you do, we're both falling off the side of this mountain."

"Haven't you heard? It's not the fall that will kill you. It's the—"

"Bounce," I say at the same time. "Yeah, I never really bought that."

He laughs. "Me either, actually." Then he squats down. "Your chariot, my lady?"

"Only you would refer to yourself as a chariot," I say with a snort as I throw the pack on my back and climb on.

"What should I refer to myself as?" he asks mildly. "A Ferrari?"

I crack up as I wrap my arms and legs around him—and ignore the way my hip flexors are protesting another several hours in this position. Not nearly as much as they'll be protesting after I slide down the mountain a time or ten, but still. They aren't happy. At all.

"Now what?" I ask once I'm as secure as I'm going to get.

"Now we climb a mountain," Hudson says. And proceeds to do just that.

57

Cliffs Notes
Got Nothing on Me
—Hudson—

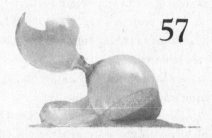

As I start to climb what feels like yet another rock wall in an endless stream of them, I finally admit to myself that I've never been this tired in my whole life.

Not even when I went on that abysmal hunger strike in my emo tween years. At the time, I was sure if I kept it up long enough, my father would cease his monthly torturing of me.

If he knew I hated being buried alive so much that I was willing to jeopardize my life to stop it, surely he would put an end to it. At least for a little while.

It didn't work. But it did teach me two lessons.

One, the only thing my father has ever loved about me is the weapon he worked so hard to turn me into. And two, it's dangerous to be this hungry.

After I'd been on the hunger strike for eight months, I slipped up. It was early morning, right after my father had me raised from the Descent, and I was still a little woozy and disoriented. I was also starving.

One of our human maids was cleaning my antechamber, and she dropped a glass dish. When she bent to pick it up, she cut herself on one of the shards. The scent of her blood filled the room, and I couldn't hold myself back. I attacked her.

Somehow, I stopped myself before I drained her, but it was too close. Even knowing that every human who works at the Court gives their consent to being fed from doesn't make my guilt about that incident any easier to bear.

She didn't fight me, didn't even try to stop me. I had her consent. And still I nearly killed her. Still I almost took too much.

I'd gone eight months without feeding then. Now I've gone two and a half years, fought a dragon, and run more than two hundred miles at the fastest clip I've ever run. Hunger is a wild animal within me, clawing at my guts. Tearing at my soul with every breath I take.

I can keep it in check, but not if I drink from Grace. Not if I taste her. She thinks I'm being stubborn, but she has no idea what's inside me at this very moment.

I've finally made it halfway up the wall, and I'm searching around for a handhold deep enough that I can use it to pull us up. I finally find one about three feet to the left of where I'd been hoping to find one. Add in that it's so high that I've got to strain to reach it, and I know this is going to be a difficult pull. Not impossible—few things are—but not easy, either.

"Hold on," I mutter to Grace, who nods just enough that her strawberry-scented hair tickles my nose.

Then she does as I instructed and tightens her arms around me. Which only succeeds in pressing the rest of her more tightly against me, too. Maybe not the best suggestion on my part.

Then again, I'm never at my best when I'm hungry.

Still, the offer she made me this afternoon touched me in a way few things ever have. She was so embarrassed even bringing it up, but she did it. For me.

As I search for another handhold, I tell myself not to read too much into it. That I know pity when I see it.

I don't want pity. Not from anyone and definitely not from Grace. Not when I know she's never looked at my brother like that.

No, Jaxon she *wants* to feed from her. Me, she'll let feed out of obligation. Guilt. *Pity.*

So many reasons that I shouldn't take what she's offering. No, not shouldn't, *won't*. I *won't* take it. No matter how hungry I am or how good she smells when she's plastered against me.

And she does smell good. Sure, there's the top odor of tago milk no one could miss, but underneath, skimming along her skin, is another, more delicate scent.

Like flowers and cinnamon and warm summer air that fills my senses with every breath I take. She feels even better, with her arms and legs wrapped around me and her sweet, perfect curves pressed against my back.

Fuck. I'm smart enough to know I shouldn't be thinking about her like this. What I don't know is if it's really me having these thoughts or if it's the hunger inside me, making me want her in all kinds of ways that I shouldn't.

Most days, we're barely friends. That doesn't change because she's spent the last two days climbing all over me while she sleeps. And it sure as hell doesn't change because she offered to let me feed.

All that proves is she's a decent fucking person, which I knew already. A little sanctimonious and a lot pain in the ass, maybe, but still a good person. That doesn't mean she's thinking about my skin pressed against hers, my fangs scraping against the delicate skin of her throat right before I finally pierce her.

Just the thought breaks my concentration, has my fingers slipping out of the tiny handhold I'd finally managed to grasp.

Fuck. Grace lets out a tiny scream as we start to slide down, but I'm not about to let either one of us plummet to our death, so I dig in with the hand that's still grasping onto the wall. Drive the tips of my fingers deep into the rock to hold us until I can get back in position and bring my other hand back up to help.

Because I'm weaker than normal, it's more of a struggle than it should be. But I finally get myself repositioned enough to keep climbing. Which I do, one hand after another.

And decide the wake-up call of nearly falling off the side of a cliff is exactly what I need to keep my head in the game.

Instead of thinking about Grace's curls or the way she smiles or how fun—and funny—she can be, I just need to focus on the fact that whatever I feel isn't special. Not when she doesn't feel anything like it for me.

And the offer she made me isn't special, either. She would make the same offer to *anyone* who needed it. I'm nothing special to Grace Foster, and she's not anything special to me.

No good will come out of imagining this as any more than a truce in the hostilities. She's in love with my brother, and I'm just the not-so-decent substitute. I'll do well to remember that.

"Almost there," she murmurs. Her breath is hot against my ear, but I ignore it—ignore her—as much as I can.

It's the only way we have a chance in hell of getting to the top.

58

I Cave It My All

—Grace—

Shaky or not, hungry or not, Hudson Vega in full action-hero mode is a sight to behold. Muscles working, body straining, just a little bit of sweat sliding down the side of his neck into the collar of his shirt...

If I wasn't so worried about him, it would be one hell of a view.

If I'm being honest, it's still one hell of a view. Especially all up close and personal like this. And especially since Hudson doesn't look like I should be worried about him at all. He's climbing these mountains like a well-oiled machine.

After he's summited the fifth sheer rock face using nothing but his bare hands, I can't keep quiet any longer. "I have to ask. Did you deliberately pick the most difficult part of this entire mountain to try to climb?"

"Hide where they least expect to find you," he answers as he finds another handhold where I swear there isn't one and pulls us up another several feet.

"*Art of War*?" I ask.

He snorts. "Common sense. And I'm not *trying* to climb this mountain. I'm climbing the fucker."

"Yeah, you are." I clear my throat and try not to notice as another trickle of sweat slides into the collar of his shirt. This is Hudson, after all. The brother of my—it's time to admit it—ex-boyfriend and my kind-of friend. Spending the last four hours with my body plastered against his doesn't mean anything. Except for the fact that he's a really decent guy.

He could have made things a lot easier for himself by ditching me anytime in the last several hours. Instead, here he is, saving us both—even if it kills him. He can say he's fine all he wants, but I can tell this is costing him more than he'll ever admit.

"When we get to the top of this cliff," Hudson grinds out as he pulls us up another several feet, "I'm going to need another break."

Finally. "I was actually going to suggest we stop for the night soon."

I wait for him to argue—I know he doesn't want to stop any sooner than we have to. He doesn't argue, though. In fact, he doesn't say a word—which tells me he's in much worse shape than he's letting on.

Then again, anyone would be tired after the day we had. Despite the sun beating solidly overhead, it's almost ten o'clock at night. We were up working the farm at six this morning, even before we went on the run for our lives. Is it any wonder we're both exhausted?

I glance up to the top of the rock wall we're currently in the middle of scaling. We're about thirty feet from the top, which means about five more minutes if Hudson stays on the pace he's been setting. And if there are decent handholds. And if we don't plummet to our deaths at any second.

The list of uncertainties is long when you're hanging on the side of a mountain. And I'm hanging on the back of a guy hanging on the side of a mountain. But I'm just really glad I'm not doing it alone. And also that Hudson is the one I'm doing this with. He may have a big mouth, but he's also got an air of steady confidence that makes me feel like even this nightmare is doable.

Five minutes later—on the dot—we reach the top of the cliff wall. Once there, I try to ignore the fact that there's another, bigger wall right in front of us. That's tomorrow's problem. Tonight's is finding some kind of shelter/protection so we're not sitting ducks out here if the Shadow Queen's soldiers actually spot us.

Oh, and finding water, because that's going to be a thing soon.

If possible, Hudson looks even more wiped than earlier, so I reach into the pack and toss him one of the few remaining bottles of water as he rests against the rock wall, then settle myself on the ground to inventory exactly what Arnst put in the backpack for us.

Turns out, the answer is quite a lot. Of course it's so heavy. Besides the water bottles, he included two tins of Maroly's homemade granola bars for me, an extra change of clothes for each of us, a couple of tiny folded-up squares that I'm pretty sure is Noromar's answer to a space blanket, a red crystal I saw Maroly light a fire with, a pocketknife, a first aid kit, and a small pouch filled with money. He also packed a few of the little sugary candies I enjoyed, and I kind of want to kiss him right now as I plop one in my mouth and continue to inventory and repack the contents of the bag.

Eventually, the hunger gnawing at my insides can't be ignored. I want to scarf down one of the granola bars so badly, my mouth won't stop watering, and I reach for the tin and have the lid open before I force myself to close it. I can't believe how hungry I am, considering I was just along for the ride for the last seven hours. I can't imagine what Hudson must be feeling, which is why I can't bring myself to eat in front of him.

I swallow hard and slide the pack over to Hudson so he can use it for a pillow again if he wants.

Except he doesn't snag it like I thought he would. In fact, he doesn't even move, which means he's sleeping heavier than I've ever seen him.

Convinced I need to find a solution to his feeding problem, I grab the first aid kit from the backpack. Then I look both ways, trying to figure out my best bet to find water or shelter and finally decide I have no freaking idea.

In the end, I choose left because why not. And because the last thing I want is for Hudson to have to come find me, I note my path with a Band-Aid from the kit every two feet or so.

This high up the mountain, it feels like I can just reach out and touch the sun. So it also feels extra hot beating down on me as I stumble around. And if I manage to find water, I'll at least get to have a sponge bath. After Hudson's experience back at the farm, I'm not exactly excited at the prospect of jumping in anything that isn't a professionally plumbed shower.

I've been walking for nearly ten minutes before I finally hit pay dirt in the form of a small cave on the side of the mountain. The entrance itself is so tiny that I nearly miss it, but something tells me to check it out.

I do have one awful moment of terror—exactly what kind of animals live in caves in the Shadow Realm anyway? And is one—or more—of them in this cave right now? The odds are good, right? I mean, how many perfectly good mountain caves go uninhabited?

Probably a lot, I tell myself. Tons, really, especially way up here, where it feels like we're the first people to ever be here. It will be fine.

We need somewhere to hide so that we can actually get some rest. This cave could be perfect. I just need to ignore every scary movie I've ever seen and get in there and actually check it out.

It's easier said than done, but Hudson climbed half a freaking mountain today with sheer will alone. Surely I can crawl inside a little cave without having a total panic attack.

I take a deep breath, let it out slowly. Take another breath and do the same thing. By the time I'm on the third breath, I'm over myself. This needs to be done. I'm going to go inside. That's all there is to it.

59

I Know a Prick
When I Smell One
—Grace—

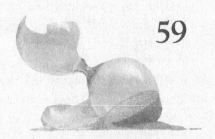

The entrance to the cave is so small that I have to drop down onto my hands and knees to fit through. Ignoring the sting of gravel against my bare palms—and the fact that the opening to the cave is very, very narrow—I pray for the best as I shimmy myself in.

No animals. No animals. Please, God, no scary animals when Hudson's not even here to benefit from it.

As soon as I make it through the ridiculously small entrance, the cave opens up a lot. Or at least it feels like it does, considering it's really dark in here and I don't have a flashlight. I know that it's tall enough for me to stand without bumping my head against the ceiling, and when I stretch my arms out, I can't touch walls in any direction.

Plus, it's about twenty degrees cooler in here than it is outside, and I'd be a fool not to appreciate that. Of course, I'd feel better if I could see the back of the cave, have some idea of what I'm really dealing with here.

I wait a few minutes for my eyes to adjust, listening the whole time for any rustle, growl, or breathing sound that might suggest that something else is in here with me. But after several minutes pass where all I hear is the fast beating of my own heart, I figure it's okay. That there's nothing in this place but me.

It's a little anticlimactic, but I'll take that over having to fight off a wild animal any day. Or a swarm of insects. Or—I shut down the line of thought before my overactive imagination gets the best of me. Again.

Knowing that the cave is empty is all I really need, so I don't bother to try to explore any more. Instead, I crawl out of the cave to head back toward Hudson. I still haven't found water—something I really need to do—but every instinct I have is screaming for me to get him out of the sun and into that cave as soon as possible.

Besides, maybe vampires have some superspecial water-finding abilities that I don't know about. Stranger things have happened to me since I found out about paranormals.

Exhaustion beats at me with every step I take back toward Hudson. I tell myself it's just an adrenaline crash from my whole "crawling into the cave" freak-out, but that doesn't make it any easier for me to keep walking. Especially when all I really want to do is curl up next to a tree and sleep.

But I can't do that, not yet. Hudson got us this far. It's my job to get us over the last little stretch to safety—or at least, relative safety. And I'm not going to drop the ball, not now when we're so close.

So I force my eyes open, force myself to keep putting one foot in front of the other as I follow the trail of Band-Aids I left for myself along the path.

Finally, finally, I see the largest bandage I stuck to the bottom of the first tree I came across, and I speed up. The sooner I get to Hudson, the sooner we can get back to the cave. The sooner we get to the cave, the sooner I can sleep.

Hudson is still asleep when I make it back to him, and waking him up is no easy feat. But once he's finally awake and I explain my plan, he's completely on board.

"Sorry I passed out like that," he tells me as he climbs to his feet.

"It's okay. I just think we really need some shade. Not hanging out in the open, waiting to be discovered, sounds like a smart idea, too."

He hands me the backpack, then starts to squat down so I can climb on his back, but I shake my head. "No way. You're still exhausted. I'll walk."

"How long did it take you to get to the cave?" he asks, brow raised.

"About ten minutes," I answer reluctantly, because I know where he's going.

"We'll be there in five if I fade us."

"Yeah, but—" I wave a hand, not wanting to say out loud what is so obvious to me. Namely, that he's completely drained, and I'm not sure he can handle fading for five seconds, let alone five minutes.

"I've got this, Grace." As if to prove it, he just swoops me up in his arms bride-style instead of arguing about it anymore. "Which way?"

I've spent enough time around Hudson at this point to know when arguing is fruitless, and this is definitely one of those times. So I shove down all my concerns, grit my teeth, and let him do his manly-man thing of getting us to the cave.

It takes three minutes to get there, not five, even with stopping to pick up the Band-Aid trail, and I'd be lying if I said I didn't appreciate that fact very much. As it is, Hudson doesn't even have the energy to tease me about it. Which is a good thing because I definitely don't have the energy to clap back.

Instead, we stumble into the cave like zombies. Hudson takes about two minutes to check the place out and deem it acceptable before collapsing on the ground. Another time, I might have been offended that he didn't trust me, but I'm the first one to admit that in the dark, vampire vision is definitely superior to human. And since I want no creepy-crawly—or any other—surprises in the middle of the night, I feel much better now that he's checked it out, too.

Not quite good enough to just lay down on the cave ground, however. Instead, I get out one of the little blankets Arnst packed for us and spread it out. Then I urge Hudson onto it. He's awake, but he's not looking good.

Pale, gaunt, exhausted. Even his breathing is shallower than normal. I know vampires are immortal, but that doesn't mean they can't still die. And Hudson is definitely looking near death's door at the moment. Which I am so not okay with.

Originally, I'd planned to wait until tomorrow to have this argument with him, but judging from how he looks at this moment, I'm not so sure waiting is the best option. Or any option, to be honest.

"Hudson—" I start, but he cuts me off.

"I'm fine, Grace."

It's such a patently absurd statement that I don't even bother arguing with him. Especially since he's slurring his words. Instead, I do the only thing I can think of that might get results. The only thing that will show him that I am totally okay with this. The only thing that he might actually believe.

Because as hard as this is for me to comprehend, now that we're in this cave and out of the sun, the only remaining reason Hudson won't feed from me is that he doesn't believe I genuinely *want* him to take what I'm offering. That I'm not feeling forced into it because he might die—although, if that *were* the case anyway, *what the fuck, Hudson Vega.*

Regardless, I lift my chin. This boy needs to know I know my own mind. If he still chooses to not feed from me with my consent assured, well, that's on him, at least.

So I pull the pocketknife out of the backpack.

Open it up.

Slice a tiny cut in my index finger—just big enough for a few drops of blood to squeeze through.

And then I wait.

60

Tastes Like
Teen Spirit
—Hudson—

I smell the blood before I realize what Grace has done. At first, I think she's injured herself, and I push to my feet, looking for the threat. Wanting to make sure she's okay.

But then I see her sitting there, her hand in her lap. And I *know*.

"You shouldn't have done that," I tell her, even as her scent permeates the room around me. More cinnamon, combined with the warmth of honey and the freshness of the sweet summer wind.

It's irresistible—she's irresistible. But the hunger inside me grows and grows until it consumes me, burning, aching, raging through my bloodstream. Slaking it is all I can think about. With Grace. Only with Grace.

"I wanted to," she whispers.

"I don't want to hurt you." I shove my trembling hands into my pockets and take a step back in a futile effort to put distance between us. My voice is rough as sandpaper as I admit, "I'm too hungry, Grace. I don't think I can control myself right now."

"You're always in control," she says. And then she's on her feet, too. Walking toward me. "I've learned that about you in the last year. And I know you won't hurt me."

"You can't know that." I tell myself to take a step back, to walk away. To go as far from here—from Grace—as I can get.

But I don't move. I can't. Not when everything inside me is yearning toward her. Needing her blood, but more. Needing her, specifically, in a way I told myself that I would never need anyone.

"It's okay, Hudson." Her voice is soft, soothing, and I feel myself sinking into it despite my best intentions. "I trust you not to go too far."

My fangs explode at her words. "You shouldn't. I'm the bad brother, remember?"

It's a test, a last-ditch effort to scare her away.

But Grace just grins. "You're nowhere near as bad as you think you are. And even if you were, it wouldn't matter. You're my friend. And I want you to do this."

Her words are the last straw, filling up a void in me that I rarely let myself think about. I stop retreating—mentally and physically—and for the first time take a step toward her.

That step, and the acceptance it signifies, must be what she's waiting for. Because just like that, she's beside me, moving into my space. "I don't know where you like to…"

"Bite?" I finish for her.

She blushes a little bit, but her eyes are steady on mine as she nods. Then she reaches up and pulls her hair to one side, exposing her jugular.

And fuck is it tempting to just go for it, to pull her close enough that I can feel all her gorgeous curves pressing against me as I drink from her. But that's not what we are to each other—not what I am to her—and I don't know if I can control myself with that much sensory overload anyway.

Plus, I'm smart enough to figure that's how Jaxon fed from her, and I'm asshole enough that I don't want my first time drinking from her to be the same as his. She's showing me a kindness, yes, but I still want her to know exactly who's drinking from her.

I don't tell her any of that, though. Instead, I just reach forward and use my fingers to gently brush her hair back where it belongs. Then, because I can, I let my fingers linger on her cheek for just a second.

She looks startled, but when I smile at her, she smiles back.

That's when I take her hand.

"What are you—"

"It's okay," I tell her as I turn her arm over to reveal the soft, delicate skin of her inner forearm.

"Oh." Her eyes grow wide.

I stroke my thumb over the web of green-blue veins that coalesce at her wrist. "Okay?" I ask, even as the hunger rises up and threatens to tear me apart. "You can still change your mind."

"I'm not changing my mind." Her mouth quirks into a mischievous little smile, and she lifts her wrist toward my mouth. "Do your worst."

"Don't I always?" Then, because I don't want her to have to awkwardly hold her arm up while I feed, I drop to my knees at her feet.

Again, she looks surprised, but she doesn't say anything. And she doesn't pull away.

Still, I bend my head slowly, giving her a chance to change her mind. She doesn't take it.

So I lift her hand to my mouth and press a soft, open-mouthed kiss against her palm in silent thanks.

A shudder works its way through her at the first brush of my lips against her skin, and she makes a small sound deep in her throat. I look up, just to be sure she's still on board.

Grace nods, whispers, "It's okay."

I nod, too, then slide my lips down her palm, over the heel of her hand to the soft, thin skin of her wrist. I lick her once, to take away the sting of the bite to come.

She shivers again, gasps, and that's when I strike.

My fangs sink deep, piercing through skin and muscle to the artery beneath. And just like that, her blood—thick, powerful, delicious—flows from her into me.

Nothing in my two hundred years of life has ever tasted as sweet.

61

Carpe Drink-Em

—Grace—

I don't know what I expect to feel when Hudson bites me, but it definitely isn't the powerful riot of feelings and sensations currently rampaging through my body.

Hot, cold, strength, weakness, certainty, confusion, power, fear, need. *So much need*. Mine? Hudson's? I can't tell the difference—or even if there is one—as our emotions build and meld, blending together into an overwhelming symphony of wants and demands that threaten to bring me to my knees.

But I know if I give in—if I let myself fall—that Hudson will stop. And it's too soon for that, way too soon, considering the restrained, gentlemanly way he is currently drinking from me.

Which begs the question, if it feels like this now, when he's being so quiet and careful, what on earth will it feel like if he ever lets go? If he lets himself drink from me the way I know that he's dying to?

I can see his need in the hands holding mine—shaking with restraint.

Can hear it in the slow, careful, even breaths that he's taking.

Can feel it in the tenseness of his body as he hovers over my arm, taking only what he has to have to survive.

And while there's a part of me that's grateful for his restraint, grateful for his care, there's another, deeper part of me that wants him to slip the chains he's wrapped around himself. That needs him to just let go.

I don't know where that part of me is coming from, and I don't question it. I can't, not when I'm drowning in the wave of our combined emotions.

"Hudson," I whisper, because I can't not say it. It's beating in my blood, sweeping through my soul, building a connection between us that I'm not sure I'm ready for but that I suddenly, desperately want.

He looks up at the sound of his name on my lips, and his gaze locks with mine. There's distance there, cordiality and, for a moment, I think I've misunderstood. That all these emotions pinging around inside me are only mine. But the longer we stare into each other's eyes, the more I realize the distance is just a ruse. Underneath it is a wild tangle of *need*, just like the one currently seething within me.

Hudson's eyes darken as we watch each other, and he stops drinking. Starts to pull away.

But it's still too soon. He's not ready and—no matter what he thinks—neither am I. So instead of letting him pull back, I reach forward and place a hand on his head.

He freezes, and a question creeps into his eyes pinned to mine. I smile in response, and for a moment—just a moment—I let him see everything burning inside me. The good. The bad. The hurt and the healing.

Hudson's response is a growl, deep in his throat. And then he's drinking—really drinking—from me in a way he hadn't been before.

Deep. Powerful. Ravenous. He drinks and drinks and drinks.

And I let him. No, I encourage him, my hand in his hair, urging him to take more from me. To take everything he needs, anything he wants. And for this one brief moment in time, he does.

I don't know what it means, and right now, I don't actually care. I'm smart enough to know I won't feel like this forever. Soon enough, I'll be back to worrying, questioning, regretting. But for now, I'm just going to hold him and let him take what I so desperately need to give.

62

Dimples and Curls

—Grace—

When he's finally drunk enough, Hudson pulls away slowly, gently. "Are you—"

"I'm fine," I interrupt him, because I am. Mostly. And the part of me that feels a little weird—a little uncertain—with all the things that just passed between us will have to wait in line. Partly because I'm exhausted and partly because it worked. Hudson looks better already.

The gray tint to his skin is gone, his breathing is no longer labored, and his face looks less gaunt and more annoyingly perfect. Even the way he moves is back to normal. There's no more hitch in his step, no more hesitation. Everything about him just flows.

He sees me looking at him and raises one perfectly sculpted brow. "You'll never get away with pretending you don't like me again," he tells me.

"Who says I'm pretending?" I shoot back, but there's no heat in it and we both know it. "Maybe I just prefer my sparring partners to have their strength—and their wits—about them?"

Hudson just laughs as he pulls my half-drunk bottle of water out of the backpack. "You need to drink some water," he tells me.

"What I need to do is go *find* some water," I tell him even as I take the bottle. "But that can wait until tomorrow morning."

"Drinking can't," he tells me as he hands me a granola bar. "And neither can eating. You need to make sure your blood sugar doesn't plummet."

"You sound like the lady who runs the bloodmobile that used to come to my old high school," I tell him with a grin. But I take the granola bar because I'm hungry. And because his advice is sound. The last thing we need is for me to take Hudson's place on the gray-and-shaky train.

After I'm done eating, I lay back down on the blanket while Hudson starts a small fire near the front of the cave, using the crystal from the backpack and the kindling I gathered earlier. I think about suggesting we each take a blanket, but I'm not particularly keen on wrapping myself up in this thing like a mummy to keep from getting dirt all over myself. Also, it seems a little ridiculous to pretend we haven't spent the last two days sleeping in the same bed. A couple more nights won't hurt anything.

Except when Hudson stretches out on the ground next to me, it doesn't feel the same as it has the last two times. *I* don't feel the same.

I try to tell myself that it's not a big deal, that nothing has changed. But I don't have enough capacity for self-delusion to pull that off. Everything has changed, whether I meant it to or not.

I close my eyes, try to think of anything else, but all I see are Hudson's bright blue eyes staring back at me.

Hudson, who has the most ridiculous sense of humor—and who is up for laughing at himself at least as often as he laughs at me.

Hudson, who worries about a little shadow's feelings simply because she's claimed him as hers.

Hudson, who would rather hurt himself than do anything that might possibly hurt me.

Damn it. How did this happen? How did I go from thinking about ways to destroy this guy to just plain thinking about him? And how do I make it stop?

Even though I know it's a bad idea, I can't resist glancing at him out of the corner of my eye. It turns out to be an even worse idea than I thought, because not only is Hudson not yet sleeping, he's actually wide awake and staring straight at me.

And now there's no pretending I wasn't looking at him, too. Fuck. My. Life.

"You okay?" I ask, hoping he'll think concern is motivating my sudden interest in looking at him.

"I was just about to ask you the same thing, actually."

"I'm fine!" I tell him a little more forcefully than is absolutely necessary. "Why wouldn't I be?"

"Oh, I don't know. Maybe because you just let a vampire drink his fill of your blood?" he answers, the corner of his mouth curling up in a crooked little grin. And what the hell? Is it the firelight or is that a freaking dimple I see?

It has to be the firelight, I decide. Or a dent. Maybe he gets a dent in his face after he sucks blood for too long.

I mean, it's doubtful, but it can happen, right? Anything's possible.

I blow out a heavy breath, decide I'm going to ignore whatever is going on with his face. Then blurt out, "What are you doing to your face right now?" despite myself.

His brows go up. "Excuse me?" Somehow, he sounds insulted and amused at the same time, which is probably why the dent grows.

"That thing on the side of your mouth. How long have you had it?"

"What thing?" he asks, and he just looks baffled. Which I can understand, considering there is absolutely no rhyme or reason to this conversation except for the fact that *Hudson has a dimple and I didn't know it.*

"The dent."

"I have a dent on the side of my face?" Now he sounds alarmed, because of course he does. You can take the boy out of the Versace underwear, but you can't take the Versace out of the boy. He runs a hand along his jawline as he asks, "What kind of dent?"

"A ridiculous one," I answer.

"Well, that narrows it down for me, thanks. You want to be a little more specific than that, or am I just supposed to…" He continues to tap a hand all over his face in an effort to find the dent.

And while it is fun to sit here and watch him feel his face and freak out, I'm going to have to put him out of his misery eventually. It might as well be now, before he gives himself a dent for real.

"You have a *dimple*," I accuse him.

"I do, yes." He narrows his eyes at me. "Is that what you've been going on about for the past five minutes? My dimple?"

I narrow my eyes right back at him. "Yeah. So what if I have?"

"So it's not a dent, that's what." His crisp British accent is out in full force—which is surefire proof that I've gotten to him.

On the plus side, he's no longer looking at me like he's thinking weird thoughts. And the funny, flippy feeling in my stomach is gone.

"I don't know about that." I pretend to study it. "Looks kind of like a dent to me."

He glares at me. "Well, it's not."

"Whatever you say," I tell him, struggling to hold back my grin. Fighting with Hudson is better than doing almost anything else with anyone else. "You would know best."

"I would know best," he agrees. "Considering it's on my face."

"Yeah, but I'm the one looking at that face right now," I counter. "And you aren't."

He opens his mouth to retort, but then he just lets out a loud sigh. "Grace."

It's a very stern, serious-sounding "Grace," so I reply in kind. "Yes, *Hudson*?"

"Why are you picking a fight with me about my dimple?"

"Honestly?" I shrug. "I have no idea."

"That's what I figured." He sighs again. "Can I go to bed now, then?"

"I suppose," I answer airily. "As long as you're not concerned about the dent in your face."

"Grace."

"Yes, Hudson?" This time I use my most angelic voice.

"Nothing." He shakes his head in resignation. "Good night."

"Good night." Then, because I can't help myself, I add, "You should probably sleep on the side that doesn't have the dent."

"You should probably quit while you're ahead," he shoots back.

He's right, so I close my eyes, feeling much better about this whole situation. At least until he wraps an arm around my waist and pulls me against his body, little spoon–style.

"Hey, what are you doing?" I ask, though I make absolutely no move to get away. Because even though the stomach flips are back, this feels good. Really good. More, it feels right.

Something Hudson obviously picks up on. "Don't act like you don't want to be here."

"Just for that, I should move."

He lifts his arm from around my waist. "Go ahead."

"I would," I tell him. "But then I'd have to look at that dent again."

"God forbid." If his voice got any drier, we'd be able to use it as kindling.

"Tomorrow, I'm going to find water," I say as I settle back against him.

"Something tells me tomorrow you're going to do a lot of things."

He's not wrong, so I let it go. And finally, finally drift off to sleep.

63

A loud screeching wakes me from a dream about Coronado Island. "Hudson!" I sit up in a rush. "What the hell is that?"

"I was about to ask you the same thing." He jumps up, starts shoving his feet into his shoes. "Where the fuck is that noise coming from?"

"It's not in here." If something was screeching like that in this cave, with these acoustics, I'm fairly certain Hudson and I would both have ruptured eardrums by now. As it is, we're just really, really uncomfortable. "Is something dying out there?"

"Surely no dying animal could make that much noise," he answers as he heads for the entrance to the cave.

I'm right behind him. If it is a wounded animal, maybe I can help. When he was alive, rescuing hurt animals was kind of a specialty of my dad's. No matter how badly hurt they were, he always found a way to nurse them back to health. I don't have his touch, but I did learn some things from him.

Except when we get there, it's to find that the noise is definitely not coming from a dying animal. In fact, it's not coming from an animal at all.

"Smokey!" Hudson exclaims.

The little shadow whirls around and runs straight into his arms.

"How did you get here?" he asks, and I have no idea if she understands him or not. But she goes off on an unintelligible rant that includes waving, jumping, and a whole lot more screeching.

"So?" I ask when she finally winds down. "How'd she get here?"

Hudson gives me a bemused look. "I can't understand her, either, you know. But my best guess is she followed my scent and then lost it when she got to the cave."

"Which is why she freaked out," I finish. "Because she thought she'd lost her precious."

"Hey, it's not my fault I'm lovable." He gives me his most charming grin—one that showcases that damn dimple perfectly.

"It's not your fault you've got a dent in your face, either," I answer with a shrug. "But you can still be blamed for it."

"Only by you."

"Is there somebody else here I should know about?" I lift a brow.

"Smokey's here," Hudson shoots back. "And she likes my dent. I mean, my dimple."

"I win." I walk closer to Hudson, but not too close, because the last thing I want to do right now is set Smokey off. "What are you going to do with her?"

Apparently, the wide berth I gave them isn't enough, because Smokey turns around and hisses at me.

"Bite me," I tell her with a roll of my eyes.

"What do you *think* I'm going to do with her?" Hudson says. "She's coming with us."

"To Adarie?" I ask. "Seriously?"

"What else am I supposed to do?" He looks offended. "Leave her here?"

I want to say yes, but if I'm honest, that's just because I hate that she hates me. And also fear that she might really bite me one day, if that's a thing that shadows do.

Even so, I know Hudson's right. We can't leave her halfway up a mountain. Besides, if we do, she'll just try to follow us again, and who knows what trouble that will bring.

"Fine." I sigh. "Why don't you change your clothes while I go find water. It'll give you two some alone time."

"That sounds about perfect, doesn't it, Smokey, my girl?"

Smokey's answer is a happy squeal that bounces off the cave walls, exactly as I'd feared this morning.

"Hurry up with those clothes," I tell him. "Or I'm leaving without them."

Ten minutes later, I'm crawling out of the cave for the second time that morning, this time with a backpack full of dirty clothes and four empty bottles to carry more water in.

I find a stream about ten minutes away from the cave. It's narrow and vertical, so the water runs fast—which is exactly what I was hoping for. I think I remember reading somewhere that there's not as much bacteria in fast-running water, and I'm definitely all for that.

I make quick work of filling the water bottles and then do the best I can to wash our clothes without soap. By the time I'm finished beating them against a rock, the clothes are clean and my hands feel frozen. But that doesn't stop me from taking a quick sponge bath, and few things have ever felt so good. Even with the frigid water, I'm so grateful to finally be clean.

When I get back to the cave, I put the clothes near the fire to dry and set the water to boiling in the empty granola tins. Then I go sit near Hudson and Smokey, who are playing tic-tac-toe on the cavern floor. "Who's winning?" I ask as Smokey makes a giant *X* in the top right-hand corner.

"She is," Hudson says glumly. "What is it, girl? Twelve games to four?"

Smokey chitters out a whole string of sounds that I don't understand. I know Hudson doesn't, either, but he waits until she's finished before saying, "My mistake. It's thirteen games to four."

Smokey settles down after that to concentrate on the game. About ninety seconds later, it's fourteen to four.

We spend the day like that, playing games with Smokey in between my trips to the stream to refill empty water bottles.

On the plus side, I get lots of sunshine on my walks and I find some wild westeberry bushes on the other side of the stream. They're purple and taste like a cross between apricots and strawberries, and I became addicted to them during my time at the farm. They also provide a nice break from granola bars, so I'm calling it a win.

And if I happen to get impatient a few times during the day, I don't let Hudson see it. It's not his fault he had to eat—all living things do. Besides, Hudson says it will only slow us down about thirty-six hours, not a week like the overly cautious Jaxon once told me. By tomorrow evening, he should be able to be out in sunlight again, and we can head straight for the top of the mountain.

Then it's down to Adarie, where please, please, please someone will be able to help us figure out our next move.

We haven't talked about it, but I know Hudson is as concerned about the Shadow Queen discovering us as I still am. She does *not* sound like someone we want to mess with at all. Best to get to Adarie and ask for sanctuary.

After that, what our lives might look like... Well, I just don't let myself think about that for now. I've accepted that this is my new home, but that doesn't mean I'm exactly excited to embrace it yet.

After a dinner of granola bars and westeberries—turns out Smokey is a huge fan of the heart-shaped purple berries—the small shadow curls up by the fire and goes to sleep.

After my multiple trips back and forth to the stream, I'm more than a little tired myself. But Hudson's been trapped in a cave all day, riding high from a fresh infusion of blood. To be honest, it's a miracle he's not bouncing off the walls.

Which is why I'm not the least surprised when he settles down next to me on the blanket and says, "Tell me your favorite memory."

64

If I Could F(lie)

—Hudson—

"**I**'m pretty sure you've seen them all," Grace tells me with a snarky look. "Not all of them," I answer. "Besides, how would I know which one was your favorite? It's not like they came with blinking lights attached, telling me which ones to pick and which ones to avoid."

She shrugs but doesn't say anything for a long time. Instead, she stares into the fire, and it feels like she's a million miles away.

I'm just about to give up and go to bed when she whispers, "I didn't like it when you looked at my memories."

Shite. I didn't know we were going to go *there* tonight. "I know," I answer quietly.

"So why'd you do it?" she asks, her voice more resigned than anything.

"Because I'm an arse, obviously. And…" I sigh, run an agitated hand through my hair. "Because I didn't like it when you read my journals."

"Yeah." She blows out a long breath, shoots me a rueful look. "That was pretty shitty on my part, wasn't it?"

"Extremely shitty, yeah," I agree. Because it was. And because I'm sick of being the bad guy in every situation.

"But how else was I going to find out the truth about you? It's not like you're exactly forthcoming."

"It's not like you gave me a reason to be forthcoming," I answer, stretching out on the blanket like I don't care about anything—especially this conversation. "You were too busy accusing me of every abomination in the book."

"To be fair, your ex-girlfriend had just tried to human sacrifice me in a deranged plot to bring you back from the dead." She rolls her eyes. "Forgive me for needing a little time to get over that."

"You're really obsessed with this human-sacrifice thing, aren't you?" I ask, just to poke at her.

"Excuse me?" Her eyebrows hit her hairline.

I hold up my palms in a "don't shoot the messenger" move. "All I'm saying is you've brought it up several times."

"Excuse me?" This time her voice is about three octaves higher than normal. "You try having your ass strapped to an altar and see how well you like it."

"Is that an offer?"

"Keep asking questions like that and it might be," she retorts.

I'm not sure why I felt the need to poke at her the way I did. Well, except maybe I regretted telling her that reading my journals bothered me. When you've spent your entire life never showing anyone weakness for fear they'd use it against you, it's hard not to feel queasy the first time you let your guard down.

She doesn't say anything as we stare at the flickering fire, and neither do I. But eventually the silence gets to me, and I say what I should have said a long time ago. "I'm sorry for looking at your memories without your permission."

She shrugs but still doesn't say anything.

Now it's my turn to be annoyed. "Seriously? You've got nothing to say to that?"

She shrugs again. Then answers, "Thank you for apologizing?" in the snidest tone imaginable.

"Yeah. That's what I was looking for." It's my turn to roll my eyes. This girl is tough as nails when she wants to be. Normally, I respect the hell out of her for it, but right now it's just pissing me off.

"Typical Hudson," she says with a huff. "You can dish it out, but you can't take it."

"What's that supposed to mean? I'm literally apologizing here—"

I break off. I don't need this, don't deserve this. Wherever I thought this conversation was going when I asked about her favorite memory, it wasn't a fight.

But then, that's where Grace goes when she's uncomfortable, isn't it?

I roll onto my side, prop my head on my hand, and hold her gaze. I don't say anything, though. I don't need to. We both know why she's acting like a brat.

Eventually her shoulders slump, the fight easing out of her as quickly as it came. "It means of course I'm sorry about the journals. It was a shit thing to do on my part, and I'd like to say I wish I hadn't done it. But that isn't true, because reading those journals is the only way I got to see the person you work so hard to keep hidden from the rest of the world. The person Smokey is crazy about, and the person I'm—" She breaks off.

But it's too late. I heard the hesitation in her voice, along with something else. Something that's got my palms going sweaty and my heart beating way too fast. "You're what?" I ask, voice hoarse and maybe even a little needy.

"The person I'm starting to think of as a very good friend."

Everything inside me deflates at her words, every hope I didn't even know I had dissolving in an instant. "Yeah," I tell her. "Me too."

Then I turn over until my back is to her. "I think I'm going to go to sleep now."

"Oh, okay. Good night." She sounds a little forlorn, a little lost. But I don't have it in me to comfort her tonight. Not when I'm feeling the need for a little comfort myself. Comfort I'm smart enough to know is never going to come—not from her and not from anybody else.

Grace sits motionless for a few more minutes before getting up to check the fire and pour the newly boiled and cooled water into our empty water bottles.

She looks at me several times as she works, but I'm an expert at pretending to be asleep—I've had nearly two hundred years to perfect the technique, after all. But when she slips outside for a couple of minutes, it takes every ounce of self-control I have not to move to the mouth of the cave to watch for her, just to make sure she's okay.

Not that there's a lot I can do for her if she isn't. One step outside in this sun, and I'll fry to a crisp.

Still, I don't take a deep breath until she's back in the cave. Not that I let her know that.

Eventually Grace comes to bed, and she, too, lays on her side so that her back is to me.

Minutes tick by with neither of us saying anything to the other. I assume she thinks I'm asleep, but I know that she's not. I can hear it in her breathing— and in the too-rapid beat of her heart.

Last night, we slept wrapped together as defense against the chill in the mountain air. Just two good friends cuddling. At least that's the story Grace is telling herself, I'm sure. It's a story I guess I've got to be on board with, too. Even if I don't believe it. Even if I don't want it to be true.

"My favorite memory," Grace says, her voice low and hesitant in the cool darkness of the cave, "is when Jaxon walked me off the parapets outside his tower. It was night and the aurora borealis was dancing through the sky all around us. Jaxon took me out there, right in the middle of them, and we danced for what felt like forever. I'd never had a moment like that in my whole life, just floating on air with a boy I was crazy about. Like it was the most natural thing in the world."

Her words aren't unexpected, but they still hit me with a force that makes me want to pull up my shirt and look for bruises. I don't, though. I can't. Not when I'm the one who asked the question. The fact that I'm not sure I can deal with the answer isn't on her. It's on me.

It's not a lesson I'm going to forget anytime soon, though.

"I didn't want to tell you about that memory because the last thing I want to do is hurt you," she continues, her voice little more than a whisper. "But I don't want to lie to you, either. I never want you to feel like you have to lie to me, so I want to give you that same courtesy."

It's hard to be angry when she puts it like that. Easy to be hurt, but not angry. And the hurt isn't her fault, either. Things are what they are. For her and for me.

"I know Jaxon was your mate," I tell her. "It's not a surprise to me that your favorite memory was with him. Why would you think you needed to hide that from me?"

"I don't know." She groans. "I guess I didn't want to bring up any bad memories between the two of you. I know there are hard feelings and—"

What bollocks. "Didn't you just say you weren't going to lie to me?" I challenge.

She sighs, then rips off the plaster. "I know it's a long shot, but we could get back to our side of the barrier, Hudson. And when we do, Jaxon will be there."

"I know," I say and pause, not sure if I should mention the blue string I saw or not. It didn't sit well with me ever since that I haven't told her about it, but to be honest, I've been scared. What if it didn't mean what I thought it meant? Worse, what if she didn't *want* it to mean what I thought it meant? That possibility slices through my chest like a knife, and it takes me a second to find my breath again. I owe her the truth, though, so I begin with, "But if we make it back, he won't be your mate anymore."

"You don't know that," she answers like a shot. "He's not my mate *here*. But even you said your magic doesn't work on this side of the divide. So maybe the bond is like that. It can't reach across whatever barrier is between the two worlds."

I start to mention how the bond never looked right to me but think better of it. No need to open myself up to being called a liar again.

"What if it's not?" I ask instead. "What if the bond is gone forever?"

She doesn't say anything for what feels like an eternity but is probably only about a minute. I hold my breath the whole time. Right up until she says, "I still love him."

"Do you? Really?" I ask, rolling over to face her. "You knew him for two weeks. Two weeks. We've been together more than a *year*. Just you and me. Do those two weeks really stand up to everything we've been through?"

I've never been skydiving before, but as I wait for Grace's answer, I imagine it probably feels exactly like this. I've willingly jumped out of a perfectly good plane, and I'm hurtling toward the earth with only a hope and a prayer that a thin string will pull open something magical that will save me. It's positively terrifying.

"I don't know," she whispers.

I swear I hear every bone in my body shatter as I hit the ground. "You don't want to know."

"Maybe you're right. Maybe I don't."

Which is all the answer I need.

I roll back to my side of the blanket and tell myself it's better this way. Better to nip in the bud whatever fucked-up things I've been feeling recently. It makes everything easier.

"Good night, Grace," I tell her softly.

"Good night," she whispers back.

Never has the three feet between us felt more like a hundred. And in between lays the remnants of a fantasy and a future that never stood a chance.

65

Live and Let's Run

—Grace—

Hudson is already out of bed when I wake up.

He's changed his clothes back to the jeans and shirt I washed in the stream yesterday, but they still look a little damp. The shirt clings to his biceps and back muscles in all the right places.

Not that I'm looking, of course, but when someone looks like Hudson, it's pretty hard to miss.

"What time is it?" I ask as I roll to my feet, keenly aware that he hasn't said good morning to me yet like he usually does.

He glances at his watch but not at me. "One o'clock."

"In the afternoon?" How could I have slept nearly twelve hours? I *never* sleep that long.

"Yeah." He draws something on the ground for Smokey. My guess is an *X* or an *O*.

"What time—" My voice breaks as the tension of last night and the discomfort of this morning—this afternoon—catches up to me.

"We should be good to leave around six or seven," he answers, and there's no rancor in his voice. No sign at all that there are any hard feelings after our conversation before bed.

But he still hasn't looked at me. And there's no warmth to anything he's said, either. I miss it. Which is ridiculous, considering I never even noticed it was there until it was gone.

"Who's winning?" I ask as I approach the fire and realize, yes, they really are playing tic-tac-toe again. "Or dare I ask?"

"Smokey's up five games."

"Is that total or just for today?" I tease.

"Does it matter?" Hudson responds, still without looking up from the game board.

His tone is completely polite, but it still feels like a slap. I don't think that's what he intended, but like he just asked me, does that actually matter when I feel like I'm reeling?

"I'm going to go change," I announce stiffly as I grab my clothes from where they've been drying before I dash outside.

I did this, I admit as I struggle to pull on my still-damp jeans. I'd said I wanted to be honest with him—but I wasn't entirely honest. I couldn't be.

I shrug on a T-shirt and slide my feet into my shoes, muttering under my breath about obstinate men. I *do* still love Jaxon. And I know in my soul I always will. Loving him is easy, has always been easy.

I don't know *what* I'm starting to feel for Hudson—but I know it's not simple.

It's wild and unpredictable and messy—and scary as fuck.

And I'm not ready to face that yet. Is that a crime?

So I said what I said and apparently broke whatever had been growing between us. I didn't mean to, but that doesn't matter, either. All that matters is I hurt him when that's the last thing I wanted to do.

But now I can't even apologize. Not when he's put giant NO TRESPASSING signs around his feelings.

I take several steadying breaths and head back inside for lunch—and get treated to so much politeness that it makes me want to rip my hair out.

Finally, I give up trying to poke a reaction out of him and curl up with my phone. I miraculously found that charger when we were in the lair, but I have no idea how to charge the device in this realm, so I've been keeping it off to preserve the charge. Still, this seems like the right time to sacrifice some battery life, so I color on the color app I downloaded before the lair.

It's not the most scintillating way to pass the afternoon, but it gets the job done. And I don't have to say a word to Hudson, which is good, considering he hasn't said one word to me all day that wasn't in direct response to something I said to him.

The universe must be on my side in this battle because my phone's battery lasts until ten minutes till six and still has some juice left. Just enough time for me to pack up a few things before we need to go. It's really Hudson who's about to do all the work, but at least I can organize the pack such that the weight distribution doesn't trouble him too much.

Then again, an hour later, I discover climbing the mountain isn't exactly a picnic for me, either. Not when I have to hold on to Hudson for hours on end as he climbs mountain walls and then fades along nonexistent trails at speeds that take my breath away.

I only thought he was fast before. Now that he's fed and is back to normal, he's practically supersonic. And I'm just along for the ride. Well, me and Smokey, who spends the whole time wrapped around his biceps.

We keep up the pace for six straight hours, with only a few five-minute breaks in between long stretches of running. I know we're on the clock, know that the longer we're out in the open, the higher our chances are of getting caught. But it's still exhausting.

We break about midnight, and I take two steps away from Hudson and fall face-first onto the ground.

"Tired?" he asks, and there's a trace of his old sarcasm in the question that I can't help but note—and run with. God knows, if I've learned anything today, it's that the only thing more annoying than a snarky Hudson is a polite one.

"I think the bigger question is, how are you not?" I answer. "I've never seen anyone move like you have since we left the cave."

"Not even Jaxon?" As soon as he says it, he looks like he wants to kick himself.

But he's the one who told me last night that we shouldn't hide from the past, so I do my best to sound normal as I answer, "No, not even Jaxon. Your speed is incomprehensible."

"Flattery will get you an extra half an hour of rest," he tells me with the little half grin that shows off his dimple.

"If I thought you meant that, I'd be tempted to hug you," I groan. "I honestly don't think I can do any more today."

"Do you want to stop?" he asks after I've roused myself enough to gulp down an entire bottle of water.

"It's up to you. You're the one doing all the work."

He watches me for a second, like he's trying to read my face. Then says, "I'd like to press on. We're almost to Adarie, probably only another twenty miles through the last of the mountains if I read Arnst's map correctly."

I can do twenty miles. "Well, then, I say we keep going."

Hudson looks from me to the map and back again. "Are you sure that's what *you* want to do? Or would you prefer to rest more and head out in the morning?"

I shoot him an exasperated look. "I thought continuing is what *you* wanted to do."

"It is," he agrees. "But I need to make sure it's what you want to do, too."

His words surprise me, and I can't help studying his face, trying to decide if he's just messing with me. But he looks as sincere as he sounds. "You really mean that, don't you?"

"Of course I mean it." Now he just looks insulted. "It's no use having a partnership if one person makes all the decisions and the other person just has to follow along. We're either in this together or we're not."

"We are," I hasten to reassure him.

"Then tell me what *you* want to do."

I don't know. I really don't. As exhausted as I am, Hudson has to be even more so—but I would love to sleep in a real bed tonight. I study his face, looking for signs that he needs a rest, but he looks like he could fade another hundred miles, honestly. "I think we should keep going and hope for the best."

Hudson's laugh is dry and more than a little pessimistic. "'The best' seems a little out of our league right about now. How about we hope for not the worst?"

"You sure do know how to instill confidence in a girl's heart," I tell him.

"Just calling it like I see it, Grace. Just calling it like I see it."

And why does that sound even more ominous?

66

Good Will Hugging

—Grace—

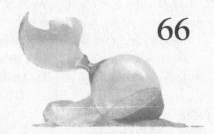

Only Hudson could turn twenty miles into an eight-hour adventure that has my teeth still rattling.

Granted, I understand he's kept up a zigzagging pattern to ensure we aren't being followed or tracked, but still—I'm about ready to pass out.

As Hudson crests the last mountain, a giant valley unfolds before us, complete with a thriving town at its base. Thank God. *Adarie.*

He must see it, too, because he slows to a stop and eases my feet back to the ground. I wobble a little, and he doesn't hesitate to reach out to steady me. I glance at his hand resting on my shoulder and sigh. I suddenly want to step closer, snake my arms around his waist, and lean into his strength and heat. Into his touch.

All day, I've missed our old intimacy. Hell, I've missed Hudson. He checked out after our discussion about Jaxon last night, and even though he's talking to me again, that friendship—that intimacy—between us is long gone.

If I had any doubt he didn't intend to freeze me out, that hope evaporates the minute he realizes I've noticed his hand still on my shoulder and he pulls away, then puts several feet between us for good measure as he pretends to study the community below.

Like nearly everything else in Noromar, the town is purple. Purple streets, purple houses, purple grass, purple people.

And while the farm—and the mountains we just went over—filled me in on what to expect, it's still hard to believe that this much purple exists in the world. Especially considering our clothes are every color but purple. It's like there was so much purple here, the people had to rebel with their clothing options. I can understand that.

I make a mental note to ask someone in town how they dye their clothes other colors, given all the plants appear to be purple. Curiosity has me turning back to Hudson to ask if he has any idea, but something in the slant of his brows has the words dying in my throat.

"I guess they really don't like strangers here," he says.

My eyes follow his line of sight and then widen.

There's a giant—and by giant I mean freaking huge—wall surrounding the entire town, at least twenty feet tall and four feet thick. I don't know how I didn't see it right away.

Probably because you were too busy mooning over Hudson, I remind myself.

I lift my chin and squint against the glaring sun, my gaze running along the edges of the wall. Eventually, I find what I was looking for and point to a faint road I can just make out in the distance leading to a pair of enormous purple gates. "Maybe we just need to say, 'Open Sesame,'" I joke.

Hudson turns to look at me with a "what the fuck" expression, and I wince, biting my lip. Ugh. Sometimes I forget he missed out on all the children's bedtime stories most kids are told growing up.

"Doesn't matter." I rush to change the subject. "What if we—"

"Why do you do that?" Hudson interrupts.

I blink up at him. "Do what?"

"Assume I need or even *want* your pity?" His lips thin.

I lean back and slam my hands on my hips. "What the hell does that mean?" I feel a lot of things for Hudson Vega, anger rising to the top of the list at the moment, but the last thing I feel for him is *pity*.

"You know exactly what it means, Grace," he snaps. "Every time you think you've said something that *might* remind me I drew the short fucking straw in life, your eyes soften like you're about to cry. Just fooking stop, will ya?"

His accent is so thick, I can't help it. I smile. The first smile I've felt since last night.

Which only seems to ratchet Hudson's anger even more if the muttered curse words rolling off his tongue are any indication. I can tell he's building a full head of steam, gearing up for an epic fight over my supposed pity stares, and I almost take him up on it. Fighting with Hudson would be infinitely more bearable than his politeness.

But I don't really want to fight right now.

I want to dance. I want to twirl and shout to the heavens that Hudson Vega still cares what I think of him. He cares a *lot*, if that *fook* was any indication.

So before he starts yelling at me again about what he thinks I may or may not feel about his *shite* childhood, I do what I've been afraid he'd never let me do again.

I take a step toward him, then another, until I can press my trembling body flush against his hard edges. He goes completely still. I'm pretty sure he even stops breathing.

But that's okay. I don't mind coming to him this time. I am the one who hurt him, after all.

So I take a deep breath, let my curves fill up the tiny cracks and crevices between us, let my softness ease past the rocky perimeter of his pain.

As I do, he finally takes that breath. And that's all I need to do what I've been wanting to do all day. I grab onto him, wrap my arms around his waist until my fingertips touch. And squeeze until his earlier distance is just an uncomfortable memory.

Still, I wait for him to bolt, for the skittishness I've seen all day to rear its ugly head.

It doesn't happen.

Instead, that one breath becomes another and another and eventually his arms come around me, too. It's not a lot, it's not even close to what that tiny voice inside me says I might want from him one day. But right here, right now, it is enough. More, it's exactly what we need.

Even Smokey must sense we need this, as she remains uncharacteristically quiet.

I know we can't stand here holding each other all night—on the side of a mountain with an army hunting us—but I want to. When Hudson's shoulders stiffen, I lean back to complain that I'm not ready. I just want to hold him for a little bit longer.

But as our gazes collide, he gives his head a quick shake for me not to speak. He doesn't release me from his embrace, just tilts his head as though listening to something in the distance. And eventually, I hear what he heard, and my heart races in my chest.

Footsteps.

Fuck.

67

The First Rule
of Fright Club
—Hudson—

Fuck, fuck, fuck! I've really cocked this up royally, haven't I?

I can't believe I was so busy listening to Grace's heartbeat, lost in the rhythm of her breathing, that I let a threat sneak up on us.

"Is it the queen's army?" Grace whispers.

She sounds so worried—but also so trusting—that I want to tear these people apart and burn the entire place to the ground, just because I can. But I'm smart enough to know that I shouldn't pick a fight until I know what we're really up against. So far, the footsteps don't sound like an army, but there could still be more soldiers moving into position.

"I don't know," I tell her, and I fucking hate to say that to her. Almost as much as I hate that I got her into this.

Yeah, we decided to do this together, but I still feel responsible. This was my plan, so I've got to find a way to get us out—one that won't end up with her or Smokey getting hurt. I should have predicted they'd know we'd likely head to Adarie, should have been more mindful of looking for signs of danger.

But we don't have time for me to worry about what I should have done. I need to focus on getting Grace and Smokey to safety—or teaching the Shadow Queen exactly what happens when you pick a fight with a vampire.

Of course, normally I'd suggest running for a while, letting them spin their wheels searching for us. But Grace looks exhausted. I don't think she's got another hour in her, if I'm being honest. She'd do it if I asked. She'd dig deep and find the strength. But that doesn't mean that's what we should do.

I need a moment to think, weigh our options.

My gaze skims over the town below, possible safety but not guaranteed. I take in the wall, the gates, the town itself with its narrow streets and rows of town houses. Plenty of places to hide—if we can get over the wall and no one sees us.

I turn left and survey the valley that stretches beyond the base of the mountains as far west as I can see. There is a river in the distance and a small forest, but not a lot of places to secure cover or hide. Not even a good place to make a stand without risking getting surrounded or pinned in.

Pivoting my gaze to the right, I groan at the sight of row after row of craggy mountaintops. We could certainly lose ourselves in their rocky terrain, but at what cost? I could use up what strength I've got left—and our best bet for long-term safety would still be to circle back around to Adarie and possibly face the same threat, only from a much weaker position.

No, our best option is to stand and fight, right here. Well, for me to fight.

As I look down into Grace's steady gaze, I know she's come to the same conclusion.

Actually, she's two steps ahead of me, if her single arched brow is any indication.

"Yes," I say.

"No," she answers, her chin tilting up in that way I know means she's going to dig her heels in.

I sigh. "Just this one time, can we not fight about this?"

"Hudson Vega, I am *not* going to go run off and hide while you fight an entire army alone!"

She looks so sincere, so *stubborn* not to leave me alone, that I want to hug her all over again. But I don't. That's not how you get Grace to do what you want…

I arch a brow right back at her. "Are you saying you think I can't beat an army *on my own*? What happened to"—I mimic Grace's voice, only higher-pitched and a little more sycophantic—"'oh, Hudson, you're like a superhero, so fast and strong'?"

When she rolls her eyes at me, I can feel the fight welling in her, and I don't hesitate to attack first.

"Grace. I *need* you to believe in me. Is that really impossible for you to do?"

She freezes, mouth half open, whatever she'd been about to say stalled on her tongue. She licks her lips, and I can see the wheels in her beautiful brain spinning, trying to find a way she can stay and fight while not hurting my feelings.

So I go in for the kill. "I've got this, Grace."

She blinks. Once. Twice. And then she nods, and I swear, I think I *could* take on an entire army alone right now.

I hope I can convince the other female in my life as easily.

I slide my hand down near my ankle, and Smokey jumps into my palm instantly, her plaintive wail a full-on warble as she's smart enough to know what's coming, and she is most definitely not happy about it.

I consider begging her to go with Grace, but Grace surprises me—and Smokey—and reaches out to rub a couple of soft pats across the top of the shadow's head before she says firmly, "He's got this, Smokey."

I can feel the umbra trembling in my hand, unsure if she can trust Grace, unsure if she *wants* to trust Grace. She gives another low, keening whine that makes my chest tighten painfully.

But when Smokey jumps into Grace's arms and lets her carry them off to hide, I can't stop the grin stretching between my cheeks, wider than ever before.

Grace tosses over her shoulder, "You're going to be insufferable now, aren't you?"

I don't even bother trying to hide it. "Most likely."

She just chuckles and replies, "Such a show-off."

Fuck taking on an entire army. I'm pretty sure I could take on *seven* armies and still have enough energy to teach the Shadow Queen a lesson.

Starting now.

68

I Have Friends in High Places
—Grace—

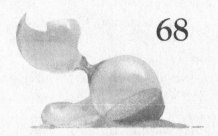

S mokey and I have only gotten about twenty yards off to the side when I hear Hudson snarl, "Who the fook are you? And what the fook do you want?"

I can't see who he's yelling at, but his hands are up, his fangs are bared, and he looks more than ready—more than capable—of tearing whoever is in front of him apart with his bare hands.

My heart is thundering in my chest, and I want to be able to help, or at least not hurt, but Hudson asked me to believe in him, and I know what that cost him. I won't let him down.

"Hey! We're just passing through, man!" a voice calls out, then a man moves forward enough that I can see him. He's in his early twenties, his light violet arms covered in tattoos that look a lot like musical notes in varying sizes. He's taller than Hudson by about four inches—even without his lavender hair shaved on both sides of his head, with a middle stripe standing straight up two inches—and a lot broader, with half a dozen earrings in his right ear and a septum piercing large enough to make me wince. He doesn't look like what I'd imagine a soldier would, but maybe this army embraces individuality—which is frankly kind of awesome. "You're the ones who look like you're in trouble."

"And you just thought you'd say hi?"

Sarcasm is rampant in Hudson's tone, and the guy's eyes narrow dangerously even as he puffs out his already barrel-size chest. "Something like that, yeah."

Despite the man's size, Hudson doesn't seem the least bit afraid of him, and I start to worry there's going to be a bloodbath before the rest of the soldiers get to us. I inch backward, give Hudson more room to do whatever impressive vampire thing he's got planned, when another man steps into view. He's roughly the same age and height as the other, but he's much skinnier, with gorgeous lilac skin tones—and has a baby strapped to his chest in a sling of some sort.

This isn't an army. It's a family.

I let out a breath I didn't know I was holding and straighten up, walk back over to Hudson's side.

"Not the queen's army?" I ask, just to confirm.

"Not unless they're recruiting babies," Hudson says, and the thinner man chuckles.

"Not yet," he says, stroking the fine purple curls on the head of the baby I can now see is sound asleep, their thick purple lashes resting against round cheeks. "We're a band of traveling troubadours called The Horizons."

The big guy puts an arm around the other man, leans down, and presses a soft kiss on the baby's forehead before adding, "I'm Orebon. And this is my husband, Lumi." He gestures to a woman who sashays up next to them and pauses with one hip thrown out so far, I worry she might have dislocated it. "This is our lead singer, Caoimhe."

Now that I'm less freaked out, I note that Orebon's got a really deep, really musical-sounding voice that fills up the space between us without him even trying. It makes me want to hear him sing.

"I'm Grace," I tell him, holding out a hand to shake his. "And this is Hudson and Smokey." I gesture to the little shadow.

"And this wee one is our daughter, Amiani," Lumi says. "Welcome to our troupe."

"Troubadours." Hudson repeats what Orebon had called themselves earlier, and he sounds a lot more skeptical than I feel.

"That's right." Orebon smiles at Hudson, then turns to me. "Why did you think we might be an army after you?"

Hudson narrows his eyes but answers, "We heard the Shadow Queen is looking for people from our world."

"Yeah, we've occasionally heard the same." Orebon pauses, as though he's not sure how much to say. He must finally decide we deserve to know why we're being hunted, because he shakes his head and continues. "The queen's sister was poisoned when she was a child by a human who crossed through the barrier, and therefore she believes her sister's cure lies in the human realm—or revenge."

My eyes widen, and a glance at Hudson shows he's as surprised by that information as I am. I'm not saying I have any intention of surrendering anytime soon, but I can't lie and say I don't feel some sympathy for her.

"But don't worry. As much as we sympathize with Queen Clio, we've never been big fans of everyone paying for the deeds of one. Or big fans of the queen's army." Lumi adjusts the baby slightly in her carrier, and as he does, I note he's got a giant case draped over his shoulder. One that looks like it belongs to a musical instrument.

"So are you on the run from the police, too?" I ask.

"Oh, no," Orebon says, then winks at me. "We're headed to a town not too far from here."

"Are you going to Adarie?" I ask, my heart beating faster at the possibility they might know how to get through those giant gates, might have some clue of the reception we could receive.

"Why?" Caoimhe gives Orebon a sly look, so quick I'm doubting I actually saw it, when she turns back to Hudson and asks, "Are you heading to the gates of Adarie?"

"Does it matter where we're going?" Hudson asks in the mild tone he uses when he's getting ready to lay a trap. Having been the victim of it numerous times in the lair, I'll admit it's got the power to make me shiver a little even when it's not directed at me.

Caoimhe doesn't pay him any mind. Instead, she just says, "Of course you're going to Adarie."

I guess it's not much of a leap. We *are* standing on a mountain overlooking the town below. Besides, surely others know this place is a safe haven for those, like us, who are trying to escape notice by the queen's army.

But then Orebon and Lumi exchange such a long glance with Caoimhe, it's clear they're not even trying to hide that they're cooking up an idea that somehow includes us. When Orebon nods, Caoimhe gives her mane of hair another impressive toss, and I can't help trying to swallow the lump that feels permanently lodged in my throat now.

And that's before Caoimhe's lips pull into an almost feline smile and she purrs at Hudson, "Perhaps we could make a deal."

69

Color Me Purple

—Hudson—

"A deal?" I ask and don't bother to try to keep the skepticism from my voice. "You want to make a deal with *us*?"

There are a million reasons why that's bollocks—including the fact that they just found out about us ten minutes ago. No way did they take one look at us fleeing from an *army* and decide they want to partner up. No fucking way.

And if they did, I don't want to be partners with them anyway.

"What kind of deal?" Grace asks, and she looks as wary as I do.

"The kind where we all get what we want," Caoimhe says. She accompanies the words with an over-the-top seductive smile that I'm guessing works on 9.5 out of 10 men between the ages of two and ninety.

But it's not going to work on me. I was raised by Delilah Vega and have seen that kind of smile in action more times than I can count. Plus, I'm more of a sucker for an obstinate chin.

"And what exactly do you think we want?" I reply with a scowl at least as impressive as her smile. And I should know—I've been practicing it for more than a century.

"Easy." She spreads her arms so wide, I can't help wondering if she's just trying to sell this or if she's auditioning for the role of a circus barker at the same time. "You want through the gates of Adarie. But *we* know you can't just waltz in without an invitation. One you have to apply for with the mayor's office first to keep crowding at the gates low and safety a top priority." Damn. No, we didn't know that. "Immigrating to Adarie is open to everyone…but it takes sixty days for approval. And that seems like it might be more time than you humans have?"

"One human, one vampire," Grace tells her.

"Nice." She looks me over, and I'd be lying if I said I didn't feel a little dirty when she was done. "I'm assuming you're the vampire."

"He is," Grace answers, and there's a bit of a growl in her tone that I'm not expecting. I'm also not expecting her to take two steps closer to me so that our arms are nearly touching. But she does.

This time when Caoimhe looks between the two of us, there's a "so that's how it is" smirk on her face. I don't bother to correct her and neither does Grace. Then again, why would she when she went out of her way to give Caoimhe that exact impression?

"Can I see your teeth later?" Caoimhe asks me, right before she runs her tongue along her own teeth.

"You can see *my* teeth," Grace tells her sweetly, and it takes all my self-control not to burst out laughing.

Obviously Lumi and Orebon don't have the same kind of self-control, because they both chuckle like fools. And get flipped off by Caoimhe for their trouble.

"Works for me." Caoimhe turns her seductive look on Grace, but Grace just rolls her eyes. Apparently, she's as good at seeing through the singer's bullshit as I am.

"The deal?" Grace urges.

"Right, the deal." Having obviously decided that she isn't going to seduce either one of us into doing her bidding, Caoimhe turns businesslike again. "As I was saying, two otherworlders, that would be you"—she points at us, just in case we couldn't figure that out—"will never get through the town gates quickly enough."

"But we just so happen to have an invitation to enter—and audition for the Starfall Festival. We are a very well-known group of troubadours," Lumi supplies.

"And?" I ask, not seeing where this is going at all.

"A very well-known group of *five* troubadours," Orebon clarifies.

"You're suggesting we can say we're in your group so that the guards let us pass through the gates as part of your invitation?" Grace asks.

Caoimhe smiles again—in a way that definitely doesn't make me feel better about their offer. "Of course."

"And in exchange for doing this, you want what exactly from us?" I cross my arms, pretend to be bored with the entire conversation.

"Well, you would join our troupe, of course," she says, then tacks on when Grace's eyebrows nearly hit her hairline, "for the audition only."

"No," I say, and Grace adds, "Hard pass." Just in case they were unsure.

"Look," Lumi pleads, "we've got two more members—it's just they're not going to make it to Adarie in time for the audition."

"When is the festival?" I ask, an idea forming that maybe we can sneak through the gates with the crowds of visitors.

But Orebon shakes his head. "Starfall isn't for two months still, but the auditions are this week. The festival coincides with Noromar's quarterly three straight days of darkness—*everyone* comes out to celebrate. The festival gig can set us up for a whole year. You'd truly be helping some fellow travelers."

"Ones with a new baby to feed," Lumi adds, rocking his hips for extra effect.

Well, hell. I shove my hands deep in my pockets as I go back to contemplating jumping over a twenty-foot wall without being noticed. I glance at Grace, though, and my stomach sinks.

Because Grace is staring at the tiny purple curls on the baby's head, the crinkles around her eyes softening, and I groan. She is one hundred percent falling for this sales pitch. This girl has got to be the most naive—and tender—person in the world.

I sigh. "What would we have to do?"

70

Way Too
Hidden Talents
—Hudson—

Caoimhe's eyes gleam, as though she'd always known we'd say yes. This woman seems very much used to getting her way, which has me stepping a little closer to Grace as she eyeballs me again, licking her lips this time.

"Surely you can sing, yes?" Lumi asks Grace.

"I mean, I sing in the shower," she tells him with a shrug.

"Anyone can sing in the shower." Orebon rolls his eyes. "The question is, are you any good at it when you *do* sing?"

"I don't know." Grace turns to me, brows raised. "Am I?"

I suddenly become very interested in the pattern of rocks on the ground.

"Oh God." Lumi cringes. "That bad?"

I go from counting the rocks to finding animal shapes in the clouds above us.

Orebon lifts a brow. "How about magic?"

Grace shakes her head.

"Whistling?" Lumi looks hopeful.

But I know the answer to that one. "Absolutely not."

"Juggling?" Orebon asks, and my snort has Grace glaring at me.

"What about dancing?" Caoimhe asks.

"I can try..." She does a little shimmy that looks great to me.

"Oh God," Lumi says again. The baby stirs at that, and he reaches into a bag and pulls out a plastic bottle filled with a creamy purple drink. He plops the nipple into the baby's mouth, and she starts sucking on it vigorously. Mission accomplished, he tosses Orebon a look of dismay. "We're never going to get this gig," he murmurs under his breath.

"We'll say she's a great singer—with a throat infection. It'll work," Orebon tells his partner with a wave of his hand, then says, "They'll just assume we'll be *even better* by the time of the festival."

Caoimhe nods and turns to me. "What about you?"

"What *about* me?" I ask back.

Caoimhe arches a brow. "Can *you* sing?"

"I can hold my own," I answer, not liking where this conversation is going one bit.

"He really can," Grace agrees. Which surprises me, considering I never knew she listened to me. Back at the lair, she always seemed to be listening to something on her earbuds when I played my albums, sometimes singing along.

"Even if I can sing, I don't know any of your tunes," I point out reasonably. "It's probably best that we just say I have a throat infection as well."

But then Grace turns to me, mischief gleaming in her eyes. "Oh, I definitely think you should sing, Hudson. Something swoony and romantic, don't you think?"

She is taking the piss, and I probably deserve it after counting rocks when they asked if *she* could sing. Still, I'm not a fan of embarrassing myself in front of strangers.

"Maybe I could just play the guitar or something," I suggest. *See*, I tell her with a look, *I am capable of being a team player.*

Grace's eyes widen. "You play the guitar?"

"Is that so hard to believe?" I cock one brow.

"I don't know. I mean, Jaxon had guitars and a drum set in his tower, so I guess I just assumed, you know, that was *his* thing." She shrugs and yeah, I can't help it. I'm insulted.

"And what, you thought only Jaxy-Waxy has a talent for anything?" I snipe back, then turn to Caoimhe and bite out, "I can sing *and* play the guitar."

The three troubadours are talking all at once, throwing out possible scenarios for how to include me in their act, but I'm not listening. I'm too busy watching Grace fight—and lose—to keep a triumphant smile from overtaking her face.

Shite. I walked right into that, didn't I?

I narrow my gaze on the treacherous girl, promising retribution later, when something Lumi says has me spinning around.

"I absolutely will *not* be juggling *anything*." A man has his pride, after all.

But when Grace giggles next to me, I know I'd juggle *kittens* if she asked me to.

I am so fucked.

71

Inn-stant Gratification

—Grace—

Turns out, getting through the gates of Adarie with a troubadour's invitation is as easy as tricking Hudson into performing with them.

I've never sweated so much in my life as I was when the guards questioned our group.

I thought for sure a troupe with two otherworlders was going to be a hard no, but looks like Caoihme was right and it's expected for troubadours to be an odd collection of people. She'd said it was common for traveling entertainers to band together with strangers from all over their world, and I have to admit, I kind of love this idea of creating a family from the people you meet.

What I really found interesting, though, is that Caoihme insisted she's met tons of otherworlders like us, and she's never heard of the queen's army hunting them to put them to death. Orebon was telling the truth, the queen *is* desperate to find a way back to our world, but Caoihme claimed she also knows that just because someone made it through the barrier doesn't always mean they know how to get back.

Which leads me to believe…the army that came to Arnst's farm was after us specifically. Why?

I make a mental note to talk to Hudson about it later. Our more immediate problem is finding the mayor and requesting sanctuary as well as securing lodging. The idea of a bed makes me a little dizzy with excitement.

As we walk along the cobblestone streets, I can't help but be charmed by the fancy village square, elaborate architecture, and miles upon miles of homes and other buildings.

The streets are still fairly empty for early morning, and I can only imagine how even more amazing this town will seem bustling with people, shop doors open and patio restaurants teeming with hungry guests.

I'm struck by the absolute beauty of this place. Old-world shops, planter boxes overflowing with flowers, winding cobblestone streets. And I kind of fall in love with all of it.

A glance at Hudson tells me he's enjoying this walk as much as I am. Even Smokey is getting in on the action. She's actually unwound herself from her seemingly permanent spot around one of Hudson's limbs and is racing through the streets, tumbling over and around herself with excitement. Apparently, she knows exactly what this place is and definitely approves.

"There's the inn," Hudson says, nodding to a building at the edge of the town square. Tall and wide, it looks like what would happen if an old German town and *The Nightmare Before Christmas* had a giant purple baby.

The architecture is all old German Bauhaus with its dark half timbering against a light background and a pointy roof. But at the same time, it has narrow towers sticking out at odd angles and looks just a little bit off-kilter. Yeah, there's definitely a little Jack Skellington in there whether it was intended or not.

"So should we check in before the auditions?" I ask. "Or try to find the mayor first?"

"Probably get settled first," Hudson says as he fishes the letter from Maroly and Arnst out of the bottom of the backpack. "Before things get too wild around here."

"There's no way they'll have an open room," Lumi tells us. "Probably completely booked up for the auditions tonight. People come from all over to preview the entertainment."

"Yeah, but—" I break off, unsure of how much to tell him. He's fun and super kind, but we literally just met. I don't know what's the right balance of information to give them.

"We've actually got a present for the manager," Hudson says smoothly. "He's related to friends of ours."

"Well, isn't that fortuitous?" Caoimhe says with a wink. "You go do that, and we'll find a good spot to set up and earn some quick change. If you're looking for us later, just follow the music—and find the biggest crowd. That will be us."

"We'll find you," I promise her, then give the troubadours a little wave before Hudson and I head across the street. "Is it wrong that I really like them?" I ask him as soon as we're out of earshot.

Sure, Caoimhe's leers at Hudson were a little much to take at first, but along the three-mile journey into Adarie, it became apparent she meant nothing by it. She has the kind of confidence that just oozes sex appeal, whether she turns it up or not. Besides, she eventually took the hint and stopped hitting on Hudson—which was neither here nor there to me, of course.

"I like them, too," he answers with a small grin. "Just not sure we can trust them. Or Maroly and Arnst, for that matter. I'd avoid her cousin's inn altogether if there was anywhere else to stay."

"Totally," I tell him with a roll of my eyes. "No one is ever that nice without a reason. Can't even be remotely trusted. Not even if they told me today was Saturday."

"Well, definitely don't trust them then," he drawls. "Considering it's Sunday."

"It is? I thought—" I break off, go over the days in my head. "How did I miss a day?"

"You didn't. I was just fucking with you."

"You know what? Some days I don't even like you," I say, mock glaring at him as he pulls the inn's front door open for me.

"Yeah you do," he shoots back.

I grin, because he's right. Despite everything, I do like him. A lot. No need to let him know that, though. "I tolerate you," I tell him with a sniff. "It's not the same thing."

"Tolerate, okay." He nods. "I'll remember that the next time you crawl all over me in the middle of the night."

"That happened once!"

"Once a night, maybe." His grin is wicked.

"Seriously?" I mock glare at him again. "You think this is the time to bring that up?"

"What better time?" he asks, brows raised. "We seem to have called a truce. Why shouldn't I take advantage of it?"

Before I can answer him, the harried-looking man at the front desk says, "Can I help you?"

"Actually, yes," I say. "We were hoping to—"

"We're all booked up," he interrupts.

"Yes, but—"

"No buts. I've got nothing. Even the small, old rooms in the back are booked up. You can try the hostel a couple of streets over—"

"Arnst and Maroly sent us." It's Hudson's turn to interrupt him. "They told us to give you this."

He hands the innkeeper the envelope, but the man doesn't open it. "Are you Grace and Hudson?"

We exchange looks. "We are."

"I'm Nyaz, Maroly's cousin. She called a couple of days ago to make sure you arrived safely. Told me to keep a room open for you, so I did. It's not a great room, but it's got a bed, so..." He turns and takes one of the old-fashioned keys hanging behind him off the wall. "You're in room 403. The stairs are that way."

He points around the corner, then turns to the door as the bell jingles on it. "How can I help you?" he asks the people who just came in.

"Wait. We didn't pay you—" I start, but he waves me away.

"We'll settle up later. About *everything*." He stresses the last word in a way that makes me think he's talking about more than the bill. Is this what Arnst meant when he said we could trust him to help us?

"Thanks," Hudson says, putting a hand on my lower back to guide me away. "We'll check back in later."

Nyaz nods, but he's already on to the next customer. By the time we get to the stairs, the lobby is filled with people either checking in or begging for a room. Wow, Caoimhe wasn't kidding about how popular these auditions were.

Once we get to our room, we take turns in the shower—and can I just say, nothing on earth feels better than a shower after a few days in the wilderness? I spend entirely too long luxuriating in the feel of shampoo in my hair and hot water coursing over my body. But I can't help it. Sponge baths in ice-cold water really don't get the job done.

I'm towel-drying my hair when Hudson steps out of the bathroom, a pair of black jogging pants low on his hips and miles of naked abs on display. "Hey, can you check my back?" Hudson asks as he steps closer and turns around. "Those leech bites feel itchy."

"You're saying the great *vampire* might need some *medicated ointment*?" I tease, running my fingers softly over the bite marks that are healing but, he's right, aren't completely gone yet. I reach into the pack and grab the ointment, squeezing some out on my fingertips and then brushing it against the marks. "I guess one bloodsucker isn't immune to another."

"Bite me," he says with absolutely no bite.

"Hey, that's my line!" I joke. "You can't just steal it."

"Sure I can," he answers, winking over his shoulder at me. "A guy has to have a dream, doesn't he?"

I start to laugh, but then my eyes meet his dark-blue ones, and the laugh sticks in my throat. As does the breath I just took. Because suddenly we're right back in that cave, my hand in his hand, my vein in his mouth.

This time I don't try to explain away the feelings bouncing around inside me. I don't try to pretend I'm not having them, either. I just stay where I am, gaze locked on Hudson's, and wonder.

Wonder what it will feel like when he does it again.

Wonder if he'll drink from my wrist next time...or somewhere else.

Wonder what I taste like to him.

I don't realize I've said the last one aloud until Hudson's eyes darken. Then he turns toward me fully and whispers, "Delicious. Like the best thing I've ever tasted. Like—" He breaks off, takes a deep breath. Then gives a rueful smile and says, "You taste good, Grace. Really good."

I know it's not what he was about to say, and I would give anything to know what his original thought was. But I don't tell *him* everything. It's hypocritical to expect him to do any different. No matter how much I want him to.

No matter how much I need to know what he's thinking.

I almost ask. But before I can work up the nerve, Hudson smiles and holds out a hand to me. "It's nearly eleven. Want to go grab some lunch?"

I almost say no, almost tell him I want to stay right here and let *him* have breakfast instead. But that isn't what anyone would call the prudent thing right now. So instead, I just nod and put my hand in his. And wait for whatever comes next.

72

Gone Wishin'

—Grace—

By the time we get back down to the street, it's bustling with people, and I'm excited to see that there are more than just wraiths in Adarie. I don't see any humans yet, but Hudson points out another vampire laughing up into the eyes of a tall, waiflike person with green skin so pale, it almost looks translucent.

There is a pack of werewolves dining at an outdoor patio—raw steak and boiled eggs, of course—and a real chupacabra, Hudson insists, who's buying a bouquet of purple daisies from a flower cart.

For the first time since the queen's army came looking for us at the farm, I feel like maybe, just maybe, we can stop running, and I look up at Hudson with hope shining in my eyes. He hands me a flaky purple roll he's bought from a food vendor, and I immediately take a bite of the warm pastry, close my eyes, and groan. It's amazing.

When I flutter my lashes open again, Hudson is staring at me strangely, but in a blink, the look is gone and he's turning us to walk down another street filled with vendors.

Smokey is super excited by all the people as well, and she's having a blast weaving in and out of the foot traffic. But the third time she almost gets stepped on, Hudson calls her back, and she winds herself around his neck so she can still have a good view of all the happenings.

We didn't have any plan when we set out except to learn the lay of the land, so we just kind of wander up and down the streets for a couple of hours. Some of the locals do give us second—and even third—looks, but everyone seems incredibly friendly.

After wandering some of the side streets, we make it back to the huge town square at the center of Adarie. The inn where we're staying is all the way at one end, but the area is so big that there's a lot between us and the hotel. Including a giant park right in the center of the square, complete with a gazebo and a wishing well filled with iridescent purple coins.

I've always been a sucker for wishing wells. When I was little, my dad used to take me to the big fountain in Balboa Park at least once a month so I could throw a penny in. I haven't done it in forever, haven't even thought about it since my parents died, but now that I'm standing here, all I want is to toss a coin in and make a wish.

Too bad I don't know what that wish would be.

Maybe that we find a way to settle in here. A way to be safe and secure and build a life in this world that's so different from our own.

But I don't make a wish.

Instead, we cut through the park to one of the ornate purple park benches that are peppered throughout the violet grass. Someone is setting up sound equipment in the center of the gazebo—probably for the auditions—and I wonder what time the troubadours are supposed to go on.

I put a hand over my mouth as I yawn, realizing we haven't slept in what feels like forever. I glance up at Hudson, and he must be thinking the same thing because he asks, "Do you suppose we have time for a quick nap before this horror show starts?"

"As much as I'd like to say yes, I doubt it," I answer as we manage to find a seat on the last empty bench. People are already crowding around the gazebo from all directions, sitting on benches and portable chairs they've brought from home. Others spread out blankets on the grass and sit on them.

"It's probably better this way," Hudson says with a grin. "I'm so tired, I'm more likely to forget it ever happened."

I chuckle as I know he intended and chuck my shoulder at his.

A few more minutes pass where we talk of nothing important while Smokey twirls and spins on the grass right in front of us. At one point, she disappears, and Hudson gets up to look for her, only to find her racing back to him loaded down with flowers from one of the planters.

"Smokey!" I tell her as she drops them at our feet. "You aren't supposed to pick flowers from the flowerpots."

She whines at me a little, and I feel bad for having to correct her, at least until she picks up all the flowers that are near me and showers Hudson with them. He cracks up, of course, and I can't fault her for doing whatever she can to make him laugh. I kind of like hearing the sound, too.

Hudson picks up a couple of flowers and hands one to Smokey, who *oohs* and *aahs* over it like he's just given her the best corsage at the prom. Which is ridiculous for so many reasons—including the fact that she's the one who brought the flowers to him.

The second bloom he gives to me, despite Smokey's hiss of disapproval.

I think of giving it right back to him, but in the end, I hand it to Smokey, too. She takes it begrudgingly, and I feel like we're at least making a little progress in our hesitant friendship.

People crowd in on us from all sides as we wait a few more minutes for the first act to start playing. Finally, the lights surrounding the gazebo turn on and bright shades of red and yellow, blue and hot pink and green, dance through the overcast air.

Seconds later, someone finally takes the stage to kick everything off. He's an old man who appears human, with flowing white hair and a craggy face, and he welcomes everyone to the festival auditions in the gravelly voice of a man who has spent his life living—and drinking—hard. He is wearing an orange-and-yellow-striped David Bowie jumpsuit—complete with gigantic fringed shoulder pads and flared legs—and he introduces himself as the mayor to anyone who might be visiting "our little oasis."

To say I'm shocked *this* is the mayor who might hold our fate in his hands would be an understatement. Hudson and I exchange looks.

"We need to meet him," Hudson murmurs to me.

I nod, because we do.

But that'll have to wait for later. Because suddenly, Lumi is rushing over to us, gesturing wildly with his arms and shouting, "Come on! Come on! We haven't much time!"

Hudson and I get to our feet as he asks, "Time for what?"

"To get your costumes on, of course."

The look on Hudson's face right now—priceless. And I send a little prayer out to the universe that his costume has sequins. The gaudier the better.

73

My Lady in Red

—Hudson—

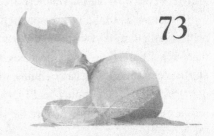

When Lumi had said *costume*, I don't know what I was imagining—but it wasn't this.

I fasten the last button, then smooth a hand down the soft lavender dress shirt, admiring the silky fabric. I'm not normally a huge fan of purple—well, except in my boxers, of course—but I have to admit this shade is really gorgeous. I shove the tails into the black dress pants Orebon had handed me, then roll up the sleeves. All in all, not too shabby.

Somehow, I don't think Grace is getting off as easy, though.

I sink my fang into my lip in an effort not to laugh as I listen to Grace argue with Caoimhe behind a folding privacy screen slash makeshift changing area set up for performers in a building behind the stage. They're in a heated debate about...well, *everything.*

Grace apparently doesn't appreciate the location of some flowers, the hem, the color, or the fit. Caoimhe insists that they will only be able to sell Grace's "throat infection" not ruining the audition if the audience is too busy looking at her outfit to notice her lack of voice.

Which means...I literally cannot wait to see what she's wear—

Grace steps out from behind the screen, and I freeze. I vaguely recognize I was about to run a hand through my hair, so that arm is now just hanging in the air. I'll bring it back down when I remember how to breathe.

Instead, I just blink. And blink again.

Holy. Hell.

Grace throws a hand on her hip and demands, "Are you even listening to me, Hudson?"

The answer to that would be no, I had no idea she was even talking, which I wisely do not tell her. I shove my hands into my pockets and rock back on my heels. Really, how am I supposed to understand *words* with Grace standing in front of me wearing the smallest dress in history?

I swallow as I take in two spaghetti straps that reach into a bouquet of brilliant silk flowers sewn around the edges of the top of the red dress. A top that has just barely enough fabric to cover her ample chest before hugging every glorious curve Grace has and ending a mere *two inches* past her ass cheeks.

"Hudson!" Grace shouts, and I jerk my gaze up to hers, a flush creeping into my cheeks as I finally take in her distress. She moans. "I cannot go out there in this."

"You look amazing," I say, because it's true.

A woman with several pencils shoved behind her ears and a clipboard in her hands rushes over and shouts, "You're on!"

Grace's eyes widen, her bottom lip trembles, and I know I can't let her go out there in that dress. Not if it makes her feel uncomfortable.

There's only one option I can think of. I turn to Orebon and say, "If you guys don't mind, I've got an idea, but it's a solo gig to warm up the crowd."

I hold his gaze, silently begging him to let me do this for Grace, until he gives me one quick nod.

Then I reach over and pick up the guitar I'd tuned earlier and head out onto the stage. Alone. Where I am more than prepared to die of embarrassment if it saves Grace the same.

My heart is pounding in my throat and I feel queasy as fuck, but I pull the guitar strap over my shoulder, approach the mic anyway.

I settle my right hand into the familiar position for a G chord.

Because even though I didn't plan to do this, now that I'm here, I know exactly what song I want to play.

Grace's favorite.

74

1D-reams Come True

—Grace—

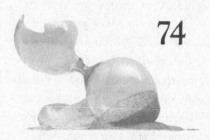

"Um, hey." Hudson's voice is hesitant as he leans into the mic. He gives a little cough to the side, then continues. "My name's Hudson, and I'm part of this amazing troubadour group called The Horizons."

I'd totally forgotten they told us that information what seems like days ago. Leave it to Hudson to have paid attention to every detail, though.

Caoimhe starts to follow him out, but Orebon places a hand on her elbow and shakes his head, whispering, "We never upstage a fellow performer."

They have some sort of silent communication before she steps back, and we all turn as one to see what Hudson does next.

He strums a couple of chords, adjusts one of the tuning knobs on the top of the guitar, before clearing his throat. "We had a little costume snafu in the back—and I couldn't let my girl come out until she was feeling confident she looked her best." He gives a half-hearted chuckle and shrugs in a "what can you do" sort of way. "So I hope you folks don't mind, but I figured I'd give her a bit more time and entertain you first."

He glances to where we're standing to the left of the stage now and winks at me. There's a sigh in the audience, and I know how they feel. He's already got all of us eating out of the palm of his hand.

A stagehand rushes over with a tall stool, and Hudson thanks him before sitting down, settling the guitar with practiced ease on one knee.

He takes a deep breath and says softly, "This is for Grace."

Then his strong fingers pluck the guitar's strings, and I recognize the song in the first three notes. And I melt. I just fucking melt.

Hudson is playing a One Direction song. For me.

Because he knew I was freaking out.

Because he knows how much I love them.

Because no matter what, he's still that little boy from his journals who would do anything, suffer anything, to save someone else pain.

So here he is, the guy who does everything in his power to stay in the shadows, taking center stage. For me.

My heart is a living beast in my chest and my palms are so sweaty, I have to rub them against the sides of this ridiculous stripper dress. What if he can't really sing? What if he gets booed? What if he forgets the words?

A zillion and one terrible outcomes rush through my head at once, and I want to shout at him to run. Forget that we promised to help the troubadours. Forget everything and save himself!

But then he leans forward and starts to sing the first line of "Little Things," and everyone—and I mean *everyone*—swoons. His voice is deep and rich and effortless, and maybe even a little boyish, as he sings about how all the little things his girl doesn't like about herself are what add up to what he loves about her.

The emotion cracks through his voice in a few places, but that only makes the song more beautiful. And I'm not the only one who feels that way, as one by one, people are now crowding closer to the stage.

Hudson doesn't seem to see it, though. He's staring off in the distance, his fingers never missing a note, the words pouring out of him like he wrote the song himself. He closes his eyes for a second, then delivers another soulful line about never letting this girl go, and when he opens them again, he's looking down at the front of the stage.

I watch as a girl of about fourteen or fifteen, with adorable blue curls falling out of her ponytail, looks like she's about to faint.

Hudson's gaze shifts to someone else in the audience then, and it's clear that he's somehow able to make every single person feel like he's singing just to them. Including me.

It's a simple song, no major vocal gymnastics involved, and that's why I love it so much. The words are so beautiful, it's like singing a love letter, and I can't help my crazy heart from wondering if that's how it feels to him, too. Especially when his voice hitches ever so slightly on the last line of the song.

I find myself wishing I were in front of the stage with everyone else right now, jostling to get closer so we can see if he's singing about us.

As the last strum of the guitar echoes around the courtyard, I notice there isn't a single other sound. There's no chattering of friends like there was in the earlier performances. Even the babies seem to have been hypnotized into reverence.

Hudson's shoulders stiffen as he moves his hands down to silence the guitar. Then he gives an awkward half smile and murmurs into the mic, "Hope that was okay."

And the courtyard goes fucking wild.

The applause is nearly overwhelming—and yet the screams of the people crowding the stage are even louder.

Orebon murmurs beside me, "I think I'm in love."

And I can't help but chuckle when Lumi agrees, "Me too."

But I can't take my eyes off Hudson. He's standing, clearly uncertain if he should walk offstage or what. He sends me a frantic look and mouths, *What now?*

What now indeed.

I take a deep breath and say to Caoimhe, "I think he's warmed up the audience enough, don't you?"

Hudson put himself out there for me. The least I can do is have his back.

So I grab up something that looks a little like a tambourine—surely even I can't screw that up—and walk onto the stage.

Orebon immediately starts playing a song we'd heard them practicing on the walk down the mountain and skips out behind me as Caoimhe and Lumi pick up the harmonies with ease. Hudson's shoulders relax as he joins the guitar playing, but he shuffles to the back of the group as quickly as he can, the troubadours clearly comfortable in the spotlight.

And they're good. Really good.

The song seems to fly by, and in no time, we're all grinning and heading back offstage to the sound of thunderous applause.

When we get backstage, Caoimhe and Lumi and Orebon are all chattering ninety miles an hour about the size of the crowd and how much fun that was. Hudson hasn't said a word yet.

He just walks over and sets his guitar down where he'd picked it up from earlier, his gaze not quite meeting mine. When he shoves his hands into his pockets, rubs the bottom of one of his shoes back and forth across the wood floor, I suddenly realize he's nervous.

It's an emotion I rarely ever associate with him, so it takes me a moment to figure it out, but once I do, I walk right up to him and slide my arms around his waist, press my cheek against his chest, and whisper, "Thank you."

He hesitates, then slowly, so very, very slowly, pulls his hands from his pockets and hugs me back. "Did I do Harry justice?" he asks, his warm breath brushing across the top of my head.

I smile. "Harry who?"

He chuckles. "I hope the troupe doesn't mind I hogged the spotlight for a bit."

"Are you kidding?" I joke, leaning back to share a smile. "Caoimhe almost threw her panties at you. So did Orebon and Lumi."

Hudson raises one brow, his turbulent blue eyes as fathomless as the ocean, and asks, "What about you?"

If nothing else, the last year I've spent with Hudson has taught me one thing: always keep this boy on his toes.

Which is why I shake my head in a poor-little-Hudson manner and murmur, "Who says I'm wearing any?"

His eyes widen for a second, just a second, and then something moves in his gaze that has me freaking out under all the cool attitude I'm trying so hard to project. Something predatory and altogether terrifying—as scary as it is exciting.

My heart beats like a wild thing and my blood roars in my ears. I take a few deep breaths, tell myself to calm down. Tell myself that he's probably just hungry.

As if he can read my thoughts still, his eyes move from my face to my lips to the pulse beating too hard at the base of my throat. They linger at that pulse point, which only makes my heart beat faster, and I swear I see the tip of a fang scrape against his lower lip.

The air between us turns tinder dry, and I know that any move on my part will be the match that burns it all to the ground.

But then Hudson takes a breath, and the predator fades away.

He takes a step back, and then another, until I can no longer feel the waves of heat rolling off his body.

I have no time to mourn the loss before his gaze centers on something over my right shoulder and he says smoothly, "And you must be the mayor."

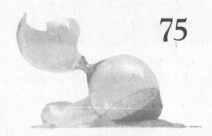

75

Café Lotta Say

—Hudson—

Bollocks.

I just walked onto a stage, in front of hundreds of strangers…*willingly.* And then, because the embarrassment factor needed to be at some monster fucking level, I didn't just sing *any* song. I picked a *love song.* Grace's favorite love song, in fact.

And then I sang it *to* her.

Like an absolute *tosser.*

When I'd walked offstage, my heart pounding and hands shaking, it took everything in me not to fade to the nearest bathroom and lose the bottle of water I'd regretted drinking earlier.

But then Grace had hugged me and fuck, I let myself hope.

Let myself want.

Then she'd teased she wasn't wearing panties…and the whole room disappeared. Just fucking fell away. In the space between one heartbeat and the next, a raging fire burned through all the oxygen in the room.

And I let myself need someone more than I needed my next breath.

So of course that wanker of a mayor decided now is the perfect time for a chitchat.

If we didn't need his permission to remain safely in Adarie, I'd scoop Grace into my arms and fade back to our room so fast, he'd question whether we'd ever even been here.

"I am indeed," the mayor says, raising his voice to be heard over the surprisingly spirited flute duel going on onstage. "Let's walk, shall we?"

I start to tell him no, but something about the way he's watching me tells me that's not an option. So I reach over and take Grace's hand and together we follow the mayor out of the park, with Smokey toddling along behind us.

I don't know where I expect him to take us, but a little bakery/coffee shop isn't it. However, as soon as we step into the sweet-smelling place with its twisted iron ice-cream shop chairs and tiny round tables, I relax just a little bit. It's doubtful the mayor would choose this place for an intense interrogation.

The mayor waves to the clerk behind the register, a woman with short purple hair, and leads us to a small pink table in the back. The clerk dashes over with some yellow cups filled with water and a tray of dainty desserts, served inside a giant swan pastry.

"What do you think he wants?" Grace whispers to me.

But I just shake my head, my poker face in full force. Which is more difficult than it should be, considering our circumstances. But it's hard to take a mayor dressed like Ziggy Stardust seriously.

Then again, it's hard to take *anyone* dressed like Ziggy Stardust seriously when we're fifty years past the seventies.

As we take our seats, he offers us both a too-broad smile. "Welcome, my friends! It's so good to have you here in Adarie." His voice booms through the small café, and everyone in it turns to stare at Grace and me.

"Thank you so much. I love pastries," Grace says as she places a cookie on a small plate. I can tell she's trying to be her most cordial, conciliatory, charming self. I make a note to ask her where this Grace is whenever she's talking to me. I figure it will piss her off to no end, so I'm going to make sure to save it for when I really need it. She adds, "And this is the cutest one I've ever seen."

"You'll find a lot of things in Adarie are the best you've ever seen," the mayor says. "Then again, that might just be me. I love this place."

He leans back in his chair and takes another sip from his tiny cup. He watches us over the rim as he does, then puts the cup down and asks, "That was some audition, eh?"

"We did okay," I tell him shortly, because bonding over swan pastries or not, I'm still not sold on this guy.

Grace tosses me a "don't be rude" look, then says, "We were actually hoping to talk to you, too, Mayor."

"Call me Souil, please," he corrects her. "Everyone around here does."

"Souil," she repeats with another smile, while I resist the urge to roll my eyes. I don't know who this super sweet Grace is, but she is sending me into pastel-colored sugar shock. And considering I'm a vampire, that's saying a lot.

"And what can I call you?" he asks with a smile.

"Oh, right." Grace practically trips over the words falling out of her mouth.

"I'm Grace, and this is Hudson."

"Nice to meet you, Grace and Hudson," Souil says. Then, after a few more seconds pass, he asks, "What brings you to our lovely town?"

"You do, actually," I tell him.

"*Moi?*" He presses a hand to his sequin-covered chest and looks completely surprised. "How did you hear about me?"

"Our friends told us about you," Grace says. "They mentioned that you might be able to help us. We've been running from the Shadow Queen's soldiers for days now, and we're just trying to find a safe place to stay."

Of course Grace just spilled everything. I have never met anyone with less trust issues than her. And, as frustrating as it is at times, I'd be lying if I didn't also admit it's what I love about her most. Well, that and her stubborn chin.

"I'm so sorry to hear that." He shakes his head, looks annoyed. "I swear, that woman is the scourge of this land. She's always trying to kill someone."

"Is she?" I raise one brow. If Orebon and Caoimhe had it right, the queen has it in specifically for us. I still haven't figured out why, but I have a sneaking suspicion it has something to do with Grace. And not because she thinks she's human, either.

I start to ask him more about the queen, but before I can, he continues. "You don't have to worry about the Shadow Queen here. Adarie is part of her realm, as she rules Noromar, but we're an independent entity. She and her soldiers have no power here, and they wouldn't dare to breach these walls. Not while I'm in charge of this village."

He takes the last bite of his pastry, then pats his mouth with his pink-polka-dotted napkin. "Is there anything else you're worried about? Maybe I can help put your minds at ease."

Grace shoots me a look, and I know she's trying to figure out if we should mention the dragon to him. So am I. If he kicks us out of here, we're pretty much fucked. But it only seems fair to tell him we've had a pissed-off dragon on our arses for more than a year.

Finally, I bite the bullet and just tell him about the dragon. Amazingly, he doesn't even look surprised. "Yes, I've heard of dragons attacking when a stranger first arrives in the Shadow Realm, but they are of no consequence." He waves his hand negligently. "You'll be safe in Adarie."

"You're not concerned?" Grace sounds surprised, and I don't blame her. This dragon is scary as hell, and the idea of him attacking Adarie and hurting a bunch of innocent people bothers the shit out of me. Why the hell doesn't it also bother the fuck out of the mayor?

"Of course not. We may be the home of the Fighting Dragons, but an actual dragon hasn't been seen here in centuries. I should know: I've been mayor here for nearly two hundred years, lived here a lot longer, and we have never had a problem on my watch."

"Never?" Grace repeats.

He looks down at his nails, rubs them absently against his chest. "Dragons aren't a problem here."

A feeling of unease skates along my spine as I study the mayor. Grace would say I'm just used to the worst in everyone, but something about his demeanor just seems *off.*

"You are human, are you not?" I ask, latching on to something else he said. "How have you lived so long?"

The mayor chuckles. "Luckily, time passes differently in the Shadow Realm, my boy."

"Y-You haven't found a way back to our world in more than two hundred years?" Grace sputters, and my stomach bottoms out as I realize she was still holding on to hope she would get back to Jaxon one day.

I drag a tight breath into my lungs, try to relieve the crushing pressure in my chest, but it's no use, so I stop trying. Vampires don't really need to breathe, right?

"Oh, I searched for a long time before I found this little gem," the mayor admits, and Grace's shoulders sink even lower. "But I stopped looking when I became mayor of Adarie. Isn't this town simply wonderful?"

The mayor is grinning as he throws his hands out in a "just look at all of this" pose.

Then he pushes away from the table and stands. "I'm afraid I have to leave now—a mayor's work is never done. But before I go…" He stops for a moment, looks back and forth between both of us before continuing. "We expect every member of our community to be productive. All right?"

Before either of us can answer, he tucks his chair in. Then calls over the counter to the woman ringing up another customer. "Gillie! Do me a favor, will you?"

"Of course, Mayor," the woman says from her spot behind the cash register.

"Grace here needs a job. Do you think you could take down that HELP

WANTED sign in your window and give her a chance?"

"For you, Mayor, anything!" She smiles at Grace. "Why don't you stop by around ten tomorrow morning, and we'll figure out what you can do. Sound good?"

"Sounds great," Grace tells her, but she sounds anything but excited. Which makes sense. Getting a job in this place is just one more signal that she's never going home again.

The mayor beams. "My pleasure. Anything else you need, you just let me know. Here in Adarie, we like to take care of our own."

"Is that what we are now?" I ask as he walks to the door. "Your own?"

He gives me a steady look. "I'm pretty sure that's up to you. Your time here—however long or short it is—will always be what you make of it. My advice is to make the best of it."

76

The Choux on the Wrong Foot
—Grace—

The mayor's advice is still ringing in my ears the next morning when Hudson and I get dressed in our last sets of clean clothes.

"We're going to need to find a Laundromat today," he says, and I'm a little surprised. He hasn't really said anything to me since we left the mayor yesterday. He said he was tired as soon as we got back to the inn, took a quick shower, and went to bed.

That was it. No teasing glances. No heated looks. No mention of the *moment* back at the audition. Nothing. Just a quick "I'm tired" and then to bed.

Actually, that isn't entirely true.

He also rolled to the very edge of his part of the bed, his back to my side, in a very clear message that he was not in the mood to talk, much less accidentally touch me.

I'd eventually drifted off to a fitful sleep, convincing myself that performing like that had just left him unsettled. He was probably feeling vulnerable, and I wanted to respect his need for space.

But by the time I woke this morning, his side of the bed was already cold. Almost as cold as the distance yawning between us. I was going to give him till dinner to work through whatever was on his mind, but after that—all bets were off. I barely made it a day with Polite Hudson. I sincerely doubted I could make it even half that long with Distant Hudson.

For now, I take a deep breath and try to act like his attitude isn't frustrating the hell out of me. "Or a store," I counter. "We could use some new clothes."

"Yeah, but I'd rather just hold on to what we have until we *both* get jobs, and then we can worry about trying to supplement our very meager wardrobe," he says.

"We'll see," I say as I tie my shoes. "I'm going to head down to the bakery and see if Gillie meant it when she told the mayor she would give me a job."

"And I'm going to see about finding a job," he tells me. He pauses, then adds, "Why don't we plan on meeting back here this afternoon and maybe taking a walk. We can check out more of the village. See what it's like."

Relief that he isn't going to shut me out forever makes me a little dizzy, and I can't help the smile lighting my face. "That sounds great, Hudson. And we still need to find Caoimhe and the guys. Make sure they didn't get into any trouble last night after the auditions."

Hudson just shakes his head. "Somehow, I'm afraid to ask that question."

"Good point," I say with a laugh. Then I wave to him and let myself out the door.

Even though Hudson and I walked these streets yesterday, I get a little turned around as I try to head across town to Gillie's bakery.

I end up on the far end of the town square—a part of town we didn't go to yesterday—and I can't help but note there's a huge statue in the center of the square. A shiver races down my spine as I realize it's comprised of two separate pieces nearly linked together—a woman holding a giant sword and shield and an enormous dragon, ribbons of fire coming from the creature's mouth and just grazing her forehead and the top of her shield. The whole thing seems impossibly balanced, and I'm careful not to walk too close.

The mayor mentioned the town mascot was the Fighting Dragons, but I had no idea they took their sports team this seriously. This is impressive as fuck, and I can't help chuckling that they're lucky their team wasn't called the Fighting Donkeys.

I backtrack a little until I see another familiar street, then hustle the rest of the way, opening the door of the bakery just as the clock tower strikes ten. Gillie is behind the counter, and she looks up with a smile when I walk in.

"There you are, Grace! Our regular help is out with a family matter for a bit, so I really hope you're still up for taking the job."

I've never wanted to work in a bakery in my life. I know nothing about pastries except that I like eating them, and almost everything I cook on my own is a total disaster—thus the now-infamous pumpkin pie that Hudson and I tried to bake together. But beggars can't exactly be choosers when they've got to pay for a room at the inn and some new, not Versace, underwear.

Right now, I need a job and this is a job.

"Absolutely," I tell her. "Where do you want me to start?"

It turns out the person she's replacing for a bit is actually one of the pastry makers, so I get stationed in the kitchen with a bunch of equipment I barely know how to use.

"One of our biggest sellers are our cream puffs and different flavored eclairs. So I thought I'd get you off with a basic choux pastry recipe." Gillie smiles at me encouragingly. "It's really easy."

"Shoe pastry?" I reply, questioning what exactly I ate last night in that swan. I knew it tasted a little funny.

"Not shoe," she tells me with a small laugh. "Choux."

"Shoe," I repeat.

I'm even more confused when she nods this time and says, "Exactly."

"Are there any particular kinds of shoes that go into the dough?" I ask, trying to figure out what the hell is happening in my life. And what I'm supposed to do about it.

"Shoes?" For the first time, Gillie looks alarmed. "Why would you put footwear in my pastries?"

"I wouldn't," I assure her. But she's looking at me a little funny and to be honest, I don't blame her. Then again, I'm pretty sure I'm looking at her funny, too.

"Have you ever baked before?" she asks as she takes out margarine, some purple egglike goo, and a lot of lavender flour.

When she doesn't put anything else on the counter, I breathe a sigh of relief. After all, how hard could it be to mix up three ingredients? Four, if you count the pitcher of ice water already sitting next to the mixer.

Very hard, it turns out, even when there are no shoes involved.

A few hours later, I'm covered in flour, margarine, and what I'm pretty sure is Smokey's weight in purple tofu pastry cream. My only clean pair of jeans is coated in whatever this egg mixture is, and my only pair of shoes might as well be choux—though the one positive I can actually say about this day is that I now know the difference between the two.

As if that's not bad enough, Gillie and the two other bakers working today keep looking back at me with varying expressions of concern. Then again, I'm concerned, too, so why shouldn't they be? After I butcher the fifth batch of choux, Gillie takes me aside and tells me that I'm being reassigned to the biscuit station, where I need to roll out the biscuit dough.

Which is already made, thank God.

This job seems right up my alley. I mean, all I have to do is grab a lump of dough, roll it out, then fold it over and roll it out again. I'm supposed to do this several times to increase the layering in the biscuits and then use a biscuit cutter to cut them out and put them on a tray.

After a morning spent in choux hell, this seems like a walk in the town square. At least for the first three seconds before my rolling pin gets stuck in the dough. And it turns out, that's actually the highlight of my day. Everything else is definitely an uphill pastry war—one where the soldiers just might have to eat choux leather if they have any hopes of survival.

The end of the day finally rolls around for me at about four o'clock. As I take off my apron—which is as useless as I am in the kitchen—Gillie comes out of her office, pulls me to the side. "You were great today, Grace. A real go-getter."

I say what we're both thinking. "But not a baker."

Gillie's eyes soften as she shakes her head. "Unfortunately, most definitely not a baker."

My shoulders sag. I got fired from my very first job. In one day.

I blink back the tears clogging my throat, but I can't fault Gillie. I actually feel like I owe her an apology. Not just for me but for every person in Adarie who might have to eat one of my choux swans today. I should probably issue a preemptive apology to them all.

I can only hope Hudson's day went better than mine. But at this point, I'm not counting on anything.

77

Ah-Choux

—Hudson—

When I get back to the room, Grace is already stretched across the bed with a pillow over her head. Her clothes from earlier are crumpled on the floor, and I'm sure there's a trail of flour or sugar or something baking-related leading from the door all the way to her spot in the bed.

"Rough day?" I ask as I bend over to untie my shoes.

"Choux," is her muffled answer.

"Gesundheit?" I lean over to try to get a better look at her face. "Are you feeling okay?"

"Not *achoo*," she groans. "Choux."

"I don't even know what that means." When she doesn't immediately answer, I pull back a little and think about it. Is she saying, shoo, like she wants me to leave? Maybe I pissed her off somehow earlier, although that hadn't been my intention. Is a guy not allowed five minutes to get over being punched in the gut?

I think back on our conversation, though, and she seemed fine when she left this morning for work. Still, I have to ask, "Are you telling me to leave?"

I really hope the answer is no, considering I've spent the last four hours trying to learn the difference between an angle sash brush and a flagged bristle brush, both of which can be used to apply any number of the 127 different shades of purple paint currently carried by the local hardware store—most of which are so close in color that I can't tell the difference.

Needless to say, it was an exciting day.

"I was telling you about the choux I made this morning, not shooing you away," Grace finally answers.

"Your morning had to do with shoes?" I ask skeptically. "What kind of bakery is this?"

"Exactly!" she agrees, then sighs. "Can you promise me that we will never talk about pastries again?"

"I'm a vampire, Grace. I *never* want to talk about pastries."

"Still, you need to promise me!"

Because she sounds just a little bit on edge, I hold my hands up in surrender. "I can absolutely promise that," I agree. "But I invoke the same courtesy for my newfound fear of drill bits."

"Drill bits?" For that, she manages to lift her head from under the pillow. "The little things that spin round and round in a drill?"

I nearly shudder just thinking about them. "Those are the ones."

Now she looks as confused as I know I did a few minutes ago. "Are you building something?"

"On the plus side, you smell good." I stretch out on the bed next to her. "And no, I don't believe anyone should ever trust me to build anything after today."

"It's hard to be covered in sugar and butter and not smell good," she answers. There's a long silence, then she continues. "Tell me about your day."

"I got a job at a hardware store today." I sigh long and low before admitting, "Let's just say I hope our friendship isn't dependent on my being handy around the house."

She laughs. "That good, huh?"

"It's not the selling that gets me. I can do that. I can stock the shelves and run the cash register. But who the fuck knows the name of every single tool, screw, nail, paintbrush, piece of wood, and who the fuck knows what else in the entire store?"

"I'm going to go out on a limb and say your boss." She lifts a brow.

"My boss," I agree.

"So after a very inauspicious start, we're both jobless again?" She raises a brow.

"Jobless? No, I go back tomorrow. Why—" I break off as the truth sinks in. "Wait a minute, you got *fired? On your first day?*"

"It was a very hard first day," she informs me with a sniff. "And that place wasn't a bakery. It was a portal to hell. I'm pretty sure that's why there's a padlock on the door in the back."

I laugh. I can't help it. "I'm sure that's what it is."

"Hey, you don't know! It could be." She makes a face at me.

"Maybe," I finally agree. "But probably not."

She sighs. "You're right. Probably not."

"Don't worry, though. You'll find a job you like," I try to reassure her.

"Forget a job I like. I'm just looking for something I can actually do." She groans. "Maybe Caoimhe can teach me how to sing."

"Orrrr maybe you should try the library before you quit your day job."

She picks up her pillow and throws it at me. "You're a real spoilsport, you know that?"

"Yeah. I'm a terrible person for trying to save the general public their eardrums." I roll my eyes.

"You don't know. I could be an amazing frontman."

"Maybe," I say, deliberately echoing my retort to her comment earlier about the portal from hell. "But probably not."

"Well, if you're going to be that way." She pushes herself out of bed and reaches for her shoes. For the first time, I realize she's wearing my last clean shirt—which looks like a dress on her—and nothing else.

"Where are you going?"

"To do laundry. And drown my sorrows in westeberry-flavored shaved ice. And maybe—just maybe—find a job that doesn't make me feel like a complete and total failure. You in?"

"When you put it like that, how could I say no?"

78

All LinkedOut

—Grace—

"**Y**ou're right," Caoimhe tells me as we walk through Adarie's shopping district two months later. "This shaved ice is incredible. I can't believe I've never had it before."

"Me either. There was a place like this where I used to live, and my best friend and I would go every day in the summer and try a different one of their hundred flavors—which was just about the same number of days we had in summer vacation, so it worked out perfectly."

She takes another quick lick of her treat and groans. "What was your favorite flavor?"

"Lemon-lime," I answer right away. "Heather always told me I was boring, but I would just say that I was a purist. Unlike her, who loved marshmallow and pickle shaved ice more than life itself."

Usually the memory of Heather and me teasing each other makes me smile, but today I have to clear my throat several times to get rid of the lump that just appeared there. I can't believe I'm never going to see her again.

I wonder what Heather is thinking right now.

At least Uncle Finn and Macy and Jaxon live in the paranormal world. At least they were there the day I disappeared and could make a hypothesis about what had happened to me. But Heather? She's got nothing.

One day we were best friends and the next day I just disappeared from her life. Is she worried that something happened to me? Or does she think I'm just a total bitch who dropped off the face of the earth when she got new friends? And if she thinks that, how hurt must she be?

Of everything that's come from us being trapped in this world, I think I hate that the most. Yes, losing Jaxon and the mating bond is pretty freaking horrible. But losing Heather isn't much better. More than a decade of best friendship gone in an instant.

"What's a pickle?" Caoimhe asks, her nose wrinkled. "It sounds funny. And so does a marshmallow."

"One's really salty and a little sour and the other is super sweet," I tell her. "Both are good on their own, but together..." I make a face.

"Unless you're Heather," she says with a smile that makes me smile, too, as I remember just how ridiculous my bestie is.

"Unless you're Heather." I take another bite of my lemony shaved ice as we weave around a couple leaning in for a quick kiss. I sigh. "Sadly, I think treats like this are going to be few and far between for me until I find another job."

She raises one eyebrow in question. "What happened to the farm?"

"Turns out I'm really, really bad at farming." I shake my head as I remember everything that happened during my two days at the nut farm. "Really, really bad."

"What about the receptionist for the doctor's office?"

"After two days, I was politely asked to reconsider my desire to work in an office setting," I tell her glumly. "I kept pressing the wrong buttons and hanging up on patients. I also maybe forgot to charge a patient before they left and then charged the next double."

She laughs, then tries to muffle it behind a cough when I mock-glare at her. "Wasn't there one more place you tried?"

"Yeah." I think back on my brief afternoon at the candle-making factory. "I don't want to talk about it."

"Okay, then." She holds her hands up in mock surrender.

"I never knew I was so incompetent," I tell her after blowing out a frustrated breath. "I mean, how can I be so bad at so many things?"

"It's okay. You'll find your thing." She dumps the last of her shaved ice in the trash can we pass. "It just takes time."

"What if I don't have a thing?" I ask as I do the same. "Because to be honest, right now I don't even care if it is my thing. I just want to get a job that I'm not absolutely terrible at. Surely that's not too much to ask."

"The guys and I could teach you how to juggle—"

"Definitely not," I cut her off with a chuckle.

"Hey, maybe you'll be really good—"

"No," I say again.

She sighs. "Okay, well, I'll keep my eyes out for any HELP WANTED signs around town. In the meantime, I've got to go meet up with the guys to practice for the festival tonight."

"You need more practice?" I ask. "You guys already sound amazing!"

She rolls her eyes. "Yes, Mother, practice makes even the best musicians better. You could tag along if you want. As long as you don't sing."

I laugh. "Tempting as that offer is, I think I'm going to keep pounding the pavement. Maybe there's some store I haven't filled out an application for yet."

"Probably a lot of stores." Caoimhe leans in for a very uncharacteristic side-armed hug. "Don't worry. You'll find something."

"Yeah, that's what Hudson says." I shake my head. "Of course, that's easy for him to say. He found his perfect forever job immediately."

And he did. He reported for duty at the hardware store for his second day, and the owner mentioned how sad she was that her daughter's teacher had retired that week. Hudson went straight to the school on his lunch break and filled out an application.

I would never have pegged the big bad vampire as a third-grade teacher—but he absolutely loved it. And he was good at it, too. Really good.

I popped by one day with a lunch basket just before class got out for recess, and he was reading a story to the kids about a giant umbra who lived in the mountains, and everyone was afraid of him. One day, a boy from the village wandered off and got lost in the mountains, and the umbra saved his life. The two became true friends, even though the boy couldn't stay in the mountains with the umbra and had to return home to his village to be with his parents.

A child with tufts of curly violet hair and round freckled cheeks raised his hand and asked, "Why wasn't the boy afraid of the umbra?"

Hudson smiled indulgently and asked, "Well, why do you think?"

And the little boy thought about this for a minute—I could tell he was really thinking—then he smiled and said, "Because he saw the umbra for *who* he was, not *what* he was."

Hudson smiled at the boy before continuing with the story, but if I'm being honest, I have no idea how the story ended. I was too busy trying my best not to blubber in front of his entire class. About how sweet Hudson is with the kids, and how they love him in return. About how he seems to have found a way to create a life in this strange new place that gives him purpose. About how effortless he makes it all look.

My thoughts drift back to the night before I turned eighteen in the lair. Hudson had asked for a truce for the evening, then tossed a gaming controller at me and we'd laughed and played Mario Kart until the wee hours of the morning. I can't help but think now that maybe he was trying to help me hold on to my childhood a little longer that day, sensed how sad I was that I'd missed so many firsts that were supposed to be a rite of passage into adulthood. Senior year. Graduation. College applications.

He bumped his shoulder into mine playfully at midnight and said, "We're the same age now."

It was such a ridiculous thought, I'd almost dropped my controller.

But then my eyes widened as it really sank in.

From what I'd read in his journals, Hudson may have been born two hundred years ago, but his father only allowed him to *live* a life outside the crypt one day a month for years, which, combined with his time at Katmere, added up to eighteen years today.

He'd just shrugged and said, "It's a long story, but when Jaxon"—he rolled his eyes dramatically—"*killed* me, I was eighteen and a senior at Katmere."

Which means Hudson missed out on all the same milestones I did, and yet, here he is, adulting like a pro. I really need to step up, stop my moaning, and figure out what I want to do for a living. Hudson is right. I can do this. Maybe.

Caoimhe wiggles her eyebrows. "You should listen to the vampire. He knows what he's talking about."

"You only say that because you think he's sexy." It's my turn to roll my eyes.

"He *is* sexy," she says. "And his brain is definitely part of that sex appeal. So listen to him. And stop worrying so much. Things will work out. They always do."

"Really?" I make a face. "You do realize you're talking to someone who accidentally crossed the barrier and is stuck in another realm forever, right?"

"And you've got me for a best friend and a sexy vampire for a...*roommate*." She wiggles her brows. "I'm just saying it could be worse."

The way she says "roommate" has little shivers racing along my skin.

Hudson and I haven't talked about what almost happened after the audition. And not because I haven't tried, either.

He's always up before me, or goes to bed after me, or—even more irritating—changes the subject. For a guy who wanted to have it out in a cave not too long ago, he seems determined now not to discuss what's going on between us at all.

And something *is* happening here.

You could cut the tension between us with a fucking chain saw.

I sigh. I should probably be thankful he's giving me space.

Ever since the mayor left no doubt that Hudson and I were never leaving Noromar, I've been trying to figure out what that means for me personally. I had dreams back home and now they're all gone, I know that. But dreams aren't something you can just throw out like the trash and not feel their loss. I need to replace them with new ones.

And getting a job that I enjoy, that I'm actually decent at, would be a good start.

Maybe then I'll be able to face how I feel about Hudson—what he's beginning to mean to me.

I glance up at the store I'm standing in front of and decide, *What the hell*. Maybe the local watchmaker needs someone to run his cash register or something.

"Hey!" Caoimhe calls from halfway down the block. "See you and your fine man at the Starfall Festival tonight?"

I'm about to tell her Hudson isn't my man, fine or otherwise, but the reminder that Noromar is about to have three straight days of darkness makes my stomach flutter like leaves in a summer wind. I swallow. Hard.

Hudson hasn't fed since the cave, and I can't help but wonder if he will tonight.

I call out, "Can't wait!" before heading into the shop and realize I mean it.

79

Getting the Red
Ribbon Treatment
—Hudson—

S mokey is so excited about going to the festival that she keeps jumping
and rolling around the room and bouncing herself off every piece of
furniture in the place.

"Hey, settle down," I say after she knocks Grace's clothes off the bed for
the third time. Grace's in the shower, but as soon as she finishes up, she'll get
dressed and we can go.

Smokey's only answer is a high-pitched yowl. Followed by a leap onto my
lap, where she bounces up and down a dozen times before winding herself
around my neck. Except she's so excited that she squeezes a little too tightly.

"Smokey, come on!" I gasp out, prying her from my throat. "You're going
to strangle me."

She mews sadly and cuddles into my chest as an apology. Then jumps
down and starts spinning like a top in the middle of the room.

"Okay, okay! If I give you the present I got you now, will you settle down
a little?"

She freezes so fast that she ends up stumbling and rolls halfway across
the room before she manages to come to a stop.

She looks up at me, obviously embarrassed, so I do my best not to laugh
as I scoop her off the ground. "Come on. It's over here."

On my way home from work today, I stopped into a boutique and bought
Grace a new dress for tonight. I haven't given it to her yet and I'm nervous
she'll hate it, but I wanted her to be able to go to the festival in something
other than her getting-raggedier-by-the-day jeans.

At the store, I also saw a couple of things I thought Smokey might like,
so I picked them up, too. "It's nothing big," I tell her as I reach for the bag.

She squeals to let me know it doesn't matter, then practically vibrates
with excitement as I open the bag and pull out her present.

Smokey screams when she sees the ribbons and snatches them out of my hands before I can even hand them to her. Then she dances around the room with them, chittering away as she twirls them with joy.

Apparently, ribbons were definitely the way to go.

I got her a pack of four different-colored ones—purple, gold, red, and rainbow—and I'm curious as to which one Smokey's going to choose for tonight.

It turns out she chooses two of them—the rainbow one and the gold one—draping them around herself like they're expensive diamonds instead of a few pieces of fabric. Once she's satisfied with how they look on her, she takes the other two ribbons and tucks them into the small nightstand drawer we gave her to use for her treasures.

Then she launches herself at me and gives me what I'm pretty sure is the world's most enthusiastic hug. She skips my throat this time, though, so at least I can breathe my way through it.

She's still hugging me when Grace comes out of the bathroom wrapped in a towel a few minutes later. She freezes when she sees the newly decorated Smokey, then grins hugely.

"You look gorgeous, Smokey!" she tells the small shadow. "That gold really brings out your coloring."

For once, Smokey preens under her attention, winding her way between Grace's feet. I, on the other hand, do my best to look anywhere but at the skimpy towel Grace currently has wrapped around her curves.

"Sorry, I forgot my—" She pauses as she catches sight of the dress on the bed. Unlike with Smokey's present, I knew this dress was for Grace the second it caught my eye.

Short (but not too short like at the audition) and flirty, with a fun skirt that she can move in easily. Back in the lair, Grace told me her prom dress had been red, so I knew she'd like this color, and I'm pretty sure it'll bring out her eyes—and the pink in her cheeks that I like so much.

"What did you do?" she whispers as she walks over to the bed to touch the dress with featherlight fingers.

"I thought you might like something new. It's…been a while."

"It has," she agrees as she continues stroking the dress. Right before she pulls a Smokey and throws herself at me, hugging me as tightly as she can. And all I can think is that if she wiggles any more, her towel—her thin, skimpy towel that is the only thing separating her body from mine—is going to fall on the floor.

I'd be lying if I said there wasn't a part of me that really, really wanted that to happen.

"Oh my gosh, Hudson, thank you so much!" she tells me. "I love it. I really love it."

"I'm glad," I answer as I awkwardly try to hug her back without doing anything to make the towel fall.

She must remember what she's wearing, though, because the second my hand touches her bare upper back, she jerks away with a gasp. "Why didn't you tell me I was in a towel?" she screeches.

"You just came from the shower," I tell her with a lifted brow. "I figured you knew."

"I forgot! Obviously!" She doesn't wait for another comeback from me. Instead, she grabs the dress and dives back into the bathroom before slamming the door between us. "I can't believe you didn't say something!" she shouts through the wood.

"Just because I'm a vampire doesn't mean I'm dead," I call back.

She cracks up, and so do I a few beats later. Which is good because it helps me convince myself that I'm fully recovered from that hug...right up until Grace opens the bathroom door and walks out in the red dress.

Which is when it hits me that no matter how hard I try, I'm never going to recover from this girl.

80

Starfalling for You

—Hudson—

Smokey is completely oblivious to the tension that has suddenly crept up between Grace and me. She takes one look at Grace and grabs onto her, then begins to pull/drag her toward the door.

"Hold on! I need my shoes, Smokey!"

The shadow yowls in impatience, but Grace just laughs. It makes my chest tighten to see them both getting along better. "One minute more, I promise."

She's as good as her word, and we're out the door moments later, even though she's being extra careful not to touch—or even look at—me.

The sun is just beginning its very slow descent as we reach the end of the inn's hallway, and I've never been so happy to see a sunset in my whole bloody life. I didn't realize how much my body craved the dark until it had to go more than two months without it.

Then again, it might be Grace's blood I crave and not the dark at all.

Stopping myself from drinking from her every day has been excruciating. Not because I'm starving but because I'm dying to taste her again. To have the sweet and spicy heat of her linger on my tongue.

"Hudson, look!" she breathes as she gazes out at the sky. "Isn't it beautiful?"

"So beautiful," I agree.

She glances up at me and her breath catches in her throat. But her voice is casual when she teases, "You aren't even looking at the sky."

I start to tell her I'm looking at something even more beautiful, but the line is so fucking cheesy, I just let it die. I need to hold on to some small shred of pride, after all.

"It's a sky. I've seen one before," I say instead.

"You are sooooo unromantic." She rolls her eyes as she reaches out to grab the stair railing. "Come on, let's go see the party."

"Baby, I am the party," I say as we reach the lobby landing.

"You and your Versace underpants."

"Um, I believe the correct term is 'boxer briefs.' And for someone who claims she doesn't like me, you certainly are obsessed with my underwear."

Grace turns to face me. "That's not true."

"Sure it is." I lift a brow. "I'm pretty sure you spend more time thinking about my former underwear than I do."

She looks surprisingly serious as she tells me, "I'm not talking about the boxers. I'm talking about the rest."

"The rest?"

"I don't dislike you. Maybe I did at the beginning, but—" She blows out a breath. "'Dislike' is definitely not one of the many, many different things you make me feel."

"Oh yeah?" Now both my brows are up and I'm leaning in, because this is getting interesting. "How do you feel?"

"Like I want to dance!" she says and takes off through the inn's cramped little lobby.

It's my turn to roll my eyes, because I really should have seen that one coming.

We hit the street just as the sun finishes going down. The moment it does, the festival springs to life around us. The lights turn on above our heads. Music fills the air. And hundreds of people pour into the street right in front of us.

"This is amazing!" Grace says as we look out at a village that's been completely transformed.

Everywhere we look, there are lights. Webs of fairy lights canopy each street, and strings of ornate, different-colored lanterns line the sidewalks. Flowers in every purple shade imaginable are woven through arches and into garlands that decorate everything from street signs to food carts to souvenir stands. They're also strewn through the streets, their perfume rising up into the air with each step people take on the cobblestones.

"What do you want to do first?" Grace shouts to be heard over the music.

"Whatever you want to do," I answer. Being with her is pretty much all I want out of this festival.

"Okay, then, I'm starving." She goes up on her tiptoes, trying to see over the crowd to where the food carts are parked. But since she's still several inches shorter than almost anybody out here—except for the kids—it doesn't do her much good.

"Come on." I take her hand so I don't lose her in the crowd—or at least that's the story I'm sticking to—and guide her across the street and down a couple of blocks to where a whole group of food vendors has set up.

"What are you in the mood for?"

"I have no idea what any of this is," she answers with a laugh. "But it sure smells good."

We stand there for several minutes as she watches what everyone orders, and eventually she steps up to a lavender cart with huge flowers painted on it and orders something on a stick and a few bottles of water.

I pay the guy, and then we walk through the crowds, her eating her stick thingy while I drink one of the water bottles. Music is playing, and she stops every minute or two to do a spin or shimmy her shoulders or shake her head and wave her curls back and forth.

She's smiling and laughing, her brown eyes sparkling in the fairy lights above us, and she's never looked more beautiful. As she finishes her strange veggie on a stick, I reach out and run the back of my finger down her face.

She stops chewing and looks at me, her eyes going from chocolate to black in an instant. I think about leaning forward and kissing her, but before I can, someone jostles her from behind and sends her careening into my chest.

Instinctively, my arms go around her and, though we've certainly touched in the last few weeks, this feels different. Better. And for a second, I forget how to breathe.

But then someone bumps into me this time, and I acknowledge I've got to get her out of this corner before she gets hurt.

So I walk us one street down to the carnival games section of the festival, which hasn't gotten busy yet. Grace grins when she sees them and asks, "Have you ever played any of these before?"

"Unless they have chess, the answer's no."

"Chess?" Her eyes go wide. "That's seriously the only game you've ever played?"

"Some people will argue that it's the only game worth playing," I counter, along with what I know is a smug smirk. But seriously. She doesn't actually think throwing Ping-Pong balls into fishbowls counts as a game, does she?

"Some people are snobs," Grace responds.

"And?" I lift a brow. "It's not like these games require any skill."

"Oh yeah? Pick one." She points a finger at me, then steps forward just enough for it to dig into my chest. "Pick one, and I will trounce you at it."

"Trounce me?" I repeat as I survey the games, weighing the pros and cons of each one. "Those are big words."

"For a girl?" she asks a little snarkily.

"For anyone," I answer mildly. "I draw the line at throwing balls at fish. It seems cruel."

"I always thought so, too. So we skip that one and go to…" She shoots me a questioning look.

"The Star-Crossed Ring Toss," I say, reading a sign above the booth with about a hundred bottles lined up.

"The ring toss?" she says, sounding surprised. "That's where you want to start?"

"That's where I want to start," I agree.

"Okay." She grins, and I get my first inkling that I might have made a mistake. Even before she says, "Let the trouncing begin."

81

All's Fair in Love and Ring Tosses
—Grace—

"**I** don't understand," Hudson says, voice rife with frustration as his fifth ring bounces off the bottles and goes flying out of bounds. "That one should have gone around the top."

"Shoulda woulda coulda," I tell him as I line up for my turn.

Everyone knows this game is rigged, but when I was younger, Heather's dad taught us a trick that *almost* never fails. You just line up the ring with the bottle you want it to land on, then take two steps to the right. And instead of throwing it up so that it can come down and land on the bottle, you throw it horizontally.

If the stars align and luck is with you, it will bounce off the bottle two away from the one you're aiming at, spin, and land directly on top of your bottle.

"You want some tips, young lady?" the old guy running the game asks as I grab my five rings.

"I think I know what to do," I answer, smiling at him sweetly. Then I stand back and let the first ring rip.

It hits the exact bottle I was aiming at, slamming down over the top and circling the bottle neck.

"Nice job!" The man makes a tally mark on the chalkboard. "That's one."

"Show me how you did that," Hudson says, eyes narrowed as he studies me.

"Oh, look! There's Lumi!" I tell him and, when he turns around to look, I let the second ring fly.

And watch with satisfaction as it, too, circles a bottle neck.

"Seriously?" Hudson demands, and I don't know if he's complaining about the fact that I've gotten two out of two or that I played a dirty trick to keep him from watching me. And honestly, I don't care. All's fair in love and ring tosses. Especially ring tosses.

"Can you do three for three?" the carnival barker asks, and now he looks a lot more interested in me.

"I can do five for five," I tell him. And turn my back just enough to obscure Hudson's view as I throw the third ring.

"Three for three," Hudson murmurs.

I throw the fourth and fifth, one right after the other, and this time I don't try to hide what I'm doing. They both land around the bottle necks, and the carnival guy crows, "Good job! I've never seen that."

Hudson just claps, a large grin on his face that makes me grin, too.

"What prize do you want?" the barker asks. "You can have anything here."

I look at the different stuffed animals, but there's really only one thing I want. "A flower crown," I say, pointing to the one I've selected.

"You get one for every two rings," he tells me. "So do you want another one?"

"I do, actually."

He hands me both, and I put one on my head before leaning down and plopping one on Smokey's. She squeals and spins, and I straighten up with a laugh. I smile at Hudson, and he looks like he's about to say something, but he shakes his head.

Instead, he adjusts the crown a little before stroking Smokey's cheek once, twice. Then he takes my hand and walks to the next game.

"Angry Clowns are my game," he says. "I can feel it."

I don't have the heart to tell him that they're weighted on the bottom, making it nearly impossible to knock them over. Then again, he is a vampire, so maybe...

Fifteen seconds later, I decide there's something to the vampire theory, considering he just hit the first clown in the line with the ball and took out the entire row.

"That's, umm, very impressive, young man," says the guy running the booth. "What prize would you like?"

Hudson looks at the bowl in front of him. "I still have two more balls."

"You do at that," the barker says, and he doesn't sound particularly thrilled by that fact. He also takes a large step back as Hudson prepares to throw.

He goes three for three and chooses a giant unicorn as his prize—which he presents to me with a smile. "Told you Angry Clowns was my game."

"They must have sensed a kindred spirit," I snark, but I hug the unicorn extra close. "What should I name her?"

"I have absolutely no idea." He looks bemused again, and I realize he's probably never had a stuffed animal—or any kind of animal—to name before.

God, he's had such a lonely, lonely life. Is it any wonder he doesn't trust anyone?

"Well, names can't be rushed," I tell him. "I'm going to have to think on it."

"What should we do now?" he asks after we've walked through all the carnival games. The festival has a couple more of my favorites, but I don't suggest we play them, because I don't want to waste the money we have left. One or two games to show Hudson what it's about, sure. Any more, and I feel careless. Only one of us has a steady income, after all.

"Maybe see if we can find the others?" I suggest.

"Sure." He turns us back toward the main square, making sure to keep his strides even with my much-shorter ones.

As we walk through the crowds in the square, a young woman, walking with the most adorable little girl in fat purple pigtails and chomping on purple cotton candy, waves at Hudson and shouts over the music, "Hey there, Mr. V!"

Then her little girl takes off and runs up to wrap her sticky hands, complete with cotton candy, around Hudson's waist. Hudson reaches down and tweaks one of her pigtails before grinning. "Well hello, Miss Ileda."

The little girl's mom rushes over and shakes her head as she tugs her daughter away from Hudson. "Now, now, Ileda, don't get Mr. V all sticky."

Ileda takes a step back and thrusts the stick with the fluffy purple candy on it up in the air as she asks Hudson, "Do you want some cotton candy, Mr. V?"

Hudson stiffens, and I know he's weighing hurting the little girl's feelings with the stomachache the treat would give him.

I lean forward and ask, "Do you mind if I have some? Hudson is allergic to sugar, remember?"

The little girl nods and gives me a big, toothy grin as I tear off a piece of the spun sugar and plop it into my mouth. I thank her, and Hudson says he'll see her next week in class, then waves and grabs my hand to lead me farther into the square.

My hand is probably sticky from the treat, but he doesn't seem to mind, so I don't mention it. His strong fingers flex around mine, and I give a gentle squeeze back as we weave through the crowd together.

We find the troubadours exactly where one would expect, in the middle of the biggest crowd in the square. Lumi and Orebon are playing and Caoimhe is singing while everyone around them laughs and dances.

Orebon spots us in the crowd and waves, but he never misses a note. And neither do the others, though they shoot us wide grins.

All around me, people are dancing and cheering and tossing money in the open instrument case lying at Lumi's and Caoimhe's feet. I start to dance, too. Swaying and spinning and shimmying in place.

I try to get Hudson to dance with me as well, but he's a steady no.

Other than holding out an arm for me to clasp while I spin, he has absolutely no interest in being my dance partner.

The longer we're there, the more raucous the crowd gets. Everyone's in great spirits, so no one gets upset or angry when they're jostled or knocked around by people dancing. But I can see Hudson growing more watchful the louder and drunker the crowd gets. And when someone falls backward into me—sending me flying forward—Hudson has had enough.

He gently grabs hold of me and slowly, inexorably moves us until we're on the edge of the crowd. More, he arranges things so he's on the inside and I'm on the outside, so that I'm free to dance and twirl and do whatever I want to while he uses his body as a wall to keep me safe.

And I feel safe, safer than I've ever felt in a situation like this. Hudson isn't taking the choice from me. He isn't trying to talk me into leaving or wrestling control out of my hands at all.

Instead, he's going out of his way to make the situation as comfortable as he can for me while still giving me ownership of what we do. No one has ever done that for me, not even Jaxon, who constantly wants to protect me by making sure I change how I behave. Hudson just makes sure that I have the space and security to do what I want when I want to do it.

It makes me like him even more.

Maybe that's why, in the space between when one song ends and another begins, I grab his hand and say, "Let's find somewhere a little quieter to hang out. Just you and me."

82

Star Light,
Star Bright
—Grace—

"O kay, you can open your eyes," Hudson tells me.

"Seriously?" I say as I open my eyes and try to get my bearings. "You brought us all the way to the top?"

"Nothing but the best for you."

"Best to push me off of, you mean?" I ask as I peer over the edge.

After convincing me to climb on his back and close my eyes, he climbed the town's immense clock tower, and now we're standing right behind the face of the clock.

The other three sides of the tower have a handrail which goes about to my waist and the rest of the area is open—giving us an incredible view of the lights and festival down below without most of the noise.

"How high is this thing anyway?" I ask as I risk another look over the edge, thinking Smokey might have been on to something when she refused to climb the tower with us. She's somewhere running around down below, probably making another bouquet of flowers to give to Hudson.

He moves to stand next to me. "Twelve or thirteen stories, why?"

"No reason. Other than wondering how long it would take me to plummet to my death if I fall off this thing."

"And people say I'm pessimistic," he adds with a shake of his head. "Don't worry, Grace. I won't let anything happen to you."

"That's what you say now," I tell him.

"I got burned rescuing you from a dragon less than an hour after we met," he reminds me. "That's what I've always said."

He's right. He did. "Did I ever thank you for that?"

"I don't want your thanks, Grace."

"What do you want?" I breathe, then am ready to kick myself because I'm not sure I should hear the answer to that question.

But it turns out I didn't have to worry because Hudson is nothing if not cagey. "What do *you* want?" he counters.

A million different answers spring to the tip of my tongue, some of them honest, some of them lies, all of them dangerous. So I swallow each but the most innocuous one back. "To dance. Come on." I hold out a hand to him. "I'll teach you."

He gives me an amused look. "I never said I couldn't dance."

"Yes, you did. Down there, when I asked you to dance, you told me you don't dance."

"Exactly. I don't dance. That doesn't mean I can't."

"Are you kidding me? You've known how to dance this whole time? That's so uncool."

"In what world would the heir to the vampire throne not know how to dance?" he asks. "Balls are still a thing in the Vampire Court—and a lot of the other courts as well."

"That's it. That settles it."

"Settles what?" he asks, but I don't answer.

Instead, I pull out my phone, which I still carry around mostly as a placebo, since the internet doesn't exist in this realm and calls can't exactly travel through the barrier. But the inn came with a handy solar charger, and the one thing the phone does still do is house things I've already downloaded. Including my music.

"What are you doing?"

"Picking out a song," I tell him. "Right here, right now, while we're on top of the freaking world, you're going to dance with me."

He looks wary. "I already told you I don't dance."

"Yeah, well, we're going to change that tonight."

He looks even warier. "Grace—"

"You know what? Pretend you're Nike and Just Do It, Vega," I tell him, right before I hit Play on the song I picked out and the first notes of Walk the Moon's "Shut Up and Dance" come through my phone's speaker.

Hudson cracks up. "This is the song you want to dance to?"

The song chooses that moment to hit the title lyrics, and I point in the air like they're hanging in a bubble above my head. Hudson shakes his head, but he grabs my hand and pulls me toward him in a very sophisticated spin.

And then he dances the hell out of me on top of that clock tower. Spinning, twisting, twirling, we cover every single inch of our makeshift dance floor. And when the song winds down, Hudson pulls me in for the big finish, a twirl and dip that would put any professional tango dancer to shame.

By the time he pulls me up, I'm laughing in pure joy. He shakes his head, then laughs along with me.

"You're freaking amazing!" I tell him. "That was so much fun!"

"Yeah?" For a second, he grins like he doesn't have a care in the world, and all I can see is his irresistible dimple.

It's so adorable—*he's* so adorable and pleased with himself—that it takes every ounce of self-control I have not to reach out and touch it. Touch *him*, in a very different way than we did while dancing.

But that's inviting something I'm not quite sure I'm ready for. Because with Jaxon, it was so easy, but I can admit now that it was easy because it was *simple*. Young love and all that. But with Hudson, I can instinctively tell it's going to be so much more. More complicated. More intense. So much more terrifying.

And so I clench my fists and use willpower I didn't even know I had. "Yeah," I tell him. "You're incredible."

"So are you." He takes a deep breath, looks like he's trying to work up to saying something. But in the end, he just blows his breath back out with a shake of his head. I feel myself relax, feel muscles I hadn't even realized were tense release in the space between one breath and the next. Even before he raises a brow and asks, "Want to do it again?"

I do, more than I want anything right now. More even than I want to get back home. "Absolutely." I reach for my phone. "Same one? It can be our song."

"Actually, I've got another idea," he tells me. "May I?" he asks, indicating my phone.

"Of course." I hand it to him.

He scrolls through my music for a second and then says, "Actually, I think this should be our song." And then he presses Play and the opening lyrics for "Rewrite the Stars" fill the night sky around us.

"Oh, Hudson," I whisper.

"Dance with me," he says. And this time when he pulls me into his arms, there's no spinning out. No twirling me around with a flick of his hand.

There's just him and me moving to the music—dancing around and around the clock tower—our bodies pressed together until his breath is mine and my heartbeat is his.

Until I forget where he begins and I end.

Until I start to believe the impossible.

When the song is over, I tell myself to step back. To move away. To pretend.

But I can't do it. I can't do anything but stare into his eyes and *want*. So I stay right where I am—in Hudson's arms—and whisper his name like it's the only thing that matters.

And so is he.

"It's okay, Grace," he whispers back. "I've got you."

And that's the thing. He does. I'm beginning to think he always has.

Maybe that's why I'm the one who makes the first move. The one who closes the small distance between us so that I can press my lips to his.

At first, he doesn't move. He holds himself completely still, like he's afraid to breathe and shatter everything. But I'm made of sterner stuff, and so is he. And as my lips move against his, he finally relaxes.

Makes a sound deep in his throat.

Lifts his hands to tangle in my curls.

And then he kisses me back. Oh God, does he kiss me back.

I expect him to ravage me, expect the tension from the last few months to explode like a supernova between us.

Instead, it builds like a song. Slow, sweet, beautiful, but no less powerful for that. And definitely no less important.

His lips are soft but firm, his breath warm and sweet, his arms hard yet gentle as he cradles me against him. And when he runs his tongue along my lower lip, I melt. I just melt and open like a secret.

He opens, too, like a memory just starting to form. His tongue brushes mine, and he tastes like magic, like a shooting star just starting to fall.

And I never want it to end. Never want to let go of this kiss, this moment, this feeling. I want to stay right here, with him, forever.

I want to hold him and devour him.

I want to comfort him and shatter him into a million pieces.

I want him to do the same to me. And I'm afraid that he might already have. Am afraid he might be doing it right now.

My hands creep up to tangle in his shirt, and I want to hold him until time stops. But he's already pulling away, already smoothing a hand over my hair as he whispers, "Okay?"

I nod because I've forgotten that sounds make words.

"Good." And then he's kissing me again. And again. And again. Until the song becomes a symphony, and the secret becomes the most powerful truth.

Then he kisses me again. And I kiss him because nothing has ever felt this right.

When he finally pulls back just far enough to look into my eyes, I feel something shift in my chest. And when he turns me around to watch as a shower of falling stars burns through the sky, I know that nothing is ever going to be the same again.

83

On Top of
the (Other)World
—Grace—

"I guess this is why they call it the Starfall Festival," Hudson murmurs as he wraps his arms around me from the back.

I stiffen a bit, because it's so new for him to touch me like this—hold me like this—but being held like this by him feels good. So good. I have no idea what that means, but it's true nonetheless.

So with a sigh, I sink back against him, relishing the solid heat of him against me.

But it turns out he stiffened when I did—I can feel the tension in him that wasn't there just a few seconds ago. I snuggle back against him, try to let him know with my body what I don't yet know how to put into words.

But this is Hudson, and he wants the words. Because of course he does.

"Okay?" he asks, for what feels like the tenth time tonight.

It doesn't bother me that he asks, because I like that he's checking in. Like even more that he wants to make sure that I'm all right with anything—and everything—that happens between us.

And the truth is, I am okay. I really am. Confused, yes. Worried, a little bit. But still okay. And for the first time since we left Katmere—I start to believe that maybe everything is going to be fine. That I'm exactly where I'm supposed to be.

"I'm good," I tell him, because it's true.

"Yeah?" Finally—finally—he relaxes against me, and it feels so good. More, it feels right. Like this is how things between us were always supposed to go.

I know it doesn't make sense, considering there was once a mating bond between Jaxon and me. But that doesn't mean it's not true. For the first time, I wonder if magic can make a mistake. Is that why the mating bond between Jaxon and me disappeared? Because it never should have been?

The thought makes me sad—thinking of Jaxon always makes me sad now—so I shove it down, into a folder of things I'll deal with when it doesn't feel like my world is on fire.

Surely there will be a time when that happens, right? I just don't know when that will be. Maybe right now. This one moment where everything feels right. New, yes. But still right.

"How about you?" I ask, because I'm not in this alone. My feelings aren't the only ones that matter. "You okay?"

I can't see him, but I can feel Hudson smile deep inside me.

"I'm bloody fantastic," he answers.

Those words, in that tone, make me feel like I could fly right off the top of this clock tower. Which is something that's never happened to me before. Not like this, like my entire body is on the brink of breaking wide open and becoming something...more, for lack of a better word.

It gives me a kind of courage that I've never had before. Maybe that's why I turn my head to look up at Hudson and, in a very flirtatious voice, say, "Oh yeah? And why is that?"

He laughs, but his blue eyes are burning with the heat of a thousand flames when he answers, "I think you know."

"Do I?" I pretend to think. "I can't remember. Maybe you should..."

"Refresh your memory?" he continues for me, brows raised and eyes somehow even more intense.

"It is an option." I shrug with pretend disinterest.

"It is," he agrees, and now that damn dimple of his is flashing. But just as he leans down to kiss me again, fireworks explode in the sky all around us.

I turn back to watch as firecrackers in shades of red and white and gold light up the purple night sky. Down below us, people clap and shout with joy.

"They really know how to throw a party, don't they?" Hudson says.

"Yeah, they do," I agree. "Then again, you throw a pretty good party yourself."

"Do I now?" His eyes are dark, his grin just a little wicked.

"You really do." This time I turn my whole body to face him and wrap my arms around his waist as I press my cheek against his chest so I can hear his heartbeat, fast as a jackhammer, beneath my ear.

"What do you want to do next?" he asks as fireworks continue to explode all around us. "We can stay up here or we can go back to the fest—"

He breaks off as flames streak across the sky.

"What was that?" I ask, terror racing through me.

It's part of the festival, I tell myself. Just another part of the celebration. After all, what shows up better at night than fire?

It's no big deal, I repeat. It's all planned. It makes so much sense that I almost believe it…right up until the people down below us start to scream.

84

It's a Knock-Down, Dragon Fight
—Hudson—

The fucking dragon is back.

How the hell did he get here? And how the hell did he find us after all this time?

I spent those days at Arnst and Maroly's farm convinced the beast was going to attack and destroy their crops. I was on red alert the whole time, determined not to let that happen.

But when he didn't even try to show his face, I decided I was wrong. I figured he'd forgotten about us and gone in search of easier prey back in that no-man's-land we were in when Grace first trapped us. That or he couldn't actually cross into Noromar, since he disappeared pretty much the second we set foot in this place all those months ago.

But here he is, looking bloody pissed off as he drops down from the sky to buzz the festival. Flames shoot out of his mouth, set fire to the big white festival organization tent.

People run out of it screaming, and the dragon grabs someone—a short, curly-haired woman in jeans—and carries her high into the air as she screams.

"Oh my God!" Grace cries. "What's he going to—"

He drops the woman right in the center of the town square. I'm grateful that we're too far away for Grace to hear the squelch and the sound of her bones breaking when she hits the ground. But I can, and it's a sound that will stick with me for a very long time.

Especially since I don't think who he picked up, a woman with light-brown skin and thick brown hair—just like Grace's—is a coincidence. I think he's hunting very specific prey.

Grace whimpers as she stares down at the woman. It's not loud, per se, but dragons have hearing almost as good as vampires, and the last thing I want is for her to attract his attention right now. Not when he's apparently holding quite the grudge from our last run-in.

Grabbing Grace's hand, I pull her down to the floor of the clock tower so that she's hidden by the wooden guardrail that goes all the way around it. It's not a huge defense, especially if he catches our scent, but it's better than just leaving her standing up there to wave when he flies on by.

"What are you doing—" She breaks off as the truth registers. "He's here looking for us, isn't he?"

"Yes." And I'm going to make damn sure he doesn't find Grace. No way is she going to end up like that woman out there.

She, however, doesn't seem to have the same attitude about that as I do.

"We have to get down there," she tells me urgently. "We did this to them. We brought that thing here. We can't just leave them to fight him alone."

I know she's right, and if it were just me, I wouldn't hesitate. I'd already be down there. But now I've got Grace to consider. And the truth is, I don't give a shit about any of those people. Not when their lives are weighed against Grace's. I've lost everyone I've ever cared about in my life. No way am I losing her, too. Not here. And not to that fucking piece-of-shit dragon.

"Hudson!" she urges when I don't respond immediately. "We have to go!"

"I don't suppose you'd consider staying here and letting me go?" I ask as someone else screams bloody murder—seconds before another sickening squelch fills the air.

"Why? Because you're the man?" she asks scornfully.

"Because I'm the *vampire*," I answer just as scornfully. "It's a lot harder to kill me than it is to kill you."

"Yeah, well, I guess we're going to have to figure out how not to let that happen," she shoots back at me. "Because there's no way I'm sitting up here like some damsel in distress while people are down there dying because of me."

"Yeah." I blow out a breath, shove a hand through my hair. "Somehow I knew you were going to say that, but it was worth a shot."

"It really wasn't." She scowls. "Now, are we coming up with a plan or are we just going to wing it? No pun intended."

"What kind of plan do you have in mind?"

"I don't know. You're the vampire." She gives me a "don't you have something up your sleeve?" look.

"I love how the vampire thing only matters when you want it to matter," I grouse.

She gives me her most innocent look. "Is that a problem?"

And fuck. Even knowing what she's doing, I fall for it. Not the sentiment that things should always be her way, but still. When she looks at me like that, it's impossible for me to say no.

"How are you with heights?" I ask as the beginning of a plan starts to come to me. It's not a good one, but it's a plan, and that has to count for something, right?

"I mean, I'm up here, aren't I?" she retorts.

"Yeah, but do you think you can get yourself down?"

Another blaze of fire illuminates the night sky behind us—and her face as she gives me a very definite "what the fuck?" look. "Are there steps? Or do you just want me to climb on over the edge?"

"I was thinking climb over the edge, but stairs would be good, too," I say as I look around for a door.

"Wow. Ten seconds ago, you wanted me to hide up here. Now you think I can just pull a King Kong on the Empire State Building? Your faith is touching."

"I have no doubt you can do anything you want to," I tell her. "I just would prefer you not die while doing it."

"You and me both," she says, peering over the edge of the clock tower at the long climb down. "Stairs would be good."

"Fair enough."

More screams fill the air, and I glance down to see the dragon narrowing in on another one of the tents. This one is the bright red one that housed children's activities for the festival.

Horror tears through me. Because *no*. That's not going to happen.

"The trapdoor's over there." I point to a small rectangle in the floor. "Take the stairs and I'll meet you down there."

"What are you going to do?" she asks suspiciously.

"Try not to die," I answer. "Now go!"

I don't wait to see if she listens to me. Not with that bloody dragon bearing down on the tent full of children. Instead, I lever myself up onto the handrail and let out the loudest, most high-pitched whistle I can manage.

It works, because the dragon pulls up almost instantly, his head whirling around as he searches for the source of the noise. I do it again, even add in a little arm wave just to make sure he sees me.

"Hudson, no!" Grace screams.

"Go!" I tell her as the dragon spots me and turns on a dime, speeding straight for me.

The dragon's almost here and fuck. Just fuck. And can I just say, this is what happens when you let yourself fucking care about someone. You end up using yourself as unarmed bait for a bloody fucking dragon.

I never thought I'd miss my powers, but now would be a really good fucking time to be able to make this thing poof. Or, you know, crawl inside his mind.

But since neither of those things is an option, I do my best to avoid his flames and end up with a nice burn on my arm for the trouble. Which puts a bloody big crimp in my plan, but at least improvisation is a thing. So when the dragon turns at the last second to avoid crashing into the clock tower, I ignore the pain in my arm and jump right onto its back.

If humans can ride bulls one-handed for eight seconds, surely I can do the same with this dragon.

It turns out, dragons are significantly stronger than bulls, and they really, really don't like to be ridden. Or at least, this one doesn't.

He lets out a scream that I'm sure the entire village can hear and then completely loses his shit. Like, full-on barrel spinning, twisting, bucking, roaring, belching flames loses his shit. And since we're still over a hundred feet in the air, it pretty much sucks for me.

But I'm not going down without a fight, not when this thing seems so desperate to get his claws into Grace. If I'm the only thing standing between this dragon and her, I'm going to make sure I take him down with me.

So, ignoring the pain in my injured arm, I dig in. I grab onto a couple of the dragon's scales that are within my reach, gouging my fingers through the hard plates to the tender muscle below.

The dragon screams and flies straight up, twisting and turning in an effort to get me to let go. But I've got a good grip, and I'm hanging on. Because the longer it's preoccupied by me, the more time people on the ground have to get to safety.

Please let Grace be one of the ones who runs to safety.

God knows I'm not doing this for my health.

Unfortunately, it doesn't take long for the dragon to figure out that he's not going to shake me anytime soon and decides to change tacks. Dropping out of his vertical climb, he dives back down toward the village.

"Don't you fucking dare, you bloody bastard," I growl as he takes aim at the red tent again.

But there's not a lot I can do from this position, except use every ounce of strength I have to dig my fingers into his sides. If I can wound him, maybe he will decide it's not worth it to attack right now.

This time, I manage to tear through the scales. Blood courses over my hands, making them slippery—and making it a lot harder for me to hang on. Especially since the dragon starts screaming in rage, his giant body shaking and jerking in pain.

I would probably feel bad about this if he hadn't spent every second he's been around us trying to flame roast Grace and me. Add in the fact that my arm is currently throbbing down to the bone as I hang on and try to direct him away from killing a tent full of *children*, and my sympathy meter is at an all-time low.

At the last second, though, the dragon swerves away from the red tent. I don't know what made him do it and honestly, I don't care as long as the children are safe. But as he barrels straight toward the side of one of the big brick buildings surrounding the square, I get an inkling of what he's about to do.

Well, shite, is all I can think before pain explodes through every inch of my body.

85

Dragon Me
Over the Coals
—Grace—

I make it down the clock-tower stairs just in time to see the dragon roll to his left and jam his back against the side of the giant library across from the stage—and in doing so, slam Hudson against him as well.

I scream and take off running, terror pounding through my every cell. The dragon is huge—at least as big as five SUVs back-to-back—and the building is made of brick and stone. With the speed that dragon was going when he slammed Hudson into the building, there's no way—no way—he survived.

Please, God, let him have survived.

The dragon hangs there for a second, almost like he hit so hard he dazed himself—which definitely isn't a good sign. I will him to move. Will him to let me see Hudson breathe. Hell, just to let me see him.

Eventually, the dragon pulls away and somehow—some way—Hudson is still on his back. He looks roughed up and definitely the worse for wear, but he's still alive. And he's still hanging on, something that seems to outrage the dragon beyond measure.

He's snorting fire now.

Screaming with fury.

Bucking like a wild thing as he tries to get Hudson off of his back.

Even worse, he's flying higher. Building up speed. And circling around like he wants to have another go at slamming Hudson against the building.

I don't think Hudson would survive it. To be honest, I have no idea how he survived the first hit, and I know I have to figure out a way for him not to take the second one.

Of course, I've got a very limited repertoire of tricks in my bag, so it's not like I have a ton of choices here. In the end, I do the only thing I can think of. I take off running toward the library, screaming as loudly as I can. If the dragon is after me, and all evidence—except for the way he's currently trying to kill Hudson—points to the fact that he is, then it stands to reason that I'm the best distraction.

I just need to get his attention. It's harder than it seems, considering everyone else in the square is running *away* from the library and I'm pretty much lost in a crowd. Add in that I'm going against the very powerful flow of guests, and it feels like every step I take forward is followed directly by two forced steps back. It's not what I would call fast progress—which is a problem, considering the dragon has finally made it back around his loop and is racing straight for the library again.

"Hey! Stop! I'm here!" I yell, jumping up and down in a futile effort to get his attention. When that doesn't work, I look around for something else to help me stand out. But it's impossible to see in the stampeding crowd, impossible to do anything but struggle forward one small step at a time.

I can't be too late.

I can't be too late.

I can't be too late.

The words run through my head in a mantra, beat in my blood like a war cry. But even as I will them into existence, I'm terrified it won't work out. Terrified that I'll be too late.

And then I hear it. The sound of a trumpet cutting through the screams, dancing above the crowds, and filling up the tense night air. It's Orebon, I just know it.

I whirl toward the sound and there he is, on top of the gazebo in the center of the square, playing his trumpet as loudly as he can. He's trying to distract the dragon, to get his attention in the middle of all this chaos. And it's working, too. The beast veers off his course for the library and circles the gazebo with flames billowing from his mouth.

Orebon was expecting that, though, and is already on the run, his trumpet hanging from a strap around his neck. As the fire reaches him, he slides across the roof of the gazebo and right off the edge. Then he grabs hold of the lip and swings himself inside the gazebo.

Seconds later, just as I make it to the gazebo, the trumpet sounds again, its bright, brassy notes spilling out into the night.

I guess dragons and trumpets don't mix, because the thing is even more pissed. He obviously hasn't forgotten that Hudson is on his back, because he's still twisting and bucking in an effort to dislodge him. But he's also so focused on the trumpet that he's no longer trying to slam Hudson into a building, and I call that a win. At least for now.

Determined not to let anyone else suffer for what is obviously the dragon's vendetta against Hudson and me, I wait for the beast to head straight for the gazebo—straight for Orebon—and then I do the only thing I can do in this situation.

I step between them and I wait for whatever comes next.

86

Go Stone
or Go Home
—Hudson—

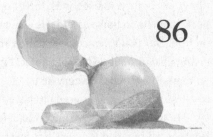

"Grace, no!" I shout as she puts herself right in front of this damn dragon. Like bait—or a sacrifice.

She made a big deal of telling me how she isn't going to do that again, and now here she is, throwing herself in front of an enraged dragon the first chance she gets? Because what? She thinks her life is worth so much less than everybody else's?

"Move! Go!" I yell, but she doesn't budge. She just stands her ground as the dragon bears down on her. More, she looks him straight in the eye as if she's daring him to attack her. Daring him to try to take her down.

It's a dare the dragon seems quite willing to take, considering he's got his head down, his wings in, and is currently laser-focused on her. I can't let that happen, though. There's no way I'm just going to sit here and watch this bastard take down the girl I lo—

I stop the thought before it can fully form. And ignore the fresh, cold slide of terror down my spine. The girl I like. No way am I going to watch him hurt the girl I like.

But no matter how good my intentions are, there's not a bloody lot I can do while sitting on this beast's back. I have to try, though. Because no other outcome is worth contemplating.

My brain races through possible tactics when I suddenly remember my old horse riding lessons and do what the instructor taught me to do on the very first day. I dig my heels into the sides of the dragon at the same time I pull back as hard as I can on the scales I'm holding.

I hated doing this to the horses, got banned from the stables for weeks because both my father and my instructor believed I was too gentle with the animals. But I'm not gentle now. Instead, I use every ounce of strength I have to bring this thing to a stop.

It works for a few seconds, the dragon bellowing in rage even as he rears back much like a horse would. He struggles, determined to overcome my hold on him. But that's Grace down there in front of us and there is no way I'm giving up without one hell of a fight. I'm not just rolling over for this animal, no matter how big and angry he is.

If he wants her, he's going to have to go through me first.

He must reach the same conclusion—and is not opposed to the idea. Because all of a sudden, he's not just rearing back. He's turning over. And I don't know what the hell kind of dragon this is, but I do know he's not the kind I grew up with. Because this one is flying upside down, but also because he does that thing he did before. The thing I wasn't sure I hadn't imagined.

He fucking skips through the air.

Through time, through space, maybe through both.

I don't know, and I don't bloody care. All I do know is that one second he's two hundred feet away from Grace and the next he's almost on top of her. And I'm not with him.

Instead, I hang in midair for about half a second—exactly where he was when he disappeared. Then I plummet toward the ground at an alarming rate. The fall won't kill me—I know that—but it sure as hell is going to hurt after that damn dragon dragged me across a building a few minutes ago.

Even worse—so much worse—he's landing in front of Grace right now, with a scream that can be heard for miles. And there's not a bloody damn thing I can do to stop him from here.

I hit the ground with a roll and a tuck that has me back on my feet in no time flat. I fade straight to Grace, determined to get between her and the dragon before it's too late.

Except I wasn't fast enough. I know that, even as I ignore the pain that's in every part of my body, and pull on all the strength I have. I'm not going to get to her in time.

But I have to try.

I lay on an extra burst of speed, aim straight for the dragon, but I'm still twenty-five feet out when he sends a spray of fire straight at Grace.

"No!" I scream, the words torn from my soul.

She doesn't move and neither does the dragon, who keeps up a steady stream of fire aimed right at her.

I'm there now, though, and I hit him in the side with every ounce of power

I've got. It works, too. The hit to his already wounded neck area knocks him sideways, has his screeches of pain and annoyance filling the night sky around us.

He turns on me and I'm trembling, terrified in a way I've never been before. Not of this damn dragon but of turning around and seeing what's become of Grace. My Grace.

But ignorance isn't bliss—it never has been for me—and I have to know.

So I turn, expecting the worst and yet totally unprepared for it at the same time. And there she is—Grace, but not.

At first, I think he's burned her so badly that he's turned her to ash right in front of me. My stomach clenches, my knees shake, and rage like I have never known wells up inside me. Rage and hate and agony—so much agony that I don't know what to do with it. I definitely don't know how to contain it.

It bursts out of me like a supernova, a wave of energy so intense, it's sure to destroy everything in its path. Then it just as quickly becomes a black hole. A pit of despair so violent, so empty, that it can swallow this world and any other it comes across. It sure as shit can take down one fucking dragon.

It's with that thought in mind that I turn back to the dragon, determined to annihilate him no matter the cost. But I've barely taken one step away from Grace when something brushes against my hand.

I turn back to her, startled, and notice it's her fingers that are brushing against mine. Except not exactly her fingers. Stone replicas of them.

Not ash, I realize as I gaze at her. As our fingers meet and join. *Stone.*

Grace is stone. And not stone as in a statue, either. This Grace, who is somehow—incomprehensibly—made of stone, is also somehow—incomprehensibly—*alive.*

87

Let Me Change into
Something a Little More Stony
—Grace—

The dragon takes off in a wild flapping of wings, his screams echoing through the square. I don't know where he's going or if he's coming back. I just know that I have a second to breathe. We all do, thankfully.

"Grace!" Hudson shouts as his hand wraps around mine. "Are you okay? Are you—" He breaks off as he stares me up and down, his blue eyes wide and wild.

And I get it. I do. Because something is really wrong with me. Or not *wrong*, but definitely different. My senses feel keener, and I feel stronger, too. Heck, I feel incredible.

"I'm okay," I tell him, because—by some miracle—I am.

I don't know how. I was sure that dragon was going to kill me, was prepared to die if it meant somehow giving the dragon what he wanted. If it meant he would leave Hudson and the rest of the people in this village alone.

Only I'm not dead—and neither is the dragon. I'm stone—except not. I can move. I can breathe. I can *talk*.

Which isn't terrifying at all. Because, yay for not being reduced to ash— this must have been how I survived that first fire attack when we left the lair—but what the fuck is happening to me?

Did the dragon's fire somehow do this? And if so, how do I fix it? I need to fix it. Like, now!

"You've got wings," Hudson says as he stares at me, slack-jawed.

"What do you mean?" I twist my head back and forth trying to see what he's talking about, and damn if he isn't right. I've got wings. Two wings. Two big freaking wings coming out of my shoulder blades. How is that possible?

What the fuck just happened to me?

"And horns." He tentatively reaches his free hand out to touch my head.

"Excuse me?" Horror rips through me as I bring my hand up to the top of my head. And realize, as my fingers tangle with Hudson's, that they are resting on a horn.

A freaking horn. Even worse, there are two of them. Sure, maybe that's better than one, because I'm not a freaking unicorn. But still.

Horns.

Stone.

Wings.

Fireproof.

And, oh yeah, did I mention I have HORNS?????

"What the hell is happening to me?" I whisper to Hudson as terror whips through me.

"Umm, I hate to be the one to interrupt what seems like a well-deserved freak-out." Lumi's voice comes from behind me. "But I feel it would be remiss of me not to point out that the dragon's coming back—with its bigger, badder older brother."

His words snap me out of the panic I'm feeling about whatever's happening to me. Or, if they don't snap me out of it, they at least refocus it. Because he's right. The dragon is coming back, and he looks pissed. And so does the friend he brought back with him.

"What do we do now?" I ask. Part of me wants to run, but can I even do that? I'm stone. I'm freaking stone. Stone can't run. Can it? "How do we fix this?"

I'm ashamed to admit that I'm not sure if I'm talking about the dragons or me.

"Hey, cool." Caoihme drops in from wherever she's been hiding. "You're not just a human. You're a *gargoyle*. That's even better."

"I'm a what?" I ask, and my voice is so high at this point, I'm pretty sure it's a dog whistle. Or it would be if the Shadow Realm had dogs.

"A gargoyle," Hudson repeats, like it makes perfect sense. "Of course you are."

"Of course I am?" I hold my hand out and stare at fingers that look familiar but not, because they're *stone*. "There's no 'of course' about any of this."

"Again." Orebon's voice sounds urgent from where he is still hiding inside the gazebo. "Dragons—plural—bearing down on us at three o'clock."

"What do we do?" I ask Hudson because my ability to think of a plan left right around the time I grew horns. "What do we do?"

"My first suggestion is to run," he answers, grabbing my hand.

"I don't know if I can do that!" I say, but then he's taking off, and I'm running right beside him. It's actually more like I'm jogging and he's dragging me along, but it works. And a quick glance back tells me our new friends are running right beside us.

"Where are we going?" I ask, breathless because running in this body is way harder than running in my own. Or maybe I'm just having a panic attack. It's a little hard to tell right now.

"Somewhere it's easier to run defense," Hudson says as we turn down a street and skid to a quick stop behind a tall building. His gaze is bouncing around the various streets, I'm sure calculating the best route for us to take next. "And somewhere without so many people around who could get hurt."

It's a good point. Even though most of the people ran at the first sign of the dragon, a lot of them didn't go far. And some are still in the square. They're hiding, but they're definitely here—and definitely dragon fodder if we don't get them out of here.

"Where exactly is that?" Orebon sounds doubtful. But that could be because a streak of fire is currently illuminating the sky above our heads.

"I'll let you know when I find it," Hudson answers, but he takes off again down a side street that leads to an alley near the outer wall, and we all follow him.

"Fantastic," Caoimhe shouts. "I've always wanted to be dragon bait."

"Well, then, you're living your best life, aren't you?" Hudson shoots back at her. "You're welcome."

Nice to know he's not too stressed out to snark. Then again, this is Hudson. When isn't he up for talking a little shit?

Except the dragons are right behind us, and I'm getting more and more terrified. Not for me, necessarily, because apparently I am now fireproof. But what about Hudson and the troubadours? They definitely aren't—as evidenced by Caoimhe letting out a shout of pain.

"Fuck!" Orebon says, and then he's on her, ripping off her military-type jacket—which happens to be on fire—before throwing it on the ground and stomping on it.

A dragon swoops by above us, and I tell Hudson, "We're running out of time."

"Yeah," he answers grimly before taking off again and leading us out of the alley and down a wide street at the other end of town. "I got that."

Up ahead of us, City Hall looms. It's a giant white marble building, complete with a dome and at least a hundred steps leading up to the front door.

"There!" Hudson shouts, pointing at it.

It's a good plan. If we make it up those steps, we're on higher ground and we've got a giant fireproof building at our backs, which will be a lot harder for the dragons to damage. Plus, we won't have to worry about a sneak attack from behind.

Add to that the fact that there's almost no one else around for the dragons to go after, and it's our best choice.

It's not perfect by any means, but it's better than the center of the town square, where the dragons could come at us from every direction. We run up the stairs—and can I say that a hundred stairs is about ninety-nine too many when you're suddenly made of stone?—with the dragons swooping around us, shooting fire.

They miss more than they hit, thankfully, but by the time we get to the top of the stairs everyone but me is a little—or a lot—singed. Looks like this gargoyle thing is good for something, at least.

"Now what?" Lumi asks, and I get it. Because I don't know what to do, and I can tell Hudson is a little off his game, too. Then again, not having his powers has to be disconcerting for him in this kind of fight.

Hudson doesn't answer. He's too busy staring down the dragon heading straight for him. Straight for us.

It's the smaller dragon, the one he injured earlier, but that doesn't make his fire any less dangerous. I move to get in front of him, terrified one good snort of flames and Hudson will be toast. But he pivots at the last second, blocking me as the dragon swoops down to get him.

And then he jumps about fifteen feet straight into the air. Because, who knew, that's a thing vampires can do.

"He's going to ride it again?" Caoimhe asks, and she sounds part awed and part exasperated—which I totally get. It didn't work out so well for him last time.

"I don't know—" I say, but it turns out Hudson has other plans. Namely kicking the dragon right in the chest with every ounce of strength he's got.

The dragon screams, but Hudson follows the first kick with a punch that has the dragon spinning backward through the air.

The second, much larger dragon swoops in with a warning snarl, and I take off running. Straight toward City Hall and the giant marble walls that make up the front of it.

The dragon is going fast—really fast—and that's what I'm counting on.

But I need to go faster, too, or she's going to catch me before I can put my plan into action.

I try to lay on the speed, but I'm no vampire and there's only so fast I can go when I'm made of *very heavy rock*—but then my wings start moving of their own volition.

"What the hell?" I whisper. But I'm not one to look a gift horse in the mouth, so I use them to propel myself even faster. I'm not brave enough to try to leave the ground yet with these things, but I'll definitely take the extra speed they give me.

Behind me, Hudson's dragon screams again, but I don't take the time to look back and see what's going on. Not when I'm almost there.

Five steps. Four. Three. Two. At the last possible second, I drop to the ground. And then I tuck my wings and roll like hell.

The dragon, who was so focused on me that she didn't see the trap I was leading her into, lets out one furious screech. She tries to pull up at the last second to avoid slamming into the giant marble wall, but the overhang on the building is huge, and she ends up crashing into it instead.

I stop rolling just in time to see her fall backward and hit the ground, feet in the air. She's so dazed, I can practically see the little cartoon birdies circling around her head, and I know that now is the time to move in for the kill. If I had a clue how I was supposed to do that...

But before I can even take a step toward her, Orebon calls my name. I turn to look and find that the smaller dragon has picked Hudson up and has him in his claws. Even worse, he's flying up, up, up, and I have a sick feeling I know what's coming.

I look to the troubadours for help, but as the dragon on the ground moves to come around, they all take off in different directions. Which I get—they've got no extra powers to deal with the thing, but still. Being abandoned sucks.

Hudson's already survived one fall tonight, plus being slammed into a giant wall. I don't know if he can survive a second, especially from the height this dragon is climbing to. Which means someone has to go after them. And since I'm the only one with wings...

I take a deep breath, check to make sure my wings are actually working on command and not just when they want to. Then mutter, "Here goes nothing," as I take a running jump off the stairs and pray that this isn't a complete and utter disaster.

88

Feather or Not, Here I Come!
—Grace—

"Grace, no!" Hudson yells. "You're made of stone! You can't fly—"

Well, shit, that would have been nice to know about two seconds ago...

I start to fall—fast. I squeeze my eyes shut because I don't want to see the ground coming—except, somehow, I'm not falling anymore. And I'm not made of stone, either.

I'm still not me—a quick glance down at my silvery hands proves that, as does the fact that I *have wings*—but I'm not solid stone anymore. Which does not, under any circumstances, mean I can fly decently. Because I absolutely cannot. I'm in no danger of hitting the ground anymore, but getting my wings to do what I want them to do is another story entirely.

I'm wobbly and can't fly in a straight line to save my life.

Every couple of flaps of my wings, I go sideways or down or straight—anywhere but where I want to go, which is a diagonal line straight at Hudson, who the dragon is still carrying higher. And higher. And higher.

And who is yelling down at me to go back to the ground, that it isn't safe for me up here. To which I want to say, *No shit, Sherlock*. Because who actually thinks it's safe for me to be doing this right now? But another thing that isn't safe is Hudson being dropped by a dragon from a thousand feet up. So if he wants to yell at anyone, he should yell at himself for getting us both into this ridiculous situation.

Of course, by the time I drop down for about the fiftieth time, I'm pretty close to yelling myself. How do people do this? Seriously. Flint made it look so easy, but this isn't easy at all. What am I doing wrong?

I try to think back to all the superhero movies I've seen. How did they fly? I think Iron Man had his hands by his sides, but I've been doing that since I got up here and it hasn't worked at all. But Superman flies with his arms out in front of him, right? It's not a look I'm confident I can pull off, but he doesn't die, so maybe I should try that.

But that's easier said than done, since the second I upset the kind-of sort-of balance I've finally manage to establish, I end up flipping upside down—which, for the record, is also not a great way to fly. Who knew?

Still, I'm not quite ready to give up on this arms-in-front thing. So I engage every core muscle I have, thrust my arms out in front of me, and use them to essentially guide where I want to go as I simultaneously imagine making powerful strokes through the air with my giant wings.

At first, it doesn't seem like anything has changed. But then I start to go up. And not just a little bit. I'm going *way* up, straight at Hudson, thank God. And this whole new arrangement makes me go *way* faster, so yay Superman.

In fact, I'm going so fast that I'm catching up to Hudson and the dragon, which is a very good thing because the dragon is leveling out, like he's finally reached cruising altitude. Which I'm terrified signifies he's about to drop Hudson.

The thought has me pushing myself even harder, to go faster, faster, *faster*.

I try not to think about how I'm not a great catcher at the best of times, so trying to snag a falling vampire in midair—while also managing to not die myself—might be a little above my skill set right now.

Still, I didn't come all this way up here for nothing. I have to try something. I just wish I knew what.

Suddenly, the dragon lets out a loud, pained screech, and I think Hudson did something to him, but then I realize he's finally caught sight of me. And he is very obviously *not* happy that I am up here in the sky with him and closing the distance.

To be fair, I'm not particularly happy to be here myself. But when life hands you fireballs, you learn how to juggle—preferably with oven mitts.

The fact that I left my oven mitts at home doesn't matter. Nothing does but getting to Hudson and making sure we don't die. Of course, that's easier said than done, considering now that the dragon has seen me, he's decided to stop climbing. And is headed straight for me—at what looks like an impossibly fast speed.

As the dragon turns, I get one second to exchange a look with Hudson, who is still clutched in his impossibly long talons.

"Go, Grace! Get out of here before—" He breaks off without finishing the statement. But then, he doesn't have to.

Get out of here before you die.

Get out of here before you crash.

Get out of here before the dragon kills you.

None of them sound particularly pleasant. But then, neither does the alternative, which goes a little something like this: get out of here and let the dragon kill me.

No, thanks. Not going to happen.

Unfortunately, I have no idea what *is* going to happen, but whatever it is, it's going to happen soon. Because I'm still going up and the dragon is still coming down—which means I am now engaged in a game of supernatural chicken. One I can't afford to lose.

Except the dragon has weapons I don't have—including the aforementioned fireballs. As our eyes meet, he snorts in outrage—and a giant billow of flames comes shooting straight at me.

Before I can even start to figure out how to dodge, my gargoyle takes over.

And I turn to solid stone—right in the middle of my high-speed, midair chase.

89

No One Wants to Catch These Cookies
—Grace—

I scream.

Hudson screams.

The dragon screams.

But that's pretty much all we can do, because the laws of physics still apply when you're a thousand feet above the earth. And it's too late to change course.

I've just registered Hudson's eyes going wide a split second before he ducks and the dragon and I crash into each other in a truly spectacular high-speed collision. And as any driver's ed class or first-year physics word problem will teach you, two high-speed objects traveling at each other hit with a lot more force than either one of them has on their own.

And when one of those objects is made of really heavy stone and the other one is made of flesh, there's only one outcome.

My outstretched arms pierce straight through the dragon's chest to his heart.

I have one moment to think, *Oh shit*. And then, just like that, I'm not solid stone anymore.

I am, however, buried up to my armpits in a dragon's freaking chest cavity. A dragon's really squishy, really squelchy, really slimy chest cavity.

I can't help it. I scream again, then realize what a truly horrible idea that was when the blood currently gushing all over me…gushes straight into my fucking mouth.

Because of course it does.

It tastes beyond horrible, and I start to gag, which has Hudson yelling in alarm all over again. And I get it, I do. This is not the optimal place or time to toss my cookies. But I am positive both Iron Man and Superman would have hurled by now. So why do *I* have to keep it together?

Well, besides the fact that I am directly above Hudson so, if I toss my cookies, he's going to catch them whether he wants to or not.

Since puking on the boy I just kissed is pretty much the last thing I want to have happen at the moment, I do the only thing I can think of to get myself out of this situation. I yank my arms back and out of the dragon as fast as I can.

I don't even have a second to blink before I regret that decision.

Blood sprays out of his chest cavity like two fire hydrants set loose and immediately coats Hudson and me in a thick, viscous orange wave from head to toe.

I barely have time to scream internally as I try to use the very tiny part of my palms that are still dry to wipe the blood out of my eyes. But as I'm doing that, the dragon's talons open and an even bloodier Hudson plummets through the air right in front of me.

Fuck!

Fuck fuck fuck fuck fuck!

I have no idea how to turn in midair, but I give it the old college try, thankful for all those months of jumping jacks Hudson and I did. And then I'm flying/falling after him, desperate to reach him before he splats on the ground.

Except the dragon is falling, too, in a full-on flat spin above us, and I'm not entirely sure he isn't going to land on top of us. Which makes it doubly important that I get to Hudson as soon as possible. We need to get the hell out of here. And we need to do it *now*.

Ignoring the blood and squick factor, I put my arms back out like Superman and aim for Hudson with every ounce of strength and concentration I've got. Except I've forgotten one thing—the other dragon. She's finally come out of whatever stunned state she was in and is gunning for us. Gunning for me.

Because of course she is. Two dragons for the price of one. Lucky, lucky me.

"Grace! Look out!" Hudson yells from down below me, like I don't see the giant dragon bearing down on me with murder in her eyes. Besides, how much "looking out" can I do when I'm focused on getting to him? I'm a good multitasker, but this is ridiculous.

I do manage to avoid the dragon's first pass at me with a midair somersault I didn't even know I could do. The somersault has another side benefit, too—it gets me closer to Hudson. But this time, the dragon isn't fooling around, and she does that weird "skipping through space" thing they do and makes up the distance between us in an instant.

Which eats up too much of the precious time I've got left to get to Hudson before he becomes a vampire pancake. So, with very little else left in my tiny repertoire of tricks, I do the only thing I can do. I fly directly beneath the dragon, then come up on her side. When I do, I grab onto her wing, will myself to solid stone again, and pull down as hard as I can.

She lets out a shriek of rage, twisting in midair in an effort to get to me. A shot of flames sluices by me as the dragon bellows again, but I ignore her as I grab onto her wing and pull again. I don't need to punch through her heart—something I never, ever, *ever* want to do again. I just need to sprain her wing so she can't fly. Surely I can manage that with what feels like a thousand pounds of concrete in my ass right now.

I pull on the wing a third time, yanking it out from her body at a weird angle, and it goes all topsy-turvy, her aerodynamics completely messed up. It's exactly what I'm trying for, so I hang on through the weird spinning roll thing she does and try one more time.

This time, though, she's so angry she shoots a long, powerful stream of flames right at me. And because I'm attached to her wing, she ends up hitting herself as well—and burning a small hole through her own wing.

Which seems really odd to me. Of all the creatures in the world, shouldn't dragons be fireproof?

It doesn't make sense to me, but then it doesn't have to make sense. All I need is for the dragon to be incapacitated for a little while, and I think this just might do the trick.

Letting go of her wing as she spins out, I instinctively lose my solid stone body and make a last-ditch dive for Hudson. This time, I manage to grab his hand, but he's so slippery from the blood—*don't think about it, don't think about it, don't think about it*—that his fingers slide right through my grasp.

"Don't worry about me!" he shouts, pointing above me at what I can only assume is a very pissed-off dragon.

I just roll my eyes at him. Because yeah, I'm not going to worry about Hudson plunging to his death. "Grab onto me," I yell back. And this time when I lunge for him, I manage to get my fingers around his wrist.

"Hold on!" I tell him, and thankfully, he does. His fingers wrap around my wrist as well, and then he drags me closer to him—which is exactly what I need right now.

Because once I'm close enough, I wrap my arms around him like a koala—not pretty or empowering but it gets the job done—and use my wings to fly as fast and as far away from both dragons as I can possibly manage.

The dying one plummets to earth, and I have a moment of feeling awful for the creature. Sure, he was hell-bent on killing me, but he didn't seem sentient as much as acting on some weird instinct that we needed to die. I don't question the feeling, but I do my best to shake the remorse and focus on not letting the second dragon finish the job.

I brace for landing—yes, that's how close it was for Hudson—but the larger dragon, with the hole in her wing, makes one last pass at us. This time Hudson is the one who reaches out and grabs onto her wing. Taking a play from my book, he yanks at the wing using a whole lot of that vampire strength of his, and there's a sickening crunch just before the eerie sound of canvas ripping fills the air.

The dragon screams and loses control, slamming into the ground. I pull my wings back in two powerful strokes, then land with Hudson as far away from the dragon as I can get. The massive creature tries to wobble to her feet again and then lets loose streams of fire in all directions.

At the same time, the troubadours come running forward, their arms full of rope, and I realize they didn't abandon us after all. But the moment they try to lasso her, she lets out a shriek of warning as she backs away. And then takes one more step before she disappears.

We have one moment to exchange wide-eyed looks before she reappears in the sky several hundred feet away. She's going slow, coasting on air currents more than she is actually flying, and I blink away the idea of going after her. About ending this once and for all.

Because I don't have it in me to attack an injured creature fleeing from me—that's no longer self-defense—so I let her go. And turn my attention to the other dragon, who is just slamming into the earth.

He hits hard, rolls until he comes to a stop in the yard of a giant house across from City Hall. Then he releases one long, shaky breath. As he does, silver droplets fill the air around him. Slowly, they start to rotate until they coalesce into something that looks like a cross between a wide double-helix DNA strand and a mini tornado. They spin, spin, spin around the dragon for several seconds before slowly rising into the night.

Sadness fills me as I follow their progress into the night sky, and I tell myself to look away. Tell myself that I don't need to see the dying last breath of this beast.

But deep inside, I don't think that's true. I killed this dragon—yes, he was trying to kill my friends and me and nearly succeeded—but still. I killed him. It is only right that I bear witness to what that means.

As I turn to watch his essence disappear into the night, for the first time I notice a man standing on a top-floor balcony of City Hall. He's wearing a hat and turned away from me, so I can't see his face—or really anything distinguishable about him. Except it's obvious that he, too, is watching the silver mist float up, up, up.

It sucks. It just sucks. But then again, everything about this sucks.

It sucks that this dragon has been determined to kill us from the moment he learned of our existence.

It sucks that Hudson and I nearly died several times tonight—and that we're both covered in sticky, nasty dragon blood.

It sucks that the dragon had to die. But, as I turn back to face Hudson, I can't help but acknowledge that it would suck even worse if we had died.

I didn't want this fight, I didn't pick it, but I'm not going to run away from it, either. Not now and not in the future, if that other dragon comes back.

Because if there is anything I've learned since I found myself in this strange and awful and miraculous paranormal world, it's that destiny has a way of finding you whether you're ready for it or not.

As Hudson comes forward and wraps one slimy arm around my shoulder, I can't help thinking that I'd better get ready.

90

Sucker Brunch Me

—Hudson—

"Are you okay?" I ask Grace, my hands still shaking as I pull her close, try to assure myself she's really here, she's alive.

She gives me a look. "Define okay."

"Good point." I laugh, because what the fuck else is there to do? "Are you injured?"

"I don't think so." She steps away to get a better look at me. "Are you? Those talons were sharp."

"I'm good."

"Good?" she repeats, her voice going higher. "You're good? Seriously?"

"I mean—"

"You've been slammed against a building," she interrupts, ticking things off on her fingers. "You've been dropped by a dragon—twice—"

"But I only hit the ground once," I say, trying to derail things before she gets even more upset.

Which is apparently the wrong move, because her voice goes even higher. "Like that matters? You are covered in blood, and so am I—"

"At least none of it's ours." I shoot her the most winning grin that I can, considering I am—indeed—covered in orange blood.

"You don't know that," she snaps back. "We'll revisit that statement after we've both had a shower and can be sure there's been no bloodshed."

I start to remind her that I'm a vampire, and I can smell blood from really far away—and distinguish human blood from, say, dragon blood, without even having to think about it. But judging from the look on her face, I'm thinking I should just let that go for now.

"Jeez, Gargoyle Girl," Caoimhe says as she and the other two musicians approach. "Who knew you were such a badass?"

"Certainly not me," Grace answers with a shudder. "Although, I've got to say, you throw a mean lasso."

Caoimhe grins. "I do know my way around a rope."

"Did you grow up on a ranch or something?" Grace asks.

Lumi and Orebon crack up at that, and Caoimhe just smiles bigger as she says, "Yeah. Let's go with that."

"You know what? Never mind. I don't want to know." Grace holds up a hand. "I don't think my heart could take it."

"Let's get you back to the inn, sweetheart," Lumi says. "So you can..."

"Bathe in bleach?" Grace fills in helpfully.

"Yeah, that."

"Good call." She walks a couple of steps, then stops. For the first time, she looks as lost and upset as I think she must be feeling. "Which way is the inn?"

"It's over here, Grace." This time I put a hand around her waist—to guide her, yes, but also to help hold her up. Adrenaline crashes aren't pretty, and I'm sure she'll be going through one any second. I want to get her to our room before hers hits too hard.

We wave to the troubadours and finally head back to the inn.

The knots still twisting my stomach aren't going anywhere until I can get Grace showered and checked out for injuries, but the walk home takes a lot longer than it should. With each step we take, more people pour out of the various buildings that line the street. And every one of them wants to talk to us and shake our hands.

That's not my scene at the best of times, and this isn't the best of anything. Somehow, rapidly drying dragon blood feels even more disgusting than wet dragon blood. Even so, I try to run interference for Grace, who looks like she wants to talk to people even less than I do.

She's too polite to tell them that, though. I'm not.

A little brusqueness gets us a long way and eventually we make it back to the inn. Only to find the mayor himself standing to the right of the front door, waiting for us.

"Grace, Hudson." He smiles hugely as he holds one hand out to each of us. "It's so good to see you again."

"You probably don't want to touch us right now," I tell him, holding up my blood-drenched hands with a smile that shows my fangs. The more tired Grace looks, the closer I get to running out of patience.

It must register on him because he goes from effusive congeniality to restraint in the blink of an eye. "I just wanted to say thank you for what you did for our village tonight. We're lucky you were here. You're real heroes."

"We're not," Grace tells him with a shake of her head. "We did what anyone would do."

I'm pretty sure that's absolute bollocks, but I'm not about to point it out to her at this moment. Instead, I pull the heavy wood door of the inn open and start to guide her inside.

"Nevertheless." Souil puts his hand on the door, holds it open for us. "I'd like to invite you to my house for brunch tomorrow. As a thank-you."

"That's not necessary—" I say.

"Of course it is, dear boy," he interrupts me with a smile and a clap that makes Grace jump a little. "Here in Adarie, we celebrate our heroes. So let's say one o'clock, hmm? I'll be looking forward to it."

He moves to let the door close between us—which is fine with me. But Grace darts her hand out at the last minute and says, "Thank you for the invitation."

Of course she does. Because even covered in dragon blood and absolutely exhausted, she's still going to be kind, still going to go out of her way to make someone else happy. Because that's who she is.

"Can we get your address?" Grace continues.

The mayor laughs at her request, and I'm surprised at how much younger it makes him look. As does the broad smile he shoots her as he waves her off. "Just ask the innkeeper for directions to my house. He'll be happy to provide them. Good night and sleep well."

He bows with a little flourish of his hand, and then he's gone, just slips into the shadows of the night, finally without a sun, with ease.

I turn around to find the innkeeper, Nyaz, staring at us from his spot behind the front desk. "It's the fancy house across from City Hall," he says, his face completely blank. "You'll recognize it by the dead dragon on the front lawn."

Before either Grace or I can figure out what to say to that, he picks up a book from the desk in front of him and goes back to reading.

"Last one to the room gets the shower second," Grace says. And then she steps on my foot—hard—before racing for the stairs. In the two seconds it takes me to recover, she's halfway up the first flight.

I chuckle and head for the stairs. If I fade, I can be in our room before she even reaches our floor, and I'm man enough to admit it might be worth beating her this one time to get to the shower first. Gentlemanly? No. But I have dragon blood in places no one should...

Before I can take off, though, the innkeeper—without looking up from his book—says, "Any woman who saves me from dying in a fiery dragon explosion gets the shower first for life."

"I wasn't going to—"

I break off when he harrumphs. And then he turns the page, making it very clear he knew exactly what I'd been about to do.

With a sigh, I walk to the stairs and head up at a very modest pace. How long can one girl spend in the shower anyway?

91

I Know How to
Hold My Drink
—Hudson—

"Seriously, Grace?" I ask as I pound on the door for the third time in the last fifteen minutes. Smokey—who is sleeping off the trauma of the dragon fight on the little rug by the window—makes a disgruntled noise before settling back down with a loud snore.

In a bid not to wake her, I lower my voice a little before knocking on the door again. "You've been in there for more than an hour. How long does it take to wash off a little bit of dragon blood?"

The door flies open, and Grace stands there in nothing but one of the T-shirts Arnst gave her and a warm, rosy-cheeked glow. "It was in my *hair*," she says, enunciating each word slowly and precisely. "Do you have any idea how long it takes to get drying dragon's blood out of every single curl of my hair?"

"I'm guessing an hour and fifteen minutes," I deadpan, "judging by how long you were in there."

"You would be correct. And pounding on the door every five minutes didn't make it go any faster."

"To be fair," I say, lifting a brow as I call her on her fib, "I only knocked three times—and those were all in the last fifteen minutes."

"Yeah, well, it seemed like more than that." She sniffs.

"I don't know what to tell you." Before she can say anything else, I step into the bathroom and close the door in her face. It won't take me an hour to get this dragon's blood off, but however long it does take, I'm anxious to get started.

Twenty minutes later, I step back into the bedroom to find Grace sitting cross-legged in the center of the bed eating a sandwich off a tray of food on her lap. "Nice towel," she says with a snort. Then, "Nyaz thought we might be hungry after our 'strenuous activity.' He sent up some food."

"We?" I ask, leaning a shoulder against the doorframe so I can watch her.

And maybe fantasize a little about what's under that nightshirt—and whether or not I'll ever get the chance to see it.

"Okay, he thought *I* might be hungry." She rolls her eyes. "But he did include some water for you."

She sends a bottle soaring across the room to me. I catch it and drain it dry—turns out I'm really bloody thirsty. And not just for water, but it will do for now.

Except Grace is watching me over the top of her sandwich, wet curls tumbling over her shoulders and big brown eyes filled with questions I can't read and probably don't have the answers to anyway.

Plus, I can't spend the whole night in a towel, so I do what I came out here to do in the first place. I grab my last clean pair of boxers—a plain black pair from the package Arnst gave me while we were staying on the farm—and my black sweatpants before I head back into the bathroom to change.

The second time I come out, Grace has already moved the tray to the dresser and is sitting at the end of the bed, looking more nervous than when she was staring down a pissed-off dragon.

"What's going on?" I ask.

It feels like she's focusing on a spot behind my shoulder when she says, "You have to be hungry, too."

I am. Really fucking hungry. But it's not like it was at the cave, not yet. I don't have to drink—I'm uncomfortable, but not in trouble. "I'm fine."

"I don't believe you." She stands up and crosses to me. "You can…you know."

It's my turn to roll my eyes. "You're not my personal blood bank, Grace."

"Yeah, but what if I want to be?" she whispers.

It's the last thing I expect to hear. Especially since she hasn't said a word about the kiss we shared earlier. Then again, neither have I.

The things that happened today that we haven't talked about yet could fill a library. That kiss. The dragons finding us. The dead dragon on the mayor's lawn. The injured dragon possibly coming back. And yeah, Grace being a badass gargoyle.

Although, I have to admit, that kiss is top of my list right now.

Since that's probably why she looks so awkward. Because we're stuck here, with no hope of going home, we just took a huge step in what I hope is our relationship, and she probably doesn't know where we stand anymore.

Then again, neither do I.

But I'm not sure if this is the right time to change that.

I don't have to be able to read her mind to know she's struggling to find her place in this new world. And that's without having to also figure out if there's a *we* in that future.

So I've given her space. Tried to respect her need for time. Tried not to take it personally that she apparently rushed into a bond with my brother at first glance but to even consider *liking me*, she needs to take her bloody sweet time.

And tonight, it's taking everything in me not to think about that glowing blue string I saw in her head before we left the lair. Part of me hoped it wasn't what I thought it might be. Part of me believed it couldn't be, since Grace was human, after all.

But the smarter side of me kept insisting Grace wasn't as human as she claimed, which meant...

I swallow the feelings clogging my throat as I stare down into her annoyingly beautiful chocolate eyes. No, now isn't the time for us to have any sort of heavy conversation about what we may or may not mean to each other.

Not with so many other questions and uncertainties swirling around us. At least, not if I really am sincere in not wanting to put any pressure on her while she figures out what she wants from me.

"What if I want you to feed from me?" she asks again, her chin rising as she bites into her soft bottom lip.

I study her for a second, trying to figure out the right thing to say in this situation. But I'm not sure there is any right thing to say when you're thinking about drinking someone's blood, so finally I settle on, "Is that what you want?" It's simple, clear, to the point.

Except Grace—in typical Grace style—still manages to squeak her way around it. "I don't want you to be hungry."

"That's not the same thing as wanting me to drink from you." Plus, I'm way too exhausted to do mental gymnastics with her right now. "Let's just go to sleep, Grace. We can talk about this another time."

She doesn't budge. And she doesn't stop looking at me with those big, soft eyes. "I think you took that the wrong way."

"How was I supposed to take it?" I lift a brow.

"Like this." She takes another step forward until her body is practically pressed against mine. Then she goes on tiptoe, loops her arms around my neck. And tilts her head to the side, exposing her jugular.

Because, seemingly, the queen of talking about *everything* no longer feels the need to talk. And fuck. Just *fuck*. How the bloody hell am I supposed to resist her? Especially when she smells so good and looks so good and I know—I fucking know—just how good she fucking tastes.

It's madness even thinking about it.

And yet I do think about it. I *do* try to resist. For both our sakes. Yes, we kissed. But it was just a kiss. I don't have a clue what that means to her. I sure as hell don't know what letting me feed from her so intimately means to her. And shouldn't I know before this goes any further? Shouldn't we both know?

"Grace—" Though it kills me, I start to take a step back.

"Don't," she tells me as her arms tighten around my neck. "I know you're confused. I'm confused, too. But please don't walk away right now. Please, just take what you need from me. I want you to do it."

Again, she tilts her head.

"Why?" I ask hoarsely, because I need the answer. But my eyes are already fixated on the pulse point at the hollow of her throat—and the way it's fluttering in and out.

"I need this, too," she whispers. "I need you."

It turns out seven little words are all it takes to obliterate a lifetime of self-control and set free the wildness within me. *I need this, too. I need you.* How can I tell her no when she puts it like that? How can I tell her no when I feel the exact same way?

The truth is, I can't. So I don't even try. Not anymore.

Instead, I wrap an arm around her waist and pull her closer, until her soft curves are pressed against the hardness of my angles. Then I bend my head, press my face into the silky, fragrant curve of her neck. And just breathe her in. Let her do the same for me.

My fangs drop the moment I'm pressed against her neck, but that doesn't matter. No one says we have to go fast. I can take as much time letting her get used to me as she needs.

She makes a needy sound low in her throat, and the self-control I have a stranglehold on begins to crumble.

But still I hesitate, until even I don't know what I'm waiting for. She's willing, more than willing, and I'm desperate for another taste of her. But it doesn't feel right yet. It doesn't—

She slides her hand up my neck, tangles her fingers in my hair. Whispers, "Hudson, please."

Turns out, that's all it takes to break the floodgates of my control. My name on her lips.

My name.

In response, I scrape the tips of my fangs along the slender length of her neck. Her skin is so thin here, so delicate, that I can feel her heartbeat right below the surface. It's mesmerizing. Irresistible.

As is the way she arches against me and whispers, "Do it."

The last vestiges of my control evaporate in an instant and I do what I've been dying to do for months. I strike, my fangs sinking deep.

Instantly, the taste of her—the strong, gorgeous, sweet and spicy taste of her—explodes across my tongue. It fills my senses, turns my knees weak and my control into a Molotov cocktail just waiting to explode.

And that's before I start to drink.

92

Drinks Are On Me

—Grace—

I'm trembling the second Hudson's fangs sink into my jugular. Not from fear or from nerves but from a need so powerful, it's all I can think about. All I can feel.

I didn't expect this. Maybe I should have, considering how that kiss in the clock tower went down. But he's fed from me before—in the cave—and while that felt good, it felt nothing like this.

Nothing in my life has ever felt like this.

Electricity sizzling along my every nerve ending.

Heat threatening to burn me alive from the inside out.

Pleasure—incredible, unbelievable, infinite pleasure—suffusing my every cell. Filling me up and wrecking me at the same time, until I want nothing more than for this to go on forever. For it to never, ever end.

Hudson shifts a little, growls deep in his throat. The arm he has wrapped around my waist pulls me even closer, until our bodies are plastered together and any distance we had between us—real or imaginary—feels like nothing more than a memory. And still, I press closer, still I want to feel more of him. Feel all of him in all the ways one person can feel another.

My fingers are already tangled in his hair, and I twist them harder, relishing the feel of the soft silk twisting around my fingertips as I bind him to me a little more with each breath we take.

Hudson's growl is louder this time, his body and his hands and his mouth—oh God, his mouth—more insistent as he holds me tighter, drinks me deeper.

And somehow, the pleasure grows even more intense, until I can't breathe under the onslaught of it all. I'm destroyed, totally ruined, my body nothing but an empty vessel begging to be filled by him.

Begging for more even though a part of me can't imagine there ever being more than this.

Begging for everything Hudson has to give me. Begging to give him everything in return.

I whimper low in my throat, and Hudson pauses for a moment to check if I'm okay. "Don't stop," I whisper urgently in his ear. "Don't stop, don't stop, please don't stop."

This time, his growl fills the room, echoing off the wall as he bites deeper, pulls harder, sending ecstasy arrowing to the very heart of me. I cry out as my body goes up and over, my hands shifting from his hair to his shoulders in an effort to hold myself while my knees turn to water and my blood turns to steam.

Nothing has ever felt this good. *Nothing else could ever feel this good.*

Hudson drinking from me is a total sensory overload, where the deepest pleasure and the sweetest pain meet and mingle inside me until there is nothing else. Until there is only Hudson and me and this one perfect moment out of time that I never want to end.

But eventually—like everything—it does.

Hudson pulls back, pulls away, and I clutch at him with desperate hands. He smiles against my skin before gently swirling his tongue over and around the bite marks he's left just below my ear.

"Okay?" he whispers against my ear when I press my hand to the back of his head to hold him in place.

"More than okay," I whisper back. Then, using every ounce of strength I have left in my body, I lean back just enough to see his face. "You?"

He grins. "Never better."

That makes me happy. "Yeah?" I ask with a little smile.

"Oh yeah."

And then he sweeps me into his arms and carries me to the bed. He lays me down gently, laughing a little as I clutch at him in an effort to keep him close.

"I'm not going anywhere, Grace," he tells me as he stretches out next to me and drops a gentle kiss on my lips.

I don't know if it's a promise or just a way to relax me, but either way, it works. Sleep rises up to claim me and, as I fall into it, I say, "Good," and give him the only promise that I can right now. "Neither am I."

He smiles against my hair, and I can't help hoping that it's enough.

93

I'm Spooning
Over You
—Grace—

I wake up slowly, warm and cozy in a way I haven't felt in way too long. It takes me a beat to realize why. I'm wrapped around Hudson, my front to his back. The big spoon to his little spoon. And judging from the way he's curled into me so that every part of my body is touching a part of his, he's enjoying every second of being that little spoon.

Which is fine with me, considering I'm enjoying the hell out of being the big one.

I cuddle even closer and start to open my eyes, but the truth is, I'm not ready to get up yet. I'm not ready to lose this safe, secure feeling I've got going on right now, and I'm definitely not ready to think about all the things I'll think about once I drift into full consciousness. Those things will hit me soon enough. I might as well enjoy these last few minutes of bliss.

But it turns out my wiggling around has woken up Hudson, and when he rolls over to look at me—smile at me—everything that happened last night comes roaring back, whether I'm ready for it to or not.

The kiss in the clock tower.

The dragon attack.

The blood.

The bite.

The whole gargoyle situation.

And just like that, the warm, fuzzy feeling goes away.

In its place is a lot of uncertainty and a whole lot of fear.

I'm not afraid of Hudson anymore—I haven't been in a very long time, if I ever really was—but I am afraid of what I'm feeling. And I'm even more afraid of what I'm not.

I know I'm never getting back to Katmere Academy, never getting back to my world. I'm never getting back to Jaxon. And the frightening thing is,

I'm not upset about it anymore.

Because I'm not the girl who fell in love with Jaxon. She doesn't exist anymore.

And it's not hard to figure out that *that* is the real reason why the mating bond is gone.

Tears bloom in my eyes—for him and for all we've lost—but I blink them away before they can fall. Because it's not just the mating bond that has disappeared. So has the girl I was when I first got to Katmere Academy.

That Grace was lost, unsure, determined to protect herself but not having a clue how to do it.

I'm a gargoyle now. A freaking gargoyle.

I fight *dragons*. Not well, mind you, but I fight them, and I win. Sometimes.

I know if I had stayed at Katmere, if this weird thing—whatever it is— hadn't happened, Jaxon and I could have had a good life together. If things had stayed the same and we had had the time to really learn each other and love each other, maybe we could have grown together and the mating bond would have held.

I'll never know, though, because that didn't happen. I ended up here, so we didn't stay together. We didn't *grow* together. The mating bond broke and so did we.

This last year and change has taken me on a different path. It's helped me grow and become, if not a different person, then at least someone who sees things differently than she used to. Someone who *is* different than she used to be.

And a lot of that growth is because of Hudson.

He pushes me, challenges me, and definitely never lets me get away with anything.

Which is why, mating bond gone or not, somewhere in the last several months, as I've changed and grown and come to accept that I will never, ever see Jaxon again, I've also fallen out of love with him. That's not something I can change. And I'm not sure it's something I'd even want to change if I could. He's a good person. He deserves someone who can love him as completely and passionately as he loves them.

The way the old Grace used to love him.

But that's life, isn't it? We change and grow and some people follow that journey with us, become an integral part of it, and others go on their own paths.

"Hey," Hudson says in a voice hoarse from sleep. "You okay?"

His smile has faded, and in its place is a blankness I haven't seen from him since those first months we were trapped together. Back then, he'd retreat behind a blank wall regularly. I never understood what caused it back then. But laying here, watching him now that I know him the way I do, I can't help but think it's a defense mechanism. That he's shielding himself from some kind of blow.

The fact that he still thinks that blow might come from me breaks my heart.

It also calms the nervousness deep inside me. The worry that things are becoming so different between us. Because it looks like I'm not the only one who feels a little anxious about it. Hudson does, too, and that makes it a million times easier for me to take a deep breath. A million times easier to tell myself that we can take this slow. See where it goes—or even if it's going to go anywhere at all.

Because it might not, and that's okay, too.

My feelings for Jaxon didn't change because I'm in love with Hudson.

They changed because of the shitty hand we were dealt.

They changed because the universe broke our bond.

They changed because of who I am now and who I am still becoming.

Hudson… Hudson is something else entirely, though. I don't know about him.

I don't know about us.

I don't know what I feel for him yet, not exactly, and I definitely don't know what he feels for me.

But the one thing I do know? Is that I'd like the chance to find out.

So instead of freaking out at the blank face he's currently giving me, I lean forward and press a soft kiss on his forehead—because morning breath is definitely a thing, and I don't want to scare the boy off before things have a chance to go somewhere.

His eyes close at the small kiss, and the arm he threw around my waist when he rolled over tightens. Pulls me closer. And while I'm feeling very mature about all the things I've just worked out in my head—or at least semi-mature—I'm not ready to talk about them yet. Or to hear him talk about them, either.

So I do the only thing I can do in this situation.

I reach under the covers, press my hand against the hard warmth of his abdomen.

And tickle the everlasting hell out of him. That he never saw it coming makes it a million times sweeter.

94

Talk Dirty to Me

—Hudson—

"You play dirty!" I squawk as I try to dodge Grace's determined tickles. The fact that I fell for that kiss shows just how gullible I've become. And how diabolical she is.

"If I do, it's because I learned it from the best," she shoots back, rolling on top of me to pin me down as she presses my wrists into the bed on either side of my head.

Maybe I should remind her that I can lift her with two fingers and not even break a sweat doing it. But since she's currently on top of me, with her legs on either side of my hips, I have no intention of issuing that reminder. Not when she's finally stopped tickling me. And not when I like her exactly where she is.

So instead, I feign ignorance. "I have no idea what you're talking about. I've been perfectly lovely since the day we met."

"Oh, right. I remember." She pretends to think. "Why don't you do your toucan impression again? I remember that being so very, very lovely."

"I knew you'd end up liking it eventually. It just took some time for you to come around to it." I give her a proud smile.

She returns it with interest. "I mean, what's not to like? It is *such* a beautiful, melodious sound."

"It really is. And if you like the toucan, just wait until you hear the white bellbird. Do you know their calls reach over one hundred and twenty-five decibels and sound like th—"

"No!" She slaps her hand over my mouth. "No, no, no! We are not doing birdcalls this morning."

I give her the most innocent look I can muster, considering she's covering half my face with her hand. And when that doesn't work—and, in fact, only has her narrowing her eyes suspiciously—I do the next best thing. I lick her palm.

"Eeeeew!" She gives me a "what the hell" look—which is fair—but then she does lift her hand. Which is also fair, in my opinion.

"Gotcha!" I tell her with a grin that might or might not be a little diabolical.

"Please." She wipes her hand on the sheet and shoots me a dirty look. "You did not."

"So you *do* want to hear the mating call of the white bellbird? It's not something you'll soon forget."

"One more birdcall," she tells me with narrowed eyes, "and you are never biting me again."

I lift a brow. "Is that a challenge?"

"It's a—" She breaks off as the alarm clock next to the bed starts ringing. "Ugh. We've got to get ready for *brunch* with the mayor."

I'm not sure which one of us was just saved by the bell, but it was definitely one of us. So instead of insisting we finish what I know is a ridiculous argument, I decide to take the conversational segue. "We could cancel. Spend the day in the village while the sun is still down."

"We could," she agrees, even as she rolls off me and out of bed. "But then we wouldn't be able to quiz him about how he was sure at the bakery the dragons wouldn't be a problem, and then they did their best to murder everyone. Besides, you saw that man. If we don't show up, I have no doubt he'll be here beating down our door ten minutes later. He seems very determined to thank us."

Smokey, disturbed by all the fuss in the room, makes an annoyed noise right before she slides under the crack in the window and shimmies down the side of the building. I think about calling her back, but it's not like she listens to me.

"He was very aggressive with his gratitude," I say after a few seconds, responding to Grace's comments about the mayor. I sit up, watching with interest as Grace bends over to rummage through the pile of dirty and semi-dirty clothes on the floor.

It's been a busy few weeks and laundry hasn't exactly been a priority. We're going to have to change that soon.

Then again, if we had clean clothes, I'd be looking at a very different view. And that would be a shame, because the way Grace looks in a T-shirt really is a thing of beauty. I've seen enough of her memories to know she disagrees, but I think she's bloody gorgeous—inside and out.

"I honestly don't think we have anything to wear that isn't covered in dragon blood or sweat," she says. "Grateful or not, I'm pretty sure old Souil is going to be unimpressed by our sartorial situation."

"Yeah, well, he doesn't need to be impressed." I walk over to the pile and pull out the pair of jeans I *wasn't* wearing last night. Yeah, they're a little dirty from school, a faint child's sticky handprint on the knee, but it's a lot better than showing up covered in blood.

Besides, we've got a brunch to attend. And like Grace said, the mayor doesn't exactly strike me as the patient type.

95

We Roll with
the Brunches
—Grace—

While I wasn't in a position to notice it last night, Souil's house is the most beautiful one on the street. Like pretty much every other house in Adarie, it's purple. But unlike many of the other houses, it's five or six different shades of purple that all work really well together. Add in the half-timbering on the front and sides and the boxes filled with cheerful flowers beneath every front-facing window, and the place radiates stately elegance and a charm I wasn't expecting.

Hudson rings the doorbell, and we're greeted by a woman with freckled purple skin the color of a field of heather and wearing a dark-purple dress and pearls. Souil's wife, I wonder, as she welcomes us in. Or his housekeeper?

"The mayor will be down soon," she says while showing us into the living room.

Housekeeper, not wife, I decide as Hudson and I take a seat on a gold velvet sofa.

"May I get you a drink?" she asks.

"I'm good for now, thank you," I tell her.

"Me too," Hudson concurs.

"All right." She smiles. "Please let me know if that changes. Brunch will be served at one thirty."

And then she glides away in the fascinating way all the people in the Shadow Realm have, as if her feet aren't quite touching the ground, although I can see that they are.

Once she leaves, Hudson turns to me with wide eyes. "This is …"

"A lot," I murmur under my breath, taking in the room. "A lot a lot."

I don't know where to look first, so I start with what's directly in front of me.

And what that is is a giant wall, wallpapered with different-size flower faces in overlapping shades of orange and red and gold. And hanging on that wall are three different paintings in opulent gold frames—two of them are portraits of Souil and one is a picture of a young girl who looks a lot like him.

One of the portraits showcases Souil holding a tennis racket, wearing the shortest white tennis shorts I've ever seen in my life. But my personal favorite—in an "oh my God that can't be real" kind of way—is the center one, where he's wearing a bright red caftan and lying down in a full centerfold pose.

The side walls are wallpapered in contrasting red and gold stripes and plenty of pictures are hanging on those walls as well—also of Souil and the mystery child. The curtains are a wild gold-red-and-orange diamond pattern that matches the giant shag rug on the floor and the pillows on the seventies modular chairs that are arranged in a separate seating area in another part of the room.

Plants are everywhere—giant trees in gaudy pots of all different colors hold court in the room's every corner while smaller houseplants are arranged on a bright orange plant stand that is very, very seventies.

And overlooking it all is a massive crystal chandelier in the shape of a disco ball. Yes, a disco ball.

I've never seen anything like it. To be honest, I'm not sure anyone has in this century. Or maybe ever.

"It looks like the seventies exploded in here—and their entrails were eaten by the eighties," he tells me in a voice even lower than mine.

"That's a very"—I search for a nonjudgmental word, but in the end, all I can come up with is—"appropriate description."

"I didn't know this many colors existed in the Shadow Realm."

"I didn't know this many colors existed in *any* realm," I counter, and I know my eyes are at least as wide as Hudson's as I look around.

"You make a good point." Hudson chuckles. "How big of a narcissist—" He continues in a nearly soundless whisper, but he breaks off just as footsteps come pounding down the stairs outside the room.

We turn as one to find Souil standing on the center landing of the circular staircase in a white disco suit à la John Travolta in *Saturday Night Fever*. Although standing might be a bit of an exaggeration, since he's currently draped along the banister like he's having a sudden attack of the vapors—or posing for *Playboy*.

"What the fuck?" Hudson whispers almost soundlessly.

I have no idea, but I'm not about to answer him when the mayor is staring down at me with the most intense expression I've ever seen on another person's face. Add in the fact that his shoulder-length white hair is slicked back into a short ponytail at the nape of his neck—à la John Travolta in *Pulp Fiction*—and I honestly have nothing to say. Except that if he suddenly bursts out in the chorus from "Greased Lightnin'" or threatens to rip one of our faces off, I wouldn't be the least bit surprised.

"Welcome, welcome!" Souil says, pushing away from the banister with a dramatic toss of his head. "I'm so sorry to keep you waiting, but duty calls."

"We've only been here a couple of minutes," I tell him, walking over to meet him at the bottom of the stairs, as he's taking his sweet time strutting down each step. "Thank you again for inviting us."

"Of course, of course." He spreads his arms wide. "Welcome to my humble abode."

I'm pretty sure Hudson chokes at that, but he doesn't say a word. Thank God. I can only imagine the snark going through his head, and right now my only goal is to get out of here without offending the most powerful man in Adarie.

"It's absolutely…fascinating," I tell him. "I particularly like the photo of you in the red caftan."

"Red *is* one of my best colors," he agrees with another toss of his head. Then he claps his hands and shouts, "Trudgey, Trudgey! We're ready for lunch!"

His voice is so loud, it bounces off the Sistine Chapel ceiling knockoff and echoes in the room. Within seconds, the housekeeper—aka Trudgey, it seems—glides into the room.

"Of course, Mayor. Let me show you to your seats."

And then she slides open the two ornate gold doors on the back wall and leads us into a dining room that just might be more garish than the living room—if that's possible, which I wasn't sure it was until this very moment.

"Have a seat," he says, beckoning to the carved marble behemoth that doubles for a table in the center of the room. "Place cards have been set up for you, so please find your name."

Place cards? There are only three of us here—and only three place settings on the giant table. How hard could it be for us to find a spot?

I don't say anything, though, and neither does Hudson, much to my surprise and relief. Instead, he simply holds out the chair in front of the place card with my name on it and waits for me to sit.

After I do, he takes his seat across the large table from me as the mayor sits down at the head.

As he does, the light from the stacked-glass, circle-cut chandelier—which just might give the disco ball in the living room a run for its money in terms of ugliness—illuminates his face, and I realize he looks different than he did the first time we met him. Younger somehow. The lines that had been so pronounced when he spoke at the festival auditions seem minimized, less craggy.

Maybe that's why he keeps these obnoxious chandeliers around—the light makes him look really, really good. That or he's had some very solid work done in the last few months.

Then again, judging by the vanity showcased in this place, I can totally believe he's recently had whatever passes for Botox in the Shadow Realm.

"Trudgey, please get our guest of honor a mimosa," he says, gesturing to me. "And some water for the gentleman."

"Of course," Trudgey answers with a smile. "What kind of mimosa would you like, dear?"

"Actually, water is fine for me, too. I'm not really much of a drinker and—"

"Nonsense!" Souil insists. "Trudgey spent an hour squeezing laranfon for you this morning, just so we'd have fresh juice. You simply must try it. It's delicious."

"Of course." I smile at Trudgey. "Thank you so much for doing that. I would love a larsa—"

"Laranfon," she helps me out. "It's a sweet and sour fruit the mayor simply loves. I'll bring you both some water as well."

"Thank you. I appreciate it."

She nods and gives me another one of her kind smiles. Then turns to Souil and says, "If you're ready, I'll send in the food."

"Of course we're ready!" he blusters. "It's after one. Grace must be starving!"

"Oh, I can—"

He waves me off. "You'll love brunch. Trudgey and her sister Tringia are amazing chefs." He puts his fingers to his mouth in a chef's kiss gesture. "Everything they make is perfect."

"I'm sure it is," Hudson says, then turns to her. "Thank you for going through all the trouble for us today."

She nods, then turns and heads back toward the kitchen. But no sooner has she left than the room fills up with people carrying serving tray after serving tray of food.

Some of the dishes I recognize—a fruit platter, for instance, even though the fruit is very different-looking than what I would eat at home. A basket of what I think are sweet rolls. Something in a pie pan that looks like it might be some kind of vegan quiche—if I ignore the fact that it seems to have been made using purple egg substitute. And finally, a steaming hot pot of what looks an awful lot like some kind of soft purple tofu.

I'm all for vegan meals—vegetables have always been one of my favorite things—but Noromar takes it to an extreme. I have nothing against normal tofu, but purple tofu? I'm not so sure about that.

"Is that a *fondue*?" I ask as one of the housekeepers puts a cast-iron pot down in the place of honor at the center of the table and someone else gives both Souil and me a little plate of bread and fruit to dip into it. A third person hands us each a long fork.

"It is! And it is just delightful! I would have it every day if I could, but Trudgey insists I watch my weight, so she reserves it for special occasions."

"Oh, we're not a special occasion—" I start, only to be cut off by another wave of his hand.

"Please, dear girl. The two of you are about as special as they come. I've been wanting to do this since you first showed up. It's been decades since I've seen another human-type visitor like you, Grace! This is a celebration! In fact—"

He gets distracted when Trudgey comes back in with a bottle of bubbly wine and a pitcher of what I'm guessing is laranfon juice.

As she pours mimosas under the mayor's watchful eye, I let my hair fall in my face and mouth to Hudson, *Human-type?*

He just shrugs and gives me a look reminding me that I'm the one who wanted to come to what is apparently a seventies-themed brunch, Noromar-style. Then again, Souil did say *decades*. Maybe that's why his house looks like an homage to disco. His last human visitor must have been from the seventies, and Souil thinks this is still the height of current human fashion.

I can't help but wonder what happened to that bell-bottomed visitor.

Which is why the second Trudgey is done pouring the purple mimosas, I turn to the mayor and ask the question that's been burning at the back of my throat since we arrived. "Why do you think the dragons attacked us? And are they coming back to finish the job?"

96

No Such Thing
as a Free Brunch
—Grace—

Hudson chokes for the second time in the last ten minutes—this time on a sip of water.

The mayor doesn't notice as he pulls in a very deliberate sip of his own drink and stares at me over the rim of the champagne flute.

"The dragons were after you specifically?" he asks once several long, uncomfortable seconds have passed. "Whatever gave you that idea?"

"Really? You didn't see how the dragon—" I lean forward in my seat, but Hudson shoots me a quick warning look.

So instead of bombarding him with the three million questions currently bouncing around inside me, I force myself to have some self-control and only ask one. "You've never said. How did you get to the Shadow Realm?"

He laughs as he spoons some fruit onto his plate before offering the serving bowl to me. I take it and do the same, even though food is the last thing on my mind right now.

"I'm pretty sure I got here the same way you did, dear."

"I don't understand." I look at Hudson for help.

"We got here accidentally," he says, finally joining the conversation.

"Accidentally?" Souil makes a face. "Is that what you're calling it?"

"What should we be calling it?" Hudson counters, and though his face is doing that impassive thing again, I can feel the watchfulness—and the impatience—deep inside him.

"Ancient magic, of course." Souil looks back and forth between us, as if trying to gauge our reactions. "I'm a time wizard. And you are a—"

"Gargoyle," I finish for him, trying not to react to the fact that the mayor just said the words "time" and "wizard" together. I'm not sure if I'm ready for what that might mean yet. So instead, I say, "Yeah, I just found that out yesterday. It's pretty wild."

"Gargoyle. Hmm." He looks at Hudson. "Is that what she thinks she is?"

"It's not what she *thinks*. It's what she *is*," Hudson counters with narrowed eyes.

Souil holds up a placating hand. "Of course, of course." But the look on his face says there's something more to the story. Maybe even a lot more.

"Is that not true?" I ask, more confused than ever but wanting to know. "Am I something else?"

"You would know that better than I, dear girl. I suppose I was just making assumptions." He takes a sip of his mimosa, then leans back in his chair. "Now, tell me, please. How can I help the two of you?"

"You're the one who invited us here," Hudson reminds him.

"I did, of course. To thank you for your truly incredible service last night. I'd like to give you something in exchange for your bravery. It was a sight to see. Such generosity is truly heartening."

"I don't know about that. I think anyone who could have would have done the same," I say.

"Well, that's the thing," he tells me. "I don't think that's necessarily true. Plus, I don't know that anyone else in Adarie could have done what you did."

"Kill a dragon?" Hudson asks doubtfully.

"Kill a guardian of the barrier," the mayor counters.

97

Time After Time Dragon
—Grace—

"**A**re you saying dragons guard the barrier between the realms?" Hudson sounds doubtful. "I've never heard that before."

"Not just dragons. Time dragons," Souil answers.

"Time dragons?" I think back on everything I've learned about the dragons. Including things that didn't make much sense before. "Is that how they can do that thing where they skip from one place to the next?"

The mayor gives me a proud smile. "It is, yes."

My heart is pounding in my chest, and I can't keep the excitement from my voice as I ask, "Can they get us home?"

Souil taps his napkin against his mouth for what feels like forever before he replies, "They can, of a sort, yes."

"And now we've killed one?" Hudson asks. "Which, I assume, is not going to encourage the rest of them to help us?"

"But he was trying to kill us. They both were," I insist. "They weren't trying to help us do anything except die."

"That's what the guardians do," Souil explains. "And there aren't hundreds of them—or even ten of them—if that's what you're thinking. Guardians—time dragons—are created when someone tears through the barrier between the realms. One dragon for every rift. Tears in the barrier mess with time itself, which is obviously not acceptable. So the God of Time created guardians to watch over the barrier and repair the rifts immediately."

"God of Time?" I blurt out because, yeah. God. Of. Time.

The mayor shrugs. "There are all sorts of gods, dear girl. Don't you know?"

I shake my head. "But why would the dragons come after us?" I ask. "What do we have to do with repairing a rift in time?"

Souil does a kind of back-and-forth thing with his head. "It's a little more complicated, but essentially, you shouldn't be here—and they won't rest until they rid the realm of you."

"And they get rid of us by—?" Hudson's eyes narrow like he's trying to figure out what happens next.

"Killing us," I whisper.

"I can't tell you that. No one can." Souil leans back in his chair and drinks the rest of his mimosa down in one long sip. After he puts the glass back on the table, he looks at each of us in turn. Then says, "What I can tell you is that the time dragons won't quit. They will keep coming after you forever, until either you're dead or they are."

That's pretty much the last thing I want to hear. Killing one time dragon was horrible. Not just the fight and the blood and the terror that went into it but the actual act of killing him itself. I didn't even *mean* to kill him, and I'm still upset that I did. Now the mayor is telling me that we need to kill a second dragon, or she will eventually kill us? Or—

"But if they kill us, we *might* end up back in our own world?" I ask on a breath, and I can sense Hudson stiffen. And I get it. Letting a time dragon kill you in the *hope* you might survive in another place seems silly as fuck, but still…if it were possible…I might be able to see Macy and Uncle Finn again. Graduate high school properly. Go to college.

"The only people who would know for sure that's what happens would, by necessity, no longer be here to tell us. Personally, I don't think anyone should risk death just to know for sure." The mayor shakes his head. "I'd imagine nothing worse than death by time dragon, honestly. If I were you, I'd not try to find out."

I don't want to believe it. I don't want to think that we're going to have to spend the rest of our time in Noromar either looking over our shoulders waiting for that giant dragon to attack or preemptively hunting her so she doesn't attack and catch us off guard. And so she doesn't kill any more innocent people like they did last night.

I think that's what makes me sickest of all about this whole situation. We managed to stop the smaller dragon—and injure the bigger one—before they injured too many people. But at the beginning, when the small one first flew into town, he killed that woman because she looked like me. He hurt other people because they were between us and him.

I hate that. I absolutely detest the idea that people in this realm died last night because of a mistake I made somehow when I trapped Hudson in my head. I detest even more the idea that other people might have to die before this is over. Because of me. Because of something I did that I don't even understand.

"Grace." Hudson calls my name just loudly enough to yank me out of my reverie. *It's not your fault*, he mouths to me.

I shake my head. Of course it's my fault. Who else's fault could it be? From the very beginning, when we were first together in the lair, Hudson has told me that I'm responsible. He doesn't get to change his tune now, just because I'm upset by the truth. And by upset, I mean pretty freaking traumatized.

"So what do we do?" Hudson asks Souil.

"There's only one thing you *can* do. You have to kill the time dragon when she comes back around in three months. It's—"

"Three months?" I ask, horrified. "We have to wait three months before she comes back?"

"Well, they only show up when it's dark, of course. And since it's only dark for three days every three months in the Shadow Realm..." He throws up his hands in a "what can I do" gesture.

There's nothing he can do. Nothing any of us can do. But knowing there's a real possibility of getting home, the idea of having to wait three more months before we can even think about trying to do so...it's not what I wanted to hear.

Souil clears his throat to pull our attention back to the conversation. When we're both looking at him, he continues. "You will kill the second dragon, won't you? You wouldn't want to hurt anyone else in our benevolent community, now would you?"

His words hit like a punch to the gut, but I lift my chin and offer another option. "We could leave Adarie before the dragon comes back."

Hudson opens his mouth to say something, probably to volunteer to lure the dragon away from town himself, but Souil blurts out, "Absolutely not."

Hudson closes his mouth, his eyes narrowing on the mayor, and my gaze bounces between the two of them.

Souil offers a kind smile and reassures us both, "This is your home now. We won't hear of you leaving." He motions for Trudgey to refill my champagne flute before adding, "You've killed one dragon. You only have one remaining to defeat, and you can live out the rest of your lives in this wonderful place." His next smile never quite reaches his eyes. "So it's settled then, yes?"

Hudson steeples his fingers. "We'll see."

And I can't help but wonder if we're going to have to fight a dragon in three months—or tonight.

98

Let's Talk About the
Time Dragon in the Room
—Hudson—

"That guy has issues," I tell Grace the minute we make it off his property and onto the street.

She presses a hand to her chest, looking shocked. "Why, Hudson, whatever do you mean? He seemed perfectly lovely to me." For one second, I think she's serious, but then she rolls her eyes. "What tipped you off?" she asks as we continue walking back toward town square.

"The fact that every room we went in had more ridiculous paintings of himself on the walls than the room before?" I suggest.

"That was a good indicator," she agrees. "Though I think the staircase pose was one for the record books."

"That was something else," I agree. And then, because *someone* has to bring it up... "So, umm, time dragons, eh?"

She doesn't say anything at first, and I let the sounds of our feet against the cobblestone road surround us, give her time to collect her thoughts. Because if I know Grace, she will have a *lot* of thoughts on the subject.

A ball rolls in front of us, and I reach down to pick it up without breaking stride and toss it to a young boy with short brown hair and dark-purple skin who'd run up after it.

"Thanks!" The kid waves, then runs back to a group of six or seven children, throwing the ball into the middle of the pack. Screams and laughter echo on the night under the strings of fairy lights as the ball is kicked from person to person in some sort of complicated rhythm, until one child holding a giant hoop tosses it over the ball. It's unlike any game I've ever seen, but they seem to be having fun.

I glance back at Grace, but she's still staring at her feet as we walk. My stomach twists a little because I think I know exactly what she's thinking—and what she's trying to work up the nerve to tell me.

"No," I say firmly. "We are not leaving Adarie."

She blinks with a "how did you know?" expression, and I roll my eyes at her.

"Because I know you would rather die than put someone else's safety at risk," I point out, and the corners of her mouth turn down.

Still, she says nothing.

Which scares the ever-loving fuck out of me.

Because right now, I can only think of one reason why Grace wouldn't be yelling at me that she's right and I'm wrong. She's thinking about jumping in front of a moving dragon instead.

"You are not bloody losing to a dragon on purpose, either." I can't help the anger leaching into my voice. "Would you really do *anything* to try to get back to Jaxon?"

Grace stops, her eyebrows hitting her hairline. "What the—" She shakes her head. "Hudson. No. I'd never even *consider* that."

"You still want to go home," I insist. "You asked about going home."

"Of course I still want to go home!" Grace shouts. "Don't you?"

And that's really the rub, I guess. I don't. "No."

She blusters for a second. "But—but—you don't even have your powers here!"

"Yeah, I know. It's bloody fantastic." I grit my teeth. "I don't have shite parents trying to use me. No pseudo friends who are actually scared of me. And honestly, no powers period to scare myself with *needing* to use. Yeah, I like it here."

I don't say the main reason I like it here, though. What it feels like waking up beside her every morning. Sharing a laugh about whatever silly thing Smokey did that day. Or hell, even fighting with her about whose turn it is to do laundry.

But I can't say any of those things. That would put too much pressure on Grace, and that's not fair.

"I never really thought of it that way before, Hudson," she murmurs and looks up at me with soft eyes. "I'm so sorry."

Well, fuck.

How did this conversation go from time dragons to a fucking pity party?

I run a hand through my hair, try to think of the words she needs me to say.

I want to tell her it's okay, that I understand. She has a life waiting for her back there. Family she misses, friends...Jaxon. Granted, we've only been here a few months, but it's been obvious from the start she's struggling to fit in. And I *want* to tell her I understand.

But I can't.

I feel like an artic is parked on my chest, and I don't want to be understanding about it.

So I don't say anything. I just shove my hands into my pockets and keep walking. I breathe a sigh of relief when she catches up and doesn't bring up shit she read in my journals.

"I can't believe there are time dragons hunting us," she says quietly.

At least, I think that's what she says. It's hard to hear anything over the blood rushing out of my heart.

"I guess," I say. There was a lot Souil said that made sense...but the things he didn't say left me with even more questions.

"Do you think that big one will come back tonight?" she asks as we turn the corner off the main square to a side street filled with little shops.

"Not likely," I say. "She probably needs to let that wing heal a bit."

Grace nods, finally looking up just as we pass a shop window filled with tiny baby clothes. She takes a deep breath, and I almost pass out from the fear of what she's building up to tell me.

Then she tosses me a half smile and asks, "So, what do you want to do tonight?"

It's so far removed from what I thought she was going to say that I just stare at her and blink. "Huh?"

She points at the still-dark sky. "We've got at least another day before we have to worry about the sun rising. What do you want to do?"

I let out the breath I didn't realize I'd been holding. Part of me wants to demand we discuss the time dragon and *not* possibly killing ourselves to go home. But in the end, a chance to spend more time with Grace without yet facing a future without her sounds like a great way to spend the evening.

"We could take advantage of the darkness to wander the shops for a while," I suggest. "Maybe I could even spend a little of my paycheck on you and Smokey."

She positively lights up at the suggestion. "That's a fantastic idea. As long as I get to spend some of *my* very pathetic paycheck on *you*."

"I don't need—" I break off when she glares at me. And even though the idea of her spending money on me grates when I want to shower her with everything she could ever dream of, I swallow the words and instead say, "That would be great."

"Excellent!" She rubs her hands together. "Then let's go do some serious damage!"

As we walk down the street, Grace laughs a little even as she shoots me a strange look.

"What's so funny?" I ask.

She shakes her head. "I was just thinking that never in a million years would I hear the great vampire prince, Hudson Vega, talking about his paycheck."

I understand what she's saying, but it still stings a little. "I'm not afraid to work."

"Of course you're not!" she rushes to say. "I saw you on the farm."

"Exactly. No regular prince would ever let himself get covered with that much tago milk."

Grace feigns confusion. "And yet you had no trouble sticking me with milking duty the next day?"

"Well, you *did* get me covered in leeches for it, so I'd say you're still winning."

She gives me a superior look. "I haven't mentioned the leeches once."

I narrow my eyes in a mock glare. "You haven't tried to throw them in my face because you know it's your fault."

"You're the one who got me covered in stinky tago milk!" she says primly.

"To which your completely proportional response was to toss me into a lake full of leeches."

She shrugs. "I didn't *toss* you. You...*launched* yourself. Besides, I liked that shirt, and now it's ruined forever."

"More than you like me, apparently." I roll my eyes at her.

"At the time, maybe." She reaches over, slips her hand into mine. And nearly makes my bloody heart explode, even before she adds, "Not anymore."

99

Distrust but Verify

—Hudson—

I can't believe it.

Two little words and I'm suddenly tongue-tied to hell and back. It'd be embarrassing if I wasn't also so…happy. It's a weird feeling, one I'm definitely not used to. Still, I'm trying to stay right here for a while and try not to borrow trouble.

I've grown adept at appreciating any small happiness I might have in the moment. Which is why I can be ecstatic Grace wants to be with me today, even if she might be thinking of how *not* to be with me tomorrow.

When Grace is by my side, it's even easier than it sounds. Definitely easier than it's ever been before. And yes, I am exactly aware of how pathetic that is. But that doesn't make it any less true.

I smile as I remember how excited I was to receive my first paycheck as a teacher, Grace dancing around our room and waving it in the air, chanting "Mr. V rocks" over and over. I can't help but think Richard would be very proud of me if he saw it, too.

It's strange to worry about money for the first time in my life. For all of Cyrus's and Delilah's flaws—of which there are a legion—they've always been generous with their money when it comes to Jaxon and me. And I always took it because I figured it was the least they could do after everything they've put me through.

Besides which, as a firstborn prince, I have a huge trust fund given to me by the Vampire Court itself. One that has nothing to do with my parents' money at all.

But that doesn't mean I mind having to work for the money to survive here—and the money to be able to pay Arnst back. I like the idea of having money only because I earned it.

We walk along, holding hands, for several minutes, taking in the different storefronts and trying to pretend the other people on the street aren't staring at us.

Then again, I imagine it's pretty normal for people to be curious about the vampire and the gargoyle who left a dead dragon on the mayor's front lawn.

On the plus side, Grace finds a candy store and a flower shop with HELP WANTED signs in the windows. I consider maybe applying for part-time work at the library, since elementary school here lets out by two every afternoon. Besides, the idea of being surrounded by books for a few hours each day sounds like heaven.

"Why don't we go in here?" Grace suggests, stopping in front of a small boutique that sells both women's and men's clothing. It doesn't have a big selection, but I consider that a bonus. I've spent the majority of my life wearing designer clothes I've got no interest in—mainly to play my part as a vampire prince for dear old Dad. This looks like the perfect change from that.

Though I would give a small ransom to have my Versace underwear back.

The second we walk in the store, I can't help wondering if we made the wrong decision. Not because there's anything wrong with the clothes but because the shopkeeper swoops down as soon as the door closes behind us.

"It's you!" she says, bustling toward us with a giant grin on her face. "Grace and Hudson! I was hoping I would get to meet you!"

Grace and I exchange an uneasy look. I take a step back, but it's already too late. The storekeeper has thrown her arms around the both of us and is squeezing us into a tight group hug.

"Thank you, thank you, thank you!" she says. "You saved us all."

"Um, I don't actually think we deserve any credit," Grace tells her awkwardly. "I'm pretty sure the dragons were here for us—"

"Nonsense! Whatever reason they came, they would have destroyed the whole village if not for you. And I'm so grateful that they didn't." She beams up at both of us. "Now, no more talk of unpleasant things. I'm Tinyati, and this is my store. What can I do for you today?"

"We're here because we're a mess," Grace tells her with the smile she has that always puts people at ease. "We had almost no clothes to begin with and last night pretty much destroyed the best things we did have. So if you have anything that might fit, we would be so grateful if you would help us find it."

Turns out those are the magic words, because it takes about five minutes for Tinyati to hustle us into dressing rooms with a pile of clothes in our arms.

Then, as we start to try them on, she keeps bringing more and more back, until it feels like we're working our way through the entire store.

I'm in nothing but a pair of unbuttoned jeans when there's yet another knock on my dressing room door. "I'll be out in a second, Tinyati!" I call.

But it's not Tinyati who answers. "It's me," Grace whispers. "Are you naked?"

"No, but—"

"Good." She yanks the door open and squeezes inside. Then sits on the tiny bench against the wall—the one currently covered in clothes I still need to try on—and pulls her feet up so that nothing is touching the ground.

"Problem?" I ask.

She focuses on me for the first time. "Seriously?" She throws a shirt at me. "Can you put some clothes on, please?"

"This is *my* dressing room. I'm supposed to be undressed in here. That's actually what it's for."

"Really?" she hisses. "You think this is the time to mansplain to me what a dressing room is for?"

"Sometimes it's just explaining, not mansplaining. And I only explained because you seem confused about the whole 'what people do in here' thing."

"For the love of God, will you please just put some clothes on?" She throws another shirt my way.

"Careful, Grace. You keep trying to cover me up, and I'm going to start thinking my half-naked physique makes you uncomfortable," I tease.

"It does," she answers, deadpan. "It makes me want to climb you like a tree, wrap my legs around your hips, and persuade you to have your way with me."

"Um." For the second time today—and pretty much the second time ever—I've got absolutely no comeback for Grace. Except, "The inn is just around the corner."

And just like that, her tone goes from joking to something charged with electricity. My mind is racing. My heart is racing. Fuck, everything is racing. I glance at the door, consider swooping Grace into my arms and fading us back to our room.

But then Tinyati is speaking, and the moment is gone. "Grace, where are you? I've got more dresses for you to try on. I can't wait to see you in the taffeta!"

Grace grabs my hand and mouths, *Be very quiet.*

"Grace?" There's a knock on the door, followed by Tinyati calling,

"Hudson, is Grace in there with you?"

"Too late. She's found me," Grace whispers huffily. "I rescind my offer, and now you'll never know why I came in here in the first place. Aren't you sorry you wasted all that time going on about your rock-hard abs?"

"To be fair, I never mentioned my rock-hard abs," I whisper back.

"Grace? Hudson?" Now Tinyati sounds concerned.

"You might as well have," Grace sniffs. Then she calls, "You can just put them in my dressing room, Tinyati! I'll be there in a second!" She turns back to me and whispers, "Taffeta. Pray for me."

"Sorry, I'm in mourning," I tell her.

She laughs. "As you should be. Next time, shut up faster." And then she walks out, leaving me alone with a pile of clothes and a bunch of thoughts that make trying on those clothes very uncomfortable.

Forty-five minutes later, we walk out of Tinyati's boutique loaded down with bags. We each decided on some new jeans, shirts, and underwear, but when we brought them up to the counter, Tinyati had a fit. I explained to her that we're pretty close to broke, which is why we're being so sparing with our purchases.

Of course that just meant she tried stuffing our bags with clothes we couldn't pay for—against our oft-repeated denials.

"They're on clearance," she kept repeating. "You'll be doing me a favor if you take them off my hands."

When I pointed out they weren't actually on clearance and that, while we appreciated the gesture, we didn't want to impose on her goodwill, I was told she had gone her entire life without having a man tell her how to run her business and she wasn't going to start now.

It's absolutely a fair point, so I retired the field and left Grace to fight. She didn't come out much better, but on the plus side—in my mind anyway—she is now the proud owner of a purple-and-hot-pink taffeta dress. Because sometimes the universe just hands you a gift.

Another plus? Grace also has a job. She starts tomorrow at eleven a.m.

Her eyes are glowing as she turns to me, and I can't help but hope that maybe this time, she's found something she'll love. I've always thought she had a great sense of style.

Although, if I'm being honest, all I can think about right now is if she was serious about climbing me like a tree. Maybe in that taffeta dress.

100

Whine and Dine

—Grace—

I can't believe I propositioned Hudson.

I mean, at first I was just trying to get a rise out of him—since he seemed completely unfazed that I'd dashed into his dressing room to avoid having to try on that taffeta dress. But then we were in that tiny space…and he was half naked. And making thinking difficult.

But then he'd suggested we head back to the inn, and my brain completely short-circuited.

I'd been deep in thought after the mayor's little brunch, worried about a time dragon attacking again, the poor people who were harmed yesterday and their families, all because of something I apparently did without realizing it.

How had I torn a rift in time in the first place? And if I did it once, can I do it again?

I'd been so thankful when Hudson suggested we go shopping. A normal activity to take my mind off the billion and one thoughts circling in my brain.

Now we have a new wardrobe, I have a job I think I might really enjoy, and…we have enough sexual tension between us to keep every fairy light in Adarie lit for weeks.

As we finish up our shopping, I'm about to suggest maybe we order some room service back at the inn when we run into the troubadours. While they all look a little worse for wear after The Great and Unfortunate Dragon Encounter, they do seem to be in good spirits and insist we have dinner with them.

Hudson and I drop our new clothes back at the inn, then head to the restaurant where we're meeting the others, right on time. They're already seated, so we join them amid a bunch of ribbing about how hard it is to make an honest living in retail.

"But seriously," Caoimhe asks after everyone's ordered. "Do you want to spend the rest of your life selling jeans and dresses?"

"Maybe," I admit. "We'll see how it goes after I try it, at least for the next three months. But at least my new boss seems super sweet, if a little bit pushy when it comes to taffeta, and I think she'll be really easy to work for."

"Three months?" Lumi asks. "What happens then?"

I shoot Hudson a look, but he just shrugs. I don't think there's any reason not to tell them about the time dragon coming back—or about it being an us-or-them kind of situation.

"The time dragon comes back," I finally say.

"Time dragon?" Orebon repeats. "Those things that attacked the festival are *time dragons*? How do you know?"

"The mayor told us," I say and then proceed to fill them in on everything we know so far about time dragons, rifts, and death warrants.

I don't know why, but I leave out the mayor mentioning he was a time wizard. That's one topic I want to talk to Hudson about later before I go blabbing it around town. Hudson hadn't seemed surprised when Souil revealed that bit of news, so I'm really hoping he's familiar with time wizards from back home and knows exactly what they're capable of doing. If nothing else, I figure it explains why the mayor looks younger today than he did yesterday. Maybe even why he's been alive so long? Could time wizards be called time wizards because they're immortal? I make a mental note to ask Hudson all the questions later tonight.

Lumi lets out a long, low whistle. "Well, that's certainly scary as hell."

And it is.

The dragon could even attack tonight, although Hudson thinks it's unlikely.

My breaths start to come short and shallow, and I realize I haven't really had a panic attack since we got to Adarie. That track record seems like it's coming to an end now.

I glance over at Hudson, but he's already reaching under the table. He rests his large hand on mine on my thigh, then absently taps his finger against the top of my hand. I can't help myself from counting along. One. Two. Three. Four. Five...

By the time I get to fifteen, I feel my chest relax and I'm able to pull a fairly decent breath into my lungs.

I mouth to him, *Thank you*, and he squeezes my hand.

We spend the rest of dinner talking about trivial things—work, which restaurant we should try next, who makes the best cookies in town. And it is soothing. But it feels like we're missing something important.

I'm still thinking about it an hour later when Lumi says they have to go relieve the babysitter. We say our goodbyes outside an ice-cream parlor, and I walk back to the inn with Hudson.

My palms are so sweaty, I have to rub them against my jeans twice before we get to our room. I keep remembering the incident in the changing room, worried Hudson is going to bring it up once we're alone. Worried he won't.

As we walk into the room, I turn and watch him slowly close the door, then face me. He shoves his hands into his pockets, and we both just stand there, staring at each other, unsure what to do next.

But then Hudson says, "I'm wiped. Night, Grace."

I stay rooted to the spot as he opens a drawer, pulls out his sweatpants, and heads to the bathroom to change.

I'm still standing in the same spot when he opens the bathroom door again and tosses his dirty clothes in the laundry basket. He leans over and drops a quick kiss on my head before continuing to his side of the bed, pulls back the sheets, and climbs in.

Then he rolls over, his back to my side of the bed, and his message couldn't be clearer if he'd shouted it.

There will be no tree climbing tonight.

101

Covering None
of the Bases
—Grace—

"**M**y stack's bigger than yours." Hudson's voice, low and teasing, floats down a library aisle to me.

I don't bother to look up from the back cover of the book in my hand. "I'm not a guy. That statement doesn't freak me out—or make me want to fight."

He laughs, then closes the twenty or so steps between us in an instant.

"You know what freaks me out?" I complain as I pop the book into my to-be-read pile and then reach for another one.

"Me walking?" He lifts a brow.

"You fading when you only have a few steps to walk. Show-off."

Of course, I'm mature enough to admit to myself that's not why it bothers me. Every time he fades, I'm reminded of what a strong and fast and powerful and—I swallow—sexy as fuck vampire this boy is.

Which, after two months, is hard enough to ignore as he swaggers in from changing into his sweats in the bathroom before bed every night *with no shirt on*.

He stopped wearing a shirt to bed when we'd first run out of clothes, before the shopping spree, and just never picked it up again. I'm not complaining, of course, or at least I wouldn't be except for the fact that Hudson seems intent on making *zero moves* on me lately.

Less than zero.

Nada.

None.

He even chucked me on the chin this morning. Chucked. Me. On. The Chin.

He shifts the pile of books in my arms to his. "Find anything interesting?"

Hudson surprised me the week after the dragon attacks by saying he'd gotten a part-time job at the library. Now I meet him here once a week to restock my TBR pile beside the bed. It's amazing how much free time you have to read when there's no Netflix—and the guy you're living with would rather read about the Shadow Realm than kiss you.

I shake my head, push thoughts of what Hudson does or doesn't want to do with me anymore down deep. So what if he hasn't kissed me again in more than a month. That's okay. He has a right to decide what he wants.

I grit my teeth. Of course, it would be great if he *told* me what he wanted, but every time I try to bring up the subject of an "us," he quickly changes it. And even worse…he hasn't picked a fight with me since the mayor's brunch. Six. Weeks. Ago.

I want to sob at the thought that I'm not worth fighting with anymore.

But I take a deep breath, plaster on a friendly smile.

"A few things, yeah." I put the book I just picked up back on the shelf and then turn to go. Eight books should keep me busy for a little while, at least. "Turns out murder mysteries are just as popular in Noromar as they are back at home."

Hudson nods sagely. "Which just goes to show that people appreciate not being dead."

"They appreciate it so much that they like to read about other people being dead?" I ask.

"That just makes them appreciate it more, doesn't it? Someone's dead. Could have been me. It's not." He does a slow twirl in the air with his index finger. "Woo-hoo."

"Woo-hoo?" I repeat incredulously.

"It's a thing. Look it up." He stops at a table and picks up what is definitely a bigger stack than mine, then heads for the library checkout desk.

"I know it's a thing," I tell him. "I just never thought it was a thing *you* would say."

He looks insulted. "Hey, I'm hip. I know what's what."

"Everything about you screams hip," I agree. "All you're missing is the bell-bottoms."

"Exactly. But I think we both know who I can borrow a pair from."

I laugh. "True story. But they'll be *Saturday Night Fever* white."

"You don't think I can rock a pair of white pants?" He pretends to be offended. "I'll have you know my ass looks great in white."

"Not sure that's saying much." I smile at the librarian, a young woman no more than a couple of years older than us, as I hand her my library card. I turn back to Hudson and mutter, "Your ass looks good in everything."

The librarian's eyes go wide, and she chokes a little—presumably on her own saliva—but she never stops scanning the books, so I figure she's okay. But I narrow my eyes on her when her gaze dips down to check out the ass in question.

"Aww, you noticed." Hudson presses a hand to his heart like he's touched. Then he turns to the girl checking us out—checking *him* out—and offers a smile. "Hey, Dolomy."

"Hi, Hudson," she says, her cheeks pinking up just a little. "You coming to the reading of Talinger's 77 *Poems of Irreconcilable Light* Saturday night?"

Hudson shakes his head. "Sadly, Saturday night is laundry night for me." He winks at her, though. "Plus, I think perhaps he should have stopped at thirty-four, don't you?"

The clerk giggles and the sound grates along my skin.

"I could do the laundry alone," I suggest sweetly.

Hudson gasps. "I could never leave the only pair of Versace underwear I have left to your tender mercies. No telling what you'd do with them if you got them alone."

"Buck up, buttercup. Surely we can find you a brand here in the Shadow Realm that's just as—" I break off when he gives me a look.

"I'm not sure what adjective you were about to use to describe my Versace underwear, but only synonyms of the words 'amazing' and 'fantastic' are acceptable." He narrows his eyes at me. "Consider yourself warned."

"Oooh, now I'm scared." I smile my thanks at the librarian as she hands me my stack, then step out of the way so she can check Hudson out, too. "But why on earth would you assume I have it in for your underwear?"

"Oh, I don't know, history? You tend to go for the jugular."

"That's one hell of an accusation coming from a vampire." But I pause, think about his words. "You don't really believe that, do you?"

"Sure I do." He snorts. "If my time with you has taught me anything, it's that you don't need to have fangs to draw blood."

Ouch. I try to think of a comeback, but before I can, the librarian hands Hudson his books. "Here you go. I think you'll really like the one on the physics of shadows. It's very interesting."

"Thank you!" He flashes her a grin. "That's the one I'm looking forward to the most, actually."

She smiles back, then reaches over and rubs his hand. "You know, a youth group meets here every Thursday evening. It's a good place to make new...friends."

I try not to be insulted by her words, but it's hard not to take them personally when she's acting like I'm not even standing here. Or when Hudson nods solemnly and says, "I'll keep it in mind. Thanks."

And oh my God. Is Hudson flirting with her?

By the time we make it back outside, I've decided we need to have this conversation once and for all. He can't dance with me and kiss me and feed from me one night and just...nothing else for weeks. And he sure as hell can't flirt with someone in front of said dance and kissing partner without some sort of explanation. 'Cause yeah, this is ridiculous.

"Would you rather be spending your time with Miss Librarian in there?" I ask, stamping my foot for good measure.

Hudson is jogging down the stairs where Smokey is waiting for him, but he pauses mid-step, turning to face me. I think he's about to deny it—hope he's about to deny it—because he looks like he's about to say something important.

At least until he starts laughing his ass off.

"Seriously?" I snap. "You think that's funny?"

"No, no, that's not why I'm laughing," he says. Or at least that's what I think he says—he's still laughing too hard for me to understand his every word.

"That girl was hitting on you right in front of me!" I snarl.

"Nah. She just wanted me to know I had prospects, that's all."

"You want prospects?" I ask, and I know I'm a little wild-eyed at this point. "Have at it. Have all the prospects."

For the first time, he seems to clue in that I'm upset. Like, really upset. "Hey, Grace. I didn't mean—"

"Don't." I throw up a hand to stop whatever BS he's going to throw my way. And end up doing something else entirely.

At first, I don't know what's happening. I just know that it's suddenly really hard to move. And then it registers. Holy shit. I just turned myself to stone.

"Did I just—"

"Yeah," Hudson says, raising one eyebrow. "You did. Looks like you'd rather be stone than talk to me right now."

"Maybe you should learn something from that, then," I tell him.

"Maybe I should." He waits for a second, but I still don't have anything to say to him, so he continues. "This mean you're planning on staying stone?"

"Maybe," I tell him.

"Oooookay. And does that mean you want to keep standing here? Or do you want to walk back to the inn?"

"We can walk back to the inn," I tell him, but I'm so mad that I end up freezing in place.

"Or we can stand here," Hudson says.

I don't answer him…because I can't. I'm completely stone now.

102

O h. My. God.
I'm as solid stone as every other gargoyle I've ever seen on buildings.

Which makes me wonder—are they people, too? All those gargoyles on the Cathedral of Notre-Dame? Are they real? The thought blows my mind, and I promise myself that once I manage to get out of this, I'll do some research into that.

In the meantime, Hudson is leaning forward and peering into my eyes like he's trying to figure out if I'm still in here. I am, obviously, but I have no way of knowing how to tell him that.

Before I can so much as attempt a squeak, a bright purple butterfly comes by and lands on my nose. And it tickles. A lot.

And I can't do anything about it.

Hudson comes to my rescue, though, shooing it away when I obviously can't.

Panic is welling up within me, and I don't know how to stop it. I try to take a deep breath, but it turns out that stone doesn't breathe all that well.

I try to count, but the counting usually comes with the breathing.

I can't dig my feet into my shoes, can't ground myself with sensory details, because there are none. I mean, I can see and I can hear, but that's about it. And I can't even see that much—only what's right in front of me, which at the moment happens to be Hudson.

The panic gets worse, starts to cloud my head. Starts to make it harder and harder for me to think. I need out of this. I just need out of it. I need—

"Hey." Hudson's voice is a little too sharp and a little too loud, but it manages to burrow through the layers of panic and get my attention. "You're okay, Grace," he says. "You're okay."

That's it? I want to tell him. *That's all you've got for me? I'm freaking*

stone over here, and you're just going to stand out there and tell me I'm okay?
I'm not okay! This is not okay!

The panic comes back double-time, and now things are about to go dark. I can't even see Hudson all that well as terror overwhelms me, starts blocking out everything but the rapid pounding of my heart. Until there's nothing and no one in the world but me and this giant stone sarcophagus I'm wrapped up in.

What do I do?

What do I do?

WHAT. DO. I. DO?

Staying in this world is one thing. Staying in it as a freaking stone statue is something else entirely. I'm not okay with this. I'm not okay with it AT. ALL.

"Hey, Grace!" Somehow, Hudson's voice manages to permeate the fear that threatens to smother me. This time he's closer, bending down a little, so that we're face-to-face. I can see the calm, focused look in his eyes even before he reaches a hand out and touches my arm.

I shouldn't be able to feel it—feel him—because I'm stone. But somehow, I do—just like I felt the butterfly.

I try to hold on to the warmth, try to ground myself in that one singular sensation, but it's not enough to beat back the panic. Not enough to help me think.

At least not until Hudson raises a brow and gives me his should-be-patented obnoxious smirk. "So, I'm thinking I should just carry you back to our room at the inn like this. What do you think? I could put you in the corner, use you as a sock rack?"

Excuse me? A sock rack?

"Or, I don't know. The way your hand is out like that makes it seem like it'd be very convenient to hang my underwear on you. I think my lone Versace pair would look great hanging from your middle finger."

Seriously? Annoyance wells up inside me. I know he won't actually do what he's saying, but him saying this shit while I'm trapped in stone makes him seem like a real jerk. And if he wants to talk about middle fingers, I've definitely got one for him.

"What else could you be good at? A doorstop maybe? Or I could put you out on the balcony. You could attract more butterflies. Maybe a few birds? You know how I love my ornithology." He snaps his fingers. "I know! I could borrow a bowl from the kitchen and put it on your head. Turn you into a birdbath! I'll get a hummingbird feeder to hang from your finger and—"

"Are you fucking kidding me?" I demand as the stone releases me. I spend about two seconds as animated stone and then I'm back in my regular Grace body. "A fucking birdbath? You know what? When we get back to the inn, I'm burning those Versace underwear. The next time you see them, they're going to be ash!"

"Grace!" He breathes a relieved sigh. "You're back!"

"No thanks to you," I snarl at him, even though I know it's not true. The only reason I got out of that stone is because of him, and I'm smart enough to know it. Just like I'm smart enough to know he said what he said on purpose.

Not that I'm about to let him know that. Not after he threatened to turn me into a hummingbird feeder, for God's sake.

"Hey." He gives a negligible shrug. "You'd make a cute birdbath. Plus, I figured it would help keep your spirits up. I didn't want you to get depressed."

"You're a real giver like that," I tell him as I start walking.

"I really am." He heaves a big sigh. "Although I am a little sad to lose my boxer stand."

"Keep it up, Vega, and I'll find a boxer stand for you. But you're not going to like what I do with it."

"Such violence, Grace." He shakes his head sadly, but I can see the amused gleam in his eyes. "I thought gargoyles were supposed to be the peaceful sort."

"I have no idea what gargoyles are supposed to be!" I snap. "I've never met one before."

"I never had, either, before you." He takes the books out of my arms and falls into step beside me, and we walk in silence for a few blocks.

Hudson keeps glancing at me out of the corner of his eye, little concerned looks that should piss me off but somehow don't. By the time we get back to the inn, I've actually calmed down enough to say what's really on my mind.

"How do I make sure that doesn't happen again?"

"Practice," he tells me, pressing a supportive hand to my lower back. "We figure it out, and then we practice. A lot."

103

Passing the Pouspous

—Grace—

So that's exactly what I do for the next week.
With Hudson's help, with Caoimhe's help, even with Nyaz's help.

I practice turning into a gargoyle and practice turning human again. Practice turning into a gargoyle, practice turning human. Over and over and over.

Sometimes it happens easily, and sometimes I can't do it at all. Sometimes I'm stuck in stone for an hour or more. But I always manage to find my way back, and eventually I get stuck less and less.

And yes, I know there's more to being a gargoyle than just changing to stone and back, but it's a good start. Especially since I'm not quite ready to try to figure out flying. I still remember turning to stone and accidentally impaling the dragon on my hands.

The last thing I want is for that to happen with a person. Or for me to fall out of the air and crush some unsuspecting passerby.

No, controlling my gargoyle shifts is definitely the first order of business. Then I'll worry about the rest.

Of course, when I get stuck, it's always at inconvenient moments. Like when I have plans with Hudson. Or when I need to get to work. Or when I'm meeting a friend.

That's what happened today, and it's why I'm fifteen minutes late when I finally settle down next to Caoimhe at a tiny table at a restaurant that's usually way out of our price range. But she invited me, told me she was springing for lunch, so here I am—albeit fifteen minutes late.

"Sorry, sorry!" I tell her as I grab one of the waters on the table and take a long drink. Being stuck in stone is thirsty work.

"No worries," she tells me with a grin. "I figured I'd give you another twenty minutes and then come looking for you. On the plus side, you're a really great listener when you're stone."

"That's what Nyaz says." I take another sip.

"So we know how gargoyle practice is going." Caoimhe smirks. "How's work?"

"Actually, it's going really well. It turns out I've got a knack for 'selling baubles.'" I put air quotes around my boss's words. "Which is great, because I love selling jewelry to people. Seeing them smile. It's a good job if you can get it."

She smiles at our approaching waiter. "I would love a glass of laranfade," she tells him. "Heavy on the -ade."

"What does that mean?" I ask. Even after four months in Adarie, there are still things I'm learning about the food and the customs.

"I want it more sweet than sour," she answers, grinning at me like it's the best day of her life. "Actually, bring us two of those," she tells the waiter. "And an order of pouspous for the table. We're celebrating."

"What exactly are we celebrating?" I ask. Because the impending Starfall Festival with even bigger impending dragon attack is definitely not something I'm up to even thinking about yet, let alone celebrating.

"What, having lunch with one of my best friends isn't reason enough?" she asks, brows raised.

"That's enough reason for a grilled veggie stick from the cart in the park. This," I say, looking around, "is another whole level."

The waiter discreetly brings our drinks and, after giving him our order, Caoimhe raises her glass and says, "To whole other levels."

"I don't know if I actually want to drink to that," I answer, considering what I know of her ulterior motives.

"Come on, live dangerously. We are celebrating life today." She clinks her glass with mine and takes a big sip before moving on. "Annnnnnd how's Hudson?"

"Same as he always is," I answer warily. "Really good."

She rolls her eyes. "That's not what I was asking, and you know it. Don't friends share boyfriend info back where you come from? I need details!"

"The details haven't changed from when we talked about them—about him—two weeks ago. I don't know what you want me to say?"

"Does he still get your panties in a twist?" she asks, wiggling her brows. "In a good way, I mean?"

I think back to what I spent the morning doing and can feel myself blushing. "Oh, there it is!" Caoimhe crows. "Come on, spill it! Some of us need to live vicariously."

"I wish there was something to share." I sigh. "I spent the morning watching him fold socks."

She blinks back at me. "And *that* made you blush just now?"

I stare out the window. Look at the lighting fixture. Rearrange my silverware.

But Caoimhe doesn't take the hint. She crosses her arms and just waits me out until I let out an exacerbated breath and admit, "He did it in only his sweatpants."

"Sweatpants get you hot and bothered?" she asks.

And I have to roll my eyes. "He wasn't wearing a shirt."

Caoimhe laughs. Hard.

When she settles back down, I decide maybe a "girlfriend rant" is exactly what I need to relieve some pressure, so I dive in. "He *never* wears a shirt! It's so annoying!"

Caoimhe's eyes twinkle and she leans forward. "Tell me more."

I take a deep breath, and I tell her. Everything. How Hudson has taken to walking around without a shirt on every minute he's in our room. Even when we're just hanging out and playing with Smokey. It's like he knows I can't look away from how his silken skin moves over the muscles and bones in his back. "And don't even get me started on his abs!"

"And you've asked him to wear a shirt and he won't?" Caoimhe asks.

"Of course not." That's not the point. "The sun is always out. He's hot."

She nods. "So you're not wearing clothes, either, then. To stay cool."

I snort. "Of course I'm always dressed! It's not *that* hot."

My friend just smiles knowingly at me. I hate it when she's right. Hudson isn't doing it on purpose. I know he's not. And he'd put a shirt on if I asked. He's just getting comfortable living in his own space. This is probably exactly how he hung out when he was back home.

I groan. "Could you please start dating someone so we can talk about an actual love life instead of this misery I'm currently living with?"

"Oh, please." She waves a hand. "Been there, done that. Found out the crunch isn't worth the patsoni chip."

"I don't even know what that means."

"Sure you do," she says, taking another sip of her drink. "You're one of the lucky ones."

"Who gets the crunch and the patsoni chip?" I ask dryly.

"Everyone gets the crunch with their patsoni chip. It's just that most patsoni is really, really bitter—and really, really dry and not worth eating."

The waiter brings our pouspous, and the dishes are sprinkled with some kind of seasoning that smells delicious.

I pop one in my mouth with a grin. Then, when I'm done chewing, I lift a brow and ask, "So what you're saying is Hudson is dry and bitter?"

"I wasn't, but if the shoe fits..." She shrugs.

"Hey! It's a good kind of dry, and he's getting less bitter by the day."

"I wouldn't know." She gives me a baleful look. "My friend won't share anything about that."

"I already told you. There's nothing to share."

She laughs. "Please. There's always something to share. I've seen how that boy looks at you."

"Oh yeah?" Now she's got my attention. "How does he look at me?"

Caoimhe's smile disappears. "Like he wants to do it for the rest of his immortal life," she answers seriously.

"Give me a break." I roll my eyes. "You can't get all that from just a look."

She seems insulted. "Of course I can. As a performer, I spend my life reading a room. And that guy is one hundred percent gone over you."

Warmth blossoms inside me at her words. I don't know if they're true or not—despite what she says about her abilities, Hudson can be a locked book most days—but I realize suddenly that I want them to be. I want Hudson to want me...the way that I'm coming to want him.

Not just for someone to hang out with. Not just for someone to kiss. I want him.

Maybe that's why I plop another pouspous in my mouth and decide here and now—Hudson and I are going to finally have that talk.

104

How to Rock and Not Roll
—Grace—

It's been a couple of weeks since that one lunch with Caoimhe, and I still haven't figured out a way to get Hudson to tell me how he feels.

Every time I bring up the subject, he says Smokey needs a walk. Or he forgot to tell Nyaz something. Or he needs a shower.

If I didn't know better, I'd think the boy was avoiding me.

No, he *was* avoiding me.

I can't even get him to feed.

Muttering under my breath, I find a seat in the middle of town square to eat my lunch. The library is right across the street from me, and as I glance at it, I wonder if I should pop in and say hi to Hudson. School is out today, so he said he had some research he wanted to do.

Time is ticking down for both of us, and I'm terrified we won't be ready when darkness falls again.

When the dragon comes again.

It's still a ways off, but I can't help thinking about it. Can't help thinking if my gargoyle will be ready to fight during the attack. Because there's no way I can just sit by and let my new friends die. Not when they've all been so amazing to me. The troubadours, my boss Tinyati, Nyaz. Even Dolomy the librarian has started to warm up to me, though Hudson is still her favorite.

Then again, he's pretty much everyone's favorite these days. Smokey rarely lets him out of her sight, even when he's at work. Nyaz invites him for his weekly card game with the guys. And Lumi is giving him lessons on the trumpet in exchange for French lessons while Caoimhe and I try out local restaurants.

All in all, we're settling in really well as we build a life.

The trash can is next to the statue of the woman and the dragon, and as I stand here looking at her, I realize something I've not really noticed before… She has *horns*.

My heart is pounding in my chest. This is a memorial of a gargoyle fighting a dragon!

I make a mental note to ask Hudson if anyone's told him anything about this statue before. Surely someone knows why it was built.

Maybe gargoyles are just naturally capable of tearing rifts in time. Maybe she came to the Shadow Realm by accident like I did.

My stomach suddenly pitches and shimmies. I'm the only gargoyle in Adarie—which means this one, whoever she was, lost to the time dragon. I swallow the bile rising in my throat and toss the rest of my uneaten sandwich into the trash.

I don't like thinking about that. Don't like imagining her losing, dying, becoming anything less than the super-fierce gargoyle standing in front of me, staring down a dragon.

Eyes defiant, mouth set, head lowered for battle, giant horns at the ready. She's a badass in every way a woman can be a badass, and there's a part of me that wants to be just like her when I grow up.

No sooner do I think it than something happens inside me.

Deep down in a place I don't recognize—a place I'm not sure I've ever felt quite like this before—there's a stirring that I can't explain. That I can't describe.

It's like a silvery inner light turns on, growing brighter with every second. Its light bathes all the dark corners inside me, all the dark spots I didn't even know existed until this moment, and fills them all with power. With strength. With a determination I've never felt before—at least not like this.

And then something else happens, too.

All those places the light is touching slowly start to turn to stone.

I've tried to make this happen for weeks, have tried to find the gargoyle inside myself ever since I changed back the night the dragon attacked. But I could never find her, could never figure out how to make this happen. I've turned to stone, sure, but I've never felt like *this*.

Now that I've found my gargoyle—sort of—I never want it to stop. I've never felt this powerful, or this peaceful, in my life.

I've never felt this whole, like all the different parts of me are finally working together. Finally becoming what I was always meant to be.

It's so strange that I had to come to another world—another realm—to find this. Even stranger to know that it's been here all along.

For a moment, I think about my parents. I wonder if they knew, wonder why they didn't tell me if they did. But then I let it go, because it doesn't matter. Not right now, when I have wings. And claws. And a body made of stone.

Now that I know what's happening and I'm not panicking over something I don't understand, it's totally kick-ass.

I take a couple of steps and right away remember how hard it is to walk as stone. So I try to focus the light inside me, try to use it to turn from stone into my other gargoyle form—the one that could fly and run and do all kinds of cool stuff.

It doesn't happen the way it did the night of the fight with the dragon. I don't just instantly become a gargoyle running around and doing badass stuff.

But as I dive inside myself, as I try to find the source of the light spreading throughout me, I finally see a bright silvery platinum-colored thread. It's in the middle of a bunch of different threads—a hot-pink one, a bright green one, an electric-blue one that seems to radiate warmth and joy.

I think about touching that one, just to see what happens, but decide to come back to it because the platinum one is calling to me. I take another deep breath, let it out to the count of ten like Heather's mom taught me, and slowly, slowly slide my fingers across it.

My stone shivers, and for a second I feel something start to happen. But the instant my fingers leave the string, it stops. So I try again, pressing my fingers against the string more forcefully this time. Again, the stone shivers. Shudders. A tingling picks up in my nerve endings, spreading through my body a little more with each moment that passes.

But again, it stops as soon as I lift my hand from the string, everything returning to the heavy stone that makes it so difficult to move.

Finally, I get tired of experimenting, tired of being so tentative. And I do the only thing I can think of. I reach in and grab the platinum-colored string as tightly as I can.

And just like that, everything changes.

105

A Whole New
Meaning to Stone-Faced
—Grace—

My whole body lights up from the inside out. The heavy stone feeling seems to fall away, and in its place is a lightness like I've only felt one time before—the night of the festival.

I glance behind me, see my wings standing up from my shoulder blades. Look down at my skin and realize it's a glossy silver.

I did it! I turned to stone, and then I turned from stone into my regular gargoyle form! And all of it in full gargoyle badassery mode, not just stone!

Excitement fills me. I did it. I really did it.

A quick glance at the clock tower tells me I've got fifteen minutes before I'm due back at the boutique, and there's only one thing I want to do. One person I want to share this with.

The library is across the crowded square, but I'm betting it's a much shorter flight. I've never taken off from the ground before—last time I flew, I jumped off the huge flight of stairs at City Hall—but I figure there's no time like the present to give it a shot.

Still, it's lunchtime in town square, so there are a lot of people walking by right now—many of whom are looking at me because they've probably never seen a gargoyle before. And while that doesn't bother me at all, the last thing I want to do is wipe out in front of all of them. Especially if it's going to take me more than once to figure this stuff out.

So instead of taking off from in front of the gazebo, I walk around the corner to the next street over, which is much less busy. And then I just do it.

I close my eyes—which is probably not the optimal way to try to fly, but it is the optimal way not to see if you're going to crash—take a deep breath, and start to run. But when I try to launch myself into the air, I end up wiping out. Hard.

It's just like riding a bike, I think as I pick myself up, running my hands along my body to check for chips or cracks. Looks like my stone is resilient as fuck. Thank God. A few more times, a few more falls, and I'll get this. Another deep breath, another run down the sidewalk, and another wipeout.

Five minutes and two scraped elbows later, I decide that maybe I should try jumping off a staircase again. The building next to me has an outside staircase running up the side of it, and it seems as good a place as any to give this a try. So I climb up the stairs, climb on top of the banister, and don't even bother to look down. If I do, I know I'll never jump, and I've got to figure this stuff out in the next few weeks.

Plus, my lunch hour is ticking away, and I really want to show Hudson what I can do. So I decide fuck it, and I jump straight off the banister.

I start to fall, just like I did a few weeks ago. But this time I manage to pull up sooner—thank God—and then I'm doing it. I'm flying. Or at least coasting on the passing breeze, which I will so take over another wipeout.

It may have taken me almost ten minutes to get off the ground, but I was right when I thought it would be a short flight to the library. I land in front of it about two minutes after I jumped off the banister. And can I just say how freaking fun it is to be able to fly?

Like an unbelievably ridiculous amount of fun, even with the scraped elbows.

Excited to share what's happened with Hudson, I rush inside the building. After doing a triple take when she sees me, the young librarian kind of laughs and points me toward the small employee courtyard in the back. Apparently, I'm not the only one on my lunch break.

But when I get to the glass door leading outside, I hesitate before opening it. Because Hudson is sitting at the employee picnic table, elbows on his knees and head in his hands. Smokey is next to him, one of the ribbons Hudson always buys her wrapped around her waist while her head is in his lap as if she's trying to comfort him.

It's such an un-Hudson-like pose that I know immediately what's going on. I also don't need to see his face to know it's bad. Or to feel the hunger and fatigue beating away at him.

As much as I've been practicing lately to try to control my stone forms, Hudson has been helping the mayor build reinforcements in Adarie for when the dragon comes back. He even faded all the way to a nearby village to bring cases of steel bolts back to reinforce the front gate. All while working two jobs and still having time to spend with me.

And I knew he was hungry—I just didn't know how bad it was. Every time I've tried to get him to feed, much like get him to talk about our relationship, he's changed the subject or insisted he was fine.

But now I know that I need to be doing something more. Because I can't leave him hurting, can't leave him suffering without trying to help him.

I also know he doesn't want me to see him like this. Otherwise, he wouldn't be fronting at home the way he is. I've not seen this level of fatigue since the mountains when he had no choice but to let me see.

I think about turning around and just going back to work before he sees me—this isn't the place for the confrontation I know is coming—but at the same time, I need to make sure he's okay. So instead of sneaking up to show him my gargoyle form as I originally intended, I make sure to cough a little as I rattle the door.

By the time I walk outside, Hudson is standing and smiling at me, no trace of distress anywhere about him. At least not if I don't look too closely. Smokey, on the other hand, is running around his feet at top speed, chittering to herself. I may not be able to talk to her, but I know when she's distressed. She's obviously as worried about Hudson as I am.

If I do look closely, I can see a shadow in his eyes and a few tiny lines of strain around the corners of his mouth.

"Look at you! I knew you'd figure it out again!" he tells me with a smile that doesn't quite chase the pained shadows from his eyes. "How did you do it?"

"I was looking inside myself and I saw all these strings—like what you must have seen when you were looking for the mating bond with Jaxon. And there, in the middle of all the different colors, was a platinum string. And I just knew, even before I touched it, that that string is for my gargoyle."

"Wait." Now he just looks stunned. "You saw the strings? All of them?"

"I did! And can you believe my gargoyle string was right there? Right at the very center of all of them?"

He leans down to pet Smokey, then he says, "Being a gargoyle suits you."

I roll my eyes. "I'm pretty sure you'd think anything suited me."

"It's a trial, I know, to have a friend who thinks you're gorgeous even when you're silver. How will you survive?"

"It is a trial," I agree with an airy sigh. "But I'll do my best to muddle through."

"Good plan." He drops a quick kiss on my forehead. "Since I don't see it changing anytime soon."

"The friend thing?" I ask with an arch of my brows.

He laughs. "I was referring to the gorgeous thing, but sure. I don't see the friend thing changing anytime soon, either."

"Wow. Such a charmer." I slip back into my human form and bat my eyes at him so hard, I get an eyelash in them.

Which cracks him up completely. So much so that when he tries to help me fish it out, we have to keep stopping because he's laughing too hard.

"Let me go." I pretend to push at his chest. "I'll get the damn eyelash out myself."

His only answer is another eye roll—right before he cups my face in his hands.

"Let me see," he says gently, and it's so Hudson-like that I go quiet right away. Seconds later, the eyelash is out of my eye, and Hudson is taking several steps back from me.

"How long do we have before you've got to head back to work?" he asks, hands shoved deep into his pockets.

"About forty-five seconds," I answer. But I use the time wisely and ask the question he uses on me all the time, whether I want to hear it or not. "You okay?"

For a beat, his eyes cloud over, turn the color of a summer rainstorm. But then he smiles and asks, "How could I not be?"

"I don't know. Just a feeling I've got." I search his face, linger supportively. Give him every opportunity to tell me the truth.

But that's not the path he chooses. Instead, he doubles down with a sexy grin that should send all kinds of feelings through me—feelings that have nothing to do with fear or anger. But that's what I should feel, not what I *do* feel. Because Hudson isn't trusting me with what's going on with him, and that makes me not trust him right back.

Especially when he says, "If those are the kinds of feelings you're having, I must be doing something wrong."

"Yeah," I agree. "You must be."

That has his eyes widening and an uncertain look flitting across his face for the first time today. "Grace?"

But it's too little, too late. I'm pissed, and I'm going to be for a while. Because we are all each other has in this world, and if he keeps lying to me about something as important as his health, then what the fuck are we doing?

And where the fuck are we supposed to go from here?

106

Always Look a Gift Mayor in the Mouth
—Grace—

I fume all the way back to the boutique. And the day only goes downhill from there. Not only are we super busy—I mean "standing room only" busy—but my boss had a fight with her husband today, too, so she's in a really bad mood.

She doesn't take it out on me, but she has absolutely no patience with the difficult customers. Which leaves me to soothe an awful lot of ruffled feathers, something I try to be good at but only really succeed at about half the time.

It's fifteen minutes from closing time and two hours *after* I was supposed to get off before things finally calm down. I'm starving from working through dinner and grumpy because the afternoon rush pretty much obliterated the shelves and the racks, and I'm the one who has to get them all organized again before I can leave tonight.

Add in the monster headache building right behind my eyes that promises to ruin the rest of my night, and I am in a fantastic mood. Especially since the fight I have to have with Hudson is already looming over my head.

Into this maelstrom of problems, both petty and real, walks Souil. He's got a congenial grin on his face and eyes full of sympathy, but I wasn't born yesterday. Those seventies suits of his don't come from this boutique. Which means the only reason he's here is because he wants to see me.

Too bad I don't feel the same way.

It's not that I have anything against him. I don't. He seems like a nice enough guy for a politician, but the last thing I want to talk about tonight is that time dragon. Especially with him.

Besides, half the reason Hudson is so wiped is Souil's fault. The mayor refuses to warn the townspeople of the impending dragon attack yet, although we did get him to promise to caution citizens to stay inside during Starfall while we confront the dragon outside the town's walls. So Hudson has been running around after work fortifying the town walls and gates and whatever buildings he can with minimum outside help.

I grit my teeth as Souil launches into another story about how he became mayor. I am too tired to listen.

He's got too many stories and too much advice and all I really want is a shower and some food. Like a pizza or a whole order of cheese fries. But since the Shadow Realm has neither of those, my night is looking grim.

"Can I help you with something, Mayor?" I finally break into his story and ask, working hard to keep it from sounding rude. It's not his fault I've had a shit day, and it's not his fault all I want is to go home.

"Oh, I need a present for a friend's daughter. Tomorrow is her sixteenth birthday party, and I thought you might be able to help me pick out something she would love. She's had a rough couple of years health-wise, so her mom is really going all out for this birthday. I want to do the same."

Well, hell. Now I don't just feel grumpy, I feel churlish, too.

"That's amazing!" I tell him, and he blinks a little—I'm pretty sure at the sudden change in my tone. But now that I know he's not here to poke around about the dragon anymore, I'm more than happy to help him out. Plus, it gets me out of scarf sorting for a while and that is always a plus.

"Were you thinking of clothes?" I ask as I lead him to the center of the store. "Jewelry? Sunglasses?"

"Honestly, it's been a long time since I've bought a present for a young woman. What do you think she would like?"

"It's hard to say, considering everyone's style is a little bit different. Would you be interested in maybe picking up a gift card for her? So she can choose what she wants?"

He scrunches up his face. "There's not much wow factor in that, you know? Plus, she's been so sick recently, I'm not sure she'll be able to come shopping for a while."

"Okay, that's fair." I glance around the shop, which still looks like a tornado came through it, and try to think. Macy and I have very different tastes, so what is something we both would like as a present?

Definitely not clothes, because he probably doesn't know what size she wears. Sunglasses are so dependent on the shape of a person's face. So, jewelry then.

"How about a bracelet?" I try, leading him over to the back wall of the store next to the cash registers. It's where we keep the jewelry that's a step up from the regular costume stuff.

"She might really like that. Her mom usually wears a lot of jewelry, now that I think about it." He sounds excited, and his smile has definitely grown. "Good idea!"

I show him several different bracelets that I think both Macy and I would like, and he ends up choosing one that is a series of linked suns, made in a purple metal that is unique to the Shadow Realm.

"That's a really great choice," Tinyati says when we bring it to the register. "Grace, why don't you check the mayor out and gift wrap the bracelet for him? Then you can head on home."

"Home?" I look around the still-messy shop. "But—"

"You've already stayed late enough," she says. "I know you and Hudson probably have plans, and I really appreciate you letting me infringe on them."

Souil jokes with me as I ring him up, then wrap the bracelet in pretty gold paper with a purple bow. When I go to hand it to him, though, our hands accidentally brush for the first time since the handshake at his house.

My fingers glance over the ring on his right index finger and the second I touch it, a zap of electricity works its way up my arm.

But then the mayor is thanking me again before taking his package and disappearing out the door with a smile and a wave.

"He's an odd one," Tinyati says once the door is firmly closed behind him.

"Why do you say that?" I know why *I* think he's odd, but she's been around him a lot longer than I have. I know Hudson doesn't trust him, but—today especially—he seems harmless. A little eccentric and a lot narcissistic, but still pretty harmless.

"Have you seen the way he dresses?" She shakes her head. "I've been telling him to come in for years. That I'll get him a whole new wardrobe—with a really good discount—but he never listens." She clucks her tongue. "He just keeps wearing those tight pants and all those chains. It's truly bizarre."

"And yet, you guys elected him mayor."

"'Elected' is a pretty strong word for what happened, from what I understand. It was before my time."

"What do you mean?" I ask as alarm bells start going off inside me. "You don't have elections in Adarie?"

"I mean, not really. When he got here, Souil decided we needed a mayor to represent our interests with the Shadow Queen. When no one stepped up for the job, he volunteered himself and passed a petition that he be appointed mayor. He got a lot of the town to sign it and then suddenly started calling himself mayor."

"How long ago was that?" I ask. "He's been mayor for two hundred years, hasn't he?"

"He was here before my great-grandparents were alive. So maybe, yeah."

I think back to his house, which looks so much like a replica from a seventies mansion. "He's been mayor for two hundred years, and no one's ever won an election against him?"

"There's never been an election. Every five years or so—at least in my lifetime—he asks around, sees if anyone wants to take his place as mayor. He does a decent job, so nobody ever decides to run against him, I guess. So he just kind of keeps at it."

"Wow." I shake my head as I try to figure out how all this works.

"Indeed." She laughs. "And speaking of long times, you've been here all day. Go find Hudson and do something fun." She wiggles her eyebrows to make sure I get her meaning.

Which, no. Just no. I am not talking about Hudson's and my sex life—or lack thereof—with my boss.

"We're not planning on having the kind of fun you mean tonight," I say as I grab my bag from where I stowed it under the counter when I got to work this morning.

"Well, why not?" she asks, throwing her hands up in exasperation. "You're young and beautiful and flexible. When is there ever going to be a better time?"

Flexible? Did she really just say we were flexible? What exactly does she think Hudson and I are getting up to in the inn, with its very thin hotel walls? Then again, I don't want to know what she's thinking. At least, beyond that we need to be flexible to do it.

"I've got to go," I tell her as I head for the door, hoping against hope that she'll take the hint and drop it. "I'll see you tomorrow."

Instead, she just gives me a thumbs-up sign and says, "That's the spirit, Grace!"

Forget walking, I dive for the door. And try not to think about what's actually going to happen when I make it back to Hudson's and my room.

107

Good Girl Gone Mad as Hell
—Hudson—

My head is fucking killing me.

Vampires aren't normally prone to weird physical ailments—part and parcel of the whole immortality thing—but since we ended up in Noromar, with nonstop fucking sunlight, that's definitely changed for me.

Needless to say, I'm not exactly impressed. Even Smokey isn't impressed, given she hopped out the window ten minutes ago to pick flowers and play with some of the kids in the square rather than be cooped up in the dark with me tonight.

I took a shower when I got home from the library, but it didn't help. Neither did trying to take a nap while I waited for Grace to get back from work.

She left a message with Nyaz earlier, telling me she had to work late. But she didn't tell me how late, so I've basically been lying here in the dark—courtesy of blackout curtains—willing this headache to go the fuck away before she gets home.

So far, it's only gotten worse.

Big surprise. Nothing seems to do what it's supposed to here in the Shadow Realm. Including my relationship with Grace.

From the minute we left the lair, things started changing, evolving, and I thought they were headed in a great direction. But after brunch at the mayor's house, I had to admit I was still Grace's second choice. And I don't want to be anyone's second choice anymore.

Even *if* they offer to climb me like a tree—although I admit, that one nearly killed me to walk away from.

So here we are. Not where I want to be but in a good place nonetheless. Certainly a better place than I ever anticipated being with her when we first got trapped in the lair together. I get to spend every day with my best friend, someone who loves spending time with me right back. How amazing is that?

I swallow the lump in my throat as I think about how all of that is going to change tonight.

She saw her strings today...and the only one she seemed happy about was her gargoyle string. By the time she left the library, it was quite clear she was upset with me about something, and it doesn't take a genius to figure out what. That fucking blue string.

Frustrated, I roll over in bed. Then instantly regret it because it only angers my already sore head even more. I don't have much time to worry about that, though, because I can hear Grace's feet at the end of the hall. Seconds later, Grace's cinnamon scent permeates the room.

She's home.

And I'm unprepared.

Leaping out of bed, I ignore the way everything spins as I smooth out the covers. It's just a headache, I remind myself. It'll go away soon enough.

I'm in the middle of yanking open the curtains when the door opens and Grace walks in.

She's back in her human form and, judging from the way her hair is spilling out of the bun she's tried to constrain it in, she's had one hell of an afternoon. Which would explain why she's more than two hours later than normal.

"Bad day?" I ask when she just closes the door and leans against it.

"Something like that," she answers, eyes narrowed as they sweep over me. "Can you *never* wear a T-shirt in here?"

"Um... I'm sorry. I didn't know it bothered you." Without taking my eyes off her, I lean over and grab my shirt, shrug it on. I try again. "How was your day?"

Instead of answering, she asks, "How was *your* day?"

It doesn't *sound* like a trap, but it definitely *feels* like one. Still, what am I supposed to say besides, "Pretty good," because it was, if you don't count the fact that my head's been trying to blow up for most of it and I think Grace is about to crush my heart into a billion tiny pieces. At least that pain will take my mind off my head, I reason.

"Is that a question?" Her voice is quiet, but that doesn't stop her words from ringing through the room.

"I don't know," I counter just as quietly. "Is it?"

She doesn't answer, only stares at me for several beats. Just when I'm about to break the silence and ask her to put me out of my misery, she walks away.

Goes into the bathroom and shuts the door. Seconds later, the shower turns on.

And yeah, message received. She is *definitely* pissed about the blue string.

I swear long and low and run a hand through my hair. Then I sit on the edge of the bed, try and reassure myself I always knew this is how it could play out. I'd hoped she was growing to feel something for me. Something to build on. I guess I got it wrong.

Despite feeling sick from her obvious anger, I call down to Nyaz and ask him to send up a grilled tago cheese and some fruit for Grace.

The minutes tick by as I wait impatiently for Grace to get out of the shower, but she's decided to take her time. I can only assume it's because psychological warfare is a thing. Cyrus taught me that a long time ago.

Briefly, I think about hauling arse out of here. About just walking away and leaving her to whatever mood she's in. Things will go better for both of us if we're calm when we have whatever argument is brewing. It's not like I planned for this. Besides, it takes two to make this happen.

As I sit here, waiting on the meltdown Grace is clearly working herself into, I start to get a little angry myself.

By the time Grace finally emerges from the bathroom, one of the waiters from downstairs knocks on the door with her grilled cheese.

"I ordered you dinner," I tell her as I set the plate on the table near the window. "I thought you might be hungry."

"What about you?" she asks, brows raised. "Are *you* hungry?"

And there it is. I barely resist the urge to wipe a frustrated hand down my face.

"No," I tell her truthfully. The thought of feeding in this moment makes me nauseous. "I'm not."

"You're not?" She quirks a brow. "I don't believe you."

The words—and the expression on her face—set me off, have all the defenses I've amassed in my long life clicking into place. "Excuse me?" My voice is cold enough to rival January in Alaska, but I don't give a fuck right now. "What do you mean you don't believe me?"

And neither does Grace, apparently, because she just lifts her chin and says, "You heard me."

"I did, yes." What the fuck else am I supposed to say to that? She's spoiling for a fight and suddenly, I don't have it in me to watch what we have go up in smoke tonight. Not while I'm already feeling so beaten down.

So instead of answering her, I simply climb back in the bed and roll over.

"Seriously?" she says, her voice approaching a whole new octave. "You're just going to go to bed without even talking to me?"

"I don't know what I'm going to do," I snap over my shoulder and watch her eyes widen as she realizes that underneath the forced calm, I'm just as pissed as she is. "Tell me what you want me to say, Grace, and I'll say it."

"I want you to tell me the truth," she answers as she walks toward me. "I want you to stop lying to me."

"I have *never* lied to you, Grace." I bite out each word.

"It's not about what you're saying," she counters. "It's about what you're not telling me that you should have."

Fine. I guess we're going to do this now. I hop out of bed. I am *not* having this fight lying down. "Do we really need to have this out right now? I have a bloody terrible headache and—"

"There! There it is!" she crows, pointing at me like she's just won the argument.

"There *what* is?" I shake my head. "Why am I a liar and to blame just because I didn't mention something you should have *seen for yourself*?"

She jerks back like I slapped her, and I almost reach out to comfort her. But then she's off the ropes and taking another swing in seconds. "How is it my fault I didn't know you were so good at hiding how weak you were without feeding?"

Well, fuck. I seriously didn't think *this* is what she wanted to fight about. I'd have left out the window had I known. But she walks closer, and I back up until I'm in the corner.

The relief almost overwhelms me that she's not upset about the blue string, but then an even worse thought comes to mind, and I can't help it—it just pisses me off. Could she have seen the string and just not cared? That all she cares about is whether I'm *feeding*?

"So what?" I explode. "Is it really such a shock that I'm not doing fantastic in this bloody sunlight while working all day and then fortifying the town all night? There's nothing we can do about it until the dragon comes back, so what the fuck good will it do either of us if I whine to you every time I have a fucking headache?"

"It's not that I need you to tell me every time that you've got a headache," she counters. "Though I honestly don't know why you wouldn't. It's that you're suffering, and you don't want to share that with me. You want to pretend that everything is great even though it isn't."

"We've got enough shit on our plate right now—why do I need to bog it down with more stuff? I don't want to bother you—"

"You don't think I *want* to be bothered," she shoots back. "It's not the same thing at all."

"There's nothing wrong with not wanting to give you more to handle. You've already got so much to deal with—"

"Actually, there *is* something wrong with it," Grace interrupts. "We're partners. Or at least I thought we were."

I don't know much, but I know that statement is a giant Grace-size trap, laid out right in front of me with neon lights, and my head and heart hurt too fucking much not to step right in it. "What do you mean 'thought we were'?"

She huffs and plops her hands on her hips. "Finally. Let's finally talk about the elephant in the bedroom."

I throw my arms wide. "By all means, Grace. Tell me exactly what you think is going on here."

"Nothing. Nothing is going on here!" Her eyebrows slam down in accusation. "And that's the problem!"

"Grace, my head is killing me." I run a hand through my hair and repeat my earlier demand. "Just tell me what it is you want me to say, and I'll say it."

"I want to know why you'd rather put yourself through this *pain*"—her hand waves up and down my body—"than feed from me." She bites her lip and tears instantly well in her eyes, but she lifts her chin and holds my gaze.

"I never said that," I tell her, and I hate that my voice has suddenly gone shaky.

"That's the point. You don't have to say it. Everything you do shouts it loud and clear." She takes a swipe at her eyes and adds, "And I'm not putting up with it anymore."

108

I Want You
to Want Me
—Grace—

"What does that mean? What are you not putting up with for one second longer?" Just like that, the fight is gone from Hudson, and in its place is a quiet uneasiness that underscores everything I've just been trying to say to him.

"It means you need to understand that I'm not going to watch this happen, Hudson. That we're in this together, no matter what."

"You don't know what you're saying," he says, and it sounds like the words have been dragged across gravel.

"Of course I know what I'm saying!" I tell him. "How can you think otherwise after everything we've been through?"

And then, because I've finally got Hudson not trying to run from the conversation, I ask the one question that's been beating like a drum inside my chest for weeks. "Do you not want me anymore?"

He laughs, but there's not an ounce of humor in it. "That's what you think this is about?"

"What else should I think it's about?" I demand. "You don't tell me anything."

"I tell you *everything*, Grace," he snaps back. "I shred my fucking pride for you on a daily basis. Give you everything you want without you having to even ask for it. And still, it's not enough?"

Whoa. "I never asked for that!"

"Of course you didn't," he says, his bright blue eyes alight with a fury from within. "You still can't bring yourself to say what you want, can you?"

"That's not—I do—" I break off when he crosses his arms over his chest and leans a shoulder against the wall. It's his defensive, "I'm not going to let you hurt me" posture, and seeing it from him now, directed at me after all this time, has me tripping over my words.

More, it has shame coursing through me. Because all this time, when I've been so sure that I know him better than anyone else, it's never occurred to me that he knows me the same way. That he's been giving me the space to decide what it is I want—*who* it is I want.

As much as I know in my heart that what I had with Jaxon was special, I have been sure for a long time now that it pales in comparison to what I feel for Hudson.

Jaxon knew the best parts of me, loved the best parts of me.

Hudson lived in my head for a year…and he saw *every* part of me. He was privy to every bad mood I've ever been in, every mean word I've every regretted, every catty thing I may have thought. He knows my every irrational fear, all the things I hate about myself or wish I could change.

And yet, he's still here. Fighting with me. Laughing with me. Building a life with me.

I remember my mom once telling me one of the reasons she loved my dad was that he put up with her snoring. She was joking, of course, but I get it now. How truly special is it to find someone who just accepts you exactly as you are. Maybe even loves you because of all those little things you try to keep hidden from others.

Which is why I've always known, for far longer than I was able to admit, that Hudson is everything I want, everything I need, and more importantly, I accept him exactly as he is, the same way he accepts me.

But in the wake of the shame burning through the heat in my veins, I realize I've never said any of this to Hudson.

"Maybe I haven't been able to," I tell him with a sigh. "Not really. Not seriously."

"Maybe not," he agrees.

But it's time I change that.

And so, with a deep breath, I stop hinting. Stop trying to get him to read my mind. And tell him exactly how I feel. What I want. What I need.

"I want you, Hudson," I say and shiver as something predatory moves in his gaze. Something I suddenly want to see how far I can push. "And I need you to take what I'm offering."

Then I pull my hair behind my shoulder, tilt my head up, and expose my neck to his starving gaze.

And wait for whatever comes next.

109

It turns out, I don't have long to wait.

Not when I'm offering myself to a furious, frustrated vampire. And not when that vampire is close enough to see just how desperately I want to give what he so frantically needs to take.

"Grace." It's a plea as much as a warning, and I can hear the truth in the tremble of his voice. The truth that's been escaping me for weeks.

Hudson needs me as much as I need him—he's just afraid. And I get it. I do. Honestly, I can't believe I didn't see it before. I read his journals. I know how his father spent a lifetime giving him things to love, then taking them away.

But that's the way fear works, doesn't it? It's insidious, coming at you from all the dark corners of your soul that you would rather not look at too deeply. But the more you try to ignore it, the deeper it sinks its claws into you. Until you aren't just afraid. You're shredded.

Hudson deserves someone willing to step into the darkness with him.

"Take it," I repeat, because there's no mercy in me tonight and, when it comes to this vampire, I let go of any hint of caution long, long ago. If he didn't know that before, he's definitely going to know it now.

"Why are you doing this?" His voice cracks on the last two words.

"I already told you why. The only question is, why aren't you taking me up on my offer?"

"I don't—" He steps backward.

"You do," I tell him, stepping forward, following him into the shadows.

This time, when he doesn't move back, I take it as the sign I need to move even closer to him. Then I reach up, brush my thumb across his lower lip hard enough to have his lips parting just a little.

His fangs have dropped—I can see them—and it's the last sign. The last little shred of proof I needed to push this all the way.

So instead of backing away, instead of being good girl Grace, I do what I've been dying to do for weeks. For months. I push my thumb into his mouth and very deliberately prick the skin on the razor-sharp tip of his fang.

I know the second my blood touches his tongue. His already huge pupils blow out in an instant, the same instant he slips the powerful hold he's had on himself since I walked in the room.

Hudson grabs my arms with a snarl, flips us around until I'm pressed against the wall, staring down a furious vampire pushed far past his limit.

Because of me. Because that's what I planned to do, what I *wanted* to do. Because these days, that's the only way Hudson will really talk to me.

It's definitely the only way he'll do what we both so desperately need him to.

And still he takes the time—the care—to say, "Tell me if you don't want this."

"I want it," I answer, my hands sliding up his smooth back to tangle in his hair. "I want you."

It must be the answer he needs, the answer he's been waiting for, because I barely get the last word out of my mouth before he's rearing forward and biting me with a sound that's very close to a roar.

His teeth slice through my skin, my vein, with a force that has me arching off the wall and into him. And as he begins to feed, it's everything—and nothing—like the other times he's bitten me.

Heat doesn't shiver along my nerve endings—it sets every inch of me ablaze.

Electricity doesn't prick along my skin—it rockets through me with the force of a missile.

Desire doesn't curl in my belly—it hits me like a two-by-four. And then it does it again. And again. And again. Until my hands are curled in Hudson's hair and tugging, until my legs are wrapped around his hips.

And still he drinks, long, sexy pulls that have my breath sticking in my lungs and my heart beating way too fast.

"Please," I murmur as he finally pulls away and licks a path across my skin. "Please, please, please."

But he's already kissing his way down my throat, nuzzling the collar of my shirt out of the way so he can have better access.

"What do you want, Grace?" he asks in a voice so deep, I have to struggle to understand the words.

Or maybe that's not him. Maybe it's the way my whole body has collapsed in on itself so that the only thing I can think to say is, "More. I want more. I want you. I want…everything."

Hudson groans low in his throat and I think his brain must have short-circuited, too, because he freezes like he doesn't know what to do first. Like he's completely overwhelmed.

But then he whispers, "Are you sure?" against the sensitive skin behind my ear, and I realize he's just being Hudson. Just taking care of me the way he always does.

Except I don't need to be taken care of right now. I just need to be taken.

"Of course I'm sure," I growl even as I grab fistfuls of his hair and yank his head back so that our gazes meet. "I want you, Hudson Vega—I want us—more than I've ever wanted anything in my whole life."

For one second, two, Hudson doesn't say anything. He doesn't move. In fact, I'm pretty sure he doesn't even breathe. But then, all of a sudden, he's spinning us away from the wall and holding me up with one hand while he uses the other to rip my sleep shirt over my head.

And just like that, his mouth is everywhere.

Racing along my jawline.

Licking its way behind my ear.

Pressing long, lingering kisses across my collarbone before sliding lower.

As he does, I let my head drop back and arch my spine to give him better access. To give him all the access.

We've been living together for what feels like forever. Been watching each other for months and dancing around each other for weeks. After all this time, after all those stolen glances, his mouth on my breast feels like spontaneous combustion. His hands on my skin feel like a promise that's finally being fulfilled.

But I want in, too. I need to touch him, need to feel his body beneath my fingertips, my hands, my lips. I've already got his shirt in my hands, so I try to pull it up and over his head the same way he did to mine. Hudson's not budging, though. His mouth is racing along my skin, and he makes it obvious that he's not planning on moving anytime soon.

When I try to scoot back, just to put enough room between us so that I can get his shirt off, he growls low in his throat and just follows me, his lips never leaving my skin.

Which means there's only one thing for me to do—because waiting a single second more isn't an option. Instead, I reach deep inside myself, brush my hand across my platinum string for a moment, and use my gargoyle's strength to rip the shirt right off him.

His eyes go wide, and he chuckles, even as the air around us crackles with the desperation burning inside us both.

"You're getting pretty good with those strings," he teases as he divests himself of the last remnants of his shirt.

"I'm going to keep getting better," I answer as I think about the web of colors deep inside me. "There are so many of them, I'm going to have to if I want to figure them all out."

His grin turns soft. "I'm so glad you're okay with the mating bond. I was worried you'd be upset or disappointed."

He dips his head again, goes back to licking and kissing his way across my skin. But I don't feel it, don't feel him. I'm too busy trying to make sense of the words that just came out of his mouth.

But I can't. They make absolutely no sense to me at all.

"What did you say?" I ask, because I'm sure I didn't hear what he said correctly. I couldn't have.

He glances up at me, confused. "I said I'm glad you're not upset about being mated to me."

"Mated to you?" I repeat as shock hits me right in the chest. "We're mated?"

"I thought you knew," he says, a wariness slowly replacing the heat in his gaze.

"What do you mean you thought I knew?" I shove at his shoulders, push him back so that I can stand without feeling his hot, hard body all over mine. "How would I know?"

"It's one of the strings you keep looking at," he answers, like it's the most obvious thing in the world.

Which it absolutely is not.

"Which string?" I demand, and now I'm getting angry. The fact that he's still looking at my body, and very obviously thinking about touching me, instead of paying attention to how upset I am is not helping the matter.

"The bright blue one. It's hard to miss."

He's right. It is hard to miss. I definitely noticed it, but that didn't mean I knew what it was. Realizing that he clearly has for a while makes me feel all kinds of things—none of them good.

"Why didn't you tell me?" I demand, moving so I'm no longer trapped between him and the wall. "How long have you known?"

When he doesn't immediately answer me, I start to freak out. "That long?" I screech. "So long that you don't even want to tell me how long?"

"Awhile, okay? I've known awhile."

"Awhile?" I throw my hands up in the air. "And you didn't think that maybe you should tell me about it?"

"Why would I tell you about it?" he snarls. "It's not like you've exactly been interested in talking about it."

"What does that even mean? I have been throwing myself at you for weeks, and you haven't so much as given me the time of day!"

"Is that what you call what you've been doing?" He lifts a brow. "Throwing yourself at me?"

"I told you I wanted to climb you like a tree! That's pretty damn clear, if you ask me."

"You did, yeah. But you never even thought about what it means that you felt that way, right? The idea of being mated to *me* is so out of your scope of thought that it never once even occurred to you that we might be mates." He shoves a frustrated hand through his hair. "How do you think that makes me feel?"

"I don't know," I shoot back. "Because you never tell me how you feel."

"Don't give me that bullshit. I never tell you because you don't want to know."

"Oh really?" I cross my arms over my chest in a "do your worst" gesture. "Please, oh great Hudson Vega, tell me how you really feel about me."

His eyes narrow. "I don't need this."

"Of course you don't," I mock. "Why would you when you could use it as one more excuse to avoid actually talking to me."

"So it's my fault now?" he asks, incredulous.

"Well, it sure as shit isn't mine," I tell him sarcastically. "All you have to do is tell me how you feel, and you can't do it. You won't do it."

"I love you!" he snarls.

110

Need You Tonight

—Grace—

Shock ricochets through me. "What did you just say?"

"You heard me," he answers as he advances on me. "I'm not going to say it again."

"You can't just drop that on me—"

"Oh yeah. I can," he tells me. "Now what are you going to do about it?"

I have no freaking idea what I'm going to do about it. How could I?

He's looking at me so intently, and I know I need to say something. I know I need to tell him something, but I can't. Because all I can think is that Hudson loves me. Hudson Vega loves me.

"You don't have an answer, now, do you?" he sneers.

But I do. I so fucking do.

Because fear goes both ways, I realize. I have been just as afraid of what has been building between us as he's obviously been. But I'm not afraid anymore. And he deserves to know that.

Reaching up, I grab him by the back of the head and drag his mouth down to mine.

He makes a surprised sound, but I don't give a damn. Not here and not now. I bite his lower lip, drag it between my teeth, and suck until he groans low in his throat.

Desperate for the taste of him against my tongue, I scrape my teeth along his shoulder, then down to his pecs.

I stroke my hands along his back, reveling in the warm hardness of his muscles beneath my palms.

I press kisses along the line of his too-perfect jaw, then let my mouth linger against the side of his neck, his shoulder, his collarbone.

And then I arch my body against his, begging for more. Begging for everything that he has to give me.

And more. Always more.

Hudson groans in response, spinning us around again until my back is once more against the wall. Then he grabs my upper thighs and gently, gently lowers my legs back to the ground, taking care to make sure I'm steady enough to stand.

"What's wrong?" I ask as I try to wrap myself around him again.

But he just grins, his fangs gleaming in the soft light of the bedside lamp. Then he drops to his knees in front of me, pulling my underwear down my legs as he goes.

And suddenly, his mouth is in a whole lot of new and interesting places. Places I didn't even know could feel the way Hudson makes them feel.

Gasping, I clutch at his shoulders with desperate fingertips as he kisses his way down my body.

"Is this okay?" he asks, lifting his head for one second to look up at me.

I laugh, because this is not even remotely okay. This is so much more than okay that I don't even think I can see okay from here. I don't say that, though. I can't. Sometime in the last sixty seconds, Hudson's mouth has rendered me completely incapable of speech.

So I just nod instead, cupping his face in my hand as I smile down at him with what I'm pretty sure is the goofiest expression on the planet.

Hudson doesn't seem to mind, though. He just smiles back at me, his heavy-lidded eyes seducing me a little more with each second they remain locked on mine.

"I love you," he whispers, and because I still can't talk, I make a high-pitched whining sound in my throat.

It's not much, but it must be enough for him, because he's lifting my leg, draping it around his body. And then kissing me in a way that has my entire body turning to molten lava.

I'm burning. Boneless. Bursting with sensations that have me calling Hudson's name like a mantra as I push back into the wall to keep from crumbling to the floor.

In the end, even that's not enough support to keep me in place, so Hudson takes my hips in his hands and holds me still as he takes me higher and higher, to a place where there are no words, no fear, no past, and no future.

Until there is nothing but us and the pleasure rolling over us like a tsunami. And drowning us in sensation after sensation until finally—finally—he takes me up and over.

And still it's not enough. Still I want more. I tug at him, pulling him up, pulling him closer so that I can fumble with what's left of his clothes as he slowly, carefully walks us over to the bed. Once there, I reach into the bedside table for the package I put there ever since that day in the dressing room—just in case.

Then, after protecting me, he presses his mouth down on mine. Scrapes his fangs across my lower lip just hard enough to draw a drop or two of blood. He licks it up in an instant, and then, when I'm still high on need and joy and love—so much love—he takes us both spinning over the edge and into an ocean of endless pleasure.

111

Amateur Astronomer

—Hudson—

Grace mumbles something in her sleep and rolls over to curl into me. I wrap an arm around her and pull her closer even as I reach for the covers she consistently kicks off in the middle of the night.

I pull them up and over her before smoothing her curls back from her face and wonder if this is what it feels like to be happy.

It's not a feeling I've ever had before, this strange lightness bubbling up inside me. Making me smile whenever I see Grace or even think about her. Making me laugh whenever she says or does something ridiculous—usually for the express purpose of teasing me.

It's an odd feeling, but not a bad one. It's definitely one I can get used to, if it means I get to keep Grace in my life. And I do. I really do.

Grace mumbles something else in her sleep, and I lean over to try to figure out what it was, but then she laughs and I decide it doesn't matter. Because it feels like she's happy, too. And that, maybe, I'm the one who made her that way.

Talk about another strange feeling.

I wait for her to say something more or to laugh again so I can see the way her eyes crinkle up at the corners and the way her cheeks flush that soft pink I like so much. During our months in the lair, I spent a lot of time thinking about that soft pink. Imagining what it tasted like. Imagining running my lips along her cheeks while I whispered things to make her blush.

Just thinking about it has me leaning down, pressing a soft kiss to her cheek just to see if it will make her talk again.

It doesn't, but it does have her kicking off the sheet and comforter I just covered her with. It's the third time she's shoved them away in the last couple of hours, so I don't try to put them on her yet again. Instead, I prop myself on my elbow and let myself do something I rarely get the chance to do when she's awake.

I study all the sweet and sexy little freckles she's got in places that aren't currently covered by her sleep shirt.

There are just enough of them—tiny little dots clustered on her cheeks and her hands, in small groupings on her upper thighs and the curves of her shoulders—that they feel like secrets left for me to discover.

I lower my head and trace my lips across a constellation of them on her inner arm.

Her only response is an incomprehensible moan before she rolls over and buries her face in her pillow. But that just gives me access to all the freckles on the backs of her thighs—a whole interstellar web just waiting for me to connect them with a soft, slow slide of my finger over her skin.

"What is it with you and my freckles?" she asks. Her voice is muffled because her face is still buried in her pillow, but she doesn't seem disturbed by my attention. Just curious.

"I love them," I tell her. "They're like my own little universe right here on your skin. A tiny piece of you that only I get to touch and kiss and appreciate."

She shakes her head, but this time when I run my finger over her freckles, the noise she makes is more purr than complaint. Which only encourages me to do it again.

I'm just starting to think I'm getting somewhere—Grace rolls over and buries her face in the curve of my neck and wraps an arm around me—when her alarm goes off.

She groans, and her breath sighs out. "I've got to get to work."

"You could call in sick, like I have to," I suggest. "Spend the day in bed with me."

I make the suggestion because I want nothing more than to spend the day in bed with Grace, but also because—after last night—I feel like it would be nice to have a chance to see where we stand. Plus, I wouldn't mind the chance to spoil her a little bit, to make sure she's okay, considering last night was her first time.

"I would love to," she says. "But Tinyati sent me home when the store was still a mess last night because she knew I was tired. It wouldn't be fair to just cancel on her now, when she needs me there this morning to help fix things up."

I nod, because I know she's right. But when I go to throw back the covers on my side of the bed so I can get up, she wraps herself around me. "Just because I have to go doesn't mean I have to go right this second."

Her words make me laugh, but they also make me feel good. I like knowing that she's as reluctant to leave as I am to have her leave. "What do you say we go out tonight?" I ask after pulling her on top of me. "I can take you to a fancy restaurant and then maybe to the concert in town square?"

"Or we can stay here where there's no sun," she reminds me. "I'll order room service, and we can play some purple strip poker."

Fuck. I can't believe I forgot—even after all this time. This fucking nonstop sun kills me with the way it never sets. It's the only bad part about being stuck in Noromar forever.

Grace misses her friends and family, but I don't have that. I mean, I have Jaxon, but it's pretty hard to miss a guy who tried to kill you—and who would do it again in an instant if he had the chance.

In so many ways, it's better for me here. I have friends—people like me and trust me and don't think I'm always one step away from sociopathy. But the fact that they're pretty much a vegan society, with nothing for me to feed on but the girl I love, is a little rough.

I love feeding from Grace, would do it every day if I wasn't afraid it would weaken her too much. And if I didn't have to have a life outside this hotel room. But I do. I have to work, I have to walk Smokey, I have to be able to build some kind of life with Grace beyond these four walls. And a sun that almost never sets really puts a fucking cramp in all of that.

"Hey!" She pushes up on an elbow so she can get a better view of my face. "Where'd you go? Not a fan of strip poker?"

"Nowhere," I say with a snort. "Which is pretty much going to be the story of my life for the next few days."

"I know. And I'm sorry about that." She nuzzles into me—trying to bring comfort, I know. "But I'm not sorry you drank from me."

"You sure about that?" I mutter even as I stroke my fingers through her hair.

She laughs, like she thinks I'm joking. "Were you here last night? Because I was, and I've got to tell you, there is absolutely nothing that went on in this hotel room that I didn't like. A lot. Especially that."

"Oh yeah?" I lift my head to get a better look at her face. Because she doesn't sound like she's placating me. Doesn't sound like she feels like she's missing out on anything. In fact, both her voice and the look on her face make it feel like she wants to go another round. With everything. Which isn't exactly a hardship on my part when wanting Grace is like breathing.

Natural, instinctive, and impossible to do without.

"Yeah," she says, and her voice is breathy and urgent. She reaches up, cups the side of my face with her hand, holds my gaze. "You know I love you, right?"

I swallow, my heart lodged in the back of my throat. "I do now."

And then we smile at each other, the kind of smile that says everything two people in love can say—and that's before the first time I feel the tug on our mating bond where she's obviously squeezing it tight. My chest feels so full with love for this girl, I get a little dizzy.

I lean over to kiss her, but as soon as my lips touch hers, the alarm goes off a second time.

Grace groans. "I really need to go." But then she takes a second—okay, sixty seconds—to give me a kiss that has me really looking forward to her coming home tonight.

She pulls away and then rushes into the bathroom for the world's quickest shower. Ten minutes later, she's dragging clothes onto her still-wet body as she races around the room gathering up all the stuff she needs for work. Shoes, hair clip, wallet.

"I'll bring Smokey with me," she says, bending down to pick up the little shadow. "She can make friends with all the shoppers today, and I can take her out to lunch—if she behaves."

To drive her point home, she gives the shadow a warning look. Which Smokey's body language says she's giving back with interest. I just laugh and shake my head. Someday the two women in my life will become best friends. But someday definitely isn't today.

"She'll be fine," I say, rubbing a hand over Smokey's head, "won't you, girl?"

Smokey wraps herself around me in delight, even as she whines a little.

"We'll be fine," Grace tells me. "Right, Smokey?"

This time, the sound she makes is more like a harrumph. But she wraps around my neck in her version of a hug, then races to the door.

Grace grins, rolls her eyes. "Progress, right? Little steps are still progress."

And then she's out the door. Gone. Taking pretty much my whole world with her.

With a groan, I settle back into bed. And begin the tedious process of counting how many hours it is before I can go back outside without killing myself.

The answer is too many. And there's not a damn thing I can do about it.

The last three weeks leading up to Starfall pass in a kind of blur of training, working, planning, and still trying to build a life with Hudson. We go to dinner, to the library, to the small community theater on the other side of town sometimes.

And some days we stay in, exploring each other more.

On the plus side, Hudson is feeling much better since he's been feeding from me regularly on Fridays (so he doesn't miss school) now.

When it comes to the dragon—and the festival—it seems the mayor has finally come through and let the citizens know this one is postponed until we deal with the beast.

Funnily enough, absolutely no one assumes we're going to lose or seems upset to miss a festival. People pat us on the back when we walk through town, shout encouragements, or give us tips. Even the troubadours come to regular planning sessions and help us train. It turns out Lumi has a lot of practice with stage fighting, and while that's not quite the same thing as real fighting, it's not nothing, either.

If nothing else, he gives Hudson—who is a hell of a fighter even without his powers—someone to demonstrate technique with and also helps keep him sharp. Tinyati regularly stops by with new planning ideas, and Nyaz keeps us all fed. Even Souil pops by at the inn a few times to check on Hudson and me.

But now, it's the beginning of a new week, the night before Starfall, and we're all a little on edge.

It's late—so late that the tavern at the inn is closed and the townspeople tucked up in bed. So it's just the troubadours, Hudson, Nyaz, Tinyati, and me sitting around a giant table in the center of the room when the mayor walks in.

"Hello, everyone! Hello!" He strides in confidently, like he owns the place, wearing psychedelic bell-bottoms and a bright red western shirt with leather fringe.

Beside me, Hudson chokes a little, but I refuse to look at him. If I do, I know I'll crack up—especially since he called it on the multicolored bell-bottoms weeks ago.

"Hi, Souil," Nyaz says, then walks behind the bar to pour him a drink. It's purple—big shock—and loaded with fruit, and when he hands it to Souil, the mayor drinks it down in one long swallow.

"Bring me another, will you?" he asks, sliding the glass down the bar to the innkeeper, who catches it smoothly. Then he walks over to the empty chair next to me and sits down, kicking his feet up on the edge of the table.

"So, how's everyone doing?" he asks. "Ready for the big night?"

"They are," Tinyati says as she gathers up her bag before leaning down to give me a hug. "I've got to get home—the kids are a bear to get to bed for my husband alone. And they need a good night's sleep for Starfall!"

"Wait, what?" I ask, confused. "You aren't really going to let them outside, are you? What if the dragon—"

"Oh, no, of course not! But if there's still a festival left on the second day—after the dragon attack—we've told them we can go."

I nod as I remember the mayor had promised everyone a light show like they'd never seen after the dragon is taken care of, to make up for the canceled festival. In fact, Hudson and I had even made tentative plans—assuming all goes well—to watch the fireworks from the clock tower together.

"Is that what everyone is doing?" Lumi asks as he taps his fingers on the table nervously. "I really hope no one is going out on the streets."

"We've warned everyone—even the tourists." Souil shrugs. "Nothing we can do if they don't heed our advice."

"Actually, there is," Hudson tells him, his voice dripping in irony. "You are the mayor. You can order a full lockdown tomorrow: a mandatory curfew."

"Yes, I tried that," Souil tells him with a blithe wave of his hand. "But the town council outvoted me. Told me there was almost no chance that our two most esteemed new citizens would allow the dragon to enter the city limits. It was hard enough to convince them to cancel the festival in the first place, as most don't believe the dragon is coming back after what Grace and Hudson did to her last time."

He doesn't sound that upset the council doesn't agree. In fact, he looks like he's relishing something going wrong so he can hold it over the council's head. At least until he glances my way and realizes I'm studying him. Then he shakes his head and puts on a disgusted face, one I'm not sure I buy.

A quick glance at Hudson tells me he feels the same. It makes me uneasy, makes me wonder if there's more at play here than we know. But in the end, does it really matter if the mayor is in a war with the town council or not? I mean, as residents of Adarie ourselves, it could make things uncomfortable for us in the long run. But for the specific purpose of killing this dragon, it doesn't really matter.

At least not if we can find a way to keep the people away from the fight and the casualties at zero, and we've put a lot of planning these last three months into doing just that.

"What happens if the town council is right?" Orebon asks. "What if we do all this and the dragon never shows?"

"The dragon will show," the mayor tells him.

"How do you know?" I ask, gaze narrowed.

"The dragon will come," Souil says in a voice that brooks no argument. "I know that for a fact. All we have to do is kill her when she does."

And by we, he means the rest of us. But I'm not going to quibble.

To be honest, wizard or not, I don't think he'd be much help out there. He's actually shown zero magical abilities in all this time, to the point that Hudson and I have joked his "time wizard" is a title he's given himself, much like "mayor." Either that or his magic only works on his wardrobe.

We spend a few more minutes talking things through, making sure we're as ready as we're ever going to be. Then, once everybody else has left, Hudson and I head up.

We don't talk on the stairs, mostly because there's not a lot to say. Not about this. And since I'm pretty sure it's the only thing either one of us is thinking about right now, there's nothing else to talk about, either.

Once we get to our floor, though, I glance out the window at the end of the hall. In Noromar, sunset can last for hours, and I revel at watching the early rays start to dip for the first time in months.

"It's beautiful, isn't it?" Hudson murmurs.

I sigh. "Yeah, it is. It sucks that thinking about it reminds me of being covered in dragon guts."

"Hopefully we won't let that happen." The fact that his tone is so serious says everything it needs to about what he expects tomorrow night to be like.

Not that I blame him. I feel the exact same way. "Yeah, hopefully."

After we get to our room, I take a quick shower before heading back into the bedroom. Hudson's already in bed, and he smiles when he sees me.

I try to smile back, but it's harder than it sounds when I'm terrified that another person I love will die tomorrow night. Tears well up behind my eyes, and I blink them away. I'm not going to cry right now. I'm just not.

"Oh, Grace." Hudson sits up in bed to wait for me, and the second I crawl between the sheets, he wraps his arm around my waist and gently pulls me across the bed until my back rests against his front. "What can I do?" he asks, voice soft and soothing against my ear.

Before I can answer, Smokey gets up from her spot on the floor and grumbles her way into the bathroom. The door closes with a slam.

"Well, she definitely knows how to make her point," he says.

"She really does."

He reaches up, smooths my curls back from my face. "You didn't answer me. What do you need me to do?"

"Nothing," I tell him in a voice that's little more than a whisper. "There's nothing to do. I'm fine."

He doesn't answer—probably because he's trying to come up with a diplomatic way to tell me that nothing about me is radiating fine at this moment. Then again, he's not looking so good himself, so maybe that's not what he's doing at all.

In the end, he just holds me and rubs a soothing hand up and down my arm for a while. Then says, "So...worried about tomorrow, then?"

"If by worried you mean absolutely terrified, then yes. I'm worried."

I can feel his smile against my cheek. "I'm worried, too."

"Bullshit." I snort. "You're never scared."

"That's not true." His smile fades.

"Yes, it is. In all the time I've known you, I've never actually seen you afraid. Pissed off, sure. Concerned, absolutely. But afraid? No, I've literally *never* seen that."

"Then you haven't been looking very closely, because there were a couple of times in particular when I was terrified," he tells me.

I narrow my eyes at him as I think back over the time we've spent together. Then ask, "When exactly were these terror-filled experiences supposed to have taken place?"

"Anytime I thought I might lose you," he answers.

"Hudson." I roll over to face him, cup his face in my hands. And kiss him with all the love and fear I have inside me.

He pulls away almost immediately. "Don't do that."

"Don't do what?"

"Don't kiss me like you think it's the last time," he whispers. And I realize, in shock, that his eyes are wet and my heart cracks. Hudson hasn't cried since he was a kid, according to his journals. That's not going to change tonight.

Still, just in case, I press myself up against him. Bat my eyes a little. And say in the most atrocious French accent I can muster up, "Tell me, monsieur. How do you want me to kiss you?"

For a second, he just stares at me like I've drunk too much. And then he starts to laugh, exactly as I intended.

When he finally stops, I put the accent back on. "You didn't answer me, monsieur."

This time he just shakes his head and says, "Like you mean it, Grace. Kiss me like you mean it."

It's the best idea I've heard all day. So that's exactly what I do.

113

One Surprise Deserves Another
—Hudson—

race, Smokey, and I hit the streets a little under three hours before the sun goes down. We'll need to head toward the gates soon and the area we've decided to confront the dragon—far enough from Adarie to be safe for the townspeople, though the troubadours have offered to meet us there and help fight—but we've got time to wander for a bit, appreciate the quiet before the coming storm.

Smokey takes off to explore the second we get outside, which leaves Grace and me walking along the cobblestone streets, wondering what happens next.

"It's so beautiful," Grace says as she looks up at all the balconies, with overflowing flower boxes and purple vines crawling along the brick exteriors. As she does, she twirls around slowly so as not to miss anything, and I'm captivated all over again.

Despite the weight of the things hanging over us, here in this moment of early twilight with fairy lights tiptoeing across her skin, she is so incredibly beautiful. Her smile is open and bright. Her eyes are filled with wonder. Even those few little freckles I love so much seem to dance across her cheeks and the bridge of her nose with every move she makes.

And when she reaches for my hand, when she pulls me in for a cuddle and a kiss, I've never been more in love with her.

My strong, radiant, powerful mate, who faces down everything that comes her way with courage and compassion. Even now, as we prepare for what we both know may be a bloodbath in every possible way, she is resolute in her determination to do what needs to be done. And still, she takes a moment to revel in the beauty of the world around her.

How could I not love her?

How could I not want her for an eternity?

She's the universe's gift to me, and if I can just have her and nothing else, then I'll be satisfied. And I'll still consider myself luckier than I have any right to be.

"Why are you looking at me like that?" she asks when our eyes finally meet.

"Just feeling grateful."

She lifts her brows. "We're about to go into the biggest fight of our lives, and you're feeling grateful?"

"Strange, I know." I reach behind her and pluck a flower from one of the many garlands draped around the town square. When I hold it out to her, I say, "I know it's not a flower crown, but—"

Her eyes go misty. "For me?"

"No, for Smokey," I tease. "She's behind you."

Grace just rolls her eyes. "Give me my flower."

"I already told you. It's for—"

She snatches it out of my hand and tucks it into the curls above her left ear. "Touch it and I'll break every bone in your hand."

It's my turn to raise a brow. "It's kind of hard to fight a dragon one handed."

"Well, then, you know what you need to do, don't you?" Her voice is prim and proper, but the look in her eyes is that of a warrior goddess who bends for no man.

"I am so ridiculously crazy about you."

She grins. "As you should be." Then she takes hold of my hand and starts pulling me through the streets.

"Where are we going?" I ask as she pulls me deeper into the square.

"I have a surprise for you."

"Oh yeah?"

She laughs. "Don't give me that look. It's not that kind of a surprise."

"A guy can dream, can't he?" But I'm just teasing her, and she knows it, even as she rolls her eyes at me.

She pulls me all the way through the square, past the closed food trucks and the empty activity tents and the quiet gazebo.

Grace makes a noise low in her throat and starts tugging me harder. "It's almost dark."

Because the surprise seems so important to her, I hurry up. Then freeze when I realize where she's brought me. The clock tower.

"What did you do?" I ask.

She smiles just a little sexily. "Guess you'll have to come inside with me if you want to find out."

"I've got a better idea." I pick her up and put her on my back.

"For old times' sake?" she asks.

"For new times' sake," I answer.

And then I start to climb.

We reach the top with still an hour before the sun goes down. I glance inside, see the blanket she's spread on the floor and covered with flowers and the fancy water she has chilling in an ice bucket.

"Grace—" I say, then stop as all hell breaks loose.

114

It takes every ounce of self-control I have not to scream as the dragon swoops into town.

We weren't expecting her this early, thought we'd have hours to kill before she finally showed up. The mayor insisted time dragons only attack at night, and the sun hasn't set yet!

As the dragon faces straight to the center of the town square and spews flames at the gazebo that is the heart of so many village events, it catches fire instantly, flames licking from the roof downward onto the actual structure as smoke spews into the air.

The streets are empty, thankfully, but Hudson doesn't hesitate to jump into action. He leaps straight off the clock tower, lands in a crouch on the cobblestone road below. And then he's fading straight for the burning gazebo without so much as a backward glance.

I take off after him, shifting into my gargoyle form and jumping off next, my wings catching the air effortlessly even as I wonder what he's doing.

We have weapons and ropes planted along the edge of a forest outside of town, so why isn't he trying to get this beast to the planned site?

As I fly after Hudson, the dragon swoops right by, and I register how big this creature is. She must be younger than we thought, because she's obviously spent the last three months healing and growing. Like really, really growing. She has to be double her size from our first encounter, and she was already close to three times as large as the dragon we killed then.

How the hell are we supposed to take her down?

"What's going on?" Orebon shouts as he falls into step beside me, a sword banging against his hip as he runs.

"What are you doing here?" I shout, panic filling my voice. "You're supposed to be inside! Orebon, no—you need to stay safe, to protect Amiani!"

But Orebon just shakes his head, yells, "This is how we protect Amiani. How we protect *everyone* who is important to us."

Then we hear Lumi and Caoimhe shouting, and I finally understand what the dragon is doing, what made Hudson take off like a bat out of hell, what Orebon is referring to.

Because I see her. Smokey. Standing next to the gazebo, completely frozen except for the fact that she's screaming her head off. And the dragon is headed straight for her.

My heart slams into my throat, and I lay on a burst of speed. Because that shadow might be difficult as hell for me to live with, but Hudson loves her. And she would do anything for him. Anything save stop screaming, apparently, because that seems to be beyond her right now. And there's something about the sound that's pulling the dragon straight to her.

Hudson's moving so fast he's practically a blur, and just as the dragon swoops down to grab Smokey, he slides in front of her and snatches the small shadow into his arms. Then he's gone again, and the dragon is screaming her displeasure to the world.

Whipping around to follow him, she lets out a stream of fire so large, it takes out two food carts in seconds.

"If a dragon's weapon is fire, shouldn't we find a way to neutralize that weapon as best we can?" Lumi had said during one of our planning sessions, and I frantically look around for one of the fire extinguishers the mayor had gotten the council to agree to spread around the village, just in case.

I spy one hiding next to a bench about fifty feet from what's left of the food courts and race for it. Orebon beats me to it. He snatches it up and races to put out the food truck fires before they spread.

Knowing Orebon has the fires taken care of, I turn back toward the square, searching for Hudson. I find him back on top of the clock tower, dropping Smokey on the blanket I'd laid out for the two of us.

Then he's jumping back down and racing across the square toward me as the dragon takes another turn around the area.

I meet him about fifteen percent of the way because fading is a thing. "I'm sorry!" he says before I even have time to yell at him for not giving me some kind of heads-up. "I couldn't just let her die."

"Of course you couldn't," I tell him but promise myself that I'll get to yell at him later for scaring the hell out of me. "What do we do now?"

Before Hudson can even say a word, the dragon lets out a screech that rips through the air like a lightning strike. Right before she pulls in her wings and starts to dive straight toward the troubadours, who are racing down the street leading outside of the square to the gates.

There's no way they'll make it.

115

The Tail End
of the Deal
—Grace—

"What the hell is with this dragon?" Hudson demands. "She's fucking evil."

And then he's fading again, racing straight to our friends. But Lumi, Caoimhe, and Orebon must realize they're not going to make it outside of town, so they duck into one of the giant tents erected in case the festival is allowed to proceed tomorrow.

She must see them, though, because the dragon changes course at the last minute. Instead of flying above the tent, she tucks her wings in and flies straight through it. She tears the tent itself to shreds and sends everything inside it flying in all directions—including our friends.

"Oh my God," I whisper as I push myself to fly faster. It's like she knows all our plans and our weaknesses—and is using both against us. I don't know how that's possible, but she's obviously so much smarter than we gave her credit for. It's terrifying in a whole new way.

Now that she's ripped the tent apart, the dragon sends a wave of fire through the whole place—and everything inside it that is now scattered through the square. It's like she wants to be sure there's nowhere for any of us to hide.

Seeing the tent go up in flames, someone comes running out of their house, fire extinguisher in their hands. It's a woman with long brown hair, and my heart is pounding in my throat as I yell at her, "Get back inside!"

But it's too late. The dragon swoops down and grabs the wraith up in her powerful jaws.

The ensuing crunch—the cracking of bones—is something I will never forget as long as I live.

I scream as horror rips through me, and for a second, my knees go weak. I hit the ground, hard, and so does the woman as the dragon flings her away with one powerful shake of her head.

The woman is dead before she hits the ground. And there's nothing any of us or any of our big plans can do about it.

I stumble back to my feet with some thought of getting to her, but before I can even take a step, the dragon snatches Lumi up in her talons and starts to climb back into the sky.

Orebon is immediately running, screaming for his spouse, but Hudson gets to the dragon first, and he leaps ten feet straight into the air to grab onto her tail. She screams in outrage, thrashes it back and forth, but he hangs on for all he's worth.

But even he can't do that forever, and as she climbs higher into the night, all I can think is, what happens when they both fall?

116

Ripping the Scales

—Hudson—

What's that quote by Einstein that used to be so popular on social media posts? "Insanity is doing the same thing over and over and expecting different results"? I probably should have remembered that before I jumped on another bloody dragon. Because there is no way I'm cowboying my way off this one. She's massive and pissed off and determined to get me off her.

Normally, I'd be more than happy to oblige, but she's also determined to drop Lumi, and that I am *not* okay with. So there's only one thing I can think of to do, as she is currently whipping me around like one of those carnival rides that makes everyone vomit.

I plaster my torso against her tail while wrapping my arms and legs around it as tightly as I can. When my arms and ankles are linked on the underside of her tail, I start to shimmy my way up it as quickly as I can. Which, sadly, is nowhere near as quickly as I would like it to be.

Lumi, in the meantime, is trying to pry his way out of the cage of the dragon's talons. But we're getting too high up for that. If he manages to escape or she just gets fed up with the annoyance of him prying at her and drops him, he'll never survive the fall.

Which means I need to go fucking faster. And hope like shit I don't fall off, either.

But it really isn't as easy as it sounds, considering she's got sharp scales going all the way up her damn tail, and I'm trying quite hard not to bloody unman myself on one of them.

By the time I finally make it to the top of her tail, I feel like I've been shaken and stirred. I take a moment to get my bearings—and swallow down the nausea. I mentally measure the distance between the top of the tail and the talons that are currently holding Lumi. And decide, fuck it, I can make it in one go.

I don't let myself think what will happen to him if I miss. Instead, I concentrate on spinning around to the underside of the dragon—not a view or position I would recommend, by the way.

Realizing my mistake a little too late, I very carefully, and very laboriously, shimmy my way back up to the side of the dragon's tail.

I'm draped over the thing now, meaning I'm only holding on with one hand and one leg. So the second she starts thrashing around again, I'm going to fly off if I don't do something quick.

As if I thought it into fruition, the dragon picks this exact moment to wag her tail, or whatever the hell dragons do with the things. I begin to slide off, just like I feared, and barely manage to grab one of the scales to hold on to.

They're even sharper on bare skin than they are through jeans, however, and it slices through the skin of my palm. As blood flows all down my hand and fingers, it becomes a hundred times harder to hold on—and that's not even counting the pain of the whole thing.

Still, there's too much at stake here to let go. So I just grit my teeth, hold on tight, and wait for the perfect opening.

It finally comes as the dragon circles the clock tower. To avoid running into the sharp spires, she pulls her talons up close to her body, with Lumi still in them.

It's the closest he's been to me this entire time, but I'm smart enough to know that I've only got a few seconds to capitalize on his proximity. As soon as we round this expanse of taller buildings, the dragon will untuck her legs and the opportunity will be lost.

With that in my head, I don't give myself any more time to think about what might go wrong. Instead, I just move. I release the scale with my hand and push off the dragon's tail with my leg as hard as I can and end up flying the eight or so feet straight into her clenched talons. And Lumi.

I bounce off as soon as I hit the talons and scramble to hold on to something, anything. That something is Lumi, my good hand tangling in his shirt as I hold on for dear life.

Lumi screams as I crash into him and start to slide down, but then he's scrambling, too. Reaching out and grabbing whatever part of me *he* can take hold of.

He grabs the wrist on my bad hand, holding on with a strength that surprises me considering how lanky he is. And then we're flying through the air with me dangling from her talons like I'm paragliding with a fucking dragon on my back.

"What do we do?" Lumi yells to be heard over the air rushing past us.

Part of me wants to say bollocks if I know, but somehow I don't think that will go over well. Besides, there's only one thing we can do at this point. Jump and bloody well pray we land somewhere soft.

I'm only going to get one chance at this, though, so I have to make sure we don't drop too early or too late. At this point, I honestly think our best bet is one of the tents set up around the square. I just need it to break our fall a little bit and I should be able to get Lumi on the ground without too much damage.

But I have to make sure I can get the dragon's talons open at just the right moment. And considering last time I had a fuck of a time, this could end really badly.

Plus, to pry them open, I need both hands, and right now my hands are the only things keeping me from falling out of the air. Well, my hands and Lumi, who still has a death grip around my wrist.

The dragon's coming around to the town square again, finally, which means I have to figure this out fast. I only hope Grace doesn't decide to try to come and rescue me. The last thing I need is the dragon taking a piece of her or setting her on fire if Grace isn't in her solid stone form. If that happens, I'm afraid I'll burn the whole fucking village to the ground just for a chance to get this damn dragon.

I start to inch my hand over on the talon to the dragon's knuckles when I happen to spot Lumi's dagger in the sheath around his waist. Grace and I encouraged everyone to take a sword—or two—for this battle, but Lumi had insisted his dagger was the only weapon he needed.

At the time, I thought he was being shortsighted, but here, now, I've never been more grateful for someone's stubbornness in my life. Because that dagger is going to save our fucking lives.

As she gets closer to the part of the square where the tents are—and fires still rage—the dragon starts to go faster. Knowing I'm about to miss my opportunity, and not sure my blood-slicked hand is going to be up for another spin around the village, I yell to Lumi to hold on to my wrist as tightly as he can.

Which leaves me with only one thing to do in this situation. I take a bloody huge leap of faith and hope I land somewhere that won't kill the both of us.

117

After spending the last five minutes holding on for dear life, it takes a couple of seconds to convince my brain to let go. When I finally manage it, I lever myself up and snag the dagger off Lumi's belt.

I glance down as the dragon approaches the tents. It's now or never, so I do what needs to be done and use the dagger to slice a large gash in the dragon's talons.

"Hold on!" I shout and am grateful when Lumi grabs me around the waist so I have both hands free again.

The dragon screams in pain at the exact same instant we start to fall. But instead of freaking out and flying away, as I expected, she gets pissed as hell and lets loose a string of fire that burns straight through every single tent in the square. Including the one I was hoping to land on. Of course.

"New plan," I shout to Lumi as we fall.

"There's a plan?" he shouts back to be heard over the rushing wind.

"Not really," I admit. With Lumi holding on, I spin around the best I can in midair. My goal is to land first and have him use me as a cushion. It's not a great plan, and I know I'm going to end up with a shit ton of broken bones, but I can't just leave him to die.

Not the fall but the bounce, I remind myself even though I still think it's bullshit. And prepare to—

All of a sudden, Grace flies right into us at what feels like one hundred miles an hour. She sends us spinning through the air, but she catches up immediately and wraps her arms around me.

"Need a ride?" she asks.

"Bless you, Grace," Lumi says, and he looks completely green.

I have one second to fear that he's going to puke on me, but somehow he manages to hold it together until we get to the ground. As soon as his feet hit grass, he stumbles away and pukes behind the nearest bench.

Not that I blame him—that was one hell of a close call.

To be honest, it's still a close call, considering the dragon has gone into a rage like nothing I've ever seen before. She's burning everything in her path, and suddenly I'm afraid there won't be any village come morning if we don't do something fast.

The only good thing—and good is a relative term here—that comes out of this latest rampage is that when she spins in midair, she catches sight of Grace and me. And once she's found us, she locks on like a heat-seeking missile and comes right at us.

"Fly!" I yell to Grace because this is the best chance we've got to get her out of town and away from all the people who live here.

"I'm on it!" she yells back, and she is, leaping into the air in a blink. We need the dragon to think she can catch us because we need her to stay interested in us and not go find another, easier target. Like poor Lumi, for example, who is currently cowering under the park bench he just puked behind.

Determined to make sure the dragon doesn't focus on Lumi, I lay on the speed just a little more. The dragon responds by sending a streak of flames straight at me. I manage to swerve out of the way in time, but it's a little too close for comfort.

I glance above and find Grace, her brown eyes narrowing dangerously as she says, "I've got an idea."

"What idea?" I ask, right before she executes a pretty impressive midair flip, turning around and flying close enough to the dragon to touch her nose before flipping again and flying straight for the town gate.

Which pisses the dragon the hell off—exactly what Grace was intending.

The flying beast goes wild and lays on speed in a wild effort to catch her. But Grace lays on speed, too. And just like that, they're caught in a high-speed chase that I'm terrified isn't going to end well for Grace.

It's a feeling that's reinforced by the fact that, as the dragon gains on Grace, she releases one stream of fire after the other. Grace—whose flying skills have improved a lot in the last several weeks—spins, ducks, and dodges away from the flames.

At least until one manages to catch the tip of her wing and throws everything out of whack.

Grace screams as she starts plummeting to the earth, the dragon hot on her tail. She tries to pull up, but the dragon either got really lucky or knew exactly where to aim, because Grace's wing has lost whatever it is that makes it aerodynamic.

She's currently in a flat spin, headed straight toward the ground.

As I fade across the terrain, I'm terrified I'm not going to make it in time. Especially since the fall isn't the biggest of her problems. The dragon is catching up to her now that she's no longer in control and the closer the creature gets, the more convinced I am that she plans to light Grace up for good.

I'm not going to let that happen.

I fade to them with only one thought in my mind—getting Grace out of the dragon's line of fire. And when the dragon lets loose another stream of flames so close to Grace that it will fry her to a crisp, I'm left with no choice. I jump straight up to intercept it, throwing my body between Grace and the fire.

I spin in midair, grabbing Grace so she doesn't plummet to the ground and bracing myself to feel all the dragon's fire. She's close enough for me to know I'm not going to get out of this, close enough that all I can do is pray that I can shield Grace—and make it to the ground so that I can save her before the dragon kills me.

But I'm not the only one who has that idea, because I'm still turning—still bracing myself—when at the very last second, Smokey comes racing through the night.

I have one millisecond to yell for her to stay back, to get down, but it's too late.

She throws herself between the dragon's fire and me.

And she takes it all.

118

It's a Hack Job but Someone's Got to Do It
—Grace—

udson screams like his heart is breaking, and I manage to look up just in time to watch Smokey get hit with a stream of fire so powerful that no one who isn't solid stone could survive it.

And it's all my fault.

If I hadn't tried to lead the dragon away, if I had been faster and not let the dragon clip my wing with her fire, none of this would have happened. Smokey would be safe. She would be alive.

And Hudson. Hudson wouldn't be free-falling with me toward the earth like his entire world just lost meaning.

We hit the ground, hard, but he doesn't flinch. He takes one second to put me down gently on the ground.

"Go!" I tell him. "Go!"

He's fading across the square before I get the first word out—and catches what's left of Smokey's poor incinerated body before it can hit the ground.

I'm right behind him, and I catch *him* as he stumbles, hold him as Smokey's ashes flutter in the air around us, the singed red ribbon falling limply to the ground.

"No," he whispers as he falls to his knees in front of me, takes the ribbon in his hand. "Please, no, no, no."

"I'm sorry." I clutch his shoulder as I, too, look at what's left of our tiny, mischievous little friend. "I'm so sorry."

He looks up at me with pain-ravaged eyes, and I want nothing more than to hold him. To comfort him. To take the last two minutes back and make this all okay.

But I can't do that. I can't do any of that. And so I do the only thing I can do to buy Hudson time to mourn. I change to stone and back again to see if maybe—just maybe—it will cure my wing.

When I change back, my wing is repaired. The pain is still there, but the tip of the wing is healed. I can fly again.

And so I do, rocketing straight into the air as the dragon bears down on Hudson and on poor Smokey's remains.

I get to the same level as the dragon one second before she lets loose another stream of flames straight at Hudson and, this time, when my fist turns to stone, it's on purpose. We connect with a powerful slam, and I hit her with an undercut beneath her jaw as hard as I can.

The power behind the stone sends the dragon reeling through the air, her fire spewing across the night sky as she tumbles backward. I fly after her, determined to bring her down this time. Determined that she's wreaked enough havoc tonight, killed and injured enough people. I'm done with her. Done with this. Even if I have to die to stop her, this ends now.

And so I chase her across the night sky.

Eventually the dragon rebounds from my punch and comes back at me, fire blazing from her nose and mouth and rage pouring from her eyes.

But that makes two of us. I may not have the flames, but I sure as hell have the fury, and I drop down so that I can fly beneath her this time. As I do, I change both my hands to stone. Then I lower myself to where she can't see me beneath her and come right back up, gathering speed as I go.

This isn't like before. I don't have the power or momentum behind me to plow right through her chest. But I do have enough power to aim for something else.

As the dragon spreads her wings wide and searches the area far below us for more prey, I take my stone fists and plow right through her thin, leathery wing—and then yank down with as much strength as I can find.

She screams again as a jagged rip appears where she once had a functioning wing. She goes into free fall, turning upside down and spinning, spinning, spinning completely out of control, and I kick away from her, my wings pulling me out of the path of her death spiral.

But still she doesn't go down without a fight. She hits the ground hard, flames spewing in all directions as she climbs shakily to her feet. But Hudson is there, too, fading up and around and under her flames as he races straight for her.

I don't know what he plans to do, don't know even if he has a plan at this point, but there's no way I'm letting my mate go after this dragon alone. Not when she's angry and hurt and cornered and has nothing left to lose.

I fly full-tilt toward them, pushing myself as hard as I possibly can in an effort to get to her before she lights Hudson up. He's not thinking straight right now, and I don't know if he's in any state of mind to take this dragon on alone.

Except he's not alone, because even before I get there, Caoimhe races out of the night with two giant purple swords.

She tosses one to Hudson, who slows down just enough to catch it on the fly, then barrels straight toward the dragon, who is screaming and clawing at the ground as she continues to shoot fire all around her.

I get there just as Hudson jumps straight into the air, sword arcing over his head. With a cry of pain and rage that equals anything the dragon is screeching out, he brings the sword down on her neck with every ounce of vampire power he has in his body.

The razor-sharp sword slices straight through her tough outer skin, straight through the muscle and bone beneath, until her severed head falls to the ground at his feet.

119

Big Disco
Ball Energy
—Grace—

Blood gushes out of the dragon's neck, where her head used to be, and soaks the purple ground around her in this strange, radioactive orange dragon blood.

Hudson is standing in it all, swinging his sword with both hands as he hacks away at the dead dragon's gaping neck wound, over and over and over with sickening thwacks. Like she died too quickly, like there's nowhere for his anger and pain to go unless she suffers as much as he is.

I reach for him, ease the sword from his clenched hands as he stumbles backward. "It's okay," I say softly, and he leans heavily on me. "It's over. It's all over."

He turns to look at me for the first time, and his face is drained of color, his brilliant blue eyes dull and shattered.

"She's gone," he chokes out, and I know he's not talking about the dragon.

"She is," I whisper back, even as my own heart breaks at the loss. "I'm so, so sorry."

"Why did she do that?" he rages. "Why did she have to get in the middle of this fight? I put her in that clock tower. I told her to stay put, told her I would come get her when it was all over. Why didn't she listen? Why didn't she—"

"Because she loved you," I say. I want to pull him close, hold him against my heart, but I know he's not ready for that yet. So I just tell him the truth. "Because she wanted to protect you as much as you ever wanted to protect her."

He nods, his jaw working, but the devastation in his eyes is as black as ever.

I promise myself when we get back to the inn—or what's left of the inn after this dragon lost her shit all over the town square—I'll hold him for as long as he'll let me.

But right now, we have a new problem. Because just like the dragon we killed last time, droplets of gold and silver are rising out of this dragon, too.

They're spinning, spinning, spinning in that same double-helix pattern I saw before. Only instead of rising into the night as I thought the other ones did, this energy stays right here between us and the dragon.

As first, I don't know what's wrong, and it creeps me out. Is this her soul circling around us? Her energy? Is this a way for her broken body to try to reassemble itself?

I hope it's not that. I really do. Because death should be respectful—even the death of our enemies—and the last thing I want is to have to fight some oddly reanimated zombie dragon after everything else that's happened tonight.

But it turns out what's actually happening is *so much worse.*

Because when I look behind me, Souil is here. He's the one pulling forth this fine gold-and-silver mist from within the dragon. And under my horrified, watchful eye, he's the one who opens his mouth and starts to pull the dragon's essence deep inside himself.

"What are you doing?" I gasp, trying to get between him and the dragon's soul. "You can't do that. You can't—"

He shoves me out of the way so hard that I stumble into the slick blood and nearly fall. But Hudson's there to catch me even as he whirls around to see what the mayor is doing.

"You sick fuck," he growls, setting me aside as he moves toward the mayor, who has almost absorbed all of the dragon's essence by this time.

No, not just the *mayor,* I remember sickly.

Souil had claimed he was a time wizard, too, but we'd laughed it off. My stomach bottoms out as I realize we may have made a terrible mistake.

For the first time in months, I remember the figure on the balcony of City Hall as the smaller dragon's essence made its way up and into the night.

I remember how almost unrecognizable Souil was when we met up with him for brunch the next day. How much younger and smoother his face had looked.

More, I remember him pushing us to kill this very dragon, telling us that it was the only way to save the village.

And here he is now, at the scene of this death, taking the last thing this dragon has to give.

Yes, I know she had to die. I know she was determined to kill us all—and, at the end, I think, to kill Hudson and me specifically. But knowing that is one thing.

Knowing that we might have been duped—that we might have been used—is another thing altogether.

Already, the mayor looks younger, taller, stronger. He definitely seems more powerful, his body alight from within by the powerful magic he's just absorbed. When he moves, when he lifts his arms in front of him, he fairly crackles with electricity and, by the time he breathes in the last of the dragon's essence, he is glowing.

"What the fuck did you do?" Hudson yells, heading toward him at a run.

But before Hudson gets there, Souil is gone.

"What the hell?" Hudson turns around, wild-eyed. "Where'd he go?"

I shake my head because I have no idea.

Long seconds pass as we spin in circles trying to figure out where he disappeared to, all to no avail.

And then, suddenly, he's back. A hundred feet from where he'd been just a moment before.

"How did he do that?" I ask, but Hudson doesn't take the time to answer. Instead, he fades toward the wizard again.

He's there in less than a second, but Souil is already gone.

Except this time it isn't for as long. A beat later, he pops up directly behind Hudson and shoves him, hard.

The push has Hudson flying forward and landing on his face. *Hudson*, who never stumbles under the weight of someone else's power.

He's back up in a split second, whirling toward Souil, who is standing in the middle of town square now, legs apart and head thrown back in laughter.

"You don't actually think you're going to be able to touch me, do you?" he queries as Hudson fades toward him.

And yet again, he disappears—only to reappear several feet away with a giant stick in his hand. But it's not just any stick. It's got two chains coming from the top of it, and attached to those chains are spiky silver balls the likes of which I have never seen before.

Oh, and he's added a cape to his ensemble—a bright white and silver sequined one, to be exact, nearly the same color as what I think might possibly be a medieval battle mace in his hand—updated, of course, with a little seventies flare.

"What the fuck is that?" Hudson shoots me a look, completely bewildered.

"I think it's—" I breaks off as Souil lifts the stick above his head and starts to spin it while his hips gyrate, Elvis style. The chains—and the balls attached to them—start to spin, too, and I gasp as the entire town square is suddenly turned into a seventies, LSD-inspired disco party.

The only thing missing is the Bee Gees singing "How Deep Is Your Love." Then again, I think Souil might be auditioning for the role as the fourth Bee Gee as we speak. He's definitely got the hip motions down—now all he needs is a little of that cross-body pointing action, and he'll be good to go.

"Are those spiked…disco balls?" Hudson whispers in horror.

"I'm pretty sure they are, yeah," I answer. Because what else is there to say at this point? If the Beatles' yellow submarine started floating down Main Street, I wouldn't be surprised.

But even though Souil looks ridiculous, there's something really creepy about his fixation with the seventies that makes me wonder… Does he have the ability to bend time? Can he skip between the past and the future whenever he wants? And if he can, is there anything he can't do? Anything he can't use in the middle of a fight? Any trap he won't be able to weasel out of?

I shake my head. No, that can't be right. If he could do that, surely others would have noticed, said something. My shoulders start to relax. Maybe this isn't as bad as it looks.

"Well, that's something you don't see every day," Orebon comments as he comes up behind us.

"Or ever," Caoimhe adds. "Thankfully."

"Come on, Hudson!" Souil calls from his spot across the square. "You were so brave before. Don't you want to get down tonight?"

"Is anyone else seeing this?" Lumi asks, shaking his head like he wants to clear it. "Or did I get hit so hard, I'm hallucinating?"

I can see why he thinks that could be the case. Because who would ever, *ever* imagine that this is an actual thing? That the seventies-obsessed mayor of the largest town in the Shadow Realm would swing disco balls around like a weapon, all while dressed like a damn Elvis impersonator?

The fact that this isn't even the weirdest thing we've seen in this realm says it all. As does the fact that it's not even the weirdest thing we've seen from him.

"Nope," Caoimhe tells him. "We're all seeing those great big glittery balls."

Lumi sighs. "I was afraid of that." But he doesn't say anything more.

And yeah, I get that it's weird as fuck, but it's not awful—as in we're-all-going-to-die bad. Maybe the dragon energy just powered up the mayor so he could possibly visit another time period. Maybe discover leg warmers and off-the-shoulder *Flashdance* apparel next. That certainly wouldn't be the worst thing to happen to this Evel Knievel reject.

But then the mayor throws his head back and laughs, the kind of laugh that causes shivers to race down your spine. "I have waited a thousand years for this moment, my dear. So thank you."

I swallow as my stomach rolls and pitches like the ocean in a storm. "Umm, you're thanking me for what, exactly?"

Please don't say something evil. Please don't say something evil.

"Why, for giving me the power to go home—and rewrite history, of course."

I have no idea what this really means, but I know it's bad. Very bad. I've watched enough Marvel movies to know that. But I'd have guessed it anyway by the way Hudson's entire body stills, the air around him turning icy cold and causing goose bumps to skate along my flesh.

I shoot a quick glance at him, but he's already launched himself straight into the air and lands several yards away, right at Souil's feet.

Except, once again, Souil is gone.

And this time when he reappears, it's three feet away from Orebon, his disco-ball mace already mid-swing.

120

Death on the Dance Floor
—Grace—

Ihave one horrified moment to register what's happening, but by then it's too late.

The swinging disco balls connect with the side of Orebon's head—and rips it half off. Flesh and brains fly everywhere, and he crumples to the ground in a pool of his own purple blood.

Caoimhe screams and rushes toward Souil, but Hudson grabs her before she reaches him.

No one could keep Lumi from launching himself at Souil, though. Not that it matters. Like every other time, the wizard's disappeared. And now he's standing on the steps of the gazebo, shaking his head.

"Consider that a warning," he tells us. "I don't want to kill any of you, but I *will* kill *all* of you if you try to get in my way." He glances down at Orebon's lifeless body with absolutely no remorse on his face. "I have something to do, and I will not fail. Not after I've waited centuries for the chance."

"Whatever it is, you'll never get away with it," I tell him, praying I'm speaking truth. "People like you never do."

"Oh, Grace, you sweet, naive little girl. I've got money. I've got power. And I've got all the time in the world on my side. There is nothing any of you can do to stop me." The mace starts to swing again. "Or do you need another demonstration?"

"Why are you doing this?" Lumi cries from where he is, holding Orebon's lifeless body. "He did nothing to you."

"He *was* nothing to me," Souil says, but even his voice is different now. Deeper, richer, it cracks like lightning across the sky, echoes all around us like the thunder that follows. "None of you are. Remember that if you choose to get in my way, because I'm warning you. I will not be thwarted."

"What exactly are we not supposed to *thwart* you in?" Hudson sounds bored, and yet again, I see the vampire prince standing in front of me as he sets Caoimhe aside. Crossed arms, mocking eyes, insolent look on his face. I can't say I'm usually all that happy to see his smart ass, but I'd be lying if I said it wasn't good to see him here, in this moment. "Besides being a seventies supervillain with delusions of grandeur, that is?"

For a second, Souil's face darkens into something ugly and dangerous, but it smooths out again almost immediately—except for the gleefully evil look in his eyes. "I don't know why we're at such odds right now. I wouldn't have been able to do any of this without you."

"You bastard." Out of nowhere, Caoimhe rushes him, dagger raised.

I start to jump in front of her, to do whatever I have to do to stop her from dying, but Souil just rolls his eyes. Then he snaps his fingers and everyone around us freezes.

Hudson, with his arms crossed over his chest.

Lumi, bent over Orebon.

Caoimhe, mid-run, with her dagger raised.

While I'm still trying to register what just happened, Souil lifts a brow at me. "Interesting," he murmurs. Then he snaps again.

I wait for the others to unfreeze, but they don't. And now Souil is looking at me like I'm a bug under a microscope—both fascinating and revolting at the same time. But all he says is, "*Very* interesting."

His words—and tone—break through the shock, send me toward Hudson to make sure he's okay.

"Calm down, Grace. I didn't hurt them. I was just tired of their incessant yammering and murder attempts. But you—you present a new challenge."

I ignore him. It's not like Souil's reassurances mean anything to me. But when I race over to Hudson, reach inside myself, I can still feel our bright blue mating string, and I let out a long sigh. Hudson is okay—if frozen.

"Do we really need to go through all this drama?" Souil asks with a studied yawn. "I have places to be, after all."

"Unfreeze them!" I demand as I whirl on him. "Unfreeze them right now. You can't leave them like this."

His eyes go from gleeful to annoyed in an instant. He disappears for one second, and this time when he reappears, he's right next to me, his mace pressing against the underside of my chin. "How many times do I need to tell you? I can do whatever I want. The sooner you get that through your little stone head, the better off you'll be. Do you understand me?"

It's hard to swallow with his mace digging into my chin and throat, harder even to speak. But since he's not relenting—every second I don't answer, the mace presses a little deeper—I finally manage to squeak out, "Yes."

"Good." He smiles ruefully before removing the mace from my throat and leaning back against one of the gazebo pillars, his weight on his forearm. "Because I've been waiting a long time for you."

"For me?" I ask, confused.

"Not for you specifically." He waves a hand, as if telling me not to get too big a head out of this. As if I would. "But I have been providing sanctuary and collecting otherworlders in Adarie for centuries, waiting for a big enough rift in space-time—and the time dragon that comes with it."

"So you really were—"

He shoots me a warning look, and I shut up. The guy is already worked up and violent. I figure there's no need to antagonize him any worse when Hudson and my friends can't defend themselves.

"At first, it was difficult to get people to come here. But after rumors spread of the Shadow Queen hunting visitors and this idyllic sanctuary city, it certainly got easier."

"So the mayorship, everything, was just a ruse to attract a time dragon to kill the people who trust you?" I ask, horrified, though I don't know why. With everything he's revealed, I kind of thought I'd be beyond horror, but nope. It just keeps coming.

"If they're foolish enough to trust me, I'm smart enough to exploit it," he answers in an oh-so-reasonable tone. "Besides, what do they have to complain about? I made their pathetic little lives amazing. Look at this place, at what I've given them!"

"I don't think that counts if you're willing to sacrifice them whenever you want."

"Not whenever I want," he thunders before lowering his voice again. "I've been here for a millennium, waiting. Just waiting for a large enough dragon, for so long that I almost gave up. I almost resigned myself to being stuck in this *realm*. But then I heard of two strangers mentioning dragons, and I knew my long wait was finally over. And boy, you really delivered, Grace."

This time his grin is happy—which somehow makes this whole experience even more macabre and terrible. What kind of person can smile like that, minutes after brutally murdering an innocent man?

"But do you know what the problem with self-sacrificing types is?" he says, rubbing his chin musingly. "You're always willing to die to protect others, but you're never willing to take the deal that will save your lives."

He leans forward and snaps his fingers, unfreezing Hudson and the others just like that. Then, in a voice barely loud enough for us to hear him, he continues. "For once, be smart," he tells us. "For once, forget about the self-sacrifice and worry about yourselves. For once, take the fucking deal I'm about to offer and be glad of it."

121

This Is How
You Skew It
—Hudson—

W hat the fuck?

For a second, I'm confused—really confused. Like, "can't remember what I was talking about" confused. Like, "everything feels off" confused.

I turn to Grace, who isn't where I remember her being, which is another "what the fuck?" question I've got. Because something isn't right.

"He froze you," she whispers.

"He what?" My blood boils as I figure out what she means.

I don't take being played for a fool so easily. I don't like my will being subverted, either. And I sure as shit don't like it when some arsehole with a god complex decides what he wants is worth the deaths of people I care about and the destruction of a place I've learned to call home.

"Exactly what deal are you referring to?" I demand, when what I really want to do is knock this bastard flat on his arse.

A quick look at Caoimhe and Grace tells me they feel the same way. Lumi, on the other hand, just looks as devastated as I feel about Orebon's death. Which pisses me off even more.

And that's before Souil says, "It's easy…" with a smile that makes my blood run cold. It's full of malice and arrogance and self-satisfaction all at the same time—and I'm very, very familiar with it. I've seen it looking back at me from my father's face more times than I want to think about. And whenever it showed up, things never ended well for me.

"All you have to do is walk away," he continues. "Take your girlfriend, and your little musician friends, and whatever's left of that poor shadow creature, and just walk away right now."

Rage nearly overwhelms me at the way he refers to Grace and Smokey and the others—especially after what he did to Orebon—but I grit my teeth in an effort to hold back the hatred. And just let him talk.

It's how I used to handle my father. The first step was always "respectful" silence as he raved on and on about how brilliant he was.

The second step was a few compliments to stroke his narcissism and make him feel like we were on the same team.

And the third step was to actively work against him while doing my best to stay out of the blast zone.

Sometimes, I stalled out on two and never got the chance to get to three because it wasn't possible. Or because he was too far gone to oppose.

Standing here, looking into Souil's eyes brimming with an unholy power that seems an awful lot like madness reminds me of those times. More, it chills my blood because I'm suddenly afraid that whatever his big plan is, I won't be able to stop him. Grace, and Adarie, will suffer because I didn't recognize the evil sooner. And Orebon and Smokey—poor, sweet Smokey—have already paid the ultimate price.

I should have recognized it. I fucking should have. I've stared it down my whole bloody life. How could I have not seen it now, when I needed to the most?

I didn't like him from the beginning, knew something was off with him. And still I fell into his trap—and took everyone I care about with me. How fucking stupid can one person be?

"What happens if we do that?" Grace asks, and I glance at her. She doesn't look back at me, though. Instead, she keeps her eyes on his, never looking away.

And that's when I know that she gets it, too. Souil is a snake, and the second we take our eyes off him, it's over. He'll strike, and we'll be collateral damage in whatever parts of this evil plot he hasn't shared with us yet.

Then again, maybe we already are, and we just don't know it yet.

"*If* you do it?" He laughs. "There is no if. You *will* do it—the only question is if you do it voluntarily or if I make you do it."

"It's one thing to jump around through time or to freeze us when we aren't expecting it," I tell him scornfully. "But do you really think you can make us do something we don't want to do?"

"Do you know how much power is coursing through my veins right this moment?" he demands. "Do you have any idea what happens when you kill a time dragon?"

Before either Grace or I can say anything, he whirls around, throws an arm out, and the clock tower disappears. It just…disappears.

It doesn't disintegrate. It doesn't blow up. It just ceases to exist.

"The God of Time, that old bastard, created them to destroy people who were arrogant enough to try to mess with how he's woven time and space together. Anyone who creates a tear in either, anyone who actually succeeds, would end up with one of these dragons on their ass. The creatures' job is to fix rifts, and they don't stop until they cauterize the tear and erase the offender from the entire timeline with dragon fire.

"Now that you've killed the last dragon, that can't happen," he continues with a negligent little shrug. "Which technically means you should be thanking me instead of standing there looking like I just kicked your shadow. My plan *did* save your lives."

Despite myself, I wince when he says it, which only makes him laugh. "Too soon?" he mocks. "She *was* a brave little thing. Foolish but brave."

"You have no idea what she was!" I growl.

The next thing I know, Souil is gone again. I whirl around, looking for where he'll land. I'm determined not to end up like Orebon, not now, when Grace and I still have to find a solution for this.

But he doesn't appear next to me at all. He shows up next to Grace and, in an instant, sweeps her legs out from under her.

She hits the ground with a startled screech, but I'm immediately fading to her, ready to take this fucker out.

But he's already gone again.

Frustration wells up inside me. No matter how fast I fade, no matter how prepared I think I am, I can't fight someone who can move through time like this. He is always one step ahead or behind where I think he is, and there's no way I can anticipate which it's going to be.

I reach down and help Grace up as Souil flashes back into existence twenty feet away from us.

"There's more where that came from, Hudson," he taunts. "Keep acting up, and I'll take back your choice to walk away and just kill you now."

I start to tell him to do it. To just do it. I'd rather get it over with than stand here and let him play with me like this for much longer. I've lived that way once, spent my whole life getting old enough and strong enough that I didn't have to live like that anymore. No way am I going back to it. Not for him. Not for anyone.

But then I look over at Grace, and I realize that's not true. I can't let him kill me, because if he takes me out, he'll take Grace out, too. And I can't let that happen. She's my mate, the love of my life, the most beautiful on the inside—and the outside—girl I could find in any realm. I won't let this bastard take her from this world.

I can't.

And so I swallow back my pride, swallow back the words that are burning me alive. And let him think he has me cowed as Grace asks, "So we accidentally made a time rift. But you're a time wizard. You know how this stuff works. What did you do to get here?"

He snorts, shakes his head. "I got here the same way you did. I tried to go back in time, tried to save my daughter from dying of such a terrible illness. No father—" For the first time, his voice breaks.

He clears his throat, looks away for several seconds, and I think back on the time we visited his house, to the paintings on his wall. Of him, yes, but also of a little girl who looked like him. The cause of all this mess, even though I doubt she ever had a clue.

Souil takes a deep breath, and this time when he turns back to me, there's a bright sheen over his eyes. One that has nothing to do with madness and everything to do with sorrow. "No father would let his only child suffer like that if there was something he could do to take the pain away."

My first thought is that that's not true. Cyrus wouldn't walk across the street to save me from hurting, let alone take on the God of Time and spend centuries exiled in a place he hates. But Souil has. Does that mean that, in some strange way, he's right for what he's done? Who the fuck are we to make that call? And who the fuck are we to stand in the way of his only chance to save his child?

I glance at Grace to see what she thinks, but all I see is her frozen expression illuminated by the fires still burning all around us. It doesn't take a genius to figure out that she's thinking about her parents—I can see it in her eyes, in the tight press of her lips, in her fists clenched by her sides. I know she's wondering if she would have done the same thing to save her mom and dad if she'd had the power to do so.

How can I understand her need, her pain, but not have the same understanding for his?

But before I can say anything—to Grace or to Souil—she steps forward. And though her fists are still clenched by her sides, her eyes are resolute. "It doesn't work that way, Souil. You can't just change the world to suit yourself.

I should know."

"That's where you're wrong. That's where you're all wrong." He makes a sweeping gesture to encompass all of us. "When you have this much power, the world works the way you want it to work."

As if to underscore his statement, the clock tower pops back up—right where it belongs.

"And fuck anybody who tells me differently," he snarls. "It wasn't the God of Time's daughter who was dying. It wasn't his precious light that was being extinguished from this world. I would have messed with anything—anyone— to save my precious Lorelei. And I would do it again, even after all the time I've wasted here."

"But what about the lives you'll mess up when you do this?" I ask as I think about the butterfly effect—and every time travel book I've ever read. "When you go home, you may save your daughter, but you're going to hurt millions of innocent, unsuspecting people."

"My daughter is innocent!" he snaps at me. "And what does it matter if things change for other people? If you never meet your previous mate in your new life, what will you care? You won't even know she existed, so you won't know to mourn her."

"Don't you mean *if* our new lives exist? If you do this, there's no guarantee any of us exist. That I do. Grace or my brother or our friends or any number of people whose lives could be obliterated or changed beyond recognition because you decided you and your daughter are more important than anyone— everyone—else."

I look at Grace, who is the love of my life. She's also my mate, the person who was made just for me. I wouldn't have to know she didn't exist to miss her. The same goes for her and for anyone else who has had a soul mate in the last thousand years. Anyone else who has ever fallen in love, who has ever had a family or a best friend. It's inconceivable.

"You can't do this," Grace tells him. "Whatever you've suffered, whatever Lorelei has suffered, you don't have the right to bring that suffering on the rest of the world."

"You don't understand because you've never had a child," he tells her. "I've waited a thousand years for this day. A thousand years for the chance to bring her back, to save her from an excruciating death. And nothing is going to stand in my way. Nothing." He eyes us like a rabid dog, just waiting until we're close enough to attack. "When the sun comes up in two days, I'm going to take all this power inside me, the power you gave me when you killed that dragon, and walk across the barrier to home. I would prefer to save this power for that walk—and for what comes next. But get in my way, and I will kill all of you. And there will be nothing you can do to stop me."

And then—as if to underscore his words about his own power—he snaps his fingers. And completely disappears.

122

Love Is a
Red-Ribboned Thing
—Grace—

After he disappears, none of us move. We just stand there, staring at one another as everything Souil said runs through my head.

That he's been here a thousand years.

That I somehow tore a hole in time and space. A *big* one.

That the big dragon attacking was the last puzzle piece Souil needed. And I gave it to him. Brought it right to his doorstep.

The thought has my stomach churning, has panic welling up inside me. My heart goes crazy, and I can't remember how to breathe.

We've been fighting time dragons, hell-bent on "cauterizing" us from this time and place. No wonder they seemed so different than the dragons I met at Katmere. They're not the same thing at all. I already knew they weren't shifters—but this? A dragon species created by the God of Time for the specific purpose of seeking and destroying anyone who messes with his creation?

Except the mayor, who somehow has managed to survive for hundreds of years in Adarie despite these dragons? And if that's true, why the hell does he look like an extra from *Saturday Night Fever*? And how the hell has he lived this long? Time wizards aren't immortal, are they? I would imagine they have life spans like witches, like other humans, so how the hell has he cheated death all this time?

It doesn't make sense. None of this makes sense.

Except...I think back on things I've heard in my time here. About people like us who have shown up through the years.

Did the time dragons eat them all? Or did Souil kill their time dragons so that he could continue to live?

A loud wail comes from behind me, interrupting my thoughts, and I turn to find a bruised and battered Lumi on the ground beside Orebon's body. He gathers his spouse up in his arms and rocks him as the most awful sobs I've ever heard tear from his chest.

Caoimhe is still there as well, holding Orebon's hand while silent tears roll down her face. "He didn't have to do this," she whispers when our gazes meet. "He didn't have to kill him."

I nod, because she's right. There was no reason for Orebon to die except that Souil wanted to make a point. And no way for us to stop him because we never even saw it coming.

"I'm sorry," I tell her and Lumi. "I'm so sorry."

But Lumi is inconsolable, his cries filling up the night sky as he rocks the body of his best friend and lover, his husband, the father of their child.

I turn to Hudson, who has walked over to Smokey's remains. Like the troubadours, he, too, sinks to his knees. He, too, gathers her in his arms and holds her to his chest.

As he does, the sparkly red ribbon she wore for tonight flutters in the breeze. And one harsh and terrible shudder rips through his body.

"I'm sorry," he whispers to her. "I'm sorry, I'm sorry, I'm sorry."

"Hudson." I crouch down next to him and wrap my arms around his shoulders. "It's not your fault. None of this is your fault."

"I didn't see it," he says. "I knew there was something off about that arsehole, but I thought he was harmless. I didn't stop him and now—" His voice breaks, so he clears his throat before trying again. "Now she's dead. And Orebon's dead. And there's nothing I can do about it."

"We can stop him," I say, talking to Hudson but also to Lumi and Caoimhe. "He doesn't have to get away with this—"

Caoimhe's snort cuts through the silent night air. "And how are we going to do that, Grace? We can't catch him. Your vampire, the fastest person in this entire realm, can't even get near him. How the fuck are we supposed to stop someone who can kill us anytime he wants in ways that we'll never see coming? It's impossible."

I want to tell him that nothing is impossible, but then I look at Orebon, at Smokey, and I know that's not true. Some problems really are insurmountable, and there's nothing we can do about that.

"I'm sorry," I whisper to Hudson as I pull him closer and press my lips to his neck.

He seems to dissolve right in front of me, his whole body shaking with the energy it takes to keep his grief inside. He doesn't cry. He doesn't sob. He just takes it all in. Absorbs the anger and sorrow and pain, like it's second nature.

It's strange to see him like this—strange and heartbreaking. Practically from the minute we met, he's been my rock—the one steady thing in my life that was there no matter what.

And who always had my back, no matter what.

To see him shaken like this—destroyed like this—wounds me in a way I never expected. I hold him tighter, try to pull his grief inside me, try to make it so he doesn't hurt so badly because he chooses to share his pain with me.

But this is Hudson, who is pretty much the definition of self-sufficient when it comes to pain. He's handled it all alone his whole life, without ever thinking to ask anyone for help or even a little support.

But that's not who he is anymore, and it's definitely not who I want to be when I'm with him. The girl who just sits back and lets her man bear all the pain. No thank you.

"I love you," I whisper as I press kisses to his cheek, to his jaw, to the sensitive skin of his neck. "I love you, I love you, I love you."

He nods against my shoulder, but my words don't seem to make an impression. Not now, when he hurts so badly.

I hate that, almost as much as I hate the fact that there's nothing we can do. No way that we can fight Souil.

"What's going to happen?" Caoimhe asks as she brushes her hands across her cheeks. "When he goes across the barrier and changes things that happened hundreds of years ago, what will that mean for us?"

"I don't know," I say, shaking my head. "Could be nothing, could be everything. I have no idea if what happens in one realm affects another."

Caoimhe looks doubtful, but Lumi looks up from Orebon for the first time. "Nothing will happen to us," he says quietly. "But what about you? You're not from this realm. Your whole existence is due to your presence in the other realm. What if he changes something that changes something else that changes your whole life—or even if you have a life at all?"

123

Grin and Grace It

—Hudson—

At first, Lumi's words don't register for me. I'm too busy thinking of everything I've done wrong in the last year, all the mistakes I've made that I shouldn't have.

I should have insisted Smokey stayed inside our room today.

I knew the dragon was coming. I knew she would be angry and dangerous. I had no business letting Smokey come out, no matter how much she insisted.

I should have figured out what was going on with Souil.

After listening to him try to justify everything he's done, I can see the sociopathy so clearly. I've always been able to see the narcissism—anyone who looks at him can see that—but I didn't realize how truly selfish he was until tonight.

I should never have agreed to let the troubadours take part in the fight.

I know they wanted to help, but they don't have any paranormal powers. And Lumi and Orebon are *parents*. They were sitting ducks out there. First Lumi, who nearly died because I wasn't prepared for him to be scooped up by the dragon. And then Orebon, who did die because I wasn't fast enough—and because I didn't predict what Souil was going to do.

I should have.

I should have been able to prevent all of this.

And now, three people are dead. The woman who tried to save Lumi. Orebon. Smokey. Just like that. Gone in the blink of an eye, and I did nothing to protect them.

Worse, I did nothing to try to save them.

"I love you," Grace whispers, and I want to ask her why. How.

I've failed her. I've failed everybody here. And worse, my failures have cost people their lives—have cost everyone here people they care about. What is there to love about me if I can't even think far enough ahead to anticipate something as major, as terrible, as this?

"You shouldn't," I tell her, pulling away from the hug that suddenly feels like torture. I know she's trying to comfort me, but every kiss, every hug, every soft word she whispers in my ear reminds me that I don't actually deserve it. Reminds me that Grace really is slumming when it comes to me, vampire prince or not.

"Don't say that," she says, but she finally gets the hint and drops her arms.

I don't have anything else to say to her—or anybody, for that matter—so I don't argue with her. I just keep my mouth shut and my eyes pinned on Smokey's red ribbon.

It's better this way. It has to be. I've already fucked up so much, what the hell do I have to offer? People died because I couldn't get my shit together, because I was too focused on being happy for the first time in my life. I dropped my guard, started to believe in fucking fairy tales and now...and now people who *trusted me* are dead.

Smokey is dead. Oh my God. *Smokey is dead.*

All she wanted in this world was to be near me. To love me.

And it was my job to protect her. To keep her safe.

I fucking let her down.

I let everyone down.

Grace reaches for me again.

She keeps talking to me, keeps touching me and kissing me and telling me how sorry she is when she's got absolutely nothing to be sorry for. She didn't do this. I did.

I start to go deeper inside myself, the way I used to while in my crypt. I try to blank my mind, try to make myself float away. If I can just disappear, I won't feel like this anymore. The guilt and pain and rage will just melt away, will become nothing as I become nothing.

I'm almost there, can feel the strange lassitude that used to invade my body right before it happened. The emptiness and the surcease of pain that makes disintegrating so worth it—whether it's for a month or for a year or maybe for even longer.

I close my eyes, try to take the last part of the journey. But before I can, Grace is there, her hands cupping my face, her voice calling to the deepest parts of me.

"I know what you're doing, Hudson," she tells me, "and this isn't the way.

This isn't like before. This isn't a way out of the pain."

I shake my head, try to shut out her words. But it doesn't work. How can it when she's so insistent about getting my attention? And once she has it, she holds it—because this is Grace, my Grace, and ignoring her is the one thing I've never been able to do.

Her arms tighten around me, grounding me when I want nothing more than to just float away. "I'm sorry, Hudson. I'm so sorry it hurts. But this kind of pain follows you. Trust me, I know."

She presses her forehead to mine, keeps her hands on my cheeks, urges herself so close to me that her breath and warmth and softness become mine. "If you go away now, the pain will just be there on the other side, waiting for you. The only way to get over it is to go through it, no matter how much it hurts.

"But that doesn't mean you'll be going through it alone. Because I'm right here." She brushes her lips against mine. "I'm right here, Hudson, and I'm not going anywhere. You just have to reach out. You just have to trust me to help you get to the other side."

She makes it sound so easy, when two hundred years of life have taught me it's anything but. My whole life I've felt too much, hurt too much, over things I couldn't change. It took years to learn how to bear the emptiness and the agony alone.

But I did it.

I learned how to handle the pain and learned how to disappear when I didn't.

It's how I survived all those years of torture. And now Grace wants me to let those lessons go? She wants me to lean into her and trust her to get me—to get us—where we need to go?

A year ago, that would have been impossible. Two years ago, it would have been a joke—and not a particularly funny one at that. But this isn't two years ago. I'm not the Hudson I was when they dragged me back. I'm not the same guy who would rather disappear than know his own brother wanted him dead.

That betrayal was so painful, I willed myself out of existence in an instant.

And it's nothing compared to the pain I feel ripping through my chest right now.

But this time…this time someone *wants* me to stay.

Someone needs me, loves me, as much as I need and love her.

I take a deep, shuddering breath.

I'm Grace's mate. She *chose* me. And she deserves more than a guy who can't get his shit together. A guy who runs away when things start to hurt. And she sure as shit deserves someone who will place the same trust in her that she places in him.

So even though life has taught me over and over again that there is no going through pain—there is only *getting* through it—I ignore the lesson, and I choose Grace. The way I've always chosen her. The way I *will* always choose her.

I let the mist go, bury my need to flee. And then I reach my hand out and say the only thing that will guarantee that Grace is mine forever.

"We can't let Souil cross the barrier. We have to find a way to stop him."

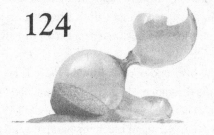

124

Grace throws her arms around my neck and holds me tight for several seconds. I hold her, too, and whisper, "Sorry," because I know I scared her.

But she just shakes her head in an "I've got you" kind of way. Then pulls back and asks, "What are we going to do? We can't let him just go back into our realm and ruin everything. We might not be there, but Uncle Finn and Macy and Jaxon and everyone else we care about still is. We can't just let him destroy the whole world because he wants to save his daughter."

"We know," Caoimhe tells her in a voice that says she's trying really, really hard to keep calm. "We just don't know what to do about it."

"Let me think," I murmur as my mind starts working again.

I've got nothing yet, and I don't think anyone else does, either, but my mind is finally moving again, the seeds of an idea beginning to form. But first, I turn to Lumi. "We've got time—at least twenty-four hours—to deal with that tosser. Right now, though, I think we should take a few minutes and… do what needs to be done."

A lump lodges in my throat at the words. Normally, I'd be a lot more direct, but I just can't bring myself to say out loud that we need to bury our loved ones.

Thankfully, the others figure out my meaning easily enough. "There's a park not far from here," Caoimhe says softly. "It's not super fancy, but I think they might like it. Plus, it doesn't get a ton of traffic the way the park at the center of town does."

Several townspeople have started to poke out of their homes, and they help us move Orebon to the park. Others came and took the woman's body, presumably to her family. The streets remain mainly deserted, which is a good thing considering our precious cargo, and we get to our destination easily.

There's a small toolshed at the back of the park, and Lumi heads over and breaks the lock so we can "borrow" a few shovels.

It only takes a few minutes for me to dig a small grave, where I drop in Smokey's ribbon, next to a bed of beautiful flowers while the other three work on Orebon's.

Fifteen minutes after we get to the park, we've buried them. But that doesn't seem enough—not for Smokey or for Orebon. I'm racking my brain for some poem that I can recite here—maybe Thomas or Dickinson, Lowell or Hardy—but before I can decide on something, Caoimhe starts to sing.

Her voice is low and haunting, a melody without words that reaches inside my soul. Squeezes my heart. And somehow makes the pain a little worse and a little better at the same time.

Grace reaches over, takes hold of my hand, and brings it to her lips. Like the song, I feel her kiss deep inside.

Tears are pouring down Caoimhe's face by the time she finishes her song, and Lumi wraps her in a hug.

"I need—" Her voice breaks.

"I know." Grace steps in. "I think we all need a moment. Let's meet up at the inn in a few hours. We'll decide what we're going to do then."

It's as good a plan as any of us are capable of right now. I'm drained and have been for a while, but I wasn't about to say that when we had things to do. I must look as bad as I feel, though, because Grace wraps her arm through mine and starts steering us back toward the inn.

The more I think about it, the more I think survival—in either realm—is an iffy proposition if Souil manages to make it back across the barrier. Which means we need to figure out a way to stop him, sooner rather than later.

I want to say that's a problem for tomorrow, when I'm feeling a little less exhausted, but the truth is there is no time. The irony of running out of time while hunting a time wizard doesn't escape me, but it's where we're at.

Grace must be thinking the same way I am, because she asks, "Do you think we'll be able to kill him?"

"Considering what he can do with just a thought?" I answer skeptically. "I'm pretty sure it's a long shot. I mean, maybe if I had my powers here…"

"So what do we have?" she asks. "If we don't have what's pretty much the best weapon in existence—"

"And the worst," I remind her. She read my journals, so she knows the only way I could disintegrate the time wizard would be to climb inside his mind, take his thoughts in my own—forever. Every gift has a cost, Richard used to say, and that was the cost of mine. I can kill anyone with a thought, but I then have to carry them with me for the rest of my life. It's half the reason it was so easy to choose torture over helping Cyrus. The other half was because yeah, not a psychopath.

"Yes, also the worst," she agrees. "So what *can* we use to defeat him?"

"Swords? Speed? Strength?" That's pretty much all I can think of based on what we've seen in Adarie, and I can't help but think the guy who just masterminded this whole thing is ready for all of that and a whole lot more.

"There's got to be something," she says. "Otherwise, what? We just give up now and let him destroy everything and everyone who has ever existed in a thousand years?"

I haven't voiced my thoughts about that out loud, but apparently Grace got there with me and figured out that Souil is so overcome by pain at his daughter's death that he doesn't see what will happen. Or he doesn't care.

Either way, not great for us.

When we pass Grace's regular smoothie place and realize it's still open, despite everything, I stop in and get the number three special—her favorite. It's purple, but then they all are, so I'm not exactly sure what distinguishes it from any of the other numbers on the menu. But I'm not about to rock the boat, not with everything she's been through tonight. And everything there still is to come.

We turn a corner—we're almost to the inn—then stop dead at what's in front of us. We're back in the town square, which is still deserted, and seeing the place after being gone for a little while makes it register what a battle zone it really was. The destruction has been cleared away, but that's about it. The burned buildings and tents are still in place, and each one we pass looks worse than the next, while flowers and lights are strewn everywhere.

Even the inn has some damage, but it's on the side of the square opposite where the battle took place, so it doesn't look too bad. Though I'm nearly certain Nyaz is going to need a new roof. And he's definitely going to need some new landscaping, because the whole yard in front of the inn is a disaster of burned trees and debris-strewn flower beds.

"This is awful," Grace whispers as we begin the familiar walk to the front door. "I feel terrible."

"We'll help him," I tell her. I've never laid a roof, but if we make it through the battle that's to come, I'm sure I can learn how.

I hold the door open for Grace and, as she walks through in front of me, all I can think about is a shower. Feeding. Holding her for a little while as we sleep and make plans for what's to come.

But the second the door closes behind us, I know that's not to be. Because for the first time ever, when Nyaz catches sight of us, he walks out from behind the desk.

Grace must realize just how odd it is, too, because she asks, "Nyaz? Are you okay?"

"I am, but I need to talk to you both." He gestures for us to precede him into the back office that I know is there, but which I've never actually seen him inhabit.

"About?" I ask, brows raised as I try to determine what's going on here.

"Do you remember what I said when you first got here, about settling up?"

Grace looks baffled, but I remember very well what he said. After we got here, it bothered me enough that I asked him about it several times later. He told me he would let us know when the time was right.

Apparently right now, in the middle of this nightmare we're currently living, is the right bloody time. Fuck all.

"I remember," I tell him wearily.

"Good. Because it's time to settle your bill."

I sigh. I really hope we're not going to be evicted before I can take a shower.

125

Kiss My Asset

—Grace—

"**S**ettle our bill?" I repeat in a questioning voice. I know what he means—have always known that we'll owe him something—but is now really the time to deal with this? When we're bloody, exhausted, scared, and so sad, it's all we can do to keep putting one foot in front of the other?

I get that Nyaz might not think we're going to survive through the next several hours till the sun rises again—God knows, that's something I'm worried about as well. But still. Couldn't he have at least waited until we cleaned up?

I start to say as much, but Hudson puts a hand on my arm and, when I glance up at him, the look he gives me urges restraint. I offer the barest nod, partly because I'm so tired that even that small amount of energy seems like too much to expend and partly because I reserve the right to tell Nyaz to back off for a few hours, no matter what Hudson thinks.

My mate looks like a breeze could blow him off his feet as easily as I could blow him a kiss, and I really want to get him upstairs. At the same time, though, Nyaz doesn't look like he can be put off.

Fine. Whatever. I'll listen to what he says, but if it takes too long, I'm getting Hudson out of here. ASAP.

With another questioning look at Hudson—which gets me a reassuring stroke down the center of my back—I walk into Nyaz's back room.

"Sit down, please," he says once he closes the door behind us. He gestures to the two chairs opposite his desk before walking to a small refrigerator in the corner of the room and pulling out three waters.

He hands one to Hudson and me before finally making his way to the chair behind his desk.

"Thank you," I tell him as I open the bottle and drink half of it down in one gulp. Fighting dragons—and evil mayors—is thirsty work.

Hudson does the same, except he finishes his bottle. Then he turns to

Nyaz and asks, "What do you need from us?"

Nyaz inclines his head in an "okay, we're cutting to the chase" kind of way. Then he says, "You weren't as alone in town square tonight as you thought you were."

"We certainly felt alone," I answer, because I did. It was just Hudson, me, and the troubadours out there trying to save the whole town. Smokey died, Orebon died, and no one came to help us.

Deep down, I know the best thing the townspeople could do was hide during all that mess and destruction. But a small part of me is bitter, because why are five people and an umbra—none of whom are from this town—on our own when it comes to the safety of this place?

"I can imagine," Nyaz tells me. "And I'm sorry about that. But rumors are spreading that the mayor has managed to absorb the power of your two time dragons and plans on using it to cross the barrier at first light."

I stare at him. "You heard all that from behind your desk?"

"I hear all I need to hear," he answers me.

"So what do rumors about the mayor have to do with us?" Hudson asks.

"It's a difficult time here in Adarie—"

"Dragon attacks will do that to a place." It comes out sounding more sarcastic than I mean it to, but I don't apologize. I'm frustrated and exhausted, and I don't understand why he's talking to us about this. We lived it—we don't need a recap.

Nyaz's gaze is steady on me as he answers, "They will. But so will having a time wizard who plans to go back to his world and reset time. There are people here who don't want him to succeed—more people than you might imagine, in fact."

"Why does it matter to you anyway?" Hudson asks. "It's our world, and our timeline, that will be completely fucked if it happens."

Hearing my worst fears voiced aloud makes me shiver. Hudson reaches over and takes my hand, strokes his fingers over my knuckles in the way he always does when he's trying to soothe me.

"That's what I want to talk to you about, actually." Nyaz steeples his hands in front of him on the desk, looks over his fingertips at us. "To be honest, I don't care what happens in your world. But if Souil is successful—if he makes it back there—he'll not only reset your timeline, but he'll also reset the curse trapping everyone here in Noromar."

"A curse?" I turn, wide-eyed, to Hudson to see if he knows what Nyaz is talking about, but he looks as confused as I feel. Maybe even more so, which makes sense considering the paranormal world has been a part of his life from the very beginning. I may not know this stuff, but him? How do he and his family not know about a cursed Shadow Realm?

"Yeah." Nyaz sighs. "Many years ago, the Shadow Queen tried to overthrow a god—"

"Which god?" Hudson interrupts, eyes narrowed.

"I don't know. A vengeful one?" Nyaz gives a half shrug. "When she failed, the god banished her and all her people into the shadows."

"Why the shadows?" Hudson asks, and I can tell—like me—he's still trying to wrap his mind around all this.

"Shadows are from where wraiths have always drawn their power, and it was those powers that they tried to use to overthrow this god. So their punishment—which I'm sure was fitting in the god's mind—was to create a Shadow Realm and trap the queen here, where the powers she'd always been so proud of could be used to imprison her as opposed to liberate her."

"That's...diabolical," I tell him.

Hudson snorts. "I take it you've never met a god."

"Personally?" I ask, brows raised. "Um, no."

"Diabolical is pretty much a thing with them."

"It is." Nyaz nods. "But seriously. You two have lived here for months. Haven't you ever wondered why everything here is purple and looks a little different, yet so much is also close in function and form to your world in so many ways? It's because the people who live in Noromar are *from* your world. We just live in the shadows of that world now, instead of in the actual world."

"You mean all of you are cursed to live in the shadows of our world without ever being able to go back?" I ask, feeling a little sick.

"That's the thing," Nyaz tells me. "Most of us don't *want* to go back. We've been here for a thousand years, and we're happy. We have families, jobs, a community we love. When our ancestors first got here, they would have done anything to go home. But we took what was supposed to be a prison and turned it into a paradise. We've built Noromar—and Adarie, in particular—into something better than a paradise. We've built it into our home. And now that there's a chance we might be forced to leave, we don't want to."

"Can't you just stay?" I ask. "Refuse to go anywhere and stay right here in the shadows and continue living your lives?"

"That's what we want to do. But some people remember stories of the old realm. They're tired of living the way we do here. Tired of eating purple vegetables growing out of purple dirt, tired of living under a purple sky." He pauses. "Tired of only seeing a sunset four times a year—of only seeing darkness every three months. They want to go home.

"Add in the fact that we've had our favorite holiday attacked and ruined by time dragons two festivals in a row, and is it any wonder some people are ready to get the hell out of here? But if they do that, how will we fit in the other world now? It's been a thousand years since we were there. It's not our home anymore. *This* is our home.

"But now that the mayor has the power he needs to cross between worlds and reset the curse, we're in real trouble. Because not only will he be risking every single person who lives in the Shadow Realm, he'll be risking Noromar itself. We can't let that happen—not to the only real home we've had in a millennium."

His voice has risen a little out of its regular, non-excitable, "take everything in stride" tone to one of urgency. But surprisingly, there's no fear to go along with that urgency. Just a fervent determination that has me taking a big mental step back. Because I don't like the way he's staring at me or what that stare might mean.

Hudson must have the same feeling that I do, because he scoots his chair a little closer to mine. He holds Nyaz's gaze with frigid blue eyes. And then he asks, "What are you trying to tell us?"

Nyaz simply whispers, "We have a secret weapon."

Hudson's face goes blank instantly. "By secret weapon, I assume you are not referring to Grace in any way."

"Yes." For the first time, Nyaz looks uncomfortable. "Grace is a gargoyle. She can turn the mayor to stone, trapping him here forever."

126

A Not-So-Tastee
Freeze
—Grace—

A chill sweeps up my spine that has nothing to do with the air-conditioning in Nyaz's office.

I don't even question if it's possible. I know it is. One evening, I'd been chasing Hudson around our room in a tickle fight—one I was soundly winning—when Smokey had hopped in the window and come to Hudson's defense by jumping straight at my head. I'd been so startled, I'd turned to solid stone—as had Smokey. She hadn't spoken to me all night after I unfroze us.

"But I would have to remain stone as well," I gasp.

"Yes, but both realms would be safe," Nyaz says.

The chill becomes icicles slicing their way down my spine.

I turn to Hudson to see how he's reacting to this very, very, very terrible idea, but he doesn't look nearly as traumatized as I feel. In fact, his eyes are narrowed and distant in that way that means he's working out a problem in his head. And that he's almost got the solution.

I want to ask him what he's thinking about, but before I can, he blinks. His gaze goes from distant to focused in an instant, and this time when he looks at me, there's an answer there that I'm not sure I'm going to like.

"You're not getting behind this idea, right?" I ask him, almost afraid of what he's going to say. I mean, I know Hudson would never agree with my becoming a statue forever. But still, I can tell by the set of his chin that he's definitely thinking something else I'm not going to like.

Instead of answering right away, he shifts to look out the window on the left side of Nyaz's office, murmuring to himself. "Yes. A gargoyle *could* turn someone to stone with them. Or some*thing*."

"You can't be serious—" I start to say.

Hudson returns his blue gaze to mine and interrupts. "What's the one thing the mayor fears?"

"Clothes without sequins," I deadpan. 'Cause I've got nothing else. Hudson only raises one brow at me, so I shrug. "The man seems impervious to everything except good fashion sense."

This time he chuckles, then drops what I'm sure he thinks is a bombshell. "Souil said once that dying by dragon is the worst death he can imagine, and I think I know why," he says, crossing his arms over his chest. "I think a time dragon is the only thing that can kill him now."

"O-kay," I draw out the word. "But how?"

"Souil showed us he could blink a building in and out of existence—out of our timeline—implying he could do the same to all of us. It was meant as a threat, but..." Hudson pauses. "Who else would be resistant to time magic other than another being made of time magic? And I think Souil knows it, because he has never appeared until *after* we've killed each dragon. I don't think his brand of power will help in a fight against a time dragon in the slightest. He'd be toast."

My heart is racing. If that's true, maybe we're not all completely fucked. Well, except for, "But where do we get another time dragon? Souil said he's waited centuries for the ones we brought," I say.

"Exactly. He waited for us to destroy *both* dragons." Hudson leans back in his chair, looks from me to Nyaz, then shakes his head. "If all he needed was the magic of a time dragon—why didn't he leave after we killed the first one? He stayed another three months, waited on us to kill a *second* dragon, and *now* he says he can go home when the sun rises."

Hudson pops to his feet and walks over to the window before continuing. "We know he killed a dragon in the past—because the dragon that followed him to the Shadow Realm isn't still attacking. That and he's somehow managed to live a thousand years. But when he killed that dragon, why didn't he leave then, either?" He turns around to face us again, one eyebrow raised. "I think he needs two. Always needed two. One to absorb enough power to reset time—and another's power to get home. Which means..."

"Which means what?" Nyaz asks, clearly not understanding.

But I do. "Souil is many things, but he wouldn't come all the way here to save his daughter without a way home. He came with someone else—someone else who caused a second dragon to follow them."

Hudson nods. "And since he's still here, since he didn't use that dragon's magic to get home, that second dragon must still be alive."

I walk over to the window Hudson had been staring out, and I can just make out the giant statue at the other end of the town square. "The statue isn't…"

"A statue?" Hudson finishes. "No, I don't think she is."

My pulse is racing. I whisper, "I'm not the only gargoyle in Noromar, am I?"

Hudson puts an arm around my shoulders, pulls me in tight by his side. "No, Grace, I don't think you are."

"The statue is an actual gargoyle," I whisper in awe. But then my eyes go wide. "A gargoyle *frozen with a time dragon.*"

"But—" Nyaz begins, understanding dawning. "*If* the gargoyle in our town square is truly a real gargoyle, how can we convince her to free the dragon? She's a statue."

I glance at Hudson.

"Grace can talk to her."

And he's right. I can. When I'd frozen Smokey with me, I could hear her chattering in my head nonstop. There's a real possibility if I touched the statue and froze with her, I could talk to the other gargoyle.

Even the idea of talking to someone else like me has my heart pounding in my chest. I have so many questions for her. I've had to figure out what it means to be a gargoyle without any help from someone else like me. To know I'm not alone, that there's someone who's had to learn the same things, who could teach me, is amazing. And not just anyone. A great warrior, if the statue is any indication.

"Yes, I think I can talk to her," I agree.

"But even if she frees the dragon, how do we get her to attack the mayor—and not kill everyone else?" Nyaz asks, running a hand along his chin.

"We lure the mayor into a trap, of course," Hudson says, and I know he's making it sound much easier than he thinks it will be. "He'll have to come out of his house at some point when the sun rises so he can travel in the shadows through the barrier—and that's when we'll attack."

I take a deep breath and blow it out slowly. My anxiety isn't rearing its ugly head—surprisingly, considering everything we've gone through tonight—but I still need to clear my head. A trap that's foolproof, of course. But none of that matters if I can't convince the gargoyle to help us.

I take one more deep breath. Then turn to Nyaz and say, "I will try to convince her—"

I break off as a loud clattering comes from directly outside the door.

Hudson's there in a second, opening it up to see what's happened—only to find one of the inn's housekeepers on the ground behind the counter trying to pick up the large executive desk pad she must have knocked down—along with everything on it, including Nyaz's book, dinner plate, and water glass.

"What's going on here?" he demands, coming out from behind his desk.

"I'm sorry, sir. I'm so sorry," the housekeeper says as she places everything back on the front desk.

"I'm not worried about what you knocked down, Yrrah," he tells her as she starts picking up the broken shards of his cup. "I'm worried about what you're doing behind my desk in the first place."

A quick glance at Hudson tells me he was wondering the same thing—as was I. We don't say anything, though, just kind of step back and let Nyaz deal with it. Which seems like an extra-smart move on our part when Yrrah begins to cry.

"I'm sorry. I came in and found my wife listening at your door. She's loyal to the queen, sir, and she's on her way out of the city to tell her of your treachery. Your plan," she quickly corrects herself. "Which she calls treachery."

As she continues to cry, Hudson fades out the inn's front door without a word to Nyaz or me.

"Why would she do such a thing?" Nyaz asks. "Aren't you happy here?"

"I am, but she wants to go home. She's always wanted to go home—to a world that's continued to grow and change. We've fought about it for a long time, and I thought she finally saw my side of the argument. But she wouldn't have done this if she did." Yrrah starts to cry harder. "I'm sorry. I really am so, so sorry."

As Nyaz comforts her, Hudson slips back through the door. I raise my brows, but he just shakes his head. "She's gone," he says quietly as he comes to stand next to me again.

"What does this mean?" I ask as my stomach twists and turns.

Nyaz looks grim. "It means the queen's army will be on us soon. She'll do anything to undo the Shadow Realm curse." He looks to me.

And I already know what I have to do. No matter how it happened, no matter how Hudson and I got to this town, we're here now. And there's no way I can let the time wizard go back and screw around with time. No way I can play roulette with Hudson's existence, Jaxon's existence, Macy's existence,

Heather's existence. A thousand years is a lot of timeline to mess up.

"I'll go talk to the gargoyle," I tell them. "But I'm warning you now. You should probably figure out a backup plan because I have absolutely no idea how this is going to go."

"You've got this, Grace," Hudson tells me. And I can tell he means it. Silly boy.

"Of course I do," I say with a wave of my hand. And a clench of terror in my belly.

Because something tells me there isn't a good enough plan in the world to make this turn out okay.

127

Statue of Limitations
—Grace—

The trip across the square is one of the loneliest I've taken since I've been here. The feeling isn't helped by the fact that the square is deserted—news of the impending attack of the Shadow Queen's army moved fast, triggering a complete lockdown.

Now I kind of wish I'd asked Hudson to come with me to do this.

He'd stayed behind to work with Nyaz on the other problem we have… Namely, even if I'm able to get the gargoyle to free the dragon, how the hell do we get her to attack Souil?

In addition, Nyaz reported that Souil was holed up in his mansion with some sort of time force field around it. Anyone who attacked got transported in time. Some only a few feet backward, others to where they were days ago. So they're working on a plan to combat the force field and get Souil out in the open where the dragon can attack him.

It's exactly what he needs to be doing at this point, but that means I'm coming out here to face another gargoyle—the first gargoyle I've ever met—all on my own. It's a scary proposition.

Not as scary as having the Shadow Queen descend on the town and do who knows what to anyone who opposes her. And definitely not as scary as letting Souil loose in the universal timeline.

But it's no picnic, either, especially since I have absolutely no idea what I'm supposed to say to her at this point.

I glance back at Hudson, who's standing at the door of the inn with Nyaz, greeting people who've come to help work on their part of the plan. Hudson grins when he sees me looking, gives me a little "go get 'em, tiger" wave. But Nyaz appears concerned, and when he leans over to say something to Hudson, I'm certain he's asking if I can do this.

Just knowing he's thinking that gets my back up, even as Hudson nods in a "hell yeah she can" kind of way.

I smile at that, wait for his eyes to come back to mine. Then I stick my chin up in the air so he knows I'm serious and call out, "I've got this."

Because I do. I really, really do. And it's nice to finally have someone who believes that as much as I do.

I've spent my whole life being underestimated.

By my parents, who didn't think I was strong enough to handle knowing who or what I am.

By Macy and Uncle Finn, who didn't trust me to be able to handle knowing what Katmere Academy was really about.

Even by Jaxon, who thinks I need to be protected against anything and everything that might pose a threat to me.

But I'm done being underestimated. I'm done being discounted. I'm done having people think I'm not good enough or strong enough or powerful enough to do what needs to be done.

I am all of those things and I am not going to fail. Not now, when it comes to talking that gargoyle into doing what we so desperately need her to do. And not later, when it comes time to fight Souil.

This is my fight and I'm going to lead it. More, I'm going to crush it.

Because Hudson deserves it.

Orebon and Smokey deserve it.

Our friends deserve it.

Adarie deserves it.

And, damn it, I fucking deserve it.

This gargoyle isn't going to know what hit her.

As I come up beside the fierce stone warrior, I raise my hand above her arm. I start to hesitate—I'm not exactly sure how to freeze like a statue *with* a statue—but really, the time for hesitating is long past. Now is the time for action.

So I take a deep breath and lay one hand on the statue gargoyle's shoulder. Then I close my eyes. Look deep inside myself until I can find all the multicolored strings. My strings that connect to I don't even know what yet. I do know that I'd like the chance to find out, though. I want to know what the hot-pink string connects me to. What the green and black and yellow and red ones mean for me. There are a bunch of other strings, too, but it's hard to pay attention to any of them when there's a blue one right in the center of the web. A bright, bright blue one that's the exact color of Hudson's eyes.

Our mating bond.

I let my hand briefly glide against it, just so he'll know that I'm thinking about him. Then I reach past it to the platinum string. Instead of brushing it like I usually do or holding it for a few seconds, I wrap my fist around it and hold it as tightly as I can. And I don't let go.

I shift quickly, like I always do, into my regular gargoyle form and then into stone.

And the longer I hold the string, the heavier the stone around me gets until I can barely lift my arms or legs. Finally, even that becomes too hard as everything goes dim and gray while I slowly, slowly, *slowly* freeze.

I have one moment to register what's happened before a voice with a decidedly Irish accent comes through a dark mist enveloping everything around me. "Well, it's about time you decided to visit."

128

Here's Your Horns, What's Your Hurry?
—Grace—

I'm pretty sure if I wasn't frozen, I'd fall over in shock right now.

Because yeah, I've been praying she was a real gargoyle, but that doesn't mean I'm not still shocked when she talks to me.

"I've been wondering what was taking you so long," she says, and already she sounds a million times more confident than I feel.

"Hello...?" I ask tentatively, to make sure I'm not manifesting what I want to hear.

"Artelya," she fills in.

"Umm...nice to meet you, Artelya." She sounds so tough that it's freaking me out more than I already was. Clearing my throat, I continue. "I'm sorry, I just can't believe I'm actually talking to another gargoyle."

"I've got horns and I'm made of stone, so I guess I'm making dreams come true today."

"Oh, right. I guess—"

"Relax." She laughs. "I'm just fucking with you, Grace."

"You know my name?"

"Of course," she says. "I heard you as soon as you arrived in Adarie. I haven't really paid attention to those walking past me all these years, since we kind of go into stasis when we're fortified too long—"

I interrupt. "Fortified?"

"Yes. Our solid stone form—" She breaks off, steps forward, and suddenly the mist around us seems to disappear. She's tall and muscular, with dark curls and brown skin. She's carrying a massive shield and sword and yeah, this woman looks like she could slay *all* the dragons. "Has no one given you any training yet?"

"Nope," I tell her. "You're the first gargoyle I've ever met."

"The *first* gargoyle?" She sounds horrified. "What are you talking about?

There are tens of thousands of us. How could you not have found any? Sure, I haven't been in my world for a while, but I can't imagine they would just leave you on your own. That's not what gargoyles are about at all."

"I don't think they knew about me," I rush to explain. "I've only found out about myself since I've been in Noromar."

"That's impossible. Gargoyles can communicate—" She shakes her head like she's trying to clear it. "I don't get it. How could things have changed so much in the time I've been here?"

I look around and realize we're no longer in Adarie. We're standing on rocky cliffs above a roiling, grayish-green ocean. The sky above us is a bright blue with clouds made of giant white fluff, and the grass we're standing on is an absolutely gorgeous bright green.

I kind of want to ask her where we are, but there's no time for that. There's too much to do.

So instead of asking about what might be the most beautiful place I've ever seen, I simply answer her question. "I think, maybe, it's because you've been here a really, *really* long time."

"How long?" she asks urgently, her brown eyes blazing with an internal fire that burns right through me. "What's the year?"

I tell her, and she blanches.

"Are you sure? It's really been that long?"

She turns to look across a field where a giant dragon—and by giant I mean makes the last one we killed look like its kid sister—is chained to the ground and resting, thankfully. Her massive green head is lying across a long, spikey tail curved around her semi-truck-size body. She pulls in powerful deep breaths through flared nostrils that bend the grass with every exhale.

Before I can answer, Artelya sighs, closes her eyes as though she's concentrating really hard on something, then eventually murmurs to herself, "Well, fuck. I thought when I fortified with the dragon I might be stuck with her forever, but I didn't expect *this*."

"Forever's a long time."

"Yeah, it is." She sighs again, then turns back to me with a calculating look in her eyes. "But you didn't come over here to talk about ancient history, did you?"

"Actually, I did. We have a big problem, and I was hoping you and the time dragon there could help."

"*That* time dragon?" Artelya laughs, nodding toward the beast. "Asuga isn't exactly what I'd call the helpful type."

"Asuga's her name?" I repeat. "That's really pretty."

"Yeah, it is. Too bad 'pretty' doesn't properly encompass her...personality, shall we say?"

"Yeah, I've found that time dragons aren't exactly the nicest."

She snorts, then props her sword across her shoulder. "That's a delicate way of saying they're arseholes, isn't it?"

I laugh, because she's absolutely nothing like I expected. But I like her a lot anyway.

"Well, *this* dragon is the worst of the lot—especially after being chained up with me all this time. She's been having to fight her nature, and I'm sad to say she's gone a bit rabid. Even if she were feeling helpful, she's nothing but instinct and hunger at this point. It's why I have to keep her chained up."

We're both staring at the great beast, and I can't help a quiver of sadness fluttering in my chest for the animal. She didn't ask to be here any more than we did.

"So," Artelya prompts as a cold wind kicks up. "You've got a problem only a time dragon can help solve?"

"Yeah." I sigh. "But I really wish I didn't."

She raises one brow. "Since you're here—and by here, I mean Noromar— I'm going to go out on a limb and ask if the problem has anything to do with a man named Souil?"

I groan, and the story pours out of me. Souil's time as mayor, the way he's turned Adarie into a sanctuary city for luring visitors in hopes of finding another time dragon whose energy he can drain, the way he plans to cross the barrier at sunrise and mess with the timeline for the last thousand years. All of it.

When I'm done talking, I take a deep breath and wait for her response. I don't have long to wait.

"Jeez. You'd think after this many years, he would have learned something." Artelya makes a displeased face.

"Oh, he's learned a lot of things," I answer. "But none of them are good."

"That I believe."

"You agree with me, though, right? He can't be allowed to cross back to our side of the barrier. If he does..."

"If he does, all hell will break loose," she finishes for me. "Yes, I most definitely agree that can't be allowed to happen."

"Oh, thank God." For the first time since I watched Souil absorb that dragon last night, I feel like there might be just a tiny bit of hope.

"Unfortunately, I cannot let Asuga kill the wizard with dragon fire."

And just like that, my stomach pitches again. "But why?" I gasp.

"Because anything the dragon's fire touches is cauterized from time."

"He said that once before, but I'm not sure what that means exactly, other than the asshole dies—which I'm perfectly fine with," I say.

Artelya shakes her head, starts walking closer to the dragon. I follow. "It means it'll be as though he never came to Adarie. This village did not exist before Souil and I arrived. In fact, it grew *around* me. I think Souil built it in case I ever released the dragon, so he'd be nearby. If dragon fire consumes him…Adarie will disappear, and all of its people will be leading different lives—if they are born at all."

My eyes widen as I think of all the friends we've made in Adarie, all the villagers who've built their homes here. Then a thought occurs to me. "But you'll still be here. Won't you be enough to hold the timeline, if the village was built around you, too?"

I hold my breath, my chest tight at the thought of so many lives destroyed. We cannot risk their timeline just to save mine.

"I don't think you realize what will happen if I unfreeze Asuga," Artelya says, and I can tell whatever she's about to say—I'm definitely not going to like it.

"That bad?" I ask.

She gives me a bracing slap on the back. It's not quite the kind of comfort I was expecting, but I'll take it—especially coming from her. Because she strikes me as the kind of woman who doesn't give false comfort.

Especially after she says, "The dragon's breath is already upon me. The minute I unfreeze her—I will die by dragon fire as well."

129

Gargoyle Girl Gang

—Grace—

My stomach feels like it just jumped off the side of the cliff, and I'm in free fall. All of our plans...*gone.*

But no, I won't let this dissuade me. Surely we can come up with something else. I lift my chin and start to tell her we will find another way, but she interrupts me.

"Though I think there is another way to defeat Souil."

Thank God. I ask, "What's that?"

"I release the dragon...and you kill her before she kills Souil."

"What? How is that any better than where we're at right now?"

She rests the tip of her sword into the ground at her feet, leans her weight on it. "You know, Faincha begged me to let her come with us. So did many other gargoyles. When Souil told us there were innocent people dying here, being attacked mercilessly by dragons after being invaded, everyone wanted to help. But Souil insisted only I should come, that their presence would create more time dragons who could terrorize the people of Noromar. And I believed him."

"Faincha?" I ask.

"My older sister." She smiles a little, a far-off look in her eyes. "I was too busy trying to make my own way in the world, so I eagerly agreed with him, told everyone that I could handle this mission alone. Of course, once I got here, I could see right away that Souil never wanted to help anyone except himself. He needed to harness the magic of time dragons, and he needed a gargoyle for that, someone immune to dragon fire. As soon as I saw him absorb the power of the first dragon I'd killed, I refused to help him kill the second. But he said he needed the second to return home, and he would kill her with or without me."

I nod, my chest tightening at Artelya's sacrifice. "So you froze the dragon so he could not have it."

Artelya laughs, but there's no humor in the sound. "I did, but only after I lost to Souil." Her brown eyes bore into mine. "He will move through space and time, lure the dragon to wherever you are—and then he will disappear just as the beast attacks."

I gasp as I realize what she's saying.

"Yes, I only froze the dragon when there was no other choice. Souil had already won. As the heat from the dragon fire licked against my flesh, I fortified. I could not defeat the time wizard, but I was able to deny him his victory."

My heart is breaking for this powerful warrior whose only choice was to spend an eternity trapped in stone to save millions of lives.

"I've had a long time to think about this," she says, "and I just can't get over how insistent Souil was that I bring no one else with us, that I not risk loosing another dragon on this realm." Her eyes narrow on mine. "When I killed the first dragon, his magic seemed to seek Souil out. Souil appeared to have no control over it. What if he's a magnet for time magic? And what if he can't help absorbing too much magic, even if it would kill him?"

My eyebrows shoot into my hairline. "Do you really think it's possible?"

She nods. "That man is arrogant as hell. I just can't believe he would only bring exactly the number of dragons he needs to increase his power and return when he could have had a sky full of them. If I'd even brought my sister with me, he'd have had a chance to return home by now. Instead, he's apparently been waiting centuries to get home." She raises one brow. "Seems kind of foolish, if you ask me."

I turn to stare at the dragon now no more than twenty feet in front of us. Could she be right? Could the answer to stopping Souil really be in simply giving him *more* time?

But before I can let myself hope, I remember that we cannot release Asuga regardless.

"I'm sorry," I say. And I am. I saw how close the flames in the statue were to her head. I can't believe it didn't even occur to me that fortifying herself with the dragon had also acted to save her from Asuga's dragon breath. My arm had been singed when I wasn't solid stone, so I know we're only impervious to the flames in our solid stone form. I shake my head. "We'll find another way. We cannot risk your life, too."

Artelya's eyebrows slash down and, if possible, she looks offended I'd even suggest such a thing. "Of course I will release the dragon if you agree to kill her."

I start, "But—"

"Will my death save innocent lives?" she asks, but we both know the answer, so she continues. "Then it will be my honor to save them."

I must look horrified at the suggestion because she squares her shoulders, turns to face me fully, the sword no longer resting casually across her shoulder but gripped in one of her powerful hands between us.

"I will forgive you this, as you say you have never known another gargoyle, but Grace—" She shakes her head at me, and I suddenly feel very small. She bangs her sword on her shield and the sound echoes against the sea as she says, "Gargoyles are protectors. It is our sacred duty to protect those who cannot protect themselves."

The words settle around me like a mantle. Strong. Powerful. Right. Like an echo in my bones. Like a destiny waiting to be claimed.

And I stand taller.

"Yes," I agree with conviction. "You are right. But—there must be another way."

Artelya shrugs. "Even if there were, I'm afraid I would not survive long anyway."

My eyes widen. "But why?"

"I don't know. I just know that I'm very sick and that I can't fight with this poison inside me. My fortification froze the poison as well as my body." She lowers her head, and thunder booms across the sky, shaking the ground. "But when I shift back, I fear it will weaken me quickly. I've never felt anything like it before and yet, being here in Noromar all these years, I know that it is some type of shadow poison."

"If it's shadow poison," I argue, "then surely we can find a cure here in the Shadow Realm."

But Artelya just shakes her head. "Shadow magic is the most ancient and powerful magic in the universe. It's older than the stars in the heavens. There is nothing more powerful. I cannot guarantee whether the poison or dragon fire will kill me first, so whatever happens, you must promise to not allow dragon fire to kill Souil. The fate of this world depends on it."

"You have my word." Artelya sacrificed everything to keep the world safe, and now she's dying anyway? It's not fair and it's not right. "I'm so, so sorry."

"Don't be sorry, Grace. I'm the one who did this." It's her turn to reach out and touch me. She does it slowly, tentatively, like the action is foreign to her. Then again, after a thousand years, it probably is.

Eventually, though, she manages to pat my hand.

I grab onto her fingers and squeeze tight, because even if this is the last time I get to talk to her, I want her to know she's not alone. I want her to know that someone in this village remembers her and cares about her and is thinking about her.

Because I am. I'll think about her for the rest of my life—which may not be long if Souil's bullshit ends up erasing me from the timeline. But still.

"What matters is that we stop Souil." She holds my gaze in her steady one. "You will have only one chance. When I release the dragon, I will immediately succumb to dragon fire. You will need to kill her instantly. At least I know you will be ending her suffering."

"How will I signal you?" I ask.

"All gargoyles can speak to their queen any time they wish," she explains, and my heart skips in my chest. This powerful warrior is my *queen*. I should have known. That day in the park, all I could think was that I hoped one day I would become as powerful as she seemed. I must have recognized even then her royal bloodline.

I lift my chin. If this queen can have the courage to sacrifice her life for our mistakes, the very least I can do is not let her death be in vain. "I will *not* let you down. That bastard will leave this realm on *my terms*—or not at all. You have my word."

The first real smile spreads across her face, crinkles the corners of her eyes. "We are a lot alike, Grace. Headstrong. Fiercely protective. Stubborn." She chuckles softly. "You will make a great leader one day."

I blink at her. "Leader?"

Then she says the oddest thing. "Of course, my queen."

I blink again.

And just like that, I'm back in town square.

130

A Shot in the Dark
—Hudson—

"So we're on the same page when it comes to the backup plan?" I ask Nyaz, just to be sure.

"You mean the fact that we're totally screwed if Grace can't wake the time dragon?" he answers, both brows raised. "Yeah, we're on the same page."

"Grace *will* wake the dragon." I give him a look, but he shrugs in return. "We need a backup plan in case the dragon is a tosser about it, though."

"I'll try to get the rest of them to come. But that's the best I can do. I don't control them—no one does."

It's not exactly a ringing endorsement of my idea, but I'll take it. Mainly because I'm preoccupied looking out the window every two minutes to check on the frozen-in-stone gargoyle Grace has currently become.

But I've got something else on my mind besides Souil and what's going to happen in that fight. So I force myself to take one last look at Grace—for now—and turn back to Nyaz, who I know has been watching me watch her for the past four hours.

"She's doing fine," he tells me after a second. "Your Grace is a smart, powerful, capable young woman."

"I know," I murmur.

"I know you do." He sits down behind the main desk in the inn's lobby and picks up his latest book. But he doesn't open it. Instead, he just watches me over the top edge, like he knows I want to say something.

Which I do.

It takes a lot for me to open up to someone—perks of being the child of an absolute sociopath—but right now I don't have a choice. Not if I'm going to have a chance to take care of Grace, of what we've become to each other.

So while Nyaz continues to watch me, I finally say what I've been wanting to say for hours. "How does shadow magic work?"

Nyaz's eyes narrow suspiciously. "What do you want to know? And why?"

"My tutor mentioned it to me once, many years ago. He said it was one of the oldest forms of magic—that it's so old, it comes from the time before time, in the first light of creation. And because of this, it's also some of the strongest, most unbreakable magic in the universe."

"Shadow magic is a lot of things," Nyaz counters. "Ancient, yes. Powerful, yes. Unbreakable? Almost always." Now he puts the book down and just watches me carefully. "Are you sure that's what you want? Something that no other magic can undo?"

"That's exactly what I want, actually."

It's Nyaz's turn to glance out the window at Grace, which tells me I'm not as smooth as I think I am. Then again, when it comes to her, I've never had a chance at smooth. From the minute we met, she's turned everything about my life upside down.

Thank God.

She hasn't just broken my walls. She's taken a sledgehammer to them and shattered them into a million tiny pieces. There's a small part of me that wants to gather a few of those pieces, to hide them and hold them so that if something goes wrong in the next forty-eight hours, I won't be completely and utterly destroyed. But the rest of me knows that isn't possible. It's already way too late for me to hold back a few pieces, too late to bury them deep and hope Grace doesn't somehow rip my heart out of my chest.

She already has, and her smile, her touch, her love, are the only things that keep it beating, even now. The truth is, there's no use holding on to a few pieces of myself, because without her, they don't matter anyway.

"What are you looking to use shadow magic for?" Nyaz asks when I don't say anything more. "Because it holds up to almost everything, but I'm not sure it will actually hold up to a time dragon. They are created by the God of Time himself, and I truly don't know if magic—even shadow magic—can stand against them."

That's what I was afraid he'd say, but it's still the best chance I've got. Especially here, in the Shadow Realm itself.

"If Grace actually manages to convince the gargoyle to release the time dragon, I'm afraid the creature won't stop at taking care of Souil," I admit. "I'm afraid she will go after Grace and me, too, because we're also out of place in this space and time. We created a time rift when we got here and the time dragon feeds on time rifts, from what I understand." I take a deep breath. "As much as I believe in Grace, we could still lose today. If not to Souil, then to the time dragon."

Nyaz nods, urges me to continue.

"Grace is my mate because she *chose* me. I still can't believe whatever miracle made me the luckiest guy in the world, but before her, I was lost. I was alone and in pain and I can't ever go back to a time when I do not remember what it feels like to love her with my very soul. And I know if I somehow survive alone...no world will be safe. If I allow the pain of her death to destroy the love in my soul for her—"

I break off, my gaze holding his. "I'm afraid the monster my father spent two hundred years forging in darkness will overtake me. I almost let the darkness take me at my friend Smokey's death, and only Grace could pull me back from the brink. What happens if she's go—" I break off because I can't say it, even to Nyaz. Even in a whisper.

"I understand," Nyaz says, and for once, it feels like he might. His stoic expression is gone, and in its place is a sympathy I don't want and don't have a fucking clue what to do with. But since it comes with his help, I'll take it.

I'll take anything that means I have a chance to keep Grace in my heart forever.

"In my opinion, your best bet is a Shadow Promise. Do you know what that is?"

I shake my head.

Nyaz continues. "A Shadow Promise is the strongest of all shadow magic, an unbreakable promise one person makes to another. There's no going back on it, no undoing it if you suddenly decide you've made a mistake. It's forever."

"That's exactly what I want," I say, and honestly, it is. "I want Grace to know that I will always love her—and I want my soul to remember it."

"Okay then." He nods and gestures out the window to the square. "I think you need to ask someone a question, if her little tête-à-tête with that gargoyle ever ends."

131

The Story of Tonight
—Grace—

Hudson comes running up to me in the center of town square. "Oh my God, Grace. Are you okay?" he asks as he slides his hand into mine. "What happened?"

Maybe it shouldn't warm me that he asks if I'm okay before he asks about the single most important thing we all need to know. But it *does* warm me. Because it's becoming more and more apparent that Hudson will always put me first—above everything.

"She's going to try to help us," I tell him, then wait for him and Nyaz to congratulate me, pat me on the back, give me a high-five...something. But they both just stare at me like I've come back from the dead.

"Grace...I was worried sick." I've never heard Hudson sound so frantic, and it makes my heart pound. "You were frozen so long, I was sure something had gone wrong in there."

My high from winning over Artelya fades away as his words register. "H-How long was I gone?" I ask. Because to me, it was a handful of minutes, max.

Hudson's eyes meet mine. "A full day, Grace."

I mull on this as the three of us head back inside the inn, Hudson and Nyaz both checking me over for injuries like a couple of mother hens. Could time pass differently when I'm frozen? And if so, what does that mean for Artelya, who's been frozen for hundreds of years?

By the time we're sitting back in Nyaz's office, I've shared the entire story of what Artelya and I talked about. Everything except that last bit. I save that to discuss with Hudson privately after all of this is over because yeah, I have no idea how I feel about being *anyone*'s queen, much less a gargoyle queen.

Once I finish with the update, the general consensus is it's the best we can count on. We'll secure the dragon with ropes, I'll signal Artelya to release

Asuga, and we'll kill the beast as quickly and humanely as possible. And then we will pray like hell that Artelya is right and the time magic finds Souil's sorry ass and stops him as well.

And that the Shadow Queen doesn't show up to slaughter us all right in the middle of it.

Easy freaking peasy.

It's a Hail Mary pass, but then, we always knew it would be. Now we just have to wait and see if it works.

After saying goodbye to Nyaz, whose main job for the next handful of hours is to recruit backup to help if the Shadow Queen attacks—or if the dragon kills us before Souil—Hudson and I make our way up to our room for what may be the last time.

It's a terrifying thought. And a sad one. Especially since we thought when we left here, it would be to move into a cute little house somewhere near the park and his school, so that we could really start our life together. And now... now, who knows what's going to happen?

Who knows if we'll have that little house or if we'll have nothing at all?

Who knows if we'll even exist in twenty-four hours?

The idea of losing Hudson—in battle or because of the vagaries of time— hurts in a way that threatens to destroy me.

But I'm not going to let it. Not now when I have no idea what the future holds. And not now, when this might very well be the last time we ever spend alone together.

We're both exhausted from being up all night wrestling a dragon and a time wizard—and then trying to figure out how to do it all over again tomorrow. Nyaz assures us the main gate will hold the Shadow Queen and her army till morning as well, since she's at her weakest without sunlight. But we've barely gotten our shoes off before there's a knock on the door.

"What now?" I ask.

Hudson just shakes his head wearily as he pulls it open.

It turns out Nyaz was kind enough to send up a cheese and fruit plate for me and several bottles of water for the both of us. I eat a few crackers and some westeberries, but my stomach is churning and I'm afraid I'll throw up if I eat too much.

Instead, Hudson and I take a long shower, reveling in the feel of the hot water rushing over us as we try to wash the nightmare of the last days off ourselves.

It's even harder than it sounds, though I do my best not to think about it.

If we survive, the horror of last night will be with me for a long time to come. I can take it out and examine it later, when I don't feel so fragile. For now, all I want to do is get through the next several hours. Then I'll worry about my grief—and about figuring out how to stop a wizard who has had centuries to plan this very moment.

When we finally get into bed, Hudson lays on his back staring up at the ceiling, one arm bent behind his head. He hasn't fed yet—he says he's not hungry, but I can feel his hunger beating at him. Can hear it in the low rumble in his chest. Can see it in the way his gaze lingers on my throat when I lean over him.

But I can also see the sorrow in his face and the way he keeps glancing over at Smokey's little bed by the window.

She hated me at least sixty percent of the time, and I *know* I'm going to miss her. I can't imagine how much Hudson is going to miss her and just how heartbroken he must be in this moment.

He still has to take care of himself, though. And he still has to eat. We don't have a clue what the last day of darkness will bring—except a whole lot of shit we don't want to deal with—and he needs to replenish his strength if we have any hope of dealing with this mess.

Instead of fighting him, though, I take a different approach, one that will comfort both of us right now. One that we both need.

I turn the bedside lamp off, then roll over and press myself against Hudson's right side. I put my head on his shoulder and reassure myself with the slow, strong sound of his heartbeat beneath my ear.

His left arm reaches over to stroke my back and tangle in the ends of my still-wet curls. Despite everything, a zing of electricity goes through me. Because this is Hudson, my mate, and I can't imagine ever being in a situation where my body—where my mind and heart and soul—don't respond to him.

"I love you," I whisper as I press soft kisses to his bare chest and collarbone.

His arm tightens around me, pulling me in closer until the only space between our bodies comes when we exhale.

He's warm from the shower and his hair is still damp as I move up to drop slow, sweet, open-mouthed kisses all the way along his jawline to the sensitive spot behind his ear that I love so much.

"Grace." My name is a low, deep rumble in his chest—part sigh, part question, all demand.

"I love you," I tell him again, and this time when I move in even closer, I go all the way, until I'm lying on his chest, my legs straddling his lean, sexy hips.

"Oh yeah?" he asks, brow raised. And though the sadness is a cloak around him, there's a spark of interest deep in his eyes. Our love has always been a beacon out of the darkness for him, and I love that I can be that for him. He's so much more to me, he just doesn't realize it. Yet.

"Yeah," I whisper, sliding my hands up his sides. There's a dip between two ribs right above his waist, a tiny ridge in the area where his elbows line up, a smooth hollow of skin over the sharp bones of his hip.

He feels right—feels perfect for me—and as I lean forward to kiss his lips, I stay awhile. I linger over the perfect V of his upper lip, the full ripeness of his lower lip. Skim my mouth along the left just a little so that I can press kisses to the dimple there.

It's just as beautiful as the day I first saw it, and a part of me wants to stay right here, exploring it forever.

But there's so much more of him to feel. So much more of him to kiss and lick and bite and love.

I skim my mouth lower, lingering at the juncture of his jaw where I can feel his pulse pounding a little harder and faster than it was a few minutes ago. From there, I coast down to the hollow of his throat, relishing the dark-amber scent of him, the rich, warm, delicious taste of him.

He whispers my name again, groaning a little deep in his throat as his hands tangle in my hair. His fingers scratch gently against my scalp, and I moan as shivers of sensation work their way down my spine. His response is to fist a hand in my hair and then—when he has a secure hold—he tugs my head back and presses kisses to the delicate skin of my throat.

It feels good. *He* feels good.

It's strange to find this—to feel this—in the middle of all this sorrow and fear. But it feels right, too, for Hudson and me to have this one moment that belongs to just us. This one moment to reaffirm not only our feelings for each other, but why we're willing to fight so hard. For our family, for our friends, *for each other.*

It's easy to be afraid of love when you see it go sideways. When you feel the pain of a bad breakup or the loss of a loved one or you see a man willing to shatter an entire world because of his love for his daughter. But moments like these—not stolen but shared, not broken but blessed—make everything else fall away. They make everything else worth it.

When Hudson finally lets go of my lips, I reach down and pull off the sleep shirt I just changed into. I toss it onto the ground beside the bed, then slide down his body a little, kissing, licking, biting, touching every tiny little patch of skin I run across.

"Hudson," I whisper. "My Hudson."

"Grace." He echoes my name as I skim my way over his body like moonlight over water. Slow and soft, dark and devastating.

Until all he can feel is me.

Until all he can see and hear and smell and taste is me.

Until the pain from earlier and the fear of later fade under the pleasure—the joy—of now.

Then, and only then, do I slide back up his body.

Then and only then do I glide my palms against the roughness of his, weaving our fingers together as I hold on tight.

Then and only then do I take him deep inside my heart, my body, my soul. And give them all to him.

He takes them as he takes me—with care, with power, with love. And as we move together, as we take each other up, up, up, all that matters is this. All that matters is us.

And for this one perfect moment in the middle of so much imperfection, it is more than enough. It is everything.

We are everything.

132

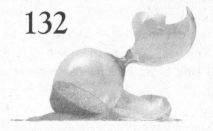

Grace wraps her arms around my neck and pulls me as close to her as I can get. Which is fine with me—when it comes to Grace, I'm always happy to be as close as she wants me.

And when she presses her lips to my cheek, I bury my face against her neck and just breathe her in. She smells so good, feels so good, that I want nothing more than to stay right here forever.

Even before she tilts her head and cups the back of my head in her hands and holds me to her throat.

It's very obviously an invitation to drink from her, and my fangs drop immediately in response. But I hold back, take my time. Because this is Grace, and I'll never get enough of her.

I'll always want more.

She sighs as I press slow kisses to the bend where her shoulder meets her neck. I smile against her throat, then slide my lips across the tiny constellation of freckles that decorates the spot right beside her collarbone. I'd say it was my favorite grouping, but there are so many, it's hard to choose.

The star on her left hip. The spiral on her right shoulder. The perfectly spaced scattering on the inside of her right thigh. So many little pieces that make up my Grace—and I love them all.

I start to think about tomorrow, about what comes next. About what it will feel like if this is the last time I get to kiss these freckles, the last time I get to taste her on my tongue.

But tomorrow will come whether I choose to think about it or not, so for these last moments, I choose to focus on Grace. Just Grace. Especially when she squirms under me, the hand on my head becoming more insistent as she presses me more tightly to her throat.

"Are you sure?" I whisper. Because I will always check when it comes to this. I will never take it for granted, no matter how many times or ways Grace tells me it's okay. She's taking care of me, but it's my job to take care of her as well.

She moves her head so that her lips are pressed against my skin and I can feel her smile. "When am I not sure?" she asks.

"I'm lucky like that." I chuckle as I run my fingers through the softness of her flower-scented hair and smooth it out of the way. Then I take a second or two to rub my thumb over her collarbone even as I scrape my fangs against her jugular.

Grace gasps and arches against me, and still I wait. Still, I let the anticipation build until she's moving restlessly against me.

Only then do I strike, my teeth piercing her skin as hunger washes through me in a wave. She tugs on my hair, tries to press me closer as I drink and drink and drink.

I take my time, going slowly to make sure I don't hurt her. To make sure I don't take too much.

She turns to warm honey against me as I lick the small wounds closed, her body wrapping around mine until I can't tell where I leave off and she begins.

"I love you," I tell her. "Forever."

Her arms tighten around me. "I love you the same way."

"I'm glad." I press a kiss to her mouth, then hold her as she slowly drifts off to sleep.

It takes me a little longer—my mind is full of what ifs and hows—but eventually I sleep, too.

I wake up early the next morning to the sound of Grace screaming. I sit straight up in bed, heart racing and hands clenched into fists, only to realize that it was all a dream. She might have been screaming in my sleep, but the real Grace is rolled onto her side right now, snoring softly.

I lay back down, will my heart to stop pounding. But even as I do, I know there's no way I'm going back to sleep. Not with everything the next twenty-four hours will bring rolling through my head like the most fucked-up montage on the planet.

I give up a few minutes later and get out of bed. Take a quick shower. Then throw on some jeans and head into town. I don't know what things look like down in the square and beyond, but I have something I need to do before Grace wakes up. I just hope some of the shopkeepers braved the burned-up streets of Adarie to try to make a living today.

But I don't even make it out of the inn before Nyaz stops me and asks if Grace and I would feel comfortable being the bait to get Souil out of his house later tonight.

I agree—mainly because I know we'd both planned to do it anyway—then head out to run my errands.

But as I walk out of the inn, I realize town square is still closed up tight due to all the damage. People from the city have started working on it, though—collecting trash, picking up the broken equipment from the hospital last night, cleaning away the ruined landscape.

I'm impressed with how quickly things are getting done, especially considering the village doesn't have a mayor anymore to direct things. As far as I know, Souil is still locked up in that massive house of his, waiting for the first rays of sunlight to destroy everything all these people are working so hard to fix.

It's infuriating, hateful, and it makes me want nothing more than to rip him apart limb from limb. I know that's not possible at the moment, considering all the power he's got bouncing around inside him, but that doesn't make it any less true. This guy is a manipulative fucking bastard, and the world would be a better fucking place without him in it.

Soon enough, I promise myself as I stride through the square to one of the side streets lined with shops. Soon enough, we'll make sure that fucker never gets to mess with anyone again.

It's a promise to myself as much as it is to everyone else he's hurt, and I tell myself I'm going to keep it.

As I walk, a few village regulars finally start to come back out onto the streets, wave at me as I pass. I make a mental note to talk to Nyaz again about ensuring everyone is inside for the coming battle.

The damn werewolves growl and posture the second I walk by, and it makes me want to give them something to growl about. But I don't have time for their bullshit—I want to get back before Grace wakes up—so I walk on by without so much as a snide look. It hurts a little, though, especially when the short, stocky one lets out a growl he thinks is going to intimidate me.

But fuck it. I've got tougher shit than them to deal with right now, so I don't even bother to flash my fangs. Instead, I just look for what I need in the shop windows.

I'm halfway down the boutique-lined street when I find the perfect shop and almost pass out when I see the shopkeeper inside. A fist clamps around my stomach as I open the door, but I ignore it and keep on walking. Nerves have no place here, not when I've already made up my mind.

It's a small shop, and I take my time, walking around slowly until I find exactly what I'm looking for. Then I stand there for a minute, looking down at it as joy and terror war inside me.

One quick conversation with the man behind the counter, plus an unavoidable fifteen-minute wait later, and I'm on my way back to the inn. I force myself not to fade, to enjoy every moment that I'm living. It's harder than it should be, considering Grace is probably still asleep.

But that doesn't matter, because soon—very soon—I'm going to find out exactly what Grace wants. And that isn't terrifying at all...

133

Cross My Heart and
Promise Not to Fry
—Grace—

I wake up alone.

The scent of Hudson's shampoo still hangs in the air, so I know he hasn't been gone long. But he didn't leave a note telling me where he was going—which isn't like him—and I start to worry. Which I admit is ridiculous, considering he's probably just running an errand. Though with everything that's going on, I don't think either of us should be out alone for any length of time.

Who knows what can happen?

To keep my mind off imagining him dead in the street like Orebon and Smokey, I get up and take a quick shower.

Hudson walks in while I'm getting dressed, and I take one look at him and my heart sinks. "What's wrong?" I ask, yanking my shirt over my head. "What happened?"

"Nothing, why?" He tries to smile at me, but his dimple doesn't show.

"Oh, I don't know. Maybe because you look pale as hell." I cross the room to him. "What's going on?"

"Nothing," he says again, and if possible, his smile is even more sickly. "I swear."

I don't believe him—at all. But I'm not going to fight with him right now, either. So I pass the time by picking up around the room, putting our dirty clothes from last night in the laundry basket I keep next to the bathroom door. Smoothing out the sheets. Straightening up the bathroom counter.

Anything to keep from staring at Hudson looking so freaked out and trying not to freak out myself.

I'm in the middle of organizing my hair products alphabetically when Hudson comes up behind me and lays a gentle hand on my shoulder. "Hey, can you stop for a second? I was kind of hoping to talk to you."

"It sure didn't seem like it a few minutes ago," I mutter.

We're standing in front of the bathroom mirror, and I glance up to see if I can gauge his reaction. Then startle a little bit when—of course—he's not there. I shake my head at my own foolishness, wonder when I'll ever get used to Hudson not having a reflection.

"I'm sorry. I'm just..." He trails off, clearing his throat, and for the first time I question if I misread something.

I thought Hudson was keeping something from me because he didn't want to worry me. Now I wonder if he's just nervous? The way he keeps drumming his hands on the counter, the way he keeps clearing his throat? That feels like nerves to me, not subterfuge.

But about what?

I turn to face him, because I want to see his face one way or the other when I ask, "What's going on?"

He takes my hand, leads me back into the bedroom, and gestures for me to sit down on the small chair in the corner.

I do, my stomach clenching uneasily as he starts to pace back and forth in front of me.

On his fourth trip by me, I reach out and grab his hand. "Hey, Hudson. You're making me nervous. Can you just tell me what's going on in your head?"

"Yeah, of course. Sorry." He stops and stands there for a second. Then he drops to his knees in front of me.

"Are you okay?" I ask, worry trumping annoyance. "Are you not feeling well?"

He laughs, but it's a tortured sound deep in his throat. "I'm fine, Grace."

"Are you sure?" I know I sound doubtful, but look at the guy. I'm pretty sure he's sweating, and I didn't even know vampires *could* sweat.

"I'm positive." He takes a page from my book and breathes in deeply. Lets it out slowly. Then reaches for my hand and holds it gently in his.

"This isn't how I thought I'd ever be doing this," he says. "Then again, before you, I never imagined I'd be doing this at all."

"Doing what?" I ask warily. A new kind of nervousness is kicking up in my stomach, one that has me looking at Hudson through different eyes.

"I love you, Grace," he tells me, and there's such sincerity—such love—shining from his eyes that I melt deep inside. Just full-on melt, turning into an ooey-gooey pile of mush right here in this chair. "I love you and—"

"I love you, too," I interrupt, and he smiles, lifting my hand to his lips so that he can press a kiss to the center of my palm.

"I love you," he says again. "In the time we've been together, I've felt things for you I never imagined feeling for another person. I am in awe of you, Grace. Of your strength and your kindness and your resilience. The way you always try to help others, the way you always get back up no matter what bad thing happens to you."

"Hudson—"

"Let me finish, please." He shakes his head, blows out a shaky breath as tears dance in his eyes. "I've never met anyone like you before. I've never had anyone make me laugh the way you do. I've never had anyone want to take care of me the way you do. I've never loved anyone the way that I love you. It's the most all-encompassing thing I've ever felt, and I can't imagine ever going back to a life without you in it."

"Oh, Hudson." I reach for him, cupping his cheeks in my hands as I pull him forward for a kiss. "It's going to be okay—"

"You don't know that," he tells me, and he's shaking now, really shaking. "I don't want Souil to destroy the timeline so badly that I have to try to build a life without you, Grace. I don't want to forget you. I don't want to go back to the way things used to be—I'd rather be locked in a crypt for another two hundred years than face a life without you in it."

I feel the same way about him. Maybe not the dark, scary crypt thing, but definitely everything else, and it breaks my heart to see him so worried. He's hurting so much, and it kills me that there's nothing I can do to fix it. Nothing I can do to make him feel more secure—not just in me but in whatever our fate is going to be.

"I'm not going anywhere, Hudson, and neither are you." I lean forward, press a gentle kiss to his lips. "We're meant to be together. You just need to have some faith."

"I wish I could," he answers. "I wish I could have the kind of faith in the world that you have—it's one of the things I love most about you. That optimistic belief you have that everything is going to be all right. And I'm trying, Grace. I'm really trying. Which is why—"

He reaches into his pocket and pulls out a small box that looks an awful lot like it should be holding a ring.

"What are you—" I break off, my hand flying to my mouth as my entire body goes hot and cold.

He smiles, like he can see what's going on in my head. "It's not an engagement ring, if that's what you're afraid of," he tells me with a roll of his eyes.

"I didn't say I was afraid of anything," I tell him with a sniff. But I still haven't taken my eyes off that box, either.

"It's a promise ring," he says. "And right here, right now, I'd like to make you a promise—if you'll have me."

"A promise?" I repeat, because I want to be sure I know what's happening here. Back home, a promise ring is kind of a symbol to each other that a couple is serious. But it doesn't require anyone to promise anything to the other—at least not the way Hudson is making it sound.

"It's a special promise," he tells me. "A Shadow Promise, made from magic as old as the universe, from me to you. It's a promise that can't be broken from my side."

"But you don't need to make me an unbreakable promise, Hudson," I assure him as I look down into the earnest blue eyes of this proud vampire prince kneeling before me. "It's enough that you love me today, and that I have faith you will love me tomorrow."

He reaches up, pushes a lock of curls behind my ear. "The promise is as much for me as a gift to you." He squeezes my hand. "I don't know much about love, Grace. But you've taught me that real love isn't about finding someone who makes you happy. It's about finding your own happiness and then sharing that with the person you love. You will always be my light out of the darkness, but not because it's your job to make me happy. Because you light the path I can follow to find my own happiness. And I want to always see that path, let it lead me back to you. Always."

With a shaky hand, he flips open the box, and my already fast-beating heart goes completely out of control. Because the ring he got me is beautiful—the most beautiful thing I've ever seen. It's a simple band made of a delicate silvery-purple metal with beautiful small symbols etched around the band.

It's gorgeous and perfect and I couldn't have picked out anything I would have liked more than this.

"Oh my God," I whisper as he slowly takes the ring out of the box.

"If you'll have me, Grace," he tells me, and for the first time I realize how vulnerable he looks, with his hair all disheveled from his nervous fingers and his face pale with worry. I love that he's resolute in his decision, wish he understood just how resolute I am, too.

"Always," I tell him with a watery laugh. Then I reach for his hand, bring his palm to my lips. "I love you, Hudson. I'll always want you."

He smiles, the first real smile I've seen since he walked in the room.

Then he slides the ring up my finger, leans forward to whisper in my ear. "'I love you with a love that shall not die, until the sun grows cold and the stars grow old.'"

The moment he finishes speaking, my finger tingles everywhere the ring is touching and it tightens for a second, like it's settling into place. Then it's done and warmth spreads from my hand to Hudson's as I reach for him and kiss him with all the love and joy and determination burning within me.

Hudson Vega is my mate, and I will fight for him with every ounce of strength I have in my body and my soul. Because he deserves someone to fight for him. He deserves someone to want him.

And I do want him. I do love him. And I'm determined that not even time itself is going to take him away from me.

When our kiss finally ends, Hudson pulls me up. He must have snagged my phone because suddenly the opening notes of Shawn Mendes's "Fallin' All in You" start playing.

"Dance with me?" he says, dimple in full attendance and blue eyes shining more brightly than the stars currently falling outside our window.

I give him my hand, and he sweeps me into a spin that takes us across the entire hotel room. "So is this our thing?" I ask as he dips me to the beginnings of the chorus. "Dancing to cheesy love songs?"

"I want us to have a lot of different things," he answers as he pulls me up and spins me out, as only a crown prince who spent his life in dancing lessons can. "But yeah, if you don't mind. I love dancing with you."

"I love being in your arms," I answer, and for once there's no snark and no teasing in our tones. There's only love and a laid-bare honesty I never would have imagined possible that first night when Hudson told me to turn on the fucking lights. "Any way that I can get here. But especially this way."

He twirls us around again, eating up the small hotel room floor in a series of complicated steps. If dancing with me gives him even a little of the joy it brings me—I'll dance with him forever, if he'll have me.

But as one of my favorite Shawn Mendes songs segues into George Ezra's slow and deep "Hold My Girl," an urgent knock sounds on our door. Hudson and I have one moment to glance at each other in alarm before the door flies open.

Nyaz is standing there, looking more shaken than I've ever seen him. "Yssah's wife must have made it to warn the Shadow Queen. Her army is at the gate. It's go time."

134

The Wheel of
Misfortune
—Grace—

My heart is beating double-time as we race down the stairs. We'd hoped the queen wouldn't breach the gate until after sunrise in an hour, so we're all panicked now.

"The first round of fighters are holding the queen off near the gate, at least for a bit," Nyaz says as he's running along right behind us. "But we need to hurry."

"We need to get Caoimhe!" I tell Hudson as we hit the landing on the second floor hard and start down our last flight of steps.

"She's already downstairs," Nyaz shouts at us. "And so is Lumi."

"Lumi?" I almost miss the bottom step as I turn to him in shock. "But the baby—"

"He's got her set up with friends. He said he wants to fight." Nyaz adds the last like that's all there is to it. And maybe it is. I know if something happened to Hudson and I had the chance to stand against the man who killed him, there'd be no way I could walk away from that. No way I could just stay home and let someone else take him on.

We burst out into the lobby, and I nearly plow straight into Gillie, the baker I worked with for a day when I first got to Adarie. She gives me a discreet thumbs-up. Thank God. The first step of the plan Hudson and Nyaz came up with is in place.

The entire first floor of the inn is filled with people from the village. Gillie and a man I'm pretty sure is her husband. Tinyati and her husband and their two adult daughters. Hudson's principal and her wife. Two of the librarians. The chupacabra. Some of the wolves who live outside the village but shop and visit here often. Even Arnst and Maroly are here, though Arnst isn't even from the village. Tiola is nowhere in sight, thank goodness.

They head straight toward us, smiles on their faces, and we rush over to meet them halfway.

"Grace! Hudson!" Arnst grabs me and pulls me into a giant bear hug. "We're so glad to find you safely in one piece. We've both had more than a few sleepless nights worrying about you since you left our farm. When Nyaz hinted what was coming the other day, we came immediately."

"We've worried about you, too," I tell them as I move to give Maroly a hug.

"How's Tiola?" Hudson asks after he exchanges a hearty handshake and back slapping with Arnst. "We miss her."

"She misses you guys, too," Maroly comments. "But she's good. Still collecting every stray umbra that comes her way." There's a question in Maroly's eyes, one I really don't want to answer right now. At least, not in front of Hudson, who carries the guilt of Smokey's death like a bruise that won't heal.

Thankfully, Caoimhe and Lumi pick this moment to join us. Caoimhe is red-eyed yet clear, but Lumi is a different story. He's a mess—not only his puffy eyes and face from the obvious crying but the dark circles under his eyes and the lank, lackluster hair.

Combined with the exhausted body language and air of sadness that radiates from him, I'm terrified to let him go into battle with us. It's not that I don't trust him, but the last thing I want is to have him make a mistake that leaves his daughter without either of her fathers.

Before I can figure out what—if anything—to say, people are gathering around Hudson and me. And I know it's time for us to get things going.

I look to Hudson, to see if he wants to say anything before I lay out the plan, but he just steps back with the others and waits for me to speak.

Which isn't terrifying at all. After surreptitiously wiping my hands on my jeans, I take a deep breath and will my anxiety to stay under control. And then I just start.

"First of all," I say, turning around as I speak so that I have a chance to look every single one of these people in the eye. They deserve that and so much more when I stand here asking them to fight. "I'd like to say thank you to all of you for being here tonight to help us make this stand. Many of you have known this was coming for a while. Known that one day you would have to stand up against the Shadow Queen and the mayor. We didn't know it would be at the same time, but at least that means our nightmare will be over that much sooner."

People murmur and nod, agreeing with me, and it helps keep the low-grade panic in my stomach in check.

"Because we can't go on worried that every day—every Starfall—will be our last. Worried that the lives and families we've built here in Noromar will disappear one day because some wizard or some queen wills it so."

"No!" shouts someone from the crowd. "We won't go!"

"You're damn right we won't!" Nyaz agrees, lending his voice to mine. "This is our village. These are our friends. These are our lives. And we will fight for them, down to the last one of us. No wizard is going to blink all of us out of existence."

Cheers go up from a lot of the people around us. Hudson and I don't cheer—I may agree with the sentiment Nyaz is expressing, but I don't think I'll ever be good with clapping and whistling for a war.

My parents raised me to believe that fighting was a last resort. Walking away from a fight that doesn't matter is always a better option than getting hurt or hurting someone. But there's a big difference between a bully calling me names on the playground or someone graffitiing my bike to letting a person follow his own selfish plans and basically ruin an entire world—and so many of the lives in it.

This isn't a fight to cheer about, but it isn't a fight to walk away from, either.

Not when losing means Souil resets the timeline, not only in Hudson's and my world but in this world as well. We can't let that happen. We *won't* let that happen. Not to our friends and not to anyone in this realm. They deserve the right to live their lives without the threat of someone choosing to take it all away, just because he can.

"I've spoken to Artelya. She's the gargoyle out front, in case any of you want to know her name. She's agreed to release the time dragon, exactly as we wanted."

More cheers go up. "But there has been a change in plans." Again, I try to look as many people in the eye as I can. Because this is the part I have to sell. The part I really need them to get behind.

I glance at Hudson, who gives me a "you've got this" nod. It's all I need to remind myself that yeah, I really do have this.

"We've got a problem with letting the time dragon loose." I still shake my head when I think of how simple his plan was. I'm also astonished by how easily it almost worked. If not for Artelya's sacrifice, that is. "The mayor is a time wizard who has been waiting for the death of two time dragons to power him up so he can go home and reset time in my world. A brave gargoyle realized what his plan was and has been frozen in time for nearly a thousand years to prevent him from succeeding. But today, she is going to make the ultimate sacrifice and free that dragon."

I look at each person as I say, "We cannot let her sacrifice be in vain. If the dragon kills him with dragon fire—*your* world's timeline will reset. Many of you, your friends and family, will cease to exist. At *all costs*, that dragon cannot kill Souil by fire."

"Why wake the dragon up at all, then?" Hudson's principal, Saniya, asks. "If we just keep him asleep, then the fire will never get him?"

"Because we can't kill the wizard without it. He's too powerful—we can't even touch him. At this point, nothing can but the energy of time itself."

Everyone's eyes widen, but then they start nodding and murmuring.

I continue. "We believe the only way that we can save both of our worlds is by killing the time dragon and forcing Souil to absorb her magic. Like a bottle already full of water, we think the extra magic will kill him. We're going to show this asshole—if you want power, we will *give* you power. More power than you can handle, and then watch as it destroys you!"

Everyone cheers and slaps one another on the back. But I raise a hand, quiet the crowd down again. "But killing this dragon is not going to be easy. She's big. She's powerful. And she's been locked in chains for a thousand years. And if that weren't bad enough...the Shadow Queen and her army will do anything to keep us from killing the dragon as well. The Shadow Queen *wants* Souil to reset time. She *wants* to destroy this home—*your* home. But we won't let her!"

When the shouting and discussing of plans dies down, Nyaz breaks in and says, "Okay. But how are we going to keep the time dragon from killing everyone else when we let her go? This village has a lot of residents—"

"I've taken care of it," Gillie speaks up. "I printed up some notices and my staff are distributing them now. Everyone is up-to-date, meaning no one will wander out into the street for hours."

"That's really smart!" Maroly says, smiling approvingly at me.

Hudson steps forward. "So plan A is simple: Grace will signal to the gargoyle to free the dragon and we will kill her instantly. The time magic will leave her, go to Souil, and destroy him, and everyone will be safe. Should the dragon not die instantly...well, we'll have to move on to plan B, which will only have two goals." He raises his pointer finger. "Do not let the dragon kill Souil with dragon fire." He raises another finger. "Kill the dragon before the sun rises."

He glances around the room, then gives a half smile as he adds, "So it goes without saying, let's try to kill the dragon immediately."

Saniya raises a brow. "I have one more question, then. Isn't the dragon going to go after the mayor the second we wake her up? That'll make it really hard to keep her from touching Souil with flames."

"Don't worry. I have a plan for that, too," I tell them. "And to make it happen, we're going to need ropes. Lots and lots of ropes."

135

BDSM: Bondage, Dragons, Stone, and Magic
—Grace—

Thanks to Nyaz and the chupacabra, whose name I learn is Polo, it only takes about five minutes for us to round up all the supplies we need. Then we head out to town square as quickly as we can. Time is ticking closer and closer toward dawn, which means the Shadow Queen's army will be too powerful to hold back. And once the queen is able to sneak in on a shadow, Souil will be able to sneak out.

We race to the other side of the square, and the wolves and Hudson start wrapping the dragon in Caoimhe's heaviest ropes while Arnst, Maroly, and I do the same to Artelya.

"Are you sure this is going to work?" Nyaz asks as we wrap them both up as tightly as we can—though for very different reasons.

"It should," Hudson tells him. "The second Artelya wakes the dragon, you'll all pull the ropes to hold the dragon down so I can kill her. In the meantime, Grace and the others will pull Artelya down so the flames that are already heading toward her won't touch her—if we're lucky. They're really close already to her, but we have to try. It'll all be a question of timing in the end."

"And your ability to kill a dragon this big and powerful," Tinyati's husband tells him as he shifts the sword we gave him back and forth in his hands. "I know we're supposed to be backup, but maybe I should be on the other side from you. Just in case. We can kill the beast together."

"I'm not going to say no." Hudson flashes a quick grin. "I'll take any help you want to give me. From what I understand, this beast is feral."

"She is," I tell him—and myself. Because even though I know it's the right thing to do, even though it's the only way to save all the people in Adarie plus who knows how many thousands of people in my realm, it's still hard to think of killing a living creature who isn't actively attacking me.

Artelya assures me that will change the second Asuga wakes up. That she's incredibly powerful, incredibly mean, and she's had a thousand years of hunger beating at her chest. There's no way I can give her a chance to be free.

"The dragon's ropes are done," the chupacabra says, stepping away.

"So are Artelya's," Arnst comments as he does the same thing.

"Okay, so this is it. We're going to do this now, and then the energy will seek out Souil at his house. And hopefully this ends quickly—"

Hudson finishes. "And you will all be free from living under the threat of him destroying Adarie forever."

"Don't underestimate the Shadow Queen, though," I warn them. "She's going to try to help him any way she can."

"Which means we need to keep her off Grace and Hudson so they can kill the dragon and end this thing once and for all," Nyaz says. "We can do that, right?"

Everyone nods their assent. And I turn back to the dragon—to Artelya— with only one thought in mind. *Please, please, let this work.*

But before I can ask Artelya to unfreeze as we've discussed, the werewolves stop dead and start sniffing the air.

They lift their noses, and I get a very bad feeling in my stomach. "What's going on?" I ask, already afraid of what the answer is going to be.

Because Hudson has tilted his head, too, as if he's listening to something with his incredible hearing. When he turns back to me, his eyes are narrowed. "The Shadow Queen has made it past the gate."

"Yeah, well, screw her," I tell him, annoyance coloring my voice. "Let's do this."

"Everybody ready?" Hudson asks as he picks up a giant sword. Tinyati's husband does the same, then positions himself on the other side of the dragon.

"As ready as we'll ever be," Gillie says grimly. She lifts her sword and clutches it in front of her with both hands.

As do the other thirty or forty people who aren't actively holding ropes.

"Okay. I'm going to talk to Artelya now. But remember, in case anything goes wrong, we cannot—"

"Let the dragon kill Souil with dragon fire," everyone repeats at the same time.

"We've got it," Tinyati tells me. "No matter what happens, we won't let her near the mayor."

Her reassurance is all I've been waiting for, and after a smile of encouragement for all of them, I take a second to center myself.

Then I close my eyes, say to myself, *"Artelya?"*

"Everything in place?" she asks, her words echoing in my head and yeah, I'm a little shocked I can hear her. No, a lot shocked. But I shake it off quickly and get to business.

"It is," I tell her. *"I've got this. I promise. And we're not going to let anything happen to you."*

I can feel her smile through our connection. *"I'm not afraid, Grace. Protecting people is what gargoyles do, no matter what the cost. It has been an honor to protect the people of Adarie for the last thousand years. And it will continue to be an honor to protect them, no matter what happens next."*

"Thank you," I whisper. *"For all of your service and all of your sacrifice. You are amazing."*

"As are you, Grace." I can hear her take a deep breath, and then she says, *"Now, I'm going to un-fortify, so get ready to kick some dragon arse."*

A blink later, she loses her stone form—and so does the dragon.

We don't even have a second to pull her out of the way of the flames as the fire turns her to dust in a blink right in front of us.

I scream in horror, but I have no time to absorb what just happened, because Hudson is bringing his sword down on the dragon, as is Tinyati's husband. Everyone else is holding on to the ropes like they are the only thing standing between them and death—which they very well might be.

But as soon as Hudson's sword starts to make contact with the dragon's neck, she blinks out of the ropes and is gone in an instant.

136

It's Darkest
Before the Dawn
—Hudson—

The dragon reappears several seconds later—in the sky.

Brilliant. This suddenly just got a whole fuck-ton harder than we'd anticipated. And we never thought it'd be anything *but* difficult.

"We need to move!" Grace shouts as she takes off running toward the other side of the square. "We can't let her get to the mayor!"

Like the dragon can smell the time rift stench on Souil, she banks hard and then heads across the square, straight for the mansion like a heat-seeking dragon missile.

"Already on it!" I shout back as I fade straight across the square toward the mayor's house. Because I can*not* let that bloody dragon get to that tosser. Not while we are so close. And not with everything we stand to lose.

But if there's one thing dear old Dad has taught me, it's that things can always get worse. And apparently today is no exception. Because I've barely gotten to the edge of the square, dodging lines of dragon fire the entire time, before Souil strides into the square in full disco king dress, complete with cape.

And everything else goes straight to hell.

Grace must have seen him before I did because she's already racing straight for him in complete gargoyle mode. He sees her coming, though, and blinks away, about three feet closer to where the first rays of sunlight will hit, yet clearly staying out of the dragon's eyeline.

We've still got an hour before the sun comes up, though, so I have no idea what Disco Man is doing rushing for the edge of the town square just yet. Nor do I care. Because at this moment, the dragon ditches chasing me and races straight toward Grace instead, coming in low and flame-hot.

Fuck no. I'm prepared for a lot of things tonight—including my own death. The one thing I'm not prepared for is Grace blinking the fuck out of existence. Not on my fucking watch.

I fade to them in an instant, then jump straight at the dragon. I hit her feet-first, knocking her back through the air—just far enough to send her flames spiraling away from Grace and straight through the town's stage.

The small area catches fire and the wolves race to put it out before it can spread. Everyone else runs toward Souil with swords raised. We never told them they couldn't try to kill him—except with dragon fire—so they must decide he just needs to die now. Too bad they don't know what we've seen... He's not going to be that easy to take down.

He tosses one look at them and blinks several feet away, then flips his hand in the air like he's spinning a record, and five of the six people chasing him freeze instantly. Interesting.

Four blinks later and Souil has evaded the sixth guy but—and this is *really* interesting—no blink is more than three feet in distance, *and* the first five people who were frozen in time unfreeze.

"Souil can't keep people frozen if he has to move himself through time and space!" I shout to Grace as I turn to face her and realize the dragon has recovered from having the vampire-shit kicked out of her. She's coming after me again. Good. She can bring it the fuck on. Because as long as she's chasing me, she's not going after Souil.

Which gives the others time to regroup. Grace can come up with another plan to kill the dragon while I keep her attention focused on me. And Souil isn't going anywhere if we keep the dragon occupied. I glance briefly at the skyline and note the black night is slowly giving way to a deep blue. Fuck. We've got less than an hour now to kill this bitch.

With that thought in mind, I run straight at the dragon again. But this time she's not distracted by anyone else. She knows I'm coming, and she's more than ready for me.

To prove it, she flies straight at me, and all I can think is fuck, she's huge. Like really, really huge. I thought the last time dragon was big, but Asuga, as Grace mentioned she was called, is monstrous. Her green scales gleam in the early-morning dusk as she races toward me, red eyes burning with rage. Her mouth is open, her huge teeth on full display as she lets loose with a stream of fire that sizzles across the square.

I jump several feet in the air to avoid it, but she just sends another wave of flames straight at me. And since I'm in the middle of the air, I don't have a lot of options other than to twist and hope for the best.

She misses once more, but she's picking up on my tricks, and the next line of flames she sends at me is impossible to avoid. I close my eyes, prepare myself to blink out of the timeline—only to have a very heavy, very stony Grace slam right into me.

We hit the ground hard, with her on top of me and dragon flames coming straight at us. I have one second to roll us away, as the dragon swoops in, before more fire comes barreling toward us.

Two of the wolves jump into the battle then, hitting the dragon from both sides with claws and teeth. She shakes them off with an outraged roar, but they both get a piece of her. Not enough to weaken her but enough to slow her down just a little.

Which is all I need.

Picking up the sword from where I dropped it, I race toward her as she tries to head back up into the air. She's fast, but I'm faster, and I manage to slice a couple of feet into her soft underbelly.

This time, her scream is pained as well as furious, and she turns her head back toward me and shoots me with what I'm pretty sure is everything she's got. I jump out of the way, and Souil—thank the fucking universe—uses his finely honed protection instinct to blink several feet away and races toward the wall around town. As dawn breaks, first light is going to hit right over there.

But Polo the chupacabra is on his arse, determined to bring the time wizard down before he can get there. Plus the dragon is flying straight at them both, flames shooting out of her mouth in all directions. Terrified his personal force field won't hold up against the flames, I fade straight at them.

The chupacabra jumps at him hard enough to shake his force field and I take over, tackling Souil and rolling with him straight under one of the oversize park benches that dot the area around the used-to-be gazebo. The benches are metal, and that should be enough to deflect the dragon's flames if she aims for us again—which I have no doubt she's going to do.

"Thanks for the save," Souil says in an obnoxious tone, then blinks out of my hold as soon as we come to a stop. I dart after him, but he keeps blinking straight back toward the wall.

The dragon has locked on to him, and I have to wonder yet again what this plonker is doing running around before dawn. Seriously.

We all knew we'd have to keep the mayor out of the path of the dragon fire, but we figured it wasn't going to be more than a few minutes between the time he'd likely run out of his protected mansion and when the dragon would disappear in the sunlight. But instead, he's apparently bought his own advertising and thinks he's invincible, given he's just running around, cape flying behind him, as he makes my job ten thousand times harder. I should be killing the damn dragon and instead I'm playing bodyguard to this overgrown cockwomble.

Speaking of which, this jumbo jet of a dragon is wicked fast in the air, much faster than she looks like she'd be given her size, and she is closing the distance on Souil much quicker than I'd like.

I grit my teeth and fade toward her, determined to get to her before she can shoot fire at him. She's not having it, though, flames spewing out of her mouth as her powerful wings bring her closer and closer to the mayor. Grace is already in the air, flying straight for Asuga in an attempt to deflect her while I fade full-out toward Souil.

But I still don't think either of us is going to make it before the fire touches him.

I lay on a little bit more speed and—

Out of what seems like nowhere, Gillie jumps in front of the mayor and takes the powerful blast of fire meant for him.

137

Where the Wild Things Really Are
—Grace—

Gillie screams when the flames hit her, and I try to reach her. I swear to God, I try. But Hudson jumps up and grabs me, pulling me out of the air.

"It's still dragon fire," he tells me as we hit the ground. "Which no one can survive. If we could save her, I'd do it in an instant. But it's too late."

I know he's right, can see that Gillie's already gone limp. But it doesn't make standing here any easier to bear. And then she's gone.

Tears roll down my face as the same wolves who put out the gazebo fire race toward her. And it feels like we should do something, feels like we should pay our respects somehow. But the dragon is circling around again, and Souil is getting closer to the wall.

Caoimhe and Lumi start chasing after him, but every time they get close, Souil blinks somewhere else. Plus, he's got that damn disco ball weapon of his, and he's swinging it around his head in obvious warning.

For a second, all I can see is Orebon moments before Souil murdered him. I scream despite myself as Hudson and I race toward our friends.

There's a shimmer of light as Souil lowers his shields—just long enough to swing the weapon straight at Caoimhe's head, and my heart is pounding in my throat. Thank God, she goes low at the last second, throwing herself at Souil and tackling him much the way Hudson did a couple of minutes ago. At the same time, Lumi raises the club he's been carrying. But right before his swing connects with Souil's head, the mayor flashes three feet away again.

And Lumi—who is definitely swinging for the fences—barely misses connecting the club with Caoimhe's head.

At just that moment, Saniya comes out of the darkness with her sword raised. Unfortunately, Souil flashes up his shield, and her sword bounces off uselessly.

The rest of the townspeople are converging on Souil, and the mayor—

always the showman—is putting on one hell of a show for all of them. Anytime someone gets near him, he flashes somewhere else, until everyone catches on and stops trying. Which is, of course, exactly what he wants to have happen as the minute hand on the clock tower ticks inexorably closer to sunrise.

Because if we don't kill this damn dragon in the next few minutes, he wins. All he needs is one patch of light and he can ride it straight out of here.

Not that I need the clock to tell me that. The fact that shadows are starting to slowly, slowly creep across the grass tells me everything I need to know. They're faint yet, almost nonexistent, but they're there. I can see them. More, I can feel them as they skitter across my feet and brush up against my legs, though I don't know how.

Just then, like the universe decided to give me a brief moment to celebrate, the dragon banks hard left and circles back around—and lays dragon fire in a giant circle around us and Souil, setting grass and trees and various structures ablaze. Bad news is, of course, there's fucking dragon fire everywhere, but good news—Souil can't flash to the creeping sunlight now. He's got to wait for it to come to him.

But the shadows appear to be growing, creeping past the fire somehow, even beyond where the first rays of light are touching the square.

My blood suddenly runs cold as I think of Smokey and all the other shadows that followed Tiola around on the farm. Not shadows at all, now that I think about it. Umbras.

Shape-shifting umbras.

Another shadow brushes against my calf, and it freaks me out enough that I whirl around even as I step closer to Hudson. What if that's what these shadows are, too? Umbras that can touch you and communicate and wreak havoc, if that's what they want to do.

Smokey certainly knew how to do all those things, even when she wasn't trying.

"Something's wrong," I tell Hudson as I watch the shadows creep farther and farther into the square.

"No shit," he snarls, but he's still focused on what's going on with Souil.

"No." I reach out and grab onto his arm. "Not with him. With the umbras."

"Umbras?" He looks confused, but then he follows my gaze and his eyes widen, too. "Holy fuck. Are those—"

"I think so, yeah."

And just like that, it's on, almost as if our recognition of the things brought them to life. Or, at least, activated them from whatever stealth maneuver they'd been pulling up until this point. Because all of a sudden, umbras are everywhere.

And they aren't just any kind of umbras, either. They certainly aren't little, cute, squishable umbras like Smokey was. No, these things are serious. And ugly. And absolutely terrifying.

At first, the ones on the grass turn into shadow bugs—shadow roaches and ants and spiders crawling and writhing over the grass in their effort to get to the people standing against Souil.

"Oh my God!" I gasp as the umbra brushing against me transforms into a wave of shadow tarantulas crawling over my feet and up my legs. "Hudson!"

It's more of a whimper than a scream, but my mate hears me. He fades to grab me and lift me up, but I'm already turning to stone. Which really doesn't help much, considering there are still bugs crawling on me.

But at least I can't feel it—not in the same way I could when I was human, anyway. And at least this way, they can't bite me, which is more than I can say for so many of the other people around me right now.

Unfortunately, I also can't move like this. At least not well. So, after screaming internally for what feels like a solid minute, I shift into my regular gargoyle form—and then lift up so I'm hovering a good two feet off the ground where Hudson is stuck, shadow roaches streaming along his legs and arms.

"Do you want me to lift you up?" I ask, reaching for him. "Get you out of this mess?"

He looks disgusted as he kicks out at the bugs, but he just shakes his head. "We've got bigger problems."

"Bigger problems than a narcissistic time wizard bent on global annihilation, a pissed-off time dragon, and an entire town square worth of creepy, crawly bugs?" I ask incredulously. "How exactly is that possible?"

Hudson doesn't answer me. Instead, he just nods toward the sky behind me. And though I really, really don't want to turn around, there isn't anything else for me to do.

And that's when I see them. Giant shadow ravens and vultures soaring through the air, dive-bombing anyone who tries to run. And anyone who gets too close to Souil—especially Caoimhe and Lumi, who are still chasing him along with the wolves.

"Is he doing this?" I ask, revulsion churning in my stomach as a pile of giant roaches scatters just beneath me.

Polo shrieks below as the shadow bugs crawl on his arms, cover his body, and rush over his face. Diving in his open mouth as he lets out another involuntary scream before taking off at an all-out run in an attempt to dislodge the bugs.

"It's the Shadow Queen," Hudson answers from between clenched teeth as the bugs start to bite him.

Of course it is. The bitch. I want to ask him more, but he shouts up to me, "Just kill the fucking dragon!"

And he's right. If we can kill the dragon, all of this ends.

I take off as Hudson fades across the square. He's leaping from balconies to rooftops, each jump taking him higher and higher to get to a greater vantage point to help with the dragon that is circling the square again. Luckily—or not, depending on how you want to look at it—we must reek of time rift as much as Souil, because the dragon has no issue leaving him be and coming after us instead.

But now we've got another problem. Because being in the air and on a rooftop means we're perfect targets for the huge freaking shadow birds that are flying around all over the place. A giant condor-like shadow flies straight at me, claws extended like the weapons they are.

Not to mention the dragon who is slowly circling overhead, looking for an opening to shoot odd bursts of dragon fire nearby.

As the condor closes in on me, I at first think it's trying to scare me or scratch me, but then I realize it's so much worse.

It's going for my eyes.

I let out another scream and dive toward the earth with this giant bird right on my ass. I'm kind of hoping if we get close enough to the ground, it will decide to go for some of the tarantulas or something—easy prey and all that. Unfortunately, the only thing it seems interested in is me.

Too bad the feeling isn't mutual.

I dive just low enough to fake a landing, then turn around and prepare to climb in an effort to distract the bird from my sudden change in direction. But Hudson is having none of it—big surprise. He drops into a crouch on a nearby rooftop. Then launches himself straight up—and snatches the shadow bird, mid-wing flap, right out of the air.

He grabs onto its wing, and there's a tearing sound before he sends the condor careening across the sky with such force that it slams into two other giant birds and takes them down, too.

I feel like maybe I should be upset about hurting the damn things, but then I remember they aren't birds. They're just shadows, giving their best Hitchcock impression—although these seem conjured by the queen more than sentient like Smokey.

Personally, I think it's a little over-the-top, and that's before the birds all fly into a circular formation right above the center of town square—right above Souil—and start attacking anyone who goes near him.

Add in the fact that daylight is slowly creeping across the sky, barely fifteen minutes away from Souil at best guess, and we've got a really serious problem. And that's before howls and snarls fill the air.

138

Buggin' the F*ck Out
—Grace—

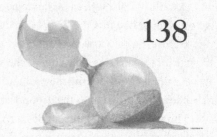

I race back toward Hudson as the snarls get closer, trying to figure out where these new noises are coming from.

He's trying to figure out the same thing, spinning around on the rooftop even as he kicks away another dead shadow bird. "What the hell is that?" Hudson asks as I swoop down next to him.

"I don't—" I break off as the snarls get worse, and I finally see what's making them.

Wolves. Dozens and dozens of shadow wolves rushing through the streets of Adarie straight toward town square. Straight toward Souil.

As if that's not bad enough, Asuga—who has been waiting patiently for us to be clear of the shadow animals—must decide this is her moment because she dives straight toward us, flames flying.

"Dragon or shadows?" Hudson asks, and I want to answer "neither." But I know we need to divide and conquer if we're going to kill the dragon. One of us needs to distract the shadow creatures while the other is free to focus on the flying dragon bitch.

So I choose, "Shadows."

He nods and leaps off the rooftop, landing superhero-style on the one rooftop across the way and racing straight toward the dragon. And though I want nothing more than to watch him, backing him up is more important right now. Which means keeping these damn shadow creatures off him so he can get to Asuga and kill her.

As he runs, a giant raven sweeps down at him, and I launch myself into the sky. I intercept it at the last second, and it rakes a claw straight down my stone cheek.

"Seriously," I shout at the bird and the universe and who knows what else. "Don't you think this is just a little overkill?"

"A little?" Polo says as he lands nearby, shaking his head. "Who thinks up something like this?"

Before I can answer, a shadow wolf launches straight at him. The chupacabra wraps one arm around the wolf's giant chest and a hand around its very unpleasant-looking muzzle before slamming the wolf up and over his shoulder, then down onto the ground so hard that it trembles all around us.

The wolf whines and trembles, too, but the second the chupacabra lets go of it, it makes another pass at him. This attack is much weaker, but it's still an attack, and I jump in the middle of them. I turn to stone in an instant and the wolf slams into me, hard.

It's the distraction the chupacabra needs to get his hands on it again, and this time he picks it up and slams it into the ground over and over again until the thing lays unmoving at his feet.

Bugs swarm it instantly and they swarm Polo, too, who grunts as they bite him over and over again.

It's the most disgusting thing I've ever seen, and I reach forward to intervene, slapping the nasty things off his back as fast as I can. But they just keep coming back, faster and more numerous every time.

As I try to get them off him, they crawl onto me, too. I'm still stone, thankfully, so they can't bite me any more than they already have. The few bites I do have burn like hellfire itself. How is Hudson doing it with all the bites he has, I wonder as I turn around slowly, hampered by the stone. How does any one of these people do it?

I look around and realize that the answer is, they don't. More than half of the people who started off this morning standing beside us are now on the ground. Wraiths and otherworlders alike, brought down by the bugs and the birds and these wolves that somehow seem like they're everywhere.

A scream rends the air and it's familiar enough that it has me turning to look. Only to find Caoimhe on the ground beneath a giant wolf. She's got her hands on its chest and is pushing it away as hard as she can, but it's snapping and biting as it tries just as hard to get to her.

I know she won't be able to hold it off much longer, so I race across the lawn in a desperate attempt to get to Caoimhe before the wolf can take her out.

At the same moment, Hudson goes spinning across the sky and crash lands into the clock tower. He ducks inside right as a stream of dragon fire rips by him and suddenly I'm terrified to look. Terrified when I do that he won't be there anymore.

But he is, thankfully, and as the dragon circles the tower, he climbs onto the roof and launches himself at her. I watch long enough to make sure he grabs onto something on her and isn't free-falling, then launch myself into the air, determined to help Caoimhe however I can.

As I fly toward her, I dodge birds and bugs and wild-looking jungle cats with giant teeth, all in an effort to help my friend.

Lumi gets there a few seconds ahead of me and slams his club into the wolf hard enough to make the thing howl. He hits it again and again, then rolls it off Caoimhe and yanks her to her feet.

As soon as he does, the two of them go back-to-back to defend themselves— and each other—from the snarling beast as it comes back at them.

I'm almost there, almost there—until something huge and heavy blindsides me and sends me careening through the air. I try to right myself, to fly back up, but something else hits me just as hard from the other side.

It knocks the breath out of me, makes it impossible for my paralyzed lungs to draw in oxygen as I tumble down, down, down to the ground. A glance to the side shows not one but two shadow wolves aiming straight for me.

And I'm trapped directly between the two, with no escape in sight.

A glance at the sky tells me we're running out of time. The mayor is positioned by the wall, force field in place as his shadow-creature guards conjured by the queen swarm the area around him. In minutes, it will be light enough for him to escape if we don't find a way to stop him. But how can we when the Shadow Queen's nightmarish familiars—or whatever the hell they are—are all around us, taking us down one by one?

It's terrifying and demoralizing and I don't know what to do about it. Don't know how to make any of the attacks stop long enough for a few of us to actually try to get to the former mayor. And that doesn't even count the fact that the dragon and Hudson are tearing the clock tower and several other buildings all to hell as they fight each other on the other side of the square.

I want nothing more than to go help him, but dawn is way too close for me to leave the mayor alone. If I get trapped up there with Hudson and the dragon, then there's no way I'll be able to get back before the sun rises enough to cast shadows. And if that happens, Souil is gone. Too many other people are out of commission to be able to stop him.

Before I can decide what to do, the choice is taken out of my hands.

One of the shadow wolves lets loose another loud, brutal snarl and I whirl around on it, prepared to do whatever I need to do to survive. But it doesn't launch itself toward me. Instead, the other one does—the one I was foolish enough to turn my back on even if it was only for a second.

I go down without a fight, but it's pretty damn hard to fight when you've been ambushed from behind. I turn to stone as I hit the ground—the last defense I've got—and it turns out, it's just in time. Because one of the wolves tries to take a giant chunk out of my back while the other goes straight for my jugular.

Both end up screaming when their teeth clench down fast and hard on stone. But that doesn't stop them from attacking again. And again. And again. And since I'm currently on the ground with them on top of me, stone remains my only defense. Even as people are injured all around me.

I'm desperate to check on Hudson, on Caoimhe and Lumi, desperate to know that the three of them are okay in the middle of all this madness. But until these damn wolves lose interest in me, I'm totally screwed.

I just hope I'm the only one, because if Hudson is busy with the dragon, and the troubadours are busy with the wolves, I can't help wondering who—if anyone—has an eye on Souil. And if he's still deflecting everyone by flashing along the wall with his force field fully intact.

For a second, the biting stops, and I think I might actually be safe. I wait another couple of beats to be sure, then start to sit up—still as stone—to see if they've actually forgotten about me. Turns out it's just a ploy and the second I stick my head up, they attack again.

Only this time, Hudson is here to save me. He grabs one wolf and sends it flying halfway across the square, then takes hold of the second one and does the same thing. I spring up, changing from stone to my regular gargoyle form as I do.

He takes off, fading back across the square to where the dragon is.

"Thank you!" I call after him as I go to take to the air so I can intercept at least one of the wolves if it decides to come back.

But then, just that easily, I'm back on the ground underneath the two wolves again. Only this time, I'm not stone.

I scream as one sinks its teeth into my left calf and the other grabs hold of my arm. I have one moment—two—of excruciating pain, and then I somehow manage to turn to stone again.

I don't know what happened, don't know how I could be free one second and then back in the same position three seconds later, even though I know there was no way the wolves attacked me again. They were all the way across the square...until they weren't.

That's when it hits me why we're having so much trouble defeating the shadow creatures. Yes, it's partly because there are so many of them and so few of us, but it's also because Souil is *turning back time*. There's absolutely no other way those wolves could have been gone and then back again so quickly. Especially since Hudson wasn't there to rip them off me the second time, even though he'd been standing right over me.

Another half a minute passes of me being these damn wolves' chew toy, and I decide I've had enough. It's hard to move as stone—very hard—but I'm going to have to figure out how to make it work. Sunrise is streaking across the sky and we're down to only minutes before Souil will be able to sneak into a shadow and get the hell out of Adarie—blowing the timeline to hell and back in the process.

With that thought in the front of my mind, I force myself to roll over—much to the shadow wolves' shock and chagrin. Then, once I'm on my back, I kick with my right leg as hard as I can while punching with my left arm just as hard.

I get one wolf in the leg hard enough that it goes down with a scream, and I get the second wolf right in the nose. It doesn't go down as easily, though, its mouth clamping down on my stone hard enough that I can feel—and hear—his teeth scraping against my stone.

I figure it's going to leave a gnarly scar, but that's the least of my worries right now. I have to get away from this wolf, have to get to Souil before it's too late.

So I do the only thing I can do in this case. I take a deep breath and turn myself back into my regular gargoyle form. As I do, I try to convince the hand that's currently being gnawed on to stay stone, but I'm prepared for what will happen if it doesn't. Or at least, I think I am—right up until I shift and the wolf's teeth dig straight into my flesh.

Fuck, that hurts! Still, I ignore the pain as best I can as I launch myself straight up and into the air. As I do, I will my hand to turn back to stone, and this time it listens to me, thankfully. Moments later, I'm soaring high, high, high above town square with a shadow wolf still attached to my stone arm.

Not for long this time, though. Because I've had enough of this bullshit, and I am done.

Willing my other hand to also turn to stone, I pull it back and hit this wolf as hard as I can in the face.

This time it lets go with a scream, and I watch—without an ounce of guilt—as it plummets straight down.

I move on before it even hits the ground, whirling around to find Soul still time jumping to his left and right, back and forth. And he's still only moving two or three feet at a time. Maybe, just maybe, that means we'll get a shot at him when he finally dives for the shadow he needs to ride his way out of here.

I start toward him, not sure what I'm going to do but knowing I need to do something. But before I fly more than a few feet myself, Hudson goes careening right past me—which is of particular concern because I am *flying*, and this vampire can't fly.

139

Don't Trust Her as Far as I Can Throw Her
—Hudson—

"Hudson!" Grace screams, flying after me as I tumble through the air. I want to tell her I'm fine, but that last hit from Asuga knocked the wind out of me and I've got no breath to say anything.

Gravity finally comes into play, and I hit the ground hard, go skidding several feet across it. The only good point about the whole debacle is, when I look up at the dragon, I realize that I got her, too, and we may—just may—have a few minutes before she comes after us again.

At the moment, she's sitting on top of one of the buildings. Or maybe "lying" is the better word, as she looks as exhausted as I feel. Blood is leaking down the roof and for a second, I think that she might be dead. But then her wings move, and I can see she's trying to get her feet under her so she can launch herself back into the air.

She's not having much luck, though. At least this gives me a couple of minutes to help Grace. I know I should head back over and try to finish Asuga off, but Grace and the few other people who are still standing are drowning over here. And dawn is creeping ever closer, which means Souil almost has his ticket out of town, so someone needs to be left standing to make sure he doesn't get a chance to use it.

I head toward Grace to see what she wants to do, but before I get there, another wolf launches itself at her and takes her down again. She fights it off valiantly, but I know another one is coming. And another one. And another one after that, because the Shadow Queen is in town now, and she's not leaving until Souil is gone and she's freed from this cursed world.

Which means, as much as I have to fight every instinct in me not to leave my mate's side, the only way to make this attack stop is to focus on the Shadow Queen and end this once and for all.

With that in mind, I toss a quick glance to make sure Grace is okay—she is—then fade straight across town square and slam myself into the Shadow Queen with her evil birds and bugs, her snakes and wolves.

Shadow creatures aside, the woman waving her arms around before me looks nothing like I expected and yet exactly as I thought she would.

She's just an average woman in a rich, "I've got way more money and power than you" outfit with a murderous look in her eyes as she picks off people she deems less important than herself. Basically, she looks like my mother with giant purple hair.

Been there, and so not interested in a repeat.

I hit her so hard, she goes flying, spinning through the air. And still that's not enough—not for what she's done, to Grace and to these people she is supposed to rule. These people who surround her, who call her queen, who do her bidding no matter what.

Because it's not enough, because I can see the way she's already gathering her shadow army around her. Before she can finish summoning them, I snatch her out of midair and slam her into the ground hard enough to make it shake. Definitely hard enough to steal the breath from her lungs.

But she's back up in an instant, and now it seems like every creature she has—every bug or scorpion or beetle or bird—is with her. And they are all focused on the same thing: eliminating me.

I try to run, but the bugs swarm me, crawling up my legs, my stomach, my chest. They bite me a thousand times over, their poison working its way through my muscles into my veins. Burning me like a thousand Shadow Realm suns searing me from the inside out.

The birds dive-bomb me, scratching at my arms, my face, my shoulders. In another world—a normal world—maybe they'd actually help me out and pick the bugs off me. But here, they're just another way to torture me. Another way to inject the Shadow Queen's poison—her venom—into me as the time dragon circles overhead.

I hate every second of this, want nothing more than to fade so fast that everything falls off me and I'm free. Free to get the fuck out of this fucked-up place. Free to forget the pain staring me down from all sides. Free to forget everything and everyone but Grace.

But if I do that, if I get the fuck out now, Grace is the one I'll be leaving in the lurch. She's the one I'll be walking away from. And I can't do that. I won't do that.

Especially not now, when a third option is forming in the back of my mind, one that none of us thought of before. Not Grace, not Nyaz, not Souil, not me. It's a long shot—the Hail Mary of Hail Marys, as Grace would probably say.

But it's something. A light in the tunnel. A second chance for someone who never knew life even provided *first* chances.

And fuck if I'm not going to take it. Or die trying.

I whirl on the queen, start advancing toward her despite the snakes wrapping themselves around my ankles and the bugs biting whatever skin they can get to. The good and bad part of being a vampire is it takes a lot to bring me down. It doesn't take that much to hurt me—the bugs and birds and snakes with their venomous fangs are doing a damn good job of that. But they're barely slowing me down, and they sure as shit aren't bringing me down.

Not even close.

As I advance toward her, the Shadow Queen tosses more and more disgusting things at me.

A giant shadow mamba races across the grass and lunges at me, but I manage to grab it just behind the head and rip it in half.

Next comes a wave of jumping spiders bigger than my head. I kick away as many as I can, but a few make it onto me. And I have to say, I have seen a lot of disgusting things in my life, but these might just be the most disgusting by far.

And when one bites me, the pain nearly brings me to my knees. Fuck. Who the bloody hell knew a spider—especially a fucking shadow spider—could do that to a man?

I grab it by one of its nasty furry legs and send it soaring high above the others as I mutter a series of expletives under my breath. Then do the same to the other spiders currently crawling up whatever part of me they can reach.

A particularly huge spider of this already large species dangles right in front of me, mouth open and venomous fangs at the ready. And fuck it. Just fuck it. I plow my fist straight through its body and rip out its slimy, nasty guts.

Which seems to be enough to send the other spiders on me scurrying away—and shit, I wish I'd thought of it sooner.

Wish I'd thought of a lot of things sooner, including this idea. Because it might work, I realize as a pack of shadow wolves comes racing toward me. It just might work.

The first wolf leaps at me and I grab hold of it by the neck and under its stomach, then send it flying the length of a football pitch.

But that's the only free shot I get before the other wolves are on me. They go for my arms and legs, biting and tearing and trying to rip me apart. A couple even leap for my jugular as I do my best to knock them away.

But there are too many of them and they are too determined. Or the Shadow Queen is—who knows and who cares.

Either way, they drag me to the ground, swarm me. But then Grace is there, fighting every disgusting creature with me, and I can't let her down. I can't let them hurt her.

So I keep swinging, tearing the wolves off me. Slamming them into the ground. Hitting them away, I even go so far as to punt one all the way out of the square and onto one of the side streets.

When I finally manage to get out from under the last of them, I decide I'm done. Done with all these bullshit animals and insects the Shadow Queen is tossing at me in an effort to slow me down.

I'm done with trying to play by rules that don't work in a game that's long been busted wide open. If Grace can be brave enough to take all the risks she has, so can I.

And fuck anyone who tries to stop me.

But to get there, I need to go through this Shadow Queen once and for all. After everything she's just put me through, taking her out isn't going to be a hardship. It's going to be a fucking delight.

Which is why, when she waves another hand at me and sends a wave of shadow dragons straight toward me, I decide I've had enough. Getting killed by one of the giant dragons I'm used to from Katmere Academy is one thing. Being eaten alive by dragons the size of large vultures is something else entirely.

I'm not going down like that.

And I'm not backing down, either. Not when I'm this close.

The closer I get to the Shadow Queen, the worse the pain from the bites and the poison gets. So that by the time I'm next to her, I can barely hear or see anything. I can barely feel anything, except the heat racing through my blood and the blood pouring out of my body through a million different wounds.

But I don't give a shit. Because I'm almost there. We're almost there. The Shadow Queen and her realm of nightmares can go fuck itself. Because I am done with all of them.

As I find the energy to fade right to her fucking face, the Shadow Queen jerks back in alarm. Her eyes grow wide, her mouth opens in what I'm pretty sure is going to be a scream. But as her creatures race toward us from all directions, ready to tear me apart for daring to touch their queen, I take the opening I've got.

I reach forward and grab hold of her waist. She squawks and balls up a fist, tries to hit me with it. But after everything I've been through, I don't even know if she connects. And I don't care.

Because I'm done and so the fuck is she.

Lifting her up—which is no easy feat considering she's kicking and hitting and squirming like a pissed-off toddler—I use every ounce of strength I have inside me, and I throw her as hard as I possibly can.

I throw her so hard that my arm hurts, so hard that my back and my spleen and my everything hurts. But I don't give a shit. Because it works.

The Shadow Queen, nightmarish hag that she is, goes soaring across the town square.

She goes flying over the shops at the edge of the square.

She goes flying over the streets behind the town square.

And then she goes flying over that goddamn wall that Souil put up to make Adarie seem like a sanctuary city. As fucking if.

If this is what he calls sanctuary, I'd rather take my chances in hell.

140

It's Not Even
My Third Rodeo
—Hudson—

Turns out hell can be arranged, because I've no sooner done away with that shadow bitch than I turn and see Grace locked in mortal combat with Asuga.

Grace is under the dragon's chest at the moment, plastered against her with her arms wrapped around the dragon's neck. Asuga, on the other hand, is screaming her head off and belching flames as she spins and spins in an effort to shake Grace off.

On the plus side, the flames can't reach Grace because she's beneath them. On the negative side, her arms don't reach all the way around Asuga's neck, and I'm pretty sure she's going to fall at any second—directly into the line of fire.

I take off running, fading as fast as I can without a spleen or feeling in my feet, really, toward the clock tower side of town square, which is where the two of them are. As I do, the dragon lets out another high-pitched scream and I realize she must notice what I do—dawn is breaking. She's running out of time, and so are we.

Grace has her arms as far around the dragon's neck as they can go, while the dragon spins and spins in an effort to knock Grace off her back. But Grace isn't letting go.

Instead, she's hanging on for dear life, as she does her best to—I think—strangle the life out of the dragon. Of course, it's not working, because her arms don't reach all the way around the dragon's neck, plus it's really freaking hard to strangle a dragon, even if your arms do reach all the way.

I'm almost there when the dragon gets completely fed up with her unwelcome passenger. She stops spinning and starts thrashing hard enough to give herself whiplash—and more than hard enough to send Grace tumbling into the night.

Of course, as soon as she's dislodged Grace, she shoots a stream of fire straight at her. And Grace is too dizzy from the shaking to notice.

My heart freezes in my chest, and I scream her name at the top of my lungs. My voice must get through, because Grace drops several feet in the air at the last second, and the flames fly right by.

The dragon screams in outrage and shoots closer to her, and in desperation I scale my way up the clock tower at a run. It's not high enough—not nearly high enough to get me to the dragon—but I have to try. I have to find a way to keep her from killing Grace.

Polo runs up the clock tower's stairs right along with me. I'm so focused on Grace that I don't pay any attention to him until we get to the roof.

"I'll throw you," he says, and I have one second to think that this is the worst plan ever.

But I don't have a better one, and the dragon is taking aim at Grace, so I nod my assent. And run straight up on the hand he's got braced on his knee. Then I jump as hard as I can as *he* pushes me up as hard as he can and somehow, somehow it works.

I get just high enough to grab onto the dragon's feet, which freaks her out enough that she forgoes spraying Grace with fire to try to shake me off. I hold on as hard as I can, though, and when she tucks in her wings and starts racing toward the nearest building—I'm guessing to scrape me off like gum on the bottom of her shoe—I do the first thing I think of.

I start to climb.

Straight up her feet to her legs, straight up her leg until I'm close enough to jump to her tail. She's waving it around like a kite in a windstorm, so I almost miss and land somewhere much, much worse.

In the end, I manage to avoid a close encounter of the unpleasant kind and get one hand on her tail. I have to dig in, gouging my fingers into her flesh to do it, and then I'm swinging myself up and onto her back.

Which is exactly where I swore I'd never be again after the last fucking time dragon. But vampires don't get to be choosers—especially when they're flying—so here I am. Back in the saddle again.

The only problem is I don't have a weapon of any kind, and Asuga is massive. She's not going down without some help.

Even worse, she's still focused on Grace, who is flying around her in circles, trying to find some way to help me...and dodging fire every few seconds as she does.

"Get out of here!" I yell after one bout of flames gets extra close. "I've got this."

But Grace just rolls her eyes and ignores me, flying back and forth in front of the dragon until the beast lets out a frustrated scream.

"You're pissing her off!" I shout at her.

"No shit, Sherlock!" she shouts back, and then she's darting to the back of the dragon.

Asuga's turning radius is much bigger than Grace's, but she still manages to turn around quickly enough that I almost fall off. More flames shoot by Grace, but she darts under the dragon just in time, and Asuga roars again and goes into a dive that turns into a somersault as Grace darts back up into the sky.

Fuck this. I need a weapon and I need to end this. Now.

Suddenly, I spot something. The church steeple directly ahead of us. It's long and pointy and metal and sharp enough to do some serious damage. I just need to get Asuga a little closer to it.

"Grace!" I shout, and when she looks up at me, I point toward the church.

For a second, she looks confused, but then her eyes widen, and she races straight for it. But those moments of broken concentration cost her, because the dragon pulls in closer, and this time her fire gets near enough to singe the ends of Grace's hair.

My heart stops as the edges smolder, but in the end, they don't catch fire—and neither does Grace as she breaks what I'm pretty sure is all speed records for gargoyles as she shoots toward the church. And its steeple.

A few somersaults and a quick dive down and we're right there. Asuga is so focused on Grace that she's barely paying attention to me at all—which is exactly what I need right now. So I lean to the side just a little bit and as we fly by, I reach down and, using every ounce of vampire strength I can muster, tear the steeple right off the roof.

At that exact second, Grace races up to the time dragon and kicks her in the nose hard enough to have her screaming and belching fire. And chasing her higher, higher, higher into the sky.

That's when I strike, taking advantage of the distraction to lean down, this time with the steeple in my hand. And as the first moments of daylight break across the sky, I ignore the feel of the sun touching—burning—my skin as I swing the steeple sideways as hard as I can, straight into the dragon's jugular.

Orange blood gushes out like a geyser, showering Grace and me with the disgusting, viscous stuff. The dragon stutters midflight, rears her head back as I pull the steeple out. Then I shift it to my other hand and raise it high above my head to gain momentum.

Again, agony shoots through me as the sun touches my skin. Burns it. But I'm almost done here, and I'm not going to let that stop me. I leap into the air and bring my whole body slamming down, stabbing the steeple straight into the dragon's skull.

Blood shoots out in an initial burst, but then it only sputters as the dragon starts to wobble in midair. I look for Grace, expecting her to swoop in and yank me off Asuga's back.

But Grace has already taken off. She's speeding toward the ground at an alarming rate, and I can't figure out what she's doing.

Until I realize she's aiming straight for Souil.

141

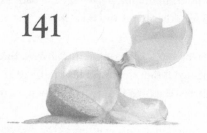

Is This a Bad Time? —Grace—

I hate to leave Hudson up there with the dragon, but she isn't dying quickly enough. A minute or two is all she's got left, but the light will be on Souil by then, and he'll be gone. All this will have been for naught.

I can't let that happen. Can't let all these people's lives end in a moment because we were thirty seconds too late. Because I couldn't get there in time. No freaking way.

We've come too far to let it all go now.

And so I dig deep, using every ounce of speed I have to race the sun across the earth. Souil is watching it also. I can see him looking back and forth, can see him trying to figure out which way to go to make sure he catches the first shadow.

I'm getting closer to him, but the sun is getting closer, too. I can feel it on my legs, can feel it washing over my back. So I push harder, harder, harder, until I pull ahead just a little.

And then just a little more.

I'm so close, so close. I just need—

Souil glances to his left one millisecond before he drops his shields, and that's all it takes. I adjust course a tiny bit and when he blinks himself three feet to the left, I'm right there.

I slam into him with every ounce of strength and built-up force I've got in me and send the two of us soaring two hundred feet to the left. It's not much, but it's enough. Maybe. Please, please, please let it be enough.

He's had the wind knocked out of him, hard, and as he struggles to take a breath, he doesn't have the strength to put his force field back up. Or to blink anywhere.

Just to make sure he stays down, I change my hand to stone and plow it as hard as I can into his chest.

His body bows up, the tiny gasp of air he'd finally managed to pull in slamming right back out of him again.

And by then, it's over.

The dragon is dead, her magic swirling through the air in droplets of gold and silver and green. The closer they get to Souil, the faster they twirl, until they form a giant ball of light that heads straight for him.

I jump off at the last second, and he staggers to his knees, arms outstretched, gasping for air.

He tries to raise his force field, tries to blink away, but he only moves a pitiful couple of inches. And then it's too late. The energy finds him and slams into his chest.

It hits him so hard, it knocks him straight into the air. He hangs there for one second, two, mouth open, gaping, as the time magic races through him. As it does, he grows brighter and brighter, until he's lighting up the early-morning dawn like the disco balls he so loves.

And then he explodes.

142

Full of Light,
Full of Grace
—Hudson—

I coast toward the ground on the back of a dead dragon, her wings still gliding across the air as she sinks closer and closer to the grass beneath us. As I feel the life leave her body, I send a request out to the universe, asking it to give her a safe, easy passing from this life to the next. And then I jump off before I crash with her, landing right in the center of the action.

People crowd around me, cheering and patting me on the back. It's embarrassing as shit, especially considering what's going on right now, but it feels nice to know I have a home, one that's filled with people who respect and appreciate me. I only have a moment to take that feeling in, though, because when I try to catch Grace's eyes, I realize she's standing too close to Souil for my comfort.

I weave through the villagers, trying to get to her, but they're all watching what's going on now, too, and not paying attention to me trying to get around them. And as Souil explodes, his own essence turning into drops of energy—of magic—just like the dragon's before him, I realize we might have a problem.

Because the tiny little dots of time magic that exploded out of Souil are re-forming, the energy looking for another place to go.

And in that moment, even before Grace focuses on the magic. Even before her eyes get wide. Even before she takes a breath and lets it out as she opens her arms, I know what it is she's going to do. She's realized—as I have—that that much power, that much magic, needs somewhere to go. And for whatever reason, she's entreating it to herself, even if it destroys her, as long as everyone else is safe.

I have one second to tell myself that she won't, that she wouldn't dare after everything we've been through. Except even as I try to convince myself of that, I know it's not true.

Because this is Grace, my beautiful, wonderful, unbelievably unselfish

Grace. And she could never do anything else, not as long as she had breath in her body.

And not as long as she knew she could somehow, some way help another person.

There's a part of me that wants to hate her for what she's about to do. That wants to blame her for leaving me after making me love her so bloody much.

But the truth is, I always knew what I was getting into. Because the girl who does this—the girl who doesn't think twice about sacrificing herself to save everyone else—that's my Grace. It's always been my Grace.

That year we were in the lair, I saw all her memories—including ones of incidents she barely remembers. They were all right there for me to see and, like her with my journals, once I got started, I couldn't stop.

Not when every memory was another piece in the puzzle of who she is. And not when every single story taught me just how kind and thoughtful and wonderful Grace really is. Even the memories she's ashamed of, even the things she thinks make her a not-so-great person, make me love her more because she has something no one in the Vampire Court has ever shown an ounce of—remorse.

I don't love Grace because she's perfect all the time. Hell, no one can make me want to pull my hair out faster than her sometimes. I love Grace because she wants to be better, always strives to be the best she can. That doesn't mean she never has a bad day. It means her bad days are not what define her. It's her stubbornness, her willingness to learn from her mistakes, and her strength to pick herself up and always do better.

She makes me want to be a better man—someone worthy of her.

She's more than I ever hoped for in a mate. And definitely more than I ever deserved.

As I watch the energy swirl around and around, getting tighter and tighter, I feel tears burn the back of my eyes. I blink them away, refusing to give in to them right now. I haven't cried in a lot of years, and I'm not going to start now. Not when Grace still needs me.

And she does need me. Even now.

Because there's no more time. It's now or never, and I can't let it be never. Can't let my Grace be erased from the timeline like she never existed. Not when I can take the hit instead and everything can go back to the way it was.

Grace, mated to Jaxon.

Me, dead or pretending to be dead, depending on how this goes.

No one remembering me at all, certainly not the woman I love.

The loss of Grace is already an emptiness inside me. It's an acid in my blood, a burning, gnawing ache that will be with me as long as I live. I've never loved anyone the way I love her, never even imagined it was possible to love someone this way.

But I do. And because I do, I'll do anything for her. Even this. Especially this. Because it's worth it. More than worth it, if it means that Grace, my beautiful, loving, perfect Grace gets to live. Even if that life doesn't include me.

I look up at the glowing energy and realize it's become an arrow now, spinning through the air as it races down, down, down toward Grace. And so I fade faster than I ever have in my entire life, slamming through the crowd like it doesn't exist.

I'm almost there. Almost there. Almost—

I jump in front of Grace, wrap myself around her.

And bam. The world explodes in a kaleidoscope of colors.

143

What Grace Around Comes Around
—Grace—

I wake up slowly, with a headache and an upset stomach that feels an awful lot like what I imagine a hangover is like. Which is strange, considering I don't remember having anything to drink last night at all. In fact, I don't really remember anything about last night, except—

Holy shit!

I roll over in a hurry, reaching a hand out for Hudson as I do. And nearly end up rolling right off the couch.

What the hell?

I hold on to the cushion for dear life.

When did we even get a couch? And why am I sleeping on it instead of in bed with Hudson? We always sleep together.

Confused, disoriented, and more than a little concerned, I sit up quickly and look around. As I do, I realize I'm not at the inn. In fact, I'm not in the Shadow Realm at all. I'm back in Hudson's lair.

How? Why?

I jump off the couch, panicked, and practically do a 360-degree turn as I search for Hudson. I finally find him—or at least a Hudson-shaped lump—in bed, with the covers yanked up to the top of his head.

Oh my God. He's here. He's here and so am I.

Relief courses through me, so powerful, so overwhelming, that I nearly break down in tears. Because Hudson and I are in his lair, and I remember everything.

I remember the Shadow Realm.

I remember falling in love with Hudson.

I remember that last horrible battle and the shadow cockroach in my mouth.

And I remember Souil exploding into a billion points of light. *Time magic.*

I remember looking up at the pretty lights, thinking how they looked like the fairy lights that Adarie strings up during the festival and how fitting it was that the mayor finally made the town square twinkle.

We won! We stopped Souil from ruining two worlds.

I start to wonder why we're in Hudson's lair again when I remember something else…

I remember the time magic floating in the sky, swirling and dancing and then re-forming. And I knew, I just knew, that energy was coming for me. Something inside me was vibrating, calling to the time magic, and it wanted to come home.

It felt right to raise my arms, to welcome the magic inside me.

But just before it could connect with me—Hudson faded in front of me and took that arrow of time magic straight through his heart and into mine.

My knees go weak, and my breath stills in my chest.

Oh my God. What if he really doesn't remember? What am I going to do?

Horror rolls through me at the thought, and I want to dive back onto the couch and wait for him to wake up. Because if he doesn't remember me— remember us—I don't know how I'll cope.

But sitting on the couch worrying about what Hudson knows or doesn't know isn't going to help me much, either. So I tell myself to stop being a baby and just go do what needs to be done.

I'm here and *I* remember, don't I? Is it such a stretch to think that Hudson might, too? Lightning has been known to strike twice…and so have miracles.

Part of me thinks I've already had my own miracle—I'm here. Healthy and relatively happy.

When I get to his bed, I pull off the pillow that's covering Hudson's head. And I look at him, just look at him.

He doesn't seem any worse for wear after everything we just went through. No bugbites, no claw marks. I look down at my own arms and realize I don't have any marks, either. The similarity has to be a good thing, right?

Not that I'll ever know unless I finally work up the nerve to just woman up and ask him.

Still, I take a minute to just stare at him, with his face relaxed and his too-long eyelashes casting shadows on his cheeks. Even though he's not smiling, his left dimple is in stark relief against his cheek and his skin looks flawless.

So yeah, this Hudson definitely hasn't been in any fights with rabid shadow wolves lately. Whether that's a good thing or not remains to be seen.

I take a deep breath, blow it out slowly. Tell myself that whatever happens, it's going to be okay. Then reach out and run soft fingers through the silky strands of Hudson's hair.

He stirs, just a little, and I hold my breath. Will him to open his eyes.

When he doesn't, I stroke his hair again and whisper his name. Then gasp when those oceanic eyes of his fly open.

144

Out of the Shadows,
Into the Light
—Grace—

A t first, confusion flashes on his face. But then he's smiling—grinning—and reaching out to touch my hand.

"Grace," he whispers as he brings my fingertips to his lips. "We made it."

"We did," I whisper back with a matching smile.

Quick as a lightning strike, his hand whips out and grabs my waist. Then he's pulling me down into bed with him.

I laugh as I land on his chest, but when I try to push myself up, he rolls us over so that we're tangled in the comforter as he settles in on top of me.

"Well, someone's feeling awfully bold this morning," I say archly, even as I hook my heels around the backs of his thighs.

"Someone is," he agrees. And then he's bending down and kissing me like it's the first time and the last time all wrapped into one.

Desperation.

Excitement.

Happiness.

Thrall.

Relief.

They're all there, clear as day. But so is need—rich, powerful, overwhelming need.

He groans low in his throat, then makes me tremble when he scrapes his fangs across the inside of my lower lip.

I do the same to him, sans fangs, then reluctantly pull away. Because I still have questions, and I really hope Hudson has the answers.

The first one of which is, "How?"

He takes my hand in his, and this time when he brings my fingers to his mouth, he kisses the promise ring he gave me in the Shadow Realm.

It's the first time I realize that *it's here*. It didn't disappear like everything else.

"How?" I ask again.

Hudson shrugs, but he gives me that careless smile I love that shows off his dimple so clearly. Or should I say his dent?

"I took a chance," he tells me. "Shadow magic is among the oldest and strongest on the planet. I researched it in the library, then talked to Nyaz about what I'd learned. He told me it was forever. Completely unbreakable except—maybe—by a time dragon's magic."

He drops another kiss on my ring, then moves to press kisses along the length of my neck because he knows I love it. And also because I think he loves it, too.

"I took a chance," he repeats. "That the shadow magic and our mating bond and the love I feel for you would be strong enough to survive anything."

"Even a massive arrow of time magic," I murmur as I take a turn kissing and licking and nibbling my way across the sharp line of his jaw.

"Even that," he agrees.

And then he's kissing me, really kissing me, and nothing has ever felt so good. Because we're free and we're us and somehow, despite all the odds, we made it through all of that together.

When Hudson's finally done kissing me—and maybe doing some other stuff as well—I glance around for my phone and realize it did not make it back from the Shadow Realm with me.

"What day is it?" he asks, glancing at his watch.

At first, I don't know what he's asking, but then I realize we were here for more than a year. The time magic could have sent us back to any one of the days we'd been here or a day in the future for all we know.

It turns out that it's March. We've been here for nearly four months, according to the regular timeline, which seems so strange, considering everything we've been through. And how long we've actually been together.

"Four months," Hudson muses. "That's not very long at all, is it?"

"It's not," I agree. And as I do, I can't help thinking about what has probably happened at Katmere Academy during those four months. About how worried Macy and Uncle Finn and Jaxon probably still are about me. And how they are all probably blaming Hudson for this mess even though it's really my fault.

"Hudson..." I broach the subject tentatively.

"Don't," he tells me as he rolls onto his back and covers his eyes with the back of his hand.

"I think we need to at least talk about it."

"Yeah, well, I don't." He throws the covers back and climbs out of bed.

I have one second to admire his body in all its perfection before he's reaching into his dresser and pulling out—big surprise—a pair of Versace boxer briefs, sans mustaches, devil horns, and peace signs.

"Look!" I tell him as I get up to rummage in the drawer. "They're all Versace all the time again."

He rolls his eyes at me, but he doesn't seem extra pleased when he reaches back in the drawer to straighten up the underwear that I had the nerve to touch.

"You know what else this means, don't you?" I ask as I, too, start to get dressed.

"What?" he asks warily.

I nod toward his turntable. "Your vinyl collection—"

"Is still in order!" he crows as he races over to his stereo area and crouches down.

He spends the next fifteen minutes pulling the perfectly organized, perfectly alphabetized albums out with such glee that I can't help but laugh along with him. At least until he settles on the vinyl edition of the soundtrack for *The Greatest Showman*.

Then I watch him with tears in my eyes as he skips to the song he told me was our song all those months ago. "Dance with me?" he asks, holding out a hand to me as the opening strains of "Rewrite the Stars" fill the lair.

And I know we need to talk about going back. I know we need to make a plan, because we can't leave our friends and family worrying about us forever. Especially not when I know how to take us home again.

But as Hudson grins down at me, his un-gelled hair falling over his forehead, I decide it can all wait just a little while longer. Because there will never be a time when this guy—my guy—asks me to dance that I will ever say no to him.

So I take his hand. I let him sweep me into his arms. And while I prepare myself to be spun and twirled and dipped, it turns out this isn't that kind of dance. Instead, it's just him and me with our arms and bodies wrapped around each other as we move to the familiar music.

Hudson does dip me at the very end of the song, and as he pulls me up, I can see the fear in his eyes. Just like I know he can see the resolution in mine.

"It's going to be okay," I tell him.

"You don't know that," he answers. "You have no idea what all of that time magic hitting us did to you—or me."

I grab his hand. "I know everything is going to be fine. How could things *not* be okay? With everything we've already gone through, everything that we've done and been to each other, how could going back do anything to ruin what we've got?"

"I don't know," he tells me as he blows out a long breath. "But I know that it's not that simple."

I try to hug him, to show him that I love him and that everything is going to work out, but he ducks out of the hug, paces several feet away.

"We could just stay here," he suggests, and there's a thread of desperation in his voice that's impossible to miss. "We could be happy here, Grace. I swear I'd make you happy."

"You'll make me happy wherever we are, Hudson," I answer firmly. "Going back to Katmere won't change that."

He doesn't look convinced, and I get that. I really do. When we were here, in his lair the first time, four months in I was still in love with Jaxon. Still mated to him even, most likely. I was trying to figure out a way home to him.

But a lot has changed since then—a lot of really important things. And when I look inside myself now, I see the brilliant blue string that connects Hudson and me. Our mating bond, glowing and healthy and beautiful. Nothing can change that now, certainly not going back to Katmere Academy.

Yes, there's still a string connecting Jaxon and me, but it's nothing like what Hudson and I have. In fact, it looks like almost all the other strings, and I know it's not a mating bond anymore. It's just a connection, because of course I still love Jaxon. Of course I still want what's best for him. But it's not the kind of love I should have for my mate, and it sure as hell isn't anything compared to what I feel for Hudson.

I tell him that, I tell him all of that, but he still doesn't look convinced. Especially when I tell him we're going to have to be careful of Jaxon's feelings for a while.

But if it's not a mating bond to me, it's not going to be one to Jaxon, either. He might need time to process what's happened, but I somehow know in my soul that he's going to ultimately be okay with us not being mated anymore. I don't know how I know that, I just do.

"Yeah, of course," he says with a whole lot of sarcasm. "By all means. Let's make sure we take care of Jaxy-Waxy."

I roll my eyes. "You're not seriously going to call him that, are you?"

"I might. If he deserves it." He snorts, shakes his head. "Who am I kidding? Of course he's going to deserve it."

"I love you," I tell him, wrapping my arms around his waist. "Not Jaxon. You, Hudson, and nothing is going to change that. You're my mate. You're my best friend." I lean into him. "You're my true north and I will always, always choose you."

"You can say that now, but how is that going to work when we're back there?" he asks. "When you see Jaxon and everyone else and they all tell you what a bastard I am."

"It'll work exactly the same. And if anyone talks shit about you, I'll set them straight. You can, too."

He laughs, but there's no humor in it. "That'll be pretty hard considering I probably won't have a body."

"At all?" I ask, alarm flooding through me. "You won't have a body like, at all? Ever?"

This time when he laughs, there's all the humor in it. "Relax, Grace. I'll still be able to—"

He breaks off as I slap a hand over his mouth. "That's not what I meant."

He lifts a brow.

"Okay," I admit as heat creeps up my cheeks. "Maybe it's a little bit about that. But not mostly. Mostly I'm just worried about you."

"I'm a little worried about me, too," he says with a grimace. "And a lot worried about that, but we can make it work for a while."

He walks over to the bookshelf with the oldest books on it, pulls off one that's got a broken spine and looks like it's about a thousand years old. "Besides, it's not like I'll be throwing slumber parties in your head for long. We just need to get a few things, and you can perform this spell and give me a body again."

"What kind of things?" I ask, curious and also a little wary. I've seen enough Disney movies to know what kind of stuff is needed to make spells, and I'm not a big fan of eyes of newt or eyes of anything else, for that matter.

"Don't worry. None of the ingredients are bad. One is hard to get, though. Really hard." He pauses. "Although, back in our world, I'll probably have my powers back, which should make it easier."

"Easier to get the ingredient?" I ask doubtfully.

"Yeah." He holds my gaze. "Although you probably won't love how I'd have to do it."

Right away, I know where he's going. And while the Grace who first arrived at the lair would have rather died than give Hudson any power over her, the Grace who has loved him for so long knows that there's no one better for her to trust in the whole world.

Which is why I sigh heavily and then say, "Fine, fine, fine. If—and it's a really big if—you need to mess with my whole mind/body thing a little bit for the express purpose of making you whole again, then fine. I give you my permission." I make a face at him. "But you have to promise to give me a heads-up before you do anything, okay? Like you've got to at least let me know what's going on."

"If there's any way for me to do that, I promise you I will," he tells me seriously. But then he grins and says, "Although I have always wondered what it would be like to fly."

We both laugh, and he tosses the book on the couch and scoops me up bride-style to carry me back to bed. I cuddle into him, lifting my face for a kiss. "If this is going to be the last one we have for a while, you need to make it good," I tell him.

"Happy to oblige," he answers with a lift of his brow. And he does oblige. He really does.

When he finally pulls away, I say, "So, I've only got one question left."

"And that is?"

"How do I get us free of the lair?" I look around at the place that was home to us for so long and feel just a little sad, because who knows if we'll ever be here again.

Hudson gives me the sweetest smile, though, and I know it won't matter if we never make it back here. Because he really is my true north, really is my home, and wherever he is is where I know I'll always want to be.

"It's easy," he tells me. "You've just got to believe in me."

"I do," I answer, going up on tiptoes to press one more kiss to his too-sexy lips. "And I always will."

Warmth spreads through me and I pull it into my chest. I pull Hudson's smile and his kindness and his sarcasm and his love into me right along with it, and then…the world goes black.

Epilogue

It's All Coming
Back to Me Now
—Grace—

"I remember," I whisper as memories flood my system. "Oh my God, Hudson. I remember *everything*."

My hands are shaking as I reach up to cup his face. But then, so is the rest of me as memory after memory—day after day—comes flooding back to me in a tidal wave of moments and emotions.

Hudson's eyes go wide—wider than I've ever seen them. And when he reaches for me, I realize his hands are shaking, too. "What do you mean? What do you remember, Grace?"

"Everything," I say again as the memories continue to pour through me like warm, sticky honey. They glom on to everything they touch, impossible to miss and even more impossible to ignore. "The Shadow Realm. The lair." I laugh a little, but it comes out sounding like a sob. "The leeches."

The shock has faded from Hudson's eyes a little more with each thing that I list, but when I get to leeches, he lifts both brows. "Seriously? The fucking leeches? That's what you want to talk to me about right now?"

"What do you want me to talk about?" I tease. "Your over-the-top love of Versace underpants?"

"Excuse me, but you have been aware of my completely normal love of Versace boxer briefs for several months now."

"You're right. I have." I go up on my tiptoes and wrap my arms around his neck. "I remember everything," I tell him again, as the joy fades and shame takes its place. "I'm sorry. Hudson, I'm so sorry."

He shakes his head, says, "Don't. Please don't do that."

"How can I not?" I ask as tears start spilling down my cheeks. "How could I treat you like that? How could you let me treat you like that?"

"Because I love you, Grace. And because I understood."

"How could you possibly understand?" I start to shake again. "It must have been so horrible for you."

He inclines his head, and because he's Hudson—my Hudson—he tells the truth, like he always does. "Sometimes it was horrible," he agrees. "Sometimes it wasn't bad. Sometimes it was downright great." His eyes gleam just a little.

"Now. Now it's great. But at the beginning? When I kept pushing you away. Telling you Jaxon was my mate. Kissing him when you were in my head?" I close my eyes. "How did you not set me on fire?"

"You mean besides the fact that I was in your head?" He grins. "You never had to worry. I'd never hurt you. Jaxon, on the other hand?" I open my eyes to see him run his tongue over the tip of his fang. "Him I wanted to light up any number of times."

"I'm sorry." I say it again. I think I'll be saying it a lot in the coming weeks and months. How can I not? After everything we'd shared and been through, if Hudson had treated me the way I treated him when we "first met" in my head, I'm pretty sure I'd be devastated. I don't know how I would ever recover. I sure as shit would have set something of his on fire—maybe the Versace boxer briefs and maybe his whole freaking world.

But he never treated me like that. No matter how much I hurt him—and looking back I know that I really did hurt him a lot—he never made me feel like that. And he always, always had my back, even when I didn't have his.

"Hey." Hudson puts a finger under my chin when I look down, tilts my face back up to his. "I didn't want you to remember so that you would feel bad, Grace. I wanted you to remember so that you could tease me about my underwear and remember our first time and..." He shakes his head. "I just wanted you to remember. But I never want you to be upset or ashamed about what happened between us or how it played out."

He presses a kiss to my forehead, then lowers his head and presses another one to my lips. He means it to be soft, sweet, but right now I don't want either of those things. Or at least, not just those things.

I slide my hands up his arms, tangle my fingers in his hair. And keep his mouth on mine as I explore all the places I've explored a hundred—no, a thousand—times before.

When he finally pulls away to look down at me, he lifts a brow. And says, "Hey, how many guys get to say their woman fell head over heels in love with them twice? It's not so bad to be me."

"By that logic, how many girls get to say their guy is so great they fell in love with him twice?" I counter.

"Exactly my point." He grins with satisfaction. "Not so bad to be me."

Except it was. It really freaking was, and he's giving me a pass anyway. Because he's Hudson.

"Why didn't you say something? At the beginning, when I was so suspicious of you? Or later, when we were getting to be friends. You could have told me then."

He takes my hand, runs his thumb over the promise ring he gave me when we were in Giant City. I've always loved this ring, even before I knew what he'd promised me, but now I find myself longing for my other ring, as well. The purple metal and shadow script that he gave me when he first made the promise to love me until the sun grew cold and the stars grew old.

Except, when he lifts his thumb, I realize there's something different about my ring now. I lift my hand up to get a closer look and my breath catches in my throat. Because in the moments between when Hudson whispered his promise to me and now, my ring has morphed into a different design.

Instead of the silver ring with the delicate runic etchings Hudson bought me at the Giant market—or the purple band with markings from the Shadow Realm—this ring is a combination of both. The two rings, one of which I thought was lost forever, have braided themselves into a beautiful new ring that I want to wear forever.

"There didn't seem to be any point." Hudson finally answers my question as I continue to examine my new ring. I look up to find him watching me and finally manage to tear my attention away from my new double promise ring.

"Shadow magic is the oldest magic in the world," he continues. "It came before light, before time, before anything. And if it couldn't stand up to us returning to Katmere, I figured what was the point. We'd never get back what we lost, so why burden you with it?"

"And yet you gave me a promise ring when we were in Giant City. You repeated the same words—the same promise to me there that you made me in the Shadow Realm."

He nods. "I did. Yes."

"But why?"

For the first time since I got my memories back, he looks confused. "Why what?"

"Why would you promise to love me again when you thought I would never love you back? Why make a promise with ancient magic that would bind you to me forever, even though you didn't know if I would ever fall back in love with you?"

He laughs. He actually laughs—and continues laughing, despite the warning I know is in my narrowed eyes.

"Really?" I demand, hands on hips. "You think this is funny?"

"I think it's funny that you have to ask," he answers. "Grace, I'm already bound to you, and not just through the mating bond. When it broke, when we came back here and the Bloodletter's ancient magic tore apart our bond and disrupted the shadow magic so that you and Jaxon would get back together... Do you actually think that made me stop loving you?"

"Well, no. But—"

"Nothing will ever make me stop loving you, Grace," he tells me as he strokes a tender hand down my cheek. "Nothing will ever make me feel anything but bound to you forever. It's nice to have the ring, and it's nice to have the mating bond. It's definitely nice to have the promise ring, since repeating the words triggered the shadow promise and somehow gave you back your memories. But I loved you without all of it once, and I'll love you without all of it forever."

"Oh, Hudson—" I start, but he stops me with a gentle finger pressed against my lips.

"Binding myself to you didn't do anything except give a physical manifestation of what I already knew. I belong to you, Grace. Heart, soul, body. I have since before we left the lair the first time. I'll be yours until the day I die, and if there's some kind of afterlife, I'll be yours then, too. Nothing will ever change that, so why wouldn't I make a promise to you?"

I'm crying now, just full-on sobbing as Hudson's words wash over me. As they soothe part of my heart even as they make another part realize that I've really messed up. Not just in forgetting him—though we figure that was the ancient magic at work, not me—but because I've never given him the same reassurances that he's given me. I've never let this brilliant, beautiful, wonderful man know that I love him the same way that he loves me.

Through anything.

Through everything.

Through eternity...no matter what.

And there seems no more perfect place to tell him than right here, in the home we're making together. No more perfect time to tell him than right now, before we head back to the Shadow Realm where we had our first home together.

So I walk to my dresser and dig in the back of the bottom drawer where I've been hiding Hudson's birthday present since I found it at an artisan fair several weeks ago. I pull out the small box and then hand it to him.

"What's this?" he asks.

"An early birthday present," I answer. But when he goes to lift the lid, a goofy smile on his lips, I stop him with a gentle hand.

"You know—" My voice cracks, and I have to stop and clear my throat. I take a deep breath and let it out slowly, willing the hummingbirds having a party in my stomach to calm the fuck down. This is Hudson, my Hudson, and there's no need for me to be nervous with him of all people.

But I am. I really am, *because* it's Hudson. The love of my life. And no one deserves a flawless declaration of love more than he does. I just don't know if I'm going to be able to give it to him.

Not when tears are still streaming down my face and panic is beating wild wings inside my rib cage. And not when the perfect words are all jumbled in my head.

I take another breath, blow it out slowly, and try to fix them into something coherent. Something that will be as beautiful and as special as he is.

Except I can't do it. I keep tripping over my tongue, tripping over my thoughts, and making a giant mess of this. The same way I've made a giant mess of so much in our relationship.

It's amazing he loves me anyway.

But he does. He does love me, despite the mess.

And maybe that's the point. To all of this.

Love isn't always easy. And it isn't always pretty. Sometimes it's messy and painful and completely fucked up. But maybe that's okay. Maybe love doesn't have to be perfect.

Maybe it just has to be real.

That thought calms me down, because nothing is messier—or more real— than my love for Hudson Vega. It's time he knows it.

"Are you okay?" he asks, and I realize I've been staring at him for a good minute as I try to work all this out in my head.

Because of course I have. Smooth, I'm definitely not.

"I am okay, actually." I tell him. Not perfect, not amazing, definitely not flawless. But I am okay. And so is he.

"You know, now that I have my memories back, there's something I need to tell you."

Hudson blinks, and just that easily, his eyes go from amused to guarded, from happy to waiting for the other shoe to drop. And that's on me...well, me and everyone else in the world who Hudson has ever cared about.

Me and everyone else in the world who has made him doubt himself.

Me and everyone else in the world who has screwed this boy over and told him that it's his own fault that it happened.

That stops now.

"You're vain," I tell him.

"Excuse me?" He lifts a brow.

"You're vain. It's true. I've known it from the first time I saw those ridiculous peacock underpants you like to wear."

"They're boxer—"

"Shh," I tell him with a glare. "It's my turn to talk now."

"Lucky me," he mutters, crossing his arms in front of his chest in that way he does when he's getting defensive.

"You're often arrogant."

"Really?" This time, the second brow joins the first.

"You are. It's because you're usually the smartest person in the room, and you know it. But still, you can be arrogant. And more than a little unsympathetic—especially if you think people aren't living their best lives."

"All right then." He tries to hand the box back, but I won't take it.

"You're also entirely too sarcastic like, ninety percent of the time—*and* you hate the fact that I was once mated to Jaxon. You try to pretend you don't, try to pretend it doesn't matter at all, but I know you get jealous sometimes when you think about the two of us together."

"If this is what you getting your memories back gets me, I vote for amnesia," he says in a voice that should cut like broken glass. But it doesn't. Not this time.

"I should probably add defensive to that list. And you're a terrible cook." I move closer to him until our bodies are pressed together so tightly that I can feel his heart beating wildly beneath my cheek. "But I love you anyway."

"What?" he snaps, like that's the last thing he expected to hear.

And it probably was, so I say it again. "I love you anyway."

"Grace?" The annoyance drains from his eyes, only to be replaced by an uncertainty that breaks my heart.

"I love you, Hudson. I love the way you make me smile and the way you're grumpy when you first wake up. I love the way you always have a quick one-liner and how you're always brutally honest, even with yourself. Even when it hurts."

"Grace." His voice breaks this time when he says my name and there are tears in his bright blue eyes. Or maybe there's not—maybe the tears are in my eyes.

"I love how protective you are and how loyal you are and how you always accuse me of having a mean streak, but you've got one, too. I love how particular you are about your things and how annoyed you get when I mess with them, even though you usually don't say anything. I love how pissy you sound when you do say something."

"What are you doing?" he asks, and yeah. Those are definitely tears in his eyes, definitely tears running down the cheeks of this boy who hasn't let himself cry in a century.

"Telling you that I love you, Hudson. The good parts and the bad. The parts you hide away because you don't think anyone will ever love you if they know about them. I see those parts and I love you anyway. More, I love you because of them. And because of your good points. And because of all the things in between.

"I love you because you can pull a dozen birdcalls out of your ass at a moment's notice. I love you because you let me sometimes cry and drip snot all over you and never complain even when you're completely grossed out. I love you because you've always got my back and I love you because you let me have yours.

"I love you, Hudson Vega." I take the box from him and lift the lid so he can see the bracelet inside. The bracelet made of giant chains knotted together at first glance, but they're really hearts when you look more closely.

"'Till the sun grows cold and the stars grow old,'" I whisper as I unclasp the bracelet and show him the engraving on the inside of the clasp. The same exact engraving that I now know is on the inside of my promise ring.

He looks shocked, even through the tears that are still falling. "How did you know?"

"I didn't," I tell him. "I just love you the same way you love me. I think I always have. I know I always will."

"Grace." This time when he says my name, it's filled with everything he's ever felt for me—everything he will ever feel for me. It's messy and wonderful and in its own imperfect way, absolutely perfect.

I fasten the bracelet around his wrist and let him kiss me. Once, twice, then again and again. But when he starts angling us toward the bed, I slap a hand against his chest and say, "Slow your roll, hot jets."

"Hot jets?" Now he's back to sounding offended. So, so offended.

"I'm just saying. We've got shit to do. We've got a vampire to save and a shadow queen's ass to kick. There's no time for anything else."

"There's always time for 'anything else,'" he tells me, lips skimming down my neck in that way he has that makes me shiver.

"Not this time," I say as I bend over and pick up my backpack. "Besides, there's something I've remembered that I think you've forgotten from our time in the Shadow Realm."

"My vanity?" he asks as he grabs his own backpack. "My arrogance? My jealousy?"

"No, no, and no." I sling my backpack over my shoulder and head for the front door. "So we didn't return to the lair because we met dragon fire. I was hit with an arrow of time magic—and now knowing that I'm the demi-god of chaos, well, that makes perfect sense why it sought me out."

"Of course it does," he snarks.

"Anywaaaay." I roll my eyes. "I think you're forgetting, though, who *was* hit with dragon fire—which, as you know, doesn't kill you. It just resets your timeline."

"Who?" he says as we walk down the stairs and let ourselves out the front door.

"Well, I'm not one hundred percent sure here, but have you considered the possibility that Smokey didn't die? I think she just went back to a different point in time."

Hudson freezes, his eyes going wide as his big, beautiful brain races through the theories and the possibilities. "Do you think?" he asks after a minute. I can't help noticing his hands are shaking again.

"I do," I tell him. "I really do. And I think we should pack some glitter ribbons, just in case."

"Fuck." He shakes his head. "I love you, Grace."

"I love you, too." I smile at him. "So let's go save Mekhi and kick that creepy bitch's ass up and down the Shadow Realm."

I reach down, intertwine my fingers in his, and add, "And let's go get our Smokey back."

ACKNOWLEDGMENTS

Writing a long-running series, especially a prequel with time travel in it, is a lot of fun, but it isn't always easy, so I have to start by thanking the two women who even made it possible: Liz Pelletier and Emily Sylvan Kim.

Liz, you are a truly incredible editor and friend and I am so, so lucky to have you in my corner. Thank you for all you did to make sure this book happened.

Emily, I hit the agent jackpot. Sincerely. We're sixty-nine books in, and I couldn't be more grateful to have you in my corner. Your support, encouragement, friendship, determination, and joy for this series has kept me going when I wasn't sure I'd be able to make it. Thank you for everything you do for me. I am so, so, so lucky that you were willing to take me on all those years ago. I wouldn't want to make this journey without you.

Stacy Cantor Abrams, I don't know how to thank you for everything you've done for me and for this book and this series. The fact that we are still working together after all these years is a matter of great pride and joy to me. I feel so lucky to have you in my corner. You really are the best!

To everyone else at Entangled who has played a part in the success of the Crave series, thank you, thank you, thank you, from the bottom of my heart. Jessica Turner, for your unfailing support. Bree Archer for making me ALL the beautiful covers and art all the time. Meredith Johnson for all your help with this series in all the different capacities. You make my job so much easier. To the fantastic proofreading team of Greta, Hannah, Jessica M., Brittany, Erin, Debbie, Lydia, and Richard, thank you for making my words shine! Zac Smith, thank you for the careful read to make sure my Britishisms were correct. Toni Kerr for the incredible care you took formatting and designing my baby. It looks amazing! Curtis Svehlak for making miracles happen on the production side over and over again—you are awesome! Katie Clapsadl for fixing my mistakes and always having my back, Angela Melamud for getting the word out about this series, Riki Cleveland for being so lovely always, Heather Riccio for your attention to detail and your help with coordinating the million different things that happen on the business side of book publishing.

A special thank-you to Valerie Esposito and the amazing Macmillan sales team for all the support they've shown this series over the years and to Beth Metrick and Grainne Daly for working so extra hard to get these books into readers' hands. And to Ellen Brescia at Prospect Agency and Julia Kniep at DTV for all the meticulous continuity reading you've both done for this series over the years.

Eden Kim, for being the best reader a writer could ever ask for. And for putting up with your mom's and my badgering of you ALL the time.

In Koo, Avery, and Phoebe Kim, thank you for lending me your wife and mom for all the late nights, early mornings, and breakfast/lunch/dinner/ midnight conversations that went into making this book possible.

Stephanie Marquez, thank you for all your love, patience, strength, and support every day of our lives together. You make everything in my life so much better.

My mother, thank you for teaching me so much about what it means to be a strong woman and a good person, lessons I've tried so hard to pass on to Grace in these books.

And my three boys, who I love with my whole heart and soul. Thank you for understanding all the evenings I had to hide in my office and work instead of hanging out, for pitching in when I needed you most, for sticking with me through all the difficult years, and for being the best kids I could ever ask for.

And finally, for fans of Grace and Hudson, plus the whole brand-new crew. Thank you, thank you, thank you for your unflagging support and enthusiasm for the Crave series. I can't tell you how much your emails and DMs and posts mean to me. I am so grateful that you've taken us into your hearts and chosen to go on this journey with me. I hope you enjoyed *Charm* as much as I enjoyed writing it. I love and am grateful for every single one of you. xoxoxoxo

Author's Note: This book depicts issues of panic attacks, death and violence, suicidal thoughts, life-and-death situations, torture, imprisonment, insect-related situations, death of a parent, and sexual content. It is my hope that these elements have been handled sensitively, but if these issues could be considered triggering to you, please take note.

A thrilling and unique fantasy based on Korean legend perfect for fans of *Iron Widow* and *These Violent Delights*

In this game of cat and mouse, there are no rules...
Turn the page for a sneak peek

CHAPTER SEVEN

One moment, I am standing on the street, my body crouched low in anticipation of an attack. The next, I am pressed against the Piper's chest.

For a brief second, I'm unable to do anything but gape as cold hands fold me into a lover's embrace, and as the frigid metal of his rings kisses the heat of my exposed skin. Somehow, my dagger has found its way back into its sheath at my side—and I'm unable to reach for it, inescapably pinned against the Dokkaebi.

As a blue flame dances in the Piper's glare, I'm reminded of the whispers that the Emperor of Dokkaebi is the only being who possesses the ability to summon a flame of indigo. To summon Dokkaebi fire, so white-hot that it is as cold as a bitter winter, and ten times as biting.

For a moment, I think he plans to summon that flame, to wield it against me...but the burning fire in his gaze quickly recedes, replaced by cold amusement. "I suggest that you close your eyes, little thief," he says in a feather-soft whisper that caresses the side of my cheek.

It's the feeling of his breath against my skin that jerks me from my reverie of terror, flooding my body with scorching adrenaline and boiling hatred. "*I suggest you let go of me,*" I snarl from behind gritted teeth before lifting myself up on my tiptoes, jerking my head back the way Yoonho taught me, and slamming my forehead against his hard enough that I see stars. A normal man would stumble backward, disoriented and weakened, leaving an opening for me to gain the upper hand and disembowel him in a few quick movements.

But as a dizzying pain racks my head, the Pied Piper merely chuckles, not at all fazed by my attack. If anything, he seems amused as I gasp weakly for breath. Dokkaebi heads, it seems, are infuriatingly resistant to blunt trauma.

A warm, wet trickle slowly makes its way down my forehead.

"And what exactly," I hear him whisper mockingly, "was that supposed to accomplish?" One of his fingers, cold with rings, slowly brushes away the droplet of blood. I can *feel* him silently laughing at me as I choke out a vicious curse—

But then the ground seems to drop beneath our feet, and we are falling— falling, falling, falling through shadows and darkness.

A scream of pure terror erupts from my lips, answered by a soft, wicked laugh as we jolt from side to side, forever tumbling through the eternal night.

Through returning vision, I glimpse flashes of Sunpo speeding by through the darkness.

The marketplace, the dingy taverns, pleasure halls, and the Blackbloods' giwajip... But then they are gone, replaced by a blinding light and a rush of heat that sends me gasping.

My boots hit ground.

Solid ground.

The impact is hard enough that it sends a wave of sickness through my body, but I shove it down as my eyes adjust to the quickly fading burst of white light—and to the Dokkaebi looking down at me, glimmers of amusement dancing across his fine features.

I swallow hard.

There is no use trying to deny that this Dokkaebi is as beautiful as he was this morning on the rooftop. His golden skin, his inky black hair, the cheekbones that could have been carved by the gods themselves... All of it is gorgeous in a way that only an inhuman can be.

I remind myself that it is very probable that this beautiful creature is about to kill me.

Red lips curve into a sly, sleek smile as I strain to break free from his arms.

A moment later, I crash to the floor as the bastard abruptly releases me, his smile quickly replaced by a look of pure boredom. My heart drops and my head throbs as my eyes meet the vast, high ceiling looming over me.

Flecks of gold dapple a dark sky. Dragons with ruby scales swim through dozens of moons, their taloned toes brushing against storm clouds. Fighting back awe, I turn my gaze to the rest of the room.

Black columns line the expanse of the room, surrounding the marble floor on which I sprawl. A silver carpet weaves its way to a throne raised on a dais. My eyes linger on the throne the longest. It's made out of dark thorns woven together and twisted into a seat.

My blood runs cold a split second later.

Next to the throne, in a glass case, is a flute.

Long, narrow, and a rich black, the flute is nearly as stunning as its owner. Delicate swirls of silver glint as they wrap in tendrils around the pipe, as if they are choking the slender neck of the instrument. Danger seems to throb through the air as I stare at the flute, entranced by its beauty.

This is the flute that the Dokkaebi emperor wields as a weapon, the flute that I have heard of, but never seen.

This is the flute that lures men and women from their beds in the middle of the night, leaving them vacant-eyed and hollow as they walk through the twisting Sunpo streets, following a haunting melody underneath an ink-black sky. Following the Pied Piper to his realm, *this* realm, where they surely meet some terrible fate.

This is the Pied Piper's flute.

"Beautiful, isn't it?" I didn't see the Pied Piper move, but he now lounges listlessly on the throne, amused as he follows my gaze. His ring-embellished fingers curl around a crystal glass of what appears to be black wine. He takes a sip, the liquid leaving a glossy stain on his lips. Something glitters in his eyes as he licks the stain away. "It was my father's flute, and his father's before him. Manpasikjeok. The Flute to Calm Ten Thousand Waves."

My lips continue to move of their own accord, even as a dull roaring fills my ears. "Only ten thousand?" I drag myself to my feet, careful not to put too much weight on my bad leg. The fall has not been good for it—spikes of sharp pain are shooting up its length. I grit my teeth and do my best to ignore it.

"You ask the oddest questions." The Dokkaebi raises a brow. "But perhaps it is because you are ill. You look unwell. Quite different from this morning." He pauses as he delicately sips again at his wine. "You also have a rather large bruise blossoming on your forehead. However did that get there?"

I fight the urge to massage my aching forehead. "If you are going to kill me, I would rather you do it without the small talk."

"So brash. And much too eager." He traces the rim of his glass with a slender finger. I watch as it circles around and around. "No, Shin Lina. I do not plan on killing you."

I blink slowly. "Why have you taken me, if not to kill me?"

The Pied Piper chuckles and leans forward. "Why, you're the Reaper of Sunpo. Word of your...*exploits*...has made its way here in the form of whispers that a wrathful spirit has deemed Sunpo's souls ripe for the reaping. Killing you, little thief, would be an awful waste of talent."

I struggle to grasp his meaning. All I can manage to think is that I am in Gyeulcheon. *Gyeulcheon.*

How did this happen? my mind chants. *How did this happen, how did this happen, how did this happen, howdidthishappenhowdidthishappenhowdidthishappen...*

The Piper cocks his head. "I would like to ask you some questions, Reaper. And I would like, very much, for you to answer them."

I release a too-shaky breath. Questions—not killing.

Not yet, anyway.

I clench my fingers around the hilt of my dagger. This is too good to be true. Something is wrong. Very, very wrong.

"The scarlet-haired is your boss."

"That is hardly a question." I hastily snap my mouth shut as the Piper's eyes darken to a storm-cloud gray. I bite my lip hard. This is no place for smart-assery. "Konrarnd Kalmin is my boss. Yes."

His brows furrow slightly. "And yet you despise him."

I freeze. *How does he—?*

"You did not fall for my little trick," he explains, waving a hand aimlessly. His rings flash underneath the light of the chandelier. "Imagine my surprise and disappointment, Shin Lina, when you did not play with me." The corners of his mouth tilt downward into what is almost a petulant pout.

"You mean fall for your bait."

"Semantics." The Pied Piper raises a shoulder in a shrug. "I suspect that you were not planning on coming to retrieve the scarlet-haired. You are not fond of him. And I now suspect that he returns the sentiment." He runs a hand across his chin in contemplation.

I slowly incline my head in a nod.

The Pied Piper's expression is inscrutable. "It is he who ordered you to steal my tapestry."

I nod again, this time fervently. "Yes. Yes, he ordered me to steal it. He desired the jewels, he's in the Oktarian jewel trade, he's greedy, he's—" I'm silenced by a sharp look.

"This is not a test of his character. And you will not escape my judgment by pinning blame on *him*. What I do find interesting, though, is where you were planning to run instead. There is something that you want very much, and it is not here in Gyeulcheon. It is somewhere else entirely, isn't it?"

Eunbi. I hold my breath.

"I watched you on the street," the Dokkaebi continues, sending hot humiliation creeping up the sides of my neck. I fight back a flinch at the knowledge that he saw me in those moments when the Thought had me entirely in its grasp. He clucks his tongue twice. "If your tears were any indication, you seem to be in a delicate situation, Reaper."

I hold his gaze. "You may remedy that delicacy by releasing me from this realm." *And letting me retrieve my sister.*

Because if thirty days go by and Kalmin has not been returned...

Eunbi will die. Because of me.

I cannot have more blood on my hands. Cannot have my little sister's blood on my hands.

Losing Eunbi would shatter me completely. She is all I have.

A brief moment passes as the Pied Piper sets aside his wineglass and laces his fingers. He props them underneath his chin, his expression concerningly contemplative. Finally, he straightens in his seat and narrows his eyes, as if staring at a puzzle he cannot quite complete. "I would like to offer you a bargain, Shin Lina."

A bargain. Every primal instinct in my body screams for me to run as far away from this Dokkaebi as possible. Yet it is impossible. I'm trapped here, and there is nowhere to go—except forward, toward the Emperor of the Dokkaebi. Steeling myself, I take another step closer to his throne. "Bargains involve promises. Agreements. Honesty. I have to wonder, Pied Piper, how much your word is worth."

"My word is worth whatever I decide it is worth." *Bastard.* I scowl, trembling with unrestrained hatred. "But your situation intrigues me," he continues. "I am eager to see how it unfolds."

My breath catches in my throat as I dare to hope. Perhaps there is a way out of this, after all. Perhaps I will escape with Kalmin unscathed, the threat to Eunbi's life null, perhaps—

"You and your crime lord—if you desire that he return with you—will be granted passage back to Sunpo...*if* you manage to assassinate the Emperor of Gyeulcheon."

What in the gods' names?

The wonderful hope warming my body gutters out, replaced by icy dread. I struggle to push words through my tight jaw. "*You're* the Emperor of Gyeulcheon."

"Yes, Reaper, I am well aware," the Pied Piper replies with a sharp, sly smile. "And I am also very bored. Such a game will keep me thoroughly entertained. There is nothing that we Dokkaebi love more than games of fortune. As for the rules..." The Piper tilts his head. "Well. I've always been fond of the number fourteen."

"Fourteen?" I rasp through a dry mouth, unable to understand the connection. My pulse thunders in my ears. I cannot think through my shock. I cannot do anything but sway where I stand.

"Fourteen," the Pied Piper confirms silkily. "It's my second favorite number, my first one being, simply, four. But four is far too small a number for my purposes."

Four. I shiver, suddenly aware of the clamminess coating my skin, the dampness under my arms, the way my heart pounds erratically as it sends wave after wave of nausea through my trembling body.

Four is an unlucky number. It brings bad fortune—at least, that's what the superstitions say, and the Eastern Continent's myths have so far proven to be true. I find it fitting that four would be the Pied Piper's favorite number.

"I could, of course, give you four days." The emperor slips a hand into the folds of his hanbok, as if looking for something. "But I am nothing if not magnanimous." A dark grin. "And so you have four*teen* days, Reaper, to kill me." He finds what he is looking for and tosses it toward me. I see only the glitter of a chain until I catch it in my hands, glass and metal cold on my skin.

It is a necklace, a small hourglass connected to the chain. The curving, eight-shaped glass is situated between two obsidian circles, the same material that makes up the elegant pillars on the hourglass's left and right. Inside, silver sand waits inside the top curve of glass, unmoving.

"Go on," says the Pied Piper. "Put it on. A fine piece of jewelry, is it not?"

My fingers tremble around the chain, and he laughs ever so softly.

"When the sand trickles out, little thief, your time is up. And if you have failed to kill me by the end of the fourteenth day... Well. I'll kill you," the Piper whispers softly. Lethally. "And I can assure you that it will not be pleasant. That tapestry was very important to me."

"Which is why it was sitting in a dust-covered box in Sunpo." The words spill out of my mouth before I can clamp my lips shut. My hands are still shaking violently around the necklace I have not donned. This game he offers me—it is impossible to win. Fear and anger have quickened my tongue, and I regret the words as soon as they are spoken.

A cold shiver kisses my sweat-dampened back as the Piper straightens indignantly. Fury radiates from the emperor in powerful waves of unbearable heat that scorch my skin as I curse my foul mouth.

His silver gaze is unforgiving. "Perhaps my absence from your kingdom has helped you forget who I am, as so many of your kind have forgotten the names of the gone gods."

I hold my chin high, refusing to cower even as fear grips my heart. "*I* have not forgotten."

The Pied Piper considers me for a long moment, his scrutiny sharp. I stop breathing altogether as he tilts his head to one side, then another, before finally settling back in his throne with an air of disinterest that now feels... calculated. "Well then." His mouth is a cruel, crooked line. "Perhaps the fact that I have let your little kingdom live a full life apart from the power I hold over it has made you think that you can let your tongue run quick. But," the Pied Piper warns, his lips curving into a frigid smile, "it is so very dangerous to forget such things."

I will my knees not to buckle under the overwhelming strength of his glare. Will my eyes to resist flickering to his flute, Manpasikjeok, only a hairsbreadth away from his ringed fingers.

"You stole from me, Shin Lina. I have not forgotten, nor will I ever. I have some compassion, as you were only under orders, but we all have choices. Orders do not always require obedience. Demands do not always hold dominance over what is right."

His eyes narrow and he watches me struggle to hold his gaze, watches me struggle not to tremble. There is no amusement on his countenance now, only cold displeasure.

"This bargain is the best deal that you will receive. Take it or don't. If you kill me, my court will ensure your and your crime lord's safe return." He smiles thinly. "It grows so dreadfully boring here. I urge you to take this bargain. If not..." The Piper flashes his teeth, showing sharp white canines. "Well. The result will be the same as if you lose. Do you prefer a beheading? Or perhaps an arrow to the heart? Although in my opinion, a beheading seems rather quicker and much more entertaining. On my part, at least."

My stomach roils and I take a deep breath, my chest tight. With this offer before me, I suddenly miss the comfort of Asina's thirty days. For now that time means nothing, and I have been handed fourteen days in their place. Fourteen days to kill the Dokkaebi emperor and save my sister. Fourteen days of cat and mouse...but I will be the cat this time.

The room is silent, save for the torrents of thoughts pounding through my mind so loudly that I worry the Dokkaebi can hear them. I lift the hourglass, staring at the glittering sand as my mouth sets into a firm line.

I am a skilled fighter, quick and agile. A weapon honed by Yoonho himself, and deadlier than any of the Talons combined.

And yet...there is no way I can kill the Dokkaebi in front of me.

But I can try.

I can bide my time. Rebuild my strength. And strike.

Except if I end up dead, Eunbi will die, too.

I choke down a whimper and fight back a desperate, keening prayer. Shin Lina does *not* cry. Pain builds in my constricting throat as I will back tears. Weak. I look weak. There is a moment of silence that seems to drag on forever, as long as time itself...

But then I fasten the necklace around my neck.

The glass is cold on my skin, and I fight back a shiver. "Fine. I'll play your godsdamned game," I rasp as the Pied Piper's lips curve. I feel my face tighten into a puzzled frown as he extends a hand. The blood from my forehead is still on his fingers, spots of red on his silver jewelry.

I frown at it. *Am I supposed to—*

"Shake it," the Piper says, arching a brow. A taunt. A dare. A challenge.

I hesitate. But... *For Eunbi. For her chiming laugh and sparkling eyes.*

I make myself walk forward. Climb the dais. Force myself to grasp his hand. *For Eunbi.*

Despite its smooth, slender appearance, his hand is callused and cold. A shock of ice floods my veins, and I gasp, flinching away.

The Pied Piper merely laughs, soft and sly. "We have a deal."

CHAPTER EIGHT

When I was fifteen, I broke my arm.

It happened so fast that I registered only the unmistakable *snap* before it all went black.

Yoonho was working me into a drench of sweat as I punched, kicked, flipped, and twisted, determined to be honed into what Yoonho envisioned for me. A living weapon, and the Talons' greatest asset. It had been only a year since Yoonho had plucked me, a sticky-fingered urchin, from the street. Yet I was strong. Ferocious. I had already killed seven men—seedy, scowling men who believed that the Talons' Sunpo belonged to them. The very sort of men who believed everything and every*one* was theirs to take with force and unforgiving brutality. I took pleasure in seeing them cowering in their final moments, took pleasure in making the kills.

But when it all went dark, I felt fear. Sharp, stabbing fear. *Yeomra*, I thought. *Please do not take me yet.*

When I awoke, Yoonho's narrowed gaze peered down at me from where I lay on my bed. He had pulled up a chair, and by the look of the circles under his eyes, he'd been there for a while. His graying hair was disheveled, and the wrinkles alongside his thin mouth and hooked nose seemed even more prominent.

I blinked blearily. "What happened?"

Yoonho was silent, yet his eyes spoke for him. I followed them to my right arm. To the heavy white bandages strapping it to my chest, immobilizing one of my body's most useful limbs.

Oh. *Oh.*

The training session, the burst of pain, the darkness... I blinked as realization struck me.

"You *broke* it," I fired, feeling tears prick at my eyes and threaten to spill out. "You broke it," I repeated quietly, furiously rubbing my eyes with the back of my left hand and fighting back those tears. "Why did you break it?"

Yoonho's face turned from haggard to steely. "You need to be lighter on your feet. Quicker. *Faster.* Had this been a real fight, you wouldn't have a broken arm. You would be dead. Do you understand, Lina?" He held my gaze, and a heavy silence settled between us, broken only as my anger reached a boiling point.

"How am I supposed to train?" I exploded. Everything I was working for, everything I'd achieved... "My arm is broken!"

"Who said anything about not training?"

"My arm," I repeated slowly, "is broken."

"And?" He sat back in his chair. "You have another arm."

"My *left* arm," I retorted, trembling with fury.

"Precisely. Your left arm could use more attention, regardless. Think of this as the perfect opportunity to strengthen dexterity on your nondominant side."

"It's not fair," I cut in, frustration making my voice small and tight. "You have both arms. Fighting you with one arm isn't fair."

"Life," Yoonho replied curtly, his patience finally slipping, "is not fair. Especially in this line of work. You want to survive? Then fight with what you have. And what you have is a perfectly good left arm. You'll have opponents bigger than you. Stronger than you. More powerful than you. Use every resource you can in order to win." He ran a hand down his face, which suddenly seemed haggard again. He looked old in that moment; a great deal older than his fifty years. And tired. So very tired. "You're on your way to becoming the Talons' greatest asset. Prove to me that you can be."

I clenched my jaw tight enough that it popped. But he was right. I knew he was. And, like any petulant fifteen-year-old, I hated him for it. "Fine," I spat out. "I will."

And I did.

. . .

Fighting the Pied Piper will be like fighting without an arm. And a leg.

And eyes, or ears.

I try to ignore the Dokkaebi's air of obvious satisfaction as he stands from his throne and gracefully makes his way down from the dais, his shoulder brushing past mine.

Heat blooms on the spot where our skin meets. "Your time starts tomorrow," he says with an air of dark satisfaction, eyes on the hourglass. "Consider this your day of rest."

I grit my teeth and imagine running him through with the dagger still strapped to my waist. But no—too risky. So I stay where I am as he once again parts his lips, which this time reveal words that are not meant for me.

"Your eavesdropping stops now," he calls, his voice tinged with dark laughter as he fixes his eyes on a point on the other side of the room, near the black doors.

There is a muffled feminine swear, followed by two low, masculine laughs—and then the heavy, dark doors slam open, accompanied by a burst of light.

My breath catches in my throat as more Dokkaebi appear, their footsteps echoing across the black marble floor. There are three, with pointed ears, and breathtaking in ways that humans can never be—one a beautiful female, tall and regal, with a waterfall of curly black hair. She carries herself with an air of haughty pride, emphasized by her narrowed eyes and upturned chin. A dress of glittering gold clings to her alabaster, freckled skin. The garment is one of the Northern style, skintight and utterly at odds with this continent's traditional hanbok.

She stands between two males, but her fingers are brushing those of a Dokkaebi who, despite his unlined face, harbors a shock of long white hair. His skin is a rich umber and his uptilted eyes—a deep emerald green—take me in with wary interest. He wears a black hanbok embellished with gray embroidery, a sash of silver secured around his waist, where a sheathed sword, along with various golden medallions, also hang. I wonder, warily, if he is some sort of general.

He scowls at me.

I scowl right back.

The final male, wearing a simple tunic and baggy pants, is clutching a staff of twisted black wood. He eyes me with a vague intrigue that unnerves me. His eyes are not a searing silver like the Pied Piper's—they are brown and rimmed with dark circles. Their depths seem to swim with infinite questions and answers, knowledge and thought, wisdom and wonder. His hair falls to his chin, the red-brown color of autumn foliage. Under my gaze, he tilts his head in what could be a greeting or a warning.

Probably the latter.

I don't return the gesture, but my fingers twitch to my dagger.

"It was hardly eavesdropping," the female Dokkaebi replies coolly. "Your voice is simply too loud to ignore."

The white-haired male to her right seems to swallow a laugh with difficulty before composing his face back into stiff stoicism.

"I see we have a guest," the staff-bearing Dokkaebi murmurs before the Piper can reply. "I hope that you have not forgotten to introduce us."

The Piper casts a sparking look over his shoulder in my direction. "Shin Lina, meet Jeong Kang, Park Hana, and Kim Chan." He cuts a look to Kang, the one with the staff. "That satisfies you, I hope."

In the presence of these intimidating immortals, I suddenly become overly aware of the grime crusting my skin and the bruises dappling my face. I straighten and say nothing, gripping the hilt of my dagger so tightly that my knuckles ache.

"An honor," Hana says icily, lips twisting into a mocking smile. Her voice is slick with a distaste that sends me scowling.

"I truly wish that I could say the same," I reply sweetly before I can stop myself.

Chan tenses as Hana's eyes flash, but before she can reply, Kang turns to the Piper with a bone-weary expression. "Haneul Rui, you owe me a great explanation."

My eyes snap to the Pied Piper, who gives Kang a bland smile. *Haneul Rui*...of course the Piper has a name other than what Sunpo dubs him. Something roils uneasily in my stomach, the danger that I am in suddenly seeming much more real.

"Lina," the Piper—*Rui*—says, "and I have struck a little bargain."

"Dear gods." Kang's face pales and his eyes dart to the hourglass upon my neck. "Rui." I take pleasure in the fact that there is genuine concern in his voice, take pleasure in the idea that perhaps, somehow, I can pose a threat after all.

The emperor ignores him. "Hana, darling." Rui turns to the dark-haired female. "Show Shin Lina to the guest wing. She could use a bath."

My cheeks burn red as he and his companions chuckle.

Kang is the only one who remains silent, his brows furrowed in quiet contemplation. He meets my gaze for a moment, and it almost seems as if sympathy swirls in those dark depths.

I scoff. I don't want his pity. Don't *need* his pity.

"This way," Hana says with an elegant tilt of her head as she begins to make her way out of the throne room, her golden dress swishing across the glossy ground.

I don't move.

Instead, I turn my gaze to the Pied Piper.

His smile falters slightly as I hold his stare and let him see every bit of the Reaper that is still in me. Let him see every murderous and predatory gleam that shines in my eyes as if to say, *You've made a fool's bargain, Your Majesty.*

The Piper just curls his lips into a razor-sharp half-moon.

I cock my head and smile an awful smile for a split second before allowing my lips to flatten, allowing my eyes to bore into his.

Seconds pass before his jaw flexes—just slightly.

And with that, I taste triumph, sweet and spiced on my tongue.

Limping past him toward Hana, I make an extra point to shove my shoulder into his. He doesn't budge, but I do not miss his scowl.

As I follow Hana out of the room, Haneul Rui's glower is a sharp sword embedded in my back.

The Da Vinci Code *meets* Riverdale *in the new YA fantasy from #1* New York Times *bestselling author Alyson Noël*

Stealing
Infinity

My life goes completely sideways the moment I meet the mysterious Braxton. Sure, he's ridiculously hot, but he's also the reason I've been kicked out of school and recruited into Gray Wolf Academy—a remote island school completely off the grid. I never should have trusted a face so perfect.

But the reality of *why* Gray Wolf wanted me is what truly blows my mind. It's a school for time travelers. *Tripping*, they call it. This place is filled with elaborate costumes and rare artifacts, where every move is strategic and the halls are filled with shadows and secrets.

Here, what you see isn't always what it appears. Including Braxton. Because even though there's an energy connecting us together, the more secrets he keeps from me, the more it feels like something is pulling us apart. Something that has to do with this place—and its darker purpose. It's all part of a guarded, elaborate puzzle of history and time...and I might be one of the missing pieces.

Now I have all the time in the world. And yet I can't shake the feeling that time is the one thing I'm about to run out of...*fast*.

She-Ra meets Thor in an epic fantasy perfect for fans of Adrienne Young.

THE
VALKYRIE'S
DAUGHTER

TIANA WARNER

From the time she was born, Sigrid has only ever been ordinary. Being paired at birth with a plain horse—instead of the powerful winged mare of a valkyrie—meant there would be no warrior path for her. No riding the skies, no glory among the nine worlds. Just the simple, unremarkable life of a stable hand.

Everything changes when a terrible enemy ambushes Vanaheim and Sigrid sees a vision of herself atop a mythical stallion, leading the valkyries into a harrowing battle. Finally, she can grab her future with her own two hands and become the hero of her own story...if she dares.

But her destiny is tied up with Mariam, a fallen valkyrie who's allied herself with the very enemy Sigrid is trying to stop.

Now Sigrid has left ordinary behind as she begins a journey with the beautiful—if treacherous—valkyrie, each step bringing her closer to answers...and to awakened feelings for Mariam.

Only, the life Sigrid has escaped may have been paradise compared to the one she's racing toward. Because her destination is the realm of the dead: the gates of Hel.

Some shadows protect you...others will kill you in this dazzling new fantasy series from award-winning author Abigail Owen.

Everything about my life is a lie. As a hidden twin princess, born second, I have only one purpose—to sacrifice my life for my sister if death comes for her. I've been living under the guise of a poor, obscure girl of no standing, slipping into the palace and into the role of the true princess when danger is present.

Now the queen is dead and the ageless King Eidolon has sent my sister a gift—an eerily familiar gift—and a proposal to wed. I don't trust him, so I do what I was born to do and secretly take her place on the eve of the coronation. Which is why, when a figure made of shadow kidnaps the new queen, he gets me by mistake.

As I try to escape, all the lies start to unravel. And not just my lies. The Shadowraith who took me has secrets of his own. He struggles to contain the shadows he wields—other faces, identities that threaten my very life.

Winter is at the walls. Darkness is looming. And the only way to save my sister and our dominion is to kill Eidolon...and the Shadowraith who has stolen my heart.

*An emotional and heartfelt coming-of-age drama perfect
for fans of Jennifer Niven*

the gravity

of missing

things

m a r i s a   u r g o

Flight 133 disappeared over the ocean. No wreckage. No distress signal. Just gone.

Suddenly, everyone on the news and social media is talking about whether the pilot intentionally crashed it—everyone but me. Because I know her. The pilot was my mom, and there's no way she would hurt anyone. No one else knows that before she left, she wrote me a note. *Trust me*, it said.

Now it feels like someone split my world—and me—in two, and the only person who believes me is Landon. I want to trust him, to let him see who I really am, but I can't. I have my secrets, the same way Mom has hers. All I know is falling for him will only make things more complicated.

Just as I start to open up, the answer to what really happened to Flight 133 could rip my world apart all over again—for good this time.

An epic angels-and-demons series full of pulse-pounding romance, epic worldbuilding, and plenty of twists and turns.

EMBER
OF
NIGHT

MOLLY E. LEE

I've never been a stranger to the darkness. But when darkness comes knocking and looks *that* good, who wouldn't invite him in?

Draven is mysterious, evasive, and hot as sin. The only thing more infuriating than his silence is how obnoxious he is every time he *does* open his mouth. But when a group of strangers attacks me and he fights back—causing them to vanish into a cloud of black dust—I know Draven is more than he seems.

Now I know the truth. There's a veil separating the world I know from a world of demons living all around us. Turns out, good and evil are just words. Some of the demons don't fall into either category. And I'm realizing just how easily I fit in among the ancient warlocks, the divine soldiers, and the twisted supernaturals...

There's so much more to me and my past that I don't know—let alone what I am truly capable of. So when all signs point to me having the ability to unleash Hell on earth? I'll have to decide if I want to do the world a solid and save it... or give it one hell of a makeover.

Let's be friends!

🐦 @EntangledTeen

📷 @EntangledTeen

f @EntangledTeen

♪ @EntangledTeen

📰 bit.ly/TeenNewsletter

Visit to learn more about the school with bite:

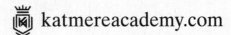 katmereacademy.com